PRAISE FOR *NEW YORK TIMES* BESTSELLING AUTHOR JULIE KAGAWA

"*The Iron King* has the...enchantment, imagination and adventure of...*Alice in Wonderland, Narnia* and *Lord of the Rings,* but with lots more romance."
—*Justine* magazine

"Fan-fun-tastic! I'm telling you guys, *The Iron King* is a blast... this book had me riveted."
—*Teens Read and Write* blog

"*The Iron King* surpasses the greater majority of dark fantasies, leaving a lot for readers to look forward to.... The romance is well done and adds to the mood of fantasy."
—*TeenReads.com*

"Meghan is a likeable heroine and her quest is fraught with danger and adventure... Expect it to be popular with teens who liked Melissa Marr's *Wicked Lovely*."
—*School Library Journal* on *The Iron King*

"*The Iron King* has it all, a lot of action and a little romance."
—*MonsterLibrarian.com*

"A full five stars to Julie Kagawa's *The Iron Daughter*. If you love action, romance and watching how characters mature through heart-wrenching trials, you will love this story as much as I do."
—*Mundie Moms* blog

"*The Iron Daughter* is a book that will keep its readers glued to the pages until the very end."
—*New York Journal of Books*

"Julie Kagawa's Iron Fey series is the next *Twilight*."
—*Teen.com*

"Julie Kagawa is one killer storyteller."
—MTV's *Hollywood Crush* blog

Books by Julie Kagawa
available from Harlequin TEEN

The Iron Fey series
(in reading order)

*The Iron King**
"Winter's Passage" (ebook novella)****
*The Iron Daughter**
The Iron Queen
"Summer's Crossing" (ebook novella)****
The Iron Knight
"Iron's Prophecy" (ebook novella)****
The Lost Prince
The Iron Traitor

*also available in print in *The Iron Fey Volume One* anthology
**Also available in print in *The Iron Legends* anthology

Blood of Eden series
(in reading order)

The Immortal Rules
The Eternity Cure

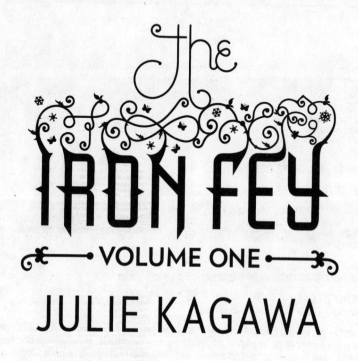

THE IRON FEY

VOLUME ONE

JULIE KAGAWA

THE IRON KING · THE IRON DAUGHTER

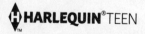

HARLEQUIN®TEEN

Recycling programs
for this product may
not exist in your area.

ISBN-13: 978-0-373-21138-8

THE IRON FEY VOLUME ONE

Copyright © 2013 by Harlequin Books S.A.

The publisher acknowledges the copyright holder of the individual works
as follows:

THE IRON KING
Copyright © 2010 by Julie Kagawa

THE IRON DAUGHTER
Copyright © 2010 by Julie Kagawa

This edition published by arrangement with Harlequin Books S.A.

For questions and comments about the quality of this book, please contact us
at CustomerService@Harlequin.com.

Printed in U.S.A.

CONTENTS

For Nick, Brandon and Villis. May we continue
to beat those dead horses into the ground.

PART ONE

CHAPTER ONE

The Ghost in the Computer

Ten years ago, on my sixth birthday, my father disappeared.

No, he didn't leave. Leaving would imply suitcases and empty drawers, and late birthday cards with ten-dollar bills stuffed inside. Leaving would imply he was unhappy with Mom and me, or that he found a new love elsewhere. None of that was true. He also did not die, because we would've heard about it. There was no car crash, no body, no police mingling about the scene of a brutal murder. It all happened very quietly.

On my sixth birthday, my father took me to the park, one of my favorite places to go at that time. It was a lonely little park in the middle of nowhere, with a running trail and a misty green pond surrounded by pine trees. We were at the edge of the pond, feeding the ducks, when I heard the jingle of an ice cream truck in the parking lot over the hill. When I begged my dad to get me a Creamsicle, he laughed, handed me a few bills, and sent me after the truck.

That was the last time I saw him.

Later, when the police searched the area, they discovered

his shoes at the edge of the water, but nothing else. They sent divers into the pond, but it was barely ten feet down, and they found nothing but branches and mud at the bottom. My father had disappeared without a trace.

For months afterward, I had a recurring nightmare about standing at the top of that hill, looking down and seeing my father walk into the pond. As the water closed over his head, I could hear the ice cream truck singing in the background, a slow, eerie song with words I could almost understand. Every time I tried to listen to them, however, I'd wake up.

Not long after my father's disappearance, Mom moved us far away, to a tiny little hick town in the middle of the Louisiana bayou. Mom said she wanted to "start over," but I always knew, deep down, that she was running from something.

It would be another ten years before I discovered what.

My name is Meghan Chase.

In less than twenty-four hours, I'll be sixteen years old.

Sweet sixteen. It has a magical ring to it. Sixteen is supposed to be the age when girls become princesses and fall in love and go to dances and proms and such. Countless stories, songs, and poems have been written about this wonderful age, when a girl finds true love and the stars shine for her and the handsome prince carries her off into the sunset.

I didn't think it would be that way for me.

The morning before my birthday, I woke up, showered, and rummaged through my dresser for something to wear. Normally, I'd just grab whatever clean-ish thing is on the floor, but today was special. Today was the day Scott Waldron would finally notice me. I wanted to look perfect. Of course, my wardrobe is sadly lacking in the popular-attire department. While other girls spend hours in front of their closets crying, "What should I wear?" my drawers basically hold three things: clothes from Goodwill, hand-me-downs, and overalls.

I wish we weren't so poor. I know pig farming isn't the most glamorous of jobs, but you'd think Mom could afford to buy me at least one pair of nice jeans. I glared at my scanty wardrobe in disgust. *Oh, well, I guess Scott will have to be wowed with my natural grace and charm, if I don't make an idiot of myself in front of him.*

I finally slipped into cargo pants, a neutral green T-shirt, and my only pair of ratty sneakers, before dragging a brush through my white-blond hair. My hair is straight and very fine, and was doing that stupid floating thing again, where it looked like I'd jammed my finger up an electrical outlet. Yanking it into a ponytail, I went downstairs.

Luke, my stepfather, sat at the table, drinking coffee and leafing through the town's tiny newspaper, which reads more like our high school gossip column than a real news source. "Five-legged calf born on Patterson's farm," the front page screamed; you get the idea. Ethan, my four-year-old half brother, sat on his father's lap, eating a Pop-Tart and getting crumbs all over Luke's overalls. He clutched Floppy, his favorite stuffed rabbit, in one arm and occasionally tried to feed it his breakfast; the rabbit's face was full of crumbs and fruit filling.

Ethan is a good kid. He has his father's curly brown hair, but like me, inherited Mom's big blue eyes. He's the type of kid old ladies stop to coo at, and total strangers smile and wave at him from across the street. Mom and Luke dote on their baby, but it doesn't seem to spoil him, thank goodness.

"Where's Mom?" I asked as I entered the kitchen. Opening the cabinet doors, I scoured the boxes of cereal for the one I liked, wondering if Mom remembered to pick it up. Of course she hadn't. Nothing but fiber squares and disgusting marshmallow cereals for Ethan. Was it so hard to remember Cheerios?

Luke ignored me and sipped his coffee. Ethan chewed his Pop-Tart and sneezed on his father's arm. I slammed the cabinet doors with a satisfying bang.

"Where's Mom?" I asked, a bit louder this time. Luke jerked his head up and finally looked at me. His lazy brown eyes, like those of a cow, registered mild surprise.

"Oh, hello, Meg," he said calmly. "I didn't hear you come in. What did you say?"

I sighed and repeated my question for the third time.

"She had a meeting with some of the ladies at church," Luke murmured, turning back to his paper. "She won't be back for a few hours, so you'll have to take the bus."

I always took the bus. I just wanted to remind Mom that she was supposed to take me to get a learner's permit this weekend. With Luke, it was hopeless. I could tell him something fourteen different times, and he'd forget it the moment I left the room. It wasn't that Luke was mean or malicious, or even stupid. He adored Ethan, and Mom seemed truly happy with him. But, every time I spoke to my stepdad, he would look at me with genuine surprise, as if he'd forgotten I lived here, too.

I grabbed a bagel from the top of the fridge and chewed it sullenly, keeping an eye on the clock. Beau, our German shepherd, wandered in and put his big head on my knee. I scratched him behind the ears and he groaned. At least the *dog* appreciated me.

Luke stood, gently placing Ethan back in his seat. "All right, big guy," he said, kissing the top of Ethan's head. "Dad has to fix the bathroom sink, so you sit there and be good. When I'm done, we'll go feed the pigs, okay?"

"'Kay," Ethan chirped, swinging his chubby legs. "Floppy wants to see if Ms. Daisy had her babies yet."

Luke's smile was so disgustingly proud, I felt nauseous.

"Hey, Luke," I said as he turned to go, "bet you can't guess what tomorrow is."

"Mmm?" He didn't even turn around. "I don't know, Meg. If you have plans for tomorrow, talk to your mother." He snapped his fingers, and Beau immediately left me to follow him. Their footsteps faded up the stairs, and I was alone with my half brother.

Ethan kicked his feet, regarding me in that solemn way of his. "I know," he announced softly, putting his Pop-Tart on the table. "Tomorrow's your birthday, isn't it? Floppy told me, and I remembered."

"Yeah," I muttered, turning and lobbing the bagel into the trash can. It hit the wall with a thump and dropped inside, leaving a greasy smear on the paint. I smirked and decided to leave it.

"Floppy says to tell you happy early birthday."

"Tell Floppy thanks." I ruffled Ethan's hair as I left the kitchen, my mood completely soured. I knew it. Mom and Luke would completely forget my birthday tomorrow. I wouldn't get a card, or a cake, or even a "happy birthday" from anyone. Except my kid brother's stupid stuffed rabbit. How pathetic was that?

Back in my room, I grabbed books, homework, gym clothes, and the iPod I'd spent a year saving for, despite Luke's disdain of those "useless, brain-numbing gadgets." In true hick fashion, my stepfather dislikes and distrusts anything that could make life easier. Cell phones? No way, we've got a perfectly good landline. Video games? They're the devil's tools, turning kids into delinquents and serial killers. I've begged

Mom over and over to buy me a laptop for school, but Luke insists that if his ancient, clunky PC is good enough for him, it's good enough for the family. Never mind that dial-up takes flipping *forever*. I mean, who uses dial-up anymore?

I checked my watch and swore. The bus would arrive shortly, and I had a good ten-minute walk to the main road. Looking out the window, I saw the sky was gray and heavy with rain, so I grabbed a jacket, as well. And, not for the first time, I wished we lived closer to town.

I swear, when I get a license and a car, I am never coming back to this place.

"Meggie?" Ethan hovered in the doorway, clutching his rabbit under his chin. His blue eyes regarded me somberly. "Can I go with you today?"

"What?" Shrugging into my jacket, I gazed around for my backpack. "No, Ethan. I'm going to school now. Big-kids school, no rug rats allowed."

I turned away, only to feel two small arms wrap around my leg. Putting my hand against the wall to avoid falling, I glared down at my half brother. Ethan clung to me doggedly, his face tilted up to mine, his jaw set. "Please?" he begged. "I'll be good, I promise. Take me with you? Just for today?"

With a sigh, I bent down and picked him up.

"What's up, squirt?" I asked, brushing his hair out of his eyes. Mom would need to cut it soon; it was starting to look like a bird's nest. "You're awfully clingy this morning. What's going on?"

"Scared," Ethan muttered, burying his face in my neck.

"You're scared?"

He shook his head. "Floppy's scared."

"What's Floppy scared of?"

"The man in the closet."

I felt a small chill slide up my back. Sometimes, Ethan was so quiet and serious, it was hard to remember he was only four. He still had childish fears of monsters under his bed and bogeymen in his closet. In Ethan's world, stuffed animals spoke to him, invisible men waved to him from the bushes, and scary creatures tapped long nails against his bedroom window. He rarely went to Mom or Luke with stories of monsters and bogeymen; from the time he was old enough to walk, he always came to me.

I sighed, knowing he wanted me to go upstairs and check, to reassure him that nothing lurked in his closet or under his bed. I kept a flashlight on his dresser for that very reason.

Outside, lightning flickered, and thunder rumbled in the distance. I winced. My walk to the bus was not going to be pleasant.

Dammit, I don't have time for this.

Ethan pulled back and looked at me, eyes pleading. I sighed again. "Fine," I muttered, putting him down. "Let's go check for monsters."

He followed me silently up the stairs, watching anxiously as I grabbed the flashlight and got down on my knees, shining it under the bed. "No monsters there," I announced, standing up. I walked to the closet door and flung it open as Ethan peeked out from behind my legs. "No monsters here, either. Think you'll be all right now?"

He nodded and gave me a faint smile. I started to close the door when I noticed a strange gray hat in the corner. It was domed on top, with a circular rim and a red band around the base: a bowler hat.

Weird. Why would that be there?

As I straightened and started to turn around, something moved out of the corner of my eye. I caught a glimpse of a figure hiding behind Ethan's bedroom door, its pale eyes watching me through the crack. I jerked my head around, but of course there was nothing there.

Jeez, now Ethan's got me *seeing imaginary monsters. I need to stop watching those late-night horror flicks.*

A thunderous boom directly overhead made me jump, and fat drops plinked against the windowpanes. Rushing past Ethan, I burst out of the house and sprinted down the driveway.

I was soaked when I reached the bus stop. The late spring rain wasn't frigid, but it was cold enough to be uncomfortable. I crossed my arms and huddled under a mossy cypress, waiting for the bus to arrive.

Wonder where Robbie is? I mused, gazing down the road. *He's usually here by now. Maybe he didn't feel like getting drenched and stayed home.* I snorted and rolled my eyes. *Skipping class again, huh? Slacker. Wish I could do that.*

If only I had a car. I knew kids whose parents gave *them* cars for their sixteenth birthday. Me, I'd be lucky if I got a cake. Most of my classmates already had licenses and could drive themselves to clubs and parties and anywhere they wanted. I was always left behind, the backward hick girl nobody wanted to invite.

Except Robbie, I amended with a small mental shrug. *At least Robbie will remember. Wonder what kooky thing he has planned for my birthday tomorrow?* I could almost guarantee it would be something strange or crazy. Last year, he snuck me out of the house for a midnight picnic in the woods. It was weird; I remembered the glen and the little pond with the fireflies drifting over it, but though I explored the woods behind my house countless times since then, I never found it again.

Something rustled in the bushes behind me. A possum or a deer, or even a fox, seeking shelter from the rain. The wildlife out here was stupidly bold and had little fear of humans. If it wasn't for Beau, Mom's vegetable garden would be a buffet for rabbits and deer, and the local raccoon family would help themselves to everything in our cupboards.

A branch snapped in the trees, closer this time. I shifted uncomfortably, determined not to turn around for some stupid squirrel or raccoon. I'm not like "inflate-a-boob" Angie, Ms. Perfect Cheerleader, who'd flip out if she saw a caged gerbil or a speck of dirt on her Hollister jeans. I've pitched hay and killed rats and driven pigs through knee-deep mud. Wild animals don't scare me.

Still, I stared down the road, hoping to see the bus turn the corner. Maybe it was the rain and my own sick imagination, but the woods felt like the set for *The Blair Witch Project*.

There are no wolves or serial killers out here, I told myself. *Stop being paranoid.*

The forest was suddenly very quiet. I leaned against the tree and shivered, trying to will the bus into appearing. A chill crawled up my back. I wasn't alone. Cautiously, I craned my neck up, peering through the leaves. An enormous black bird perched on a branch, feathers spiked out against the rain, sitting as motionless as a statue. As I watched, it turned its head and met my gaze, with eyes as green as colored glass.

And then, something reached around the tree and grabbed me.

I screamed and leaped away, my heart hammering in my ears. Whirling around, I tensed to run, my mind filled with rapists and murderers and Leatherface from *The Texas Chainsaw Massacre*.

Laughter exploded behind me.

Robbie Goodfell, my closest neighbor—meaning he lived nearly two miles away—slouched against the tree trunk, gasping with mirth. Lanky and tall, in tattered jeans and an old

T-shirt, he paused to look at my pale face, before cracking up again. His spiky red hair lay plastered to his forehead and his clothes clung to his skin, emphasizing his lean, bony frame, as though his limbs didn't fit quite right. Being drenched and covered in twigs, leaves, and mud didn't seem to bother him. Few things did.

"Dammit, Robbie!" I raged, stomping up and aiming a kick at him. He dodged and staggered into the road, his face red from laughter. "That wasn't funny, you idiot. You nearly gave me a heart attack."

"S-sorry, princess," Robbie gasped, clutching his heart as he sucked in air. "It was just too perfect." He gave a final chortle and straightened, holding his ribs. "Man, that was impressive. You must've jumped three feet in the air. What, did you think I was Leatherface or something?"

"Of course not, stupid." I turned away with a huff to hide my burning face. "And I told you to stop calling me that! I'm not ten anymore."

"Sure thing, princess."

I rolled my eyes. "Has anyone told you you have the maturity level of a four-year-old?"

He laughed cheerfully. "Look who's talking. I'm not the one who stayed up all night with the lights on after watching *The Texas Chainsaw Massacre*. I tried to warn you." He made a grotesque face and staggered toward me, arms outstretched. "Ooooh, look out, it's Leatherface."

I scowled and kicked water at him. He kicked some back, laughing. By the time the bus showed up a few minutes later, we were both covered in mud, dripping wet, and the bus driver told us to sit in the back.

"What are you doing after school?" Robbie asked as we huddled in the far backseat. Around us, students talked, joked, laughed, and generally paid us no attention. "Wanna grab a coffee later? Or we could sneak into the theater and see a movie."

"Not today, Rob," I replied, trying to wring water from my shirt. Now that it was over, I dearly regretted our little mud battle. I was going to look like the Creature from the Black Lagoon in front of Scott. "You'll have to do your sneaking without me this time. I'm tutoring someone after class."

Robbie's green eyes narrowed. "Tutoring someone? Who?"

My stomach fluttered, and I tried not to grin. "Scott Waldron."

"What?" Robbie's lip curled in a grimace of disgust. "The jockstrap? Why, does he need you to teach him how to read?"

I scowled at him. "Just because he's captain of the football team doesn't mean you can be a jerk. Or are you jealous?"

"Oh, of course, that's it," Robbie said with a sneer. "I've always wanted the IQ of a rock. No, wait. That would be an insult to the rock." He snorted. "I can't believe you're going for the jockstrap. You can do so much better, princess."

"Don't call me that." I turned away to hide my burning face. "And it's just a tutoring session. He's not going to ask me to the prom. Jeez."

"Right." Robbie sounded unconvinced. "He's not, but you're *hoping* he will. Admit it. You're drooling over him just like every empty-headed cheerleader on campus."

"So what if I am?" I snapped, spinning around. "It's none of your business, Rob. What do you care, anyway?"

He got very quiet, muttering something unintelligible under his breath. I turned my back on him and stared out the window. I didn't care what Robbie said. This afternoon, for one glorious hour, Scott Waldron would be mine alone, and no one would distract me from that.

★ ★ ★

School dragged. The teachers all spoke gibberish, and the clocks seemed to be moving backward. The afternoon crept by in a daze. Finally, finally, the last bell rang, freeing me from the endless torture of X equals Y problems.

Today is the day, I told myself as I maneuvered the crowded hallways, keeping to the edge of the teeming mass. Wet sneakers squeaked over tile, and a miasma of sweat, smoke, and body odor hung thick in the air. Nervousness fluttered inside me. *You can do this. Don't think about it. Just go in and get it over with.*

Dodging students, I wove my way down the hall and peeked into the computer room.

There he was, sitting at one of the desks with both feet up on another chair. Scott Waldron, captain of the football team. Gorgeous Scott. King-of-the-school Scott. He wore a red-and-white letterman jacket that showed off his broad chest, and his thick dark blond hair brushed the top of his collar.

My heart pounded. *A whole hour in the same room with Scott Waldron, with no one to get in the way.* Normally, I couldn't even get close to Scott; he was either surrounded by Angie and her cheerleader groupies, or his football buddies. There were other students in the computer lab with us, but they were nerds and academic types, beneath Scott Waldron's notice. The jocks and cheerleaders wouldn't be caught dead in here if they could help it. I took a deep breath and stepped into the room.

He didn't glance at me when I walked up beside him. He lounged in the chair with his feet up and his head back, tossing an invisible ball across the room. I cleared my throat. Nothing. I cleared it a little louder. Still nothing.

Gathering my courage, I stepped in front of him and waved. His coffee-brown eyes finally jerked up to mine. For a moment, he looked startled. Then an eyebrow rose in a lazy arc, as if he couldn't figure out why I wanted to talk to him.

Uh-oh. Say something, Meg. Something intelligent.

"Um…" I stammered. "Hi. I'm Meghan. I sit behind you. In computer class." He was still giving me that blank stare, and I felt my cheeks getting hot. "Uh…I really don't watch a lot of sports, but I think you're an awesome quarterback, not that I've seen many—well, just you, actually. But you really seem to know what you're doing. I go to all your games, you know. I'm usually in the very back, so you probably don't see me." *Oh, God. Shut up, Meg. Shut up now.* I clamped my mouth closed to stop the incessant babbling, wanting to crawl into a hole and die. What was I thinking, agreeing to this? Better to be invisible than to look like a complete and total moron, especially in front of Scott.

He blinked lazily, reached up, and pulled the earphones from his ears. "Sorry, babe," he drawled in that wonderful, deep voice of his. "I couldn't hear you." He gave me a once-over and smirked. "Are you supposed to be the tutor?"

"Um, yes." I straightened and smoothed out my remaining shreds of dignity. "I'm Meghan. Mr. Sanders asked me to help you out with your programming project."

He continued to smirk at me. "Aren't you that hick girl who lives out in the swamp? Do you even know what a computer is?"

My face flamed, and my stomach contracted into a tight little ball. Okay, so I didn't have a great computer at home. That was why I spent most of my after-school time here, in the lab, doing homework or just surfing online. In fact, I was hoping to make it into ITT Tech in a couple of years. Programming and Web design came easily to me. I knew how to work a computer, dammit.

But, in the face of Scott's criticism, I could only stammer:

"Y-yes, I do. I mean, I know a lot." He gave me a dubious look, and I felt the sting of wounded pride. I had to prove to him that I wasn't the backward hillbilly he thought I was. "Here, I'll show you," I offered, and reached toward the keyboard on the table.

Then something weird happened.

I hadn't even touched the keys when the computer screen blipped on. When I paused, my fingers hovering over the board, words began to scroll across the blue screen.

Meghan Chase. We see you. We're coming for you.

I froze. The words continued, those three sentences, over and over. *Meghan Chase. We see you. We're coming for you. Meghan Chase we see you we're coming for you. Meghan Chase we seeyou we'recoming for you...* over and over until it completely filled the screen.

Scott leaned back in his seat, glaring at me, then at the computer. "What is this?" he asked, scowling. "What the hell are you doing, freak?" Pushing him aside, I shook the mouse, punched Escape, and pressed Ctrl/Alt/Del to stop the endless string of words. Nothing worked.

Suddenly, without warning, the words stopped, and the screen went blank for a moment. Then, in giant letters, another message flashed into view.

SCOTT WALDRON PEEKS AT GUYS IN THE SHOWER ROOM, ROFL.

I gasped. The message began to scroll across all the computer screens, wending its way around the room, with me powerless to stop it. The other students at the desks paused, shocked for a moment, then began to point and laugh.

I could feel Scott's gaze like a knife in my back. Fearfully, I turned to find him glaring at me, chest heaving. His face was crimson, probably from rage or embarrassment, and he jabbed a finger in my direction.

"You think that's funny, swamp girl? Do you? Just wait. I'll show you funny. You just dug your own grave, bitch."

He stormed out of the room with the echo of laughter trailing behind him. A few of the students gave me grins, applause, and thumbs-up; one of them even winked at me.

My knees were shaking. I dropped into a chair and stared blankly at the computer screen, which suddenly flicked off, taking the offensive message with it, but the damage was already done. My stomach roiled, and there was a stinging sensation behind my eyes.

I buried my face in my hands. *I'm dead. I'm so dead. That's it, game over, Meghan. I wonder if Mom will let me move to a boarding school in Canada?*

A faint snicker cut through my bleak thoughts, and I raised my head.

Crouched atop the monitor, silhouetted black against the open window, was a tiny, misshapen *thing*. Spindly and emaciated, it had long, thin arms and huge batlike ears. Slitted green eyes regarded me across the table, gleaming with intelligence. It grinned, showing off a mouthful of pointed teeth that glowed with neon-blue light, before it vanished, like an image on the computer screen.

I sat there a moment, staring at the spot where the creature had been, my mind spinning in a dozen directions at once. *Okay. Great. Not only does Scott hate me, I'm starting to hallucinate, as well. Meghan Chase, victim of a nervous breakdown the day before she turned sixteen. Just send me off to the loony bin, 'cause I sure won't survive another day at school.*

Dragging myself upright, I shuffled, zombielike, into the hall. Robbie waited for me by the lockers, a soda bottle in each hand. "Hey, princess," he greeted as I shambled past. "You're out early. How'd the tutoring session go?"

"Don't call me that," I muttered, banging my forehead into my locker. "And the tutoring session went fabulous. Please kill me now."

"That good, huh?" He tossed me a diet soda, which I barely caught, and twisted open his root beer in a hiss of foam. I could hear the grin in his voice. "Well, I suppose I could say 'I told you so—'"

I glared daggers at him, daring him to continue.

The smile vanished from his face. "—but…I won't." He pursed his lips, trying not to grin. "'Cause…that would just be wrong."

"What are you doing here, anyway?" I demanded. "The buses have all left by now. Were you *lurking* by the computer lab, like some creepy stalker guy?"

Rob coughed loudly and took a long sip of his root beer. "Hey, I was wondering," he continued brightly, "what are you doing for your birthday tomorrow?"

Hiding in my room, with the covers over my head, I thought, but shrugged and yanked open my rusty locker. "I dunno. Whatever. I don't have anything planned." I grabbed my books, stuffed them in my bag, and slammed the locker door. "Why?"

Robbie gave me that smile that always makes me nervous, a grin that stretched his entire face so that his eyes narrowed to green slits. "I've got a bottle of champagne I managed to swipe from the wine cabinet," he said in a low voice, waggling his eyebrows. "How 'bout I come by your place tomorrow? We can celebrate your birthday in style."

I'd never had champagne. I did try a sip of Luke's beer once, and thought I was going to throw up. Mom sometimes brought home wine in a box, and that wasn't terrible, but I wasn't much of an alcohol drinker.

What the hell? You're only sixteen once, right? "Sure," I told Robbie, and gave a resigned shrug. "Sounds good. Might as well go out with a bang."

He cocked his head at me. "You okay, princess?"

What could I tell him? That the captain of the football team, whom I'd been crushing on for two years, was out to get me, that I was seeing monsters at every turn, and that the school computers were either hacked or possessed? Yeah, right. I'd get no sympathy from the school's greatest prankster. Knowing Robbie, he'd think it was a brilliant joke and congratulate me. If I didn't know him better, I might even think he set it up.

I just gave him a tired smile and nodded. "I'm fine. I'll see you tomorrow, Robbie."

"See you then, princess."

Mom was late picking me up, again. The tutoring session was only supposed to be an hour, but I sat on the curb, in the drizzling rain, for another good half hour, contemplating my miserable life and watching cars pull in and out of the parking lot. Finally, her blue station wagon turned the corner and pulled to a stop in front of me. The front seat was filled with grocery bags and newspapers, so I slid into the back.

"Meg, you're sopping wet," cried my mother, watching me from the rearview mirror. "Don't sit on the upholstery—get a towel or something. Didn't you bring an umbrella?"

Nice to see you, too, Mom, I thought, scowling as I grabbed a newspaper off the floor to put on the seat. No "how was your day?" or "sorry I'm late." I should've abandoned the stupid tutoring session with Scott and taken the bus home.

We drove in silence. People used to tell me I looked like

her, that is, before Ethan came along and swallowed up the spotlight. To this day, I don't know where they saw the resemblance. Mom is one of those ladies who looks natural in a three-piece suit and heels; me, I like baggy cargo pants and sneakers. Mom's hair hangs in thick golden ringlets; mine is limp and fine, almost silver if it catches the light just right. She looks regal and graceful and slender; I just look skinny.

Mom could've married anyone in the world—a movie star, a rich business tycoon—but she chose Luke the pig farmer and a shabby little farm out in the sticks. Which reminded me…

"Hey, Mom. Don't forget, you have to take me to get a permit this weekend."

"Oh, Meg." Mom sighed. "I don't know. I've got a lot of work this week, and your father wants me to help him fix the barn. Maybe next week."

"Mom, you promised!"

"Meghan, please. I've had a long day." Mom sighed again and looked back at me in the mirror. Her eyes were bloodshot and ringed with smeared mascara. I shifted uncomfortably. Had Mom been crying?

"What's up?" I asked cautiously.

She hesitated. "There was an…accident at home," she began, and her voice made my insides squirm. "Your father had to take Ethan to the hospital this afternoon." She paused again, blinking rapidly, and took a short breath. "Beau attacked him."

"What?" My outburst made her start. *Our* German shepherd? Attacking Ethan? "Is Ethan all right?" I demanded, feeling my stomach twist in fear.

"Yes." Mom gave me a tired smile. "Very shaken up, but nothing serious, thank God."

I breathed a sigh of relief. "What happened?" I asked, still unable to believe our dog actually attacked a family member. Beau adored Ethan; he got upset if anyone even scolded my half brother. I'd seen Ethan yanking on Beau's fur, ears, and tail, and the dog barely responded with a lick. I'd seen Beau take Ethan's sleeve and gently tug him back from the drive-way. Our German shepherd might be a terror to squirrels and deer, but he'd never even shown teeth to anyone in the house. "Why did Beau go crazy like that?"

Mom shook her head. "I don't know. Luke saw Beau run up the stairs, then heard Ethan screaming. When he got to his room, he found the dog dragging Ethan across the floor. His face was badly scratched, and there were bite marks on his arm."

My blood ran cold. I saw Ethan being mauled, imagined his absolute terror when our previously trustworthy shepherd turned on him. It was so hard to believe, like something out of a horror movie. I knew Mom was just as stunned as I was; she'd trusted Beau completely.

Still, Mom was holding back, I could tell by the way she pressed her lips together. There was something she wasn't tell-ing me, and I was afraid I knew what it was.

"What will happen to Beau?"

Her eyes filled with tears, and my heart sank. "We can't have a dangerous dog running around, Meg," she said, and I heard the plea for understanding. "If Ethan asks, tell him that we found Beau another home." She took a deep breath and gripped the steering wheel tightly, not looking at me. "It's for the safety of the family, Meghan. Don't blame your father. But, after Luke brought Ethan home, he took Beau to the pound."

CHAPTER TWO

Ring Tone of Doom

Dinner was tense that night. I was furious at both my parents: Luke for doing the deed, and Mom for allowing him to do it. I refused to speak to either of them. Mom and Luke talked between themselves about useless, trivial stuff, and Ethan sat clutching Floppy in silence. It was weird not having Beau pacing round the table like he always did, looking for crumbs. I excused myself early and retreated to my room, slamming the door behind me.

I flopped back on my bed, remembering all the times Beau had curled up here with me, a solid, warm presence. He never asked anyone for anything, content just to be near, making sure his charges were safe. Now he was gone, and the house seemed emptier for it.

I wished I could talk to someone. I wanted to call Robbie and rant about the total unfairness of it all, but his parents—who were even more backward than mine, apparently—didn't have a phone, or even a computer. Talk about living in the Dark Ages. Rob and I made our plans at school, or sometimes he would just show up outside my window, having walked the two miles to my house. It was a total pain in the ass, something I fully intended to fix once I got my own car. Mom and Luke couldn't keep me in this isolated bubble forever. Maybe my next big purchase would be cell phones for *both* of us, and screw what Luke thought about that. This whole "technology is evil" thing was getting really old.

I'd talk to Robbie tomorrow. I couldn't do it tonight. Besides, the only phone in my house was the landline in the kitchen, and I didn't want to vent about grown-up stupidity with them in the same room. That would be pushing it.

There was a timid knock on the door, and Ethan's head peeked inside.

"Hey, squirt." I sat up on the bed, swiping at a few stray tears. A dinosaur Band-Aid covered his forehead, and his right arm was wrapped in gauze. "What's up?"

"Mommy and Daddy sent Beau away." His lower lip trembled, and he hiccuped, wiping his eyes on Floppy's fur. I sighed and patted the bed.

"They had to," I explained as he clambered up and snuggled into my lap, rabbit and all. "They didn't want Beau to bite you again. They were afraid you'd get hurt."

"Beau didn't bite me." Ethan gazed back at me with wide, teary eyes. I saw fear in them, and an understanding that went way beyond his years. "Beau didn't hurt me," he insisted. "Beau was trying to save me from the man in the closet."

Monsters again? I sighed, wanting to dismiss it, but a part of me hesitated. What if Ethan was right? I'd been seeing weird things, too, lately. What if…what if Beau really was protecting Ethan from something horrible and terrifying…?

No! I shook my head. This was ridiculous! I'd be turning sixteen in a few hours; that was way too old to believe in monsters. And it was high time Ethan grew up, as well. He was a smart kid, and I was getting tired of him blaming imaginary bogeymen whenever something went wrong.

"Ethan." I sighed again, trying not to appear cranky. If I was too harsh, he'd probably start bawling, and I didn't want to upset him after all he'd gone through today. Still, this had gone far enough. "There are no monsters in your closet, Ethan. There's no such thing as monsters, okay?"

"Yes, there are!" He scowled and kicked his feet into the covers. "I've seen them. They talk to me. They say the king wants to see me." He held out his arm, showing me the bandage. "The man in the closet grabbed me here. He was pulling me under the bed when Beau came in and scared him off."

Clearly, I wasn't going to change his mind. And I really didn't want a temper tantrum in my room right now. "Okay, fine," I relented, wrapping my arms around him. "Let's say something other than Beau grabbed you today. Why don't you tell Mom and Luke?"

"They're grown-ups," Ethan said, as if it was perfectly clear. "They won't believe me. They can't see the monsters." He sighed and looked at me with the gravest expression I'd ever seen on a kid. "But Floppy says *you* can see them. If you try hard enough. You can see through the Mist and the glamour, Floppy says so."

"The what and the what?"

"Ethan?" Mom's voice floated outside the door, and her silhouette appeared in the frame. "Are you in here?" Seeing us together, she blinked and offered a tentative smile. I glared back stonily.

Mom ignored me. "Ethan, honey, time to get ready for bed. It's been a long day." She held out her hand, and Ethan hopped down to pad across the room, dragging his rabbit behind him.

"Can I sleep with you and Daddy?" I heard him ask, his voice small and scared.

"Oh, I guess so. Just for tonight, okay?"

"'Kay." Their voices faded away down the hall, and I kicked my door shut.

That night, I had a strange dream about waking up and seeing Floppy, Ethan's stuffed rabbit, at the foot of my bed. In the dream, the rabbit was speaking to me, words that were grave and terrifying, filled with danger. It wanted to warn me, or it wanted me to help. I might have promised it something. The next morning, however, I couldn't remember much of the dream at all.

I woke to the sound of rain drumming on the roof. My birthday seemed destined to be cold, ugly, and wet. For a moment, a heavy weight pressed at the back of my mind, though I didn't know why I felt so depressed. Then everything from the previous day came back to me, and I groaned.

Happy birthday to me, I thought, burrowing under the covers. *I'll be spending the rest of the week in bed, thanks.*

"Meghan?" Mom's voice sounded outside my door, followed by a timid knock. "It's getting late. Are you up yet?"

I ignored her and curled up farther into the covers. Resentment simmered as I thought of poor Beau, carted off to the pound. Mom knew I was mad at her, but she could stew in her guilt for a while. I wasn't ready to forgive and make up just yet.

"Meghan, get up. You're going to miss the bus," said Mom, poking her head in the room. Her tone was matter-of-fact, and I snorted. So much for making up.

"I'm not going to school," I muttered from beneath the covers. "I don't feel good. I think I've got the flu."

"Sick? On your birthday? That's unfortunate." Mom came into the room, and I peeked at her through a crack in the blankets. She remembered?

"Very sad," Mom continued, smiling at me and crossing her arms. "I was going to take you to get a learner's permit after school today, but if you're sick…"

I popped up. "Really? Um…well, I guess I don't feel all that bad. I'll just take some aspirin or something."

"I thought so." Mom shook her head as I bounced to my feet. "I'm helping your father fix the barn this afternoon, so I can't pick you up. But, as soon as you get home, we'll go to the license bureau together. That sound like a good birthday present?"

I barely heard her. I was too busy racing around the room, grabbing clothes and getting my stuff together. The sooner I got through the day, the better.

I was stuffing homework into my backpack when the door creaked open again. Ethan peeked in the doorway, his hands behind his back, a shy, expectant smile on his face.

I blinked at him and pushed back my hair. "What do you need, squirt?"

With a grin, he stepped forward and held out a folded piece of paper. Bright crayon drawings decorated the front; a smiley-faced sun hovered over a little house with smoke curling from the chimney.

"Happy birthday, Meggie," he said, quite pleased with himself. "See how I remembered?"

Smiling, I took the homemade card and opened it. Inside, a simple crayon drawing of our family smiled back: stick figures of Mom and Luke, me and Ethan holding hands, and a four-legged critter that had to be Beau. I felt a lump in my throat, and my eyes watered for just a moment.

"You like it?" Ethan asked, watching me anxiously.

"I love it," I said, ruffling his hair. "Thank you. Here, why don't you put it on the fridge, so everyone can see what a great artist you are."

He grinned and scampered off, clutching the card, and I felt my heart get a little bit lighter. Maybe today wouldn't be so terrible, after all.

"So, your mom is taking you to get a permit today?" Robbie asked as the bus pulled into the school parking lot. "That's cool. You can finally drive us downtown and to the movies. We won't have to depend on the bus, or spend another evening watching VHS tapes on your twelve-inch screen."

"It's only a permit, Rob." I gathered my backpack as the bus lurched to a halt. "I won't have my license yet. Knowing Mom, it'll be another sixteen years before I can drive the car on my own. Ethan will probably get a license before I do."

The thought of my half brother sent an unexpected chill through me. I remembered his words from the night before: *You can see through the Mist and the glamour, Floppy says so.*

Stuffed rabbit aside, I had no idea what he was talking about.

As I walked down the bus steps, a familiar figure broke away from a large group and came striding toward me. Scott. My stomach twisted, and I gazed around for a suitable escape route, but before I could flee into the crowd, he was already in front of me.

"Hey." His voice, drawling and deep, made me shiver. Terrified as I was, he was still gorgeous, with his damp blond hair falling in unruly waves and curls on his forehead. For some reason, he seemed nervous today, running his hands through his bangs and gazing around. "Um…" He hesitated, narrowing his eyes. "What was your name again?"

"Meghan," I whispered.

"Oh, yeah." Stepping closer, he glanced back at his friends and lowered his voice. "Listen, I feel bad about the way I treated you yesterday. It was uncalled-for. I'm sorry."

For a moment, I didn't understand what he was saying. I'd been expecting threats, taunts, or accusations. Then a great balloon of relief swelled inside me as his words finally registered. "O-oh," I stammered, feeling my face heat, "that's okay. Forget about it."

"I can't," he muttered. "You've been on my mind since yesterday. I was a real jerk, and I'd like to make it up to you. Do…" He stopped, chewing his lip, then got it all out in a rush. "Do you want to eat lunch with me this afternoon?"

My heart pounded. Butterflies swarmed madly in my stomach, and my feet felt like they were floating an inch off the ground. I barely had the voice to squeak a breathless "Sure." Scott grinned, showing blindingly white teeth, and gave me a wink.

"Hey, guys! Over here!" One of Scott's football buddies stood a few feet away, a camera-phone in hand, pointed at us. "Smile for the birdie."

Before I knew what was happening, Scott put a hand around my shoulders and pulled me close to his side. I blinked up at him, stunned, as my heart began racing around my chest. He flashed his dazzling grin at the camera, but I could only stare, stupefied, like a moron.

"Thanks, Meg," Scott said, breaking away from me. "See you at lunch." He smiled and trotted off toward the school with one final wink. The cameraman chuckled and sprinted after him, leaving me dazed and confused at the edge of the parking lot.

For a moment, I stood there, staring like an idiot as my classmates surged around me. Then a grin spread across my face and I whooped, leaping into the air. Scott Waldron wanted to see me! He wanted to have lunch with me, just me, in the cafeteria. Maybe my luck was finally turning around. My best birthday ever might just be starting.

As a silvery curtain of rain crept over the parking lot, I felt eyes on me. Turning, I saw Robbie a few paces away, watching me through the crowd.

Through the rain, his eyes glittered, a too-bright green. As water pounded the concrete and students rushed toward the school, I saw a hint of something on his face: a long muzzle, slitted eyes, a tongue lolling out between pointed fangs. My stomach twisted, but I blinked and Robbie was himself again—normal, grinning, unconcerned that he was getting drenched.

And so was I.

With a little yelp, I sprinted beneath the overhang and ducked inside the school. Robbie followed, laughing, pulling at my limp strands of hair until I smacked him and he stopped.

All through the first class, I kept glancing at Robbie, looking for that eerie, predatory hint on his face, wondering if I was crazy. All it got me was a sore neck and a brusque comment from my English teacher to pay attention and stop staring at boys.

When the lunch bell rang, I leaped up, my heart fluttering a hundred miles a minute. Scott was waiting for me in the cafeteria. I grabbed my books, stuffed them into my backpack, whirled around—

And came face-to-face with Robbie, standing behind me.

I shrieked. "Rob, I'm going to smack you if you don't stop doing that! Now, move. I have to get somewhere."

"Don't go." His voice was quiet, serious. Surprised, I looked up at him. The perpetual goofy grin was gone, and his jaw was set. The look in his eyes was almost frightening. "This is bad, I can feel it. Jockstrap is up to something—he and his buddies were hanging around the yearbook department for a long time after he talked to you. I don't like it. Promise me you won't go."

I recoiled. "Were you eavesdropping on us?" I demanded, scowling. "What's wrong with you? Ever hear of a 'private conversation'?"

"Waldron doesn't care about you." Robbie crossed his arms, daring me to contradict him. "He'll break your heart, princess. Trust me, I've seen enough of his kind to know."

Anger flared, anger that he dared stick his nose into my affairs, anger that he could be right. "Again, it's none of your business, Rob!" I snapped, making his eyebrows arch. "And I can take care of myself, okay? Quit butting in where you're not wanted."

Hurt glimmered briefly, but then it was gone. "Fine, princess." He smirked, holding up his hands. "Don't get your royal pink panties in a twist. Forget I said anything."

"I will." Tossing my head, I flounced out of the room without looking back.

Guilt gnawed at me as I wove through the halls toward the cafeteria. I regretted snapping at Robbie, but sometimes his Big Brother act went too far. Still, Robbie had always been that way—jealous, overprotective, forever looking out for me, like it was his job. I couldn't remember when I first met him; it felt like he'd always been there.

The cafeteria was noisy and dim. I hovered just inside the door, looking for Scott, only to see him at a table in the middle of the floor, surrounded by cheerleaders and football jocks. I hesitated. I couldn't just march up to that table and sit down; Angie Whitmond and her cheerleading squad would rip me to shreds.

Scott glanced up and saw me, and a lazy smile spread over his face. Taking that as an invitation, I started toward him, weaving my way past the tables. He flipped out his iPhone, pressed a button, and looked at me with half-lidded eyes, still grinning.

A phone rang close by.

I jumped a bit, but continued walking. Behind me, there were gasps, and then hysterical giggles. And then, the whispered conversation that always makes you think they're talking about you. I felt eyes on the back of my head. Trying to ignore it, I continued down the aisle.

Another phone rang.

And another.

And now, whispers and laughter were spreading like wildfire. For some reason, I felt horribly exposed, as if a spotlight shone right on me and I was on display. The laughter couldn't be directed at me, could it? I saw several people point in my direction, whispering among themselves, and tried my best to ignore them. Scott's table was only a few feet away.

"Hey, hot cheeks!" A hand smacked my ass and I shrieked. Spinning around, I glared at Dan Ottoman, a blond, pimply clarinet player from band. He leered back at me and winked. "Never took you for a player, girl," he said, trying to ooze charm but reminding me of a dirty Kermit the Frog. "Come down to band sometime. I've got a flute you can play."

"What are you talking about?" I snarled, but he snickered and held up his phone.

At first, the screen was blank. But then a message flashed across it in bright yellow. *"How is Meghan Chase like a cold beer?"* it read. I gasped, and the words disappeared as a picture flashed into view.

Me. Me with Scott in the parking lot, his arm around my shoulders, a wide leer on his face. Only now—my mouth dropped open—I was butt naked, staring at him in wonder, my eyes blank and stupid. He'd obviously used Photoshop; my "body" was obscenely skinny and featureless, like a doll's, my chest as flat as a twelve-year-old's. I froze, and my heart stopped beating as the second part of the message scrolled over the screen.

"She's smooth and goes down easy!"

The bottom dropped out of my stomach, and my cheeks flamed. Horrified, I looked up at Scott, to see his whole table roaring with laughter and pointing at me. Ring tones echoed through the cafeteria, and laughter pounded me like physical waves. I started trembling, and my eyes burned.

Covering my face, I turned and fled the cafeteria before I started wailing like a two-year-old. Shrieking laughter echoed around me, and tears stung my eyes like poison. I managed to cross the room without tripping over benches or my feet, bashed open the doors, and escaped into the hallway.

I spent nearly an hour in the corner stall of the girls' bathroom, sobbing my eyes out and planning my move to Canada, or possibly Fiji—somewhere far, far away. I didn't dare show my face to anyone in this state ever again. Finally, as the tears slowed and my gasping breaths returned to normal, I reflected on how miserable my life had become.

I guess I should feel honored, I thought bitterly, holding my breath as a group of girls flocked into the bathroom. *Scott took the time to personally ruin my life. I bet he's never done that to anyone else. Lucky me, I'm the world's biggest loser.* Tears threatened again, but I was tired of bawling and held them back.

At first, I planned to hole up in the bathroom until school ended. But, if anyone missed me from class, this would be the first place they'd look. So, I finally gathered the courage to tiptoe down to the nurse's office and fake a horrid stomachache so I could hide out there.

The nurse stood about four feet in thick-heeled loafers, but the look she gave me when I peered through the door suggested she wasn't going to take any teenage foolishness. Her skin looked like that of a shrunken walnut, her white hair was pulled into a severe bun, and she wore tiny gold glasses on the end of her nose.

"Well, now, Ms. Chase," she said in a gravelly, high-pitched voice, setting aside her clipboard. "What are you doing here?" I blinked, wondering how she knew me. I'd only been to the nurse's office once before, when a stray soccer ball hit me in the nose. Back then, the nurse was bony and tall, with an overbite that made her look like a horse. This plump, shriveled little woman was new, and slightly unnerving, with the way she stared at me.

"I have a stomachache," I complained, holding my navel like it was about to burst. "I just need to lie down for a few minutes."

"Of course, Ms. Chase. There are some cots in the back. I'll bring you something to make you feel better."

I nodded and moved into a room divided by several huge sheets. Except for myself and the nurse, the room was empty. Perfect. I chose a corner cot and lay back on the paper-covered mattress.

Moments later, the nurse appeared, handing me a Dixie cup full of something that bubbled and steamed. "Take this, you'll feel better," she said, pressing the cup into my hand.

I stared at it. The fizzling white liquid smelled like chocolate and herbs, except stronger, somehow, a mix so potent it made my eyes water. "What is it?" I asked.

The nurse just smiled and left the room.

I took a cautious sip and felt warmth spread from my throat down to my stomach. The taste was incredible, like the richest chocolate in the world, with just a hint of bitter aftertaste. I quaffed the rest in two gulps, holding the cup upside down to get the last drops.

Almost immediately, I felt sleepy. Lying back on the crinkly mattress, I closed my eyes for just a moment, and everything faded away.

I awoke to low voices, talking in furtive tones, just beyond the curtains. I tried to move, but it felt like my body was wrapped in cotton, my head filled with gauze. I struggled to keep my eyes open. On the other side of the sheets, I saw two silhouettes.

"Don't do anything reckless," warned a low, gravelly voice. *The nurse,* I thought, wondering, in my delirium, if she would give me more of that chocolaty stuff. "Remember, your duty is to watch the girl. You must not do anything that will draw attention."

"Me?" asked a tantalizingly familiar voice. "Draw attention to myself? Would I do such a thing?"

The nurse snorted. "If the entire cheerleading squad turns into mice, Robin, I will be very upset with you. Mortal adolescents are blind and cruel. You know that. You mustn't take revenge, no matter how you feel about the girl. Especially now. There are more worrisome things on the move."

I'm dreaming, I decided. *That must be it. What was in that drink, anyway?* In the dim light, the silhouettes playing across the curtain looked confusing and strange. The nurse, it seemed, was even smaller, barely three feet in height. The other shadow was even more peculiar: normal-size, but with strange protrusions on the side of his head that looked like horns, or ears.

The taller shadow sighed and moved to sit in a chair, crossing his long legs. "I've heard the same," he muttered. "Dark rumors are stirring. The Courts are restless. Seems like something is out there that has both of them scared."

"Which is why you must continue to be both her shield and her guardian." The nurse turned, putting both hands on her hips, her voice chiding. "I'm surprised you haven't given her the mistwine yet. She is sixteen today. The veil is beginning to lift."

"I know, I know. I'm getting to it." The shadow sighed, putting his head in his hands. "I'll take care of that later this afternoon. How is she?"

"Resting," said the nurse. "Poor thing, she was traumatized. I gave her a mild sleep potion that will knock her out until she goes home."

A chuckle. "The last kid who drank one of your 'mild' sleep potions didn't wake up for two weeks. You're one to talk about being inconspicuous."

The nurse's reply was garbled and broken, but I was almost sure she said, "She's her father's daughter. She'll be fine." Or maybe it was just me. The world went fuzzy, like an out-of-focus camera, and I knew nothing for a time.

"Meghan!"

Someone was shaking me awake. I cursed and flailed, momentarily confused, and finally lifted my head. My eyes felt

like they had ten pounds of sand in them, and sleep gook
crusted the corners, making it impossible to focus. Groaning, I wiped my lids and stared blearily into Robbie's face.
For a moment, his brow was furrowed with concern. Then I
blinked and he was his normal, grinning self.

"Wakey wakey, sleeping beauty," he teased as I struggled
to a sitting position. "Lucky you, school is out. It's time to
go home."

"Huh?" I muttered intelligently, wiping the last traces of
sleep snot from my eyes. Robbie snorted and pulled me to my
feet.

"Here," he said, handing me my backpack, heavy with
books. "You're lucky I'm such a great friend. I got notes for
all the classes you missed after lunch. Oh, and you're forgiven,
by the way. I won't even say 'I told you so.'"

He was speaking too fast. My brain was still asleep, my
mind foggy and disconnected. "What are you talking about?"
I mumbled, shrugging into my pack.

And then I remembered.

"I need to call my mom," I said, dropping back on the cot.
Robbie frowned and looked confused. "She has to come pick
me up," I elaborated. "No way am I getting on the bus, ever
again." Despair settled on me, and I hid my face in my hands.

"Look, Meghan," Robbie said, "I heard what happened.
It's not a big deal."

"Are you on crack?" I asked, glaring at him through my
fingers. "The whole school is talking about me. This will
probably go in the school paper. I'll be crucified if I show my
face in public. And you say it's not a big deal?"

I drew my knees to my chest and buried my head in them.
Everything was so horribly unfair. "It's my birthday," I moaned

into my jeans. "This isn't supposed to happen to people on their birthdays."

Robbie sighed. Dropping his bag, he sat down and put his arms around me, pulling me to his chest. I sniffled and shed a few tears into his jacket, listening to his heartbeat through his shirt. It thudded rapidly against his chest, like he'd been sprinting several miles.

"Come on." Robbie stood, pulling me up with him. "You can do this. And I promise, no one will care what happened today. By tomorrow, everyone will have forgotten about it." He smiled, squeezing my arm. "Besides, don't you have a driver's permit to get?"

That one bright spark in the black misery of my life gave me hope. I nodded, steeling myself for what was to come. We left the nurse's office together, Robbie's hand clasped firmly around mine.

"Just stick close," he muttered as we neared the crowded part of the hallway. Angie and three of her groupies stood in front of the lockers, chattering away and snapping their gum. My stomach tensed and my heart began to pound. Robbie squeezed my hand. "It's okay. Don't let go of me, and don't say anything to anyone. They won't even notice we're here."

As we neared the cluster of girls, I prepared for them to turn on me with their laughter and their ugly remarks. But we swept by them without so much as a glance, though Angie was in the midst of describing my shameful retreat from the cafeteria.

"And then she, like, started bawling," Angie said, her nasal voice cutting through the hall. "And I was like, omygod she's *such* a loser. But what can you expect from an inbred hillbilly?" Her voice dropped to a whisper and she leaned forward. "I heard her mom has an unnatural obsession with pigs, if you know what I mean."

The girls broke into a chorus of shocked giggles, and I almost snapped. Robbie, however, tightened his grip and pulled me away. I heard him mutter something under his breath, and felt a shudder go through the air, like thunder with no sound.

Behind us, Angie started to scream.

I tried to turn back, but Robbie yanked me onward, weaving through the crowd as the rest of the students jerked their heads toward the shrieking. But, for a split second, I saw Angie covering her nose with her hands, and her screams were sounding more and more like the squeals of a pig.

CHAPTER THREE

The Changeling

The bus ride home was silent, at least between Robbie and me. Partly because I didn't want to draw attention to myself, but mainly because I had a lot on my mind. We sat in the back corner, with me crushed against the window, staring at the trees flashing by. I had my iPod out and my headphones blasting my eardrums, but it was mostly an excuse not to talk to anyone.

Angie's piglike screams still echoed through my head. It was probably the most horrible sound I'd ever heard, and though she was a total bitch, I couldn't help but feel a little guilty. There was no doubt in my mind that Robbie had done something to her, though I couldn't prove it. I was actually afraid to bring it up. Robbie seemed like a different person now, quiet, brooding, watching the kids on the bus with predator-like intensity. He was acting weird—weird and creepy—and I wondered what was wrong with him.

Then there was that strange dream, which I was beginning to think hadn't really been a dream at all. The more I thought about it, the more I realized that the familiar voice talking to the nurse had been Robbie's.

Something was happening, something strange and creepy and terrifying, and the scariest part of all was that it wore a familiar, ordinary face. I snuck a glance at Robbie. How well did I know him, really know him? He'd been my friend for longer than I could remember, and yet I'd never been to his house, or met his parents. The few times I suggested meeting at his place, he'd always had some excuse not to; his folks were out of town, or they were remodeling the kitchen, a kitchen I'd never seen. That was strange, but what was weirder was the fact that I'd never wondered about it, never questioned it, until now. Robbie was simply *there,* like he'd been conjured out of nothing, with no background, no home, and no past. What was his favorite music? Did he have goals in life? Had he ever fallen in love?

Not at all, my mind whispered, disturbingly. *You don't know him at all.*

I shivered and looked out the window again.

The bus lurched to a halt at a four-way stop, and I saw we'd left the outskirts of town and were now heading into the boondocks. My neighborhood. Rain still spattered the windows, making the swampy marshlands blurry and indistinct, the trees fuzzy dark shapes through the glass.

I blinked and straightened up in my seat. Deep in the swamp, a horse and rider stood beneath the limbs of an enormous oak, as still as the trees themselves. The horse was a huge black animal with a mane and tail that rippled behind it, even drenched as it was. Its rider was tall and lean, garbed in silver and black. A dark cape fluttered from its shoulders. Through the rain, I caught the barest glimpse of a face: young, pale, strikingly handsome...staring right at me. My stomach lurched and I caught my breath.

"Rob," I murmured, pulling my headphones out, "look at tha—"

Robbie's face was inches from mine, staring out the window, his eyes narrowed to green slits, hard and dangerous. My stomach twisted and I leaned away from him, but he didn't notice me. His lips moved, and he whispered one word, so soft I barely caught it, even as close as we were.

"Ash."

"Ash?" I repeated. "Who's Ash?"

The bus coughed and lurched forward again. Robbie leaned back, his face so still it could've been carved from stone. Swallowing, I looked out the window, but the space beneath the oak was empty. Horse and rider were gone, like they'd never existed.

The weirdness kept getting weirder.

"Who's Ash?" I repeated, turning back to Robbie, who seemed to be in his own world. "Robbie? Hey!" I poked him in the shoulder. He twitched and finally looked at me. "Who is Ash?"

"Ash?" For a moment, his eyes were bright and feral, his face like that of a wild dog. Then he blinked and was normal again. "Oh, he's just an old buddy of mine, from long ago. Don't worry about it, princess."

His words slid over me strangely, like he was willing me to forget simply by requesting it. I felt a prickle of annoyance that he was hiding something, but it quickly faded, because I couldn't remember what we were talking about.

At our curb, Robbie leaped up as if the seat was on fire and rushed out the door. Blinking at his abrupt departure, I put my iPod safely in my backpack before leaving the bus. The last thing I wanted was for the expensive thing to get wet.

"I have to go," Robbie announced when I joined him on the pavement. His green eyes swept through the trees, as if he expected something to come crashing out of the woods. I gazed around, but except for some bird trilling overhead, the forest was quiet and still. "I...um...forgot something at home." He turned to me then with an apologetic look. "See you tonight, princess? I'll bring that champagne over later, okay?"

"Oh." I'd forgotten about that. "Sure."

"Go straight home, okay?" Robbie narrowed his eyes, his face intense. "Don't stop, and don't talk to anyone you meet, got it?"

I laughed nervously. "What are you, my mom? Are you going to tell me not to run with scissors and to look both ways before crossing the street? Besides," I continued as Robbie smirked, looking more like his normal self, "who would I meet way out here in the boondocks?" The image of the boy on the horse suddenly came to mind, and my stomach did that strange little flop again. Who was he? And why couldn't I stop thinking about him, if he even existed at all? Things were getting really odd. If it wasn't for Robbie's weird reaction on the bus, I would think the boy was another of my crazy hallucinations.

"Fine." Robbie waved, flashing his mischievous grin. "See you later, princess. Don't let Leatherface catch you on your way home."

I kicked at him. He laughed, bounced away, and sprinted off down the road. Shouldering my backpack, I trudged up the driveway.

"Mom?" I called, opening the front door. "Mom, I'm home."

Silence greeted me, echoing off the walls and floor, hanging heavy in the air. The stillness was almost a living thing, crouched in the center of the room, watching me with cold eyes. My heart began a loud, irregular thud in my chest. Something was wrong.

"Mom?" I called again, venturing into the house. "Luke? Anybody home?" The door creaked as I crept in farther. The television blared and flickered, playing a rerun of an old black-and-white sitcom, though the couch in front of it was empty. I switched it off and continued down the hall, into the kitchen.

For a moment, everything looked normal, except for the refrigerator door, swinging on its hinges. A small object on the floor caught my attention. At first, I thought it was a dirty rag. But, looking closer, I saw it was Floppy, Ethan's rabbit. The stuffed animal's head had been torn off, and cotton spilled from the hole in the neck.

Straightening, I heard a small noise on the other side of the dining table. I walked around, and my stomach twisted so violently that bile rose to my throat.

My mother lay on her back on the checkered tile floor, arms and legs flung akimbo, one side of her face covered in glistening crimson. Her purse, its contents scattered everywhere, lay beside one limp white hand. Standing over her in the doorway, his head cocked to one side like a curious cat, was Ethan.

And he was smiling.

"Mom!" I screamed, flinging myself down beside her. "Mom, are you okay?" I grabbed one shoulder and shook her, but it was like shaking a dead fish. Her skin was still warm, though, so she couldn't be dead. Right?

Where the hell is Luke? I shook her again, watching her head flop limply. It made my stomach turn. "Mom, wake up! Can you hear me? It's Meghan." I looked around frantically, then snatched a washrag off the sink. As I dabbed it over her bloodied face, I became aware again of Ethan standing in the doorway, his blue eyes now wide and teary.

"Mommy slipped," he whispered, and I noticed a clear, slick puddle on the floor in front of the refrigerator. Hand trembling, I dipped a finger in the goo and sniffed. Vegetable oil? What the hell? I wiped more blood off her face and noticed a small gash on her temple, nearly invisible beneath blood and hair.

"Will she die?" Ethan asked, and I glanced at him sharply. Though his eyes were huge and round, and tears brimmed in the corners, he sounded more curious than anything.

I wrenched my gaze away from my half brother. I had to get help. Luke was gone, so the only thing left would be to call for an ambulance. But, just as I stood to get the phone, Mom groaned, stirred, and opened her eyes.

My heart leaped. "Mom," I said as she struggled into a sitting position, a dazed look on her face. "Don't move. I'll call 911."

"Meghan?" Mom looked around, blinking. A hand came up to touch her cheek, and she stared at the blood on her fingers. "What happened? I…I must've fallen…"

"You hit your head," I replied, standing up and looking around for the phone. "You might have a concussion. Hold on, I'm calling the ambulance."

"The ambulance? No, no." Mom sat up, looking a little clearer. "Don't do that, honey. I'm fine. I'll just clean up and put on a Band-Aid. There's no need to go to that trouble."

"But, Mom—"

"I'm fine, Meg." Mom snatched the forgotten washrag and began wiping the blood off her face. "I'm sorry if I frightened you, but I'll be fine. It's only blood, nothing serious. Besides, we can't afford a big doctor's bill." She abruptly straightened and looked around the room. "Where's your brother?"

Startled, I looked back to the doorway, but Ethan was gone.

Mom's protests were wasted when Luke got home. He took one look at her pale, bandaged face, threw a fit, and insisted they go to the hospital. Luke can be stubbornly persistent when he needs to be, and Mom eventually buckled under the pressure. She was still calling out instructions to me—take care of Ethan, don't let him stay up too late, there's frozen pizza in the fridge—as Luke bundled her into his battered Ford and roared off down the driveway.

As the truck turned a corner and vanished from sight, the chilly silence descended on the house once more. I shivered, rubbing my arms, feeling it creep into the room and breathe down my neck. The house where I'd lived most of my life seemed unfamiliar and frightening, as if things lurked in the cupboards and around corners, waiting to grab me as I walked past. My gaze lingered on the crumpled remains of Floppy, strewn across the floor, and for some reason, it made me very sad and scared. No one in this house would rip up Ethan's favorite stuffed animal. Something was very wrong.

Footsteps padded over the floor. I turned to find Ethan in the doorway, staring at me. He looked strange without the rabbit in his arms, and I wondered why he wasn't upset about it.

"I'm hungry," he announced, making me blink. "Cook me something, Meggie."

I scowled at the demanding tone.

"It's not dinnertime yet, squirt," I told him, crossing my arms. "You can wait a couple hours."

His eyes narrowed, and his lips curled back from his teeth. For just a moment, I imagined they were jagged and sharp.

"I'm hungry *now*," he growled, taking a step forward. Dread shot through me and I recoiled.

Almost immediately, his face smoothed out again, his eyes enormous and pleading. "Please, Meggie?" he whined. "Please? I'm so hungry." He pouted, and his voice turned menacing. "Mommy didn't make me food, either."

"All right, fine! If it'll shut you up, fine." The angry words erupted from fear, and from a hot embarrassment because I was afraid. Of Ethan. Of my stupid, four-year-old half brother. I didn't know where these demonic mood swings of his were coming from, but I hoped they weren't the start of a trend. Maybe he was just upset because of Mom's accident. Maybe if I fed the brat, he'd fall asleep and leave me alone for the night. I stalked to the freezer, grabbed the pizza, and shoved it in the oven.

While the pizza cooked, I tried to clean up the puddle of vegetable oil in front of the refrigerator. I wondered how the stuff had ended up on the floor, especially when I found the empty bottle stuffed in the trash. I smelled like Crisco when I was done, and the floor still had a slick spot, but it was the best I could do.

The creak of the oven door startled me. I turned to see Ethan pulling it open and reaching inside.

"Ethan!" Grabbing his wrist, I yanked him back, ignoring his scream of protest. "What are you doing, you idiot? You want to burn yourself?"

"Hungry!"

"Sit down!" I snapped, plunking him into a dining chair. He actually tried to hit me, the little ingrate. I resisted the urge to smack him. "God, you're being snotty today. Sit there and be quiet. I'll get your food in a second."

When the pizza came out, he fell on it like a wild thing,

not waiting for it to cool. Astonished, I could only stare as he tore through the slices like a starved dog, barely stopping to chew as he gulped it down. Soon, his face and hands were smeared with sauce and cheese, and the pizza was rapidly diminished. In less than two minutes, he had consumed it all, down to the last crumb.

Ethan licked his hands, then raised his eyes to me and frowned. "Still hungry."

"You are not," I told him, snapping out of my daze. "If you eat anything else you'll get sick. Go play in your room or something."

He stared at me with a baleful expression, and it seemed that his skin grew darker, wrinkled, and shriveled beneath his baby fat. Without warning, he leaped off the chair, rushed me, and sank his teeth into my leg.

"Ow!" Pain lanced through my calf like an electrical shock. Grabbing his hair, I tried prying his teeth from my skin, but he clung to me like a leech and bit down harder. It felt like glass shards stabbing into my leg. Tears blurred my vision, and my knees almost buckled from the pain.

"Meghan!"

Robbie stood inside the front door, a backpack flung over his shoulder, his green eyes wide with shock.

Ethan released me, jerking his head toward the shout. Blood smeared his lips. Seeing Robbie, he hissed and—there's no other way to put it—*scuttled* away from us and up the stairs, vanishing from sight.

I shook so hard I had to sit down on the couch. My leg throbbed, and my breath came in short, uneven gasps. Blood, bright and vivid, seeped through my jeans like an unfurling blossom. Dazed, I stared at it, numbness deadening my limbs, freezing them in shock.

Robbie crossed the room in three strides and knelt beside me. Briskly, as if he'd done this kind of thing before, he began rolling up the cuff of one pant leg.

"Robbie," I whispered as he bent over his task, his long fingers surprisingly gentle. "What's happening? Everything's going crazy. Ethan just attacked me…like a wild dog."

"That wasn't your brother," Robbie muttered as he pushed back the material, revealing a bloody mess below my knee. An oval of jagged puncture wounds marred my leg, seeping blood, and the skin around them was already purpling. Rob whistled softly. "Nasty. Wait here. I'll be right back."

"Like I'm going anywhere," I replied automatically, and then his previous statement sank in. "Wait a minute. What do you mean, that wasn't Ethan? Who the hell else could it be?"

Rob ignored me. Walking to his backpack, he opened it and pulled out a long, green-tinted bottle and a tiny crystal cup. I frowned. Why was he going for champagne now? I was hurt, in pain, and my kid brother had turned into a monster. I was certainly not in the mood for celebrating.

With the utmost care, Robbie poured the champagne into the cup and walked back, being careful not to spill a single drop.

"Here," he said, giving it to me. The cup sparkled in his hand. "Drink this. Where do you keep the towels?"

I took it suspiciously. "In the bathroom. Just don't use Mom's good white ones." As Rob walked off, I peered into the tiny cup. There was barely enough for a swallow. It didn't look like champagne to me. I was expecting something fizzy white or pink, sparkling in the glass. The liquid in the cup was a deep, dark red, the color of blood. A fine mist writhed and danced on the surface.

"What is this?"

Robbie, returning from the bathroom with a white towel, rolled his eyes. "Do you have to question everything? It will help you forget the pain. Just drink it already."

I sniffed experimentally, expecting hints of roses or berries or some type of sweet scent mixed in with the alcohol.

It smelled of nothing. Nothing at all.

Oh, well. I raised the glass in a silent toast. "Happy birthday to me."

The wine filled my mouth, flooding my senses. It tasted of nothing, and everything. It tasted of twilight and mist, moonlight and frost, emptiness and longing. The room swayed, and I fell back against the couch, it was so strong. Reality blurred at the edges, wrapping me in a fuzzy haze. I felt sick and sleepy all at once.

By the time my senses cleared, Robbie was tying a bandage around my leg. I didn't remember him cleaning or dressing the wound. I felt numb and dazed, like a blanket had dropped over my thoughts, making it hard to concentrate.

"There," Robbie said, straightening up. "That's done. At least your leg won't fall off." His eyes swept up to mine, anxious and assessing. "How're you feeling, princess?"

"Un," I said intelligently, and tried to sweep the cobwebs from my brain. There was something I wasn't remembering, something important. Why was Robbie binding my leg? Had I hurt myself somehow?

I bolted upright.

"Ethan bit me!" I exclaimed, indignant and furious all over again. I turned on Robbie. "And you...you said that wasn't Ethan at all! What were you talking about? What's going on?"

"Relax, princess." Robbie tossed the bloody towel onto the floor and plopped onto a footstool. He sighed. "I was hoping it wouldn't come to this. My fault, I suppose. I shouldn't have left you alone today."

"What are you talking about?"

"You weren't supposed to see this, any of this," Robbie went on, to my utter confusion. He seemed to be talking more to himself than me. "Your Sight has always been strong, that was a given. Still, I didn't expect them to go after your family, too. This changes things."

"Rob, if you don't tell me what's going on—"

Robbie looked at me. His eyes gleamed, impish and feral. "Tell you? Are you sure?" His voice went soft and dangerous, and goose bumps crawled up my arms. "Once you start seeing things, you won't be able to stop. People have gone mad with too much knowledge." He sighed, and the menace dropped from his eyes. "I don't want that to happen to you, princess. It doesn't have to be this way, you know. I can make you forget all of this."

"Forget?"

He nodded and held up the wine bottle. "This is mistwine. You just had a swallow. A cup will make everything go back to normal." He balanced the bottle on two fingers, watching it sway back and forth. "One cup, and you'll be normal again. Your brother's behavior will not seem strange, and you won't remember anything weird or scary. You know what they say—ignorance is bliss, right?"

Despite my uneasiness, I felt a slow flame of anger burning my chest. "So, you want me to drink that…that stuff, and just forget about Ethan. Just forget about my only brother. That's what you're saying."

He raised an eyebrow. "Well, when you put it like that…"

The burning grew hot and furious, searing away the fear.

I clenched my fists. "Of course I won't forget about Ethan! He's my brother! Are you really that inhuman, or just stupid?"

To my surprise, a grin spread over his face. He dropped the bottle, caught it, and put it on the floor. "The first," he said, very softly.

That threw me. "What?"

"Inhuman." He was still grinning at me, the smile stretching his whole mouth so that his teeth gleamed in the fading light. "I warned you, princess. I'm not like you. And now, neither is your brother."

Despite the fear prickling my stomach, I leaned forward. "Ethan? What do you mean? What's wrong with him?"

"That wasn't Ethan." Robbie leaned back, crossing his arms. "The thing that attacked you today is a changeling."

CHAPTER FOUR

Puck

I stared at Robbie, wondering if this was another one of his stupid pranks. He sat there, observing me calmly, watching my reaction. Though he still wore a half grin, his eyes were hard and serious. He wasn't joking around.

"Ch-changeling?" I finally stammered, looking at him like he was insane. "Isn't that some kind of…of…"

"Faery," Robbie finished for me. "A changeling is a faery offspring that has been switched with a human child. Usually, a troll's or goblin's, though the sidhe—the faery nobility—have been known to make the switch, as well. Your brother has been replaced. That thing is not Ethan, any more than I am."

"You're crazy," I whispered. If I wasn't sitting, I'd be backing away from him toward the door. "You've gone off the deep end. Time to cut back on the anime, Rob. There's no such thing as faeries."

Robbie sighed. "Really? That's what you're going with? How predictable." He leaned back and crossed his arms. "I thought better of you, princess."

"Thought better of *me?*" I cried, leaping off the couch.

"Listen to yourself! You really expect me to believe that my brother is some kind of pixie with glitter dust and butterfly wings?"

"Don't be stupid," Rob said mildly. "You have no idea what you're talking about. You're thinking 'Tinker Bell,' which is a typical human response to the word *faery*. The real fey aren't like that at all." He paused a moment. "Well, except for the piskies, of course, but that's a different story altogether."

I shook my head, my thoughts spinning in several directions at once. "I can't deal with this right now," I muttered and staggered away from him. "I have to check on Ethan."

Robbie only shrugged, leaned back against the wall, and put his hands behind his head. After one final glare at him, I rushed up the stairs and opened the door to Ethan's bedroom.

It was a mess, a war zone of broken toys, books, and scattered clothes. I looked around for Ethan, but the room appeared empty, until I heard a faint scratching noise under his bed.

"Ethan?" Kneeling down, pushing away broken action figures and snapped Tinkertoys, I peered into the space between the mattress and the floor. In the shadows, I could just make out a small lump huddled in the corner with his back to me. He was trembling.

"Ethan," I called softly. "Are you all right? Why don't you come out a second? I'm not mad at you." Well, that was a lie, but I was more shaken than angry. I wanted to drag Ethan downstairs and prove that he wasn't a troll or a changeling or whatever Robbie said he was.

The lump stirred a little, and Ethan's voice drifted out of the gap. "Is the scary man still here?" he asked in a small, frightened voice. I might've been sympathetic, if my calf wasn't throbbing so much.

"No," I lied. "He's gone now. You can come out." Ethan didn't move, and my irritation sparked. "Ethan, this is ridiculous. Get out of there already, will you?" I stuck my head farther under the mattress and reached for him.

Ethan turned on me with a hiss, eyes burning yellow, and lunged at my arm. I jerked it back as his teeth, jaggedly pointed like a shark's, snapped together with a horrid clicking sound. Ethan snarled, his skin the ghastly blue of a drowned infant's, bared teeth shining in the darkness. I shrieked, scrabbling back, Lego blocks and Tinkertoys biting into my palms. Hitting the wall, I leaped to my feet, turned, and fled the room.

And ran smack into Robbie, standing outside the door.

He grabbed my shoulders as I screamed and started hitting him, barely conscious of what I was doing. He bore the attack wordlessly, simply holding me in place, until I collapsed against him and buried my head in his chest. And he held me as I sobbed out my fear and anger.

At last, the tears stopped, leaving me drained and utterly exhausted. I sniffed and backed away, wiping my eyes on my palm, shaking. Robbie still stood there quietly, his shirt damp with my tears. The door to Ethan's bedroom was shut, but I could hear faint thumps and cackling laughter beyond the door.

I shivered, looking up at Robbie. "Ethan is really gone?" I whispered. "He's not just hiding somewhere? He's really gone?"

Robbie nodded gravely. I looked at Ethan's bedroom door and bit my lip. "Where is he now?"

"Probably in Faeryland." Stated so simply, I almost laughed from the sheer ridiculousness of it all. Ethan had been stolen by faeries and replaced with an evil doppelgänger. *Faeries* kidnapped my brother. I was tempted to pinch myself to see if this was a twisted dream or hallucination. Maybe I had fallen into a drunken stupor on the couch. On impulse, I bit the inside of my cheek, hard. The sharp pain and taste of blood told me this was, indeed, real.

I looked to Robbie, and his grave expression banished the last of my doubts. A sick feeling rose to my stomach, making me nauseous and afraid.

"So…" I swallowed and forced myself to be calm. Okay, Ethan was kidnapped by faeries; I could deal with this. "What do we do now?"

Robbie raised one shoulder. "That's up to you, princess. There are human families that have raised changelings as their own, though they are usually unaware of the child's true nature. Generally speaking, if you feed it and leave it alone, it will settle into its new home without too much trouble. Changelings make a nuisance of themselves at first, but most families adapt." Robbie grinned, but it was an attempt at lightheartedness rather than humor. "Hopefully, your folks will think he's just going through a late terrible twos."

"Robbie, that thing bit me, and probably made Mom slip and fall in the kitchen. It's more than a nuisance, it's dangerous." I glared at Ethan's closed door and shuddered. "I want it gone. I want my brother back. How do we get rid of it?"

Robbie sobered. "Well, there are ways of getting rid of changelings," he began, looking uncomfortable. "One old method is to brew beer or cook stew in eggshells, and that will make the changeling comment on the weirdness of it. But that method was for infants who'd been switched—since the baby was too young to speak, the parents knew that the impostor was a changeling and the real parents had to take it back. I don't think it'll work for someone older, like your brother."

"Great. What's another way?"

"Er, the other way is to beat the changeling near to death, until the screams force the fey parents to return the real child. Barring that, you could stick him in the oven and cook him alive—"

"Stop." I felt sick. "I can't do any of those things, Robbie. I just can't. There has to be another way."

"Well…" Rob looked hesitant and scratched the back of his neck. "The only other way is to travel into the faery lands and take him back. Bringing the real child into the home again will force the changeling to leave. But…" He paused, as if on the verge of saying something, only to think better of it.

"But what?"

"But…you don't know who took your brother. And without that knowledge, you'll just be walking in circles. And, if you're wondering, walking in circles in Faeryland is a very, very bad idea."

I narrowed my eyes. "I don't know who took him," I agreed, staring hard at Robbie, "but you do."

Robbie shuffled nervously. "I have a guess."

"Who?"

"It's just a guess, mind you. I could be wrong. Don't go jumping to conclusions."

"Robbie!"

He sighed. "The Unseelie Court."

"The what?"

"The Unseelie Court," Robbie repeated. "The Court of Mab, Queen of Air and Darkness. Sworn enemies of King Oberon and Queen Titania. Very powerful. Very nasty."

"Wait, wait, wait." I held up my hands. "Oberon? Titania? Like from *A Midsummer Night's Dream*? Aren't those just ancient myths?"

"Ancient, yes," Robbie said. "Myths, no. The faery lords

are immortal. Those who have songs, ballads, and stories written about them never die. Belief, worship, imagination—we were born of the dreams and fears of mortals, and if we are remembered, even in some small way, we will always exist."

"You keep saying 'we,'" I pointed out. "As though you're one of those immortal faeries. As though you're one of them." Robbie smiled, a proud, impish smile, and I gulped. "Who are you, anyway?"

"Ah, well." Robbie shrugged, trying to look modest and failing entirely. "If you've read *A Midsummer Night's Dream,* you might remember me. There was this unfortunate incident, completely unplanned, where I gave someone a donkey's head and made Titania fall in love with him."

I ran through the play in my mind. I'd read it in the seventh grade, but had forgotten most of the plot. There were so many characters, so many names to sift through, people falling in and out of love so often it was ridiculous. I remembered a few human names: Hermia, Helena, Demetrius. On the faery side, there was Oberon and Titania and...

"Shit," I whispered, falling back against the wall. I stared at Robbie with new eyes. "Robbie Goodfell. Robin...you're Robin Goodfellow."

Robbie grinned. "Call me Puck."

Puck. *The* Puck was standing in my hallway.

"No way," I whispered, shaking my head. This was Robbie, my closest friend. I would've known if he was an ancient faery. Wouldn't I?

Frighteningly, the more I thought about it, the more likely it seemed. I'd never seen Robbie's house, or his parents. The teachers all loved him, though he never did a lick of schoolwork and slept through most of the classes. And strange things happened when he was around: mice and frogs ended up in desks, or names were switched around on term papers. Though Robbie Goodfell thought these scenarios absolutely hilarious, no one ever suspected him.

"No," I muttered again, backing away toward my room. "That's impossible. Puck is a legend, a myth. I don't believe it."

Robbie gave me that eerie smile. "Then, princess, by all means, let me assure you."

His arms rose from his sides, as if he might levitate into the air. From downstairs, I heard the front door creak open, and I hoped Mom and Luke weren't home yet. *Yeah, Mom, Ethan's turned into a monster and my best friend thinks he's a faery. How was your day?*

An enormous black bird swooped into the hallway. I yelped and ducked as the raven, or crow or whatever it was, made a beeline straight for Robbie and perched on his arm. They watched me, the pair of them, with glittering eyes, and Robbie smiled.

A rush of wind, and suddenly, the air was filled with screaming black birds, swooping in from the open door. I gasped and ducked as the cloud of ravens filled the hallway, their raucous cries nearly deafening me. They swirled around Robbie, a tornado of beating wings and sharp claws, tearing at him with talons and beaks. Feathers flew everywhere, and Robbie disappeared within the swirling mass. Then, as one, the birds scattered, flying out the open door as swiftly as they had come. As the last bird swooped outside, the door slammed behind it, and silence descended once more. I caught my breath and glanced at Rob.

Robbie was gone. Only a swirl of black feathers and dust motes remained in the place where he'd stood.

It was too much. I felt my sanity unravel like frayed cloth.

With a choked scream, I turned and fled into my room, slamming the door behind me. Flinging myself under my bed-covers, I put the pillow over my head and shook, hoping that when I woke up, things would be normal.

My door opened, and the sound of wings fluttered into my room. I didn't want to look and pulled the covers tighter around me, willing the nightmare to end. I heard a sigh, and footsteps padded over the floor.

"Well, I tried to warn you, princess."

I peeked out. Robbie stood there, looking down at me, a pained smile on his face. Seeing him, I felt relieved, angry, and terrified at the same time. I threw off the covers and sat up, narrowing my eyes as I stared at him. Robbie waited, hands in the pockets of his jeans, as if daring me to contradict him some more.

"You really are Puck?" I said finally. "*The* Puck? Like in the stories?"

Robbie/Puck gave a little bow. "The one and only."

My heart was still pounding. I took a deep breath to calm it and glared at the stranger in my room. My emotions churned; I didn't know what to feel. I settled on anger; Robbie had been my best friend for years, and he never saw fit to share his secret with me. "You could have told me sooner," I said, trying not to sound hurt. "I would have kept your secret." He only smirked and raised an eyebrow, infuriating me even more. "Fine. Go back to Faeryland, or wherever you come from. Aren't you supposed to be Oberon's jester or something? Why were you hanging around *me* so long?"

"You wound me, princess." Robbie sounded anything but hurt. "And after I made up my mind to help you get your brother back."

My anger vanished instantly, replaced with fear. With all the talk of fey and faery lords, I'd nearly forgotten about Ethan.

I shivered as my stomach twisted into a tight little ball. This still felt like something out of a nightmare. But Ethan was gone, and faeries were real. I had to accept that now. Robbie stood there, gazing at me expectantly. A black feather dropped from his hair, spiraling down to the bed. Gingerly, I picked it up, twirling it in my fingers. It felt solid and real.

"You'll help me?" I whispered.

He gave me a shrewd look, one corner of his mouth turning up. "Do you know a way into Faery by yourself?"

"No."

"Then you need my help." Robbie smiled and rubbed his hands together. "Besides, it's been a while since I've gone home, and nothing ever happens here. Storming the Unseelie Court sounds like fun."

I didn't share his enthusiasm. "When do we leave?" I asked.

"Now," Robbie replied. "The sooner the better. Do you have anything you want to take, princess? You might not be back for a while."

I nodded, trying to stay calm. "Just give me a minute."

Robbie nodded and walked into the hallway. I snatched my bright orange backpack and tossed it on the bed, wondering what to take. What did one need for an overnight trip to Faeryland? I grabbed jeans and an extra shirt, a flashlight, and a bottle of aspirin, stuffing them into the pack. Walking down to the kitchen, I tossed in a Coke and a couple of bags of chips, hoping Robbie would know where to find food on the journey. Finally, not even knowing why, I grabbed my iPod, zipping it into the side pocket.

Mom was supposed to take me to the DMV today. I hesitated, biting my lip. What would Mom and Luke think when they found me gone? I'd always followed the rules, never sneaking out—except that one time with Robbie—never staying up past curfew. I wondered what Rob meant when he said we'd be gone "awhile." Luke might not even notice I'd left, but Mom would worry. Grabbing an old homework sheet, I started to write her a quick note, but stopped, my pen hovering over the paper.

What are you going to tell her? "Dear Mom, Ethan's been kidnapped by faeries. Gone to get him back. Oh, and don't trust the Ethan that's here—he's really a faery changeling." It sounded insane even to me. I hesitated, thinking, then scrawled a quick:

Mom, there's something I have to take care of. I'll be back soon, I promise. Don't worry about me. Meghan

I stuck the note on the refrigerator door, trying not to think that I might never see home again. Shouldering the pack, feeling my insides squirm like a nest of snakes, I climbed the stairs.

Robbie waited on the landing, arms crossed over his chest, wearing a lazy grin. "Ready?"

Apprehension tickled my stomach. "Will it be very dangerous?"

"Oh, extremely," Robbie said, walking up to Ethan's bedroom door. "That's what makes it fun. You can die in so many interesting ways—skewered on a glass sword, dragged underwater and eaten by a kelpie, turned into a spider or a rosebush for all time—" He looked back at me. "Well, are you coming or not?"

I noticed my hands were shaking and held them to my chest. "Why are you saying these things?" I whispered. "Are you trying to scare me?"

"Yes," Robbie replied, unabashed. He paused at Ethan's

door, one hand on the knob, and stared at me. "These are the things you're going to face, princess. I'm giving you fair warning now. Still think you want to go? My previous offer still stands."

I remembered the taste of the mistwine, the desperate longing for more, and shivered. "No," I said quickly. "I won't leave Ethan with a bunch of monsters. I've lost a father already—I won't lose a brother, as well."

And then, something occurred to me, something that left me breathless, wondering why I didn't think of it before. *Dad.* My heart pounded, recalling half-remembered dreams, where my father vanished beneath a pond and never resurfaced. What if he'd been kidnapped by faeries, as well? I could find Ethan *and* my dad, and bring them *both* home!

"Let's go," I demanded, looking Robbie in the eyes. "Come on, we've wasted enough time here. If we're gonna do this, let's get it over with."

Rob blinked, and a strange look passed over his face. For a moment, it seemed like he wanted to say something. But then he shook himself, like he was coming out of a trance, and the moment was gone.

"All right, then. Don't say I didn't warn you." He grinned, and the gleam in his eyes grew brighter. "First things first. We have to find an entrance to the Nevernever. That's Faeryland to you. It's not a place you can just walk to, and the doors are usually very well hidden. Fortunately, I have a good idea of where one is lurking." He grinned, turned away, and pounded on Ethan's bedroom door. "Knock, knock!" he called in a high, singsong voice.

For a moment, silence. Then came a thud and a crash, as if something heavy had been hurled at the door. "Go away!" snarled the voice from within.

"Ah, no. That's not how the joke goes," called Rob. "I say 'knock, knock,' and you're supposed to answer with 'who's there?'"

"Fuck off!"

"Nope, that's still wrong." Robbie seemed unperturbed. I, however, was horrified at Ethan's language, though I knew it wasn't him. "Here," continued Rob in an amiable voice, "I'll go through the whole thing, so you'll know how to an-swer next time." He cleared his throat and pounded the door again. "Knock, knock!" he bellowed. "Who's there? Puck! Puck who? Puck, who will turn you into a squealing pig and stuff you in the oven if you don't get out of our way!" And with that, he banged open the door.

The thing that looked like Ethan stood on the bed, a book in each hand. With a hiss, he hurled them at the doorway. Robbie dodged, but one paperback hit me in the stomach and I grunted.

"Please," I heard Rob mutter, and a ripple went through the air. Suddenly, all the books in the room flapped their covers, rose off the floor and shelves, and began dive-bombing Ethan like a flock of enraged seagulls. I could only stare, feeling my life get more surreal by the second. The fake Ethan hissed and snarled, swatting at the books as they buzzed around him, until one hit him smack in the face and tumbled him off the mattress. Spitting in fury, he darted under the bed. I heard claws scrabbling against the wood as his feet vanished into the crawl space. Curses and growls drifted out from the darkness.

Robbie shook his head. "Amateurs." He sighed as the books swooping around the room froze midflight and rained to the floor with echoing thuds. "Let's go, princess."

I shook myself and picked my way over fallen books, join-ing Robbie in the middle of the room. "So," I ventured, trying to sound casual, as if flying books and faeries were something I encountered every day. "Where's this entrance to Faeryland? Will you have to make a magic ring or cast a spell or something?"

Rob snickered. "Not exactly, princess. You're making it too complicated. Doorways to the Nevernever tend to appear in places where there is a lot of belief, creativity, or imagination. Often you can find one in a child's bedroom closet, or under his bed."

Floppy's afraid of the man in the closet. I shivered, mentally apologizing to my half brother. When I found him again, I'd be sure to tell him I believed in the monsters, too.

"The closet, then," I murmured, stepping over books and toys to reach it. My hand shook a bit as I grabbed the doorknob. *No turning back now,* I told myself, and pulled it open.

A tall, emaciated figure with a narrow face and sunken eyes stared at me as the door swung open. A black suit clung to its rail-thin body, and a bowler hat perched atop its pointed head. It blinked wide, staring at me, and bloodless lips pulled back in a grimace, revealing thin, pointed teeth. I leaped back with a shriek.

"My closet!" hissed the figure. A spiderlike hand darted out and grabbed the doorknob. "My closet! Mine!" And it slammed the door with a bang.

Robbie gave an exasperated sigh as I skittered behind him, my heart careening around my rib cage like a bat. "Bogeys," he muttered, shaking his head. He strode to the door, tapped on it three times, and flung it open.

This time, the space stood empty, except for hanging shirts, stacked boxes, and normal closet things. Robbie shoved aside the clothes, maneuvered around the boxes, and put a hand to the back wall, tracing his fingers along the wood. Curious, I edged closer.

"Where are you?" he muttered, feeling along the wall. I crept to the doorway and peered over his shoulder. "I know you're here. Where is… Aha."

Crouching down, he took a breath and blew against the wall. Instantly, a cloud of dust arose, billowing around him and sparkling like orange glitter.

When he straightened, I saw a gold handle on the back wall, and the faint outline of a door, pale light shining through the bottom crack.

"Come on, princess." Rob turned and beckoned me forward. His eyes glowed green in the darkness. "This is our ride. Your one-way ticket to the Nevernever."

I hesitated, waiting for my pulse to slow to something resembling normal. It didn't. *This is insane,* a small, scared part of me whispered. Who knew what waited through that doorway, what horrors lurked in the shadows? I might never come home again. This was my last chance to turn back.

No, I told myself. *I can't turn back. Ethan is out there, somewhere. Ethan is counting on me.* I took a deep breath and one step forward.

A wrinkled hand shot from beneath the bed, latching on to my ankle. It yanked savagely and I nearly fell, as a snarl echoed from the dark space beneath. With a shriek, I kicked free of the flailing claw, charged blindly into the closet, and slammed the door behind me.

CHAPTER FIVE

The Nevernever

In the musty darkness of Ethan's closet, I pressed a hand to my chest and waited once more for my heartbeat to return to normal. Blackness surrounded me, except for the thin rectangle of light outlined against the far wall. I couldn't see Robbie, but I felt his presence close by, heard his quiet breathing in my ear.

"Ready?" he whispered, his breath warm on my skin. And before I could answer, he pushed the door back with a creak, revealing the Nevernever.

Pale silver light flooded the room. The clearing beyond the door frame was surrounded by enormous trees, so thick and tangled I couldn't see the sky through the branches. A curling mist crept along the ground, and the woods were dark and still, as if the forest was trapped in perpetual twilight. Here and there, brilliant splashes of color stood out among the gray. A patch of flowers, their petals a shocking electric-blue, waved gently in the mist. A creeper vine snaked around the trunk of a dying oak, long red thorns a stark contrast to the tree it was killing.

A warm breeze blew into the closet, carrying with it a

shocking assortment of smells—smells that should not be together in one place. Crushed leaves and cinnamon, smoke
and apples, fresh earth, lavender, and the faint, cloying scent
of rot and decay. For a moment, I caught a tang of something
metallic and coppery, wrapped around the smell of rot, but it
was gone in the next breath. Clouds of insects swarmed overhead, and if I listened hard I could almost imagine I heard
singing. The forest was still at first, but I then caught movement deep in the shadows, and heard leaves rustle all around
us. Invisible eyes seemed to watch me from every angle, boring into my skin.

Robbie, his hair a bright flame atop his head, stepped
through the doorway, gazed around, and laughed. "Home."
He sighed, flinging his arms wide, as if to embrace it all. "I'm
finally home." He spun in place and, with another laugh, fell
backward into the mist, like he was making a snow angel,
and vanished.

I gulped and took a cautious step forward. Mist swirled
around my ankles like a living thing, caressing my skin with
damp fingers. "Rob?"

The silence mocked me. Out of the corner of my eye,
something big and white darted into the trees like quicksil-
ver. "Rob?" I called again, edging to the place he had fallen.
"Where are you? Robbie?"

"Boo." Rob appeared behind me, rising out of the mist
like a vampire from its coffin. To say I screamed was a bit of
an understatement.

"A little jumpy today, aren't we?" Robbie laughed and
darted out of reach before I could kill him. "Time to switch
to decaf, princess. If you're going to shriek at every bogey that
jumps out and says 'boo,' you'll be exhausted before we reach
the edge of the woods."

He had changed. Hunter-green pants and a thick brown hoodie replaced his jeans and ratty T-shirt. I couldn't see his feet very well in the mist, but it looked like he'd traded his sneakers for soft leather boots. His face was leaner, harsher, with sharp angles and pointed features. Combined with his bright auburn hair and green eyes, he reminded me of a grinning fox.

But the most noticeable difference was his ears. Slender and pointed, they jutted out from the sides of his head, like… well, like an elf's. And, in that moment, all traces of Robbie Goodfell disappeared. The boy I'd known for most of my life was gone, like he never existed, and only Puck remained.

"What's the matter, princess?" Puck yawned, stretching his long limbs. Was it my imagination, or had he gotten taller, too? "You look like you lost your best friend."

I ignored the question, not wanting to dwell on it. "How did you do that?" I asked, to steer the conversation elsewhere. "Your clothes, I mean. They're different. And the way you made the books fly around the room. Was it magic?"

Puck grinned. "Glamour," he said, as if that meant anything to me at all. I frowned at him, and he sighed. "I didn't have time to change before we came here, and my lord King Oberon frowns on wearing mortal clothes to court. So I used glamour to make myself presentable. Just like I used glamour to make myself look human."

"Wait a minute." I thought back to the dream conversation between Robbie and the nurse. "Are there others like you… you faery-types, walking around back home? Right under everyone's noses?"

Puck gave me a very eerie smile. "We're everywhere, princess," he said firmly. "Under your bed, in your attic, walking past you on the street." His smile grew wider, more wolfish.

"Glamour is fueled by the dreams and imagination of mortals. Writers, artists, little boys pretending to be knights—the fey are drawn to them like moths to a flame. Why do you think so many children have imaginary friends? Even your brother had one. Floppy, I think he called it, though that wasn't its true name. A pity the changeling managed to kill it."

My stomach felt tight. "And...no one can see you?"

"We're invisible, or we use glamour to hide our true nature." Puck leaned against a tree, lacing his hands behind his head in a very Robbie-like fashion. "Don't look so shocked, princess. Mortals have perfected the art of not seeing what they don't expect to be there. Though, there are a few rare humans who can see through the mist and the glamour. Usually, these are very special individuals—innocent, naive dreamers—and the fey are even more attracted to them."

"Like Ethan," I murmured.

Puck gave me a strange look, one corner of his mouth quirked up. "Like you, princess." He seemed about to say something else, but then a branch snapped somewhere in the tangled darkness.

He straightened quickly. "Whoops, time to go. It's dangerous to linger in any one place. We'll attract unwanted attention."

"What?" I exclaimed as he strode across the clearing, moving as gracefully as a deer. "I thought you said this was home."

"The Nevernever is home to all fey," Puck said without looking back. "It's divided into territories, or more technically, Courts. The Seelie Court is Oberon's domain, while Mab rules the Unseelie territories. While in the Courts, it is usually forbidden to torment, maim, or kill another fey without permission from its rulers.

"However," he continued, looking back at me, "right now,

we are in neutral territory, home of the wild fey. Here, as you humans put it, all bets are off. The things coming at us now could be a herd of satyrs who will make you dance until you're exhausted, then rape you one by one, or it could be a pack of hedge wolves that will tear us both apart. Either way, I don't think you want to hang around."

I was afraid again. It seemed I was always afraid. I didn't want to be here, in this eerie forest, with this person I only thought I knew. I wanted to go home. Only, home had become a frightening place as well, almost as much as the Nevernever. I felt lost and betrayed, out of place in a world that wished me harm.

Ethan, I reminded myself. *You're doing this for Ethan. Once you get him, you can go home and everything will go back to normal.*

The rustling grew louder, and twigs snapped as whatever was out there drew closer. "Princess," Puck snapped, right next to me. I jumped and bit down a shriek as he grabbed my wrist. "The aforementioned nasties have picked up our scent and are coming for us." Though his voice was casual, I could see the strain in his eyes. "If you don't want your first day in the Nevernever to be your last, I suggest we move."

I looked back and saw the door we came through standing upright in the middle of the clearing. "Will we be able to get back home this way?" I asked as Puck pulled me along.

"Nope." When I stared at him in horror, he shrugged. "Well, you can't expect the doors to stand around in one place, princess. Don't worry, though. You have me, remember? When the time comes, we'll find the way home."

We ran for the far side of the clearing, straight for a tangle of bushes with hooked yellow thorns as long as my thumb. I held back, sure we'd be sliced to ribbons, but as we neared, the branches shivered and peeled away from us, revealing a narrow path cutting through the trees. As we stepped through, the bushes knitted together again, hiding the trail and protecting our retreat.

We walked for hours, or at least it felt that way to me. Puck kept up a steady pace, neither hurrying nor slowing down, and in time the sounds of pursuit faded away. Sometimes the trail split, wending off in different directions, but Puck always chose a path without hesitation. Many times, I'd catch movement from the corner of my eye—a flash of color in the brush, a figure silhouetted between the trees—but when I turned, there'd be nothing. Sometimes, I almost swore I heard singing or music, but, of course, it would fade when I tried to focus on it. The sickly luminescence of the forest never dimmed or brightened, and when I asked Puck what time night would fall, he cocked an eyebrow at me and said night would come when it was ready.

Annoyed, I checked my watch, wondering how long we'd been traveling. I received an unpleasant shock. The slender hands were frozen in place. Either the watch's battery was dead, or something else was interfering.

Or maybe time doesn't exist in this place. I don't know why I found that immensely disturbing, but I did.

My feet were aching, my stomach hurt, and my legs were burning with exhaustion when the eternal twilight finally began to dim. Puck stopped, gazing up at the sky, where an enormous moon glimmered over the treetops, so close you could see pits and craters marring the surface.

"I suppose we should rest for the night." Puck sounded reluctant. He gave me a sideways grin as I collapsed on a moldy log. "We wouldn't want you stumbling onto a dancing mound, or following a white bunny down a dark hole.

Come on, I know a place not far from here where we can sleep undisturbed."

He took my hand and pulled me to my feet. My limbs screamed in protest, and I almost sat down again. I was tired, cranky, and the last thing I wanted was more hiking. Gazing around, I saw a lovely little pond through a stand of trees. The water shimmered in the moonlight, and I paused, gazing out over the mirrored surface. "Why not stop there?" I asked.

Puck took one look at the pond, grimaced, and pulled me onward. "Ah, no," he said quickly. "Too many nasties lurking underwater—kelpies and glaistigs and mermaids and such. Best not to risk it."

I looked back and saw a dark shape breach the perfect surface of the pond, sending ripples across the still water. The top of a horse's head, coal-black and slick like a seal, watched me with baleful white eyes. With a gasp, I hurried on.

A few minutes later, we came to the trunk of a huge, gnarled tree. The bark was so knobby and rough that I could almost see faces peering out of the trunk. It reminded me of wrinkled old men, stacked atop each other and waving their crooked arms indignantly.

Puck knelt among the roots and knocked on the wood. I peered over his shoulder and, with a start, saw a tiny door, barely a foot tall, near the base of the tree. As I watched, wide-eyed, the door creaked open, and a head peered out suspiciously.

"Eh? Who's there?" a rough, squeaky voice asked as I stared in wonder. The little man's skin was the color of walnuts; his hair looked like a bundle of twigs sticking out of his scalp. He wore a brown tunic and brown leggings, and looked like a stick come to life, except for the eyes peering out of his face, black and shiny like a beetle's.

"Good evening, Twiggs," Puck greeted politely.

The little man blinked, squinting up at the figure towering over him. "Robin Goodfellow?" he squeaked at last. "Haven't seen you round these parts in a while. What brings you to my humble tree?"

"Escort service," Puck replied, shifting to the side so that Twiggs could get a clear view of me. Those beady eyes fixed on me, blinking in confusion. Then, suddenly, they got huge and round, as Twiggs looked back at Puck.

"Is…is that…?"

"It is."

"Does she…?"

"No."

"Oh, my." Twiggs opened the door wide, beckoning with a sticklike arm. "Come in, come in. Quickly, now. Before the dryads catch sight of you, the irritating gossips." He vanished inside, and Puck turned to me.

"I'll never be able to fit in there," I told him before he could say a word. "There's no way I'm going to squeeze through, unless you've got a magic toadstool that'll shrink me to the size of a wasp. And I'm not eating anything like that. I've seen *Alice in Wonderland,* you know."

Puck grinned and took my hand.

"Close your eyes," he told me, "and just walk."

I did, half expecting to walk nose first into the tree, courtesy of a great Robbie-prank. When nothing happened, I almost peeked but thought better of it. The air turned warm, and I heard a door slam behind me, when Puck said I could open my eyes again.

I stood in a cozy, round room, the walls made of smooth red wood, the floor covered with mossy carpet. A flat rock on three stumps served as a table in the center of the room, displaying berries the size of soccer balls. A rope ladder hung on the far wall, and when my gaze followed it up, I nearly fainted. Dozens of insects crawled on the walls or hovered in the air high above us, for the trunk extended farther than I could see. Each bug was the size of a cocker spaniel, and their rear ends glowed a luminescent yellow-green.

"You've been renovating, Twiggs," Puck said, sitting on a bundle of furs that passed for a couch. I looked closer and saw the head of a squirrel still attached to the skin, and had to look away. "This place was barely a hole in the tree when I saw it last."

Twiggs looked pleased. He was our height now—actually, I guess we were more *his* height—and up close he smelled of cedar and moss.

"Yes, I've grown quite fond of it," Twiggs said, walking over to the table. He picked up a knife and split a berry into thirds, arranging the pieces on wooden plates. "Still, I might have to move soon. The dryads whisper to me, tell me dark things. They say parts of the wyldwood are dying, vanishing more every day. No one knows what is causing it."

"You know what's causing it," Puck said, draping the squirrel tail over his lap. "We all do. This is nothing new."

"No." Twiggs shook his head. "Mortal disbelief has always taken a bit of the Nevernever, but not like this. This is…different. It's hard to explain. You'll see what I mean if you go any farther."

He handed us each a plate with a huge slab of red berry, half an acorn, and a pile of what looked like steamed white grubs. Despite the weirdness of the day, I was ravenous after hours of hiking. The berry wedge tasted tart and sweet, but I wasn't about to touch the maggoty-looking things and gave them all to Puck. After dinner, Twiggs made me a bed of squirrel hides and chipmunk fur, and though I was mildly grossed out, I fell asleep immediately.

That night, I dreamed.

In my dream, my house was dark and still, the living room cloaked in shadow. A brief glimpse of the wall clock pronounced it 3:19 a.m. I floated through the living room past the kitchen and made my way up the stairs. The door to my room was closed, and I heard Luke's grizzly-bear snores coming from the master bedroom, but at the end of the hall, Ethan's door stood slightly ajar. I padded down the hallway and peeked in through the crack.

A stranger stood in Ethan's bedroom, a tall, lean figure dressed in silver and black. A boy, perhaps a little older than me, though it was impossible to tell his exact age. His body was youthful, but there was a stillness to him that hinted at something far older, something incredibly dangerous. With a shock, I recognized him as the boy on the horse, who had watched me through the forest that day. Why was he here now, in my house? How did he even get in? I toyed with the idea of confronting him, knowing this was all a dream, when I noticed something else, something that made my blood run cold. Thick, raven-wing hair tumbled to his shoulders, not quite covering the delicate, pointed ears.

He wasn't human. He was one of *them,* one of the fey. Standing in my house, in my brother's bedroom. I shuddered and began to ease back down the hall.

He turned then, looking right through me, and I would've gasped if I had the breath. He was gorgeous. More than gorgeous, he was beautiful. Regal beautiful, prince-of-a-foreign-nation beautiful. If he walked into my classroom during finals, students and teachers alike would be throwing themselves at his feet. Still, it was a cold, hard beauty, like that of a marble statue, inhuman and otherworldly. His slanted eyes, beneath long, jagged bangs, glimmered like chips of steel.

The changeling was nowhere to be seen, but I could hear faint noises coming from beneath the bed, the thud of a rapidly beating heart. The fey boy didn't seem to notice. He turned and placed one pale hand on the closet door, running his fingers down the faded wood. A ghost of a smile touched his lips.

In one smooth motion, he pushed the door open and walked through. The door shut behind him with a soft click, and he was gone.

Warily, I edged toward the closet door, keeping a careful eye on the space beneath the bed. I still heard muffled heartbeats, but nothing reached out to grab at me. I crossed the room without incident. As quietly as I could, I grasped the closet doorknob, turned it, and pulled the door open.

"My closet!" shrieked the bowler hat man, leaping out at me. "Mine!"

I screamed and jerked myself awake.

For a moment, I glared wildly around the room, not knowing where I was. My heart pounded, and a cold sweat made my forehead clammy and slick. Scenes from a vivid nightmare danced across my mind: Ethan attacking me, Robbie making books fly around the room, a portal opening to an eerie new world.

A loud snore caught my attention, and I turned. Puck was sprawled out on the couch across from me, one arm flung over his eyes, his torso wrapped in a squirrel blanket.

My heart sank as the memories came flooding back. This wasn't a nightmare. I hadn't been dreaming this. Ethan was gone; a monster had replaced him. Robbie was a faery. And I was in the middle of the Nevernever searching for my brother, though I had no idea where to look, and no real hope of finding him.

I lay back, shivering. It was dark in Twiggs's home; the fireflies or whatever they were had stopped blinking and were now clinging to the walls, apparently asleep. The only light came from a flickering orange glow outside the window. Maybe Twiggs had the porch light on or something.

I bolted upright. That glow was actually candlelight, and above it, a face was peering into the room from outside. I opened my mouth to yell for Puck, when those blue eyes turned to me, and a face I knew all too well backed away into the night.

Ethan.

I scrambled out of bed and sprinted across the floor, not bothering to put on my shoes. Puck snorted and shifted under his mound of furs, but I ignored him. Ethan was out there! If I could get to him, we could go home and forget this mess ever existed.

I yanked on the door and stepped out, scanning the woods for my brother. Only later did it occur to me that I was normal-size again, and that the door was still only a foot tall. All I could think about was Ethan and getting him home, getting us both home.

Darkness greeted me, but up ahead, I saw a flickering orange glow bouncing along, getting steadily farther away. "Ethan!" I called, my voice echoing into the stillness. "Ethan, wait!"

I started to run, my bare feet slapping against leaves and branches, slipping on rocks and mud. My toe hit something sharp, and it should've hurt, but my mind didn't register the pain. I could see him up ahead, a small figure making his way through the trees, holding a candle out before him. I ran as fast as I could, branches scraping my skin and tearing at my hair and clothes, but it seemed he was always the same distance away.

Then he stopped and looked back over his shoulder, smiling. The flickering candlelight cast his features in an eerie glow. I put on a burst of speed, and was just a few feet away when the ground suddenly dropped away from me. With a shriek, I plummeted like a stone, landing with a splash in icy water that closed over my head, flooding my nose and mouth.

Gasping, I floundered to the surface, my face stinging and my limbs already numb. Above me, a giggle rang out, and a glowing ball of light hovered overhead. It dangled there a moment, as if enjoying my humiliation, then sped away into the trees, high-pitched laughter echoing behind it.

Treading water, I gazed around. A muddy bank rose above me, slick and treacherous. There were several old trees growing out over the water, but their branches were too high for me to reach. I tried finding handholds in the bank to pull myself out, but my feet slipped in the mud, and the plants I grabbed came loose from the soil, dumping me into the lake with a noisy splash. I'd have to find another way out.

And then I heard another splash, farther out, and knew I wasn't alone.

Moonlight shone upon the water, painting everything in a relief of silver and black. Except for the buzzing of insects, the night was very still. On the far side of the lake, fireflies danced and whirled above the surface, some glowing pink and blue instead of yellow. Maybe I'd only imagined I'd heard a noise. Nothing seemed to be moving except for an old log drifting toward me.

I blinked and looked again. That log suddenly looked a lot

like the top half of a horse's head, if a horse could swim like an alligator. And then I saw the dead white eyes, the thin shiny teeth, and panic rose up in me like a black tide.

"Puck!" I screamed, scrabbling at the bank. Mud tore loose in clumps; I'd find a handhold only to slip back again. I could feel the thing draw closer. "Puck, help me!"

I looked over my shoulder. The horse thing was only a few feet away, raising its neck out of the water to expose a mouthful of needlelike teeth. *Oh, God, I'm going to die! That thing is going to eat me! Somebody, help!* I clawed frantically at the bank—and felt a solid branch under my fingers. Grasping it, I yanked with all my strength, and felt the branch lift me out of the water, just as the horse monster lunged with a roar. Its wet, rubbery nose hit the bottom of my foot, jaws snapping with an evil *snick.* Then the branch flung me, gasping and crying, to the bank, and the horse thing sank below the surface once more.

Puck found me minutes later, curled into a ball several yards from the bank, wet to the skin and shaking like a leaf. His eyes were a mix of sympathy and exasperation as he pulled me upright.

"Are you all right?" He ran his hands up my arms, making sure I was still in one piece. "Still in there, princess? Talk to me."

I nodded, shivering. "I saw...Ethan," I stammered, trying to make sense of it all. "I followed him, but he turned into a light and flew away, and then this horse thing tried to *eat* me...." I trailed off. "That wasn't Ethan, was it? That was just another faery, playing with my emotions. And I fell for it."

Puck sighed and led me back down the trail. "Yeah," he muttered, glancing back at me. "Wisps are like that, making you see what you want to see, before leading you off the path. Though, that one seemed particularly spiteful, leading you right to a kelpie's pond. I suppose I could tell you never to go off alone, but I think it'd be a waste of breath. Oh, what the hell." He stopped and whirled around, stopping me in my tracks. *"Don't go off alone, princess.* Under any circumstances, understand? In this world, you're viewed as either a plaything or a light snack. Don't forget that."

"Yeah," I muttered. "Yeah, I get that now."

We continued down the trail. The door in the knobby tree was gone, but my sneakers and backpack lay outside, a clear sign our welcome was over. Shivering, I slipped the shoes over my bloody feet, hating this world and everything in it, wanting only to go home.

"Well," Puck said too cheerfully, "if you're done playing with will-o'-the-wisps and kelpies, I think we should continue. Oh, but do tell me the next time you want to have tea with an ogre. I'll be sure to bring my club."

I shot him a poisonous glare. He only grinned. Above us, the sky was lightening into that eerie gray twilight, silent and still as death, as we ventured deeper into the Nevernever.

CHAPTER SIX

The Wild Hunt

We hadn't gone far when we came upon the patch of death in the middle of the forest.

The wyldwood was an eerie, quiet place, but it was still alive. Trees stood ancient and tall, plants bloomed, and splashes of vibrant color pierced the grayness, indicating life. Animals slipped through the trees, and strange creatures moved about in the shadows; you never got a clear view of them, but you knew they were there. You could feel them watching you.

Then, all of a sudden, the trees dropped away, and we stood at the edge of a barren clearing.

What little grass remained was yellow and dying, sparse patches of vegetation in the rocky ground. A few trees were scattered here and there, but they were withered, twisted things, empty of leaves and blackened. From a distance, the branches glinted, jagged and sharp, like weird metal sculptures. The hot wind smelled of copper and dust.

Puck stared at the dead forest for a long time. "Twiggs was right," he muttered, staring at a withered tree. He made as if to touch one of the branches, but withdrew his hand with a shudder. "This isn't natural. Something is poisoning the wyldwood."

I reached up to touch one of the glittering branches, and jerked back with a gasp. "Ouch!"

Puck whirled on me. "What?"

I showed him my hand. Blood welled from a slice in my finger, thin as a paper cut. "The tree. It cut me."

Puck examined my finger and frowned. "Metallic trees," he mused, pulling a hankie from his pocket and wrapping it around my finger. "That's new. If you see any steel dryads, be sure to tell me so I can run away screaming."

I scowled and looked back at the tree. A single drop of blood glistened on the offending branch before dropping to the cracked earth. The twigs gleamed along their edges, as if honed to fine blades.

"Oberon must know about this," Puck muttered, crouching to examine a circle of dry grass. "Twiggs said it was spreading, but where is it coming from?" He rose quickly and swayed on his feet, putting out a hand to steady himself. I grabbed his arm.

"Are you all right?" I asked.

"I'm fine, princess." He nodded and gave me a pained smile. "A little perturbed about the state of my home, but what can you do?" He coughed and waved a hand in front of his face, as if he smelled something foul. "But this air is making me sick. Let's get out of here."

I sniffed, but smelled nothing bad, just dirt and the sharp tang of something metallic, like rust. But Puck was already leaving, his brow furrowed in anger or pain, and I hurried to catch up.

The howling began a few hours later.

Puck stopped in the middle of the trail, so abruptly that I

nearly ran into him. He held up a hand, silencing me, before I could ask what was going on.

I heard it then, drifting over the breeze, a chorus of chilling bays and howls echoing behind us. My heart revved up, and I inched closer to my companion.

"What is that?"

"A hunt," Puck replied, looking off into the distance. He grimaced. "You know, I was just thinking we needed to be run down like rabbits and torn apart. My day just isn't complete without something trying to kill me."

I grew cold. "Something's after us?"

"You've never seen a wild hunt, have you." Puck groaned, running his fingers through his hair. "Damn. Well, this will complicate things. I was hoping to give you the grand tour of the Nevernever, princess, but I guess I'll have to put it on hold."

The baying grew closer, deep, throaty howls. Whatever was coming at us, it was big. "Shouldn't we run?" I whispered.

"You'll never be able to outrun them," Puck said, backing away. "They've got our scent now, and no mortal has ever escaped a wild hunt." He sighed and dramatically flung his arm over his eyes. "I guess the sacrifice of my dignity is the only thing that will save us now. The things I endure for love. The Fates laugh at my torment."

"What are you talking about?"

Puck smiled his eerie little grin and began to change.

His face stretched out, becoming longer and narrower, as his neck began to grow. His arms spasmed, fingers turning black and fusing into hooves. He arched his back, spine expanding, as his legs became hindquarters bunched with muscle. Fur covered his skin as he dropped to all fours, no longer a boy but a sleek gray horse with a shaggy mane and tail. The transformation had taken less than ten seconds.

I backed up, remembering my encounter with the thing in the water, but the dappled horse stamped its foreleg and swished its tail impatiently. I saw its eyes, shining like emeralds through the dangling forelocks, and my fear abated somewhat.

The howling was very close now, growing more and more frenzied. I ran to horse-Puck and threw myself on his back, grabbing his mane to heave myself up. Despite living on a farm, I'd only been on horseback once or twice, and it took me a couple of tries to get up. Puck snorted and tossed his head, annoyed with my lack of equestrian skills.

Struggling upright, I grasped the mane and saw Puck's eyes roll back at me. Then, with a half rear, we plunged into the bushes and were off.

Riding bareback is not fun, especially when you have no control over your mount or where it's going. I can honestly say this was the most terrifying ride of my life. The trees flashed by in a blur, branches slapped at me, and my legs burned from gripping the horse's sides with my knees. My fingers were locked around his mane in a death grip, but that didn't keep me from sliding halfway off whenever Puck changed direction. The wind shrieked in my ears, but I could still hear the terrifying bays of our pursuers, seemingly right on our heels. I didn't dare look back.

I lost track of time. Puck never slowed or grew winded, but sweat darkened his body and made my seating slick and even more terrifying. My legs grew numb, and my hands seemed to belong to somebody else.

And then a huge black creature burst from the ferns to our right and lunged at the horse, snapping its jaws. It was a hound, bigger than any I'd seen, with eyes of blue fire. Puck leaped aside to avoid it and reared, nearly spilling me to the forest floor. As I screamed, one foreleg slashed out, striking the hound in the chest midleap, and the dog yelped as it was hurled away.

The bushes exploded, and five more monstrous dogs spilled into the road. Surrounding us, they snarled and howled, snapping at the horse's legs and leaping back as he kicked at them. I was frozen, clinging to Puck's back, watching as those massive jaws clicked shut inches from my dangling feet.

Then, through the trees, I saw him, a lean figure on a huge black horse. The boy from my dream, the one I saw from the bus that day. His cruel, angelic face wore a smile as he drew back a large bow, an arrow glistening at the tip.

"Puck!" I screeched, knowing it was already too late. "Look out!"

The leaves above the hunter rustled, and then a large branch swept down, striking the boy in the arm just as he released the string. I felt the hum as the arrow zipped past my head and lodged into a pine tree. A spiderweb of frost spread out from where the arrow hit, and Puck's equine head whipped toward the source. The hunter fit another arrow to the string, and with a shrill whinny, Puck reared and leaped over the dogs, somehow avoiding their snapping teeth. When his hooves struck dirt again, he fled, the hounds barking and snapping at his heels.

An arrow whistled past, and I looked back to see the other horse pursuing us through the trees, its rider reaching back for another shot. Puck snorted and switched directions, nearly unseating me, plunging into a deeper part of the forest.

The trees here were monsters, and grew so close together that Puck had to swerve and weave around them. The hounds fell back, but I still heard their bays and occasionally caught a glimpse of their lean black bodies, hurtling through the undergrowth. The rider had disappeared, but I knew he still followed, his deadly arrows ready to pierce our hearts.

As we passed under the boughs of an enormous oak, Puck skidded to a halt, then bucked so violently that I flew off his back, my hands torn from his mane. I soared over his head, my stomach in my throat, and landed with a jarring impact in a crossbeam of connecting branches. My breath exploded from my lungs, and a stab of pain shot through my ribs, bringing tears to my eyes. With a snort, Puck galloped on, the dogs following him into the shadows.

Moments later, the black horse and rider passed under the tree.

He slowed for a chilling heartbeat, and I held my breath, sure he would look up and see me. Then the excited howl of one of the dogs rang through the air, and he spurred his horse onward, following the hunt into the trees. In a moment, the sounds had faded. Silence fell through the branches, and I was alone.

"Well," someone said, very close by. "That was interesting."

CHAPTER SEVEN

Of Goblins and Grimalkin

I didn't scream this time, but came very close. As it was, I nearly fell out of the tree. Hugging a branch, I looked around wildly, trying to determine the owner of the voice, but I glimpsed nothing but leaves and sickly gray light shining through the branches.

"Where are you?" I gasped. "Show yourself."

"I am not hiding, little girl." The voice sounded amused. "Perhaps…if you open your eyes a bit wider. Like this."

Directly in front of me, not five feet away, a pair of saucer-like eyes opened up out of nowhere, and I stared into the face of an enormous gray cat.

"There," it purred, regarding me with a lazy yellow gaze. Its fur was long and wispy, blending perfectly into the tree and the entire landscape. "See me now?"

"You're a cat," I blurted stupidly, and I swore it arched a brow at me.

"In the crudest sense of the word, I suppose you could call me that." The feline rose, arching its back, before sitting and curling its plumed tail around its legs. Now that my shock was fading, I realized the cat was a *he,* not an it. "Others have called me Cait Sith, Grimalkin, and Devil's Cat, but since they all mean the same, I suppose you would be correct."

I gaped at him, but the sharp throb of my ribs returned my mind to other things. Namely, that Puck had left me alone in this world that viewed me as a snack, and I had no idea how to survive.

Shock and anger came first—Puck had really *left* me, to save his own skin—and after that came a fear so real and terrifying it was all I could do not to hug the branch and sob. How could Puck do this to me? I'd never make it out on my own. I'd end up as dessert for a carnivorous horse monster, torn apart by a pack of wolves, or hopelessly lost for decades, because I was sure time had ceased to exist and I'd be stuck here forever.

I took a deep breath, forcing myself to be calm. *No, Robbie wouldn't do that to me. I'm sure of it.* Perhaps he ditched me to lead the hunt away, to make sure the hunt followed him and left me alone. Maybe he thought he was saving my life. Maybe he *had* saved my life. If that was the case, I hoped he came back soon; I didn't think I would get out of the Nevernever without him.

Grimalkin, or whatever his name was, continued to observe me as if I was a particularly interesting insect. I eyed him with new feelings of suspicion. Sure, he looked like an enormous, slightly plump house cat, but horses weren't generally meat-eaters and normal trees did not have little men living inside. This feline could be sizing me up for its next meal. I gulped and met his eerie, intelligent gaze head-on.

"W-what do you want?" I asked, thankful that my voice only trembled a little bit.

The cat didn't blink. "Human," he said, and if a cat could

sound patronizing, this one nailed it, "think about the absurdity of that question. I am resting in my tree, minding my own business and wondering if I should hunt today, when you come flying in like a bean sidhe and scare off every bird for miles around. Then, you have the audacity to ask what *I* want." He sniffed and gave me a very catlike stare of disdain. "I am aware that mortals are rude and barbaric, but still."

"I'm sorry," I muttered automatically. "I didn't mean to offend you."

Grimalkin twitched his tail, and then turned to groom his hindquarters.

"Um," I continued after a moment of silence, "I was wondering if, maybe...you could help me."

Grimalkin paused midlick, then continued without looking up. "And why would I want to do that?" he asked, weaving words and grooming together without missing a beat. He still didn't look at me.

"I'm trying to find my brother," I replied, stung by Grimalkin's casual refusal. "He's been stolen by the Unseelie Court."

"Mmm. How terribly uninteresting."

"Please," I begged. "Help me. Give me a hint, or just point me in the right direction. Anything. I'll make it up to you, I swear."

Grimalkin yawned, showing off long canines and a bright pink tongue, and finally looked at me.

"Are you suggesting I do you a favor?"

"Yes. Look, I'll pay you back somehow, I promise."

He twitched an ear, looking amused. "Be careful throwing those words around so casually," he warned. "Doing this will put you in my debt. Are you sure you wish to continue?"

I didn't think about it. I was so desperate for help, I'd agree to anything. "Yes! Please, I need to find Puck. The horse I was riding when he bucked me off. He's not really a horse, you know. He's a—"

"I know what he is," Grimalkin said quietly.

"Really? Oh, that's great. Do you know where he could've gone?"

He fixed me with an unblinking stare, and then lashed his tail, once. Without a word, he rose, leaped gracefully onto a lower limb, and dropped to the ground. He stretched, arching his bushy tail over his spine, and vanished into the bushes without looking back.

I yelped, scrambling to untangle myself from the branches, wincing at the shard of pain between my ribs. I more or less fell out of the tree, landing with a thump on my backside that sparked a word Mom would ground me for. Dusting off my rear, I looked around for Grimalkin.

"Human." He appeared like a gray ghost sliding out of the bushes, big glowing eyes the only evidence he was there. "This is our agreement. I will lead you to your Puck, and you will owe me a small favor in return, yes?"

Something about the way he said *agreement* caused my skin to prickle, but I nodded.

"Very well, then. Follow me. And do try to keep up."

Easier said than done.

If you've ever tried following a cat through a dense forest filled with briars, bushes, and tangled undergrowth, you'll know how impossible it is. I lost track of the times Grimalkin vanished from sight, and I'd spend a few heart-pounding minutes searching for him, hoping I was going the right way. I always felt a desperate relief when I'd finally catch a glimpse of him slinking through the trees ahead, only to go through the same thing minutes later.

It didn't help that my mind was occupied with what could've happened to Puck. Was he dead, shot down by the dark fey boy and ripped apart by the hounds? Or had he really fled, already resolved that he wasn't coming back for me, and I could take my chances on my own?

Fear and anger welled, and my sullen thoughts shifted to my present guide. Grimalkin seemed to know the path we should take, but how did he know where Puck would be? Why should I trust him? What if the devious feline was leading me into some sort of trap?

As I was entertaining these bleak thoughts, Grimalkin disappeared again.

Dammit, I'm going to tie a bell around the stupid thing's neck if it doesn't stop that. The light was fading, and the forest was even more gray. I stopped and squinted at the bushes, searching for the elusive feline. Up ahead, the bushes rustled, which surprised me. Grimalkin had been completely silent up until now.

"Human!" whispered a familiar voice, somewhere above me. "Hide!"

"What?" I said, but it was too late. Twigs snapped, bushes parted, and a slew of creatures spilled into view.

They were short, ugly things, standing two to three feet high, with knobby yellow-green skin and bulbous noses. Their ears were large and pointed. They wore tattered clothing and carried bone-tipped spears in yellow claws. Their faces were mean and cruel, with beady eyes and mouths full of broken, jagged teeth.

For a moment, they stopped, blinking in surprise. Then the whole pack of them screeched and swarmed forward, jabbing at me with their spears.

"What is it? What is it?" snarled one, as I cringed away

from the stabbing points. Laughter and jeers filled the air as they surrounded me.

"It's an elf," hissed another, giving me a toothy leer. "An elf what lost its ears, maybe."

"No, a goat-girl," cried yet a third. "Good eatin', them."

"She ain't no goat, cretin! Lookit, she ain't got no 'ooves!"

I trembled and looked around for an escape route, but wherever I turned, those sharp bony points were thrust at me.

"Take 'er to the chief," someone suggested at last. "The chief'll know what she is, and if she's safe to eat."

"Right! The chief'll know!"

A couple of them rushed me from behind, and I felt a blow to the backs of my knees. With a shriek, I collapsed, and the whole pack of them swarmed me, hooting and hollering. I screamed and kicked, flailing my arms, thrashing under the weight of the creatures. A few went flying into the bushes, but they bounced up with shrill cries and pounced on me again. Blows rained down on me.

Then something struck me behind the head, making lights explode behind my eyes, and I knew nothing for a time.

I woke with the mother of all headaches doing a jig inside my skull. I was in a sitting position, and something that felt like broom handles pressed uncomfortably into my back. Groaning, I probed around my skull, searching for anything cracked or broken. Except for a massive lump just above my hairline, everything seemed to be intact.

When I was sure I was still in one piece, I opened my eyes. And regretted it immediately.

I was in a cage. A very small cage, made of branches lashed together with leather bindings. There was barely enough room for me to raise my head, and when I moved, something sharp poked me in the arm, drawing blood. I looked closer and saw that many of the branches were covered in thorns about an inch long.

Beyond the bars, several mud huts sat in no particular arrangement around a large fire pit. The squat, ugly little creatures scampered to and fro around the camp, fighting, arguing, or gnawing on bones. A group of them sat around my backpack, pulling things out one by one. My extra clothes they just tossed in the dirt, but the chips and bottle of aspirin they immediately ripped open, tasted, and squabbled over. One managed to open the soda can and spray fizzy liquid everywhere, to the angry shrieks of his companions.

One of them, shorter than its fellows and wearing a muddy red vest, saw that I was awake. With a hiss, it scuttled up to the cage and thrust its spear through the bars. I cringed back, but there was nowhere to go; the thorns stung my flesh as the spear jabbed me in the thigh.

"Ouch, stop it!" I cried, which only encouraged it further. Cackling, it poked and prodded me, until I reached down and grabbed the head of the spear. Snarling and cursing, the creature tried yanking it back, and we held a ridiculous tug-of-war until another goblin saw what we were doing. It rushed up and stabbed me through the bars on the opposite side, and I released the spear with a yelp.

"Greertig, stop pokin' the meat," snapped the second, taller creature. "Ain't no good if all the blood runs out."

"Pah, I was just makin' sure it was tender, is all." The other snorted and spit on the ground, then glared at me with greedy red eyes. "Why we waitin' about? Let's just eat it already."

"The chief ain't back yet." The taller creature looked at me, and to my horror, a long string of drool dripped down its chin. "He 'as to make sure this thing is safe to eat."

They gave me a last longing glare, then stomped back to the fire pit, arguing and spitting at each other. I drew my knees to my chest and tried to control my shaking.

"If you are going to cry, please do it quietly," murmured a familiar voice at my back. "Goblins can smell fear. They will only torment you more if you give them a reason."

"Grimalkin?" Squirming in my cage, I glanced around to see the nearly invisible gray cat crouched by one corner. His eyes were narrowed in concentration, and his strong, sharp teeth were chewing at one of the leather bindings.

"Idiot, do not look at me!" he spat, and I quickly glanced away. The cat growled, tugging on one of the bars. "Goblins are not very smart, but even they will notice if you start talking to nobody. Just sit tight and I will have you out of here in a minute."

"Thank you for coming back," I whispered, watching two goblins fight over some unfortunate beast's rib cage. The quarrel ended when one goblin bashed the other over the head with a club and scampered off with its trophy. The other goblin lay stunned for a moment, then leaped to its feet in pursuit.

Grimalkin sniffed and began chewing the bindings again. "Do not put yourself even more in debt," he said around a mouthful of leather. "We have already made a contract. I agreed to take you to Puck, and I always keep my end of the bargain. Now, shut up so I can work."

I nodded and fell silent, but suddenly there was a great cry in the goblin camp. Goblins leaped to their feet, hissing and scuttling about, as a large creature sauntered out of the forest into the middle of the encampment.

It was another goblin, only bigger, broader, and meaner-looking than its fellows. It wore a crimson uniform with brass buttons, the sleeves rolled up and the tails dragging along the ground. It also carried a curved blade, rusty bronze and jagged along the edge. It snarled and swaggered into the camp, the other goblins cringing away from it, and I knew this must be the chief.

"Shut up, ya pack of jabberin' dogs," the chief roared, aiming a blow at a couple of goblins who didn't get out of his way quick enough. "Worthless, the lot of ya! I been hard at work, raidin' the borderlands, an' what have you lot got to show me, eh? Nothin'! Not even a rabbit fer the stewpot. Ya make me sick."

"Chief, chief!" cried several goblins at once, dancing around and pointing. "Lookit, lookit! We caught something! We brought it back for you!"

"Eh?" The chief's gaze flashed across the camp, his evil eyes fastening on me. "What's this? Did you miserable louts actually manage to catch a high an' mighty elf?"

He sauntered toward the cage. I couldn't help myself and snuck a quick glance at Grimalkin, hoping the cat would flee. But Grimalkin was nowhere to be seen.

Swallowing hard, I looked up and met the chief's beady red eyes.

"What in Pan's privates is this?" the goblin chief snorted. "This ain't no elf, you cretins. Not unless she bartered away her ears! Besides—" he sniffed the air, wrinkling his snotty nose "—it smells different. Ey, funny elf-thing." He smacked the cage with the flat of his sword, making me jump. "What are ya?"

I took a deep breath as the rest of the goblin tribe crowded around the cage, watching me, some curious, most hungry-looking. "I'm a…an otaku faery," I said, drawing a confused scowl from the chief and bewildered looks from the rest of the camp. Whispers began to erupt from the crowd, gaining strength like wildfire.

"A what?"

"Ain't never 'erd of that before."

"Is it tasty?"

"Can we eat it?"

The chief frowned. "I admit, I ain't never come across no otaku faery before," he growled, scratching his head. "Ah, but that ain't important. Ya look young an' juicy enough, I figure you'll feed me crew fer several nights. So, what's yer preference, otaku?" He grinned and raised his sword. "Boiled alive, or skewered over the fire?"

I clenched my hands to stop them from shaking. "Either way is fine with me," I said, trying to sound casual. "Tomorrow it won't matter at all. There's a deadly poison running through my veins. If you swallow one bite of me, your blood will boil, your insides will melt, and you'll dissolve into a steaming pile of muck." Hisses went around the tribe; several goblins bared their teeth at me and snarled. I crossed my arms and raised my chin, staring down the goblin chief. "So, go ahead and eat me. Tomorrow you'll be a big puddle of goo, sinking into the ground."

Many of the goblins were backing away now, but the chief stood firm. "Shut up, you sniveling lot!" he snarled at the nervous goblins. Giving me a sour look, he spat on the ground. "So, we can't eat ya." He sounded unimpressed. "Pity, that is. But don't think that'll save ya, girl. If yer so deadly, I'll just kill ya now, except I'll bleed ya slow, so yer poison blood won't hurt me. Then I'll skin ya and hang yer hide on me door, and use yer bones fer arrowheads. As me grandmother always said, waste not."

"Wait!" I cried as he stepped forward, raising his sword.

"It—it would be a shame for me to go to waste like that," I stammered as he glared at me with suspicious eyes. "There *is* a way to purify the poison from my blood so that I'm safe to eat. If I'm going to die anyway, I'd rather be eaten than tortured."

The goblin chief smiled. "I knew you'd see it my way," he gloated. Turning to his minions, he puffed out his chest. "See there, dogs? Yer chief is still lookin' out fer ya! We feast tonight!"

A raucous cheer went up, and the chief turned to me again, leveling his sword at my face. "So then, otaku girl. What's yer secret?"

I thought quickly. "To cleanse the poison from my blood, you have to boil me in a big pot with several purifying ingredients. Spring water from a waterfall, an acorn from the tallest oak tree, blue mushrooms, and...um..."

"Don't tell me ya forgot," the chief said in a menacing tone, and poked the sword tip through the bars of the cage. "Maybe I can help ya remember."

"Pixie dust!" I blurted desperately, making him blink. "From a live pixie," I added. "Not dead. If it dies, the recipe won't work." I prayed that there were pixies in this world. If not, I was as good as dead.

"Huh," the chief grunted, and turned to the waiting tribe. "All right, louts, you heard it! I want those ingredients back here before dawn! Anyone who don't work, don't eat! Now, get movin'."

The tribe scattered. Hissing, jabbering, and cursing at one another, they vanished into the forest until only one guard remained, leaning on a crooked spear.

The chief eyed me warily and pointed his sword through the bars.

"Don't think ya can trick me by givin' false ingredients,"

he threatened. "I plan to cut off yer finger, toss it in the stew, an' have one of me mates taste it. If he dies, or melts into a puddle, it be a long, slow death fer you. Understand?"

Chilled, I nodded. I knew none of the goblins would die, because my claim of poison and the recipe for the stew was, of course, completely bogus. Still, I wasn't thrilled about losing one of my fingers. *Terrified* would be a better word.

The chief spat and looked around the near-deserted campsite. "Bah, none of them dogs will know how to catch a piskie," he muttered, scratching his ear. "They'd probably eat the damn thing if they caught it. Arg, I'd better find one myself. Bugrat!"

A few yards away, the lone guard snapped to attention. "Chief?"

"Keep an eye on our dinner," the chief ordered, sheathing his sword. "If it tries to escape, cut off its feet."

"You got it, chief."

"I'm goin' huntin'." The chief shot me one last warning glare, then bounded off into the undergrowth.

"That was clever," Grimalkin murmured, sounding reluctantly impressed.

I nodded, too breathless to answer. After a moment, the sound of chewing recommenced.

It took a while, during which time I chewed my lip, wrung my hands, and tried not to ask how Grimalkin was doing every twenty seconds. As the minutes stretched, I cast anxious glances at the trees and the forest, expecting the chief or the goblin horde to come bursting through. The lone guard stalked the perimeter of the camp, shooting me an evil look as it walked by and triggering Grimalkin's vanishing act. Finally, on the eighth or ninth circle, Grimalkin's voice floated up after the guard had passed.

"There. I think you can get through now."

I wiggled around as best I could. Peering at the bars, I saw that several of the bindings were chewed in half, testament to Grim's strong jaws and sharp teeth.

"Come on, come on, let us go," Grimalkin hissed, lashing its tail. "You can gawk later—they are coming back."

Bushes rustled around me, and harsh laughter filled the air, getting closer. Heart pounding, I grasped the bars, being careful to avoid the thorns, and pushed. They resisted me, held in place by interlocking branches, and I shoved harder. It was like trying to push through a heavy briar patch; the bars shifted a bit, teasing me with freedom, but stubbornly gave little ground.

The goblin chief stepped out of the trees, followed by three more goblins. He clutched something small and wriggling in one fist, and his followers' arms were filled with pale blue toadstools.

"Mushrooms were the easy part," the chief snorted, casting a derisive glance back at the others. "Any idiot can collect plants. If I'd left these dogs ta catch a piskie, we'd be nothin' but bones before—"

He stopped, and his gaze snapped to me. For a moment, he stood there, blinking, then his eyes narrowed and he clenched his fists. The creature in his grasp gave a high-pitched squeal as the goblin crushed the life from it and flung it to the ground. With a roar of outrage, the chief drew his sword. I screamed and shoved on the cage as hard as I could.

With a great snapping of twigs and thorns, the back of the cage came loose, and I was free.

"Run!" Grimalkin yelled, and I didn't need encouragement. We bolted into the forest, the enraged cries of the goblins on our heels.

CHAPTER EIGHT

Moonlit Grove

I tore through the forest, branches and leaves slapping at my face, following Grimalkin's shadowy form as best I could. Behind me, twigs snapped, snarls echoed, and the angry cursing of the goblin chief grew louder in my ears. My breath rasped in my chest, my lungs burned, but I forced my legs to keep moving, knowing that if I stumbled or fell, I would die.

"This way!" I heard Grimalkin shout, darting into a patch of bramble. "If we can get to the river, we will be safe! Goblins cannot swim!"

I followed him into the briars, bracing myself for thorns tearing at my flesh and ripping at my clothes. But the branches parted easily for me, as they had when I was with Puck, and I slipped through with minimal scrapes. As I exited the bramble patch, a great crashing noise echoed behind me, followed by loud yelps and swearing. It seemed the goblins weren't finding the path as easy to navigate, and I thanked whatever forces were at work as I continued on.

Over the roaring in my ears and my own ragged breaths, I heard the sound of rushing water. When I staggered out of

the trees, the ground abruptly dropped away into a rocky em-
bankment. A great river loomed before me, nearly a hundred
yards across, with no bridges or rafts in sight. I couldn't see
the other side because a coiling wall of mist hovered over the
water, stretching as far as I could see. Grimalkin stood at the
edge, almost invisible in the fog, lashing his tail impatiently.

"Hurry!" he ordered as I stumbled down the bank, exhaustion burning my legs. "The Erlking's territory is on the other
side. You must swim, quickly!"

I hesitated. If monster horses lurked in quiet ponds, what
would great black rivers hold? Images of giant fish and sea
monsters flashed across my mind.

Something flew past my arm, startling me, bouncing off the
rocks with a clatter. It was a goblin spear, the bone-white tip
gleaming against the stones. The blood drained from my face.
I could either stay put and be skewered, or take my chances
with the river.

Scrambling down the bank, I flung myself into the water.

The cold shocked me, and I gasped, struggling against the
current as it pulled me downstream. I'm a fairly strong swim-
mer, but my limbs felt like jelly, and my lungs were gasping to
suck in enough oxygen. I floundered and went under, snorting
water up my nose and making my lungs scream. The current
pulled me farther away, and I fought down panic.

Another lance zipped over my head. I looked back and saw
the goblins following me along the bank, scrambling over the
rocks and hurling spears. Terror shot through me, giving me
new strength. I struck out for the opposite shore, arms and
legs churning madly, fighting the current for all I was worth.
More spears splashed around me, but thankfully, the goblins'
aim seemed to match their intelligence.

As I drew close to the wall of mist, something struck my

shoulder with jarring force, sending a flare of agony across my back. I gasped and went under. Pain paralyzed my arm, and as the undertow dragged me down, I was sure I was going to die.

Something grabbed my waist, and I felt myself pulled upward. My head broke water and I gasped air into my starving lungs, fighting the blackness on the edge of my vision. As my senses returned, I realized someone was pulling me through the water, but I could see nothing around me because of the mist. Then my feet touched solid ground, and the next thing I knew, I was lying in the grass, the sun shining warmly on my face. My eyes were closed, and I cracked them open cautiously.

A girl's face hovered over mine, blond hair brushing my cheeks, wide green eyes both anxious and curious. Her skin was the color of summer grass, and tiny scales gleamed silver around her neck. She grinned, and her teeth flashed as sharp and pointed as an eel's.

A scream welled in my throat, but I swallowed it down. This…girl?…had just saved my life, even if it meant she wanted to eat me herself. It would be rude if I just shrieked in her face, plus any sudden moves might spark an aggressive feeding frenzy. I couldn't show any fear. With a deep breath, I sat up, wincing as a bolt of pain lanced through my shoulder.

"Um…hello," I stammered, watching her sit back and blink. I was surprised that she had legs instead of a fishtail, though webbing spanned her fingers and toes, and her claws were very, very sharp. A small white dress clung to her body, the hem of it dripping wet. "I'm Meghan. What's your name?"

She cocked her head, reminding me of a cat that couldn't decide whether to eat the mouse or play with it. "You're funny-looking," she stated, her voice rippling like water over rocks. "What are you?"

"Me? I'm human." The moment I said it, I wished I hadn't.

In the old fairy tales, which I was remembering more and more of, humans were always food, playthings, or the tragic love interest. And as I was quickly discovering, the inhabitants here had no qualms about eating a speaking, sentient creature. I held the same rung on the food chain as a rabbit or squirrel. It was a scary, rather humbling thought.

"Human?" The girl cocked her head the other way. I caught a glimpse of pink gills under her chin. "My sisters told me stories of humans. They said they sometimes sing to them to lure them underwater." She grinned, showing off her sharp needle-teeth. "I've been practicing. Want to hear?"

"No, she certainly does not." Grimalkin came stalking through the grass, bottlebrush tail held high in the air. The feline was soaked, water dripping off his fur in rivulets, and he did not look pleased.

"Shoo," he growled at the girl, and she drew back, hissing and baring her teeth. Grimalkin seemed unimpressed. "Go away. I am in no mood to play games with nixies. Now, get!"

The girl hissed once more and fled, sliding into the water like a seal. She glared at us from the middle of the river, then vanished in a spray of mist.

"Irritating sirens," Grimalkin fumed, turning to glare at me, eyes narrowed. "You did not promise her anything, did you?"

"No." I bristled. I was happy to see the cat, of course, but didn't appreciate the attitude. It wasn't my fault the goblins were chasing us. "You didn't have to scare her off, Grim. She did save my life."

The cat flicked his tail, spraying me with drops. "The only reason she pulled you out of the river was curiosity. If I had not come along, she would have either sung you underwater to drown, or she would have eaten you. Fortunately, nixies are not very brave. They would much prefer a fight beneath the water where they have all the advantages. Now, I suggest we find somewhere to rest. You are wounded, and the swim took a lot out of me. If you can walk, I encourage you to do so."

Grimacing, I pulled myself to my feet. My shoulder felt like it was on fire, but if I held my arm close to my chest, the pain receded to a dull throb. Biting my lip, I followed Grimalkin, away from the river and into the lands of the Erlking.

Even wet, tired, and in pain, I still had the energy to gawk. Pretty soon, my eyes felt huge and swollen from staring so long without blinking. The land on this side of the river was a far cry from the eerie gray forest of the wild fey. Rather than colors being faded and washed out, everything was overly vibrant and vivid. The trees were too green, the flowers screamingly colorful. Leaves glittered, razor sharp in the light, and petals flashed like jewels as they caught the sun. It was all very beautiful, but I couldn't shake the feeling of apprehension as I took it in. Everything seemed…fake somehow, as if this was a fancy coating over reality, as if I wasn't looking at the real world at all.

My shoulder burned, and the skin around it felt puffy and hot. As the sun rose higher in the sky, the throbbing heat leeched down my arm and spread through my back. Sweat ran down my face, making my eyes sting, and my legs trembled.

I finally collapsed under a pine tree, gasping, my body hot and cold at the same time. Grimalkin circled around and trotted back, his tail held high in the air. For a moment, there were two Grimalkins, but then I blinked sweat out of my eyes and there was only one.

"There's something wrong with me," I panted as the cat regarded me coolly. His eyes abruptly floated off his face and hovered in the air between us. I blinked, hard, and they were normal again.

Grimalkin nodded. "Dreamlace venom," he said, to my confusion. "Goblins poison their spears and arrows. When the hallucinations start coming, you do not have long."

I took a ragged breath. "Isn't there a cure?" I whispered, ignoring the fern that started crawling toward me like a leafy spider. "Someone who can help?"

"That is where we are going." Grimalkin stood, looking back at me. "Not far now, human. Keep your eyes on me, and try to ignore everything else, no matter what comes at you."

It took three tries to get back on my feet, but at last I managed to pull myself up and hold my balance long enough to take a step. And then another. And another. I followed Grimalkin for miles, or at least it seemed that way. After the first tree lunged at me, rattling its branches, it became difficult to concentrate. I nearly lost Grimalkin several times, as the landscape twisted into terrifying versions of itself, reaching for me with twiggy fingers. Distant shapes beckoned from the shadows, calling my name. The ground turned into a writhing mass of spiders and centipedes, crawling up my legs. A deer stepped into the middle of the path, cocked its head, and asked me for the time.

Grimalkin paused. Jumping onto a rock, ignoring the boulder's indignant shouts for him to get off, he turned to face me. "You are on your own from here, human," he said, or at least that's what I heard over the rock's bellowing. "Just keep walking until *he* shows himself. He owes me a favor, but also tends to distrust humans, so the chances that he will help you are about fifty-fifty. Unfortunately, he is the only one who can cure you now."

I frowned, trying to follow his words, but they buzzed

around like flies and I couldn't follow. "What are you talking about?" I asked.

"You will know what I mean when you find him, if you find him." The cat cocked his head and gave me a scrutinizing look. "You are still a virgin, right?"

I decided that last part was a figment of my delirium. Grimalkin slipped away before I could ask him anything else, leaving me confused and disoriented. Waving away a swarm of wasps that circled my head, I stumbled after him.

A vine reached up and snagged my foot. I fell, bursting through the ground, to land on a bed of yellow flowers. They turned their tiny faces to me and screamed, filling the air with pollen. I sat up and found myself in a moonlit grove, the ground carpeted with flowers. Trees danced, rocks laughed at me, and tiny lights zipped through the air.

My limbs were numb, and I was suddenly very tired. Blackness crawled on the edge of my vision. I lay back against a tree and watched the lights swarm through the air. Vaguely, some part of me realized I'd stopped breathing, but the rest of me didn't really care.

A strand of moonlight broke away from the trees and glided toward me. I watched without interest, knowing it was a hallucination. As it got closer, it shimmered and changed shape, sometimes resembling a deer, sometimes a goat or a pony. A horn of light grew from its head, as it regarded me with ancient golden eyes.

"Hello, Meghan Chase."

"Hello," I replied, though my lips didn't move and I had no breath to speak. "Am I dead?"

"Not quite." The moonlight creature laughed softly, shaking its mane. "It is not your destiny to die here, princess."

"Oh." I pondered that, my thoughts swirling muzzily in my head. "How do you know who I am?"

The creature snorted, swishing a lionlike tail. "Those of us who watch the sky have seen your coming for a long time, Meghan Chase. Catalysts always burn brightly, and your light shines unlike any I've seen before. Now, the only question remaining is, what path will you take, and how will you choose to rule?"

"I don't understand."

"You aren't supposed to." The moonlight creature stepped forward and breathed. Silver air washed over me, and my eyelids fluttered shut. "Now, sleep, my princess. Your father awaits you. And tell Grimalkin that I choose to help, not as a favor, but for reasons of my own. The next time he calls on me will be the last."

I didn't want to sleep. Questions swirled to mind, buzzing and insistent. I opened my mouth to ask about my father, but the creature's horn touched my chest, sending a rush of heat through my body. I gasped and opened my eyes.

The moonlit grove had disappeared. A meadow surrounded me, tall grasses waving in the wind, a faint pink glow lighting the horizon. The last traces of a weird dream fluttered across my mind: moving trees, talking deer, a creature made of frost and moonlight. I wondered what was real, and what had just been the effects of the delirium. I felt fine now—better than fine. Some of it must have been real.

Then the grass rustled, as if something crept up behind me.

I whipped around and saw my backpack sitting a few feet away, bright orange against the green. Snatching it up, I pulled it open. The food was gone, of course, as were the flashlight and the aspirin, but my extra clothes were there, crumpled into a ball and sopping wet.

Confused, I stared at the pack. What could have brought it here all the way from the goblins' camp? I didn't think Grimalkin would have gone back for it, especially since that would have meant crossing the river again. But, here was my pack—moldy and wet, but still here. At least the clothes would dry.

And then I remembered something else. Something that made me wince.

Unzipping the side pouch, I pulled out my dripping, waterlogged iPod.

"Dammit." I sighed, looking it over. The screen was blurry and warped, totally ruined, a year's savings down the drain. I shook it and heard water sloshing inside. Not good. Just to be sure, I plugged in the headphones and turned it on. Nothing. Not even a buzz. It was well and truly dead.

Sadly, I replaced it in the pocket and zipped it back up. So much for listening to Aerosmith in Faeryland. I was about to go looking for Grimalkin when a giggle overhead made me glance up.

Something crouched in the branches. Something small and misshapen, watching me with glowing green eyes. I saw the outline of a sinewy body, long thin arms, and goblinlike ears. Only it wasn't a goblin. It was too small for that, and more disturbing, it seemed intelligent.

The monster saw me watching it and offered a slow smile. Its teeth, pointed and razor sharp, glimmered with neon-blue fire, just before it vanished. And I don't mean it scuttled off or faded away like a ghost. It *blipped* out of sight, like the image on a computer screen.

Like that thing I saw in the computer lab.

Definitely time to go.

I found Grimalkin sunning himself on a rock, eyes shut,

purring deep in his throat. He cracked open a lazy eye as I
came rushing up.

"We're leaving," I told him, shrugging into my backpack.
"You're going to take me to Puck, I'm going to rescue Ethan,
and we're going home. And if I never see another goblin,
nixie, cait sith or whatever, it'll be too soon."

Grimalkin yawned. Infuriatingly, he took his sweet time
getting up, stretching, yawning, scratching his ears, making sure every hair was in place. I stood, nearly dancing with
impatience, wanting to grab him by the scruff of the neck,
though I knew I'd probably be shredded for it.

"Arcadia, the Summer Court, is close," Grimalkin said as
he finally deemed himself ready to start. "Remember, you
owe me a small debt when we find your Puck." He leaped
from the rock to the ground, looking back at me solemnly.
"I will claim my price as soon as we find him. Don't forget."

We walked for hours, through a forest that seemed to
be constantly closing in on us. In the corners of my eyes,
branches, leaves, even tree trunks moved and shifted, reaching out for me. Sometimes I'd pass a tree or bush, only to see
the same one farther down the path. Laughter echoed from
the canopy overhead, and strange lights winked and bobbed
in the distance. Once, a fox peeked at us from beneath a fallen
log, a human skull perched on its head. None of this bothered
Grimalkin, who trotted down the forest trail with his tail up,
never looking back to see if I followed.

Night had descended, and the enormous blue moon was
high overhead, when Grimalkin stopped, flattening his ears.
With a hiss, he slipped off the trail and vanished into a patch
of ferns. Startled, I looked up to see a pair of riders approaching, glowing bright in the darkness. Their mounts were gray

and silver, and the hooves didn't touch the ground as they broke into a canter, straight for me.

I stood my ground as they approached. There was no use trying to outrun hunters on horseback. As they got closer, I saw the riders: tall and elegant, with sharp features and coppery hair tied into a tail. They wore silver mail that flashed in the moonlight, and carried long, thin blades at their sides.

The horses surrounded me, snorting steam, their breath hanging in the air like clouds. Atop their mounts, the knights glared down with unnatural beauty, their features too fine and delicate to be real. "Are you Meghan Chase?" one of them asked, his voice high and clear like a flute. His eyes flashed, the color of the summer sky.

I swallowed. "Yes."

"You will come with us. His Majesty King Oberon, Lord of the Summer Court, has sent for you."

CHAPTER NINE

In the Seelie Court

I rode in front of an elven knight, who had one arm wrapped securely around my waist while the other held the reins. Grimalkin dozed in my lap, a warm, heavy weight, and refused to talk to me. The knights wouldn't answer any of my questions, either: where we were going, if they knew Puck, or why King Oberon wanted me. I didn't even know if I was a prisoner or a guest of these people, though I supposed I would find out soon enough. The horses flew over the forest floor, and I saw up ahead that the trees were beginning to thin.

We broke through the tree line, and ahead of us rose an enormous mound. It towered above us in ancient, grassy splendor, the pinnacle seeming to brush the sky. Thorny trees and brambles grew everywhere, especially near the top, so the whole thing resembled a large bearded head. Around it grew a hedge bristling with thorns, some longer than my arm. The knights spurred their horses toward the thickest part of the hedge. I wasn't surprised when the brambles parted for them, forming an arch that they rode beneath, before settling back with a loud crunching sound.

I *was* surprised when the horses rode straight at the side of the hill without slowing, and I clutched Grimalkin tightly, making him growl in protest. The mound neither opened up nor moved aside in any way; we rode *into* the hill and through, sending a shiver all the way down my spine to my toes.

Blinking, I gazed around at total chaos.

A massive courtyard stretched before me, a great circular plat-form of ivory pillars, marble statues, and flowering trees. Fountains hurled geysers of water into the air, multicolored lights danced over the pools, and flowers in the full spectrum of the rainbow bloomed everywhere. Strains of music reached my ears, a combination of harps and drums, strings and flutes, bells and whistles, somehow lively and melancholy at the same time. It brought tears to my eyes, and suddenly all I wanted to do was slide off the horse and dance until the music consumed me and I was lost in it. Thankfully, Grimalkin muttered something like "Get hold of yourself" and dug his claws into my wrist, snapping me out of it.

Faeries were everywhere, sitting on the marble steps or benches, dancing together in small groups, or just wandering around. My eyes could not take it in fast enough. A man with a bare chest and shaggy legs ending in hooves winked at me from the shade of a bush. A willowy girl with green-tinted skin stepped out of a tree, scolding a child hanging from the branches. The boy stuck out his tongue, flicked his squirrel tail, and darted higher into the foliage.

I felt a sharp tug on my hair. A tiny figure hovered near my shoulder, gossamer wings buzzing like a hummingbird's. I gasped, but the knight holding me didn't so much as glance at it. She grinned and held out what looked like a plump grape, except the skin of the fruit was bright blue and speckled with orange. I smiled politely and nodded, but she frowned and pointed at my hand. Confused, I held up my palm. She dropped the fruit into it, gave a delighted giggle, and sped away.

"Be careful," Grimalkin rumbled, as a heady aroma rose from the little fruit, making my mouth water. "Eating or drinking certain things in Faery could have unpleasant consequences for someone like you. Do not eat anything. In fact, until we find your Puck, I would not talk to anyone. And whatever you do, do not accept gifts of any sort. This is going to be a long night."

I swallowed and dropped the fruit into one of the fountains as we rode by, watching huge green-and-gold fish swarm around it, mouths gaping. The knights scattered faeries as we rode through the courtyard toward a high stone wall with a pair of silver gates in front. Two massive creatures, each ten feet tall, blue-skinned and tusked, guarded the doors. Their eyes glimmered yellow beneath ropey black hair and heavy brows. Even dressed up, their arms and chests bulging through the fabric of their red uniforms, popping the brass buttons, they were still terrifying. "Trolls," muttered Grimalkin, as I shrank against the unyielding frame of the elven knight. "Be thankful we're in Oberon's land. The Winter Court employs ogres."

The knights stopped and let me down a few feet from the gate. "Be courteous when you speak to the Erlking, child," the knight I'd ridden with told me, and wheeled his mount away. I was left facing two giant trolls with nothing but a cat and my backpack.

Grimalkin squirmed in my arms, and I let him drop to the stones. "Come on." The cat sighed, lashing his tail. "Let us meet Lord Pointy Ears and get this over with."

The two trolls blinked as the cat fearlessly approached the gate, looking like a gray bug scuttling around their clawed feet. One of them moved, and I braced myself, expecting him to stomp Grimalkin into kitty pudding. But the troll only reached over and pulled the gate open as the other did the same on his side. Grimalkin shot me a backward glance, twitched his tail, and slipped through the archway. I took a deep breath, smoothed down my tangled hair, and followed.

The forest grew thick on the other side of the gates, as if the wall had been built to keep it in check. A tunnel of flowering trees and branches stretched away from me, fully in bloom, the scent so overpowering I felt light-headed.

The tunnel ended with a curtain of vines, opening up into a vast clearing surrounded by giant trees. The ancient trunks and interlocking branches made a sort of cathedral, a living palace of giant columns and a leafy vaulted ceiling. Even though I knew we were underground, and it was night outside, sunlight dappled the forest floor, slanting in through tiny cracks in the canopy. Glowing balls of light danced in the air, and a waterfall cascaded gently into a nearby pool. The colors here were dazzling.

A hundred faeries clustered around the middle of the clearing, dressed in brilliant, alien finery. By the look of it, I guessed these were the nobles of the court. Their hair hung long and flowing, or was styled in impossible fashions atop their heads. Satyrs, easily recognized by their shaggy goat legs, and furry little men padded back and forth, serving drinks and trays of food. Slender hounds with moss-green fur milled about, hoping for dropped crumbs. Elven knights in silvery chain armor stood stiffly around the room; a few held hawks or even tiny dragons.

In the center of this gathering sat a pair of thrones, seemingly grown out of the forest floor and flanked by two liveried centaurs. One of the thrones stood empty, except for a caged raven on one of the arms. The great black bird cawed and beat its wings against its prison, its beady eyes bright and green. However, in the throne on the left...

King Oberon, for I could only assume this was him, sat with his fingers steepled together, gazing out at the crowd. Like the rest of the fey nobles, he was tall and slender, with silver hair that fell to his waist and eyes like green ice. An antlered crown rested on his brow, casting a long shadow over the court, like grasping talons. Power radiated from him, as subtle as a thunderstorm.

Over the colorful sea of nobles, our gazes met. Oberon raised one eyebrow, graceful as the curve of a hawk's wing, but no expression showed on his face. And at that moment, every faery in the room stopped what it was doing and turned to stare at me.

"Great," muttered Grimalkin, forgotten beside me. "Now they all know we are here. Well, come on, human. Let us play nicies with the court."

My legs felt weak, my mouth dry, but I forced myself to walk. Fey lords and ladies parted for me, but whether out of respect or disdain, I couldn't tell. Their eyes, cold and amused, gave nothing away. A green faery hound sniffed me and growled as I passed, but other than that, the place was silent.

What was I doing here? I didn't even know. Grimalkin was supposed to be leading me to Puck, but now Oberon wanted to see me. It seemed I was getting further and further from my goal of rescuing Ethan. Unless, of course, Oberon knew where Ethan was.

Unless Oberon was holding him hostage.

I reached the foot of the throne. Heart pounding, not knowing what else to do, I dropped to one knee and bowed. I felt the Erlking's eyes on the back of my neck, as ancient as the forest surrounding us. Finally, he spoke.

"Rise, Meghan Chase."

His voice was soft, yet the lilting undertone made me think of roaring oceans and savage storms. The ground trembled beneath my fingers. Controlling my fear, I stood and looked at him and saw something flicker across his masklike face. Pride? Amusement? It was gone before I could tell.

"You have trespassed in our lands," he told me, sending a

murmur down the faery court. "You were never meant to see the Nevernever, and yet you tricked a member of this court into bringing you across the barrier. Why?"

Not knowing what else to do, I told him the truth. "I'm searching for my brother, sir. Ethan Chase."

"And you have reason to believe he is here?"

"I don't know." I cast a desperate look at Grimalkin, who was grooming a back leg and paying no attention to me. "My friend Robbie…Puck…he told me that Ethan was kidnapped by faeries. That they left a changeling in his place."

"I see." Oberon turned his head slightly, regarding the caged bird on his throne. "And that is yet another transgression, Robin."

I gaped, my mouth dropping open. "Puck?"

The raven looked at me with bright green eyes, cawed softly, and seemed to shrug. I glared back at Oberon. "What are you doing to him?"

"He was commanded never to bring you to our land." Oberon's voice was calm but pitiless. "He was ordered to keep you blind to our ways, our life, our very existence. I punished him for his disobedience. Perhaps I will turn him back in a few centuries, after he has had time to think on his transgressions."

"He was trying to help me!"

Oberon smiled, but it was cold, empty. "We immortals do not think of life in the same way as humans. Puck should have had no interest in rescuing a human child, especially if it conflicted with my direct orders. That he caved to your demands suggests he may be spending too much time with mortals, learning their ways and their capricious emotions. It is time he remembers how to be fey."

I swallowed. "But what about Ethan?"

"I know not." Oberon leaned back, shrugging his lean

shoulders. "He is not here, within my territories. That much I can tell you."

Despair crushed me like a ten-ton weight. Oberon didn't know where Ethan was, and worse, didn't care. Now I'd lost Puck as a guide, as well. It was back to square one. I'd have to find the other court—the Unseelie one—sneak in and rescue my brother, all by myself. That is, if I could get there in one piece. Maybe Grimalkin would agree to help me. I looked down at the cat, who was completely absorbed in washing his tail, and my heart sank. Probably not. Well, then. I was on my own.

The enormity of my task loomed ahead, and I fought back tears. Where would I go now? How would I even survive?

"Fine." I didn't mean to sound surly, but I wasn't feeling very positive at the moment. "I'll be leaving now. If you won't help me, I'll just have to keep looking."

"I'm afraid," said Oberon, "that I can't let you go just yet."

"What?" I recoiled. "Why?"

"Much of the land knows you are here," the Erlking continued. "Outside this court, I have many enemies. Now that you are here, now that you are *aware,* they would use you to get to me. I'm afraid I cannot allow that."

"I don't get it." I looked around at the fey nobles; many of them looked grim, unfriendly. The stares they leveled at me now glittered with dislike. I turned back to Oberon, pleading. "Why would they want me? I'm just a human. I don't have anything to do with you people. I just want my brother back."

"On the contrary." Oberon sighed, and for the first time, age seemed to weigh him down. He looked old; still deadly and extremely powerful, but ancient and tired. "You are more connected to our world than you know, Meghan Chase. You see, you are my daughter."

CHAPTER TEN

The Erlking's Daughter

I stared at Oberon as the world fell away beneath me. The Erlking gazed back, his expression cool and unruffled, his eyes blank once more. The silence around us was absolute. I didn't see anyone except Oberon; the rest of the court faded into the background, until we were the only two in the whole world.

Puck gave an indignant *caw* and flapped his wings against the cage.

That broke the spell. *"What?"* I choked out. The Erlking didn't so much as blink, which somehow infuriated me even more. "That's not true! Mom was married to my dad. She stayed with him until he disappeared, and she remarried Luke."

"That is true." Oberon nodded. "But that man is not your father, Meghan. I am." He stood, his courtly robes billowing around him. "You are half-fey, half my blood. Why do you think I had Puck guard you, keep you from seeing our world? Because it comes naturally to you. Most mortals are blind, but you could see through the Mist from the beginning."

I thought back to all those times I almost saw something, out of the corner of my eye, or silhouetted in the trees. Glimpses of things not quite there. I shook my head. "No, I don't believe you. My mom loved my dad. She wouldn't—" I broke off, not wanting to think about the implications.

"Your mother was a beautiful woman," Oberon continued softly. "And quite extraordinary, for a mortal. Artistic people can always see a bit of the fey world around them. She would often go to the park to paint and draw. It was there, beside the pond, that we first met."

"Stop it," I gritted out. "You're lying. I'm not one of you. I can't be."

"Only half," Oberon said, and from the corner of my eye I caught looks of disgust and contempt from the rest of the court. "Still, that is enough for my enemies to attempt to control me through you. Or, perhaps, to turn you against me. You are more dangerous than you know, daughter. Because of the threat you represent, you must remain here."

My world seemed to be collapsing around me. "For how long?" I whispered, thinking of Mom, Luke, school, everything I left behind in my world. Had I been missed already? Would I return to find a hundred years had passed while I was gone, and everyone I knew was long dead?

"Until I deem otherwise," Oberon said, in the tone my mother often used when she settled the matter. *Because I said so.* "At the very least, until Elysium is through. The Winter Court will be arriving in a few days, and I will have you where I can see you." He clapped, and a female satyr broke away from the crowd to bow before him. "Take my daughter to her room," he ordered, sitting back on his throne. "See that she is made comfortable."

"Yes, my lord," murmured the satyr, and began to clop

away, glancing back to see if I was coming. Oberon leaned back, not looking at me, his face blank and stony.

My audience with the Erlking was over.

I had stumbled back, prepared to follow the goat-girl out of the court, when Grimalkin's voice floated up from the ground. I'd completely forgotten about the cat. "Begging your pardon, my lord," Grimalkin said, sitting up and curling his tail around himself, "but our business is not yet complete. You see, the girl is in my debt. She promised me a favor for bringing her safely here, and that obligation has yet to be paid."

I glared at the feline, wondering why it was bringing that up now. Oberon, however, looked at me with a grim expression. "Is this true?"

I nodded, wondering why the nobles were giving me looks of horror and pity. "Grim helped me escape the goblins," I explained. "He saved my life. I wouldn't be here if it weren't for…" My voice trailed off as I saw the look in Oberon's eyes.

"A life debt, then." He sighed. "Very well, Cait Sith. What would you have of me?"

Grimalkin lowered his eyelids. It was easy to see that the cat was purring. "A small favor, great lord," he rumbled, "to be called in at a later time."

"Granted." The Erlking nodded, and yet he seemed to grow bigger in his chair. His shadow loomed over the cat, who blinked and flattened his ears. Thunder growled overhead, the light in the forest dimmed, and a cold wind rattled the branches in the trees, showering us with petals. The rest of the court shrank away; some vanished from sight completely. In the sudden darkness, Oberon's eyes glowed amber. "But be warned, feline," he boomed, his voice making the ground quiver. "I am not to be trifled with. Do not think to make a fool out of me, for I can grant your request in insurmountably unpleasant ways."

"Of course, great Erlking," Grimalkin soothed, his fur whipping about in the gale. "I am always your servant."

"I would be foolish indeed to trust the flattering words of a cait sith." Oberon leaned back, his face an expressionless mask once more. The wind died down, the sun returned, and things were normal again. "You have your favor. Now go."

Grimalkin bowed his head, turned, and trotted back to me, bottlebrush tail held high.

"What was that about, Grim?" I demanded, scowling at the feline. "I thought you wanted a favor from me. What was all that with Oberon?"

Grimalkin didn't so much as pause. Tail up, he passed me without comment, slipped into the tunnel of trees, and vanished from sight.

The satyr touched my arm. "This way," she murmured, and led me away from the court. I felt the eyes of the nobles and the hounds on my back as we left the presence of the Erlking.

"I don't understand," I said miserably, following the satyr girl across the clearing. My brain had gone numb; I felt awash in a sea of confusion, moments away from drowning. I just wanted to find my brother. How had it come to this?

The satyr gave me a sympathetic glance. She was shorter than me by a foot, with large hazel eyes that matched her curly hair. I tried to keep my eyes away from her furry lower half, but it was difficult, especially when she smelled faintly like a petting zoo.

"It is not so bad," she said, leading me not through the tunnel, but to a far side of the clearing. The trees here were so thick the sunlight didn't permeate the branches, shadowing everything in emerald darkness. "You might enjoy it here. Your father does you a great honor."

"He's not my father," I snapped. She blinked wide, liquid brown eyes, and her lower lip quivered. I sighed, regretting my harsh tone. "Sorry. It's just a lot to take in. Two days ago, I was home, sleeping in my own bed. I didn't believe in goblins or elves or talking cats, and I certainly didn't ask for any of this."

"King Oberon took a great chance for you," the satyr said, her voice a bit firmer. "The cait sith held a life debt over you, which meant it could've asked for anything. My lord Oberon took it and made it his, so Grimalkin can't request you to poison anyone or to give up your first child."

I recoiled in horror. "He would have?"

"Who knows what goes on in the mind of a cat?" The satyr shrugged, picking her way over a tangle of roots. "Just… be careful what you say around here. If you make a promise, you're bound to it, and wars have been fought over 'small favors.' Be especially careful around the high lords and ladies— they are all adept at the game of politics and pawn-making." She suddenly paled and put a hand to her mouth. "I've said too much. Please forgive me. If that gets back to King Oberon…"

"I won't say anything," I promised.

She looked relieved. "I am grateful, Meghan Chase. Others might have used that against me. I am still learning the ways of the court."

"What's your name?"

"Tansy."

"Well, you're the only one who has treated me nicely without expecting anything in return," I told her. "Thank you."

She looked embarrassed. "Truly, you do not need to put

yourself in my debt, Meghan Chase. Here, let me show you your room."

We were standing at the edge of the trees. A wall of flowering bramble, so thick I couldn't see to the other side, loomed above us. Between the pink-and-purple flowers, thorns bristled menacingly.

Tansy reached out and brushed one of the petals. The hedge shuddered, then curled in and rearranged itself, forming a tunnel not unlike the one leading into the court. At the end of the prickly tube stood a small red door.

In a daze, I followed Tansy into the briar tunnel and through the door as she opened it for me. Inside, a dazzling bedroom greeted my senses. The floor was white marble, inlaid with patterns of flowers, birds, and animals. Under my disbelieving stare, some of them moved. A fountain bubbled in the middle of the room, and a small table stood nearby, covered with cakes, tea, and bottles of wine. A massive, silk-covered bed dominated one wall, while a fireplace stood at the other. The flames crackling in the hearth changed color, from green to blue to pink and back again.

"This is the guest-of-honor suite," Tansy announced, gazing around enviously. "Only important guests of the Seelie Court are allowed here. Your father really is giving you a great honor."

"Tansy, please stop calling him that." I sighed, looking around the massive room. "My dad was an insurance salesman from Brooklyn. I'd know if I wasn't fully human, wouldn't I? Wouldn't there be some sort of sign, pointed ears or wings or something like that?"

Tansy blinked, and the look she gave me sent chills up my back. Hooves clopping, she crossed the room to stand beside a large dresser with a mirror overhead. Looking back, she beckoned me with a finger.

Anxiously, I moved to stand beside her. Somewhere deep inside, a voice began screaming that I didn't want to see what would be revealed next. I didn't listen in time. With a solemn look, Tansy pointed to the mirror, and for the second time that day, my world turned upside down.

I hadn't seen myself since the day I stepped through the closet with Puck. I knew my clothes were filthy, sweat-stained, and ripped to shreds by branches, thorns, and claws. From the neck down, I looked how I expected to look: like a bum that had been tramping through the wilderness for two days without a bath.

I didn't recognize my face.

I mean, I knew it was me. The reflection moved its lips when I did, and blinked when I blinked. But my skin was paler, the bones of my face sharper, and my eyes seemed enormous, those of a deer caught in headlights. And through my matted, tangled hair, where nothing had been yesterday, two long pointed ears jutted up from both sides of my head.

I gaped at the reflection, feeling dizzy, unable to comprehend the meaning. *No!* my brain screamed, violently rejecting the image before it, *that isn't you! It isn't!*

The floor swayed under my feet. I couldn't catch my breath. And then, all the shock, adrenaline, fear, and horror of the past two days descended on me at once. The world spun, tilted on its axis, and I fell away into oblivion.

PART TWO

CHAPTER ELEVEN

Titania's Promise

"Meghan," Mom called from the other side of the door. "Get up. You're going to be late for school."

I groaned and peeked out from under the covers. Was it morning already? Apparently so. A hazy gray light filtered in my bedroom window, shining on my alarm clock, which read 6:48 a.m.

"Meghan!" Mom called, and this time a sharp rapping accompanied her voice. "Are you up?"

"Ye-es!" I hollered from the bed, wishing she'd go away.

"Well, hurry up! You're going to miss the bus."

I shambled to my feet, threw on clothes from the cleanest pile on the floor, and grabbed my backpack. My iPod tumbled out, landing with a splat on my bed. I frowned. Why was it wet?

"Meghan!" came Mom's voice yet again, and I rolled my eyes. "It's almost seven! If I have to drive you to school because you missed the bus, you're grounded for a month!"

"All right, all right! I'm coming, dammit!" Stomping to the door, I threw it open.

Ethan stood there, his face blue and wrinkled, his lips pulled into a rictus grin. In one hand, he clutched a butcher knife. Blood spattered his hands and face.

"Mommy slipped," he whispered, and plunged the knife into my leg.

I woke up screaming.

Green flames sputtered in the hearth, casting the room in an eerie glow. Panting, I lay back against cool silk pillows, the nightmare ebbing away into reality.

I was in the Seelie king's court, as much a prisoner here as poor Puck, trapped in his cage. Ethan, the real Ethan, was still out there somewhere, waiting to be rescued. I wondered if he was all right, if he was as terrified as I was. I wondered if Mom and Luke were okay with that demon changeling in the house. I prayed Mom's injury wasn't serious, and that the changeling wouldn't cause harm to anyone else.

And then, lying in a strange bed in the faery kingdom, another thought came to me. A thought sparked by something Oberon said. *That man is not your father, Meghan. I am.*

Is your father, not *was.* As if Oberon knew where he was. As if he was still alive. The thought made my heart pound in excitement. I knew it. My dad must be in Faeryland, somewhere. Maybe somewhere close. If only I could reach him.

First things first, though. I had to get out of here.

I sat up…and met the impassive green eyes of the Erlking.

He stood by the hearth, the shifting light of the flames washing over his face, making him even more eerie and spectral. His long shadow crept over the room, the horned crown branching over the bedcovers like grasping fingers. In the darkness, his eyes glowed green like a cat's. Seeing I was awake, he nodded and beckoned to me with an elegant, long-fingered hand.

"Come." His voice, though soft, was steely with authority. "Approach me. Let us talk, my daughter."

I'm not your daughter, I wanted to say, but the words stuck in my throat. Out of the corner of my eye, I saw the mirror atop the dresser, and my long-eared reflection within. I shuddered and turned away.

Throwing off the bedcovers, I saw that my clothes had changed. Instead of the ripped, disgusting shirt and pants I'd worn for the past two days, I was clean and draped in a lacy white nightgown. Not only that, but there was an outfit laid out for me at the foot of the bed: a ridiculously fancy gown encrusted with emeralds and sapphires, as well as a cloak and long, elbow-length gloves. I wrinkled my nose at the whole ensemble.

"Where are my clothes?" I asked, turning to Oberon. "My real ones."

The Erlking sniffed. "I dislike mortal clothes within my court," he stated quietly. "I believe you should wear something suited for your heritage, as you are to stay here awhile. I had your mortal rags burned."

"You *what?*"

Oberon narrowed his eyes, and I realized I might've gone too far. I figured the King of the Seelie Court wasn't used to being questioned. "Um…sorry," I murmured, sliding out of bed. I'd worry about clothes later. "So, what did you want to talk about?"

The Erlking sighed and studied me uncomfortably. "You put me in a difficult position, daughter," he murmured at last, turning back to the hearth. "You are the only one of my offspring to venture into our world. I must say, I was a bit surprised that you managed to survive this long, even with Robin looking after you."

"Offspring?" I blinked. "You mean, I have other brothers and sisters? Half siblings?"

"None that are alive." Oberon made a dismissive gesture. "And none within this century, I assure you. Your mother was the only human to catch my eye in nearly two hundred years."

My mouth was suddenly dry. I stared at Oberon in growing anger. "Why?" I demanded, making him arch a slender eyebrow. "Why her? Wasn't she already married to my dad? Did you even care about that?"

"I did not." Oberon's look was pitiless, unrepentant. "What do I care for human rituals? I need no permission to take what I want. Besides, had she been truly happy, I would not have been able to sway her."

Bastard. I bit my tongue to keep the angry word from coming out. Furious as I might be, I wasn't suicidal. But Oberon's gaze sharpened, as if he knew what I was thinking. He gave me a long, level stare, challenging me to defy him. We glared at each other for several heartbeats, the shadows curling around us, as I struggled to keep my gaze steady. It was no use; staring at Oberon was like facing down an approaching tornado. I shivered and dropped my eyes first.

After a moment, Oberon's face softened, and a faint smile curled his lips. "You are a lot like her, daughter," he continued, his voice split between pride and resignation. "Your mother was a remarkable mortal. If she had been fey, her paintings would have come to life, so much care was put into them. When I watched her at the park, I sensed her longing, her loneliness and isolation. She wanted more from her life than what she was getting. She wanted something extraordinary to happen."

I didn't want to hear this. I didn't want anything ruining my perfect memory of our life before. I wanted to keep believing that my mom loved my dad, that we were happy and content, and she was his whole life. I didn't want to hear about a mother who was lonely, who fell prey to faery tricks and glamour. With one casual statement, my past had shattered into an unfamiliar mess, and I felt I didn't know my mother at all.

"I waited a month before I made myself known to her," Oberon went on, oblivious to my torment. I slumped against the bed as he continued. "I grew to know her habits, her emotions, every inch of her. And when I did reveal myself, I showed her only a glimpse of my true nature, curious to see if she would approach the extraordinary, or if she would cling to her mortal disbelief. She accepted me eagerly, with unrestrained joy, as if she had been waiting for me all along."

"Stop," I choked. My stomach churned; I closed my eyes to avoid being sick. "I don't want to hear this. Where was my dad when all this was happening?"

"Your *mother's husband* was away most nights," Oberon replied, putting emphasis on those two words, to remind me that man was not my father. "Perhaps that was why your mother yearned for something more. I gave her that; one night of magic, of the passion she was missing. Just one, before I returned to Arcadia, and the memory of us faded from her mind."

"She doesn't remember you?" I looked up at him. "Is that why she never told me?"

Oberon nodded. "Mortals tend to forget their encounters with our kind," he said softly. "At best, it seems like a vivid dream. Most times, we fade from memory completely. Surely you've noticed this. How even the people you live with, who see you every day, cannot seem to remember you. Though, I always suspected your mother knew more, remembered more, than she let on. Especially after you were born." A dark tone crept into his voice; his slanted eyes turned black and pupilless. I trembled as the shadow crept over the floor, reaching for me with pointed fingers. "She tried to take you away," he said in a terrible voice. "She wanted to hide you from us. From me." Oberon paused, looking utterly inhuman, though he hadn't moved. The fire leaped in the hearth, dancing madly in the eyes of the Erlking.

"And yet, here you are." Oberon blinked, his tone softening, and the fire flickered low again. "Standing before me, your human mien faded at last. The moment you set foot in the Nevernever, it was only a matter of time before your heritage began to show itself. But now I must be very cautious." He drew himself up, gathering his robes around him, as if to leave. "I cannot be too wary, Meghan Chase," he warned. "There are many who would use you against me, some within this very court. Be careful, daughter. Even I cannot protect you from everything."

I sagged on the bed, my thoughts spinning crazily. Oberon watched me a moment longer, his mouth set in a grim line, then crossed the room without looking back. When I looked up, the Erlking was gone. I hadn't even heard the door close.

A knock on the door startled me upright. I didn't know how much time had passed since Oberon's visit. I still lay on the bed. The colored flames burned low, flickering erratically in the hearth. Everything seemed surreal and foggy and dreamlike, as if I'd imagined the whole encounter.

The knock came again, and I roused myself. "Come in!"

The door creaked open, and Tansy entered, smiling. "Good evening, Meghan Chase. How do you feel today?"

I slipped to the floor, realizing I was still in the nightgown. "Fine, I guess," I muttered, looking around the room. "Where are my clothes?"

"King Oberon has given you a gown." Tansy smiled and pointed to the gown on the bed. "He had it designed especially for you."

I scowled. "No. No way. I want my real clothes."

The little satyr blinked. She clopped over and picked up the hem of the dress, running it between her fingers. "But...my lord Oberon wishes you to wear this." She seemed bewildered that I would defy Oberon's wishes. "Does this not please you?"

"Tansy, I am *not* wearing that."

"Why not?"

I recoiled at the thought of parading around in that circus tent. My whole life, I had worn ratty jeans and T-shirts. My family was poor and couldn't afford designer clothes and name brands. Rather than bemoan the fact that I never got nice things, I flaunted my grunginess and sneered at the shallow rich girls who spent hours in the bathroom perfecting their makeup. The only dress I'd ever worn was to someone's wedding.

Besides, if I wore the fancy outfit Oberon picked for me, it would be like admitting to being his daughter. And I wasn't about to do that.

"I—I just don't want to," I stammered lamely. "I'd rather wear my own clothes."

"Your clothing was burned."

"Where's my backpack?" I suddenly remembered the change of clothes I'd shoved inside. They'd be damp, moldy, and disgusting, but better that than wearing faery finery.

I found my backpack, stuffed carelessly behind the dresser, and unzipped it. A sour, dank smell rose from within as I dumped the contents onto the floor. The wadded ball of clothes rolled out, wrinkled and smelly, but mine. The broken iPod also tumbled free, skidded across the marble floor, and came to a stop a few feet from Tansy.

The satyr girl yelped, and in one fantastic bound, leaped onto the bed. Clutching the bedpost, she stared wide-eyed at the device on the floor.

"What is *that?*"

"What? This? It's an iPod." Blinking, I retrieved the device and held it up. "It's a machine that plays music, but it's broken now, so I can't show you how it works. Sorry."

"It stinks of iron!"

I didn't know what to say to that, so I opted for a confused frown.

Tansy stared at me with huge brown eyes, very slowly coming down from her perch. "You…you can hold it?" she whispered. "Without burning your flesh? Without poisoning your blood?"

"Um." I glanced at the iPod, lying harmlessly in my palm. "Yes?"

She shuddered. "Please, put it away." I shrugged, grabbed my backpack, and stuffed it into a side pocket. Tansy sighed and relaxed. "Forgive me, I did not wish to upset you. King Oberon has bid me keep you company until Elysium. Would you care to see more of the court?"

Not really, but it was better than being cooped up in here with nothing to do. *And maybe I'll find a way out of this place.*

"All right," I told the satyr girl. "But I want to change first."

She cast a glance at my mortal clothes, lying wrinkled on the floor, and her nostrils flared. I could tell she wanted to say something but was polite enough not to comment on it. "As you wish. I will wait outside."

★ ★ ★

I slipped into the baggy jeans and the wrinkled, smelly T-shirt, feeling a nasty glow of satisfaction as they slid comfortably over my skin. *Burn my things, will he?* I thought, dragging my sneakers out and shoving my feet into them. *I'm not part of his court, and I'm certainly not claiming to be his daughter. No matter what he says.*

There was a brush lying on the dresser, and I grabbed it to run through my hair. As I looked in the mirror, my stomach twisted. I seemed less recognizable than before, in ways that I couldn't even put a finger on. I knew only that the longer I stayed here, the more I was fading away.

Shivering, I grabbed my backpack, happy for the familiar, comfortable weight, and slung it over my shoulders. Even though it carried nothing but a broken iPod, it was still mine. Refusing to glance at the mirror, feeling eyes on the back of my neck, I opened the door and slipped into the briar tunnel.

Moonlight filtered through the branches, dappling the path with silver shadows. I wondered how long I'd been asleep. The night was warm, and faint strings of music drifted on the breeze. Tansy approached, and in the darkness, her face looked less human and more staring-black-goat. A strand of moonlight fell over her, and she was normal again. Smiling, she took my hand and led me forward.

The bramble tunnel seemed longer this time, filled with twists and turns I didn't remember. I looked back once and saw the thorns closing behind us, the tunnel vanishing from sight.

"Um…"

"It's all right," said Tansy, pulling me forward. "The Hedge can take you wherever you want to go within the court. You just have to know the right paths."

"Where are we going?"

"You'll see."

The tunnel opened into a moonlit grove. Music drifted on the breeze, played by a willowy green girl on an elegant golden harp. A small group of elven girls clustered around a tall, vine-backed chair with white roses growing out of the arms.

Sitting at the foot of the chair was a human. I blinked, rubbing my eyes to make sure they weren't playing tricks on me. No, it was a human, a young man with curly blond hair, his eyes blank and bemused. He was shirtless, and a golden collar encircled his neck, attached to a thin silver chain. The group of fey girls swarmed around him, kissing his bare shoulders, rubbing their hands over his chest, whispering things in his ear. One of them ran a pink tongue up his neck, her fingernails drawing bloody gouges down his back, making him arch with ecstasy. My stomach turned and I looked away. A moment later, I forgot all about them.

On the throne was a woman of such otherworldly beauty, I was instantly mortified by my ratty clothes and casual appearance. Her long hair shifted colors in the moonlight, sometimes silver, sometimes brightest gold. Arrogance warred with the aura of power surrounding her. As Tansy pulled me forward and bowed, the woman narrowed glittering blue eyes and regarded me as though examining a slug found beneath a log.

"So," she said at last, her voice dripping poisoned icicles, "this is Oberon's little bastard."

Oh, crap. I knew who this was. She sat the second, empty throne in Oberon's court. She was the other driving force in *A Midsummer Night's Dream*. She was nearly as powerful as Oberon himself.

"Queen Titania." I gulped, bowing.

"It speaks," the lady went on, feigning surprise, "as if it knows me. As if being Oberon's throwback will protect it from my wrath." Her eyes glittered like chips of diamond, and she smiled, making her even more beautiful and terrifying. "But I am feeling merciful tonight. Perhaps I will not cut out its tongue and feed it to the hounds. Perhaps." Titania looked past me to Tansy, still bowed low, and crooked one elegant finger. "Come forward, goat-child."

Keeping her head bowed, Tansy edged forward until she stood at the faery queen's arm. Queen Titania leaned forward, as though whispering to the satyr, but spoke loud enough for me to hear. "I will allow you to be the voice for this conversation," she explained, as if to a small child. "I will direct all questions to you, and you will speak for the bastard over there. If, at any point, it attempts to speak to me directly, I will turn it into a hart and set my hounds after it until it collapses from exhaustion or is torn apart. Is this perfectly clear?"

"Yes, my lady," Tansy whispered.

Perfectly clear, bitch-queen, I echoed in my thoughts.

"Excellent." Titania leaned back, looking pleased. She shot me a brittle smile, as hostile as a snarling dog, then turned to Tansy. "Now, goat-girl, why is the bastard here?"

"Why are you here?" Tansy repeated, directing the question to me.

"I'm looking for my brother," I replied, being careful to keep my gaze on Tansy and not the vindictive ice-hag next to her.

"She's looking for her brother," Tansy confirmed, turning again to the faery queen. Good God, this was going to take forever.

"He was stolen and brought into the Nevernever," I said, plunging on before Titania could ask another question. "Puck led me here through the closet. I came to get my brother and take him home, and be rid of the changeling left in his place. That's all I want. I'll leave as soon as I find him."

"Puck?" mused the lady. "Aah, that is where he has been all this time. How very clever of Oberon, hiding you like that. And then you have to ruin his little deception by coming here." She *tsked* and shook her head. "Goat-girl," she said, looking at Tansy once more, "ask the bastard this—would she prefer being a rabbit or a hart?"

"M-my lady?" Tansy stammered as I felt the shadows closing in on me. My heart pounded and I looked around for an escape route. Thorny briars surrounded us; there was nowhere to run.

"It is a simple question," Titania went on, her tone perfectly conversational. "What would she prefer I change her into—a rabbit or a hart?"

Looking like a trapped rabbit herself, Tansy turned and met my eyes. "M-my lady would like to know if you—"

"Yes, I heard," I interrupted. "A rabbit or a hart. How about neither?" I dared look up and meet the faery queen's eyes. "Look, I know you hate me, but just let me rescue my brother and go home. He's only four, and he must be terrified. Please, I know he's waiting for me. Once I find him, we'll leave and you'll never see us again, I swear."

Titania's face glowed with angry triumph. "The creature dares to speak to me! Very well. She has chosen her fate." The faery queen raised a gloved hand, and lightning flashed overhead. "A hart it is, then. Set free the hounds. We will have a merry hunt!"

Her hand swept down, pointing at me, and spasms rocked my body. I screamed and arched my back, feeling my spine lengthen and pop. Invisible pliers grabbed my face and pulled, stretching my lips into a muzzle. I felt my legs getting longer, thinner, my fingers turning into cloven hooves. I screamed again, but what left my throat was the agonized bleat of a deer.

Then, suddenly, it stopped. My body snapped into the proper shape, like a taut rubber band, and I collapsed, gasping, to the forest floor.

Through my blurry vision, I saw Oberon standing at the mouth of the tunnel, a pair of faery knights behind him, his arm outstretched. For a moment, I was sure I saw Grimalkin standing by his feet, but I blinked and the shadows were empty. With his appearance, the lilting harp music ground to a halt. The fey girls surrounding the collared human flung themselves to the floor and bowed their heads.

"Wife," Oberon said calmly, stepping into the clearing. "You will not do this."

Titania rose, her face a mask of fury. "You dare speak to me that way," she spat, and wind rattled the branches of the trees. "You dare, after you hid her from me, after you sent your little pet to protect her!" Titania sneered, and lightning crackled overhead. "You deny me a consort, and yet you flaunt your half-breed abomination in the court for all to see. You are a disgrace. The court mocks you in secret, and you still protect her."

"Nonetheless." Somehow, Oberon's composed voice rose above the howling of the wind. "She is my blood, and you will not touch her. If you have any grievances, my lady, cast them on me, not on the girl. It is not her fault."

"Perhaps I shall turn her into a cabbage," the queen mused, shooting me a look of black hatred, "and plant her in my garden for the rabbits to enjoy. Then she would be useful and wanted."

"You will *not* touch her," Oberon said again, his voice rising in authority. His cloak billowed out, and he grew taller, his shadow lengthening on the ground. "I command it, wife. I have given my word that she shall not come to harm within my court, and you will follow me on this. Do I make myself clear?"

Lightning sizzled, and the ground shook under the intensity of the rulers' gazes. The girls at the foot of the throne cringed, and Oberon's guards grasped the hilts of their swords. A branch snapped nearby, barely missing the harp girl, who cowered under the trunk. I pressed myself to the earth and tried to make myself as small as possible.

"Very well, husband." Titania's voice was as cold as ice, but the wind gradually died and the earth stopped moving. "As you command. I will not harm the half-breed while she is within the court."

Oberon gave a curt nod. "And your servants will not do her ill, either."

The queen pursed her lips as if she'd swallowed a lemon. "No, husband."

The Erlking sighed. "Very well. We will speak on this later. I bid you good-night, my lady." He turned, his cloak billowing behind him, and left the clearing, the guards trailing in his wake. I wanted to call after him, but I didn't want it to look like I was running after Daddy's protection, especially after he put the smackdown on Titania.

Speaking of which…

I swallowed and turned to face the faery queen, who glared at me as if hoping the blood would boil in my veins. "Well, you heard His Majesty, half-breed," she cooed, her voice laced with poison. "Get out of my sight before I forget my promise and change you into a snail."

I was only too happy to leave. However, no sooner did I stand up and prepare to flee than Titania snapped her fingers.

"Wait!" she ordered. "I've a better idea. Goat-girl, come here."

Tansy appeared at her side. The satyr looked terrified; her eyes were bulging out of her head and her furry legs trembled. The queen flicked a finger at me. "Take Oberon's bastard to the kitchens. Tell Sarah we've found her a new serving girl. If the bastard must stay, she might as well work."

"B-but, my lady," Tansy stammered, and I marveled that she had the courage to contradict the queen, "King Oberon said—"

"Ah, but King Oberon is no longer here, is he?" Titania's eyes gleamed, and she smiled. "And what Oberon does not know will not hurt him. Now, go, before I truly lose my patience."

We went, trying not to trip over each other as we fled the queen's presence and went back into the tunnel.

As we reached the edge of the brambles, a ripple of power shook the air, and the girls behind us gave cries of dismay. A moment later, a fox darted into the tunnel with a flash of red fur. It stopped a few yards away and looked at us, amber eyes wide with confusion and fear. I saw the gleam of a golden collar around its throat, before it gave a frightened bark and vanished into the thorns.

In silence, I followed Tansy through the twisting maze of briars, trying to process all that had happened. Okay, so Titania had a serious grudge against me; that was really, really bad. As the record of "Enemies-I-did-not-want" went, the Queen of the Faeries would probably top the list. I would have to be really careful from now on, or risk ending up a mushroom in somebody's soup.

Tansy didn't say a word until we came to a pair of large

stone doors in the hedge. Tendrils of steam curled out beneath the cracks, and the air was hot and greasy.

Pushing the doors open released a blast of hot, smoky air. Blinking tears from my eyes, I stared into an enormous kitchen. Brick ovens roared, copper kettles bubbled over fires, and a dozen aromas flooded my senses. Furry little men in aprons scuttled back and forth between several long counters, cooking, baking, testing the contents of the kettles. A bloody boar carcass lay on a table, and hacking into it was a huge, green-skinned woman with thick tusks and brown hair pulled into a braid.

She saw us in the doorway and came stomping over, blood and bits of meat clinging to her apron.

"No loafers in my kitchen," she growled, waving a large bronze butcher knife at me. "I got no scraps for the likes of you. Take your sneaky, thieving fingers elsewhere."

"S-Sarah Skinflayer, this is Meghan Chase." As Tansy introduced us, I gave the troll woman a sickly, please-don't-kill-me smile. "She's to help you in the kitchen by order of the queen."

"I don't need help from a skinny half-human whelp," Sarah Skinflayer growled, eyeing me disdainfully. "She'd only slow us down, and we're running ourselves into the ground, getting ready for Elysium." Looking me over, she sighed and scratched her head with the blunt end of the knife. "I guess I could find a place for her. But tell Her Majesty that if she wants to torture someone else, try the stables or the kennel runs. I've got all the help I need here."

Tansy nodded and left quickly, leaving me alone with the giantess. I felt sweat dripping down my back, and it wasn't from the fires. "All right, whelp," Sarah Skinflayer barked, pointing at me with her knife. "I don't care if you are His Majesty's throwback, you're in my kitchen now. Rules here

are simple—you don't work, you don't eat. And I have a little fun with the horsewhip in the corner. They don't call me
Sarah Skinflayer for nothing."

The rest of the night passed in a blur of scrubbing and cleaning. I mopped blood and bits of flesh from the stone floor. I
swept ashes from the brick ovens. I washed mountains of plates,
goblets, pots, and pans. Every time I paused to rub my aching
limbs, the troll woman would be there, barking orders and
pushing me to my next chore. Toward the end of the night,
after catching me sitting on a stool, she growled something
about "lazy humans," snatched the broom from my hands,
and gave me the one she was carrying. As soon as my hands
closed around the handle, the broom leaped to life and began
sweeping vigorously, brisk, hard strokes, while my feet carried me around the room. I tried letting go of the thing, but
my fingers seemed glued to the handle, and I couldn't open
my hands. I swept the floor until my legs ached and my arms
burned, until I couldn't see for the sweat in my eyes. Finally,
the troll woman snapped her fingers and the broom stopped
its mad sweeping. I collapsed, my knees buckling underneath
me, tempted to hurl the sadistic broom into the nearest oven.

"Did you enjoy that, half-breed?" Sarah Skinflayer asked,
and I was too winded to answer. "There will be more of the
same tomorrow, I guarantee it. Here." Two pieces of bread
and a lump of cheese hit the ground. "That's the dinner you
earned tonight. It should be safe for you to eat. Maybe tomorrow you'll get something better."

"Fine," I muttered, ready to crawl back to my room, thinking there was no way I was ever coming back here. I planned
to conveniently "forget" about my forced servitude tomorrow, maybe even find a way out of the Seelie Court. "See
you tomorrow."

The troll blocked my path. "Where do you think you're going, half-breed? You're part of my workforce now, so that means you're *mine.*" She pointed to a wooden door in the corner. "The servants' quarters are full. You can take the pantry closet there." She smiled at me, fierce and terrible, showing blunt yellow teeth and tusks. "We start work at dawn. See you tomorrow, whelp."

I ate my measly dinner and crawled beneath shelves of onions, turnips, and strange blue vegetables to sleep. I had no blanket, but the kitchens were uncomfortably warm. I was trying to turn a sack of grain into a pillow, when I remembered my backpack, tossed onto a shelf, and crawled out to retrieve it. There was nothing in the orange pack now but a broken iPod, but still, it was mine, the only reminder of my old life.

I snatched the backpack off the shelf and was walking back toward my tiny room when I felt something wriggle inside the pack. Startled, I nearly dropped it, and heard a soft snicker coming from inside. Edging over to the counter, I put the bag down, grabbed a knife, and unzipped it, ready to plunge the blade into whatever jumped out.

My iPod lay there, dead and silent. With a sigh, I zipped the pack up and carried it into the pantry with me. Tossing it into a corner, I curled up on the floor, put my head on the bag of grain, and let my thoughts drift. I thought of Ethan, and Mom, and school. Was anyone missing me back home? Were there search parties being sent out for me, police and dogs sniffing around the last places I was seen? Or had Mom forgotten me, as I was sure Luke had? Would I even have a home to go back to, if I did manage to find Ethan?

I started to shake, and my eyes grew misty. Soon, tears flowed down my cheeks, staining the sack under my head and making my hair sticky. I turned my face into the rough fabric and sobbed. I'd hit rock bottom. Lying in a dark pantry, with no hope of rescuing Ethan and nothing to look forward to but fear, pain, and exhaustion, I was ready to give up.

Gradually, as my sobs stilled and my breathing grew calmer, I realized I was not alone.

Raising my head, I first saw my backpack, where I'd flung it in the corner. It was unzipped, lying open like a gaping maw. I saw the glint of the iPod inside.

Then, I saw the eyes.

My heart stopped, and I sat up quickly, banging my head against the shelf. Dust showered me as I scooted to the far corner, gasping. I'd seen those eyes before, glowing green and intelligent. The creature was small, smaller than the goblins, with oily black skin and long, spindly arms. Except for the large, goblinlike ears, it looked like a horrible cross between a monkey and a spider.

The creature smiled, and its teeth lit the corner with pale blue light.

Then it spoke.

Its voice echoed flatly in the gloom, like a radio speaker hissing static. I couldn't understand it at first. Then, as if it were changing the station, the static cleared away and I heard words.

"—are waiting," it crackled, its voice still buzzing with static. "Come to…iron…your brother…held in…"

"Ethan?" I bolted upright, banging my head again. "Where is he? What do you know about him?"

"…Iron Court…we…waiting for…" The creature flickered in the darkness, going fuzzy like a weak signal. It hissed and blipped out of sight, plunging the room into blackness again.

I lay there in the gloom, my heart pounding, thinking

about what the creature had said. I couldn't glean much from the eerie conversation, except that my brother was alive, and something called the Iron Court was waiting for something.

All right, I told myself, taking a deep breath. *They're still out there, Meghan. Ethan and your dad. You can't give up now. Time to stop being a crybaby and get your act together.*

I snatched the iPod and stuffed it into my back pocket. If that monster-thing came to me with any more news of Ethan, I wanted to be ready. Lying back on the cold floor, I closed my eyes and started to plan.

The next two days passed in a blur. I did everything the troll woman told me to do: washed dishes, scrubbed floors, sliced meat off animal carcasses until my hands were stained red. No more spells were cast on me, and Sarah Skinflayer began to eye me with grudging respect. The food they offered was simple fare: bread and cheese and water. The troll woman informed me anything more exotic might wreak havoc with my delicate half-human system. At night, I would crawl, exhausted, into my bed in the pantry and fall asleep immediately. The spindly creature visited me no more after that first night, and my sleep was blissfully free of nightmares.

All the while, I kept my eyes and ears open, gleaning information that would help me when I finally made my escape. In the kitchen, under the hawk eye of Sarah Skinflayer, escape was impossible. The troll woman had a habit of appearing whenever I thought about taking a break, or striding into a room just as I finished a task. I did try to sneak out of the kitchen one night, but when I pulled open the front door, a small storage room greeted me instead of the tunnel of thorns. I almost despaired at that point, but forced myself to be patient. The time would come, I told myself; I would just have to be ready when it did.

I spoke with the other kitchen workers when I could, creatures called brownies and house gnomes, but they were so busy I gained little information from them. I did discover something that made my heart pound excitedly. Elysium, the event that had everyone in the kitchen running around like mad things, would be held in a few days. As tradition dictated, the Seelie and Unseelie courts would meet on neutral ground, to discuss politics, sign new accords, and maintain their very uneasy truce. Since it was spring, the Unseelie Court would be traveling to Oberon's territory for Elysium; in winter, the Unseelie would play host. Everyone in the court was invited, and as kitchen staff, we were required to be there.

I continued working hard, my own plans for Elysium running around in my head.

Then, three days after my sentence to the kitchens, we had visitors.

I was standing over a basket of tiny dead quail, plucking them after Sarah Skinflayer broke their necks and passed them to me. I tried to ignore the troll as she reached into a cage, grabbed a flapping, bright-eyed bird, and twisted its neck with a faint popping sound. She then tossed the lifeless body into the basket like a plucked fruit and reached for another.

The doors swung open abruptly, streaming light into the room, and three faery knights walked in. Long silver hair, pulled into simple ponytails, glimmered in the dimness of the room, and their faces were haughty and arrogant.

"We have come for the half-breed," one of them announced, his voice ringing through the kitchen. "By order of King Oberon, she will come with us."

Sarah Skinflayer glanced my way, snorted, and picked up

another quail. "That's fine with me. The brat's been nothing but deadweight since she came here. Take her out of my kitchens, and good riddance to her." She punctured the statement with the sharp crack of the bird's neck, and a brownie left the oven to take my place, shooing me away as it hopped onto a stool.

I started to follow them, but remembered my backpack, lying on the floor of the pantry closet. Muttering an apology, I hurried to grab it, slinging it over my back as I returned. None of the brownies looked up at me as I left, though Sarah Skinflayer glowered as she wrung a bird's neck. Battling relief and an odd sense of guilt, I followed the knights out of the room.

They led me through the twisting brambles to yet another door, opening it without preamble. I walked into a small bedroom, not nearly as fancy as my first, but nice enough. I glimpsed a round, steaming pool through a side-room door, and thought longingly of a bath.

I heard muffled clops on the carpeted floor, and turned to see a pair of satyr girls enter behind a tall, willowy woman with pure white skin and straight raven hair. She wore a dress so black it sucked in the light, and her fingers were long and spiderlike.

One of the satyr girls peeked at me from behind the woman's dress. I recognized Tansy, who gave me a timid smile, as if she feared I was mad about the encounter with Titania. I wasn't; she had been a pawn in the faery queen's game, just like me. But before I could say anything, the tall woman swept up and grabbed me, holding my chin in her bony fingers. Black eyes, with no iris or pupil, scanned my face.

"Filthy," she rasped, her voice like silk over a steel blade. "What a plain, dirty little specimen. What does Oberon expect me to do with this? I'm not a miracle worker."

I wrenched my face from her grasp, and the satyr girls squeaked. The lady, however, seemed amused. "Well, I suppose we shall have to try. Half-breed—"

"My name is not 'half-breed,'" I snapped, tired of hearing the word. "It's Meghan. Meghan Chase."

The woman didn't blink. "You give out your full name so easily, child," she stated, making me frown in confusion. "You are lucky that it is not your True Name, else you might find yourself in a dire situation. Very well, Meghan Chase. I am Lady Weaver, and you will listen to me carefully. King Oberon has asked me to make you presentable for Elysium tonight. He will not have his half-breed daughter parading around in peasant rags, or worse, mortal clothes, in front of the Unseelie Court. I told him I would do my best and not to expect miracles, but we shall try. Now—" she gestured to the side room "—first things first. You reek of human, troll, and blood. Go take a bath." She clapped once, and the two satyrs trotted around to face me. "Tansy and Clarissa will attend you. Now I must design something for you to wear that will not make a laughingstock of your father."

I glanced at Tansy, who wasn't meeting my eyes. Silently, I followed them to the pool, stripped off my disgusting clothes, and sank into the hot water.

Bliss. I floated for several minutes, letting the heat soak into my bones, easing the aches and pains from the past three days. I wondered if faeries ever got dirty or sweaty; I'd never seen any of the nobles look anything less than elegant.

The heat was making me sleepy. I must've dozed, for I had disturbing dreams of spiders crawling over my body in great black swarms, covering me with webs as if I were a giant fly. When I awoke, shuddering and itchy, I was lying on the bed and Lady Weaver stood over me.

"Well." She sighed as I struggled to my feet. "It's not my greatest work, but I suppose it will have to do. Come here, girl. Stand before the mirror a moment."

I did as she asked, and gaped at the reflection it showed me. A shimmering silver dress covered me, the material lighter than silk. It rippled like water with the slightest movement, lacy sleeves billowing out from my arms, barely touching my skin. My hair had been elegantly curled and twisted into a graceful swirl atop my head, held in place by sparkling pins. A sapphire the size of a baby's fist flashed blue fire at my throat.

"Well?" Lady Weaver gently touched one of my sleeves, admiring it like an artist would a favorite painting. "What do you think?"

"It's beautiful," I managed to say, staring at the elven princess in the glass. "I don't even recognize myself." An image flashed through my head and I giggled with slight hysteria. "I won't turn into a pumpkin when midnight comes, will I?"

"If you annoy the wrong people, you might." Lady Weaver turned away, clapping her hands. Like clockwork, Tansy and Clarissa appeared wearing simple white dresses, their curly hair brushed out. I caught a glimpse of horns beneath Tansy's hazel bangs. She held my orange backpack in two fingers, as if afraid it would bite her.

"I had the girls wash your mortal clothes," Lady Weaver said, turning away from the mirror. "Oberon would have them destroyed, but then that would mean more work for me, so I put them in your bag. Once Elysium is over, I'll be taking that dress back, so you'll want to hang on to your own clothes."

"Um, okay," I said, taking the backpack from Tansy. A quick inspection showed my jeans and shirt folded inside, and the iPod still hidden in a side pocket. For a moment, I thought to leave the pack behind, but decided against it. Oberon might find it offensive and have someone burn it without my knowledge. It was still mine, and held everything I owned in this world. Feeling slightly embarrassed, I swung it over one shoulder, the hillbilly princess with a bright orange pack.

"Let us go," Lady Weaver rasped, wrapping a gauzy black shawl around her throat. "Elysium awaits. And, half-breed, I worked hard on that dress. Do try not to get yourself killed."

CHAPTER TWELVE

Elysium

We walked through the briar tunnels into the courtyard. As before, it was packed with fey, but the mood had changed into something dark. Music played, haunting and feral, and faeries danced, leaped, and cavorted in wild abandon. A satyr knelt behind an unresisting girl with red skin, running his hands up her ribs and kissing her neck. Two women with fox ears circled a dazed-looking brownie, their golden eyes bright with hunger. A group of fey nobles danced in hypnotic patterns, their movements erotic, sensual, lost in music and passion.

I felt the wild urge to join them, to throw back my head and spin into the music, not caring where it took me. I closed my eyes for a moment, feeling the lilting strains lift my soul and make it soar toward the heavens. My throat tightened, and my body began to sway in tune with the music. I opened my eyes with a start. Without meaning to, I'd begun walking toward the circle of dancers.

I bit my lip hard, tasting blood, and the sharp pain brought me back to my senses. *Get it together, Meghan. You can't let down your guard. That means no eating, dancing, or talking to strangers. Focus on what you have to do.*

I saw Oberon and Titania sitting at a long table, surrounded by Seelie knights and trolls. The king and queen sat side by side, but were actively ignoring each other. Oberon's chin rested on his hands as he gazed out over his court; Titania sat like she had an icy pole shoved up her backside.

Puck was nowhere to be seen. I wondered if Oberon had freed him yet.

"Enjoying the festivities?" asked a familiar voice.

"Grimalkin!" I cried, spotting the gray cat perched on the edge of a raised pool, tail curled around his legs. His golden eyes regarded me with the same lazy disinterest. "What are you doing here?"

He yawned. "I was taking a nap, but it appears things might get interesting soon, so I think I will stick around." Rising, the cat stretched, arching his back, and gave me a sideways look. "So, human, how is life in Oberon's court?"

"You knew," I accused him as he sat down and licked a paw. "You knew who I was all along. That's why you agreed to take me to Puck—you were hoping to blackmail Oberon."

"*Blackmail,*" said Grimalkin, blinking languid yellow eyes, "is a barbaric word. And you have much to learn about the fey, Meghan Chase. You think others would not have done the same? Everything here has a price. Ask Oberon. For that matter, ask your Puck."

I wanted to ask what he meant, but at that moment, a shadow fell over my back and I turned to see Lady Weaver looming over me.

"The Winter Court will arrive soon," she rasped, pencil-thin fingers closing on my shoulder. "You must take your

place at the table, beside King Oberon. He has requested your
presence. Go, go."

Her grip tightened, and she steered me to the table where
Oberon and the lords of the Summer Court waited. Oberon's
gaze was carefully neutral, but Titania's glare of utter hatred
made me want to run and hide. Between scary spider lady
and the Queen of the Seelie Court, I was pretty sure I would
end the night as a mouse or cockroach.

"Pay your respects to your father," Lady Weaver hissed
in my ear, before giving me a small push toward the Erlking. I swallowed and, under the stark gazes of the nobles, approached the table.

I didn't know what to say. I didn't know what to do. I felt
like I was giving a speech before the school auditorium and
had forgotten my notes. Pleading silently for a clue, I met
Oberon's empty green eyes and dropped into a clumsy curtsy.

The Erlking shifted in his seat. I saw his eyes flicker to the
bright orange backpack and narrow slightly. My cheeks flamed,
but I couldn't take it off now. "The Court welcomes Meghan
Chase," Oberon said in a stiff, formal voice. He paused, as if
waiting for me to say something, but my voice caught in my
throat. Silence stretched between us, and someone in the crowd
snickered. Finally, Oberon gestured toward an empty chair
near the end of the table, and I sat, red and blushing under the
eyes of the entire court.

"That was impressive," mused a voice near my feet. Grimalkin leaped into the chair beside me, just as I was about
to put my backpack where he stood. "You definitely inherited your father's rapier wit. Lady Weaver must be so proud."

"Shut up, Grim," I muttered, and shoved the pack under
my seat. I would've said more, but at that moment the music
stopped and a loud trumpeting began.

"They've arrived," Grimalkin stated, eyes narrowing to golden slits. The cat almost seemed to smile. "This should be very interesting."

The trumpeting grew louder, and at one end of the court, the ever-present wall of thorns shifted, curled back, and formed a grand archway, much taller and more elegant than any I'd seen before. Black roses burst into bloom among the thorns, and an icy wind hissed through the gate, coating nearby trees with frost.

A creature padded through the arch, and I shuddered from more than the cold. It was a goblin, green and warty, dressed in a fancy black coat with gold buttons. It cast a sly look around the waiting court, puffed out its chest, and cried in a clear yet gravelly voice:

"Her Majesty, Queen Mab, Lady of the Winter Court, Sovereign of the Autumn Territories, and Queen of Air and Darkness!"

And the Unseelie came.

At first glance, they looked very similar to the Seelie fey. The little men carrying the Unseelie banner looked like gnomes in fancy cloaks and red caps. Then I noticed their jagged, sharklike grins and the bright madness in their eyes, and knew these were not friendly garden gnomes, not in any sense of the word.

"Redcaps," Grimalkin mused, wrinkling his nose. "You will want to stay away from them, human. Last time they came, a not-too-bright phouka challenged one to a rigged shell game and won. It did not go well."

"What happened?" I asked, wondering what a phouka was.

"They ate him."

He pointed out the ogres next, great hulking beasts with thick, stupid faces and tusks slick with drool. Manacles bound their wrists, and silver chains were wrapped about their huge necks. They shambled into court like drugged gorillas, knuckles dragging on the ground, oblivious to the murderous glares they were receiving from the trolls.

More Unseelie spilled into the clearing. Thin, skulking bogeys like the one in Ethan's closet, creeping along the ground like spindly spiders. Snarling, hissing goblins. A man with the head and chest of a shaggy black goat, his horns sweeping into wicked points that caught the light. And more creatures, each one more nightmarish than the first. They leered when they caught sight of me, licking their lips and teeth. Thankfully, under the stern glares of Oberon and Titania, none of them approached the table.

Finally, as the court swelled to nearly twice its number, Queen Mab made her appearance.

The first hint I received was that the temperature in the clearing dropped about ten degrees. Goose bumps rose along my arms, and I shivered, wishing I had something heavier than a dress made of spider silk and gauze. I was about to move my chair a few feet down the table, out of the wind, when a cloud of snow burst from the mouth of the tunnel, and in walked the kind of woman that made ladies weep in envy and men launch wars.

She wasn't tall, like Oberon, or willowy-thin like Titania, but her presence drew every eye in the courtyard. Her hair was so black it appeared blue in places, and it spilled down her back like a waterfall of ink. Her eyes were of the void, of a night without stars, a sharp contrast to her marble skin and pale mulberry lips. She wore a dress that writhed around her like shadow incarnate. And, like Oberon and Titania, she radiated power.

The amount of fey in the courtyard, both Seelie and Unseelie, was making me very, very nervous. But just as I thought things couldn't get any eerier, Mab's entourage walked in.

The first two were tall and beautiful like the rest of their kind, all sharp angles and graceful limbs. They wore their black-and-silver suits with the easy confidence of nobles, raven hair pulled back to highlight their proud, cruel features. Like dark princes, they marched behind Mab with all the arrogance of the queen, thin hands resting on their swords, their capes flapping behind them.

The third noble, walking behind them, was also dressed in black and silver. Like the other two, he carried a sword, resting comfortably on his hip, and his face bore the fine lines of an aristocrat. But, unlike the others, he looked disinterested, almost bored, with the entire event. His eyes caught the moonlight and glittered like silver coins.

My heart turned to ice, and my stomach threatened to crawl up my throat. It was him, the boy from my dreams, the one who had chased Puck and me through the forest. I glanced around wildly, wondering if I could hide before he saw me. Grimalkin gave me a bemused stare and twitched his tail.

"It's him!" I whispered, cutting my gaze to the nobles approaching behind the queen. "That boy! He was hunting me that day in the forest, when I landed in your tree. He tried to kill me!"

Grimalkin blinked. "That is Prince Ash, youngest son of Queen Mab. They say he is quite the hunter, and spends much of his time in the wyldwood, instead of at court with his brothers."

"I don't care who he is," I hissed, ducking down in my seat. "I can't let him see me. How do I get out of here?"

Grimalkin's snort sounded suspiciously like laughter. "I wouldn't worry about that, human. Ash would not risk Oberon's fury by attacking you in his own court. The rules of Elysium prevent violence of any kind. Besides—" the cat sniffed "—that hunt was days ago. It is likely he has forgotten all about you."

I scowled at Grimalkin and kept the fey boy in my sights as he bowed to Oberon and Titania, murmuring something I couldn't hear. Oberon nodded, and the prince stepped back, still bowing. When he straightened and turned around, his gaze swept over the table—

—to rest solely on me. His eyes narrowed, and he smiled, giving me a small nod. My heart sped up and I shivered.

Ash hadn't forgotten me, not by a long shot.

As the night wore on, I thought longingly of my days in the kitchens.

Not just because of Prince Ash, though that was the main reason I tried to avoid notice. The minions of the Unseelie Court made me jumpy and uncomfortable, and I wasn't the only one. Tension ran high among the ranks of Seelie and Unseelie; it was plain that these were ancient enemies. Only the fey's devotion to rules and proper etiquette—and the power of their sidhe masters—kept things from erupting into a bloodbath.

Or so Grimalkin told me. I took his word for it and remained very still in my seat, trying not to attract attention.

Oberon, Titania, and Mab stayed at the table all night. The three princes sat to Mab's left, with Ash farthest down the table, much to my relief. Food was served, wine was poured, and the sidhe rulers spoke among themselves. Grimalkin yawned, bored with it all, and left my side, vanishing into the crowds. After what seemed like hours, the entertainment began.

Three brightly dressed boys with monkey tails swung onto

the stage set before the table. They performed amazing leaps and tumbles over, onto, and through one another. A satyr played his pipes, and a human danced to the tune until her feet bled, her face a mixture of terror and ecstasy. A stunning woman with goat hooves and piranha teeth sang a ballad about a man who followed his lover beneath the waters of the lake, never to be seen again. At the end of the song, I gasped air into my burning lungs and sat up, unaware that I'd been unable to breathe.

Sometime during the course of the festivities, Ash disappeared.

Frowning, I scanned the courtyard for him, searching for a pale face and dark hair among the chaotic sea of fey. He wasn't in the courtyard, as far as I could see, and he wasn't at the table with Mab and Oberon....

There was a soft chuckle beside me, and my heart stopped.

"So this is Oberon's famous half-blood," Ash mused as I whirled around. His eyes, cold and inhuman, glimmered with amusement. Up close, he was even more beautiful, with high cheekbones and dark tousled hair falling into his eyes. My traitor hands itched, longing to run my fingers through those bangs. Horrified, I clenched them in my lap, trying to concentrate on what Ash was saying. "And to think," the prince continued, smiling, "I lost you that day in the forest and didn't even know what I was chasing."

I shrank back, eyeing Oberon and Queen Mab. They were deep in conversation and did not notice me. I didn't want to interrupt them simply because a prince of the Unseelie Court was talking to me.

Besides, I was a faery princess now. Even if I didn't quite believe it, Ash certainly did. I took a deep breath, raised my chin, and looked him straight in the eye.

"I warn you," I said, pleased that my voice didn't tremble,

"that if you try anything, my father will remove your head and stick it to a plaque on his wall."

He shrugged one lean shoulder. "There are worse things." At my horrified look, he offered a faint, self-derogatory smile. "Don't worry, princess, I won't break the rules of Elysium. I have no intention of facing Mab's wrath should I embarrass her. That's not why I'm here."

"Then what do you want?"

He bowed. "A dance."

"What!" I stared at him in disbelief. "You tried to kill me!"

"Technically, I was trying to kill Puck. You just happened to be there. But yes, if I'd had the shot, I would have taken it."

"Then why the hell would you think I'd dance with you?"

"That was then." He regarded me blandly. "This is now. And it's tradition in Elysium that a son and daughter of opposite territories dance with each other, to demonstrate the goodwill between the courts."

"Well, it's a stupid tradition." I crossed my arms and glared. "And you can forget it. I am not going anywhere with you."

He raised an eyebrow. "Would you insult my monarch, Queen Mab, by refusing? She would take it very personally, and blame Oberon for the offense. And Mab can hold a grudge for a very, very long time."

Oh, damn. I was stuck. If I said no, I would insult the faery queen of the Unseelie Court. I'd also be on the shit lists of both Mab *and* Titania, and between them, my chances of survival were easily and completely nil.

"So, you're saying you're not giving me a choice."

"There is always a choice." Ash held out his hand. "I will not force you. I only follow the orders of my queen. But know that the rest of the court is expecting us." He smiled then, bit-

ter and self-mocking. "And I promise to be a perfect gentleman until the night is done. You have my word."

"Dammit." I hugged my arms, trying to think of something to get me out of this. "I'll just embarrass you, anyway,"
I told him defiantly. "I can't dance."

"You're Oberon's blood." A cool note of amusement colored his voice. "Of course you can dance."

I struggled with myself a moment longer. *This is the prince of
the Unseelie Court,* I thought, my mind racing. *Maybe he'll know
something about Ethan. Or your dad! The least you can do is ask.*

I took a deep breath. Ash waited patiently with his hand
outstretched, and when I finally put my fingers into his palm,
he offered a faint smile. His skin was cold as he smoothly
moved my hand to his arm, and I shivered at the nearness of
him. He smelled sharply of frost and something alien—not
unpleasant, but strange.

We left the table together, and my stomach twisted as I saw
hundreds of glowing fey eyes watching us. Seelie and Unseelie
alike parted for us, bowing, as we approached the open stage.

My knees trembled. "I can't do this," I whispered, clutching Ash's arm for support. "Let me go. I think I'm going to
be sick."

"You'll be fine." Ash didn't look at me as we stepped onto
the dance floor. He faced the trio of fey rulers with his head
up and his expression blank. I looked over the sea of faces and
shook in terror.

Ash tightened his grip on my hand. "Just follow my lead."

He bowed to Oberon's table, and I curtsied. The Erlking
gave a solemn nod, and Ash turned to face me, taking one of
my hands and guiding the other to his shoulder.

The music started.

Ash stepped forward, and I almost tripped, biting my lip

as I tried to match his steps. We more or less minced around
the stage, me concentrating on not falling or stepping on toes,
Ash moving with tigerlike grace. Thankfully, no one booed
or threw things, but I stumbled forward and back in a daze,
only wanting the humiliation to end.

Somewhere in this waking nightmare, I heard a chuckle.
"Stop thinking," Ash muttered, pulling me into a spin that ended
with me against his chest. "The audience doesn't matter. The
steps don't matter. Just close your eyes and listen to the music."

"Easy for you to say," I growled, but he spun me again, so
quickly that the stage whirled and I closed my eyes. *Remember
why you're doing this,* my mind hissed. *This is for Ethan.*

Right. I opened my eyes and faced the dark prince. "So,"
I muttered, trying to sound conversational, "you're Queen
Mab's son, right?"

"I think we've established that, yes."

"Does she like to...collect things?" Ash looked at me
strangely, and I hurried on. "Humans, I mean? Does she have
a lot of humans in her court?"

"A few." Ash spun me again, and this time I went with it.
His eyes were bright as I came back to his arms. "Mab usually gets bored with mortals after a few years. She either releases them or turns them into something more interesting,
depending on her mood. Why?"

My heart pounded. "Does she have a little boy in her
court?" I asked as we swirled around the stage. "Four years
old, curly brown hair, blue eyes? Quiet most of the time?"

Ash regarded me strangely. "I don't know," he said, to my
disappointment. "I haven't been to court lately. Even if I had,
I cannot keep track of all the mortals the queen acquires and
releases over the years."

"Oh," I muttered, lowering my eyes. Well, that idea was shot. "Well, if you're not in court, where are you, then?"

Ash gave me a chilling smile. "The wyldwood," he replied, spinning me away. "Hunting. I rarely let my prey escape, so be grateful Puck is such a coward." Before I could answer, he pulled me close again, his mouth against my ear. "Although, I am happy I didn't kill you then. I told you a daughter of Oberon could dance."

I'd forgotten about the music, and realized my body was acting on autopilot, sweeping over the dance floor as if I'd done it a thousand times. For a long moment, we said nothing, lost in the music and the dance. My emotions soared as the crescendo rose into the night, and there was no one except us, spinning around and around.

The music ceased as Ash pulled me into a final spin. I ended up pressed against him, his face inches from mine, his gray eyes bright and intense. We stood there a moment, frozen in time, our hearts thrumming wildly between us. The rest of the world had disappeared. Ash blinked and offered a tiny smile. It would take only a half step to meet his lips.

A scream shattered the night, jerking us back to our senses. The prince released me and stepped away, his face shutting into that blank mask once more.

The scream came again, followed by a thunderous roar that rattled the tables and sent fine crystal goblets crashing to the floor. Over the crowd of spectators, I saw the bramble wall shaking wildly as something large tore its way through. Fey began shouting and pushing one another, and Oberon stood, his ringing voice calling for order. For just a moment, everyone froze.

The brambles parted with deafening snaps, and something huge clawed its way free. Blood streaked the tawny hide of a monster—not a shadowy, under-your-bed bogey that jumped out at you, but a real monster that would rip open your stomach and eat your entrails. It had three horrible heads: a lion with a bloody satyr in its jaws, a goat with mad white eyes, and a hissing dragon with molten flame dripping from its teeth. A chimera.

For a heartbeat, it paused, staring at the party it had just interrupted, the heads blinking in unison. The dead satyr, now a chewed, mangled mess, dropped to the ground, and someone in the crowd screamed.

The chimera roared, three voices rising to a deafening shriek. The crowd scattered as the monster gathered its hindquarters under it and leaped into the fray. It came down beside a fleeing redcap and lashed out with a claw-tipped paw, catching the faery in the stomach and disemboweling it instantly. As the redcap staggered and fell, holding its intestines, the chimera turned and pounced on a troll, bearing it to the ground. The troll snarled and grabbed the lion's throat, holding it away, but then the dragon head came down, clamping its jaws around the troll's neck and twisting. Dark blood exploded in a fine spray, filling the air with a sickening coppery smell. The troll shuddered and went limp.

Gore dripping from its snout, the chimera looked up and saw me, still frozen on the stage. With a roar, it sprang, landing on the edge of the dance floor. My brain screamed at me to run, but I couldn't move. I could only stare in detached fascination as it crouched, muscles rippling under its bloody fur. Its hot breath washed over me, stinking of blood and rotten meat, and I saw a scrap of red clothing on the lion's tooth.

With a shriek, the chimera pounced, and I closed my eyes, hoping it'd be quick.

CHAPTER THIRTEEN

Escape from the Seelie Court

Something slammed into me, pushing me away. Pain shot up my arm as I landed on my shoulder, and I opened my eyes with a gasp.

Ash stood between me and the chimera, his sword unsheathed. The blade glowed an icy-blue, wreathed in frost and mist. The monster roared and swatted at him, but he leaped aside, slashing with his blade. The frozen edge bit into the chimera's paw, drawing a humanlike scream from the monster. It pounced, and Ash rolled away. On his feet again, he raised an arm, bluish light sparkling from his fingers. As the monster whirled on him, he flung his hand out, and the chimera shrieked as a flurry of glistening ice shards ripped into its hide.

"To arms!" Oberon's booming voice rose above the roars of the chimera. "Knights, hold the beast back! Protect the envoys! Quickly!"

Mab's voice joined the chaos, ordering her subjects to attack. Now more fey were arriving, leaping onto the stage with weapons and battle cries, fangs and teeth bared. Less warrior-type fey scurried off the stage, fleeing for their lives as the others attacked. Trolls and ogres slammed great spiked clubs onto the beast's hide, redcaps sliced at it with tarnished bronze knives, and Seelie knights brandishing swords of flame cut at its flanks. I saw Ash's brothers join the fray, their ice blades stabbing at the monster's back. The chimera roared again, badly wounded, momentarily cowed by its attackers.

Then the dragon's head came up, steam billowing from its jaws, and blasted a stream of liquid fire at the fey surrounding it. The molten spittle covered several of its attackers, who screamed and fell to the ground, thrashing wildly as the flesh melted from their bones. The monster tried to leave the dance floor, but the fey pressed closer, jabbing at it with their weapons, keeping it in place.

As the last of the civilian fey left the stage, the Seelie King stood, his face alien and terrifying, long silver hair whipping behind him. He raised his hands, and a great rumbling shook the ground. Plates clattered and smashed to the ground, trees trembled, and the fey backed away from the snarling monster. The chimera growled and snapped at the air, its eyes wary and confused, as if it were unable to understand what was happening.

The stage—four feet of solid marble—splintered with a deafening crack, and huge roots unfurled through the surface. Thick and ancient, covered in gleaming thorns, they wrapped around the chimera like giant snakes, digging into its hide. The monster roared, raking the living wood with its claws, but the coils continued to tighten.

The fey swarmed the monster again, hacking and cutting. The chimera fought on, lashing out with deadly claws and fangs, catching those who ventured too close. An ogre smashed his club into the beast's side, but took a savage blow from the monster's paw that tore his shoulder open. A Seelie knight cut at the dragon's head, but the jaws opened and it blasted the faery with molten fire. Screaming, the knight wheeled back, and the dragon raised its head to glare at the Erlking standing at the table, his eyes half closed in concentration. Its lips curled, and it took a breath. I yelled at Oberon, but my voice was lost in the cacophony, and I knew my warning would come too late.

And then Ash was there, dodging the beast's claws, his sword streaking down in an icy blur. It sliced clean through the dragon's neck, severing it, and the head struck the marble with a revolting splat. Ash danced away as the neck continued to writhe, spraying blood and liquid fire from the stump. Fey howled in pain. As Ash retreated from the lava spray, a troll rammed his spear through the lion's open maw and out the back of its head, and a trio of redcaps managed to dodge the flailing claws to swarm the goat's head, biting and stabbing. The chimera jerked, thrashed, and finally slumped in the web of branches, twitching sporadically. Even as it died, the redcaps continued to rip out its flesh.

The battle was over, but the carnage remained. Charred, mangled, mutilated bodies lay like broken toys around the fractured stage. Gravely wounded fey clutched at their injuries, their faces twisted in agony. The smell of blood and burning flesh was overwhelming.

My stomach heaved. Twisting my head from the gruesome sight, I crawled to the edge of the stage and vomited into the rose bushes.

"Oberon!"

The shriek sent chills through me. Queen Mab was on her feet, eyes blazing, pointing a gloved finger at the Erlking.

"How dare you!" she rasped, and I shivered as the temperature dropped to freezing. Frost coated the branches and crept along the ground. "How dare you set this monster on us during Elysium, when we come to you under the banner of trust! You've broken the covenant, and I will not forgive this heresy!"

Oberon looked pained, but Queen Titania leaped to her feet. "You dare?" she cried, as lightning crackled overhead. "You dare accuse us of summoning this creature? This is obviously the work of the Unseelie Court to weaken us in our own home!"

Fey began to mutter among themselves, casting suspicious glances at those from another court, though seconds ago they'd fought side by side. A redcap, its mouth dripping black chimera blood, hopped down from the stage to leer at me, beady eyes bright with hunger.

"I smell a human," it cackled, running a purple tongue over its fangs. "I smell young girl blood, and sweeter flesh than a monster's." I hurried away, walking around the stage, but it followed. "Come to me, little girl," it crooned. "Monster flesh is bitter, not like sweet young humans. I just want a nibble. Maybe just a finger."

"Back off." Ash appeared out of nowhere, looking dangerous with dark blood speckling his face. "We're in enough trouble without you eating Oberon's daughter. Get out of here."

The redcap sneered and scurried off. The fey boy sighed and turned to me, his gaze scanning the length of my dress. "Are you hurt?"

I shook my head. "You saved my life," I murmured. I was about to say "thank you," but caught myself, since those words seemed to indebt you in Faery. A thought came, unbidden and disturbing. "I...I'm not bound to you or anything like that, am I?" I asked fearfully. He raised an eyebrow, and I swallowed. "No life debt, or having to become your wife, right?"

"Not unless our sires made a deal without our knowledge." Ash glanced back at the arguing rulers. Oberon was trying to silence Titania, but she would have none of it, turning her anger on him as well as Mab. "And I'd say any contracts they made are officially broken now. This will probably mean war."

"War?" Something cold touched my cheek, and I glanced up to see snowflakes swirling in a lightning-riddled sky. It was eerily beautiful, and I shivered. "What will happen then?"

Ash stepped closer. His fingers came up to brush the hair from my face, sending an electric shock through me from my spine to my toes. His cool breath tickled my ear as he leaned in.

"I'll kill you," he whispered, and walked away, joining his brothers at the table. He did not look back.

I touched the place where his fingers had brushed my skin, giddy and terrified at the same time.

"Careful, human." Grimalkin appeared on the corner of the stage, overshadowed by the dead chimera. "Do not lose your heart to a faery prince. It never ends well."

"Who asked you?" I glared at him. "And why do you always pop up when you're not wanted? You got your payment. Why are you still following me?"

"You are amusing," purred Grimalkin. Golden eyes flicked to the bickering rulers and back again. "And of great interest to the king and queens. That makes you a valuable pawn, indeed. I wonder what you will do next, now that your brother is not in Oberon's territory?"

I looked at Ash, standing beside his brothers, stone-faced as the argument between Mab and Titania raged on. Oberon was trying to calm them both, but with little success.

"I have to go to the Unseelie Court," I whispered as Grimalkin smiled. "I'll have to look for Ethan in Queen Mab's territory."

"I would imagine so," Grimalkin purred, slitting his eyes at me. "Only, you don't know where the Unseelie Court is, do you? Mab's entourage came here in flying carriages. How will you find it?"

"I could sneak into one of the carriages, maybe. Disguise myself."

Grimalkin snorted with laughter. "If the redcaps do not smell you out, the ogres will. There would be nothing left but bones by the time you reached Tir Na Nog." The cat yawned and licked a forepaw. "Too bad you lack a guide. Someone who knows the way."

I stared at the cat, a slow anger building as I realized what it was saying. "You know the way to the Unseelie Court," I said quietly.

Grimalkin scrubbed a paw over his ears. "Perhaps."

"And you'll take me there," I continued, "for a small favor."

"No," Grimalkin said, looking up at me. "There is nothing small about going into Unseelie territory. My price will be steep, human, make no mistake about that. So, you must ask yourself, how much is your brother worth to you?"

I fell silent, staring at the table, where the queens were still going at it.

"Why would I summon the beast?" Mab questioned with a sneer in Titania's direction. "I've lost loyal subjects, as well. Why would I set the creature against my own?"

Titania matched the other queen's disdain. "You don't care who you murder," she said with a sniff, "as long as you get what you want in the end. This is a clever ploy to weaken our court without casting suspicion on yourself."

Mab swelled in fury, and the snow turned to sleet. "Now

you accuse me of murdering my own subjects! I will not listen to this a moment longer! Oberon!" She turned to the Erlking with her teeth bared. "Find the one who did this!" she hissed, her hair writhing around her like snakes. "Find them and give them to me, or face the wrath of the Unseelie Court."

"Lady Mab," Oberon said, holding up his hand, "do not be hasty. Surely you realize what this will mean for both of us."

Mab's face didn't change. "I will wait until Midsummer's Eve," she announced, her expression stony. "If the Seelie Court does not turn over those responsible for this atrocity to me, then you will prepare yourselves for war." She turned to her sons, who awaited her orders silently. "Send for our healers," she told them. "Gather our wounded and dead. We will return to Tir Na Nog tonight."

"If you are going to decide," Grimalkin said softly, "decide quickly. Once they leave, Oberon will not let you go. You are too valuable a pawn to lose to the Unseelie Court. He will keep you here against your will, under lock and key if he has to, to keep you out of Mab's clutches. After tonight, you may not get another chance to escape, and you will never find your brother."

I watched Ash and his brothers disappear into the crowd of dark fey, saw the grim, terrifying look on the Erlking's face, and made my decision.

I took a deep breath. "All right, then. Let's get out of here."

Grimalkin stood. "Good," he said. "We leave now. Before the chaos dies down and Oberon remembers you." He looked over my elegant gown and sniffed, wrinkling his nose. "I will fetch your clothes and belongings. Wait here, and try not to draw attention to yourself." He twitched his tail, slipped into the shadows, and vanished.

I stood by the dead chimera, looking around nervously and trying to keep out of Oberon's sight.

Something small dropped from the lion's mane, glimmering briefly as it caught the light, hitting the marble with a faint clink. Curious, I approached warily, keeping my eye on the huge carcass and the few redcaps still gnawing on it. The object on the ground winked metallically as I knelt and picked it up, turning it over in my palm.

It looked like a tiny metal bug, round and ticklike, about the size of my pinkie nail. Its spindly metal legs were curled up over its belly, the way insects' legs do when they die. It was covered in black ooze, which I realized with horror was chimera blood.

As I stared at it, the legs wiggled, and it flipped over in my hand. I yelped and hurled the bug to the ground, where it scuttled over the marble stage, squeezed into a crack, and vanished from sight.

I was wiping the chimera blood from my hands, discovering it stained flesh, when Grimalkin appeared, materializing from nowhere with my bright orange backpack. "This way," the cat muttered, and led me from the courtyard into a cluster of trees. "Hurry and change," he ordered as we ducked beneath the shadowy limbs. "We don't have much time."

I unzipped the pack and dumped my clothes to the ground. I started to wriggle out of the dress, when I noticed Grimalkin still watching me, eyes glowing in the dark. "Could I get a little privacy?" I asked. The cat hissed.

"You have nothing I'd be interested in, human. Hurry up."

Scowling, I shed the gown and changed into my old, comfortable clothes. As I jammed my feet into my sneakers, I noticed Grimalkin staring back at the courtyard. A trio of Seelie knights wandered toward us across the lawn, and it appeared they were looking for someone.

Grimalkin flattened his ears. "You have already been missed. This way!"

I followed the cat through the shadows toward the hedge wall surrounding the courtyard. The brambles peeled back as we approached, revealing a narrow hole in the hedge, just big enough for me to squeeze into on my hands and knees. Grimalkin slipped through without looking back. I grimaced, knelt down, and crawled in after the cat, dragging my backpack behind me.

The tunnel was dark and winding. I pricked myself a dozen times as I maneuvered my way through the twisting maze of thorns. Squeezing through a particularly narrow stretch, I cursed as the thorns kept snagging my hair, clothes, and skin. Grimalkin looked over his shoulder, blinking luminous glowing eyes as I struggled.

"Try not to bleed so much on the thorns," he said as I jabbed myself in the palm and hissed in pain. "Right now, anyone could follow us, and you are leaving a very easy trail."

"Right, 'cause I'm bleeding all over the place for shits and giggles." A bramble caught my hair, and I yanked it free with a painful tearing sound. "How much farther till we're out?"

"Not far. We are taking a shortcut."

"This is a shortcut? What, does it lead into Mab's garden or something?"

"Not really." Grimalkin sat down and scratched his ear. "This path actually leads us back to your world."

I jerked my head up, jabbing myself in the skull and bringing tears to my eyes. "What? Are you serious?" Relief and excitement flared; I could go home! I could see my mom;

she must be worried sick about me. I could go to my own room and—

I stopped, the balloon of happiness deflating as suddenly as it had come. "No. I can't go home yet," I said, feeling my throat tighten. "Not without Ethan." I bit my lip, resolved, then glared at the cat. "I thought you were taking me to the Unseelie Court, Grim."

Grimalkin yawned, sounding bored with it all. "I am. The Unseelie Court sits much closer to your world than the Seelie territories. It is faster to enter the mortal lands and slip into Tir Na Nog from there."

"Oh." I thought about that for a moment. "Well, then, why did Puck take me through the wyldwood? If it's easier to reach the Unseelie Court from my world, why didn't he use that way?"

"Who knows? Trods—the paths into the Nevernever— are difficult to find. Some are constantly shifting. Most lead directly into the wyldwood. Only a very few will take you to the Seelie or Unseelie territories, and they have powerful guardians protecting them. The trod we are using now is a one-way trip. Once we are through, we will not be able to find it again."

"Isn't there another way in?"

Grimalkin sighed. "There are other paths to Tir Na Nog from the wyldwood, but you would have to deal with the crea- tures that live there, as you found out with the goblins, and they are not the worst things you could meet. Also, Oberon's guards will be hunting for you, and the wyldwood will be the first place they'll look. The fastest way to the Unseelie Court is the way I am taking you now. So, decide, human. Do you still want to go?"

"Doesn't look like I have a choice, does it?"

"You keep saying that," Grimalkin observed, "but there is always a choice. And I suggest we stop talking and keep moving. We are being followed."

We kept going, wending our way through the briar tunnel, picking through the thorns until I lost all sense of time and direction. At first, I tried avoiding the brambles scratching at me, but continued to be pricked and poked, until I finally gave in and stopped bothering about it. Strangely, once I did, I was scratched a lot less. Once I stopped moving like a snail, Grimalkin set a steady pace through the brambles, and I followed as best I could. Occasionally, I saw side tunnels spin off in other directions, and caught glimpses of shapes moving through the brush, though I never got a clear look.

We turned a corner, and suddenly found a large cement tube in our path. It was a drainage pipe; I could see open air and blue sky through the hole. Oddly, it was sunny on the other side.

"The mortal world is through here," Grimalkin informed me. "Remember, once we are through, we will not be able to return to the Nevernever this way. We will have to find another trod to go back."

"I know," I said.

Grimalkin gave me a long, uncomfortable stare. "Also, remember, human—you have been to the Nevernever. The glamour over your eyes is gone. Though other mortals will not see anything strange about you, you will see things a little...differently. So, try not to overreact."

"Differently? Like how?"

Grimalkin smiled. "You will see."

We emerged from the drainage pipe to the sounds of car engines and street traffic, a shock after being in the wilderness for so long. We were in a downtown area, with build-ings looming over us on either side. A sidewalk extended over the drainage pipe; beyond that, rush-hour traffic clogged the roads, and people shuffled down the walkway, absorbed in their own small worlds. No one seemed to notice a cat and a scruffy, slightly bloodied teenager crawl out of a drainage ditch.

"Okay." Despite my worry, I was thrilled to be back in my own familiar world, and astounded by the huge glass-and-metal buildings towering above me. The air here was cold, uncomfortably so, and dirty slush clogged the sidewalks and drains. Craning my neck, I gazed up at the looming skyscrap-ers, feeling slightly dizzy as they seemed to sway against the sky. There was nothing like this in my tiny Louisiana town. "Where are we?"

"Detroit." Grimalkin half closed his eyes, peering around the town and the people rushing by us. "One moment. It has been a while since I have been here. Let me think."

"Detroit, *Michigan?*"

"Hush."

As he was thinking, a large figure in a tattered red hoodie lurched out of the crowd and came toward us, clutching a bottle in a sack. He looked like a homeless person, though I'd never actually seen one. I wasn't *too* worried; we were on a well-traveled street, with a lot of witnesses to hear me scream should he try anything. He would probably ask me for change or a cigarette, and keep going.

However, as he got close, he raised his head, and I saw a wrinkled, bearded face with fangs jutting crookedly from its jaw. In the shadows of the hood, his eyes were yellow and slitted like a cat's. I jumped as the stranger leered and stepped closer. His stench nearly knocked me down; he smelled of roadkill and bad eggs and fish rotting in the sun. I gagged and nearly lost my breakfast.

"Pretty girl," the stranger growled, reaching out with a claw. "You came from *there,* didn't you? Send me back, now. Send me back!"

I backed away, but Grimalkin leaped between us, fluffed out to twice his size. His yowling screech jerked the man to a halt, and the bum's eyes widened in terror. With a gurgling cry, he turned and ran, knocking people aside as he fled. People cursed and looked around, glaring at one another, but none seemed to notice the fleeing bum.

"What was that?" I asked Grimalkin.

"A norrgen." The cat sighed. "Disgusting things. Terrified of cats, if you can believe it. He was probably banished from the Nevernever at some point. That would explain his words to you, wanting you to send him back."

I looked for the norrgen, but it had vanished into the crowd. "Are all the fey walking around the human world outcasts?" I wondered.

"Of course not." Grimalkin's look was scornful, and no one does scornful better than a cat. "Many choose to be here, going back and forth between this world and the Nevernever at will, so long as they can find a trod. Some, like brownies or bogarts, haunt a house forever. Others blend in to human society, posing as mortals, feeding off dreams, emotions, and talent. Some have even been known to marry a particularly exceptional mortal, though their children are shunned by faery society, and the fey parent usually leaves if things get too tough.

"Of course, there are those who *have* been banished to the mortal world. They make their way as best they can, but spending too much time in the human world does strange things to them. Perhaps it is the amount of iron and technology that is so fatal to their existence. They start to lose themselves, a little at a time, until they are only shadows of their former selves, empty husks covered in glamour to make them look real. Eventually, they simply cease to exist."

I looked at Grimalkin in alarm. "Could that happen to you? To me?" I thought of my iPod, remembering the way Tansy leaped away from it in terror. I suddenly recalled the way Robbie was mysteriously absent from all of his computer classes. I'd simply thought he hated typing. I had no idea it was deadly to him.

Grimalkin seemed unconcerned. "If I stay here long enough, perhaps. Maybe in two or three decades, though I certainly do not plan to stay that long. As for you, you are half-human. Your mortal blood protects you from iron and the banal effects of your science and technology. I would not worry too much if I were you."

"What's wrong with science and technology?"

Grimalkin actually rolled his eyes. "If I thought this would turn into a history lesson, I would have picked a better classroom than a city street." His tail lashed, and he sat down. "You will never find a faery at a science fair. Why? Because science is all about proving theories and understanding the universe. Science folds everything into neat, logical, well-explained packages. The fey are magical, capricious, illogical, and unexplainable. Science cannot prove the existence of faeries, so naturally, we do not exist. That type of nonbelief is fatal to faeries."

"What about Robbie...er...Puck?" I asked, not knowing why he suddenly popped into my head. "How did he stay so close to me, going to school and everything, with all the iron around?"

Grimalkin yawned. "Robin Goodfellow is a very old faerie," he said, and I squirmed to think of him like that. "Not only that, he has ballads, poems, and stories written about him, so he is very near immortal, as long as humans remember them. Not to say he is immune to iron and technology—far from it. Puck is strong, but even he cannot resist the effects."

"It would kill him?"

"Slowly, over time." Grimalkin stared at me with solemn eyes. "The Nevernever is dying, human. It grows smaller and smaller every decade. Too much progress, too much technology. Mortals are losing their faith in anything but science. Even the children of man are consumed by progress. They sneer at the old stories and are drawn to the newest gadgets, computers, or video games. They no longer believe in monsters or magic. As cities grow and technology takes over the world, belief and imagination fade away, and so do we."

"What can we do to stop it?" I whispered.

"Nothing." Grimalkin raised a hind leg and scratched an ear. "Maybe the Nevernever will hold out till the end of the world. Maybe it will disappear in a few centuries. Everything dies eventually, human. Now, if you are quite done with the questions, we should keep moving."

"But if the Nevernever dies, won't you disappear, as well?"

"I am a cat," Grimalkin replied, as if that explained anything.

I followed Grimalkin down the sidewalk as the sun set over the horizon and the streetlamps flickered to life.

I caught glimpses of fey everywhere, walking past us, hanging out in dark alleys, stealing over the rooftops or skipping along the power lines. I wondered how I could've been so blind before. And I remembered a conversation with Robbie, in my living room so long ago, a lifetime ago. *Once you start seeing things, you won't be able to stop. You know what they say—ignorance is bliss, right?*

If only I'd listened to him then.

Grimalkin led me down several more streets and suddenly stopped. Across the street a two-story dance club, lit with pink-and-blue neon lights, radiated in the darkness. The sign proclaimed it Blue Chaos. Young men and women lined up outside the club, the lights sparkling off earrings, metal studs, and bleached hair. Music pounded the walls outside.

"Here we are," Grimalkin said, sounding pleased with himself. "The energy around a trod never changes, though when I was here last this place was different."

"The trod thingy is the dance club?"

"*Inside* the dance club," Grimalkin said with a great show of patience.

"I'll never get in there," I told the feline, looking at the club. "The line is, like, a mile long, and I don't think this is a minor-friendly place. I won't make it past the front door."

"I would think your Puck taught you better than this." Grimalkin sighed and slipped into a nearby alley. Confused, I followed, wondering if we were going in another way.

But Grimalkin leaped atop an overflowing Dumpster and faced me, his eyes floating yellow orbs in the dark. "Now," he began, lashing his tail, "listen closely, human. You are half fey. More important, you are Oberon's daughter, and it is high time you learned to access some of that power everyone is so worried about."

"I don't have any—"

"Of course you do." Grimalkin's eyes narrowed. "You stink of power, which is why fey react to you so strongly. You just do not know how to use it. Well, I shall teach you, because it will be easier than having to sneak you into the club myself. Are you ready?"

"I don't know."

"Good enough. First—" and Grimalkin's eyes disappeared "—close your eyes."

Feeling not a little apprehensive, I did so.

"Now, reach out and feel the glamour around you. We are very close to the dance club, so glamour is in ready supply from the emotions inside. Glamour is what fuels our power. It is how we change shape, sing someone to their death, and appear invisible to mortal eyes. Can you feel it?"

"I don't—"

"Stop talking and just *feel*."

I tried, though I didn't know what I was supposed to experience, sensing nothing but my own discomfort and fear.

And then, like an explosion of light on the inside of my eyes, I *felt* it.

It was like color given emotion: orange passion, vermillion lust, crimson anger, blue sorrow, a swirling, hypnotic play of sensations in my mind. I gasped, and heard Grimalkin's approving purr.

"Yes, that is glamour. The dreams and emotions of mortals. Now open your eyes. We are going to start with the simplest of faery glamour, the power to fade from human sight, to become invisible."

Still groggy from the torrent of swirling emotions, I nodded. "All right, becoming invisible. Sounds easy."

Grimalkin glared at me. "Your disbelief will cripple you if you think like that, human. Do not believe this impossible, or it *will* be."

"All right, all right, I'm sorry." I held up my hands. "So, how will I do this?"

"Picture the glamour in your mind." The cat half slitted its eyes again. "Imagine it is a cloak that covers you completely. You can shape the glamour to resemble anything you wish, including an empty space in the air, a spot where no one is standing. As you drape the glamour over yourself, you must believe that no one can see you. Just, so."

The eyes vanished, along with the rest of the cat. Even knowing Grimalkin was capable of it, it was still eerie seeing him fade from sight right before my eyes.

"Now." The eyes opened again, and the cat's body followed. "Your turn. When you believe you are invisible, we will go."

"What? Don't I get a practice run or something?"

"All it takes is belief, human. If you do not believe you are invisible on the first try, it only gets more difficult. Let us go. And remember, no doubts."

"Right. No doubts." I took a breath and closed my eyes, willing the glamour to come. I pictured myself fading from sight, swirling a cloak of light and air around my shoulders and pulling up the hood. *No one can see me,* I thought, trying not to feel foolish. *I'm invisible now.*

I opened my eyes and looked down at my hands.

They were still there.

Grimalkin shook his head as I looked up in disappointment. "I will never understand humans," he muttered. "With everything you have seen, magic, fey, monsters, and miracles, you still could not believe you could become invisible." He sighed heavily, leaping off the Dumpster. "Very well. I suppose *I* will have to get us in."

CHAPTER FOURTEEN

Blue Chaos

We stood in line for nearly an hour.

"All this could have been avoided if you just did what I told you," Grimalkin hissed for about the hundredth time. His claws dug into my arm, and I resisted the urge to drop-kick him over the fence like a football.

"Give me a break, Grim. I tried, okay? Just drop it already." I ignored the odd stares I was getting from the people around me, listening to the crazy girl muttering to herself. I didn't know what they saw when they looked at Grim, but it certainly wasn't a live, talking cat. And a heavy one at that.

"A simple invisibility spell. There is nothing easier. Kittens can do it before they walk."

I would've said something, but we were approaching the bouncer, who guarded the front doors to Blue Chaos. Dark, muscular, and massive, he checked the ID of the couple in front of us before waving them through. Grim pricked my arm with his claws, and I stepped up.

Cold black eyes raked me up and down. "I don't think so, honey," the bouncer said, flexing a muscle in his arm. "Why don't you turn around and leave? You have school tomorrow."

My mouth was dry, but Grim spoke up, his voice low and soothing. "You are not looking at me right," he purred, though the bouncer didn't glance at him at all. "I am actually much older than I look."

"Yeah?" He didn't seem convinced, but at least he wasn't throwing me out by the scruff of my neck. "Let's see some ID, then."

"Of course." Grim poked me, and I shifted his weight to one hand so I could hand my Blockbuster card to the bouncer. He snatched it, peering at it suspiciously, while my stomach roiled and cold sweat dripped down my neck. But Grimalkin continued to purr in my arms, completely undisturbed, and the bouncer handed the card back with a grudging look.

"Yeah, fine. Go on, then." He waved a huge hand at me, and we were through.

Inside *was* chaos. I'd never been to a club before, and was momentarily stupefied by the lights and the noise. Dry-ice smoke writhed along the floor, reminding me of the mist that crept through the wyldwood. Colored lights turned the dance floor into an electric fantasyland of pink, blue, and gold. Music rattled my ears; I could feel the vibrations in my chest, and wondered how anyone could communicate in such a cacophony.

Dancers spun, twisted, and swayed on the stage, bouncing in time to the music, sweat and energy pouring off them as they danced. Some danced alone, some in pairs that could not keep their hands off each other, their energy turning to passion.

Among them, writhing and twisting in near frenzies, feeding off the outpouring of glamour, danced the fey.

I saw faeries in leather pants and outfits that sparkled, slinked, and were half-torn, far different from the medieval finery of the Summer Court. A girl with birdlike talons and feathers for hair fluttered through the crowd, slashing young skin and licking the blood. A stick-thin boy with triple-jointed arms wrapped them around a dancing couple, long fingers entwined in their hair. Two fox-eared girls danced together, a mortal between them, their bodies pressed against his. The human's face was flung back in ecstasy, unaware of the hands running over his butt and between his legs.

Grimalkin squirmed and jumped out of my arms. He trotted toward the back of the club, his tail looking like a fuzzy periscope navigating the ocean of mist. I followed, trying not to stare at the unearthly dancers spinning among the mass of humanity.

Near the bar, a small door with the words Staff Only stood near the back of the club. I could see the shimmer of glamour around it, making the door difficult to look at; my gaze wanted to slide past. Casually, I approached the door, but before I got too close, the bartender rose up from behind the counter and narrowed his eyes.

"You don't wanna do that, love," he warned. His dark hair was pulled back in a tail, and horns curled up from his brow. He moved to the edge of the bar, and I heard hooves clopping over the wood. "Why don't you come over here and I'll fix you something nice? On the house, what'd you say?"

Grimalkin leaped onto a bar stool and put his front paws on the counter. A human on the stool next to him sipped his drink like nothing was happening. "We're looking for Shard," Grim said as the bartender shot him an irritated look, turning away from me.

"Shard is busy," the satyr replied, but he didn't meet Grim's eyes as he said it, and a moment later he began wiping down the bar. Grim continued to stare at him, until the satyr looked up. His eyes slitted dangerously. "I said, she's busy. Now, why don't you beat it, before I get the redcaps to stuff you into a bottle?"

"David, that's no way to treat customers," a cool female voice breathed from behind me, and I jumped. "Especially if one is an old friend."

The woman behind us was small and slight, with pale skin and neon-blue lips that curled sardonically at the edges. Her spiky hair stuck out at every angle, its dyed shades of blue, green, and white resembling ice crystals growing out of her scalp. She wore tight leather pants, a midriff tee that barely covered her breasts, and a dagger on one thigh. Her face glittered from countless piercings: eyebrows, nose, lips, and cheeks, all silver or gold. Her long ears sparkled with rings, studs, and bars, enough to make any metalhead weep from envy. A silver bar lanced through her belly button, and a tiny dragon pendant dangled from it.

"Hello, Grimalkin," the woman said, sounding resigned. "It's been a while, hasn't it? What brings you to my humble club? And with the Summer whelp in tow?" Her eyes, scintillating blue and green, looked me over curiously.

"We need passage into Tir Na Nog," Grimalkin said without hesitation. "Tonight, if you can."

"Don't ask for much, do you?" Shard grinned, motioning us into a corner booth. Once seated, she leaned back and snapped her fingers. A human, lean and gangly, melted out of the shadows to stand beside her, his face slack with adoration.

"Appletini," she told him. "Spill it, and spend the rest of your days as a roach. Do you two want anything?"

"No," Grimalkin said firmly. I shook my head.

The human scurried off, and Shard leaned forward. Her blue lips curved in a smile.

"So. Passage to Winter's territory. You want to use my trod, is that correct?"

"It is not your trod," Grimalkin said, thumping his tail against the booth cushions.

"But it is under *my* dance club," Shard replied. "And the Winter Queen won't be pleased if I let the Summer whelp into her territory unannounced. Don't look at me like that, Grim. I'm not stupid. I know the daughter of the Erlking when I see her. So, the question is, what do I get out of this?"

"A favor repaid." Grimalkin narrowed his eyes at her. "Your debt to me canceled."

"That's fine for you," Shard said, and turned her leer on me, "but what about this one? What can she offer?"

I swallowed. "What do you want?" I asked before Grimalkin could say anything. The cat shot me an exasperated glare, but I ignored him. If anyone would barter away my fate, it would be me. I didn't want Grimalkin promising this woman my firstborn child without my consent.

Shard leaned back again, crossing her legs with a smile. The gangly boy appeared with her drink, a green concoction with a tiny umbrella, and she sipped it slowly, her eyes never leaving mine.

"Hmm, that's a good question," Shard murmured, swirling her 'tini thoughtfully. "What do I want of you? It must be awfully important for you to get into Mab's territory. What would that be worth?"

She took another sip, appearing deep in thought. "How about...your name?" she offered at last. I blinked.

"My...my name?"

"That's right." Shard smiled disarmingly. "Nothing much. Just promise me the use of your name, your True Name, and we'll call it even, yes?"

"The girl is young, Shard," Grimalkin said, watching us both with slitted eyes. "She might not even know her true calling yet."

"That's all right." Shard smiled at me. "Just give me the name you call yourself now, and we'll make do, yes? I'm sure I can find *some* use for it."

"No," I told her. "No deal. You're not getting my name."

"Oh, well." Shard shrugged and raised the glass to her lips. "I guess you'll have to find another way into Mab's territory, then." She shifted toward the end of the booth. "It has been a pleasure. Now, if you'll excuse me, I've a club to run."

"Wait!" I blurted out.

Shard paused, watching me expectantly.

"All right," I whispered. "All right, I'll give you a name. After that, you'll open the trod, right?"

The faery smiled, showing her teeth. "Of course."

"Are you sure you want to do this?" Grimalkin asked softly. "Do you know what happens when you give a faery your name?"

I ignored him. "Swear it," I told Shard. "Promise that you'll open the trod once I give you the name. Say the words."

The faery's smile turned vicious. "Not as stupid as she first appears," she muttered, and shrugged. "Very well. I, Shard, keeper of the Chaos trod, do swear to open the path once I have received payment in the form of a single name, spoken by the requesting party." She broke off and smirked at me. "Good enough?"

I nodded.

"Fine." Shard licked her lips, looking inhumanly eager, as her eyes gleamed. "Now, give me the name."

"All right." I took a deep breath as my stomach twisted wildly. "Fred Flintstone."

Shard's face went blank. "What?" For one glorious moment, she looked utterly bewildered. "That is not your name, half-blood. That's not what we agreed on."

My heart pounded. "Yes, it is," I told her, keeping my voice firm. "I promised to give you *a* name, not *my* name. I've upheld my end of the contract. You have your name. Now, show us the trod."

Beside me, Grimalkin started sneezing, a sudden explosion of feline laughter. Shard's face remained blank a moment longer, then cold rage crept into her features and her eyes turned black. Her quills bristled, and ice coated the glass in her hand before it shattered into a million sparkling pieces.

"You." Her gaze stabbed into me, cold and terrifying. I fought the urge to run screaming out of the club. "You will regret this insolence, half-breed. I will not forget this, and will make you beg for mercy until your throat is raw from it."

My legs trembled, but I stood and faced her. "Not before you show us the trod."

Grimalkin stopped laughing and jumped onto the table. "You have been out-negotiated, Shard," he said, his voice still thick with amusement. "Cut your losses and try again some other time. Right now, we need to be going."

The faery's eyes still glimmered black, but she made a visible effort to control herself. "Very well," she said with great dignity. "I will uphold my end of the bargain. Wait here a moment. I need to inform David that I'll be gone for a bit."

She stalked away with her chin in the air, her spines quivering like icicles.

"Very clever," Grimalkin said softly as the faery marched toward the bar. "Shard has always been too rash, never pausing to listen for important details. She thinks she is too smart for that. Still, it is never wise to anger a Winter sidhe. You might regret your little battle of wits before this is over. The fey never forget an insult."

I remained silent, watching Shard lean over and whisper something to the satyr. David looked up at me, eyes narrowing, before jerking his head once and turning to wipe the counter.

Shard returned. Her eyes were normal again, though they still glared at me with cold dislike. "This way," she announced frostily, and led us across the room, toward the Staff Only door on the far wall.

We followed her down five or six flights of stairs, pausing at another door with the words *Danger! Keep Out!* painted on the surface in bright red. Shard looked back at me with an evil little smile.

"Don't mind Grumly. He's our last deterrent against those who poke their noses where they don't belong. Occasionally, some phouka or redcap will think themselves clever, and sneak past David to see what's down here. Obviously, I can't have that. So, I use Grumly to dissuade them." She chuckled. "Sometimes, a mortal will find his way down here, as well. That's the best entertainment. It cuts down on his food bill, too."

She gave me a razor-sharp grin and pushed the door open.

The stench hit me like a giant hammer, a revolting mix of rot and sweat and excrement. I recoiled, and my stomach heaved. Bones littered the stone floor, some human, some decidedly not. A pile of dirty straw lay in one corner, next to a door on the far wall. I knew that was the entrance to the Unseelie territory, but reaching it would be a real challenge.

Chained to a ring in the floor, manacled by one tree-stump leg, was the biggest ogre I'd ever seen. His skin was bruise purple, and four yellow tusks curled from his lower jaw. His

torso was massive, muscles and tendons rippling under his mot-
tled hide, and his thick fingers ended in curved black claws.

He also wore a heavy collar around his throat, the skin underneath red and raw, showing old scars where he'd clawed at
it. A moment later, I realized both the collar and the manacles
were made of iron. The ogre limped across the room, favoring
the chained leg as he moved, his ankle festering with blisters
and open sores. Grimalkin gave a small hiss.

"Interesting," he said. "Is the ogre really that strong, to be
bound that way?"

"He's escaped a few times in the past, before we started
using the iron," Shard replied, looking pleased with herself.
"Smashed the club to bits, and ate a few patrons before we
stopped him. I thought drastic measures were called for. Now
he behaves himself."

"It is killing him." Grimalkin's voice was flat. "You must
realize this will considerably shorten his life span."

"Don't lecture me, Grimalkin." Shard gave the cat a dis-
gusted look and stepped through the door. "If I didn't keep
him here, he'd only be rampaging somewhere else. The iron
won't kill him right away. Ogres heal so fast."

She sauntered up to the ogre, who glared at her with pain-
filled yellow eyes. "Move," she ordered it, pointing toward the
pile of straw in the corner. "Go to your bed, Grumly. Now."

The ogre stared at her, snarled feebly, and shuffled to his
bed, the chain clinking behind him. I couldn't help but feel
a little sorry for him.

Shard opened the door. A long hallway stretched beyond
the door, and mist flowed through the opening into the room.
"Well?" she called back to us. "Here's your trod to the Winter
territory. Are you going to stand there or what?"

Keeping a wary eye on Grumly, I started forward.

"Wait," Grimalkin muttered.

"What's the matter?" I turned and found him scanning the room, eyes narrowed to slits. "Afraid of the ogre? Shard will keep him off us, right?"

"Not at all," the cat replied. "Her bargain is done. She just opened the path to Tir Na Nog for us. She never promised us protection."

I looked into the room again and found Grumly staring at us, drool dripping to the floor from his teeth. On the other side, Shard was smirking at me.

There was a sudden clatter on the stairs, the sound of many feet skipping down the steps. Over the railing, a wrinkled, evil face peered down at me, shark-teeth gleaming. A red bandanna fell off its head to land at my feet.

"Redcaps," I gasped, stepping into the room without thinking.

Grumly roared, surging to the end of his chain, raking the ground with his claws. I yelped and flattened myself against the wall as the ogre snarled and slashed at the air, straining to reach me. His huge fists pounded the floor not ten feet away, and he bellowed in frustration. I couldn't move. Grimalkin had disappeared. Shard's laughter rang in the air as a dozen redcaps swarmed into the room.

"Now," she said, leaning against the door frame, "this is entertainment."

CHAPTER FIFTEEN

Puck's Return

The redcaps crowded through the doorway, teeth flashing in the dim light. They wore biker jackets and leather pants, and sported crimson bandannas instead of their trademark caps. Snarling and gnashing their teeth, they spotted Grumly at the same time the ogre noticed them, and leaped back as a huge fist pounded the pavement.

Snarls and curses rose in the air. The redcaps danced madly out of the ogre's reach, brandishing bronze knives and wooden baseball bats. "What is this?" I heard one of them screech. "Goat-man promised us young flesh if we followed the stairs. Where's our meat?"

"There!" snarled another, pointing at me with what looked like a tarnished shiv. "In the corner. Don't let the monster get our meat!"

They slid toward me, hugging the wall as I had done, keeping out of the ogre's grasp. Grumly roared and slashed the ground, raking deep trenches into the cement floor, but the redcaps were small and quick, and he couldn't reach them. I watched in horror as the hideous fey swarmed toward me, laughing and waving their weapons, and I couldn't move. I was about to be eaten alive, but if I ventured any farther into the room, Grumly would tear me apart.

Through it all, I was aware of Shard, lounging in the other doorway, a self-satisfied smirk on her face. "Do you like where our contract has gone, little bitch?" she called over the bellows of Grumly and the clattering teeth of the redcaps. "Throw me your real name, and I might call them off."

One of the redcaps leaped at me, jaws gaping, springing right for my face. I threw up my arm, and the jagged teeth sank into my flesh, clamping down like a steel trap. Shrieking, I flailed wildly, dislodging the repulsive weight and flinging it at the ogre. The redcap hit the ground and leaped to his feet snarling, just as Grumly's fist smashed him into bloody paste.

Time seemed to slow down. I guess that happens when you're about to die. The redcaps surged forward, shark teeth grinning and clacking, Grumly bellowed at the end of his chain, and Shard leaned against the door frame and laughed.

A huge black bird flapped through the open door.

The redcaps leaped.

The bird dove, sinking its talons into a redcap's face, shrieking and flapping its wings. Startled and confused, the redcaps hesitated as the bird thrashed about, beating its wings and stabbing at the faery's eyes with its beak. The pack hooted and slugged at it with their bats, but the bird darted up at the last second, and the redcap howled as the weapons slammed into him instead.

In the confusion, the bird exploded, changing shape in mid-air. A body dropped between me and the redcaps, shedding black feathers and giving me a familiar grin.

"Hi, princess. Sorry I'm late. Traffic was a bitch."

"Puck!"

He winked at me, then shot a glance at the Winter sidhe, standing in the doorway. "Hey, Shard." He waved. "Nice place you've got here. I'll have to remember it, so I can give it the special 'Puck touch.'"

"It's an honor to have you, Robin Goodfellow," Shard answered, grinning evilly. "If the redcaps leave your head intact, I'll mount it over the bar so everyone can see it when they come in. Kill him!"

Snarling, the redcaps leaped, teeth flashing like piranhas swarming a drowning bird. Puck pulled something out of his pocket and tossed it. It exploded into a thick log, and the redcaps clamped their jaws around the wood, teeth sinking into the bark. With muffled yelps, they clattered to the floor.

"Fetch," Puck called.

Shrieking with rage, the redcaps splintered the log, shredding it like buzz saws. Teeth chattering, they spit wood chips and glared at us murderously. Puck turned to me with an apologetic look. "Excuse me a moment, princess. I have to go play with the puppies."

He stepped toward them, grinning, and the redcaps lunged, brandishing knives and baseball bats. Puck waited until the last second before he dodged, *into* the room and away from the wall. The pack followed. I gasped as Grumly's fist hammered down, but Puck leaped aside just in time, and a redcap was smashed flatter than a pancake.

"Whoops," Puck exclaimed, putting both hands to his mouth, even as he sidestepped Grumly's second swing. "Clumsy of me."

The redcaps snarled curses and lunged at him again.

They continued this deadly dance around the room, Puck leading the redcaps on with taunts, laughter, and cheers. Grumly roared and smashed his fists at the little men scurrying around his feet, but the redcaps were quick, and now wary to the danger. This didn't stop them from launching an all-out attack on Puck, who danced, dodged, and pirouetted his way around the ogre, almost seeming to enjoy himself. My heart stayed lodged in my throat the whole time; one wrong move, one miscalculation, and Puck would be a bloody smear on the floor.

The air around me chilled. I'd been so focused on Puck, I didn't realize Shard had slipped away from the door frame and was now a few feet away. Her eyes glimmered black, and her lips curled in a smile as she raised a hand. A long spear of ice formed overhead, angled at me.

There was a yowl, and an invisible weight must have thumped onto her back, for she staggered and nearly fell. Something flashed golden on her chest: a key, attached to a thin silver chain. With a curse, Shard flung the invisible assailant into the wall; there was a thud and a hiss of pain as Grimalkin materialized for a split second and winked out of sight again.

In that moment of distraction, I lunged, grabbing the key around her neck. She turned with blinding speed, and a pale white hand clamped around my throat. I gasped, clawing at her arm with my free hand, but it seemed to be made of stone. Her skin burned with cold; ice crystals formed on my neck as Shard slowly tightened her grip, smiling. I sank to my knees as the room began to dim.

With a fierce screech, Grimalkin landed on her back, sinking claws and teeth into her neck. Shard screamed, and the pressure on my throat disappeared. Lurching upright, I shoved the sidhe with all my might, pushing her away. There was a jerk and a tinny snap, and the key came loose in my hand.

Coughing, I staggered away from the wall, looking up at the ogre. "Grumly!" I yelled, my voice raw and hoarse. "Grumly, look at me! Listen to me!"

The ogre stopped pounding the floor and swung his tormented gaze to me. Behind me, a feline yowl cut through the
air, and Grimalkin's body tumbled to the floor.

"Help us!" I cried, holding up the key. It winked golden
in the light. "Help us, Grumly, and we'll free you! We'll set
you free!"

"Free…me?"

Something smashed into the back of my head, nearly knocking me out. I collapsed, clutching the key, as pain raged across
my senses. Something kicked me in the ribs, flipping me to my
back. Shard loomed overhead, her dagger in one raised hand.

"No!"

Grumly's bellow filled the room. Startled, Shard looked
up, just realizing she was within the ogre's reach. Too late.
Grumly's backhand smashed into her chest, hurling her into
the wall with a nasty thud. Even the redcaps stopped chasing
Puck around and looked back.

I scrambled to my feet, ignoring the way my muscles
screamed in protest. I staggered toward Grumly, hoping the
ogre wouldn't forget and smash me into pudding. He didn't
move as I reached the chains, the cruel iron manacle digging
into his flesh. Shoving the key into the hole, I turned it until
it clicked. The iron band loosened and dropped away.

Grumly roared, a roar filled with triumph and rage. He
spun, surprisingly quick for his bulk, and kicked a redcap
into the wall. Puck scrambled out of the way as the ogre
raised a foot and stomped two more like roaches. The redcaps went berserk. Snarling and screeching, they swarmed
Grumly's feet, pounding them with bats and sinking teeth
into his ankles. Grumly stomped and kicked, barely missing
me, and the ground shook with his blows, but I didn't have
the strength to move.

Dodging the carnage, Puck grabbed me and pulled me away from the battle. "Let's go," he muttered, looking back over his shoulder. "While they're distracted. Head for the trod."

"What about Grimalkin?"

"I am here," the cat said, appearing beside me. His voice sounded strained, and he favored his left forepaw, but otherwise seemed fine. "It is definitely time to leave."

We staggered toward the open door, but found our path blocked by Shard. "No," the sidhe growled. Her left arm hung limp, but she raised an ice spear and angled it at my chest. "You will not pass. You will die here, and I will nail you to the wall for everyone to see."

A rumbling growl echoed behind us, and heavy footsteps shook the ground.

"Grumly," Shard said without taking her eyes from me, "kill them. All is forgiven. Rip them apart, slowly. Do it, now."

Grumly growled again, and a thick leg landed next to me. "Frrriends," the ogre rumbled, standing over us. "Free Grumly. Grumly's friends." He took another step, the raw, chafed wound on his leg smelling of gangrene and rot. "Kill mistress," he growled.

"What?" Shard backed away, her eyes widening. Grumly shuffled forward, raising his huge fists. "What are you doing? Get back, you stupid thing. I command you! No, no!"

"Let's go," Puck whispered, tugging my arm. We ducked under Grumly's legs and sprinted for the open door. The last thing I saw, as the door closed behind us, was Grumly looming over his former master, and Shard bringing up her spear as she backed away.

The corridor stretched away before us, filled with mist and flickering lights. I slumped against the wall, shaking as the adrenaline wore off.

"You all right, princess?" Puck asked, green eyes bright with concern. I staggered forward and threw my arms around him, hugging him tightly. He wrapped his arms around me and pulled me close. I felt his warmth and the rapid beat of his heart, his breath against my ear. Finally, I pulled away and sank back against the wall, drawing him down with me.

"I thought Oberon changed you into a bird," I whispered.

"He did," Puck answered with a shrug. "But when he discovered you had run away, he sent me to find you."

"So, it was you I heard following us," Grimalkin said, nearly invisible in the mist.

Puck nodded. "I figured you were heading for the Unseelie Court. Who do you think created that shortcut? Anyway, once I was out, I sniffed around and a piskie told me he saw you heading for this part of town. I knew Shard owned a club here, and the rest, as the mortals say, is history."

"I'm glad you came," I said, standing up. My legs felt a bit stronger now, and the shaking had almost stopped. "You saved my life. Again. I know you might not want to hear it, but thanks."

Puck gave me a sidelong glance that I didn't like at all. "Don't thank me just yet, princess. Oberon was quite upset that you had left the safety of the Seelie territories." He rubbed his hands and looked uncomfortable. "I'm supposed to bring you back to Court."

I stared at him, feeling as though he'd just kicked me in the stomach. "But...you won't, right?" I stammered. He looked away, and my desperation grew. "Puck, you can't. I have to find Ethan. I have to go to the Unseelie Court and bring him home."

Puck scrubbed a hand through his hair, a strangely human gesture. "You don't understand," he said, sounding uncharacteristically unsure. "I'm Oberon's favorite lackey, but I can only push him so far. If I fail him again, I might end up a lot worse than a raven for two centuries. He could banish me from the Nevernever for all time. I'd never be able to go home."

"Please," I begged, taking his hand. He still didn't look at me. "Help us. Puck, I've known you forever. Don't do this." I dropped his hand and stared at him, narrowing my eyes. "You realize you'll have to drag me back kicking and screaming, and I'll never speak to you again."

"Don't be like that." Puck finally looked up. "You don't realize what you're doing. If Mab finds you...you don't know what she's capable of."

"I don't care. All I know is, my brother is still out there, in trouble. I have to find him. And I'm going to do it with or without your help."

Puck's eyes glittered. "I could cast a charm spell over you," he mused, one corner of his lip quirking up. "That would solve a lot of problems."

"No," Grimalkin spoke up before I could explode, "you will not. And you know you will not, so stop posturing. Besides, I have something that might solve this little problem."

"Oh?"

"A favor." Grimalkin waved his tail languidly. "From the king."

"That won't stop Oberon from banishing me."

"No," Grimalkin agreed. "But I could request that you be banished for a limited time only. A few decades or so. It is better than nothing."

"Uh-huh." Puck sounded unconvinced. "And this would just cost me a small favor in return, is that right?"

"You pulled me into this conflict the moment you dropped this girl into my tree," Grimalkin said, blinking lazily. "I cannot believe that was an act of coincidence, not from the infamous Robin Goodfellow. You should have known it might come to this."

"I know better than to make deals with a cait sith," Puck shot back, then sighed, scrubbing a hand over his eyes. "Fine," he said at last. "You win, princess. Freedom is highly overrated, anyway. If I'm going to do anything, I might as well do it big."

My heart lifted. "So, you'll help us?"

"Sure, why not?" Puck gave me a resigned smile. "You'd get eaten alive without me. Besides, storming the Unseelie Court?" His grin widened. "Can't pass that up for anything."

"Then let us go," Grimalkin said as Puck pulled me to my feet. "The longer we tarry, the farther word will spread about our intentions. Tir Na Nog is not far now." He turned and trotted down the corridor, his tail help upright in the fog.

We followed the hallway for several minutes. After a while, the air turned cold and sharp; frost coated the walls of the corridor, and icicles dangled from the ceiling.

"We are getting close," came Grimalkin's disembodied voice in the mist.

The hallway ended with a simple wooden door. A thin powder of snow lined the bottom crack, and the door trembled and creaked in the wind howling just outside.

Puck stepped forward. "Ladies and felines," he stated grandly, grasping the doorknob, "welcome to Tir Na Nog. Land of endless winter and shitloads of snow."

A billow of freezing powder caressed my face as he pulled the door open. Blinking away ice crystals, I stepped forward.

I stood in a frozen garden, the thornbushes on the fence coated with ice, a cherub fountain in the center of the yard spouting frozen water. In the distance, beyond the barren trees and thorny scrub, I saw the pointed roof of a huge Victorian estate. I glanced back for Grim and Puck and saw them standing under a trellis hung with purple vines and crystal blue flowers. As they stepped through, the corridor vanished behind them.

"Charming," Puck commented, gazing around in distaste. "I love the barren, dead feel they're going for. Who's the gardener, I wonder? I'd love to get some tips."

I was already shivering. "H-how far are we from Queen Mab's court?" I asked, my teeth chattering.

"The Winter Court is maybe two days' walk from here," Grimalkin said, leaping onto a tree stump. He shook his paws, one by one, and sat down carefully. "We should find shelter soon. I am uncomfortable in this weather, and the girl will certainly freeze to death."

A dark chuckle echoed across the garden. "I wouldn't worry about that now."

A figure stepped out from behind a tree, sword held loosely in one hand. My heart skipped a beat, and then picked up again, louder and more irregular than before. The breeze ruffled the figure's black hair as he moved toward us, graceful and silent as a shadow. Grimalkin hissed and disappeared, and Puck shoved me behind him.

"I've been waiting for you," Ash murmured into the silence.

CHAPTER SIXTEEN

The Iron Fey

"Ash," I whispered as the lean, stealthy figure glided toward us, his boots making no sound in the snow. He was devastatingly gorgeous, dressed all in black, his pale face seeming to float over the ground. I remembered the way he smiled, the look in his silver eyes as we danced. He wasn't smiling now, and his eyes were cold. This wasn't the prince I'd danced with Elysium night; this wasn't anything but a predator.

"Ash," Puck repeated in a conversational tone, though his face had gone hard and feral. "What a surprise to see you here. How did you find us?"

"It wasn't difficult." Ash sounded bored. "The princess mentioned that she was looking for someone within Mab's court. There are only so many ways into Tir Na Nog from the mortal world, and Shard doesn't exactly make it a secret that she guards the trod. I figured it was only a matter of time before you came here."

"Very clever," Puck said, smirking. "But then, you were always the strategist, weren't you? What do you want, Ash?"

"Your head," Ash answered softly. "On a pike. But what I

want doesn't matter this time." He pointed his sword at me. "I've come for her."

I gasped as my heart and stomach began careening around my chest. *He's here for me, to kill me, like he promised at Elysium.*

"Over my dead body." Puck smiled, as if this was a friendly conversation on the street, but I felt muscles coiling under his skin.

"That was part of the plan." The prince raised his sword, the icy blade wreathed in mist. "I will avenge her today, and put her memory to rest." For a moment, a shadow of anguish flitted across his face, and he closed his eyes. When he opened them, they were cold and glittered with malice. "Prepare yourself."

"Stay back, princess," Puck warned, pushing me out of the way. He reached into his boot and pulled out a dagger, the curved blade clear as glass. "This might get a little rough."

"Puck, no." I clutched at his sleeve. "Don't fight him. Someone could die."

"Duels to the death tend to end that way." Puck grinned, but it was a savage thing, grim and frightening. "But I'm touched that you care. One moment, princeling," he called to Ash, who inclined his head. Taking my wrist, Puck steered me behind the fountain and bent close, his breath warm on my face.

"I have to do this, princess," he said firmly. "Ash won't let us go without a fight, and this has been coming for a long time now." For a moment, a shadow of regret flickered across his face, but then it was gone.

"So," he murmured, grinning as he tilted my chin up, "before I march off to battle, how 'bout a kiss for luck?"

I hesitated, wondering why now, of all times, he would ask for a kiss. He certainly didn't think of me in that way...

did he? I shook myself. There was no time to wonder about that. Leaning forward, I kissed him on the cheek. His skin was warm, and bristly with stubble. "Don't die," I whispered, pulling back.

Puck looked disappointed, but only for a second. "Me? Die? Didn't they tell you, princess? I'm Robin Goodfellow."

With a whoop, he flourished his knife and charged the waiting prince.

Ash lunged, a dark blur across the snow, his sword hissing down in a vicious arc. Puck leaped out of the way, and the blow sent a miniature blizzard arching toward me. I gasped, the freezing spray stinging like needles, and rubbed at my burning eyes. When I could open them again, Ash and Puck were deep in battle, and it looked like each was intent on killing the other.

Puck ducked a savage blow and tossed Ash something from his pocket. It erupted into a large boar, squealing madly as it charged the prince, tusks gleaming. The ice sword hammered into it, and the boar exploded in a swirl of dry leaves. Ash flung out his arm, and a spray of glittering ice shards flew toward Puck like daggers. I cried out, but Puck inhaled and blew in their direction, like he was blowing out a birthday candle. The shards shimmered into daisies, raining harmlessly around him, and he grinned.

Ash attacked viciously, his blade singing as he bore down on his opponent. Puck dodged and parried with his dagger, retreating before the onslaught of the Winter prince. Diving away, Puck snatched a handful of twigs from the base of the tree, blew on them, and tossed them into the air—

—and now there were *three* Pucks, grinning wickedly as they set upon their opponent. Three knives flashed, three bodies surrounded the dark prince, as the real Puck leaned against the tree and watched Ash struggle.

But Ash was far from beaten. He spun away from the Pucks, his sword a blur as he dodged and parried, whirling from one attack to the next. He ducked beneath an opponent's guard, ripped his blade up, and sliced cleanly through a Puck's stomach. The doppelgänger split in two, changing into a severed stick that dropped away. Ash spun to meet the Puck rushing up from the side. His sword whirled, and Puck's head dropped from his shoulders before reverting to a twig. The last Puck charged the prince from behind, dagger raised high. Ash didn't even turn, but rammed his blade backward, point up. Puck's lunge carried him onto the blade and drove it through his stomach, the point erupting out his back. The prince yanked the sword free without turning, and a shattered twig dropped to the snow.

Ash lowered his sword, gazing around warily. Following his gaze, I gave a start. Puck had disappeared, pulling a Grimalkin while we were distracted. Instantly wary, the Winter prince scanned the garden, edging forward with his sword raised. His gaze flicked to me, and I tensed, but he dismissed me almost as quickly, stepping beneath the boughs of a frozen pine.

As Ash stepped under the branches, something leaped out of the snow, howling. The prince dodged, the knife barely missing him, and Puck overbalanced, stumbling forward. With a snarl, Ash drove the point of the sword through Puck's back and out his chest, pinning him to the ground.

I screamed, but as I did, the body vanished. For a split second, Ash stared at the pierced leaf on his sword tip, then threw himself to the side as something dropped from the tree, dagger flashing in the light.

Puck's laughter rang out as Ash rolled to his feet, clutching his arm. Blood seeped between pale fingers. "Almost too slow that time, prince," Puck mocked, balancing the dagger on two fingers. "Really, that's the oldest trick in the book. I know, 'cause I *wrote* the book. I've got a million more, if you want to keep playing."

"I'm getting tired of sparring with copies." Ash straightened, dropping his hand. "I guess honor isn't as prevalent in the Seelie Court as I thought. Are you the real Puck, or is he too cowardly to face me himself?"

Puck regarded him disdainfully, before shimmering into nothingness. Another Puck stepped out from behind a tree, a nasty grin on his face.

"All right, then, prince," he said, smirking as he approached, "if that's what you want, I'll kill you the old-fashioned way." And they flew at each other again.

I watched the battle, my heart in my throat, wishing I could do something. I didn't want either of them to die, but I had no idea how to stop this. Shouting or rushing between them seemed like a really bad idea; one could be distracted, and the other would waste no time finishing him off. A sick despair churned in my stomach. I hadn't realized Puck was so bloodthirsty, but the mad gleam in his eyes told me he would kill the Winter prince if he could.

They have a history, I realized, watching Ash cut viciously at Puck's face, barely missing as his opponent ducked. *Something happened between them, to make them hate each other. I wonder if they were ever friends.*

My skin prickled, an uneasy shiver from more than the cold. Over the clang and screech of metal, I heard something else, a faint rustling, as if a thousand insects were scuttling toward us.

"Run!" Grimalkin's voice made me jump. Tracks appeared in the snow, rushing toward me, and invisible claws scrabbled against bark as the feline fled up a tree. "Something is coming! Hide, quickly!"

I glanced at Puck and Ash, still locked in combat. The rustling grew louder, accompanied by static and faint, high-pitched laughter. Suddenly, through the trees, hundreds of eyes glowed electric-green in the darkness, surrounding us. Puck and Ash stopped fighting and broke apart, finally aware that something was wrong, but it was too late.

They poured over the ground like a living carpet, appearing from everywhere: small, black-skinned creatures with spindly arms, huge ears, and razor grins that shone blue-white in the darkness. I heard the boys' cries of shock, and Grimalkin's yowl of horror as he fled farther up the tree. The creatures spotted me, and I had no time to react. They swarmed me like angry wasps, crawling up my legs, hurling themselves onto my back. I felt claws dig into my skin, my ears filled with loud buzzing and shrieking laughter, and I screamed, thrashing wildly. I couldn't see, didn't know which way was up. The weight of their bodies bore me down, and I fell onto a grasping, wriggling mass. Hundreds of hands lifted me up, like ants carrying a grasshopper, and began to cart me away.

"Puck!" I screamed, struggling to free myself. But whenever I rolled away from one group, a dozen more slid in to take their place, bearing me up. I never touched the ground. "Grimalkin! Help!"

Their cries seemed distant and far away. Carried on a buzzing, living mattress, I glided rapidly over the ground and into the waiting darkness.

I don't know how long they carried me. When I struggled, the claws gripping me would dig into my skin, turning the mattress into a bed of needles. I soon ceased thrashing about, and tried to concentrate on where they were taking me. But it was difficult; being carried on my back, the only thing I saw clearly was the sky. I tried to turn my head, but the creatures had their claws sunk into my hair and would yank on it until tears formed in my eyes. I resigned myself to lying still, shivering with cold, waiting to see what would happen. The cold and the gnawing worry drained me.... I allowed my eyes to slip closed, and found solace in the darkness.

When I opened my eyes again, the night sky had disappeared, replaced by a ceiling of solid ice. I realized we were traveling underground. The air grew even colder as the tunnel opened up into a magnificent ice cavern, glistening with a jagged, alien beauty. Huge icicles dripped from the ceiling, some longer than I was tall and wickedly sharp. It was a tad disturbing passing under those bristling spikes, watching them sparkle like crystal chandeliers, praying they wouldn't fall.

My teeth chattered, and my lips were numb with cold. However, as we traveled deeper into the cave, the air gradually warmed. A faint noise echoed through the lower caverns: a roaring, hissing sound, like steam escaping a cracked pipe. Water dripped from the ceiling in rivulets now, soaking my clothes, and some of the ice shards looked dangerously unstable.

The hissing grew louder, punctuated with great roaring coughs and the acrid smell of smoke. Now I saw that some of the icicles had indeed fallen, smashed to pieces on the ground and glittering like broken glass.

My abductors brought me into a large cavern littered with shattered shards of ice. Puddles saturated the floor, and water fell like rain from the ceiling. The creatures dropped me to the icy ground and scuttled off. I rubbed my numb, aching limbs and looked around, wondering where I was. The cave was mostly empty, save for a wooden box filled with black rocks—coal?—in one corner. More were stacked along the far wall, next to a wooden archway that led off into the darkness.

A piercing whistle, like a steam engine roaring into the station, erupted from the tunnel, and black smoke churned from the opening. I smelled ashes and brimstone, and then a deep voice echoed throughout the cavern. "HAVE YOU BROUGHT HER?"

The scuttling creatures scattered, and several icicles smashed to the floor with an almost musical chime. I ducked behind an ice column as heavy footsteps clanked down the tunnel. Through the smoke, I saw something huge and grossly distorted, something definitely not human, and shook in terror.

A massive black horse emerged from the writhing smoke, eyes glowing like hot coals, flared nostrils blowing steam. It was as big as the horses that pulled the Budweiser wagon, but there the resemblance ended. At first, I thought it was covered in iron plates; its hide was bulky with metal, rusted and black, and it moved awkwardly with the weight. Then I realized its body was *made* of iron. Pistons and gears jutted out from its ribs. Its mane and tail were steel cables, and a great fire burned in its belly, visible through the chinks in its hide. Its face was a terrifying mask as it turned to me, blasting flame from its nostrils.

I fell back, certain I was going to die.

"ARE YOU MEGHAN CHASE?" The horse's voice shook the room. More icicles committed suicide, but they were the least of my worries. I cringed back as the iron monster loomed over me, tossing its head and snorting flame. "ANSWER ME, HUMAN. ARE YOU MEGHAN CHASE, DAUGHTER OF THE SUMMER KING?"

"Yes," I whispered as the horse moved closer, iron hooves pounding the ice. "Who are you? What do you want with me?"

"I AM IRONHORSE," the beast replied, "ONE OF KING MACHINA'S LIEUTENANTS. I HAVE BROUGHT YOU HERE BECAUSE MY LORD HAS REQUESTED IT. YOU WILL COME WITH ME TO SEE THE IRON KING."

The booming voice was giving me a headache. I tried to focus through the pounding in my skull. "The Iron King?" I asked stupidly. "Who—?"

"KING MACHINA," Ironhorse confirmed. "SOVEREIGN LORD OF THE IRON COURT, AND RULER OF THE IRON FEY."

Iron fey?

A chill slid up my spine. I looked around, at the countless eyes of the gremlinlike monsters, to the massive bulk of Ironhorse, and felt dizzy at the implications. Iron fey? Could there be such a thing? In all the stories, poems, and plays, I'd never encountered anything like this. Where did they come from? And who was this Machina, ruler of the Iron Fey? More important…

"What does he want with me?"

"IT IS NOT MINE TO KNOW." Ironhorse snorted, swishing its tail with a clanking sound. "I ONLY OBEY. HOWEVER, YOU WOULD BE WISE TO COME WITH US, IF YOU WISH TO SEE YOUR BROTHER AGAIN."

"Ethan?" I jerked my head up, glaring at Ironhorse's expressionless mask. "How do you know about him?" I demanded. "Is he all right? Where is he?"

"COME WITH ME, AND ALL YOUR QUESTIONS WILL BE ANSWERED. THE IRON COURT AND MY LORD MACHINA AWAIT."

I stood as Ironhorse turned, clanking back toward the tunnel. Its pistons creaked and the gears complained loudly as it shuffled forward. It was old, I realized, watching a bolt come loose and fall to the ground. A relic of days gone by. I wondered if there were newer, sleeker models out there, and what they looked like. Faster, better, more superior iron fey. After a moment, I decided I didn't want to find out.

Ironhorse stood at the mouth of the tunnel, stamping impatiently. Sparks flew from its hooves as it glowered at me. "COME," it ordered, with a blast of steam from its nostrils. "FOLLOW THE TROD TO THE IRON COURT. IF YOU WILL NOT WALK, THE GREMLINS WILL CARRY YOU." It tossed its head and reared, flames shooting out its muzzle. "OR PERHAPS I WILL RUN BEHIND YOU, BREATHING FIRE—"

An ice spear flew through the air, striking Ironhorse between the ribs, bursting into steam as the fire engulfed it. The horse screamed, a high-pitched whistle, and whirled, hooves sparking as they struck the ice. The gremlins skittered forward, gazing wildly about, searching for intruders.

"Hey, ugly!" called a familiar voice. "Nice place you got here! Here's a thought, though. Next time, try a hideout a little more resistant to fire than an ice cave!"

"Puck!" I cried, and the red-haired elf waved at me, grinning from the far side of the cavern. Ironhorse screamed and charged, scattering gremlins like birds as he bore down on Puck. Puck didn't move, and the great iron beast knocked him flat in the ice, trampling him with his steel hooves.

"Oh, that looked painful," called another Puck, a little farther down. "We really need to talk about your anger-management issues."

With a roar, Ironhorse charged the second Puck, moving

farther away from me and the trod. The gremlins followed, laughing and hissing, but kept a fair distance from the raging beast and its hooves.

A cool hand clamped over my mouth, muffling my startled shriek. I turned to gaze into glittering silver eyes.

"Ash?"

"This way," he said in a low voice, tugging on my hand, "while the idiot has them distracted."

"No, wait," I whispered, pulling back. "He knows about Ethan. I have to find my brother—"

Ash narrowed his eyes. "Hesitate now, and Goodfellow will die. Besides…" He reached out and took my hand again. "I'm not giving you a choice."

Dazed, I followed the Winter prince along the wall of the cavern, too stunned to ask why he was helping me. Didn't he want to kill me? Was this rescue just to get me alone to finish the job in peace? But that didn't make any sense; he could have just killed me while Puck was distracted with Ironhorse.

"Hellooooooooo." Puck's voice echoed farther down the cavern. "Sorry, ugly, wrong me! Keep going, I'm sure you'll get it right next time!"

Ironhorse looked up from stomping a fake Puck into the ground, crimson eyes blazing with hate. Seeing yet another Puck, it tensed iron muscles to charge, when one of the gremlins spotted us sneaking along the wall and gave a yelp of alarm.

Ironhorse whirled, eyes flaring as they settled on us. Ash muttered a curse. With a bellow and a blast of flame from its nostrils, it charged, bearing down on us like the steam engine it was named for. Ash drew his sword and flung a shower of ice shards at the monster. They shattered harmlessly on its armored hide, doing nothing but enraging it further. As the roaring, flaming bulk of metal descended, Ash shoved me out of the way and dove forward, the flailing hooves missing him by inches. Rolling to his feet behind the monster, he cut at its flank, but Ironhorse plunged its head down and kicked him in the ribs. There was a sickening crack, and Ash was hurled away, crumpling to the floor in a heap.

A screaming flock of ravens descended on Ironhorse before it could stomp Ash into the ground. They swirled around its head, pecking and clawing, and Ironhorse roared as it lashed out at the flock, blasting them to cindery bits. Ash staggered to his feet as Puck appeared beside us, grabbing my hand.

"Time to go," he announced cheerfully. "Prince, either keep up or get left behind. We're leaving."

We ran through the caverns, slipping on ice and slush, the insane roars of Ironhorse and the hissing of the gremlins on our heels. I didn't dare look back. The cavern shook, and icicles smashed to the ground all around us, spraying me with stinging shards, but we kept going.

A fuzzy gray shape bounded toward us, tail held high. "You found her," Grimalkin said, stopping to glare at Puck. "Idiot. I told you not to fight the horse thing."

"Can't talk now, little busy at the moment!" Puck gasped as we tore past the feline, continuing down the tunnel. Grimalkin flattened his ears and joined us as the shrieks of the gremlins ricocheted off the walls. I could see the mouth of the cave, dripping with icicles, and put on a burst of speed.

Ironhorse bellowed, and an ice shard smashed down inches from my face.

"Collapse the cave!" Grimalkin shouted, bounding along beside us. "Bring the ceiling down on their heads! Do it!" He zipped away, through the cave entrance, and was gone.

We burst out of the cave moments later, gasping, stumbling

in the snow. Looking back, I saw dozens of green eyes skittering forward, heard the pounding hooves of Ironhorse as he
followed close behind.

"Keep going!" Ash cried, and whirled around. Closing his
eyes, he brought a fist to his face and bowed his head. The
gremlins swarmed toward him, and the red glow of Ironhorse
appeared, flames streaming in the darkness.

Ash opened his eyes and flung out a hand.

A low rumble shook the ground, and the cave trembled.
Huge clumps of icicles shivered, wobbling back and forth. As
the gremlins reached the mouth of the cave, the entire ceiling
collapsed with a roar and a sound like breaking glass. Gremlins shrieked as they were crushed under several tons of ice
and rock, and the dismayed bellow of Ironhorse rose above
the cacophony.

The noise died away, and silence fell. Ash, standing two
feet from the solid wall of ice sealing the cave, collapsed into
the snow.

Puck grabbed my arm as I rushed forward. "Whoa, whoa,
princess," he said as I tried yanking free. "What do you think
you're doing? In case you forgot, princeling there is the enemy.
We don't help the enemy."

"He's hurt."

"All the more reason to leave now."

"He just saved our lives!"

"Technically, he was saving his own life," Puck replied, still
not letting go. I shoved him, hard, and he finally released me.
"Look, princess." He sighed as I glared at him. "Do you think
Ash will play nice now? The only reason he helped—the only
reason he agreed to a truce—was so he could bring you to
Mab. She wants you alive, to use as leverage against Oberon.

That's the *only* reason he came along. If he wasn't hurt, he'd be trying to kill me now."

I looked at Ash, lying motionless in the snow. Flakes speckled his body—soon they would hide him completely. "We can't just leave him to die."

"He's a Winter prince, Meghan. He won't freeze to death, trust me."

I scowled at him. "You're just as bad as they are." He blinked, startled, and I turned away from him. "I'm going to see if he's all right, at least. Either come along or get out of my way."

Puck threw up his hands. "Fine, princess. I'll help the son of Mab, eternal enemy of our court. Even though he'll probably stick a sword in my back the second my guard is down."

"I wouldn't worry about that," Ash muttered, rising slowly to his feet. One hand gripped his sword; the other arm was wrapped around his ribs. He shook the snow from his hair and raised his weapon. "We can continue now, if you like."

Grinning, Puck pulled his dagger. "I'd be thrilled," he muttered, taking a step forward. "This won't take long at all."

I threw myself between them.

"Stop it!" I hissed, glaring at both in turn. "Stop it right now! Put your weapons up, both of you! Ash, you're in no condition to fight, and, Puck, shame on you, agreeing to duel him when he's obviously hurt. Sit down and shut up."

They blinked at me, astounded, but slowly lowered their weapons. A sneezing laugh rang out in the branches of a tree, and Grimalkin peered down, swishing his tail in mirth.

"A daughter of Oberon after all," he called, baring his teeth in a feline grin. "Queen Titania would be proud."

Puck shrugged and flopped down on a log, crossing his arms and legs. Ash continued to stand, watching me with an unreadable expression. Ignoring Puck, I walked up to him. His eyes narrowed, and he tensed, raising his sword, but I wasn't afraid. For the first time since I came here, I wasn't afraid at all.

"Prince Ash," I murmured, drawing closer, "I propose we make a deal."

Surprise flickered across his face.

"We need your help," I continued, gazing straight into his eyes. "I don't know what those things were, but they called themselves iron fey. They also mentioned someone called Machina, the Iron King. Do you know who that is?"

"The Iron King?" Ash shook his head. "There is no one by that name in the courts. If this King Machina exists, he is a danger to all of us. Both courts will want to know about him and these…iron fey."

"I need to find him," I said, forcing as much determination into my voice as I could. "He's got my brother. I need you to help us escape the Unseelie territory and find the court of the Iron King."

Ash raised an eyebrow. "And why would I do that?" he asked softly. Not mocking, but dead serious.

I swallowed. "You're injured," I pointed out, holding his gaze. "You won't be able to take me by force, not with Puck so eager to stick a knife in your ribs." I glanced back at Puck, sulking on the log, and lowered my voice. "Here's my bargain. If you help me find my brother and get him safely home, then I'll go with you to the Unseelie Court. Without a fight, from me or Puck."

Ash's eyes gleamed. "He means that much to you? You would exchange your freedom for his safety?"

I took a deep breath and nodded. "Yes." The word hung in the air between us, and I hurried on before I could take it back. "So, do we have a deal?"

He inclined his head, as if still trying to puzzle me out. "No, Meghan Chase. We have a contract."

"Good." My legs trembled. I backed away from him, needing to sit before I fell over. "And no trying to kill Puck, either."

"That wasn't part of the bargain," Ash said, before he grimaced and sank to his knees, arms around his middle. Dark blood trickled between his lips.

"Puck!" I called, turning to glare at the faery on the log. "Get over here and help."

"Oh, we're playing nice now?" Puck remained seated, looking anything but compliant. "Shall we have tea first? Brew up a nice pot of kiss-my-ass?"

"Puck!" I shouted in exasperation, but Ash raised his head and stared at his enemy.

"Truce, Goodfellow," he grated out. "The Chillsorrow manor is a few miles east of here. Right now, the lady of the house is away at court, so we'll be safe there. I suggest we postpone our duel until we arrive and the princess is out of the cold. Unless you'd like to kill me now."

"No, no. We can kill each other later." Puck hopped off the stump and padded up, shoving his dagger into his boot. Putting the prince's arm over his shoulders, he jerked him to his feet. Ash grunted and pursed his lips but didn't cry out. I glared at Puck. He ignored me.

"Off we go." Puck sighed. "You coming, Grimalkin?"

"Oh, definitely." Grimalkin landed with a soft thump in the snow. His golden eyes, bright with amusement, regarded me knowingly. "I would not miss this for the world."

CHAPTER SEVENTEEN

The Oracle

The Chillsorrow manor lived up to its name. The outside of the sprawling estate was blanketed in ice, the lawn was frozen, the numerous thorn trees were encased in crystallized water. Inside wasn't much better. The stairways were slick, the floors resembled ice rinks, and my breath hung in the air as we made our way through the frigid, narrow halls. At least the servants were helpful, if extremely creepy; skeleton-thin gnomes with pure white skin and long, long fingers glided silently around the house, not saying a word. Their pupil-less black eyes seemed too big for their faces, and they had the unnerving habit of staring at you mournfully, as if you had a fatal disease and were not long for the world.

Still, they welcomed us into the house, bowing respectfully to Ash, making him comfortable in one of the rooms. The biting chill didn't affect the Winter prince, though I was shaking, teeth chattering, until one of the servants offered me a heavy quilt and padded off without a word.

Clutching the quilt gratefully, I peeked into the room where Ash sat on a bed surrounded by ice gnomes. His shirt was off, showing his lean, muscular arms and chest. He was built more like a dancer or martial artist than a bodybuilder, the elegant frame hinting at a grace a human simply could not match. His tousled black hair fell into his eyes, and he absently raked it out of his face.

My stomach fluttered weirdly, and I backed out into the hall. *What are you doing?* I asked myself, appalled. *That is Ash, prince of the Unseelie Court. He tried to kill Puck, and he might try to kill you, as well. He is not sexy. He's not.*

But he was, extremely, and it was useless to deny it. My heart and my brain were at odds, and I knew I'd better come to terms with this quickly. *Okay, fine,* I told myself, *he's gorgeous, I'll admit it. I'm just reacting to his good looks, that's all. All the sidhe are stunning and beautiful. It doesn't mean anything.*

With that thought to buoy me, I stepped back into the room.

Ash glanced up as I approached, the quilt wrapped around my shoulders. A pair of gnomes were wrapping his torso in bandages, but above his stomach, I could see an angry black welt.

"Is that where—?"

Ash nodded, once. I continued to stare at it, noting how the flesh was blackened and crusted with scabs. I shuddered and looked away.

"It looks almost burned."

"The creature's hooves were made of iron," Ash replied. "Iron tends to burn, when it doesn't kill outright. I was lucky the blow wasn't over my heart." The gnomes tugged the bandages tight, and he winced.

"How bad are you hurt?"

He gave me an appraising look. "The fey heal faster than you mortals," he answered, and rose gracefully to his feet, scattering gnomes. "Especially if we're within our own territories. Except for this—" he lightly touched the iron burn on his ribs "—I should be fine by tomorrow."

"Oh." I was a bit breathless, suddenly unable to take my eyes from him. "That's...good, then."

He smiled then, a cold, humorless gesture, and stepped closer.

"Good?" His voice was mocking. "You shouldn't wish for my good health, princess. It would've been easier for you if Puck had killed me when he had the chance."

I resisted the urge to back away from him. "No, it wouldn't." His shadow loomed over me, prickling my skin, but I stood my ground. "I need your help, both to get out of Unseelie territory, and to find my brother. Besides, I couldn't let him kill you in cold blood."

"Why not?" He was very close now, so close I could see the pale scars on his chest. "He seems very devoted to you. Perhaps you'll wait until we leave Tir Na Nog to have him stab me in the back? What would happen if we fought again, and I killed him?"

"Stop it." I glared at him, meeting his eyes. "Why are you doing this? I gave you my word. Why are you pulling this crap now?"

"Just want to see where you stand, princess." Ash backed up a step, no longer smiling. "I like to get a feel for my enemies before we engage in combat. See what their strengths and weaknesses are."

"We aren't in combat—"

"Combat doesn't have to be with swords." Ash walked back to the bed, drawing his blade and examining the gleaming length. "Emotions can be deadly weapons, and knowing your enemy's breaking point can be key to winning a battle.

For example…" He turned and pointed the sword, staring at me down the polished edge. "You would do anything to find your brother—put yourself in danger, bargain with the enemy, give up your own freedom—if it means saving him. You'd likely do the same for your friends, or anyone else you care about. Your personal loyalty is your breaking point, and your enemies will certainly use it against you. *That* is your weakness, princess. That is the most dangerous aspect in your life."

"So what?" I challenged, pulling the quilt tighter around myself. "All you're telling me is I won't betray my friends or family. If that's a weakness, it's one I want."

He regarded me with glittering eyes, the expression on his face unreadable. "And, if the choice was between saving your brother and letting me die, which would you choose? The answer should be obvious, but could you do it?"

I chewed my lip and remained silent. Ash nodded slowly and turned away. "I'm tired," he said, sitting down on the bed. "You should find Puck and decide where we go from here. Unless, of course, you know where this Machina's court is. I do not. If I'm going to help you, I need to rest."

He lay back and put an arm over his eyes, dismissing me. I backed out and left the room, dark doubts swirling around my head.

In the hallway I met Puck, leaning against the wall with his arms crossed. "So, how is the handsome princeling?" he mocked, shoving away from the wall. "Will he survive his ordeal to fight another day?"

"He's fine," I muttered as Puck fell into step beside me. "He's got a nasty-looking burn where the horse kicked him, and I think his ribs were broken, but he wouldn't say."

"Forgive me if my heart doesn't bleed for him," Puck replied, rolling his eyes. "I don't know how you got him to help, princess, but I wouldn't trust him further than I could throw him. Deals with the Winter Court are bad news. What did you promise him?"

"Nothing," I said, not meeting his eyes. I could feel his disbelieving stare, and went on the offensive to distract him. "Look, what's your deal with him, anyway? He said you stabbed him in the back once. What's up with that?"

"That..." Puck hesitated, and I could see I'd hit a sore spot. "That was a mistake," he went on in a quiet voice. "I didn't mean for that to happen." He shook himself, and the self-doubt dropped away, replaced by his irritating smirk. "Anyway, it doesn't matter. I'm not the bad guy here, princess."

"No," I admitted. "You're not. But I'm going to need both of you to help get Ethan back. Especially now. Especially since this Iron King wants me so bad. Do you know anything about him?"

Puck sobered. "I've never heard of him before," he murmured as we entered the dining hall. A long table stood in the center of the room, with a magnificent ice sculpture as a centerpiece. Grimalkin crouched on the table with his head in a bowl, eating something that smelled strongly of fish. He glanced up as we entered, licking his jaws with a bright pink tongue.

"Heard of who before?"

"King Machina." I pulled up a chair and sat down, resting my chin in my hands. "That horse thing—Ironhorse—called him the ruler of the iron fey."

"Hmm. I have never heard of him." Grimalkin put his head back in the bowl, chewing loudly. Puck sat down beside me.

"It doesn't seem possible," he muttered, mirroring my pose with his chin in his hands. "Iron fey? It's blasphemous! It goes against everything we know." He touched his fingers to his brow, narrowing his eyes. "And yet, Ironhorse was most definitely fey. I could sense that. If there are more like him and those gremlin things, Oberon must be informed immediately. If this King Machina brings his iron fey against us, he could destroy the courts before we knew what hit us."

"But you know nothing about him," Grimalkin said, his voice echoing inside the bowl. "You have no idea where he is, what his motives are, how many iron fey are actually out there. What would you tell Oberon now? Especially since you have…ahem…fallen out of favor by disobeying him."

"He's right," I said. "We should find out more about this Machina before we tell the courts. What if they decide to confront him now? He might fight back, or he might go into hiding. I can't risk losing Ethan."

"Meghan—"

"No telling the courts," I said firmly, looking him in the eye. "That's final."

Puck sighed and threw me a grudging smirk. "Fine, princess," he said, raising his hands. "We'll do it your way."

Grimalkin snickered into the bowl.

"So, how do we find this Machina, anyway?" I asked, voicing the question that had bothered me all evening. "The only trod to his kingdom that we know of is buried under a ton of ice. Where do we start looking for him? He could be anywhere."

Grimalkin raised his head. "I might know somebody who could help us," he purred, slitting his eyes. "An oracle of sorts, living within your world. Very old, older even than Puck. Older than Oberon. Almost as old as cats. If anyone could tell you where this Iron King might be, she could."

My heart leaped. If this oracle could tell me about the Iron

King, maybe she would know where my dad was, as well. It couldn't hurt to ask.

"I thought she died," Puck said. "If it's the same oracle I'm thinking of, she vanished ages ago."

Grimalkin yawned and licked his whiskers. "Not dead," he replied. "Hardly dead. But she changed her name and appearance so many times, even the oldest fey would hardly remember her. She likes to keep a low profile, you know."

Puck frowned, knitting his brows together. "Then how is it *you* remember her?" he demanded, sounding indignant.

"I am a cat," purred Grimalkin.

I didn't sleep well that night. The numerous quilts didn't quite protect me from the incessant chill; it crept into whatever cracks it could find, stealing away the heat with frozen fingers. Also, Grimalkin slept on top of me under the blankets, his furry body a blessed warmth, but he kept digging his claws into my skin. Near dawn, after being poked awake yet again, I rose, wrapped a quilt around my shoulders, and went looking for Puck.

Instead, I found Ash in the dining hall, practicing sword drills by the gray light of dawn. His lean, honed body glided over the tiles, sword sweeping gracefully through the air, eyes closed in concentration. I stood in the doorway and watched for several minutes, unable to tear my gaze away. It was a dance, beautiful and hypnotic. I lost track of the time I stood watching him, and would have happily stayed there all morning, when he opened his eyes and saw me.

I squeaked and straightened guiltily. "Don't mind me," I said as he relaxed his stance. "I didn't mean to interrupt. Please, continue."

"I'm finished, anyway." Sheathing his sword, he regarded me solemnly. "Did you need something?"

I realized I was staring and blushed, turning my gaze away. "Um, no. That is... I'm glad you're feeling better."

He gave me a weird little smile. "I have to be on top of my game if I'm going to kill things for you, right?"

I was saved a reply as Puck strolled in, humming, carrying a bowl of strange golden fruit, each about the size of a golf ball. "Mornin', princess," he said with his mouth full, plunking the bowl on the table. "Look what I found."

Ash blinked. "Are you raiding the cellars now, Goodfellow?"

"Me? Stealing?" Puck flashed a devious grin and popped another fruit into his mouth. "In the house of my ancient enemy? What gave you that idea?" He plucked another fruit and tossed it to me with a wink. It was warm and soft, and had the texture of an overripe pear.

Grimalkin leaped onto the table and sniffed. "Summer-pod," he stated, wrapping his tail around himself. "I did not think they grew in the Winter territories." He turned to me with a serious expression. "Better not eat too many of those," he warned. "They make faery wine out of that. Your human side will not handle it well."

"Oh, let her try one," Puck snorted, rolling his eyes. "She's been in Faery long enough, eating our food. It won't turn her into a rat or anything."

"Where are we going?" Ash questioned, sounding bored with us all. "Did you manage to come up with a plan to find the Iron King, or are we going to paint targets on our backs and wander in circles until he notices?"

I bit into the fruit, and warmth flooded my mouth. I swallowed, and it filled my whole body, driving away the cold.

The quilt was suffocatingly hot; I draped it over one of the chairs and gulped the rest of the fruit in one bite.

"You're awfully eager to help," Puck drawled, leaning back against the table. "And here I was getting ready for a duel first thing in the morning. Why the change of heart, prince?"

The effects of the summerpod were fading; cold prickled my arms, and my cheeks tingled. Ignoring Grimalkin's warning glare, I snatched another fruit and popped it into my mouth like Puck had done. Wonderful, delicious warmth surged into me, and I sighed in pleasure.

Ash's outline blurred at the edges as he faced Puck. "Your princess and I made a bargain," he said. "I agreed to help her find the Iron King, though I won't bore you with the details. While I will uphold my end of the contract, it did not involve you in any way. I only promised to help *her*."

"Which means we're still free to duel each other anytime we want."

"Exactly."

The room swayed slightly. I plunked into a chair and grabbed another summerpod from the bowl, shoving the whole thing in my mouth. Again, I felt that wonderful rush of heat and headiness. Somewhere far away, Puck and Ash were holding a dangerous conversation, but I couldn't bring myself to care. Hooking the edge of the bowl, I pulled the whole thing to me and began popping them like candy.

"Well, why wait?" Puck sounded eager. "We could step outside right now, Your Highness, and get this over with."

Grimalkin sighed loudly, interrupting the conversation. Both faeries turned and glared at him. "This is all quite fascinating," Grimalkin said, his voice slurring in my ears, "but instead of posing and scratching the ground like rutting peacocks, perhaps you should look to the girl."

Both boys glanced at me, and Puck's eyes got huge. "Princess!" he yelped, springing over and tugging the bowl from my grasping fingers. "You're not supposed to... Not all of them.... How many of those did you eat?"

"How very like you, Puck." Ash's voice came from a great distance, and the room started to spin. "Offer them a taste of faery wine, and act surprised when they're consumed by it."

That struck me as hilarious, and I broke into hysterical giggles. And once I began, I couldn't stop. I laughed until I was gasping for breath, tears streaming down my face. My feet itched and my skin crawled. I needed to move, to do something. I tried standing up, wanting to spin and dance, but the room tilted violently and I fell, still shrieking with laughter.

Somebody caught me, scooping me off my feet and into their arms. I smelled frost and winter, and heard an exasperated sigh from somewhere above my head.

"What are you doing, Ash?" I heard someone ask. A familiar voice, though I couldn't think of his name, or why he sounded so suspicious.

"I'm taking her back to her room." The person above me sounded wonderfully calm and deep. I sighed and settled into his arms. "She'll have to sleep off the effects of the fruit. We'll likely be here another day because of your idiocy."

The other voice said something garbled and unintelligible. I was suddenly too sleepy and light-headed to care. Relaxing against the mysterious person's chest, I fell into a heady sleep.

I stood in a dark room, surrounded by machinery. Steel cables as thick as my arm dangled overhead, house-size computers lined the walls, blinking with millions of flashing lights, and thousands of broken televisions, ancient PCs, out-of-date game consoles, and VHS players lay in drifts and heaps throughout the room. Wires covered everything, writhing and slithering along the walls, over the mountains of forgotten technology, dropping in tangled clumps from the ceiling. A loud thrumming filled the area, making the floor vibrate and my teeth buzz.

"Meggie."

The strangled whisper came from behind me. I turned to see a small shape dangling from the wires. They coiled around his arms, chest, and legs, holding him spread-eagled near the ceiling. With horror, I saw some of the wires stabbing *into* him, plugged into his face, neck, and forehead like electrical outlets. He dangled weakly, blue eyes beseeching mine.

"Meggie," Ethan whispered, as something huge and monstrous rose up behind him. "Save me."

I bolted upright, screaming, the image of Ethan dangling from the wires burned into my mind. Grimalkin leaped away with a yowl, sharp claws stabbing into my chest as he fled. I barely felt them. Flinging aside the bedcovers, I raced for the door.

A dark shape rose from a chair against the wall, intercepting me as I tried to bolt through. It caught my upper arms, holding me still as I struggled with it. All I could see was Ethan's face, contorted in agony, dying in front of me.

"Let go!" I screamed, jerking my arm free and trying to claw my opponent's eyes. "Ethan is out there! I have to save him! Let me go!"

"You don't even know where he is." A hand caught my flailing wrist and pinned it to his chest. Silver eyes glared into mine as he shook me, once. "Listen to me! If you go charging out there without a plan, you'll kill us all and your brother will die. Is that what you want?"

I sagged against him. "No," I whispered, all the fight going out of me. Tears welled, and I shook with the effort of holding them back. I couldn't be weak, not anymore. If I was going to have any hope of saving my brother, I couldn't stand in a corner and cry. I had to be strong.

With a shaky breath, I straightened and wiped my eyes. "Sorry," I whispered, embarrassed. "I'm okay now. No more freaking out, I promise."

Ash still held my hand. Gently, I tried pulling back, but he wasn't letting go. I glanced up and found his face inches from mine, his eyes searingly bright in the shadows of the room.

Time froze around us. My heart stumbled a bit, then picked up, louder and faster than before. Ash's expression was blank; nothing showed on his face or in his eyes, but his body had gone very still. I knew I was blushing like a fire engine. His fingers came up and gently brushed a tear from my cheek, sending a tingle through my skin. I shivered, frightened by the pressure mounting between us, needing to break the tension.

I licked my lips and whispered, "Is this where you say you'll kill me?"

One corner of his lip curled. "If you like," he murmured, a flicker of amusement finally crossing his face. "Though it's gotten far too interesting for that."

Footsteps sounded outside in the hall, and Ash moved away, dropping my hand. He crossed his arms and leaned against the wall as Puck entered, Grimalkin loping lazily behind him.

I took a deep, furtive breath and hoped my burning face was lost in the shadows. Puck shot Ash a suspicious glare before looking at me. A sheepish grin crossed his lips.

"Er, how're you feeling, princess?" he asked, lacing both hands behind his head, a sure sign that he was nervous. "Those summerpod fruits pack quite a punch, don't they? Hey, at least it wasn't bristlewort. You would've spent the rest of the evening as a hedgehog."

I sighed, knowing that was as close to an apology as I would get. "I'm fine," I told him, rolling my eyes. "When do we leave?"

Puck blinked, but Ash answered as if nothing had happened. "Tonight," he said, coming away from the wall, stretching like a panther. "We've wasted enough time here. I assume the cait sith knows the way to this oracle?"

Grimalkin yawned, showing off fangs and a bright pink tongue. "Obviously."

"How far is it?" I asked him.

The cat looked from me to Ash and purred knowingly. "The oracle lives in the human world," he said, "in a large city that sits below sea level. Every year, people dress in costume and throw an enormous fiasco. They dance and eat and toss beads at others for removing their clothing."

"New Orleans," I said, frowning. "You're talking about New Orleans." I groaned, thinking about what it would take to get there. New Orleans was the closest city to our tiny little hick town, but it was still a long drive. I knew, because I'd fantasized about driving to the near-mythical city when I finally got my license. "That's hundreds of miles away!" I protested. "I have no car and no money for a plane ticket. How are we going to get there—or were we planning to hitchhike?"

"Human, the Nevernever touches all borders of the human world." Grimalkin shook his head, sounding impatient. "It has no physical boundaries—you could get to Bora Bora from here if you knew the right trod. Stop thinking in human terms. I am sure the prince knows a path to the city."

"Oh, sure he does," Puck broke in. "Or a path right into

the center of the Unseelie Court. Not that I'd mind crashing Mab's party, but I'd like for it to be on my own terms."

"He won't lead us into a trap," I snapped at Puck, who blinked at me. "He promised to help us find the Iron King. He'd be breaking his word if he handed us over to Mab. Right, Ash?"

Ash looked uncomfortable but nodded.

"Right," I repeated, forcing a bravado I didn't feel. I hoped Ash wouldn't betray us, but, as I'd learned, deals with faeries tended to bite you in the ass. I shook off my hesitation and turned to the prince. "So," I demanded, trying to sound confident, "where can we find this trod to New Orleans?"

"The frost giant ruins," Ash replied, looking thoughtful. "Very close to Mab's court." At Puck's glare, he shrugged and offered a tiny, rueful smirk. "She goes to Mardi Gras every year."

I pictured the Queen of the Unseelie Court flashing a couple of drunken partygoers, and giggled uncontrollably. All three shot me a strange look. "Sorry," I gasped, biting my lip. "Still kind of giddy, I guess. Shall we go, then?"

Puck grinned. "Just let me borrow some supplies."

Later, the four of us walked down a narrow, ice-slick trail, the Chillsorrow manor growing smaller and smaller behind us. Sometime during the night, the gnomes had disappeared; the house was empty when we left, as if it had been that way for a hundred years. I wore a long robe of gray fur that tinkled musically when I walked, like tiny wind chimes. Puck had given it to me when we were clear of the manor, under the disapproving glare of Ash, and I didn't dare ask him where he got it. But it kept me perfectly warm and comfortable as we traveled through Mab's cold, frozen domain.

As we walked, I began to realize that the icy landscape of the Unseelie territory was just as beautiful—and dangerous—as Oberon's domain. Icicles dangled from the trees, sparkling like diamonds in the light. Occasionally, a skeleton lay beneath them, spears of ice between its bones. Crystal flowers bloomed along the road, petals as hard and delicate as glass, thorns angling toward me as I approached. Once I thought I saw a white bear watching us from atop a hill, a tiny figure perched on its back, but a tree passed in front of my vision and they were gone.

Ash and Puck didn't say a word to each other as we traveled, which was probably a good thing. The last thing I wanted was another duel to the death. The prince kept a steady, silent march ahead of us, rarely looking back, while Puck entertained me with jokes and useless chatter. I think he was attempting to keep my spirits up, to make me forget about Machina and my brother, and I was grateful for the distraction. Grimalkin vanished periodically, bounding off into the trees, only to reappear minutes or hours later with no explanation of where he'd been.

Later that afternoon, we reached a range of jagged, ice-covered peaks, and the trek turned sharply uphill. The path grew slick and treacherous, and I had to watch where I put my feet. Puck had fallen back on the trail; he kept casting suspicious looks over his shoulder, as if he feared an ambush from behind. I glanced back at him again, and in that moment, my feet hit a patch of ice and slid out from under me. I flailed, losing my balance on the narrow trail, trying desperately to stay upright and not go tumbling back down the mountain.

Something grabbed my wrist, pulling me forward. I collapsed against a solid chest, my fingers digging into the fabric to keep myself upright. As the adrenaline surge faded and my heartbeat returned to normal, I glanced up and found Ash's face inches from mine, so close I could see my reflection in his silvery eyes.

His nearness made my senses spin, and I couldn't look away. This close, his face was carefully guarded, but I felt the rapid thud of his heart beneath my palm. My own heartbeat picked up in response. He held me a moment longer, just long enough to make my stomach lurch wildly, then stepped away, leaving me breathless in the middle of the trail.

I looked back and found Puck glaring at me. Embarrassed and feeling strangely guilty, I dusted off my clothes and straightened my hair with an indignant huff before following Ash up the mountain.

Puck didn't speak to me after that.

By late evening, it had begun to snow, big, soft flakes drifting lazily from the sky. They literally sang as they fell past my ears, tiny voices dancing on the wind.

Ash stopped in the middle of the path, looking back at us. Flakes dusted his hair and clothes, swirling around him as if alive. "The Unseelie Court isn't far ahead," he said, ignoring the eddies that spun around him. "We should break from the road. Mab has others besides me looking for you, as well."

As he finished, the snow whirled madly around us, shrieking and tearing at our clothes. My fur coat clanged as the blizzard pelted me with snow, burning my cheeks and blinding me. I couldn't breathe; my limbs were frozen stiff to my sides. As the whirlwind calmed, I found myself encased in ice from the neck down, unable to move. Puck was similarly frozen, except his whole head was covered in crystal glass, his features frozen in shock.

Ash was unharmed, staring at us blankly.

"Dammit, Ash!" I yelled, struggling to free myself. I couldn't even wiggle a finger. "I thought we had a deal."

"A deal?" whispered another voice. The whirlwind of snow solidified, merging into a tall woman with long white hair and blue-tinged skin. A white gown draped her elegant body, and her black lips curled into a smile.

"A deal?" she repeated, turning to Ash with a mock horrified look. "Do tell. Ash, darling, I believe you've been hiding things from us."

CHAPTER EIGHTEEN

The Voodoo Museum

"Narissa," Ash murmured. He sounded disinterested, bored even, though I saw his fingers twitch toward his sword. "To what do I owe the pleasure of this visit?"

The snow faery regarded me like a spider watching an insect in its web, before turning pupil-less black eyes on Ash. "Did I hear her right, darling?" she purred, drifting over the ground toward the prince. "Did you actually make a bargain with the half-breed? As I recall, our queen ordered us to bring the daughter of Oberon to her. Are you fraternizing with the enemy now?"

"Don't be ridiculous." Ash's voice was flat as he leveled a sneer in my direction. "I would never betray my queen. She wants Oberon's daughter, I will bring her Oberon's daughter. And I was in the middle of doing so, until you showed up and interrupted my progress."

Narissa looked unconvinced. "A pretty speech," she crooned, running a finger down Ash's cheek, leaving a trail of frost. "But what of the girl's companion? I believe you swore to kill Robin Goodfellow, Ash darling, and yet you bring him into the heart of our territory. If the queen knew he was here—"

"She would allow me to deal with him on my terms," Ash interrupted, narrowing his eyes. The anger on his face was real now. "I've brought Puck along because I want to kill him slowly, take my time with him. After I've delivered the half-breed, I'll have centuries to exact my vengeance on Robin Goodfellow. And *no one* will deny me that pleasure when it comes."

Narissa floated back. "Of course not, darling," she placated. "But perhaps I should take the half-breed on to court from here. You know how impatient the queen can be, and it really isn't fitting for the prince to be the escort." She smiled and drifted toward me. "I'll just take this burden off your hands."

Ash's sword rasped free, stopping the faery in her tracks. "Take another step and it will be your last."

"How dare you threaten me!" Narissa whirled back, snow flurrying around her. "I offer to help, and this is my reward! Your brother will hear of this."

"I'm sure he will." Ash smiled coldly and didn't lower his sword. "And you can tell Rowan that if he wants to gain Mab's favor, he should capture the half-breed himself, not send you to steal her from me. While you're at it, you can inform Queen Mab that I *will* deliver Oberon's daughter to her, I give my word on that.

"Now," he continued, making a shooing motion with his blade, "it's time for you to leave."

Narissa glared at him a moment longer, her hair billowing around her face. Then she smiled. "Very well, darling. I shall enjoy watching Rowan tear you limb from limb. Until we meet again." She twirled in place, her body dissipating into snow and wind, and blew away into the trees.

Ash sighed, shaking his head. "We need to move fast," he muttered, striding over to me. "Narissa will tell Rowan where we are, and he'll come speeding over to claim you for himself. Hold still."

He raised his sword hilt and brought it smashing down on the ice. The frozen shell cracked and began to chip in places. He sliced down again, and the cracks widened.

"D-don't worry about m-me," I said through chattering teeth. "Help P-Puck. He'll suffocate in th-there!"

"My bargain isn't with Goodfellow," Ash muttered, not looking up from his task. "I don't make a habit of aiding mortal enemies. Besides, he'll be fine. He's survived far worse than being frozen solid. Unfortunately."

I glared at him. "Are you really h-helping us?" I demanded as more bits of the ice shell began to crack. "What you said to Narissa—"

"I told her nothing that wasn't true," Ash interrupted, staring back at me. "I will not betray my queen. When this is over, I will deliver Oberon's half-blood daughter to her, as I promised." He broke eye contact and placed his hand over the ice, where the cracking was the greatest. "I'll just do it a little later than she expects. Close your eyes."

I did, and felt the ice column vibrate. The thrumming grew louder and stronger until, with the sound of breaking glass, the ice shattered into a million pieces and I was free.

I sagged to the ground, shaking uncontrollably. My robe was coated in ice, the chiming fur silenced. Ash knelt down to help me up, but I slapped his hand away.

"I'm not going anywhere," I growled, "until you get Puck out."

He sighed irritably but rose and walked over to the second frozen mound, putting his hand on it. This time, the ice shattered violently, flying in all directions like crystal shrapnel. Several pieces lodged in a nearby tree trunk, glittering ice daggers sunk deep into the bark. I cringed at the vicious explosion. If he had done that to me, I would've been shredded.

Puck staggered forward, his face bloody, his clothing in tatters. He swayed on his feet, eyes glazed over, and started to fall. I shrieked his name and raced over as he collapsed into my arms.

And disappeared. His body vanished the moment I caught him, and I was left staring at a frayed leaf, spiraling to the ground. Beside me, Ash snorted and shook his head.

"Did you hear everything you wanted, Goodfellow?" he called to the empty air.

"I did," came Puck's disembodied voice, floating out of the trees, "but I'm not sure I believe my ears."

He dropped from the branches of a pine, landing with a thump in the snow. When he straightened, his green eyes blazed with anger. Not directed at Ash, but at me.

"*That's* what you promised him, princess?" he shouted, throwing up his hands. "That was your bargain? You would offer yourself to the Unseelie Court?" He turned and punched a tree, sending twigs and icicles to the ground. "Of all the *stupid* ideas! What is wrong with you?"

I shrank back. This was the first time I'd seen him angry. Not just Puck, but Robbie, too. He never got mad, viewing everything as a colossal joke. Now he looked ready to tear my head off.

"We needed help," I said, watching in horror as his eyes glowed and his hair writhed like flames atop his head. "We have to get out of Unseelie territory and into Machina's realm."

"*I* would have gotten you there!" Puck roared. "Me! You don't need his help! Don't you trust me to keep you safe? I would've given everything for you. Why didn't you think I'd be enough?"

I was struck speechless. Puck sounded *hurt,* glaring at me like I'd just stabbed him in the back. I didn't know what to say. I didn't dare look at Ash, but I sensed he was vastly amused by this whole display.

As we stared at each other, Grimalkin slid out of the brush, a patch of smoke gliding over the snow. His eyes bore that half-lidded, amused look as he glanced at the fuming Puck, then back to me. "It gets more entertaining every day," he purred with his feline grin.

I wasn't in the mood for his sarcasm. "Do you have anything helpful to say, Grim?" I snapped, watching his eyes slit even more.

The cat yawned and sat down to lick himself. "Actually, yes," he murmured, bending to his flanks. "I do have something you might be interested in." He continued washing his tail for several heartbeats, while I fought the urge to grab that tail and swing him around my head like a bolo. Finally, he stretched and looked up, blinking lazily.

"I believe," he purred, stretching it out, "I have found the trod you are looking for."

We followed Grimalkin to the base of an ancient ruined castle, where shattered pillars and broken gargoyles lay scattered about the courtyard. Bones littered the area as well, poking up through the snow, making me nervous. Puck trailed behind, not speaking to any of us, wrapped in angry silence. I made a promise to talk to him later when he'd cooled down, but for now, I was anxious to get out of Unseelie territory.

"There," Grimalkin said, nodding to a large stone pillar broken in two. One half rested on the other, forming an arch between them.

There was also a body lying in front of it. A body that was at least twelve feet tall, covered in hides and furs, with blue-white skin and a tangled white beard. It lay sprawled on its back with its face turned away, one meaty hand clutching a stone club.

Ash grimaced. "That's right," he muttered as we ducked behind a low stone wall. "Mab leaves her pet giant here to guard the place. Cold Tom doesn't listen to anyone but the queen."

I glared at the cat, who looked unconcerned. "You could have mentioned something, Grim. Did you forget that small but ever-so-important detail? Or did you just not see the twelve-foot giant in the middle of the floor?"

Puck, his animosity forgotten, or suppressed, peeked out from behind a boulder. "Looks like its Tom's nappy time," he said. "Maybe we can sneak around him."

Grimalkin regarded each of us in turn and blinked slowly. "In times like these, I am even more grateful that I am a cat." He sighed, and trotted toward the huge body.

"Grim! Stop!" I hissed after him. "What are you doing?"

The cat ignored me. My heart caught in my throat as he sauntered up to the giant, looking like a fuzzy mouse compared to Tom's bulk. Gazing up at the body, he twitched his tail, crouched, and leaped onto the giant's chest.

I stopped breathing, but the giant didn't move. Perhaps Grimalkin was too light for him to even notice. The cat turned and sat down, curling his tail around his feet and watching us bemusedly.

"Dead," he called to us. "Quite dead, in fact. You can stop cringing in abject terror if you like. I swear, how you survive with noses like that, I will never know. I could smell his stink a mile away."

"He's dead?" Ash immediately walked forward, brow furrowing. "Strange. Cold Tom was one of the strongest in his clan. How did he die?"

Grimalkin yawned. "Perhaps he ate something that disagreed with him."

I edged forward cautiously. Maybe I'd watched too many horror flicks, but I almost expected the "dead" giant to open his eyes and take a swing at us. "What does it matter?" I called to Ash, still keeping a careful eye on the body. "If it's dead, then we can get out of here without having to fight the thing."

"You know nothing," Ash replied. His gaze swept over the corpse, eyes narrowed. "This giant was strong, one of the strongest. Something killed him, within our territory. I want to know what could've taken Cold Tom down like this."

I was close to the giant's head now, close enough to see the blank, bulging eyes, the gray tongue lolling partway out of his mouth. Blue veins stood out around his eye sockets and in his neck. Whatever killed him, it wasn't quick.

Then a metal spider crawled out of his mouth.

I screamed and leaped back. Puck and Ash rushed to my side as the huge arachnid skittered away, over Tom's face and up a wall. Ash drew his sword, but Puck gave a shout and hurled a rock at it. The stone hit the spider dead on; with a flash of sparks the bug plummeted to the ground, landing with a metallic clink on the flagstones.

We approached cautiously, Ash with his sword drawn, Puck with a good-size rock. But the insect thing lay broken and motionless on the ground, almost smashed in two. Up close, it looked less spidery and more like those face-hugger things from *Aliens,* except it was made of metal. Gingerly, I picked it up by its whiplike tail.

"What *is* that?" Ash muttered. For once, the unflappable fey sounded almost...terrified. "Another of Machina's iron fey?"

Something clicked in my head. "It's a bug," I whispered. The boys gave me puzzled frowns, and I plunged on. "Iron-

horse, gremlins, bugs—it's starting to make sense to me now."
I whirled on Puck, who blinked and stepped back. "Puck,
didn't you tell me once that the fey were born from the dreams
of mortals?"

"Yeah?" Puck said, not getting it.

"Well, what if these things—" I jiggled the metal insect
"—are born from different dreams? Dreams of technology, and
progress? Dreams of science? What if the pursuit of ideas that
once seemed impossible—flight, steam engines, the World-
wide Web—gave birth to a whole different species of faery?
Mankind has made huge leaps in technology over the past
hundred years. And with each success, we've kept reaching—
dreaming—for more. These iron fey could be the result."

Puck blanched, and Ash looked incredibly disturbed. "If
that's true," he murmured, his gray eyes darkening like thun-
derclouds, "then all fey could be in danger. Not just the Seelie
and Unseelie Courts. The Nevernever itself would be affected,
the entire fey world."

Puck nodded, looking more serious than I'd ever seen.
"This is a war," he said, locking gazes with Ash. "If the Iron
King is killing the guardians of the trods, he must be plan-
ning to invade. We have to find Machina and destroy him.
Perhaps he's the heart of these iron fey. If we kill him, his fol-
lowers could scatter."

"I agree." Ash sheathed his sword, giving the bug a revolted
look. "We will bring Meghan to the Iron Court and rescue
her brother by killing the ruler of the iron fey."

"Bravo," said Grimalkin, peering down from Cold Tom's
chest. "The Winter prince and Oberon's jester agreeing on
something. The world must be ending."

We all glared at him. The cat sneezed a laugh and hopped

down from the body, gazing up at the bug in my hand. He wrinkled his nose.

"Interesting," he mused. "That thing stinks of iron and steel, and yet it does not burn you. I suppose being half-human has perks, after all."

"What do you mean?" I asked.

"Mmm. Toss it to Ash, would you?"

"No!" Ash stepped back, his hand going to his sword. Grimalkin smiled.

"You see? Even the mighty Winter prince cannot stand the touch of iron. You, on the other hand, can handle it with no ill effects. Now do you see why the courts are scrambling to find you? Think of what Mab could do if she had you under her control."

I dropped the bug with a shudder. "Is that why Mab wants me?" I asked Ash, who still stood a few feet away. "As a weapon?"

"Ridiculous, isn't it?" Grimalkin purred. "She cannot even use glamour. She would be a horrible assassin."

"I don't know why Mab wants you," Ash said slowly, meeting my eyes. "I don't question the orders of my queen. I only obey."

"It doesn't matter now," Puck broke in, stabbing a glare at the Winter prince. "First, we have to find Machina and take him out. Then we'll decide matters from there." His voice hinted that the matters he spoke of would be decided with a fight.

Ash looked like he wanted to say something else, but he nodded. Grimalkin yawned noisily and trotted toward the gate.

"Human, do not leave the bug here when we leave," he called without looking back. "It might corrupt the land around it. You can dump it in your world and it will not make any difference."

Tail waving, he trotted beneath the pillar and disappeared. Pinching the bug between thumb and forefinger, I stuffed it into my backpack. With Ash and Puck flanking me like wary guard dogs, I stepped under the pillars and everything went white.

As the brightness faded, I gazed around, first in confusion, then in horror. I stood in the middle of an open mouth, with blunt teeth lining either side and a red tongue below my feet. I squawked in terror and leaped out, tripping over the bottom lip and sprawling flat on my stomach.

Twisting around, I saw Ash and Puck step through the gaping maw of a cartoonish blue whale. Sitting atop the whale statue, smiling and pointing off into the distance, was Pinocchio, his wooden features frozen in plaster and fiberglass.

"'Scuse me, lady!" A little girl in pink overalls stepped over me to rush into the whale's mouth, followed by her two friends. Ash and Puck stepped aside, and the kids paid them no attention as they screamed and cavorted inside the whale's jaws.

"Interesting place," Puck mused as he pulled me to my feet. I didn't answer, too busy gaping at our surroundings. It seemed we had stepped into the middle of a fantasyland. A giant pink shoe sat a few yards away, and a bright blue castle lay beyond, with kids swarming over both of them. Between park benches and shady trees, a pirate ship hosted a mob of miniature swashbucklers, and a magnificent green dragon reared on its hind legs, breathing plastic fire. The flame shooting from its mouth was an actual slide. I watched a small boy clamber up the steps of the dragon's back and zip down the slide, hollering with delight, and smiled sadly.

Ethan would love this place, I thought, watching the boy dart off toward a pumpkin coach. *Maybe, when this is all over, I'll bring him here.*

"Let us go," Grimalkin said, leaping onto a giant pink mushroom. The cat's tail bristled, and his eyes darted about. "The oracle is not far, but we should hurry."

"Why so nervous, Grim?" Puck drawled, gazing around the park. "I think we should stay for a bit, soak up the atmosphere." He grinned and waved at a small girl peeking at him from behind a cottage, and she ducked out of sight.

"Too many kids here," Grimalkin said, glancing nervously over his shoulder. "Too much imagination. They can see us, you know. As we really are. And unlike the hob over there, I do not relish the attention."

I followed his gaze and saw a short faery playing on the shoe with several children. He had curly brown hair, a battered trench coat, and furry ears poking from the sides of his head. He laughed and chased the kids around him, and the parents sitting on the benches didn't seem to notice.

A boy of about three saw us and approached, his eyes on Grimalkin. "Kitty, kitty," he crooned, holding out both hands. Grimalkin flattened his ears and hissed, baring his teeth, and the boy recoiled. "Beat it, kid," he spat, and the boy burst into tears, running toward a couple on a bench. They frowned at their son's wailing about a mean kitty, and glanced up at us.

"Right, time to go," Puck said, striding away. We followed, with Grimalkin taking the lead. We left Storyland, as it was called on a sign by the exit, through a gate guarded by Humpty Dumpty and Little Bo Peep, and walked through a park filled with truly giant oak trees draped in moss and vines. I caught faces peering at us from the trunks, women with beady black eyes. Puck blew kisses at a few of them, and

Ash bowed his head respectfully as we passed. Even Grimalkin nodded to the faces in the trees, making me wonder why
they were so important.

After nearly an hour of walking, we reached the city streets.

I paused and gazed around, wishing we had more time to
explore. I'd always wanted to go to New Orleans, particularly during Mardi Gras, though I knew Mom would never
permit it. Even now, New Orleans pulsed with life and activ-
ity. Rustic shops and buildings lined the street, many stacked
two or three stories atop one another, with railings and ve-
randas overlooking the sidewalk. Strains of jazz music drifted
into the street, and the spicy smell of Cajun food made my
stomach growl.

"Gawk later." Grimalkin poked me in the shin with a claw.
"We are not here to sightsee. We have to get to the French
Quarter. One of you, find us some transportation."

"Where exactly are we going?" Ash questioned as Puck
flagged down a carriage pulled by a sleepy-looking red mule.
The mule snorted and pinned his ears as we piled inside, but
the driver smiled and nodded. Grimalkin leaped onto the
front seat.

"The Historic Voodoo Museum," he told the driver, who
didn't look at all fazed by a talking cat. "And step on it."

Voodoo Museum? I wasn't sure what to expect when the
carriage pulled up to a shabby-looking building in the French
Quarter. A pair of simple black doors stood beneath the overhang, and a humble wooden sign proclaimed it the New Orleans Historic Voodoo Museum. Dusk had fallen, and the sign
in the grimy window read Closed. Grimalkin nodded to Puck,
who muttered a few words under his breath and tapped on
the door. It opened with a soft creak, and we stepped inside.

The inside was musty and warm. I tripped over a bump in the carpet and stumbled into Ash, who steadied me with a sigh. Puck closed the door behind us, plunging the room into blackness. I groped for the wall, but Ash spoke a quick word, and a globe of blue fire appeared over his head, illuminating the darkness.

The pale light washed over a grisly collection of horror. A skeleton in a top hat stood along the far wall beside a mannequin with an alligator head. Skulls of humans and animals decorated the room, along with grinning masks and numerous wooden dolls. Glass cases bore jars of snakes and frogs floating in amber liquid, teeth, pestles, drums, turtle shells, and other oddities.

"This way," came Grimalkin's voice, unnaturally loud in the looming silence. We trailed him down a dark hall, where portraits of men and women stared at us from the walls. I felt eyes following me as I ducked into a room cluttered with more grisly paraphernalia and a round table in the center covered with a black tablecloth. Four chairs stood around it, as if someone were expecting us.

As we approached the table, one of the desiccated faces in the corner stirred and floated away from the wall. I screamed and leaped behind Puck as a skeletal woman with tangled white hair shambled toward us, her eyes hollow pits in a withered face.

"Hello, children," the hag whispered, her voice like sand hissing through a pipe. "Come to visit old Anna, have you? Puck is here, and Grimalkin, as well. What a pleasure." She gestured to the table, and the nails on her knobby hands glinted like steel. "Please, have a seat."

We sat down around the table as the hag came to stand before us. She smelled of dust and decay, of old newspapers that

had been left in the attic for years. She smiled at me, revealing yellow, needlelike teeth.

"I smell need," she rasped, sinking into a chair. "Need, and
desire. You, child." She crooked a finger at me. "You have
come seeking knowledge. You search for something that must
be found, yes?"

"Yes," I whispered.

The hag nodded her withered head. "Ask, then, child of
two worlds. But remember…" She fixed me with a hollow
glare. "All knowledge must be paid for. I will give you the
answers you seek, but I desire something in return. Will you
accept the price?"

Defeat crushed me. More faery bargains. More prices to
pay. I was so much in debt already, I would never see the end
of it. "I don't have much left to give," I told her. She laughed,
a sibilant hissing sound.

"There is always something, dear child. So far, only your
freedom has been claimed by another." She sniffed, as a dog
might when catching a scent. "You still have your youth, your
talents, your voice. Your future child. All these are of interest to me."

"You're not getting my future child," I said automatically.

"Really?" The oracle tapped her fingers together. "You
will not give it up, even though it will bring you nothing
but grief?"

"Enough." Ash's strong voice broke through the darkness.
"We're not here to debate the what-ifs of the future. Name
your price, oracle, and let the girl decide if she wants to pay it."

The oracle sniffed and settled back. "A memory," she stated.

"A what?"

"A memory," the hag said again. "One that you recall with

great affection. The happiest memory of your childhood. I've precious few of my own, you see."

"Really?" I asked. "That's it? You just want one of my memories, and we have a deal?"

"Meghan—" Puck broke in "—don't take this so lightly. Your memories are a part of you. Losing one of your memories is like losing a piece of your soul."

That sounded a bit more ominous. *Still,* I thought, *one memory is a lot easier to pay than my voice, or my firstborn child. And it's not like I'll miss it, especially if I can't remember.* I thought about the happiest moments in my life: birthday parties, my first bike, Beau as a puppy. None of them seemed important enough to keep. "All right," I told the oracle, and took a seat across from her. "You're on. You get one memory of mine, one, and then you tell me what I want to know. Deal?"

The hag bared her teeth in a smile. "Yessssssss."

She rose up over the table, framing my face with both her claws. I shivered and closed my eyes as her nails gently scratched my cheeks.

"This might feel a bit…unpleasant," the oracle hissed, and I gasped as she sank her claws into my mind, ripping it open like a paper sack. I felt her shuffling through my head, sorting through memories like photographs, examining them before tossing them aside. Discarded images fluttered around me: memories, emotions, and old wounds rose up again, fresh and painful. I wanted to pull back, to make it stop, but I couldn't move. Finally, the oracle paused, reaching toward a bright spot of happiness, and in horror I saw what she was going for.

No! I wanted to scream. *No, not that one! Leave it alone, please!*

"Yesssssss," the oracle hissed, sinking her claws into the memory. "I will take this one. Now it is mine."

There was a ripping sensation, and a bolt of pain through my head. I stiffened, my jaw locking around a shriek, and slumped in my chair, feeling like my head had been split open.

I sat up, wincing at the throbbing in my skull. The oracle watched me over the tablecloth, a pleased smile on her face. Puck was murmuring something that I couldn't make out, and Ash regarded me with a look of pity. I felt tired, drained, and empty for some reason, like there was a gaping hole deep inside me.

Hesitantly, I probed my memories, wondering which one the oracle took. After a moment, I realized how absurd that was.

"It is done," the oracle murmured. She lay her hands, palms up, on the table between us. "And now I will uphold my end of the bargain. Place your hands in mine, child, and ask."

Swallowing my revulsion, I put my palms gently over hers, shivering as those long nails curled around my fingers. The hag closed her pitted eyes. "Three questions," she rasped, her voice seeming to come from a great distance away. "That is the standard bargain. Three questions will I answer, and I am done. Choose wisely."

I took a deep breath, glanced at Puck and Ash, and whispered: "Where can I find my brother?"

Silence for a moment. The hag's eyes opened, and I jumped. They were no longer hollow, but burned with flame, as black and depthless as the void. Her mouth opened, stretching impossibly wide, as she breathed:

Within the iron mountain
a stolen child waits.
A king no longer on his throne
shall guide you past the gates.

"Oh, fabulous," Puck muttered, sitting back in his chair and rolling his eyes. "I love riddles. And they rhyme so nicely. Ask her where we can find the Iron King."

I nodded. "Where is Machina, the Iron King?"

The oracle sighed, voices erupting from her throat to whisper:

In Blight's heart
a tower sings
upon whose thrones
sit Iron Kings.

"Blight." Puck nodded, arching his eyebrows. "And singing towers. Well, this gets better and better. I'm sure glad we decided to come here. Prince, can you think of anything you want to ask our most obliging oracle?"

Ash, deep in thought with his chin in his hands, raised his head. His eyes narrowed. "Ask her how we can kill him," he demanded.

I squirmed, uncomfortable with the thought of having to kill. I only wanted to rescue Ethan. I didn't know how this turned into a holy war. "Ash—"

"Just do it."

I swallowed and turned back to the oracle. "How do we kill the Iron King?" I whispered reluctantly. The oracle's mouth opened.

The King of Iron cannot be slain
by mortal man or fey.
Seek out the Keepers of the trees.
Their hearts will show the way.

No sooner were the last words out of her mouth than the oracle collapsed on the table. For a moment she lay there, a desiccated old woman, and then she just…disintegrated. Dust flew everywhere, stinging my eyes and throat. I turned away, coughing and hacking, and when I could breathe again, the oracle was gone. Only a few floating dust motes showed she had been there at all.

"I believe," Grimalkin said, peering over the table rim, "that our audience is over."

"So where to now?" I asked as we left the Voodoo Museum, stepping into the dimly lit streets of the French Quarter. "The oracle didn't give us much to go on."

"On the contrary," Grimalkin said, looking back at me, "she gave us a great deal. One, we know your brother is with Machina. That was a given, but confirmation is always beneficial. Two, we know Machina is supposedly invincible, and his lair is in the middle of a blighted land. And, most important, three, we know there is someone who knows how to kill him."

"Yeah, but who?" I rubbed a hand over my eyes. I was so tired—tired of searching, tired of running in circles with no answers to anything. I wanted it all to end.

"Really, human, were you not listening?" Grimalkin sighed, exasperated again, but I didn't care. "It was not even much of a riddle, really. What about you two?" he asked, looking to the boys. "Did our mighty protectors glean any bits of knowledge, or was I the only one paying attention?"

Ash didn't reply, too busy staring down the street, eyes narrowed. Puck shrugged. "Seek out the Keepers of the trees," he muttered. "That's easy enough. I assume we should go back to the park."

"Very good, Goodfellow."

"I try."

"I'm so lost," I groaned, sitting down on the curb. "Why are we going back to the park? We just came from there. There are other trees in New Orleans."

"Because, princess—"

"Explain later." Ash appeared beside me. His voice was low and harsh. "We need to go. Now."

"Why?" I asked, just as the streetlamps—and every artificial light on the block—sputtered and went out.

Faery lights glowed overhead as both Ash and Puck called them into existence. Footsteps echoed in the shadows, getting closer, coming from all directions. Grimalkin muttered something and disappeared. Puck and Ash stepped back to flank me, their eyes scanning the darkness.

Beyond the ring of light, dark shapes shuffled toward us. As they came into the light, the faery fire washed over the faces of humans—normal men and women—their features blank as they lurched forward. Most of them carried weapons: iron pipes and metal baseball bats and knives. Every zombie movie I'd ever seen sprang to mind, and I pressed close to Ash, feeling the muscles coil under his skin.

"Humans," Ash muttered, his hand dropping to his sword. "What are they doing? They shouldn't be able to see us."

A dark chuckle rose from the ranks shambling toward us, and the mob abruptly stopped. They moved aside as a woman floated between them, hands on her slender hips. She wore a business suit of poison green, three-inch heels, and green lipstick that glowed with radioactive brightness. Her hair appeared to be made of wires, thin network cables of various color: greens, blacks, and reds.

"Here you are at last." Her voice buzzed, like millions of bees given speech. "I'm shocked that Ironhorse had such a problem with you, but then again, he's so *old*. Past his usefulness, I'd say. You will not have such an easy time with me."

"Who are you?" growled Ash. Puck moved beside him, and together they formed a living shield in front of me. The lady giggled, like a mosquito humming in your ear, and held out a green-nailed hand.

"I am Virus, second of King Machina's lieutenants." She blew me a kiss that made my skin crawl. "Pleased to meet you, Meghan Chase."

"What have you done to these people?" I demanded.

"Oh, don't worry about them." Virus twirled in place, smiling. "They've just caught a little bug. These little bugs, to be exact." She held up her hand, and a tiny insect swarm flew out of her sleeve to hover over her palm, like sparkling silver dust. "Cute little things, aren't they? Quite harmless, but they allow me to get inside a brain and rewrite its programming. Allow me to demonstrate." She gestured to the nearest human, and the man dropped to all fours and started to bark. Virus tittered, clapping her hands. "See? Now he thinks he's a dog."

"Brilliant," Puck said. "Can you make him crow like a rooster, too?"

Ash and I glared at him. He blinked. "What?"

I started, a memory dropping into place, and spun back on Virus. "You...you're the one who set the chimera loose on Elysium!"

"Why, yes, that was my work." Virus looked pleased, though her face fell a moment later. "Although, as an experiment, it didn't quite work out as I'd hoped. The normal fey don't react well to my bugs. That whole aversion-to-iron thing, you know. It drove the stupid beast mad, and probably would have killed it, if it hadn't been sliced to pieces. Mortals, though!" She pirouetted in the air, flinging out her arms, as if to embrace the crowd. "They make wonderful drones. So devoted to their computers and technology, they were slaves to it long before I came along."

"Let them go," I told her.

Virus regarded me with glittering green eyes. "I don't think so, dearie." She snapped her fingers, and the mob shambled forward again, arms reaching. "Bring me the girl," she ordered as the circle tightened around us. "Kill the rest."

Ash drew his sword.

"No!" I cried, grabbing his arm. "Don't hurt them. They're just ordinary humans. They don't know what they're doing."

Ash shot me a wild glare over his shoulder. "Then what do you want me to do?"

"I suggest we run," Puck offered, taking something from his pocket. He tossed it at the crowd, and it exploded into a log, pinning two startled zombie men to the ground, creating a hole in the ring surrounding us.

"Let's go!" Puck yelled, and we didn't need encouraging. We leaped over the thrashing bodies, dodging the pipes they swung at us, and tore down the street.

CHAPTER NINETEEN

The Dryad of City Park

Pounding footsteps told us we were being followed. A twirling pipe flew over my shoulder, smashing the window of a shop. I yelped and almost fell, but Ash grabbed my hand and hauled me upright.

"This is ridiculous," I heard him growl, pulling me along. "Running from a mob, a human mob. I could take them out with one sweep of my hand."

"Perhaps you didn't see the copious amounts of iron they're carrying," Puck said, wincing as a knife hurled past him, skidding into the street. "Of course, if you want to make a suicide stand, I certainly won't stop you. Though, I'd be disappointed you wouldn't be there for our last duel."

"Scared, Goodfellow?"

"In your dreams, princeling."

I couldn't believe they were bantering while we were running for our lives. I wanted to tell them to knock it off, when a pipe hurled through the air, striking Puck in the shoulder. He gasped and staggered, barely catching himself in time, and I cried out in fear.

Buzzing laughter echoed behind us. I turned my head to see Virus floating above the crowd, her bugs swirling around her like a diamond blizzard. "You can run, little faery boys, but you can't hide," she called. "There are humans everywhere, and all can be my puppets. If you stop now and hand over the girl, I'll even let you choose how you want to die."

Ash snarled. Pushing me on, he spun and hurled a spray of ice shards at the woman overhead. She gasped, and a zombie leaped into the air to block the attack, the shards tearing through his chest. He collapsed, twitching, and Virus hissed like a furious wasp.

"Oh, nice going, prince," Puck called as the zombies lurched forward with angry cries. "Way to piss her off."

"You killed him!" I stared at Ash, horrified. "You just killed a person, and it wasn't even his fault!"

"There are casualties in every war," Ash replied coldly, pulling me around a corner. "He would have killed us if he could. One less soldier to worry about."

"This isn't a war!" I screamed at him. "And it's different when the humans don't even know what's happening. They're only after us because some crazy faery is screwing with their heads!"

"Either way, we'd still be dead."

"No more killing," I snarled, wishing we could stop so I could look at him straight. "Do you hear me, Ash? Find another way to stop them. You don't have to kill."

He glared at me out of the corner of his eye, then sighed with irritation. "As you wish, princess. Though you might regret it before the night is out."

We burst into a brightly lit square with a marble fountain in the center. People wandered down the sidewalks, and I relaxed a bit. Surely, Virus wouldn't attack us here, in front of all these eyewitnesses. Faeries could blend in or go invisible, but humans, especially mobs of humans, had no such power.

Ash slowed, catching my hand and drawing me beside him. "Walk," he murmured, tugging my arm to slow me down. "Don't run, it'll attract their attention."

The crowd chasing us broke apart at the edge of the street, wandering around as if they had always meant to do so. My heart pounded, but I forced myself to walk, holding on to Ash's hand as if we were out for a stroll.

Virus floated into the square, her bugs swarming out in all directions, and my nervousness increased. I spotted a policeman leaning beside his squad car and broke away from Ash, sprinting up to him.

Virus's laughter cut through the night. "I see you," she called, just as I reached the officer.

"Excuse me, sir!" I gasped as the policeman turned to me. "Could you help me? There's a gang chasing—"

I stumbled back in horror. The officer regarded me blankly, his jaw hanging slack, his eyes empty of reason. He lunged and grabbed my arm, and I yelped, kicking him in the shin. It didn't faze him, and he grabbed my other wrist.

The pedestrians in the square lurched toward us with renewed vigor. I snarled a curse and lashed out at the policeman, driving my knee into his groin. He winced and struck me across the face, making my head spin. The mob closed in, clawing at my hair and clothes.

And Ash was there, smashing his hilt into the policeman's jaw, knocking him back. Puck grabbed me and leaped over the police car, dragging me over the hood. We broke free of the mob and ran, Virus's laughter following us into the street.

"There!" Grimalkin appeared beside us, his tail fluffed out and his eyes wild. "Dead ahead! A carriage. Use it, quickly."

I looked across the street and saw an unattended horse and open-top buggy, waiting on the curb to pick up passengers.

It wasn't a getaway car, but it was better than nothing. We crossed the street and ran toward the carriage.

A gunshot rang out behind us.

Puck jerked weirdly and fell, collapsing to the pavement with a howl of agony. I screamed, and Ash immediately hauled him upright, forcing him to move. They staggered across the street, Ash dragging Puck with him, as another shot shattered the night. The horse whinnied and half reared at the noise, rolling its eyes. I grabbed its bridle before the beast fled in terror. Behind me, walking toward us with that zombielike shuffle, I saw the police officer, one arm extended, pointing his revolver at us.

Ash shouldered Puck into the carriage and jumped into the driver's seat, Grimalkin bounding up beside him. I scrambled inside and crouched beside Puck, sprawled on the floor of the carriage, gasping. Horrified, I watched dark blood blossom around his ribs, seeping over the floorboards.

"Hold on!" Ash yelled, and brought the reins down on the horse's flanks with a loud "Hiya!" The horse leaped forward with a squeal. We galloped through a red light, barely dodging a honking taxi. Cars blared, people shouted and cursed, and the sounds of pursuit faded behind us.

"Ash!" I cried a few minutes later. "Puck's not moving!"

Preoccupied with driving the carriage, Ash barely looked back, but Grimalkin leaped to the floor and trotted up to the body. Puck's face was the color of eggshells, his skin cool and clammy. I'd tried to stanch the bleeding using a sleeve of his hoodie, but there was so much blood. My best friend was dying, and I couldn't do anything to help.

"He needs a doctor," I called up to Ash. "We need to find a hospital—"

"No," Grimalkin interrupted. "Think, human! No faery

would survive a hospital. With all those sharp metal instruments, he would be dead before the night was out."

"Then what can we do?" I cried, on the verge of hysteria.

Grimalkin jumped up beside Ash again. "The park," he said calmly. "We take him to the park. The dryads should be able to help him."

"*Should?* What if they can't?"

"Then, human, I would start praying for a miracle."

Ash didn't stop at the edge of the park, but instead drove the carriage over the curb and into the grass beneath the trees. Worried for Puck, I didn't notice we'd stopped until the prince knelt beside me, swung Puck onto a shoulder, and dropped down. Numbly, I followed.

We'd stopped under the boughs of two enormous oaks, their gnarled branches completely shutting out the night sky. Ash carried Puck beneath the twisted giants and eased him down to the grass.

And we waited.

Two figures stepped out of the tree trunks, materializing into view. They were both slender women, with moss-green hair and skin like polished mahogany. Beetle-black eyes peered out as the dryads stepped forward, the smell of fresh earth and bark thick in the air. Grimalkin and Ash nodded respectfully, but I was too worried to catch the movement in time.

"We know why you have come," one dryad said, her voice the sigh of wind through the leaves. "The breeze carries whispers to us, news of faraway places. We know of your plight with the Iron King. We have been waiting for you, child of two worlds."

"Please," I asked, stepping forward, "can you help Puck? He was shot on the way here. I'll bargain with you, give you anything you want, if you can save him."

Out of the corner of my eye, I saw Ash shoot me a dark glare, but I ignored it.

"We will not bargain with you, child," the second dryad murmured, and I felt a sinking despair. "It is not our way. We are not like the sidhe or the cait sith, seeking endless ways to empower themselves. We simply are."

"As a favor, then," I pleaded, refusing to give up. "Please, he'll die if you don't help him."

"Death is a part of life." The dryad regarded me with pitiless black eyes. "All things fade eventually, even one as long-lived as Puck. People will forget his stories, forget he ever was, and he will cease to be. It is the way of things."

I fought the urge to scream. The dryads wouldn't help; they'd just doomed Puck to die. Clenching my fists, I glared at the tree women, wanting to shake them, throttle them until they agreed to help. I felt a rush of...something...and the trees above me groaned and shook, showering us with leaves. Ash and Grimalkin took a step back, and the dryads exchanged glances.

"She is strong," one whispered.

"Her power sleeps," the other replied. "The trees hear her, the earth answers her call."

"Perhaps it will be enough."

They nodded again, and one of them lifted Puck around the waist, dragging him toward her tree. They both melted into the bark and disappeared. I jerked in alarm.

"What are you doing?"

"Do not worry," the remaining dryad said, turning back to me. "We cannot heal him, but we can halt the damage. Puck will sleep until he is well enough to rejoin you. Whether that takes a night or several years will be entirely up to him."

She tilted her head at me, shedding moss. "You and your

companions may stay here tonight. It is safe. Within these boundaries, the iron fey will not venture. Our power over tree and land keeps them out. Rest, and we will call for you when it is time."

With that, she melted back into the tree, leaving us alone, with one less companion than when we started out.

I wanted to sleep. I wanted to lie down and black out, and wake up to a world where best friends were never shot and little brothers never kidnapped. I wanted everything to be over and my life to go back to normal.

But, as exhausted as I was, I couldn't sleep. I wandered the park in a daze, numb to everything. Ash was off speaking with the resident park fey, and Grimalkin had disappeared, so I was alone. In the scattered moonlight, faeries danced and sang and laughed, calling out to me from a distance. Satyrs whistled tunes on their pipes, piskies buzzed through the air on gossamer wings, and willowy dryads danced through the trees, their slender bodies waving like grass in the wind. I ignored them all.

At the edge of a pond, under the drooping limbs of another giant oak, I sank down, pulled my knees to my chest, and sobbed.

Mermaids broke the surface of the pond to stare at me, and a ring of piskies gathered round, tiny lights hovering in confusion. I barely saw them. The constant worry for Ethan, the fear of losing Puck, and the ill-fated promise to Ash were too much for me. I cried until I was gasping for breath, hiccuping so hard my lungs ached.

But, of course, the fey couldn't let me be miserable in peace. As my tears slowed, I became aware I wasn't alone. A herd of satyrs surrounded me, their eyes bright in the gloom.

"Pretty flower," one of them said, stepping forward. He

had a dark face, a goatee, and horns curling through his thick black hair. His voice was low and soft, and had a faint Creole accent. "Why so sad, lovely one? Come with me, and we will make you laugh again."

I shivered and rose shakily to my feet. "No, thank y— No. I'm fine. I just want to be alone for a while."

"Alone is a terrible thing to be," the satyr said, moving closer. He smiled, charming and attractive. Glamour shimmered around him, and I saw his mortal guise for a split second: a handsome college boy, out walking with his friends. "Why don't we get some coffee, and you can tell me all about it?"

He sounded so sincere, I almost believed him. Then I caught the glint of raw lust in his eyes, in the eyes of his friends, and my stomach contracted in fear.

"I really have to go," I said, backing away. They followed me, their gazes hungry and intense. I smelled something strong in the air and realized it was musk. "Please, please leave me alone."

"You'll thank us afterward," the satyr promised, and lunged.

I ran.

The herd pursued me, whooping and shouting promises: that I would enjoy it, that I needed to loosen up a bit. They were much faster, and the lead goat grabbed me from behind, arms around my waist. I screamed as he lifted me off my feet, kicking and flailing. The other satyrs closed in, grabbing and pawing, tearing at my clothes.

A rush of power, the same I'd felt earlier, and suddenly the oak above us moved. With a deafening creak, a gnarled branch as thick as my waist swung down and struck the lead satyr in the head. He dropped me and staggered back, and the limb swung back to hit him again in the stomach, knocking him sprawling. The other satyrs backed away.

Goat-boy got his feet under him and stood, glaring at me. "I see you like it a little rough," he wheezed, brushing himself off. Shaking his head, he ran a tongue over his lips and stepped forward. "That's okay, we can do rough, right, boys?"

"So can I." A dark shape glided out of the trees, a portion of shadow come to life. The satyrs blinked and hastily stepped back as Ash strode into the middle of the herd. Looming up behind me, he slid an arm around my shoulders and pulled me to his chest. My heart sped up, and my stomach did a backflip. "This one," Ash growled, "is off-limits."

"Prince Ash?" gasped the lead satyr, as the rest of the herd bowed their heads. He paled and held up his hands. "Sorry, Your Highness, I didn't know she was yours. My apologies. No harm done, okay?"

"No one touches her," Ash said, his voice coated with frost. "Touch her, and I'll freeze your testicles and put them in a jar. Understand?"

The satyrs cringed. Stammering apologies to both Ash and me, they bowed and scurried away. Ash shot a glare at two piskies hovering nearby to watch, and they sped into the trees with high-pitched giggles. Silence fell, and we were alone.

"Are you all right?" Ash murmured, releasing me. "Did they hurt you?"

I was shaking. That exhilarating rush of power was gone; now I felt completely drained. "No," I whispered, moving away. "I'm all right." I might've cried, but I had no more tears left in me. My knees trembled and I stumbled, putting a hand against a tree to steady myself.

Ash moved closer. Catching my wrist, he gently pulled me to him and wrapped his arms around me, holding me tight. I was startled, but only for a moment. Sniffling, I closed my eyes and buried my face in his chest, letting all the fear and anger seep away under his touch. I heard his rapid heartbeat, and felt the chill prickling my skin through his shirt. Strangely, it wasn't uncomfortable at all.

We stood like that for a long moment. Ash didn't speak, didn't ask questions, didn't do anything but hold me. I sighed and relaxed into him, and for a little while, everything was okay. Ethan and Puck still lingered in the back of my mind, but for now, this was good. This was enough.

Then I made a stupid mistake and looked up at him.

His eyes met mine, and for a moment, his face was open and vulnerable in the moonlight. I caught a hint of wonder there as we stared at each other. Slowly, he leaned forward. I caught my breath, a tiny gasp escaping.

He stiffened, and his expression shuttered closed, eyes going hard and frosty.

Pushing me away, he stepped back, and my heart sank. Ash looked into the trees, the shadows, the pond, anywhere but at me. Wanting to reclaim that lost moment, I reached for him, but he slid away.

"This is getting old," he said in a voice that matched his eyes. He crossed his arms and stepped away, putting even more distance between us. "I'm not here to play nursemaid, princess. Perhaps you shouldn't go wandering about on your own. I wouldn't want you damaged before you ever reached the Unseelie Court."

My cheeks burned, and I clenched my fists. The memory of being humiliated in the cafeteria, so long ago, rose to my mind to taunt me. "That's all I am to you, isn't it?" I snarled at him. "Your chance to gain favor from your queen. That's all you care about."

"Yes," he replied calmly, infuriating me even more. "I've

never pretended anything else. You knew my motivations from the beginning."

Angry tears stung my eyes. I thought I was all cried out, but I was wrong. "Bastard," I hissed. "Puck was right about you."

He smiled coldly. "Maybe you should ask Puck why I've vowed to kill him someday," he said, eyes glinting. "See if he has the courage to tell you that bit of history between us." He smirked and crossed his arms. "That is, if he ever wakes up."

I opened my mouth to reply, but with a rustle of leaves, two dryads melted out of a nearby trunk. Ash faded into the darkness as they approached, leaving me with my angry words unsaid. I fisted my hands, wanting to smack the arrogance right off his perfect face. I turned and kicked a log instead.

The dryads bowed to me, unconcerned with my mild temper tantrum.

"Meghan Chase, the Elder will see you now."

I followed them to the base of a single oak tree, its branches so draped in moss, it looked like it was hung with moldy curtains. Ash and Grimalkin were already there, though Ash didn't even look my way as I approached. I glared at him, but he continued to ignore me. With the cat on one side and the Winter prince flanking the other, I stepped beneath the boughs of the huge oak and waited.

The bark rippled, and an ancient woman stepped out of the tree. Her skin flaked, like wrinkled bark, and her long hair was the brownish-green of old moss. She was stooped and bent, covered in a robe of lichens that shivered with thousands of insects and spiders. Her face resembled a walnut, lined and wrinkled, and when she moved, her joints creaked like branches in the wind. But her beady eyes were sharp and clear as she looked me over and beckoned with one gnarled, twiggy hand.

"Come closer, child," she whispered, her voice rustling like dry leaves. I swallowed and moved forward, until I could see the insects boring into her skin, smell the earthy scent of her. "Yes, you are the daughter of Oberon, the one whom the wind whispers about. I know why you are here. You seek the one called the Iron King, yes? You wish to find the entrance into his realm."

"Yes," I murmured. "I'm looking for my brother. Machina kidnapped him, and I'm going to get him back."

"As you are, you will not be able to save him," the Elder told me, and my stomach dropped to my toes. "The Iron King waits for you in his lair of steel. He knows you are coming, and you will not be able to stop him. No weapon forged by mortal or fey can harm the Iron King. He fears nothing."

Ash stepped forward, bowing his head respectfully. "Elder," he murmured, "we were told you might know the secret to slaying the Iron King."

The ancient dryad regarded him solemnly. "Yes, young prince," she whispered. "You heard true. There is a way to kill Machina and end his reign. You need a special weapon, one that cannot be forged with tools, something as natural as a flower growing in the sunlight."

Ash leaned forward eagerly. "Where can we find this weapon?"

The Elder Dryad sighed, and seemed to shrink in on herself. "Here," she murmured, looking back at the great oak, her voice tinged with sadness. "The weapon you require is Witchwood, from the heart of the most ancient of trees, as deadly to Machina as iron is to normal fey. A living wood containing the spirit of nature and the power of the natural earth—

a bane to the faeries of progress and technology. Without it, you cannot hope to defeat him and save the human child."

Ash fell silent, his face grim. Bewildered, I looked to him, then back at the Elder Dryad. "You'll give it to us, won't you?" I asked. "If it's the only way to save Ethan—"

"Meghan," Grimalkin murmured from the grass, "you do not know what you are asking. Witchwood is the heart of the Elder's tree. Without it, the oak will die, and so will the dryad connected to it."

Dismayed, I looked at the Elder Dryad, whose lips curled in a faint smile. "It's true," she whispered. "Without its heart, the tree will slowly wither and die. And yet, I knew what you came for, Meghan Chase. I planned to offer it from the beginning."

"No," I said automatically. "I don't want it. Not like this. There has to be another way."

"There is no other way, child." The Elder shook her head at me. "And if you do not defeat the Iron King, we will perish all the same. His influence grows. The stronger he becomes, the more the Nevernever fades. Eventually we will all wither and die in a wasteland of logic and science."

"But I can't kill him," I protested. "I'm not a warrior. I just want Ethan back, that's all."

"You won't have to worry about that." The dryad nodded to Ash, standing silently nearby. "The Winter prince can fight for you, I imagine. He smells of blood and sorrow. I will happily grant the Witchwood to him."

"Please." I looked at her, pleading, wanting her to understand. Puck had already possibly given his life for my quest; I didn't want another's death on my hands. "I don't want you to do this. It's too much. You shouldn't have to die for me."

"I give my life for all fey," the dryad replied solemnly.

"You will simply be my instrument of salvation. Besides, death comes for us all, in the end. I have lived a long life, longer than most. I have no regrets."

She smiled at me, an old, grandmotherly smile, and faded back into her oak. Ash, Grim, and the other dryads stood silently, their expressions somber and grave. A moment later, the Elder reemerged, clutching something in her withered hands—a long, straight stick, so pale it was almost white, with reddish veins running down its length. When she stepped up and offered it to me, seconds passed before I could take it. It was warm and smooth in my hands, pulsing with a life of its own, and I almost hurled it away.

The Elder placed a withered, knobby hand on my arm. "One more thing, child," she added as I struggled with holding the living wood. "You are powerful, much more so than you realize. Oberon's blood flows through your veins, and the Nevernever itself responds to your whims. Your talent still sleeps within you, but it is beginning to stir. How you use it will shape the future of the courts, the fey, your own destiny, everything.

"Now," she continued, sounding weaker than before, "go and rescue your brother. The trod to Machina's realm is an abandoned factory down by the wharfs. A guide will lead you there tomorrow. Kill the Iron King and bring peace to both our worlds."

"What if I can't?" I whispered. "What if the Iron King truly is invincible?"

"Then we will all die," said the Elder Dryad, and faded back into her oak. The other dryads left, leaving me alone with a cat, a prince, and a stick. I sighed and looked down at the wood in my hands.

"No pressure or anything," I muttered.

PART THREE

CHAPTER TWENTY

Iron Dragons and Packrats

We left at dawn. Time enough for me to catch maybe two hours of sleep on the lumpy ground, and say my last goodbyes to Puck. He was still sleeping, deep within the tree, when I woke up in the still hours before sunrise. The dryad attached to the oak told me he still lived, but she didn't have any idea when he would wake.

I stood beside the oak for several minutes, my hand against the bark, trying to feel his heartbeat through the wood. I missed him. Ash and Grimalkin might be allies, but they were not friends. They wanted to use me for their own ends. Only Puck truly cared, and now he was gone.

"Meghan." Ash appeared behind me, his voice surprisingly gentle. "We should go. We can't afford to wait for him, not if it could be months before he wakes up. We don't have that time."

"I know." I pressed my palm into the bark, feeling the rough edges scrape my skin. *Wake up quickly,* I told him, wondering if he dreamed, if he could feel my touch through the tree. *Wake up quickly, and find me. I'll be waiting.*

I turned to Ash, who was dressed for battle, with his sword

at his waist and a bow slung across his back. Looking at him made my skin tingle.

"Do you have it?" I asked, to hide the burning in my cheeks.

He nodded, and held up a gleaming white arrow with red veins curling around it. He'd asked for the Witchwood the previous night, claiming he could turn it into a suitable weapon, and I gave it to him without hesitation. Now I stared at the dart, feeling my apprehension grow. It seemed like such a small, fragile thing to take down the supposedly invincible King of the Iron Fey.

"Can I hold it?" I asked, and Ash immediately placed the arrow in my palm, his fingers lingering on mine. The wood throbbed in my hand, a rhythmic *pulse-pulse,* like a heartbeat; I shuddered and held it out, waiting for him to take it back.

"Hold on to it for me," Ash said softly, his gaze never leaving mine. "This is your quest. You decide when I'm supposed to use it."

I blushed and opened my backpack, shoving the dart inside. The shaft of the arrow stuck out of the pack, and I closed the zippers around it, securing it in place before swinging the thing over my shoulders. The bag was heavier now; last night, I'd raided a park fountain and scraped up enough change to buy food and bottled water for the rest of the journey. The clerk at the nearby gas station seemed a bit annoyed at having to count handfuls of dimes and quarters at one in the morning, but I didn't want to start the final leg of our journey empty-handed. I hoped Ash and Grim liked beef jerky, trail mix, and Skittles.

"You'll only get one shot," I murmured. Ash smiled without humor.

"Then I'll have to make it count."

He sounded so confident. I wondered if he was ever afraid,

or had second thoughts about what he had to do. Holding a grudge seemed foolish now, since he was about to follow me into mortal danger. "Look, I'm sorry about last night," I offered. "I didn't mean to be a psycho. I was just worried about Ethan. And with Puck getting shot and everything—"

"Don't worry about it, Meghan."

I blinked, my stomach fluttering. That was the first time he'd called me by name. "Ash, I—"

"I have been thinking," Grimalkin announced, leaping onto a rock. I glared and bit down a sigh, cursing his timing. The cat plowed on without notice. "Perhaps we should rethink our strategy," he said, looking at each of us. "It occurs to me that charging headlong into Machina's realm is a singularly bad idea."

"What do you mean?"

"Well." The cat sat down and licked his back toes. "Given that he keeps sending his officers after us, I would guess that he probably knows we are coming. Why did he kidnap your brother in the first place? He must have known you would come after him."

"Overconfident?" I guessed. Grimalkin shook his head.

"No. Something is missing. Or maybe we are just not seeing it. The Iron King would have no use for a child. Unless..." The cat looked up at us, narrowing his eyes. "I am leaving."

"What? Why?"

"I have a theory." Grimalkin stood, waving his tail. "I think I might know another way into Machina's realm. You are welcome to join me."

"A theory?" Ash crossed his arms. "We can't break plan on a hunch, Cait Sith."

"Even if the way you are going leads straight into a trap?"

I shook my head. "We have to risk it. We're so close, Grim.

We can't turn back now." I knelt to face Grimalkin eye to eye. "Come with us. We need you. You've always pointed us in the right direction."

"I am not a fighter, human." Grimalkin shook his head and blinked. "You have the prince for that. I accompanied you to show you the way to your brother, and for my own amusement. But I know my limitations." He looked at Ash and pinned his ears. "I would be no help to you in there. Not the way you are going. So, it is time we settled our debts and parted ways."

That's right. I still owed the cat a favor. Uneasiness stirred. I hoped the cat wouldn't ask for my voice, or my future kid. I still didn't know what went on in that devious little head of his. "Right." I sighed, trying to keep my voice from shaking. Ash moved to stand behind me, a quiet, confident presence. "A deal's a deal. What do you want, Grim?"

Grimalkin's gaze bore into me. He sat up straight, flicking his tail. "My price is this," he stated. "I want to be able to call on you, once, at a time of my choosing, no questions asked. That is my debt."

Relief washed through me. That didn't sound so bad. Ash, however, made a thoughtful noise and crossed his arms.

"A summoning?" The prince sounded puzzled. "Odd for you, Cait Sith. What do you hope to accomplish with her?"

Grimalkin ignored him. "When I call," he continued, staring at me, "you must come straightaway without pause. And you must help me in any way you are able. Those are the terms of our contract. You are bound to me until they are fulfilled."

"All right." I nodded. "I can live with that. But if you call, how will I know where to find you?"

Grimalkin sneezed a laugh. "Do not worry about that, human. You will know. But for now, I must leave you." He stood, nodding once to me, then to Ash. "Until we meet again."

Then he slipped into the grass, his bottlebrush tail held straight up, and disappeared.

I smiled sadly. "And then there were two."

Ash moved closer and touched my arm, a brief, featherlight caress. I glanced at him and he offered that tiny, endearing smile, one of apology and encouragement, and a silent promise that he would not leave me. I gave him a shaky grin and resisted the urge to lean into him, wanting to feel his arms around me once more.

A piskie spiraled down from the branches, hovering a few inches from my face. Blue-skinned, with dandelion hair and gossamer wings, she stuck out her tongue at me and zipped to Ash, alighting on his shoulder. Ash cocked his head as the piskie whispered something in his ear. One corner of his mouth turned up; he glanced at me and shook his head. The piskie giggled and spun into the air again. I scowled, wondering what they were saying about me, then decided I didn't care.

"This is Seedlit," Ash said as the piskie spiraled through the air like a drunken hummingbird. "She'll lead us to the wharfs, and then to the factory. Beyond that, we're on our own."

I nodded, my heart hammering in my ears. This was it, the last leg of the journey. At the end was Machina and Ethan, or death. I smirked with rash bravado and raised my chin. "All right, Tinker Bell," I told the piskie, who gave an indignant buzz. "Lead on."

We followed the bobbing light toward the banks of the river, where the cold, slow waters of the Mississippi churned under a slate-gray sky. We didn't speak much. Ash walked beside me, our shoulders almost touching. After several silent minutes, I brushed his hand. He curled his fingers around mine, and we walked like that until we reached the factory.

A corrugated-steel building squatted behind a chain-link fence, a dark smudge against the sky. Seedlit jabbered something to Ash, who nodded gravely, before she zipped away out of sight. She had brought us as far as she could go; now we were on our own.

As we approached the gate, Ash hung back a little, a pained look on his face.

"What's the matter?"

He grimaced. "Nothing. Just…" He nodded to the fence. "Too much iron. I can feel it from here."

"Does it hurt?"

"No." He shook his head. "I'd have to touch it for that. But it's draining." He looked uncomfortable admitting it. "It makes it difficult to use glamour."

I shook the gate experimentally. It wouldn't budge. Heavy chains were wrapped around the entrance, padlocked together, and barbed wire coiled along the top of the fence.

"Give me your sword," I told Ash. He blinked at me. "What?"

"Give me your sword," I repeated. "We have to get in, and you don't like touching iron, right? Let me have it, and I'll take care of it."

He looked dubious but pulled his blade and offered it to me, hilt up. I took the weapon gingerly. The hilt was painfully cold, the blade throwing off a frozen blue aura. I raised it over my head and brought it slashing down on the chain binding the gate. The links snapped like they were made of glass, shattering with a metallic ringing sound. Pleased, I grabbed the chain to yank it free, but the metal burned like fire and I dropped it with a cry.

Ash was beside me, reclaiming his sword as I shook my singed fingers, dancing about in pain. After sheathing the weapon, he snatched my flailing hand and turned it palm up. A line of red slashed across my fingers, numb and tingly to the touch.

"I thought I was immune to iron." I sniffed. Ash sighed.

"You are," he murmured, moving me away from the fence and its glamour-draining qualities. His expression teetered between amusement and exasperation. "However, grabbing superchilled metal is still very unpleasant for Summer fey, no matter who you are."

"Oh."

He shook his head, examining the wound again. "It's not frostbitten," he muttered. "It'll blister, but you should be fine. You might only lose a couple fingers."

I glanced at him sharply, but he was smirking. For a moment, I was speechless. Good God, the Ice Prince was making jokes now; the world *must* be ending. "That's not funny," I hissed, swatting at him with my other hand. He dodged easily, the amusement still on his face.

"You're a lot like her," he mused, so softly I barely heard him. And before I could say anything, he turned, drew his sword, and swept the chains off the gate. It swung open with a creak, and Ash scanned the compound warily.

"Stay close to me," he muttered, and we eased our way inside.

Large mounds of scrap metal lay piled about the yard as we walked through, the sharp edges glinting in the faint rays of dawn. Ash winced each time we passed one, keeping a wary eye on it, as if it would leap up and attack him. Strange creatures scampered about the metal drifts, tiny men with rat-like features and naked tails. When they nibbled on a piece of metal, it rusted away under their teeth. They didn't bother us, though Ash shuddered whenever he saw one, and his hand never left his sword.

The iron doors had more chains around them, but the ice blade cut through them easily. Stepping inside, I gazed around slowly, my eyes adjusting to the dim light. It looked like an ordinary warehouse, empty and dark, though I heard skittering noises in the corners. More mountains of scrap metal littered the gloom, some larger than I was tall.

Where's the trod? I wondered, stepping farther inside. Metal grates covered the floor, pressing through my sneakers. Ash hesitated, hanging back in the doorway.

Steam drifted over the ground, coiling around my legs. Against the far wall, I saw that one of the grates had been pried up, leaving a square, gaping hole. Smoke boiled out of the opening. *There!*

I started toward the hole. From the doorway, Ash called for me to stop. Before my nerves could jangle a warning, a pile of scrap metal shifted. Then, with a screech that set my teeth on edge, the mound uncurled, sending sparks into the air as it dragged along the floor. From the jumbled mess, a long neck rose up, made of iron, wire, and broken glass. A reptilian head glared down at me, shards of metal bristling from its skull. Then the entire mound lurched up, shifting into a huge lizard of iron and steel, with curved metal talons and a jagged, spiked tail.

The dragon roared, a deafening metallic screech that made my eyes want to pop out of my skull. It lunged, and I scrambled behind another mound, praying this one wasn't a dragon, too. The dragon hissed and followed, steam erupting from its gaping jaws, steel talons clanking over the floor.

A volley of ice darts flew through the air, striking the

dragon in the head and shattering harmlessly off its skull. It screamed and reared up, glaring at Ash, who stood at the far end of the room with his sword drawn. Lashing its tail, the dragon charged, sparks flying from its claws as it bore down on Ash. My heart jumped to my throat.

Ash closed his eyes for a moment, then knelt and drove his sword point down into the floor. There was a flash of blue light, and ice spread rapidly from the tip, covering the ground and coating everything in crystal. My breath hung in the air, and icicles formed on the overhead beams. I shivered violently in the sudden chill as the scrap metal frosted over, radiating absolute cold.

Ash leaped aside as the dragon reached him, moving as easily on ice as normal ground. Unable to stop itself, the dragon slammed into the wall, bits of metal flying everywhere. It hissed and struggled to rise, sliding on the slick floor, tail thrashing. Ash jumped forward and blew out a long whistle, sending an icy whirlwind spinning through the air. The dragon shrieked as the blizzard whipped around it, coating it with frost and snow. A hoary rime caked its metal body, its struggles growing weaker as ice weighed it down.

Ash stopped, panting heavily. He staggered away from the frozen dragon and leaned back against a post, closing his eyes. I half ran, half stumbled over, slipping on the ice, until I reached him.

"Are you all right?"

"Never again," he muttered, almost to himself. His eyes were still closed, and I wasn't sure he knew I was there. "I will *not* watch that happen again. I won't…lose another…like that. I can't…"

"Ash?" I whispered, touching his arm.

His eyes opened and his gaze dropped to mine. "Meghan,"

he murmured, seeming a bit confused that I was still there. He blinked and shook his head. "Why didn't you run? I tried to buy you some time. You should've gone ahead."

"Are you crazy? I couldn't leave you to that thing. Now, come on." I took his hand, tugging him off the post while glancing nervously at the frozen dragon. "Let's get out of here. I think that thing just blinked at us."

His fingers tightened on mine and pulled me forward. Startled and overbalanced, I looked up at him, and then he was kissing me.

I froze in shock, but only for a moment. Wrapping my arms around his neck, I rose on my tiptoes to meet him, kissing him back with a hunger that surprised us both. He crushed me close, and I ran my hands through his silky hair, sliding it through my fingers. His lips were cool on mine, and my mouth tingled. And for a moment, there was no Ethan, no Puck, no Iron King. Only this.

He pulled back, slightly out of breath. My blood raced, and I leaned my head on his shoulder, feeling the steely muscles through his back. I felt him tremble.

"This isn't good," he murmured, his voice curiously shaken. But he still didn't release me. I closed my eyes and listened to his rapid heartbeat.

"I know," I whispered back.

"The Courts would kill us if they found out."

"Yeah."

"Mab would accuse me of treason. Oberon would believe I'm turning you against him. They'd both see grounds for banishment, or execution."

"I'm sorry."

He sighed, burying his face in my hair. His breath was cool

on my neck, and I shivered. Neither of us said anything for what seemed a long time.

"We'll think of something," I ventured.

He nodded wordlessly and pulled away, but stumbled as he took a step back. I caught his arm again.

"Are you all right?"

"I'll be fine." He released my elbow. "Too much iron. The spell took a lot out of me."

"Ash—"

A piercing crack interrupted us. The dragon freed a forepaw and smashed it to the floor. More cracks appeared as it struggled to rise, shedding ice. Ash grabbed my hand and ran.

With an enraged shriek, the dragon shattered its ice prison, sending shards flying. We pelted across the room, hearing the dragon give chase, its claws digging into the icy ground. The hole with its missing grate loomed ahead, and we flung ourselves toward it, leaping through the steam and plummeting into the unknown. The dragon's frustrated bellow rang overhead, as clouds of steam enveloped us, and everything went white.

I didn't remember landing, though I was aware of Ash holding my hand as the steam cleared around us. Eyes widening, we both stared around in horror.

A twisted landscape stretched out before us, barren and dark, the sky a sickly yellow-gray. Mountains of rubble dominated the land: ancient computers, rusty cars, televisions, dial phones, radios, all piled into huge mounds that loomed over everything. Some of the piles were alight, burning with a thick, choking smog. A hot wind howled through the wasteland, stirring dust into glittering eddies, spinning the wheel of an ancient bicycle lying on a trash heap. Scraps of aluminum, old cans, and foam cups rolled over the ground, and a sharp, coppery smell hung in the air, clogging the back of my throat. The trees here were sickly things, bent and withered. A few bore lightbulbs and batteries that hung like glittering fruit.

"This is the Nevernever," Ash muttered. His voice was grim. "Somewhere in the Deep Tangle, if I had to guess. No wonder the wyldwood is dying."

"*This* is the Nevernever?" I asked, gazing around in shock. I remembered the frigid, pristine beauty of Tir Na Nog, the blinding colors of the Summer Court. "No way. How could it get like this?"

"Machina," Ash replied. "The territories take on the aspects of their rulers. I'm guessing his realm is very small right now, but if it expands, it'll swallow the wyldwood and eventually destroy the Nevernever."

I thought I hated Faeryland, and everything in it, but that was before Ash. This was his home. If the Nevernever died, he would die, too. So would Puck and Grim, and everyone else I met on my strange journey here. "We have to stop it," I exclaimed, gazing around the dead landscape. Smog tickled my throat, making me want to cough. "We can't let this spread."

Ash smiled, cold and frightening. "That's why we're here."

Slowly, we made our way through the mountains of junk, keeping a wary eye on any that might come to life and attack. Out of the corner of my eye I caught movement and spun toward it, fearful of another dragon disguised as harmless debris. It wasn't a dragon this time, but several small, hunchbacked creatures waddling to and fro between the mounds. They looked like withered gnomes, bent over by the huge amount of stuff piled on their backs, like giant hermit crabs. When they found an item they liked—a broken toy, the spokes of a bicycle—they attached it to the collection on their backs and shuffled to the next mound. Some of their humps were large and quite impressive, in a sad kind of way.

A few of the creatures saw us and came waddling up, beady eyes bright and curious. Ash went for his sword, but I laid a hand on his arm. I sensed these beings weren't dangerous, and perhaps they could point us in the right direction.

"Hello," I greeted softly as they surrounded us, snuffling like eager dogs. "We don't want any trouble. We're just a little lost."

They cocked their heads but didn't say anything. A few pressed closer, and several long fingers reached out to poke my backpack, tugging on the bright material. Not maliciously, but curious, like seagulls pecking at a button. Two of them crowded Ash, pawing at his sword sheath. He shifted uneasily and stepped away.

"I need to find King Machina," I said. "Can you show us where he lives?"

But the creatures weren't paying attention, too busy pawing at my backpack, jabbering among themselves. One gave it an experimental yank that nearly toppled me off my feet.

In a flash of blue light, Ash drew his sword. The creatures scuttled back, their eyes wide and fixated to the glowing blade. A few twitched their fingers, like they wanted to touch it, but knew better than to approach.

"Come on," Ash muttered, pointing his sword at any gnome that edged forward. "They're not going to help us. Let's get out of here."

"Wait." I grabbed his sleeve as he turned. "I've got an idea."

Taking off my pack, I unzipped the side pocket, reached inside, and pulled out the broken iPod from so long ago. Stepping forward, I raised it high, seeing the gnomes follow it with wide, unbroken stares.

"A deal," I called into the silence. They watched me without blinking. "Do you see this?" I said, waving the iPod back and forth. They followed it, like dogs eyeing a cookie. "I'll give it to you, but in return, you take me to the Iron King."

The gnomes turned and jabbered to one another, occasionally peeking back to make sure I was still there. Finally, one of them stepped forward. A whole tricycle teetered at the top of his hump. He fixed me with an unblinking stare, and beckoned me to follow.

We trailed the odd little creatures—whom I secretly dubbed the pack rats—through the wasteland of junk, drawing curious stares from the other residents living there. I saw more of the ratlike men whose teeth rusted metal, a few scrawny dogs wandering about, and swarms of iron bugs crawling over everything. Once, in the distance, I caught a terrifying glimpse of another dragon, unfurling from a mound of trash. Thankfully, it only shifted into a more comfortable sleeping position and returned to its perfect disguise as a pile of debris.

At last, the mountains of garbage fell away, and the lead pack rat pointed a long finger down a barren plain. Across a cracked, gray plateau, spiderwebbed with lava and millions of blinking lights, a railroad stretched away into the distance. Hulking machines, like enormous iron beetles, sat beside it, snorting steam. And silhouetted against the sky, a jagged black tower stabbed up from the earth, wreathed in smog and billowing smoke.

Machina's fortress.

Ash drew in a quiet breath. I stared at the imposing tower, my stomach contracting with fear, until a tug on my backpack snapped me out of my daze. The pack rat stood there, an expectant look on his face, fingers twitching.

"Oh, yeah." Fishing out the iPod, I handed it to him solemnly. "A deal's a deal. Hope you enjoy it."

The pack rat chittered with joy. Clutching the device to his chest, he scuttled off like an enormous crab, vanishing back into the wasteland of junk. I heard excited jabbering, and imagined him showing off his trophy for all to see. Then the voices faded and we were alone.

Ash turned to me, and I was struck with how awful he looked. His skin was ashen; there were shadows under his eyes, and his hair was damp with sweat.

"Will you be all right?" I whispered. One corner of his mouth curled up.

"We'll see, won't we?"

I reached for his hand, wrapped my fingers around his, and squeezed. He put my hand to his face and closed his eyes, as if drawing strength from my touch. Together, we descended into the heart of Machina's realm.

CHAPTER TWENTY-ONE

Knights of the Iron Crown

"Don't look now," Ash muttered after hours of walking, "but we're being followed."

I craned my head over my shoulder. We were following the railroad—walking beside it, instead of directly on the iron tracks—toward the looming fortress, and hadn't encountered a single creature, faery or otherwise, on the journey. Streetlamps grew out of the ground, lighting the way, and iron behemoths, reminding me of vehicles in a steam-punk anime, crouched along the tracks, hissing smoke. Through the writhing steam, it was difficult to see more than a few yards away.

But then, a small, familiar creature scuttled across the tracks, vanishing into the smoke. I caught a glimpse of a tricycle poking up from a mound of junk and frowned. "Why are the pack rats following us?"

"Pack rats?" Ash smirked at me.

"Yeah, you know, they collect shiny stuff, hoard it in their dens? Pack rats? Oh, never mind." I mock glared at him, too worried to be irritated. Ash never complained, but I could see the iron everywhere was taking a toll on him. "Do you want to stop somewhere and rest?"

"No." He pressed a palm to one eye, as if trying to squelch a headache. "It won't make any difference."

The twisted landscape went on. We passed pools of molten lava, bubbling and shimmering with heat. Smokestacks loomed overhead, belching great spouts of black pollution that writhed into the yellow-gray sky. Lightning arched and crackled across blinking metal towers, and the air hummed with electricity. Pipes crisscrossed the ground, leaking steam from joints and valves, and black wires slashed the sky overhead. The tang of iron, rust, and smog clogged my throat and burned my nose.

Ash spoke very little, stumbling on with grim determination. My worry for him was a constant knot in my stomach. I was doing this to him; it was my contract that bound him to help, even though it was slowly killing him. But we couldn't turn back, and I could only watch, helpless, as Ash struggled to continue. His breath rasped painfully in his throat, and he grew paler by the hour. Fear clawed my insides. I was terrified he would die and leave me alone in this dark, twisted place.

A day passed, and the iron tower loomed black and menacing overhead, though it was still far in the distance. The sickly yellow-gray of the sky darkened, and the hazy outline of a moon shimmered behind the clouds. I stopped, looking up at the sky. No stars. None at all. The artificial lights reflected off the haze, making the night nearly as bright as the day.

Ash began coughing, putting a hand against a crumbling wall to steady himself. I slipped my arms around him, holding him steady as he leaned into me. The harsh explosions made my heart constrict. "We should rest," I muttered, gazing around for a place to camp. A huge cement tube lay half

buried in the dirt at the bottom of the tracks, covered in graffiti, and I motioned him toward it. "Come on."

He didn't argue this time, but followed me down the slope
and into the cement shelter. It wasn't tall enough for us to
stand up straight, and the floor was sprinkled with chips of
colored glass. Not the best of campsites, but at least it wasn't
iron. I kicked away a broken bottle and sat down carefully,
shrugging off my backpack.

Pulling the sword from his belt, Ash sank down opposite
me with a barely concealed groan. The Witchwood arrow
throbbed as I unzipped the pack and reached around it for the
food and bottled water.

Ripping open a bag of jerky, I offered some to Ash. He
shook his head, his eyes weary and dull.

"You should eat something," I chided, gnawing on the dried
meat. I wasn't particularly hungry myself, too tired, hot, and
worried to have an appetite, but I wanted something in my
stomach. "I have trail mix or candy if you want something
else. Here." I waggled a bag of peanut mix at him. He eyed it
dubiously, and I frowned. "I'm sorry, but they don't sell faery
food at mini-marts. Eat."

Mutely, he accepted the bag and poured out a handful of
peanuts and raisins. I gazed into the distance, where the looming black tower stabbed into the clouds. "How long do you
think until we reach it?" I murmured, just to get him talking again.

Ash tossed the whole handful back, chewed, and swallowed
without interest. "I'd guess a day at most," he replied, setting
down the bag. "Beyond that…" He sighed, and his eyes darkened. "I doubt I'd be of much use anymore."

My stomach convulsed with dread. I couldn't lose him
now. I'd lost so much already; it seemed especially cruel that

Ash might not reach the end of our adventure. I needed him as I'd never needed anyone before. *I'll protect you,* I thought, surprising myself. *You'll get through this, I promise. Just don't die on me, Ash.*

Ash met my gaze, as if he could tell what I was thinking, his gray eyes solemn in the shadows of the pipe. I wondered if my emotions were giving away my thoughts, if Ash could read the glamour aura that surrounded me. For a moment, he hesitated, as if fighting a battle within himself. Then with a resigned sigh, he smiled faintly and held out his hand. I took it, and he pulled me close, settling me in front of him and wrapping his arms around my stomach. I leaned back against his chest and listened to his beating heart. With every thump, it told me that this was real, that Ash was here, and alive, and still with me.

The wind picked up, smelling of ozone and some other weird, chemical scent. A drop of rain hit the edge of the pipe, and a tiny wisp of smoke curled into the air. Except for his slow breathing, Ash was perfectly still, as if he feared that any sudden movement would scare me away. I reached down and traced idle patterns on his arm, marveling at the cool, smooth skin under my fingers, like living ice. I felt him shiver, heard his ragged intake of breath.

"Ash?"

"Hmm?"

I licked my lips. "Why did you vow to kill Puck?"

He jerked. I felt his eyes on the back of my neck and bit the inside of my cheek, wishing I could take it back, wondering what made me ask in the first place. "Never mind," I told him, waving a hand. "Forget it. You don't have to tell me. I was just wondering—"

Who you really are. What Puck has done to make you hate him. I want to understand. I feel I don't know either of you.

A few more drops of rain hit the ground, hissing in the silence. I chewed my jerky strips and stared out into the rain, hyperaware of Ash's body, of his arms around my waist. I heard him shift to a more comfortable position and sigh.

"It was a long time ago," he murmured, his voice almost lost in the rising wind, "before you were even born. Winter and Summer had been at peace for several seasons. There were always minor skirmishes between the courts, but for the longest time in centuries, we actually left each other alone.

"Near the end of summer," he went on, a bit of pain creeping into his voice, "things began to change. The fey don't deal well with boredom, and some of the more impatient members started mischief with Summer again. I should've known there would be trouble, but that season, I wasn't thinking of politics. The entire court was bored and restless, but I..." His voice broke, only for a moment, before continuing. "I was with my lady, Ariella Tularyn."

I felt the breath sucked out of me. His lady. Ash had been involved, once. And, judging from the veiled hurt in his voice, he'd loved her a lot. I stiffened, suddenly too aware of my breath, of his arms around my waist. Ash didn't seem to notice.

"We were hunting in the wyldwood," he went on, resting his chin atop my head. "Following the rumor of a golden fox that had been seen in the area. There were three of us that day, hunting together. Ariella, myself, and...and Robin Goodfellow."

"Puck?"

Ash shifted uncomfortably. Thunder growled in the distance, shooting threads of green lightning across the sky. "Yes," he muttered, as if it pained him to say it. "Puck. Puck was…he was a friend, once. I wasn't ashamed to call him that. Back then, the three of us would often meet one another in the wyldwood, away from the condemnation of the courts. We didn't care about the rules. Back then, Puck and Ariella were my closest companions. I trusted them completely."

"What happened?"

Ash's voice was soft with memory as he continued. "We were hunting," he explained again, "following our quarry into a territory none of us had seen. The wyldwood is huge, and some parts are constantly shifting, so it can be dangerous, even for us. We tracked the golden fox for three days, through unfamiliar woods and forest, making bets on whose arrow would finally take it down. Puck boasted that Winter would surely lose to Summer, and Ariella and I made the same boast in reverse. All the while, the forest around us grew dark and wild. Our horses were fey steeds whose hooves didn't touch the ground, but they were growing increasingly nervous. We should have listened to them, but we didn't, stubborn pride leading us on like fools.

"Finally, on the fourth day, we came to a rise that plunged down into a vast hollow. On the other side, trotting along the ridge, was the golden fox. The hollow separating us wasn't deep, but it was wide and filled with tangled shadows and undergrowth, making it difficult to see what was down there.

"Ariella wanted to go around, even though it would take us longer. Puck disagreed, insisting we would lose our quarry unless we rode straight through. We argued. I sided with Ariella—though I didn't see the reason for her apprehension, if she wasn't willing to go forward, I wasn't going to make her.

"Puck, however, had other ideas. As I turned my horse around, he let out a whoop, slapped Ariella's horse on the rump, and kicked his own steed forward. They plunged over the edge, racing down the slope, with Puck yelling at me to catch up if I could. I had no choice but to follow."

Ash fell silent, his eyes dark and haunted. He gazed off into the distance, until I couldn't take it anymore. "What happened?" I whispered.

He gave a bitter laugh. "Ariella was right, of course. Puck had led us straight into a wyvern nest."

I felt stupid for asking but… "What's a wyvern?"

"It's cousin to a dragon," Ash replied. "Not as intelligent, but still extremely dangerous. And highly territorial. The thing rose up out of nowhere, all scales and teeth and wings, lashing at us with its poisoned stinger. It was enormous, an ancient drake, vicious and powerful. We fought our way free, the three of us, side by side. We'd been together so long we knew one another's fighting styles, and used them to take down the enemy. It was Ariella who landed the killing blow. But, as it was dying, the wyvern whipped its tail out one last time, striking her in the chest. Wyvern poison is extremely potent, and we were miles from any healers. We…we tried to save her, but…"

He paused, taking a shaky breath. I squeezed his arm to console him.

"She died in my arms," he finished, making an audible effort to compose himself. "She died with my name on her lips, begging me to save her. As I held her, watched the life fade from her eyes, I could only think one thing—that Puck had caused this. If it wasn't for him, she would still be alive."

"I'm so sorry, Ash."

Ash nodded once. His voice turned steely. "I swore, on that day, to avenge Ariella's death, to kill Robin Goodfellow, or die trying. We've clashed several times since, but Goodfellow always manages to slip away, or throw me some trick that

ends our duels. I cannot rest while he lives. I promised Ariella that I would continue hunting Robin Goodfellow until
one of us lies dead."

"Puck told me it was a mistake. He didn't mean for that
to happen." The words were sour in my mouth. It didn't feel
right, defending him. Ash had lost someone he loved because
of Puck's actions, a prank that finally went too far.

"It doesn't matter." Ash shifted away from me, his voice
cold. "My vow is binding. I cannot rest until I've completed
my oath."

I didn't know what to say, so I stared into the rain, miserable and torn in two. Ash and Puck, two enemies locked in
a struggle that would end only when one of them killed the
other. How could you stand between two people like that,
knowing that one day, one of them would succeed? I knew
faery oaths were binding, and Ash had good reason to hate
Puck, but I still felt trapped. I couldn't stop this, but I didn't
want either of them to die.

Ash sighed and leaned forward again, brushing my hand,
tracing the skin with his fingertips. "I'm sorry," he murmured.
A shiver went up my arm. "I wish you didn't have to be involved. There is no way to unmake a vow, once it has been
spoken. But know this—were I aware then that I would meet
you, perhaps my oath would not have been so hasty."

My throat closed up. I wanted to say something, but at that
moment, a sharp blast of wind blew a few drops of rain into
the tube. Water splashed over my jeans, and I yelped as something burned my skin.

We examined my leg. Tiny holes marred my jeans where
the drops had hit, the material seared away, the skin underneath red and burned. It throbbed as if I'd jabbed needles
into my flesh.

"What the heck?" I muttered, glaring into the storm. It looked like ordinary rain—gray, misty, somewhat depressing. Almost compulsively, I stuck my hand toward the opening, where water dripped over the edge of the tube.

Ash grabbed my wrist, snatching it back. "Yes, it will burn your hand as well as your leg," he said in a bland voice. "And here I thought you learned your lesson with the chains."

Embarrassed, I dropped my hand and scooted farther into the tube, away from the rim and the acid rain dripping from it. "Guess I'm staying up all night," I muttered, crossing my arms. "Wouldn't want to doze off and find half my face melted off when I wake up."

Ash pulled me back against him, brushing my hair from my neck. His mouth skimmed my shoulder, up my neck, sending butterflies swarming through my insides. "If you want to rest, then do so," he murmured against my skin. "The rain will not touch you, I promise."

"What about you?"

"I wasn't planning to sleep." He made a casual gesture at a trickle of rainwater seeping into the tube, and the water turned to ice. "I fear I wouldn't be able to wake up."

My worry spiked. "Ash—"

His lips brushed my ear. "Sleep, Meghan Chase," he whispered, and suddenly I couldn't keep my eyes open. Half my consciousness still struggled as darkness pulled me under and I sank into his waiting arms.

When I awoke, the rain had stopped and everything had dried, though the ground still steamed. There was no visible sun through the choking clouds, but the air still blistered with heat. I grabbed my backpack and crawled out of the pipe, looking around for Ash. He sat against the outside of the tube, head back, sword resting on his knees. Seeing him, I felt a rush of anger and fear. He'd enchanted me last night, spelled me to sleep without my consent. Which meant he'd probably used glamour, though his own body was getting weaker and weaker. Fuming and afraid, I stomped up to him and put my hands on his hips. Gray eyes cracked open and regarded me blearily.

"Don't do that again." I'd intended to yell at him, but his vulnerability made me pause. He blinked, but had the grace not to ask what I was talking about.

"My apologies," he murmured, bowing his head. "I thought at least one of us could benefit from a few hours' sleep."

God, he looked awful. His cheeks were hollow, dark circles crouched under his eyes, and his skin was almost translucent. I needed to find Ethan and get us all out of here, before Ash turned into a walking skeleton and collapsed dead at my feet.

Ash looked past me to the tower, seeming to draw strength from it. "Not far now," he murmured, as if it were a mantra that kept him going. I held out my hand, and he let me pull him to his feet.

We started following the tracks again.

The smokestacks and metal towers slowly fell away behind us as we continued across Machina's realm. The land grew flat and barren, and steam billowed out of cracks in the ground, coiling around us like wraiths. Colossal machines, with enormous iron wheels and armored shells, lay beside the tracks. They looked like a cross between modern-day tanks and the mecha vehicles of anime. They were old and rusty, and reminded me strangely of Ironhorse.

Ash grunted suddenly and fell, his legs buckling underneath him. I grabbed his arm as he pulled himself upright, panting. He felt so thin.

"Should we stop and rest?" I asked.

"No," he gritted out. "Keep going. We have to—"

Suddenly he straightened, his hand going to his sword.

Ahead of us, the steam cleared, parting enough to reveal a hulking figure standing on the tracks. A horse made of iron and snorting flame, steel hooves pawing the ground. His glowing eyes watched us balefully.

"Ironhorse!" I gasped, wondering, for a surreal moment, if my earlier thoughts had summoned him here.

"THOUGHT YOU GOT RID OF ME, DID YOU?" Ironhorse boomed, his voice reverberating off the machines around us. "IT WILL TAKE MORE THAN A CAVE-IN TO KILL ME. I MADE THE MISTAKE OF UNDERESTIMATING YOU BEFORE. THAT WON'T HAPPEN AGAIN."

Movement surged around us as hundreds of gremlins crawled into view, hissing and crackling. They swarmed over the machines like spiders, laughing and chittering, and scuttled along the ground. In seconds, they had us surrounded, a living black carpet. Ash drew his sword, and the gremlins hissed at him nastily.

Two figures appeared through the steam on either side of us. They marched forward in unison, and the gremlins parted to let them through. Warriors in full battle armor, with helmets and masks covering their faces, stepped into the circle. Their insectlike suits looked like something from a science-fiction movie, somehow ancient and modern at the same time. Their breastplates bore the insignia of a barbed-wire crown. Drawing their swords, they stepped forward.

"Meghan, get back," Ash muttered, squaring off against the armored pair coming at him.

"Are you crazy? You can't fight like this—"

"Go!"

Reluctantly, I backed away, but was suddenly grabbed from behind. I yelped and kicked, but was dragged to the edge of the circle, where the gremlins jabbered at me. I twisted around and saw that my captor was a third warrior.

"Meghan!" Ash tried to follow, but the first two knights blocked his way, the sickly light glinting off their iron blades. Glaring at them, Ash flourished his sword and sank into a battle stance.

They lunged at him, swords sweeping down in a blur, coming both low and high. Ash leaped over the first and parried the second, knocking it away with a flurry of ice and sparks. He landed, spun to his left to block the savage back strike, and ducked as the second blade hissed overhead. Whirling around, his sword lashed out, slicing across one armored chest with a grinding screech. The knight staggered back, the image of the wire crown cut through and coated with frost.

They broke away for a moment, facing each other, swords at the ready. Ash was panting, his eyes narrowed in concentration. He didn't look good, and my stomach tightened in fear. The other knights slowly began to circle him, coming at him from different sides like stalking wolves. But before they could get into position, Ash snarled and lunged.

For a moment, the knight he engaged was driven back by the ferocity of the attack. Ash hammered into him relentlessly, his blade slipping through his enemy's guard to smash at his armor. Sparks flew, and the knight stumbled, almost falling. Ash's blade swept up and struck a vicious blow to the side of his head, ripping the helmet clean off.

I gasped. The face beneath the helmet was Ash, or at least a long-lost brother. Same gray eyes, same ebony hair, same pointed ears. The face was a little older, and a scar slashed its way down his cheek, but the similarities were almost perfect.

The real Ash hesitated, just as stunned as I, and that cost him dearly. The second knight rushed up behind him, his sword slashing down, and Ash whirled—too late. His blade caught his opponent's sword, but the blow knocked the weapon from his hands. At the same time, his companion backhanded Ash with his metal gauntlet, striking him behind the ear. Ash crumpled to the ground on his back, and two iron swords were pressed against his throat.

"No!" I tried to run to him, but the third warrior held me and twisted my arms behind my back. Manacles were snapped around my wrists. The two knights kicked Ash onto his stomach and wrenched his arms behind him, binding him similarly. I heard him gasp as the metal touched his flesh, and his doppelgänger jerked him savagely to his feet.

They shoved us toward Ironhorse, who waited for us in the middle of the tracks, swishing his tail. His iron mask gave nothing away.

"GOOD," he snorted. "KING MACHINA WILL BE PLEASED." His red eyes fastened on Ash, who was barely able to stand, and he pinned back his ears. "DISPOSE OF THEIR WEAPONS," he ordered disdainfully.

Ash's face was twisted in agony. Sweat trickled down his brow, and he clenched his teeth. He watched the iron knight take his sword to the edge of the tracks and toss it into a ditch. There was a soft splash as the blade hit the oily water and sank from view. A second knight did the same with the bow. I held my breath, praying they wouldn't see the most important weapon of all.

"THE ARROW, TOO."

My heart sank and despair rose up in me. Ash's doppelgän-

ger approached, yanked the Witchwood arrow from my backpack, and tossed it into the ditch with the rest of the weapons.
My heart plummeted even further, and the tiny sliver of hope
shriveled into a ball and died. That was it, then. Game over.
We had failed.

Ironhorse looked us both over and snorted steam. "NO
FUNNY BUSINESS FROM YOU, PRINCESS," he
warned, blowing smoke at me. "OR MY KNIGHTS WILL
WRAP SO MUCH IRON AROUND THE WINTER
PRINCE THAT HIS SKIN WILL PEEL OFF HIS BONES."
He coughed flame, singeing my eyebrows, and swung his head
toward the waiting fortress. "LET'S GO. KING MACHINA
AWAITS."

CHAPTER TWENTY-TWO

Ash's Final Stand

It was a torturous, nightmare march toward Machina's tower.

A length of chain had been wrapped around my waist, attaching me to Ironhorse, who walked briskly down the tracks without pausing or looking back. Beside me, Ash wore another, and I knew it was hurting him. He kept stumbling, barely managing to keep his feet as we followed Ironhorse down the railroad tracks. Gremlins cavorted around us, poking and pinching and laughing at our torment. The knights walked to either side and refused to let Ash step off the iron tracks, shoving him back if he tried. Once, he fell, and was dragged several yards before he finally got his feet under him again. Angry red burns crisscrossed his face where his skin had touched the metal tracks, and I ached for him.

The sky clouded over, changing from yellow-gray to an ominous reddish-black in a matter of moments. Ironhorse stopped and craned his neck, flaring his nostrils.

"DAMN," he muttered, stomping a hoof. "IT'S GOING TO RAIN SOON."

My stomach turned at the thought of the acid rain. Lightning flashed, filling the air with a sharp tang.

"QUICKLY, BEFORE THE STORM HITS." The horse stepped off the tracks, breaking into a trot as thunder growled overhead. My legs burned as I broke into an awkward sprint behind him, every muscle screaming in protest, but it was either keep up or be dragged. Ash stumbled and fell, and this time he did not get up.

A drop of rain spattered against my leg, and a searing pain lanced through me. I gasped. More drops fell, hissing as they struck the ground. The air reeked of chemicals, and I heard a few gremlins screech as the raindrops hit them, as well.

A silvery curtain of rain crept toward us. It caught up to a few of the slower gremlins, engulfing them. They screamed and writhed, sparks leaping off their bodies, until they gave a final twitch and were still. The rain came on.

Panicked, I looked up to see Ironhorse leading us into a mine shaft. We ducked under the roof just as the storm swept over us, catching a few more gremlins, who squealed and danced around in agony, holes burned through their skin. The rest of the gremlins jeered and laughed. I turned away before I was sick

Ash lay motionless on the ground, covered in dust and blood from where he'd been dragged. Steam curled off his body where the raindrops had hit. He groaned and tried to get up, but didn't quite make it off his back. Snickering, a few gremlins started poking him, climbing onto his chest to slap his face. He flinched and turned away, but this only encouraged them further.

"Stop it!" I lunged and kicked a gremlin with all my might, launching it away from Ash like a football. The others turned on me, and I lashed out at them all, kicking and stomping.

Hissing, they swarmed up my pant legs, pulling my hair and raking me with their claws. One sank its razor-sharp teeth into my shoulder, and I screamed.

"ENOUGH!" Ironhorse's shout made the ceiling tremble. Dirt showered us, and the gremlins skittered back. Blood ran down my skin from a dozen tiny wounds, and my shoulder throbbed where the gremlin had bitten it. Ironhorse glared at me, swishing his tail against his flanks, then tossed his head at the knights.

"TAKE THEM INTO THE TUNNELS," he ordered with a hint of exasperation. "MAKE SURE THEY DO NOT ESCAPE. IF THE STORM DOES NOT ABATE, WE MIGHT BE HERE AWHILE."

The chains binding us to Ironhorse were released. Two knights pulled Ash to his feet and half dragged him away down a tunnel. The last knight, the one with Ash's face, took me by the arm and led me after his brothers.

We paused at a junction where several tunnels merged. Wooden tracks led off into the darkness, and rickety cars half-filled with ore sat off to the sides. Thick wooden beams held up the ceiling, standing along the tracks every few feet. A few lanterns had been nailed into the wood, though most were broken and dark. In the flickering torchlight, glimmering veins of iron snaked across the walls.

We continued down a tunnel that dead-ended in a small room, where two wooden posts stood side by side in the middle of the room. A few crates and an abandoned pickax lay stacked in a corner. The knights pushed Ash against one post, unlocked a cuff, and reattached it behind the beam, securing him in place. The flesh under the metal band was red and burned, and he jerked when they snapped it around his wrist again. I bit my lip in sympathy.

The knight who'd first caught me straightened and patted Ash on the cheek, chuckling as Ash flinched away from the steel gauntlet. "Feels good, don't it, worm?" he said, and I started in surprise. This was the first time I'd heard one of them speak. "You oldbloods are completely weak, aren't you? It's high time you moved over. You're obsolete now, ancient. Your time is done."

Ash raised his head and stared the other faery in the eye. "Bold words for someone who stood aside and wrestled a girl while his brothers fought for him."

The knight backhanded him. I cried out in fury and started forward, but the knight behind me grabbed my arm. "Leave him alone, Quintus," he said in a calm voice.

Quintus sneered. "Feeling sorry for him, Tertius? Maybe some brotherly affection for your twin here?"

"We're not supposed to speak to the oldbloods," Tertius replied in the same cool tone. "You know that. Or should I inform Ironhorse?"

Quintus spat on the ground. "You were always weak, Tertius," he snarled. "Too softhearted to be made of iron. You're a disgrace to the brotherhood." He spun on a heel and marched up the tunnel, the last knight following behind. Their boots rang loudly on the stone floor, then faded into silence.

"Jerk," I muttered as the remaining knight maneuvered me against the post. "Your name's Tertius, right?"

He unlocked a shackle and wound the chain around the beam, not looking at me. "Yes."

"Help us," I pleaded. "You're not like them, I can feel it. Please, I have to rescue my brother and get him out of here. I'll make a deal with you, if that's what it takes. Please, help us."

For a moment, he met my eyes. I was struck again by how much he resembled Ash. His eyes were gunmetal-gray instead of silver, and the scar made him look older, but he had that same intense, honorable face. He paused, and for a moment, I dared to hope. But then he snapped the cuff around my wrist and stepped away, his eyes darkening to black.

"I'm a Knight of the Iron Crown," he said, his voice as hard as steel. "I will not betray my brothers, or my king."

He turned and walked away without looking back.

In the flickering darkness of the tunnel, I heard Ash's raspy breathing, the shift of gravel as he sank into a sitting position. "Ash?" I called softly, my voice echoing down the shafts. "You all right?"

Silence for a moment. When Ash finally spoke, his voice was so low I could barely hear it. "Sorry, princess," he murmured, almost to himself. "Looks like I won't be able to uphold our contract after all."

"Don't give up," I told him, feeling like a hypocrite as I struggled with my own despair. "We'll get out of this somehow. We just have to keep our heads." A thought came to me, and I lowered my voice. "Can't you freeze the chains until they shatter, like you did in the factory?"

A low, humorless chuckle. "Right now, it's taking everything I have not to pass out," Ash muttered, sounding pained. "If you have any of that power the Elder Dryad was talking about, now would be the time to use it."

I nodded. What did we have to lose? Closing my eyes, I concentrated on feeling the glamour around us, trying to remember what Grimalkin had taught me.

Nothing. Except for a flicker of raw determination from Ash, there were no emotions to draw from, no hopes or dreams or anything. Everything here was dead, devoid of life, passionless. The iron fey were too machinelike—cold, logical, and calculating—and their world reflected that.

Refusing to give up, I pushed deeper, trying to get past the banal surface. This had been the Nevernever once. There had to be something left untouched by Machina's influence.

I felt a pulse of life, somewhere deep below. A lone tree, poisoned and dying, but still clinging to life. Its branches were slowly turning to metal, but the roots, and the heart of the tree, were not yet corrupted. It stirred to my presence, a tiny piece of the Nevernever in the void of nothingness. But before I could do anything, shuffling footsteps broke my concentration, and the link faded away.

I opened my eyes. The light in the tunnel had gone out, leaving us in pitch blackness. I heard creatures moving toward us, surrounding us, and I couldn't see a thing. My mind jumped to all sorts of terrifying conclusions: giant rats, huge cockroaches, massive underground spiders. I almost fainted when something patted my arm, but then I heard the low babble of familiar voices.

A yellowish beam clicked on in the darkness: a flashlight. It illuminated the curious, wrinkled faces of a half-dozen pack rats, blinking in the sudden light. Surprised, I stared at them as they chittered at me in their odd language. Several surrounded Ash, pulling at his sleeves.

"What are you doing here?" I whispered. They jabbered nonsense and tugged on my clothes, as if trying to drag me away. "Are you trying to help?"

The pack rat with the tricycle stepped forward. He pointed at me, then at the back of the room. In the flashlight beam, I saw the mouth of another tunnel, nearly invisible in the shadows. It was only partly formed, as if the miners had started digging only to abandon it. A way out? My heart leaped. The pack rat jibbered impatiently and beckoned me forward.

"I can't," I told him, rattling my chain. "I can't move."

He chattered at the rest of them, and they shuffled forward. One by one, they reached behind them, to the lumps of trash on their backs, and began pulling things out.

"What are they doing?" Ash muttered.

I couldn't begin to answer. One of the pack rats produced an electric drill, showing it to the leader, who shook his head. Another pulled out a butterfly knife, but the leader declined that, too, as well as a lighter, a hammer, and a round alarm clock. Then one of the smaller pack rats chittered excitedly and stepped forward, holding something long and metallic.

A pair of bolt cutters.

The lead pack rat jabbered and pointed. But at the same time, I heard the clank of steel boots coming down the tunnel, and the scuttling of thousands of claws on rock. My stomach twisted. The knights were coming back, and so were the gremlins.

"Hurry!" I urged, as the pack rat waddled over and began sawing at the chain. Lights appeared in the distance, bobbing along the ground; gremlins with lanterns or flashlights. Laughter drifted into the room, and my stomach churned. *Hurry!* I thought, furious with the pack rat's slow progress. *We're not going to make it! They'll be here any second!*

I felt the snap of links as they parted, and I was free.

Grabbing the bolt cutters, I raced over to Ash. The lights moved closer and closer, and the hissing of gremlins could be heard down the tunnel. I inserted the chain between the metal jaws and squeezed the handles, but the tool was rusty and hard to use. Snarling curses, I gripped the handles and pushed.

"Leave me," Ash muttered as I strained to close the jaws. "I won't be able to help, and I'll only slow you down. Just go."

"I'm not leaving you," I panted, gritting my teeth and pushing with all my might.

"Meghan..."

"I'm not leaving you!" I snapped, fighting angry tears. Stupid chain! Why wouldn't it break already? I threw my whole weight against it, sawing with a fury born of fear.

"Remember when I told you about your weakness?" Ash murmured, craning his head to look at me. Though his eyes were hard, glazed over with pain, his voice was gentle. "You have to make that choice now. What is most important to you?"

"Shut up!" Tears blinded me, and I blinked them away. "You can't ask me to make that decision. You're important to me, too, dammit. I'm not leaving you behind, so just shut up."

The first wave of gremlins entered the tunnel and shrieked in alarm when they saw me. With a snarl of fear and terror, I gave the bolt cutters a final jerk, and the chain finally snapped. Ash pulled himself to his feet as the gremlins howled with outrage and surged forward.

We ran for the hidden tunnel, following the pack rats as they scuttled through. The corridor was low and narrow; I had to duck my head to avoid the ceiling, and the walls scraped my arms as we fled. Behind us, gremlins poured through the opening like ants, skittering along the walls and ceiling, hissing as they pursued.

Ash suddenly stopped. Turning to face the horde, he raised a pickax like a baseball bat, bracing himself against the wall. I gave a start; he must've snatched it from the crates, right before we reached the tunnel. The broken chains, still dangling from his wrists, trembled as his arms shook. The gremlins halted a few yards away, their eyes bright as they analyzed this new threat. As one they began edging forward.

"Ash!" I called. "What are you doing? Come on!"

"Meghan." Ash's voice, despite the pain below the surface, was calm. "I hope you find your brother. If you see Puck again, tell him I regret having to step out of our duel."

"Ash, no! Don't do this!"

I felt him smile. "You made me feel alive again," he murmured.

Screeching, the gremlins attacked.

Ash smashed two of them senseless with the pickax, ducked as another leaped at his head, and was overwhelmed. They swarmed over him, clinging to his legs and arms, biting and clawing. He staggered and dropped to a knee, and they skittered up his back, until I could no longer see him through the writhing mass of gremlins. Still, Ash fought on; with a snarl, he surged back to his feet, sending several gremlins flying only to have a dozen more take their place.

"Meghan, go!" His voice was a hoarse rasp as he slammed a gremlin into the wall. *"Now!"*

Choking on tears, I turned and fled. I followed the beckoning pack rats until the tunnel split and branched off in several directions. A pack rat pulled something from his lump and waved it at the leader. I gasped when I saw that it was a stick of dynamite. The leader snarled something, and another pack rat scuttled forward with a lighter.

I couldn't help but look back, just in time to see Ash finally pulled under the sea of gremlins and lost from view. The gremlins screeched in triumph and flowed toward us.

The fuse sputtered to life. The lead pack rat hissed at me and pointed to the tunnels, where the rest of them were vanishing.

Tears flowing down my cheeks, I followed, and the pack rat holding the dynamite flung it toward the oncoming gremlins.

The *boom* shook the ceiling. Dirt and rocks rained down on me, filling the air with grit. I coughed and sagged against the wall, waiting for the chaos to die down. When everything was still, I looked up to see that the entrance to the tunnel had caved in. The pack rats were moaning softly. One of their own hadn't made it through in time.

Sagging down the wall, I pulled my knees to my chest and joined them in their grieving, feeling I'd left my heart in the tunnel where Ash had fallen.

CHAPTER TWENTY-THREE

The Iron King

For several minutes, I sat there, too numb to even cry. I couldn't believe that Ash was really dead. I kept staring at the caved-in wall, half expecting him to somehow, miraculously, push through the rubble, bruised and bloody, but alive.

How long I sat there, I don't know. But eventually, the lead pack rat tugged gently on my sleeve. His eyes, solemn and sad, met mine, before he turned away and beckoned me to follow. With one final look at the cave-in behind us, I trailed them into the tunnels.

We walked for hours, and gradually, the tunnels turned into natural caverns, dripping with water and stalactites. The pack rats loaned me a flashlight, and as I shined it about the caves, I saw that the floor was littered with strange items, a fender here, a toy robot there. It seemed we were heading deep into the pack rats' nest, for the farther we went, the more junk lay strewn about.

At last, we entered a cathedral-like cave, where the ceiling soared up into blackness, and the walls were piled with mountains of trash, resembling the Wasteland in miniature.

In the center of the room, sitting on a throne made entirely of junk, was an old, old man. His skin was gray, and I don't mean pale or ashen, but metallic-gray, mercury-gray. His white hair flowed past his feet, nearly touching the floor, as if he hadn't moved from his chair in centuries. The pack rats shuffled around him, holding up various items, placing them at his feet. I saw my iPod among them. The old man smiled as the pack rats chittered and milled around him like eager dogs, then his pale green eyes looked up at me.

He blinked several times, as if he couldn't trust what he was seeing. I held my breath. Was this Machina? Had the pack rats brought me straight to the Iron King? For an all-powerful ruler, I didn't expect him to be so...old.

"Well," he wheezed at last, "my subjects have brought me many curious things over the years, but I do believe this is the most unusual. Who are you, girl? Why are you here?"

"I... My name is Meghan, sir. Meghan Chase. I'm looking for my brother."

"Your brother?" The old man looked at the pack rats, aghast. "I don't recall you bringing home a child. What has gotten into you?"

The pack rats chittered, shaking their heads. The old man frowned at them as they jabbered and bounced around, then looked back at me. "My subjects tell me they have not encountered anyone except you and your friend out in the Wasteland. Why do you think your brother would be here?"

"I..." I stopped, gazing around at the dingy cavern, the pack rats, the frail old man. This couldn't be right. "I'm sorry," I continued, feeling stupid and confused, "but...are you Machina, the Iron King?"

"Ah." The old man settled back, lacing his hands together.

"Now I understand. Machina has your brother, yes? And you are on your way to rescue him."

"Yes." I relaxed, breathing a sigh of relief. "Then, I guess you're not the Iron King?"

"Oh, I wouldn't say that." The old man smiled, and my guard went back up. He chuckled. "Worry not, child. I mean you no harm. But you would do well to abandon your plan to rescue your brother. Machina is too strong. No weapon can hurt him. You'd be throwing your life away."

I remembered the Witchwood arrow, lying at the bottom of a ditch, and my heart constricted. "I know," I whispered. "But I have to try. I've come this far. I'm not giving up now."

"If Machina has stolen your brother, he must be waiting for you," the old man said, leaning forward. "He wants you for something. I can feel the power in you, my girl, but it will not be enough. The Iron King is a master of manipulation. He will use you to further his own schemes, and you will not be able to resist. Go home, girl. Forget what you have lost and go home."

"Forget?" I thought of my friends, who had sacrificed everything to see me this far. Puck. The Elder Dryad. Ash. "No," I murmured, a lump forming in my throat. "I can never forget. Even if it's hopeless, I have to go on. I owe everyone that much."

"Foolish girl," the old man growled. "I know more about Machina than anyone—his ways, his power, the way his mind works—and yet you still will not hear me. Very well. Rush to your doom, like everyone who came before you. You will see, as I did, far too late. Machina cannot be defeated. I only wish I'd listened to my councilors when they told me as much."

"*You* tried to defeat him?" I stared, trying to imagine the frail old man fighting anyone and failing. "When? Why?"

"Because," the old man explained patiently, "I was once the Iron King.

"My name is Ferrum," the old man explained into my shocked silence. "As you no doubt noticed, I am old. Older than that whelp Machina, older than all of the iron fey. I was the first, you see, born of the forges, when mankind first began to experiment with iron. I rose from their imagination, from their ambition to conquer the world with a metal that could slice through bronze like paper. I was there when the world started to shift, when humans took their first steps out of the Dark Ages into civilization.

"For many years, I thought I was alone. But mankind is never satisfied—he is always reaching, always trying for something better. Others came, others like me, risen from these dreams of a new world. They accepted me as their king, and for centuries, we remained hidden, isolated from the rest of the fey. I realized, beyond a doubt, that if the courts knew of our existence, they would unite to destroy us.

"Then, with the invention of computers, the gremlins came, and the bugs. Given life by the fear of monsters lurking in machines, these were more chaotic than the other fey, violent and destructive. They spread to every part of the world. As technology became a driving force in every country, powerful new fey rose into existence. Virus. Glitch. And Machina, the most powerful of all. He was not content to sit and hide. His plan was conquest, to spread throughout the Nevernever like a virus, destroying all who opposed him. He was my First— my most powerful lieutenant—and we clashed on several occasions. My advisers told me to banish him, to imprison him, even to kill him. They were afraid of him, and rightly so, but I was blind to the danger.

"Of course, it was only a matter of time before Machina

turned on me. Gathering an army of like-minded fey to his side, he attacked the fortress from within, slaughtering all who were loyal to me. My forces fought back, but we were old and obsolete, no match for Machina's cruel army.

"In the end, I sat on my throne and watched him approach, knowing I was going to die. But, as Machina threw me to the floor, he laughed and said he would not kill me. He would let me fade away a bit at a time, becoming obscure and forgotten, until no one remembered my name or who I was. And, as he settled back upon my throne, I felt my power slip away and flow into Machina, acknowledging him as the new Iron King.

"So, now I live here." Ferrum gestured to the cavern and the pack rats milling about. "In a forgotten cave, sitting on a throne made of garbage, king of the mighty trash collectors. A noble title, is it not?" His lips twisted into a bitter smile. "These creatures are very loyal, bringing me offerings that I cannot use, making me ruler of this junk heap. They have accepted me as their king, but what good is that? They cannot give me back my throne, and yet they are the only ones that keep me from fading away. I cannot die, but I can hardly bear to live, knowing what I've lost. What was stolen from me. And Machina is the one who designed it all!"

He slumped on his throne and buried his face in his hands. The pack rats shuffled forward, patting him, making worried chittering sounds. Watching him, I felt a surge of sympathy and disgust.

"I've lost things, too," I said, over the sound of his quiet sobbing. "Machina has stolen a lot from me. But I'm not going to sit on a chair and wait for him. I'll confront him, invincible or not, and somehow I'll take back what's mine. Or I'll die trying. Either way, I'm not giving up."

He stared at me through his fingers, his frail form shaking

with tears. He sniffed and lowered his hands, his face sullen and dark.

"Go, then," Ferrum whispered, shooing me away. "I cannot sway you. Perhaps a single unarmed girl will succeed where an entire army has failed." He laughed then, bitter and petulant, and I felt a flicker of annoyance. "Good luck to you, foolish one. If you will not listen to me, you are welcome here no longer. My subjects will take you under his fortress, through the secret tunnels that honeycomb the land. It's the quickest way to rush to your destruction. Now, go. I am through with you."

I didn't bow. I didn't thank him for his help. I only turned and followed the pack rats out of the cave, feeling the hateful glare of the deposed king on my back.

More tunnels. The brief respite with the last Iron King wasn't enough to stave off my exhaustion. We rested infrequently, and I caught what little sleep I could. The pack rats gave me some strange mushrooms to chew on, tiny white things that glowed in the dark and tasted like mold, but allowed me to see in pitch blackness as if it were twilight. This was a good thing, because my flashlight eventually flickered and died, and no one offered fresh batteries.

I lost track of time. All the caverns and tunnels seemed to meld together into one giant, impossible maze. I knew that, even if I did get into Machina's fortress and rescue Ethan, I wouldn't be getting out the same way.

The tunnel fell away, and suddenly I stood on a stone bridge across a vast precipice, jagged rocks spearing up from the bottom. Around me, on the walls and ceiling, hanging precariously close to the bridge, massive iron gears turned and creaked, making the ground vibrate. The closest gears were

JULIE KAGAWA

easily three times my height; some were even larger. It was like being inside a giant clock, and the noise was deafening.

We must be under Machina's fortress, I thought, gazing around in awe. *Wonder what those huge gears are for?*

There was a tug on my arm, and I turned to see the lead pack rat point across the bridge, his jabbering lost in the grinding noise of the room. I understood. They had taken me as far as they could go. Now the last part of the trek would be on my own.

I nodded to show I understood and started forward, when he grabbed my hand. Holding my wrist, he beckoned to his pack rats, chattering at them. Two waddled forward, reaching back for some item on their humps.

"It's okay," I told them. "I don't need any—"

My voice died away. The first pack rat drew out a long sheath with a familiar hilt, gleaming blue-black in the darkness. I caught my breath. "Is that...?"

He handed it over solemnly. Grasping the hilt, I pulled the blade free, washing the chamber in pale blue light. Steam writhed on the edge of Ash's blade, and a lump caught in my throat.

Oh, Ash.

I sheathed the blade and fastened it around my waist, grimly tightening the belt. "I appreciate this," I told the pack rats, unsure if they understood. They chattered at me and still didn't move, and the leader pointed at the second, smaller pack rat who'd approached. He blinked and reached back, drawing forward a slightly battered bow and—

For the second time, my heart stopped. The pack rat held up the Witchwood arrow, slimy and covered with oil, but otherwise intact. I took it reverently, my mind spinning. They could have given it to Ferrum, but they hadn't, saving it for me all this time. The arrow pulsed in my hands, still alive and deadly.

I didn't think. I dropped to my knees and hugged the pack rats, both the leader and the small one. They squeaked in surprise. Their lumps poked my skin, making it impossible to get my arms around them completely, but I didn't care. When I rose, I thought the leader was blushing, though it was difficult to see in the darkness, and the small one grinned from ear to ear.

"Thank you," I said, putting as much sincerity into my voice as I could. "Really, 'thank you' isn't enough, but it's all I have. You guys are amazing."

They jabbered at me and patted my hands. I wished I knew what they were saying. Then, with a sharp bark from the leader, they turned and faded into the tunnels. The small one looked back once, his eyes bright in the gloom, and then they were gone.

I straightened, tucking the arrow into my belt much as Ash had done. Gripping the bow, and with Ash's sword hanging from my waist, I stepped beneath Machina's tower.

I followed the walkway, which turned from stone to iron grating, through the giant maze of clockwork, setting my teeth against the grinding of metal on metal. I found a twisting iron staircase and followed it up to a trapdoor, which opened with a ringing bang. I winced and peeked out cautiously.

Nothing. The room I stared into was empty, save for the enormous boiler ovens that glowed red and filled the air with hissing steam.

"All right," I muttered, climbing out of the floor. My face and shirt were already drenched with sweat from the shimmering heat. "I'm inside. Where to now, I wonder?"

Up.

The thought came unbidden, and yet I knew it was right. Machina, and Ethan, would be at the top of the tower.

Clanking footsteps caught my attention, and I ducked behind one of the boilers, ignoring the searing heat radiating from the metal. Several figures entered the room, short and stocky and dressed in bulky canvas suits like firemen. They wore breathing apparatus that covered their entire faces, a pair of tubes snaking from the mouth to some kind of tank on their back. They stomped among the boilers, pinging on them with wrenches, checking the numerous pipes and valves. A large ring of keys dangled from each of their belts, jingling as they moved. As I scrambled back to an isolated corner, an idea floated to mind.

I followed them, staying hidden in the steam and shadows, observing how they worked. The workers didn't converse or speak to one another, being too caught up in their own work, which suited me fine. One broke off from the rest of the group, which paid him no attention as he wandered off into the steam. I trailed him down a hallway made of pipes, watching as he bent to check a hissing crack in the metal, and snuck up behind him.

Drawing Ash's sword, I waited until he turned around before stepping up and pressing the point of the blade against his chest. The worker jumped and scuttled backward, but the network of pipes trapped him between me and the exit. I stepped forward and angled the blade at his throat.

"Don't move," I snarled as fiercely as I could. He nodded and held up his gloved hands. My heart pounded, but I rushed on, poking at him with the blade. "Do exactly as I say and I won't kill you, all right? Take off your suit."

He obeyed, shedding his outer clothes and taking off the

mask, revealing a sweaty little man with a thick black beard.
A dwarf, and an ordinary-looking one at that; no steel skin,
no cables coming out of his head, nothing to mark him as an
iron fey. He glared at me with coal-black eyes, his arms rippling with muscle, and broke into a sneer.

"Come at last, have you?" He spat on the ground near a
pipe, where it sizzled noisily. "We were all wondering what
route you'd end up taking. Well, if you're going to kill me,
girl, get it over with."

"I'm not here to kill anyone," I said carefully, keeping the
sword trained on him as I'd seen Ash do. "I'm only here for
my brother."

The dwarf snorted. "He's upstairs in the throne room with
Machina. Top west tower. Good luck getting to him."

I narrowed my eyes. "You're being awfully helpful. Why
should I believe you?"

"Bah, we don't care about Machina or your whiny brother,
girl." The dwarf hawked and spat on a pipe, where it bubbled
like acid. "Our job is to keep this place running, not play
court with a bunch of snotty aristocrats. Machina's business
is his own, and I'll ask you to keep me out of it."

"So, you're not going to stop me?"

"Do you have lead in your ears? I don't care what you do,
girl! So kill me or leave me the hell alone, would you? I won't
get in your way, if you don't get in mine."

"All right." I lowered the sword. "But I'll need your suit."

"Fine, take it." The dwarf kicked it toward me with a steel-
toed boot. "We've got several. Now, can I get back to work, or
do you have more inane demands to keep me from my job?"

I hesitated. I didn't want to hurt him, but I couldn't leave
him running loose. No matter what he said, he could tell the
other workers, and I was pretty sure I couldn't fight off all of

them. I looked around and saw another trapdoor, like the one I'd come up from a few feet away.

I pointed at it with the sword. "Open that and get down there."

"Into the Cogworks?"

"Leave your boots. And your keys."

He glowered, and I raised my sword, ready to slash if he lunged at me. But the dwarf growled a curse, stalked over to the metal grate, and shoved a key into the lock. Pushing it open with a bang, he wrenched off his boots and stomped down the twisting staircase, making it ring with every step. With the dwarf glaring up at me, I shut the door and locked it, ignoring the guilt that gnawed my insides.

I dressed in the dwarf's suit, which was hot and heavy and reeked of sweat. I gagged as I slipped it on. It was too short, but between the suit's bagginess and my skinny frame, I made it work. My calves stuck out of the pant legs, but I shoved my sneakers into the dwarf's boots and it wasn't so noticeable. At least, I hoped it wasn't. I heaved the tank onto my back, finding it surprisingly light, and put on the mask. Cool, sweet air hit my face, and I sighed in relief.

Now the only problem was the sword and the bow. I figured the workmen of the tower didn't stomp around with weapons, so I found a piece of canvas and wrapped them up in it, tucking it under my arm. The Witchwood arrow was still secured to my belt inside the suit.

Heart pounding, I returned to the boiler room, where the other dwarfs were shuffling out in a broken line. Taking a deep breath to calm my twisting stomach, I joined them, keeping my head down and not making eye contact. No one paid any attention to me, and I followed them up a long flight of stairs, until we reached the main tower.

★ ★ ★

Machina's fortress was huge, metallic, and sharp. Thorned creepers crawled over the ramparts, their barbs made of metal. Jagged shards jutted away from the walls for no apparent reason. Everything was harsh lines and sharp edges, even the fey that lived here. Besides the ever-present gremlins, I saw more armored knights, hounds made of clockwork, and creatures that looked like metallic praying mantises, their bladed arms and silvery antennae glinting in the dim light.

The dwarfs scattered as they left the staircase, breaking away in little groups of twos and threes. I drifted away from the rapidly diminishing crowd and followed the wall, trying to look as if I had a purpose. Gremlins scuttled along the walls, chasing one another and tormenting the other fey. Computer mice with tiny ears, feet, and blinking red eyes scurried away as I approached. Once, a gremlin landed on one, eliciting a high-pitched squeak, before stuffing the tiny creature into its mouth and crunching the sparks. It grinned at me, the mouse's tail hanging between its pointed teeth, and scuttled off again. Wrinkling my nose, I continued walking.

At last I discovered a staircase, spiraling up hundreds of feet along the tower walls. Gazing up at the infinite number of stairs, I felt a pull in my stomach. This was the one. Ethan was up there. And Machina.

I felt a pain in my heart, as if there was something…someone else I should remember. But the memory skipped away, out of reach. With my heart fluttering around my ribs like a crazed bat, I started the last leg of my journey.

There were small, narrow windows every twenty steps up the stairs. I peered out once and saw the open sky, with strange glittering birds soaring on the wind. At the top of the stairs stood an iron door, bearing the insignia of a barbed crown. I quickly shed the dwarf's clothing, relieved to be out of the bulky, smelly garments. Taking off the bow, I carefully fit the Witchwood arrow to the string. When the arrow was nocked, it began to throb even faster, as if its heartbeat raced in excitement.

And, standing at the last door in the Iron King's tower, I hesitated. Could I really do this, kill a living creature? I wasn't a warrior like Ash or a brilliant trickster like Puck. I wasn't smart like Grim, and I certainly didn't have the power of my father, Oberon. I was just me, Meghan Chase, an ordinary high school student. Nothing special.

No. The voice in my head was mine, and it wasn't. *You're more than that. You're the daughter of Oberon and Melissa Chase. You're the key to preventing a faery war. Friend of Puck; sister to Ethan; beloved of Ash: you are much more than you think. You have everything you need. All that is left is to step forward.*

Step forward. I could do that. Taking a deep breath, I pushed the door open.

I stood at the entrance of an enormous garden, the door creaking as it swung away from me. The smooth iron walls surrounding me were topped with jagged spines, silhouetted black against the open sky. Trees lined a stony path, but they were all made of metal, their branches twisted and sharp. Birds watched me from the steel limbs. When they fluttered their wings, it sounded like knives scraping against one another.

In the center of the garden, where all the paths converged, a fountain stood. Made not of marble or plaster, but of different-size gearheads, turning sluggishly with the water's flow. I squinted and looked closer. On the bottom cog, lying on his back as the gear slowly spun him around, was a figure.

It was Ash.

I didn't scream his name. I didn't run to him, though every

fiber in my body was telling me to do so. Forcing myself to be calm, I looked around the garden, wary of traps and sudden ambushes. But there weren't many places for attackers to hide; except for the metal trees and a few thorny vines, the garden seemed empty.

Only when I'd made sure I was alone did I sprint across the stony ground to the fountain.

Don't be dead. Please, don't be dead. My heart plummeted when I saw him. He'd been chained to the cog, wrapped in metal links, spinning round and round in an endless circle. One leg dangled over the edge; the other was folded beneath him. His shirt had been ripped to shreds, the skin a shocking contrast of pale flesh and vivid red claw marks. The flesh where the chains touched him was raw and crimson. He didn't appear to be breathing.

Hands trembling, I drew the sword. The first slash shattered most of the links, the second cracked the gearhead nearly in two. The chains slid away, and the cog squealed as it ground to a halt. I dropped the blade and pulled Ash off the fountain, his body limp and cold in my arms.

"Ash." I cradled him in my lap, beyond tears, beyond anything but an awful, yawning emptiness. "Ash, come on." I shook him a little. "Don't do this to me. Open your eyes. Wake up. Please…"

His body was limp, unresponsive. I bit my lip hard enough to taste blood, and buried my face in his neck. "I'm sorry," I whispered, and now I did start to cry. Tears ran from my closed eyelids and down his clammy skin. "I'm so sorry. I wish you hadn't come. I wish I never agreed to that stupid contract. This is my fault, all of it. Puck and the dryad and Grim, and now you—" It was getting hard to speak, my voice was so choked with tears. "I'm sorry," I murmured again, for lack of anything else to say. "Sorry, so sorry—"

Something fluttered under my cheek. Blinking, hiccuping, I pulled back and looked at his face. The skin was still pale, but I caught a flicker of movement beneath his eyelids. Heart pounding, I lowered my head and brushed a kiss to his mouth. His lips parted, and a broken sigh escaped him.

I breathed his name in relief. His eyes opened and flickered to mine, confused, as if he wasn't sure if he was dreaming or not. He moved his lips, but it was a few tries before anything came out.

"Meghan?"

"Yes," I whispered immediately. "I'm here."

His hand came up, fingers resting on my cheek, trailing down my skin. "I...dreamed you...would come," he murmured, before his eyes cleared a bit and his face darkened. "You shouldn't...be here," he gasped, digging his fingers into my arm. "This...a trap."

And then, I heard it—horrible, dark laughter, rising up from the wall behind us. The gears in the fountain shivered, then began to turn backward. With a loud clanking and grinding, the wall behind us sank into the ground, revealing another part of the garden. Metal trees lined the path to an enormous iron throne, spiking into the sky. A squadron of armored knights stood at the foot of the throne with weapons drawn, pointed at me. Another squad entered through the door and slammed it shut, trapping us between them.

Standing at the top of his throne, surveying us all with a look of grim satisfaction, was Machina, the Iron King.

CHAPTER TWENTY-FOUR

Machina

The figure on the throne threw me a smile as sharp as razors. "Meghan Chase," he murmured, his scintillating voice echoing over the garden. "Welcome. I've been expecting you."

I gently laid Ash down, ignoring his protests, and stepped forward, shielding him behind me. My heart pounded. I didn't know what I expected the Iron King to look like, but it wasn't this. The figure on the throne stood tall and elegant, with flowing silver hair and the pointed ears of the fey nobility. He faintly resembled Oberon, refined and graceful, yet incredibly powerful. Unlike Oberon and the finery of the Summer Court, the Iron King wore a stark black coat that flapped in the wind. Energy crackled around him, like thunder with no sound, and I caught flashes of lightning in his slanted black eyes. A metal stud glittered in one ear, a Bluetooth phone in the other. His face was beautiful and arrogant, all sharp planes and angles; I felt I could cut myself on his cheek if I got too close. And yet, when he smiled, it lit up the whole room. A strange, silvery cloak lay across his shoulders, wriggling slightly as if it were alive.

I snatched the bow and arrow off the ground, bringing it to bear on the Iron King. This might be the only chance I got. The Witchwood pulsed in my hands as I drew back the string, aiming the tip at Machina's chest. The knights shouted in alarm and started forward, but they were too late. I released the string with a yell of triumph, seeing it speed right on target, toward the heart of the Iron King.

And Machina's cloak came alive.

Silvery cables unraveled with lightning speed, springing from his shoulders and spine. They spread around Machina like a halo of metal wings, wickedly barbed on one end, needle points glinting in the light. They whipped forward to protect the Iron King, knocking the Witchwood away, sending it flying in another direction. I watched the arrow strike a metal tree and snap in two, fluttering to the ground in pieces. Someone screamed in rage and horror, and I realized it was me.

The guards rushed us, their swords raised, and I watched them come with a certain detachment. I was aware of Ash, trying to get to his feet to protect me, and knew it was too late. The arrow had failed, and we were about to die.

"Stop."

Machina's voice wasn't loud. He didn't scream or bellow the order, but every knight jerked to a halt as if pulled by invisible string. The Iron King floated down from his throne, the cables writhing slowly behind him like hungry snakes. His feet touched the floor, and he smiled at me, completely unconcerned with the fact that I had just tried to kill him.

"Leave," he told the knights without taking his eyes from me. Several of them jerked their heads up in surprise.

"My king?" stammered one, and I recognized his voice. Quintus, one of the knights who'd been with Ironhorse in the mines. I wondered if Tertius was here, too.

"The lady is uncomfortable with your presence," Machina went on, not looking away from me. "I do not wish her to be uncomfortable. Go. I will take care of her, and the Winter prince."

"But, sire—"

Machina didn't move. One of his cables whipped out, almost too fast to see, punching through the knight's armor and out his back. The cable lifted Quintus high in the air and threw him into the wall. Quintus clanged against the metal and slumped motionless to the ground, a jagged hole through his breastplate. Dark, oily blood pooled beneath him.

"Leave," Machina repeated softly, and the knights scrambled to obey. They filed out through the door and slammed it shut, and we were alone with the Iron King.

Machina regarded me with depthless black eyes. "You are as beautiful as I imagined," he said, walking forward, his cables coiling behind him. "Beautiful, fiery, determined." He stopped a few yards away, the cables settling back into that living cloak. "Perfect."

With a final glance at Ash, still slumped next to the fountain, I stepped forward. "I'm here for my brother," I said, relieved that my voice didn't tremble. "Please, let him go. Let me take him home."

Machina regarded me silently, then gestured behind him. A loud clanking began, and something rose out of the ground beside his throne, as if it was borne on an elevator. A large, wrought-iron birdcage came into view. Inside…

"Ethan!" I started forward, but Machina's cables whipped out, blocking my path. Ethan gripped the bars of the cage, peering out with frightened blue eyes. His voice rang shrilly over the courtyard.

"Meggie!"

Behind me, Ash growled a curse and tried to stand. I turned on Machina furiously. "Let him go! He's only a little kid! What do you want with him, anyway?"

"My dear, you misunderstand me." Machina's cables waved threateningly, moving me back. "I did not take your brother because I wanted him. I did it because I knew it would bring you here."

"Why?" I demanded, whirling on him. "Why kidnap Ethan? Why not just take me instead? Why drag him into all this?"

Machina smiled. "You were well protected, Meghan Chase. Robin Goodfellow is a formidable bodyguard, and I could not risk taking you without drawing attention to myself and my realm. Fortunately, your brother had no such protection. Better to draw you here, of your own volition, than risk the wrath of Oberon and the Seelie Court. Besides…" Machina's eyes narrowed to black slits, though he still smiled at me. "I needed to test you, make certain you were truly the one. If you could not reach my tower on your own, you were not worthy."

"Worthy of what?" Suddenly, I was very tired. Tired and desperate to save my brother, take him away from this madness before it consumed him. I couldn't win; Machina had us at checkmate, but I would get Ethan home, at least. "What do you want, Machina?" I asked wearily, feeling the Iron King step closer. "Whatever it is, just let me take Ethan back to our world. You said you wanted me. Here I am. But let me take my brother home."

"Of course," Machina soothed. "But first, let us make a deal."

I froze, everything going still inside me. A deal with the Iron King, in exchange for my brother's life. I wondered what he would ask for. Somehow, I knew it would cost me either way.

"Meghan, don't," Ash growled, pulling himself up by the fountain, ignoring the burns to his hands. Machina ignored him.

"What kind of deal?" I asked softly.

The Iron King stepped closer. His cables caressed my face and arms, making me shiver. "I've watched you for sixteen years," he murmured, "waiting for the day you would finally open your eyes and see us. Waiting for the day you would come to me. Your father would have blinded you to this world forever. He is afraid of your power, afraid of your potential—a half-fey who is immune to iron, yet has the blood of the Summer King in her veins. *So* much potential." His gaze lingered on Ash, finally on his feet, and dismissed him just as quickly. "Mab realized your power, which is why she wants you so much. Which is why she sent her best to capture you. But even she cannot offer what I can."

Machina closed the last few steps between us and took my hand. His touch was cool, and I felt power humming through him, like currents of electricity. "I want you to be my queen, Meghan Chase. I offer you my kingdom, my subjects, myself. I want you to rule at my side. The oldbloods are obsolete. Their time is done. It is time for a new order to rise up, stronger and better than the ancient ones. Only say yes, and you will live forever, Queen of the Fey. Your brother can go home. I'll even let you keep your prince if you wish, though I fear he may not adapt well to our kingdom. Regardless, you belong here, at my side. Isn't that what you've always wanted? To belong?"

I hesitated. To rule with Machina, to become a queen. No one would tease or mock me anymore, I would have scores of creatures ready to jump at my bidding, and I would finally be the one on top. I would finally be the most loved. But then

I saw the trees, twisted and metallic, and remembered the terrible, barren wasteland in the wyldwood. Machina would corrupt the entire Nevernever. All the plants would die, or become twisted versions of themselves. Oberon, Grimalkin, Puck: they would fade away with the rest of the Nevernever, until only gremlins, bugs, and the iron fey remained.

I swallowed. And, even though I already knew the answer, I asked, "What if I refuse?"

Machina's expression didn't falter. "Then your prince will die. And your brother will die. Or, perhaps, I will make him one of my playthings, half human, half machine. The eradication of the oldbloods will begin with or without you, my dear. I am giving you the choice of leading it or being consumed by it."

My desperation grew. Machina reached up and stroked my face, running his fingers down my cheek. "Is it really so terrible to rule, my love?" he asked, tilting my chin up to look at him. "Throughout millennia, both humans and fey have done it. Weeded out the weak to make room for the strong. The oldbloods and the iron fey cannot exist together, you know this. Oberon and Mab would destroy us if they knew about us. How is that any different?" He brushed a kiss over my lips, featherlight and vibrating with energy. "Come. One word, that is all you have to say. One word to send your brother home, to save the prince that you love. Look." He waved a hand, and a great iron archway rose out of the ground. On the other side, I could see my house, shimmering through the portal, before it faded from view. I gasped, and Machina smiled. "I will send him home now, if you only say yes. One word, and you will be my queen, forever."

I took a breath. "I—"

And Ash was there. How he could even stand, let alone

move, was a mystery. But he shoved me aside, his face feral, as Machina's eyebrows rose in surprise. The cables flared, stabbing toward Ash as the prince lunged forward and slammed his blade into Machina's chest.

Machina staggered back, his face contorted with agony. Lightning crackled around the blade in his chest. His cables thrashed wildly, striking Ash and hurling him into a metal tree with a sickening crunch. Ash collapsed against the trunk as Machina straightened, giving him a look of white rage.

Reaching down, the Iron King grasped the hilt and pulled, sliding the blade out of his chest. Lightning sizzled, melting the ice around the hole, and thin wires wove themselves around the wound, knitting it together. Machina tossed the sword away and looked at me, his black eyes sparking with fury.

"I am losing patience with you, my dear." One of his cables shot forward, coiling around Ash's throat and lifting him off his feet. Ash choked and struggled weakly as Machina dangled him several feet overhead. Ethan wailed in his cage. "Rule with me, or let them die. Make your choice."

I sank to my knees as my legs buckled, trembling. The stone floor was cold against my palms. *What can I do?* I thought desperately. *How can I choose? Either way, people will die. I can't allow that. I won't.*

The ground pulsed under my hands. I closed my eyes and let my consciousness flow into the earth, searching for that spark of life. I felt the trees in Machina's court, their branches lifeless and dead, but their roots and hearts uncorrupted. *Just like last time.* I gave them a nudge and felt them respond, writhing to meet me, pushing up through the dirt, like the trees of the Summer Court had for Oberon with the chimera.

Like father, like daughter.

I took a deep breath, and *pulled.*

The ground rumbled, and suddenly, live roots broke through the surface, pushing up through the pavement, snapping and coiling about. Machina gave a shout of alarm, and the roots flew to meet him, wrapping around his body, entangling the cables. He roared and lashed out, lightning streaking from his hands, blasting away the wood. Roots and iron cables twined around one another like maddened snakes, swirling in a hypnotic dance of fury.

Ash dropped from the cables, hitting the ground by a metal tree, winded and dazed but still trying to get to his feet, staggering after his weapon. I saw a strip of pale wood beneath the trunk—one half of the snapped Witchwood arrow—and lunged after it.

A cable wrapped around my leg, jerking me off my feet. I twisted around to see Machina glaring at me, his arm outstretched as he fought the web of roots. The cable tightened around my leg and dragged me toward him. I screamed and clawed at the ground, tearing my nails and bloodying my fingers, but I couldn't stop. The furious face of the Iron King loomed closer.

Ash's blade slashed down once more, cutting into the cable, severing it. More cables whipped toward him, but the Winter prince stood his ground, sword flashing as iron tentacles writhed around us.

"Go," he snarled, slashing the end of a cable out of the air. "I'll hold them back. Go!"

I leaped to my feet, rushing for the trunk and the arrow beneath. My hand closed over the wood and I spun back, only to see a cable slice through Ash's defenses and slam into his shoulder, staking him to the ground. Ash howled, swinging his sword weakly, but another cable knocked it from his grasp.

I charged the Iron King, dodging cables and snaking roots.

For a moment, his attention was riveted on Ash, but then his gaze snapped to me, lightning flashing in the depths of his eyes. Shrieking a battle cry, I lunged.

Just as I reached him, something slammed into my back, driving the breath from me. I couldn't move, and realized that one of the cables had stabbed me from behind. Strangely, there was no pain.

Machina drew me to him as roots and cables waged their war overhead. Everything else faded away, and there was just us.

"I would have made you a queen," he muttered, reaching a hand to me. The roots circling his torso, pinning his other arm, tightened around him, but he didn't seem to notice. "I would have given you everything. Why reject such an offer?"

My hand tightened on the Witchwood, feeling a faint beat of life still within. "Because," I whispered, raising my arm, "I already have everything I need."

I drove my arm forward, sinking the arrow into his chest.

Machina's lips gaped in a soundless scream. He arched his head back, still screaming, and green shoots erupted from his mouth, spreading down his neck. A strange pulse of energy, like an electrical jolt, coursed through my body, making my muscles spasm. The cable flung me away; I hit the ground and bit back a shriek as pain lanced up my spine. Clawing myself upright, I looked around, grabbed the sword, and rushed to Ethan's cage. One stroke of the ice blade smashed the door open, and I hugged my brother to me, feeling him sob into my hair.

"Meghan!" Ash staggered toward me, holding his shoulder, dark blood streaming down his skin. Behind him, the door burst open, and dozens of knights poured inside. For a moment, they froze in shock, staring at their king in the center of the garden.

Machina still writhed in his prison, but weakly. Branches grew from his chest, his cables turning into vines that bloomed with tiny white flowers. As we watched, he split apart, as the trunk of a brand-new oak burst from his chest, rising into the air. The Bluetooth phone dropped from the branches and lay, winking, at the roots of the tree.

"Wow," I whispered into the silence.

The knights turned on us with a roar. They rushed forward, but suddenly, the ground trembled. Rumblings filled the air as the iron throne began to collapse, shedding jagged shrapnel like scales. A tremor shook the ground, causing everyone to stagger.

Then, a huge chunk of the garden cracked and fell away, taking several knights with it into oblivion. More cracks appeared as the courtyard began to come apart. The knights howled and scattered, and screams rose into the air.

"The whole tower's coming down!" Ash yelled, dodging a falling beam. "We have to get out of here, now!"

I ran to the iron archway, stumbling as more cracks slashed across the ground, and ducked through, only to reappear on the other side. Nothing happened. Despair rose up, and I gazed around wildly.

"Human," said a familiar voice, and Grimalkin appeared, twitching his tail. I gaped at him, hardly believing my eyes. "This way. Hurry."

"I thought you weren't coming," I gasped, following him across the garden to where two metal trees grew together, the trunks forming an archway between them. Grimalkin looked back at me and snorted.

"Trust you to take the hardest route possible," he said,

lashing his tail. "If you had only listened to me, I would have shown you an easier way. Now, hurry. This air is making me sick."

A deafening roar shook the ground, and the garden crumbled away altogether. Clutching Ethan tightly, I dived between the trunks, Ash right on my heels. I felt the tingle of magic as we passed through the barrier, and realized I was falling, before everything went completely black.

CHAPTER TWENTY-FIVE

Homecoming

I awoke slowly, a hard tile floor cold against my cheek. Wincing, I sat up, testing my body for any lingering pain. I was vaguely aware that there should be some; I remembered Machina stabbing me through the back with his iron cables, felt the blaze of agony as he ripped them from my flesh—but there was no pain. In fact, I felt better than I had in a long time, my senses buzzing with energy as I gazed around. I lay in a long, dim room filled with desks and computers. The school computer lab!

With a jerk, I sat up and looked around for my brother, wondering, for one heart-stopping instant, if everything had been a horrible dream. A moment later, I relaxed. Ethan lay under a nearby desk, his face peaceful, his breath slow and deep. I brushed a stray curl from his forehead and smiled, then got to my feet.

Ash was nowhere to be seen, but Grimalkin lay on a desk beneath a dingy window, purring in the sunlight coming through the glass. Careful not to disturb Ethan, I rose and joined him.

"There you are." The cat yawned, cracking open one golden eye to stare at me. "I was beginning to think you would sleep forever. You snore, you know."

I ignored that comment, hopping up on the desk beside him. "Where's Ash?"

"Gone." Grimalkin sat up and stretched, wrapping his tail around himself. "He took off earlier, before you woke up. He said he had some things to take care of. Told me to tell you not to wait for him."

"Oh." I let that sink in, not knowing what to feel. I could've been upset, angry, resentful that he left so suddenly, but all I felt was tired. And a little sad. "He was hurt pretty bad, Grim. Will he be all right?"

Grimalkin yawned, obviously unconcerned. I wasn't reassured, but Ash was strong: strong enough to make it all the way to the heart of the Iron Kingdom and back. A lesser faery would've died. He almost did die. Had he been drawing glamour from me, in that desolate place? Or was it something else that enabled him to survive? I wondered if I'd ever get the chance to ask him.

After a moment, I turned to gaze around the room, marveling that the trod to the Iron Kingdom had been so close. Did one of the computers hide the path to Machina's realm? Had we come flying out of a monitor, or had we just blipped into existence, like the gremlins?

"So." I turned back to the cat. "You found us the path home. Congratulations. What do I owe you for this one? Another favor or life debt? My firstborn child?"

"No." Grimalkin's eyes slitted in amusement. "We will let this one go. This once."

We sat in silence for a bit, enjoying the sunlight, content just to be alive. Still, as I watched Ethan, sleeping under the desk, a strange heaviness filled me, as if I was missing something. As if I'd forgotten something vitally important, back in Faery.

"So," Grimalkin mused, licking his front paw, "what will you do now?"

I shrugged. "I don't know. Take Ethan home, I guess. Go back to school. Try to get on with my life." I thought of Puck, and a lump rose to my throat. School wouldn't be the same without him. I hoped he was all right, and that I would see him again. I thought of Ash, and wondered if the prince of the Unseelie Court would consent to dinner and a movie.

"Hope springs eternal," the cat muttered.

"Yeah." I sighed, and we fell silent again.

"What I have been wondering," Grimalkin went on, "is how Machina kidnapped your brother in the first place. He used a changeling, yes, but that wasn't an iron faery. How did he make the switch, if it was not one of his own?"

I thought about it and frowned. "Somebody must've helped him," I guessed.

Grimalkin nodded. "I would imagine so. Which means Machina had normal fey working for him as well, and now that he is gone, they will be none too happy with you."

I shivered, feeling hope for a normal life slipping rapidly away. I imagined knives on the floor, my hair tied to the bedpost, missing items, and irate faeries lurking in my closet or under my bed, ready to pounce. I'd never be able to sleep again, that much was certain. I wondered how I would protect my family.

A groan came from the sleeping form in the corner. Ethan was waking up.

"Go on, then," Grimalkin purred as I rose. "Take him home."

I wanted to say thank-you, but there was no way I was putting myself even more in the cat's debt. Instead, I went to gather Ethan, and we started across the room, weaving around desks and dark, silent computers. At the door, which was thankfully unlocked, I looked back to the window and the shaft of sunlight, but Grimalkin was no longer there.

The school halls were empty and dark. Puzzled, I made my way down the dingy corridors, clutching Ethan's hand and wondering where everyone was. Perhaps it was the weekend, but that didn't explain the dusty floors and lockers, the feeling of complete emptiness as we passed one locked classroom after another. Even on Saturdays, there would be at least one extracurricular class going on. It felt like the school had been empty for weeks.

The front doors were closed and locked, so I had to open a window. After hoisting Ethan up, I wiggled out after him, dropping to the pavement and gazing around. No cars stood in the parking lot, even though it was the middle of the day. The place looked completely deserted.

Ethan gazed around in silence, round blue eyes taking everything in. There was a wariness to him that seemed terribly out of place, like he was older now but his body remained the same. It worried me, and I gently squeezed his hand.

"We'll be home soon, okay?" I whispered as we started across the parking lot. "Just one short bus ride, and you can see Mom again, and Luke. Are you excited?"

He regarded me solemnly and nodded once. He didn't smile.

We left the school campus, following the sidewalk until we reached the nearest bus stop. Around us, cars sped by, weaving in and out of late-afternoon traffic, and people milled around us. Some older ladies smiled and waved to Ethan, but he paid them no attention. My concern for him knotted my stomach. I tried cheering him up, asking questions, telling him little stories about my adventures, but he just stared at me with those mournful blue eyes and didn't say a word.

So we stood on the corner, waiting for the bus to come, watching the people surge around us. I saw faeries, slipping through the crowds, entering the little shops lining the street, following humans like stalking wolves. A fey boy with leathery black wings grinned and waved to Ethan from an alley across the street. Ethan shivered, and his fingers tightened on mine.

"Meghan?"

I turned at the sound of my name. A girl had come out of the coffee shop behind us, and was staring at me in amazement and disbelief. I frowned, shifting uncomfortably. She looked familiar, with her long dark hair and cheerleader-thin waist, but I couldn't remember where I knew her from. Was she a classmate? If so, I think I would have recognized her. She would have been very pretty, if it wasn't for the huge, distorted nose marring her otherwise perfect face.

And then it hit me.

"Angie," I whispered, feeling the shock punch me in the stomach. I remembered then: the cheerleader's mocking laughter, Puck muttering something under his breath, Angie's horrified screams. Her nose was flat and shiny, with two large nostrils that looked very much like a pig's. Was this faery vengeance? An awful sense of guilt gnawed at my insides, and I tore my gaze from her face. "What do you want?"

"Oh my God, it *is* you!" Angie gaped at me, nostrils flaring. I saw Ethan staring unabashed at her nose. "Everyone thought you were dead! There have been police and detectives looking for you. They said you ran away. Where have you been?"

I blinked at her. This was new. Angie had never spoken to me before, except to mock me in front of her friends. "I…

How long have I been gone?" I stammered, not knowing what else to say.

"More than three months now," she replied, and I stared at her. *Three months?* My trek to the Nevernever hadn't taken that long, had it? A week or two, at most. But I remembered how my watch stopped while in the wyldwood, and a sick feeling rose to my stomach. Time flowed differently in Faery. No wonder the school was locked and empty; it was summer vacation by now. I really had been gone three months.

Angie was still staring at me curiously, and I floundered for a reply that wouldn't sound insane. Before I could think of anything, a trio of blondes heading for the coffee shop stopped and gaped at us.

"Oh my God!" one of them screeched. "It's the swamp slut! She's back!" Shrill laughter rang out, echoing over the sidewalk, causing several people to stop and stare. "Hey, we heard you got knocked up and your folks shipped you off to some military school. Is that true?"

"Oh my God!" one of her friends yelled, pointing to Ethan. "Look at that! She's already had her kid!" They collapsed into hysterical giggles, shooting me subtle looks to see my reaction. I gazed at them calmly and smiled. *Sorry to disappoint you,* I thought, seeing their brows knit with confusion. *But after facing homicidal goblins, redcaps, gremlins, knights, and evil faeries, you just aren't that scary anymore.*

But then, to my surprise, Angie scowled and took a step forward. "Knock it off," she snapped, as I recognized the blond trio from her old cheerleading squad. "She just got back to town. Give her a break already."

They shot her evil glares. "I'm sorry, Pigface, were you talking to us?" one asked sweetly. "I don't believe I was speaking to you at all. Why don't you go home with the little swamp bitch? I'm sure she can find a place for you on the farm."

"She can't understand you," another piped up. "You have to speak her language. Like this." She broke into a chorus of oinks and squeals, and the other two took up the cry. The street echoed with high-pitched grunts, and Angie's face flushed crimson.

I stood there, stunned. It was so weird, seeing the most popular girl in school standing in my shoes. I should've been happy; the perfect cheerleader was finally getting a taste of her own medicine. But my instincts also said this treatment wasn't new. It started the day Puck had pulled his cruel joke, and all I felt was empathy. If he were here, I would twist his arm until he changed her back.

If he were here…

I quickly pushed those thoughts away. If I kept thinking about him, I would start to cry, and that was the *last* thing I wanted to do in front of the cheerleaders. For a second, I thought Angie herself would burst into tears and flee. But, after a moment, she took a deep breath and turned to me, rolling her eyes.

"Let's get out of here," she whispered, jerking her head toward a nearby parking lot. "Have you been home yet? I can drive you, if you want."

"Um…" Shocked again, I glanced down at Ethan. He gazed up at me, his face wan and tired. Despite my hesitation, I wanted to get him home as soon as possible. Though I still had my doubts, Angie certainly seemed different now. Briefly, I wondered if it was great adversity that made a person stronger. "Sure."

She asked a lot of questions on the drive home: where I had been, what made me leave, was it really a pregnancy that drove me off. I answered as vaguely as I could, leaving out the parts with the homicidal faeries, of course. Ethan curled up beside me and fell asleep, and soon his faint snores were the only sounds besides the hum of the engine.

Angie finally pulled up alongside a familiar gravel road, and my stomach twisted nervously as I opened the door, pulling Ethan out with me. The sun had gone down, and an owl hooted somewhere overhead. In the distance, a porch light glimmered like a beacon in the twilight.

"I appreciate the ride," I told Angie, slamming the car door. She nodded, and I made myself say those two little words. "Thank you." Guilt stabbed me again as I looked at her face. "I'm sorry about…you know."

She shrugged. "Don't worry about it. I'm going to a plastic surgeon in a couple weeks. He should take care of it." She went to put the car in gear, but stopped, turning back to me. "You know," she said, frowning, "I don't even remember how it got like this. Sometimes, I think I've always been this way, you know? But then, people look at me weird, like they can't figure it out. Like they're scared, because I'm so different." She blinked at me, shadows under her eyes. Her nose seemed to leap off her face. "But you know what that's like, don't you?"

I nodded breathlessly. Angie blinked again, like she was seeing me for the first time. "Well, then…" Slightly embarrassed, she waved to Ethan and gave me a brisk nod. "See you around."

"Bye." I watched her pull away, her taillights growing smaller and smaller, until they rounded a corner and disappeared. The night suddenly seemed dark and still.

Ethan took my hand, and I looked down at him in concern. He still wasn't talking. My brother had always been a quiet kid, but this complete, brooding silence was disturbing. I hoped he wasn't too traumatized by his ordeal.

"Home, kiddo." I sighed, looking up the long, long drive-way. "Think you can make it?"

"Meggie?"

Relieved, I looked down at him. "Yeah?"

"Are you one of Them now?"

I sucked in a breath, feeling as if he had punched me. "What?"

"You look different." Ethan fingered his ear, gazing up at mine. "Like the bad king. Like one of Them." He sniffled. "Are you going to live with Them now?"

"Of course not. I don't belong with Them." I squeezed his hand. "I'll live with you and Mom and Luke, just like always."

"The dark person talked to me. He said I'd forget about Them in a year or two, that I won't be able to see Them any-more. Does that mean I'll forget you, too?"

I knelt and looked him in the eye. "I don't know, Ethan. But, you know what? It doesn't matter. Whatever happens, we're still a family, right?"

He nodded solemnly, far too old for his age. Together, we continued walking.

The outline of our house grew larger as we approached. It looked familiar and strange all at once. I could see Luke's beat-up truck in the driveway, and Mom's floral curtains waving in the windows. My bedroom was dark and still, but a night-light shone out of Ethan's room, flickering orange. It made my stomach churn, to think what slept up there. A single light shone in the bottom window, and I picked up my pace.

Mom was asleep on the couch when I opened the door. The television was on, and she held a box of tissues in her lap, one twisted up in her fingers. She stirred when I shut the door behind me, but before I could say anything, Ethan wailed, "Mommy!" and flung himself into her lap.

"What?" Mom jerked awake, startled by the shaking child in her arms. "Ethan? What are you doing downstairs? Did you have a nightmare?"

She glanced up at me then, and her face went pale. I tried for a smile, but my lips wouldn't work right, and the lump in my throat made it hard to speak. She rose, still holding on to Ethan, and we fell into each other. I sobbed into her neck, and she held me tightly, her own tears staining my cheek.

"Meghan." At last, she pulled back and looked at me, a spark of anger warring with the relief in her eyes. "Where have you been?" she demanded with a little shake. "We've had the police looking for you, detectives, the whole town. No one could find any trace of you, and I've been worried sick. Where have you *been* for three months?"

"Where's Luke?" I asked, not really knowing why. Maybe I felt that he didn't need to hear this, that this was between me and Mom alone. I wondered if Luke had even noticed that I was gone. Mom frowned, as if she knew what I was thinking.

"He's upstairs, asleep," she replied, pulling back. "I should wake him up, tell him you've come home. Every night for the past three months, he's taken his truck down the back roads, looking for you. Sometimes he doesn't come home until morning."

Stunned, I blinked back tears. Mom gave me a stern look, the one I got right before I was grounded. "You wait right here until I get him, and then, young lady, you can tell us where you've been while we've been going crazy. Ethan, honey, let's put you to bed."

"Wait," I said as she turned away, Ethan still clinging to

her robe. "I'll come with you. Ethan, too. I think everyone should hear this."

She hesitated, looking down at Ethan, but finally nodded. We turned to leave together, when a noise on the stairs froze us in our tracks.

The changeling stood there, his eyes narrowed, his lips peeled back in a snarl. He wore Ethan's bunny pajamas, and his small fists were clenched in rage. The real Ethan whimpered and pressed into Mom's side, hiding his face. Mom gasped, her hand going to her mouth, as the changeling hissed at me.

"Damn you!" it shrieked, stamping a foot into the ground. "Stupid, stupid girl! Why'd you have to bring him back? I hate you! I hate you! I—"

Smoke erupted from its feet, and the changeling wailed. Twisting in on itself, it disappeared into the smoke, shouting curses as it grew smaller and smaller, and finally vanished altogether.

I allowed myself a small smirk of triumph.

Mom lowered her hand. When she turned to me again, I saw understanding in her eyes, and a terrible, terrible fear. "I see," she whispered, glancing at Ethan. She trembled, and her face was ashen. She knew. She knew all about Them.

I stared at her. Questions rose to mind, too jumbled and tangled to make out. Mom seemed different now, frail and frightened, not the mother I knew at all. "Why didn't you tell me?" I whispered.

Mom sat on the couch, pulling Ethan up with her. He snuggled into her side like he was never going to let go. "Meghan, I... That was years ago, when I met...him...your father. I barely remember it—it seemed more like a dream than anything." She didn't look at me as she spoke, lost in her own world. I perched on the edge of the armchair as she continued in a faint voice.

"For months, I convinced myself that it hadn't happened. It didn't seem real, what we did, the things he showed me. It was just one time, and I never saw him again. When I discovered I was pregnant, I was a little nervous, but Paul was so happy. The doctors had told us we would never have children."

Paul. My mind stirred uneasily at that name. It felt like I should recognize it. Then Mom's words sank in and it hit me: Paul had been my father, or at least married to my mom. I didn't remember him, not in the slightest. I had no idea who he was, what he looked like. He must've died when I was very young.

The thought made me sad, and angry. Here was another father that Mom had tried to hide from me.

"Then you were born," Mom continued, still in that distant, faraway voice, "and strange things started happening. I'd often find you out of your crib, on the floor or even outside, though you couldn't walk yet. Doors would open and close on their own. Items went missing, only to show up in the oddest places. Paul thought the house was haunted, but I knew *They* were lurking about. I could feel Them, even though I couldn't see Them. It terrified me. I was afraid They were after you, and I couldn't even tell my husband what was going on.

"We decided to move, and for a while, things were normal. You grew into an ordinary, happy child, and I thought everything was behind us. Then…" Mom's voice trembled, and tears filled her eyes. "Then there was that incident in the park, and I knew They had found us again. Afterward, after everything had died down, we came here, and I met Luke. You know the rest."

I frowned. I remembered the park, with its tall trees and

little green pond, but I couldn't recall what "incident" Mom was talking about. Before I could ask, Mom leaned forward and gripped my hand.

"I wanted to tell you for so long," she whispered, her eyes wide and teary. "But I was afraid. Not that you wouldn't believe me, but that you *would*. I wanted you to have a normal life, not to live in fear of Them, to wake up every morning dreading that They had found you."

"Didn't really work, did it?" My voice came out hoarse and raspy. Anger simmered, and I glared at her. "Not only did *They* come for me, but Ethan got pulled in, as well. What are we going to do now, Mom? Run away, just like the last two times? You saw how well that worked."

She leaned back, hugging Ethan protectively. "I…I don't know," she stammered, wiping her eyes, and I immediately felt guilty. Mom had gone through the same things I had. "We'll think of something. Right now, I'm just glad you're safe. Both of you."

She gave me a tentative smile, and I returned it, though I knew this wasn't over. We couldn't stick our heads in the sand and pretend the fey weren't out there. Machina might be gone, but the Iron Kingdom would continue to grow, poisoning the Nevernever, little by little. There was no way to stop progress or technology. Somehow, I knew we couldn't escape them. Running away just didn't work—they were too stubborn and persistent. They could hold a grudge forever. Sooner or later, we would have to face the fey once more.

Of course, sooner came more quickly than I expected.

"Ethan," Mom said after a while, once the adrenaline had worn off and the house was still, "why don't you run upstairs and wake Daddy? He'll want to know that Meghan is home. Then you can sleep between us if you want."

Ethan nodded, but at that moment, the front door creaked open, and a cold breeze shivered across the room. The moonlight beyond the door shimmered, consolidating into something solid and real.

Ash stepped over the threshold.

Mom didn't look up, but Ethan and I jumped as my heart began to thud loudly in my chest. Ash looked different now, the cuts and burns healed, his hair falling softly around his face. He wore simple dark pants and a white shirt, and his sword hung at his side. Still dangerous. Still inhuman and deadly. Still the most beautiful being I'd ever seen. His mercury eyes found mine, and he inclined his head.

"It's time," he murmured.

For a moment, I stared at him, not understanding. Then it hit me all at once. *Oh, God. The contract. He's here to take me to the Winter Court.*

"Meghan?" Mom looked from me to the door, not seeing the Winter prince silhouetted against the frame. But her face was tight; she knew *something* was there. "What's happening? Who's there?"

I can't go now, I raged silently. *I just got home! I want to be normal; I want to go to school and learn to drive and go to prom next year. I want to forget faeries ever existed.*

But I gave my word. And Ash had upheld his end of the bargain, though he almost died for it.

Ash waited quietly, his eyes never leaving mine. I nodded at him and turned back to my family.

"Mom," I whispered, sitting on the couch, "I…I have to go. I made a promise to someone that I would stay with Them for a while. Please don't worry or be sad. I'll be back, I swear.

360 · JULIE KAGAWA

But this is something I gotta do, or else They might come looking for you or Ethan again."

"Meghan, no." Mom gripped my hand, squeezing hard. "We can do something. There has to be a way to...keep Them back. We can move again, all of us. We—"

"Mom." And I let my glamour fade away, revealing my true self to her. It wasn't difficult this time, to manipulate the glamour surrounding me. Like the roots in Machina's domain, it came so naturally I wondered how I ever thought it hard. Mom's eyes widened, and she jerked her hand back, pulling Ethan close. "I'm one of Them now," I whispered. "I can't run from this. You should know that. I have to go."

Mom didn't answer. She kept staring at me with a mix of sorrow, guilt, and horror. I sighed and rose to my feet, letting the glamour settle on me again. It felt like the weight of the entire world.

"Ready?" Ash murmured, and I paused, glancing up toward my room. Did I want to take anything with me? I had my clothes, my music, little personal items collected in my sixteen years.

No. I didn't need them. That person was gone, if she had been real in the first place. I needed to figure out who I really was, before I came back. If I came back. Glancing at Mom, still frozen on the couch, I wondered if this would ever be home again.

"Meggie?" Ethan slid off the couch and padded up to me. I knelt, and he hugged me around the neck with all the strength a four-year-old could muster.

"I won't forget," he whispered, and I swallowed the lump in my throat. Standing up, I ruffled his hair and turned to Ash, still waiting silently at the door.

"You have everything?" he asked as I approached. I nodded.

"Everything I need," I murmured back. "Let's go."

He bowed, not to me, but to Mom and Ethan, and walked out. Ethan sniffled loudly and waved, trying hard not to cry. And I smiled, seeing their emotions as clearly as a beautiful painting: blue sorrow, emerald hope, scarlet love. We were connected, all of us. Nothing, fey, god, or immortal, could sever that.

I waved to Ethan, nodded forgiveness at Mom, and shut the door, following Ash into the silver moonlight.

★ ★ ★ ★ ★

ACKNOWLEDGMENTS

The road to publication is a long and arduous one, and I have many people to thank for seeing me through to the end. My parents, for encouraging me to go for my dreams instead of getting a real job. My sister, Kimiko, and my brother-in-law, Mike, for their willingness to read those horrible first drafts. My mentor, Julianne Lee, and the wonderful authors, teachers, and students at Green River Writers of Louisville, KY. My fabulous agent, Laurie McLean, for giving me a chance, and my editor, Natashya Wilson, for making the dream happen. My writing group, for all the weekends we've spent together, bleeding on one another's manuscripts, shredding one another's characters, and beating dead horses.

But mostly, I want to thank my amazing husband, Nick, who has been my writing partner, cheerleader, editor, sounding board, proofreader, voice of reason, and always willing to talk story, plot, and character whenever I got myself stuck. I couldn't have done it without him.

The Iron Daughter

To Nick, my inspiration

PART ONE

CHAPTER ONE

The Winter Court

The Iron King stood before me, magnificent in his beauty, silver hair whipping about like an unruly waterfall. His long black coat billowed behind him, accenting the pale, angular face and translucent skin, the blue-green veins glowing beneath the surface. Lightning flickered in the depths of his jet-black eyes, and the steel tentacles running the length of his spine and shoulders coiled around him like a cloak of wings, glinting in the light. Like an avenging angel, he floated toward me, hand outstretched, a sad, tender smile on his lips.

I stepped forward to meet him as the iron cables wrapped gently around me, drawing me close. "Meghan Chase," Machina murmured, running a hand through my hair. I shivered, keeping my hands at my sides as the tentacles caressed my skin. "You have come. What is it you want?"

I frowned. What did I want? What had I come for? "My brother," I answered, remembering. "You kidnapped my brother, Ethan, to draw me here. I want him back."

"No." Machina shook his head, moving closer. "You did not come for your brother, Meghan Chase. Nor did you come for the Unseelie prince you claim to love. You came here for one thing only. Power."

My head throbbed and I tried backing away, but the cables held me fast. "No," I muttered, struggling against the iron net. "This…this is wrong. This isn't how it went."

"Show me, then." Machina opened his arms wide. "How was it 'supposed' to go? What did you come here to do? Show me, Meghan Chase."

"No!"

"Show me!"

Something throbbed in my hand: the beating pulse of the Witchwood arrow. With a yell, I raised my arm and drove the sharpened point through Machina's chest, sinking the arrow into his heart.

Machina staggered back, giving me a look of shocked horror. Only it wasn't Machina anymore but a faery prince with midnight hair and bright silver eyes. Lean and dangerous, silhouetted all in black, his hand went to the sword at his belt before he realized it was too late. He swayed, fighting to stay on his feet, and I bit down a scream.

"Meghan," Ash whispered, a thin line of red trickling from his mouth. His hands clutched at the arrow in his chest as he fell to his knees, pale gaze beseeching mine. "Why?"

Shaking, I raised my hands and saw they were covered in glistening crimson, running rivulets down my arms, dripping to the ground. Below the slick coating, things wiggled beneath my skin, pushing up through the surface, like leeches in blood. Somewhere in the back of my mind, I knew I should be terrified, appalled, majorly grossed out. I wasn't. I felt powerful, powerful and strong, as if electricity surged beneath my skin, as if I could do anything I wanted and no one could stop me.

I looked down at the Unseelie prince and sneered at the

pathetic figure. Could I really have loved such a weakling once upon a time?

"Meghan." Ash knelt there, the life fading from him bit by bit, even as he struggled to hold on. For a brief moment, I admired his stubborn tenacity, but it wouldn't save him in the end. "What about your brother?" he pleaded. "And your family? They're waiting for you to come home."

Iron cables unfurled from my back and shoulders, spreading around me like glittering wings. Gazing down at the Unseelie prince, helpless before me, I gave him a patient smile.

"I *am* home."

The cables slashed down in a silver blur, slamming into the faery's chest and staking him to the ground. Ash jerked, his mouth gaping silently, before his head lolled back and he shattered like crystal on concrete.

Surrounded by the glittering remains of the Unseelie prince, I threw back my head and laughed, and it turned into a ragged scream as I wrenched myself awake.

My name is Meghan Chase.

I've been in the palace of the Winter fey for a while now. How long exactly? I don't know. Time doesn't flow right in this place. While I've been stuck in the Nevernever, the outside world, the mortal world, has gone on without me. If I ever get out of here, if I ever make it home, I might find a hundred years have passed while I was gone, like Rip van Winkle, and all my family and friends are long dead.

I try not to think of that too often, but sometimes, I can't help but wonder.

My room was cold. It was always cold. *I* was always cold. Not even the sapphire flames in the hearth were enough to drive out the incessant chill. The walls and ceiling were made of opaque, smoky ice; even the chandelier sparkled with a thousand icicles. Tonight, I wore sweatpants, gloves, a thick sweater and a wool hat, but it wasn't enough. Outside my window, the underground city of the Winter fey sparkled with icy radiance. Dark forms leaped and fluttered in the shadows, flashing claws, teeth and wings. I shivered and gazed up at the sky. The ceiling of the vast cavern was too far away to see through the darkness, but thousands of tiny lights, balls of faery fire or faeries themselves, twinkled like a blanket of stars.

There was a rap at my door.

I didn't call out *Come in.* I'd learned not to do so in the past. This was the Unseelie Court, and inviting them into your room was a very, very bad idea. I couldn't keep them out completely, but the fey follow rules above all else, and by order of their queen, I was not to be bothered unless I requested it.

Letting them into my room could almost sound like such a request.

I crossed the floor, my breath streaming around me, and cracked open the door.

A slinky black cat sat on the floor with its tail curled around itself, gazing up at me with unblinking yellow eyes. Before I could say anything, it hissed and darted through the crack like a streak of shadow.

"Hey!"

I spun around, but the cat was no longer a cat. Tiaothin the phouka stood there, grinning at me, canines glinting. Of course. It would be the phouka; they didn't follow social rules. In fact, they seemed to take great pleasure in breaking them. Furred ears peeked out of her dreadlocked hair, twitching sporadically. She wore a gaudy jacket that sparkled with fake gems and studs, ripped jeans and combat boots. Unlike the Seelie Court, the Unseelie fey actually preferred "mor-

tal" clothing. Whether it was in direct defiance of the Seelie
Court, or because they wanted to blend in more with humans, I wasn't sure.

"What do you want?" I asked cautiously. Tiaothin had
taken a keen interest in me when I was brought to court, the
insatiable curiosity of a phouka, I suppose. We'd talked a few
times, but she wasn't exactly what I'd call a friend. The way
she stared at me, unblinking, like she was sizing me up for her
next meal, always made me nervous.

The phouka hissed, running her tongue along her teeth.
"You're not ready," she said in her sibilant voice, looking me
over skeptically. "Hurry. Hurry and change. We should go,
quickly."

I frowned. Tiaothin had always been difficult to understand,
bouncing from one subject to the next so quickly it was hard
to keep up. "Go where?" I asked, and she giggled.

"The queen," Tiaothin purred, flicking her ears back and
forth. "The queen has called for you."

My stomach twisted into a tight ball. Ever since I'd come
to the Winter Court with Ash, I'd been dreading this moment. When we'd first arrived at the palace, the queen regarded me with a predatory smile and dismissed me, saying
that she wished to speak to her son alone and would call for
me soon. Of course, "soon" was a relative term in Faery, and
I'd been on pins and needles ever since, waiting for Mab to
remember me.

That was also the last time I saw Ash.

Thinking of Ash sent a flutter through my stomach, reminding me how much had changed. When I first came to
Faery, searching for my kidnapped brother, Ash had been the
enemy, the cold, dangerous son of Mab, Queen of the Unseelie Court. When war threatened the courts, Mab sent Ash

to capture me, hoping to use me as leverage against my father, King Oberon. But, frantic to save my brother, I made a bargain with the Winter prince, instead: if he helped me rescue Ethan, I would return with him to the Unseelie Court without a fight. At that point, it was a desperate gamble; I needed all the help I could get to face down the Iron King and save my brother. But, somewhere in that blasted wasteland of dust and iron, watching Ash battle the realm that was poisoning his very essence, I realized I was in love with him.

Ash had gotten me there, but he almost didn't survive his brush with Machina. The King of the Iron fey was insanely strong, almost invincible. Against all odds, I managed to defeat Machina, rescue my brother, and take him home.

That night as per our contract, Ash came for me. It was time to honor my end of the bargain. Leaving my family behind once more, I followed Ash into Tir Na Nog, the land of Winter.

The journey through Tir Na Nog was cold, dark, and terrifying. Even with the Winter prince at my side, Faery was still savage and inhospitable, especially to humans. Ash was the perfect bodyguard, dangerous, alert and protective, but he seemed distant at times, distracted. And the farther we went into Winter, the more he drew away, sealing himself off from me and the world. And he wouldn't tell me why.

On the last night of our journey we were attacked. A monstrous wolf, sent by Oberon himself, tracked us down, intent on killing Ash and spiriting me back to the Summer Court. We managed to escape, but Ash was wounded fighting the creature, so we took refuge in an abandoned ice cave to rest and bind his wounds.

He was silent as I wrapped a makeshift bandage around his arm, but I could feel his eyes on me as I tied it off. Releasing his arm, I looked up to meet his silvery gaze. Ash blinked slowly, giving me that look that meant he was trying to figure me out. I waited, hoping I would finally glean some insight into his sudden aloofness.

"Why didn't you run?" he asked softly. "If that thing had killed me, you wouldn't have to come back to Tir Na Nog. You would've been free."

I scowled at him.

"I agreed to that contract, same as you," I muttered, tying off the bandage with a jerk, but Ash didn't even grunt. Angry now, I glared up at him, meeting his eyes. "What, you think just because I'm human I was going to back out? I knew what I was getting into, and I am going to uphold my end of the bargain, no matter what happens. And if you think I'd leave you just so I wouldn't have to meet Mab, then you don't know me at all."

"It's *because* you're human," Ash continued in that same quiet voice, holding my gaze, "that you missed a tactical opportunity. A Winter fey in your position wouldn't have come back. They wouldn't let their emotions get in the way. If you're going to survive in the Unseelie Court, you have to start thinking like them."

"Well, I'm *not* like them." I rose and took a step back, trying to ignore the feeling of hurt and betrayal, the stupid angry tears pressing at the corners of my eyes. "I'm not a Winter faery. I'm human, with human feelings and emotions. And if you want me to apologize for that, you can forget it. I can't just shut off my feelings like you can."

I whirled to stalk away in a huff, but Ash rose with blinding speed and gripped my upper arms. I stiffened, locking my knees and keeping my back straight, but struggling with him would have been useless. Even wounded and bleeding, he was much stronger than me.

"I'm not ungrateful," he murmured against my ear, making my stomach flutter despite itself. "I just want you to understand. The Winter Court preys on the weak. It's their nature. They will try to tear you apart, physically and emotionally, and I won't always be there to protect you."

I shivered, anger melting away, as my own doubts and fears came rushing back. Ash sighed, and I felt his forehead touch the back of my hair, his breath fanning my neck. "I don't want to do this," he admitted in a low, anguished voice. "I don't want to see what they'll try to do to you. A Summer fey in the Winter Court doesn't stand much of a chance. But I vowed that I would bring you back, and I'm bound to that promise." He raised his head, squeezing my shoulders in an almost painful grip as his voice dropped a few octaves, turning grim and cold. "So you have to be stronger than they are. You can't let down your guard, no matter what. They will lead you on, with games and pretty words, and they will take pleasure in your misery. Don't let them get to you. And don't trust anyone." He paused, and his voice went even lower. "Not even me."

"I'll always trust you," I whispered without thinking, and his hands tightened, turning me almost savagely to face him.

"No," he said, narrowing his eyes. "You won't. I'm your enemy, Meghan. Never forget that. If Mab tells me to kill you in front of the entire court, it's my duty to obey. If she orders Rowan or Sage to carve you up slowly, making sure you suffer every second of it, I'm expected to stand there and let them do it. Do you understand? My feelings for you don't matter in the Winter Court. Summer and Winter will always be on opposite sides, and nothing will change that."

I knew I should be afraid of him. He was an Unseelie

prince, after all, and had in no uncertain terms admitted he would kill me if Mab ordered him to. But he also admitted to having feelings for me, feelings that didn't matter, but it still made my stomach squirm when I heard it. And maybe I was being naive, but I couldn't believe Ash would willingly hurt me, even in the Winter Court. Not with the way he was looking at me now, his silver eyes conflicted and angry.

He stared at me a moment longer, then sighed. "You didn't hear a word I said, did you?" he murmured, closing his eyes.

"I'm not afraid," I told him, which was a lie: I was terrified of Mab and the Unseelie Court that waited at the end of this journey. But if Ash was there, I would be all right.

"You are infuriatingly stubborn," Ash muttered, raking a hand through his hair. "I don't know how I'm going to protect you when you have no concept of self-preservation."

I stepped close to him, placing a hand on his chest, feeling his heart beat under his shirt. "I trust you," I said, rising so our faces were inches apart, trailing my fingers down his stomach. "I know you'll find a way."

His breath hitched, and he regarded me hungrily. "You're playing with fire, you know that?"

"That's weird, considering you're an ice prin—" I didn't get any further, as Ash leaned in and kissed me. I looped my arms around his neck as his snaked around my waist, and for a few moments the cold couldn't touch me.

The next morning, he was back to being distant and aloof, barely speaking to me no matter how much I prodded. That night, we reached the underground palace of the Winter Court, and Mab dismissed me almost immediately. A servant showed me to my quarters, and I sat in the small, chilly room waiting for Ash to find me again.

He never returned from his meeting with the queen, and after several hours of waiting, I finally ventured into the halls of the Winter Court, looking for him. That's when I found Tiaothin, or rather, she found me in the library, playing keep-away with a hulking Jack-in-Irons as he stalked me between the aisles. After getting rid of the giant, she informed me that Prince Ash was no longer in the palace, and no one had any idea when he would be back.

"But that's just Ash," she'd said, grinning at me from atop a bookcase. "He's hardly ever at court. You catch a glimpse of him and *poof!* He's gone for another few months."

Why would Ash just leave like that? I wondered for about the billionth time. *He could've at least told me where he was going, and when he'd be back. He didn't have to leave me hanging.*

Unless he was deliberately avoiding me. Unless everything he'd said, the kiss we'd shared, the emotions in his eyes and voice, meant nothing to him. Maybe everything he'd done was only to bring me to the Winter Court.

"You're going to be late," Tiaothin purred, jerking me back to the present, watching me with glowing cat eyes. "Mab doesn't like to be kept waiting."

"Right," I said faintly, shaken out of my dark mood. *Oops, that's right. I've got an audience with the Faery Queen of Winter.* "Just give me a minute to change." I waited, but when Tiaothin didn't move, I scowled at her. "Uh, a little privacy, please?"

Tiaothin giggled, and in one shivery motion, became a shaggy black goat, who bounced out of the room on all fours. I shut the door and leaned against it, feeling my heart thud in my chest. Mab wanted to see me. The Queen of the Unseelie Court was finally calling on me. I shivered and pushed away from the door, walking to my dresser and the icy mirror on top.

My reflection stared back at me, slightly distorted by the cracks in the ice. Sometimes, I still didn't recognize myself. My straight blond hair was almost silver in the darkness of the room, and my eyes seemed far too big for my face. And there were other things, a thousand little details I couldn't put my finger on, that told me I wasn't human, that I was something to be feared. And of course, there was the most obvious difference. Pointed ears knifed up from the sides of my head, a screaming reminder of how unnormal I was.

I broke eye contact with my reflection and looked down at my clothes. They were warm and comfortable, but I was pretty sure meeting the Queen of the Unseelie Court dressed in sweatpants and a baggy sweater was a bad idea.

Great. I'm supposed to meet the Queen of the Winter fey in five minutes. What do I wear?

Closing my eyes, I tried collecting the glamour around me and shaping it over my clothes. Nothing. The massive rush of power I'd drawn on while battling the Iron King seemed to have faded, so much that I couldn't craft even the simplest illusion anymore. And not for lack of trying. Recalling my lessons with Grimalkin, a faery cat I'd met on my first trip to the Nevernever, I'd tried to become invisible, make shoes levitate and create faery fire. All failures. I couldn't even feel the glamour anymore, though I knew it was all around me. Glamour is fueled by emotion, and the wilder and more passionate the emotion—rage, lust, love—the easier it is to draw on. Yet I couldn't access it like I used to. It seemed I was back to being plain, nonmagical Meghan Chase. With pointy ears.

It was strange; for years, I hadn't even known I was half-fey. It was just a few months ago, on my sixteenth birthday, that my best friend Robbie had revealed himself to be Robin Goodfellow, the infamous Puck from *A Midsummer Night's Dream*. My kid brother, Ethan, had been kidnapped by faeries and I needed to rescue him. Oh, and by the way, I was the half-human daughter of King Oberon, Lord of the Summer fey. It took some getting used to, both the knowledge that I was half-faery and that I could use the magic of the fey—faery glamour—to work my own spells. Not that I was very good at it—I sucked, much to Grimalkin's irritation—but that wasn't the point. I hadn't even believed in faeries back then, but now that my magic was gone, it felt like pieces of me were missing.

With a sigh, I opened the dresser and pulled out jeans, a white shirt and a long black coat, shrugging into them as quickly as I could to avoid freezing to death. For a moment, I wondered if I should dress in something fancy, like an evening gown. After a moment I decided against it. The Unseelie spurned formal attire. I'd have a better chance of survival if I tried fitting in.

When I opened the door, Tiaothin, no longer a goat or cat, stared at me and broke into a toothy leer. "This way," she hissed, backing into the icy corridor. Her yellow eyes seemed to float in the darkness. "The queen awaits."

I followed Tiaothin down the dark, twisted hallways, trying to keep my gaze straight ahead. Out of the corners of my eyes, however, I still caught glimpses of the nightmares lurking in the halls the Unseelie Court.

A spindly bogey crouched behind a door like a giant spider, the pale, emaciated face staring at me through the crack. An enormous black hound with glowing eyes trailed us down the hallways, making no noise at all, until Tiaothin hissed at it and it slunk away. Two goblins and a shark-toothed redcap huddled in a corner, rolling dice made of teeth and tiny bones. As I passed, an argument broke out, the goblins pointing to the redcap and crying "Cheat, cheat!" in high-pitched voices. I didn't look back, but a shriek rang out behind me, followed by the wet sound of snapping bones. I shuddered and followed Tiaothin around a corner.

The corridor ended, opening into a massive room with icicles dangling from the ceiling like glittering chandeliers. Will-o'-the-wisps and globes of faery fire drifted between them, sending shards of fractured light over the walls and floor. The floor was shrouded in ice and mist, and my breath steamed in the air as we entered. Icy columns held up the ceiling, sparkling like translucent crystal and adding to the dazzling, confusing array of light and colors swirling around the room. Dark, wild music echoed throughout the chamber, played by a group of humans on a corner stage. The musicians' eyes were glazed over as they sawed and beat at their instruments, their bodies frighteningly thin. Their hair hung long and lank, as if they hadn't cut it for years. Yet, they didn't seem to be distressed or unhappy, playing their instruments with zombielike fervor, seemingly blind to their inhuman audience.

Dozens of Unseelie fey milled about the chamber, each one a creature straight out of a nightmare. Ogres and redcaps, goblins and spriggans, kobolds, phoukas, hobs and faeries I didn't have a name for, all wandering to and fro in the shifting darkness.

I quickly scanned the room, searching for tousled black hair and bright silver eyes. My heart fell. He wasn't here.

On the far side of the room, a throne of ice hovered in the air, glowing with frigid brilliance. Sitting on that throne, poised with the power of a massive glacier, was Mab, Queen of the Unseelie Court.

The Winter Queen was stunning, plain and simple. When I was in Oberon's court I'd seen her beside her rival, Titania, the Summer Queen, who was also beautiful but in an evil socialite type of way. Titania also held a grudge against me for being Oberon's daughter, and had tried to turn me into a deer once, so she wasn't my favorite person. Though they were complete opposites, the two queens were insanely powerful. Titania was a summer storm, beautiful and deadly and prone to frying something with lightning if it pissed her off. Mab was the coldest day in winter, where everything lies still and dead, held in fear of the unforgiving ice that killed the world before and could again.

The queen lounged in her chair, surrounded by several fey gentry—the sidhe—dressed in expensive, modern-day clothes, crisp white business suits and pin-striped Armani. When I saw her last, in Oberon's court, Mab had worn a flowing black dress that writhed like living shadows. Today, she was dressed in white: a white pantsuit, opal-tinted nails and ivory heels, her dark hair styled elegantly atop her head. Depthless black eyes, like a night without stars, looked up and spotted me, and her pale mulberry lips curved in a slow smile.

A chill slithered up my back. Fey care little for mortals. Humans are merely playthings to be used up and discarded. Both the Seelie and Unseelie Courts are subject to this. Even if I was half-fey and Oberon's daughter, I was all alone in the court of my father's ancient enemies. If I irritated Mab, there was no telling what the queen would do. Maybe turn me into a white rabbit and sic the goblins on me, though that seemed more Titania's style. I had a feeling Mab could come up with something infinitely more awful and twisted, and that made me very afraid.

Tiaothin ambled through the crowds of Unseelie fey, who

paid her little attention. Most of their interest was directed at me as I followed, my heart thudding against my ribs. I felt the hungry stares, the eager grins and the eyes on the back of my neck, and concentrated on keeping my head up and my step confident. Nothing attracts faeries more than fear. A sidhe noble with a face that was all sharp angles caught my gaze and smiled, and my heart contracted painfully. He reminded me of Ash, who wasn't here, who had left me alone in this court of monsters.

The Winter Queen's chill grew more pronounced the closer we got; soon it was so cold it hurt to breathe. Tiaothin reached the foot of the throne and bowed. I did the same, though it was hard to do so without my teeth chattering. The Unseelie fey crowded behind us, their breath and murmuring voices making my skin crawl.

"Meghan Chase." The queen's voice rasped over the assembly, making my hair stand on end. Tiaothin slunk away and disappeared into the crowd, leaving me truly alone. "How good of you to join us."

"It's an honor to be here, my lady," I replied, using every ounce of my willpower to keep my voice from shaking. A tremor slipped out anyway, and not just from the cold. Mab smiled, amused, and leaned back, observing me with emotionless black eyes. Silence fell for a few heartbeats.

"So." The queen tapped her nails with a rhythmic clicking sound, making me jump. "Here we are. You must think you are very clever, daughter of Oberon."

"I—I'm sorry?" I stammered, as an icy fist gripped my heart. This wasn't starting well, not at all.

"You're not," Mab continued, giving me a patient smile. "But you will be. Make no mistake about that." She leaned forward, looking utterly inhuman, and I fought the urge to run screaming from the throne room. "I have heard of your exploits, Meghan Chase," the queen rasped, narrowing her eyes. "Did you not think I would find out? You tricked a prince of the Unseelie Court into following you into the Iron Realm. You made him fight your enemies for you. You bound him to a contract that nearly killed him. My precious boy, almost lost to me forever, because of you. How do you think that makes me feel?" Mab's smile grew more predatory, as my stomach twisted in fear. What could she do to me? Encase me in ice? Freeze me from the inside out? Chill my blood so I would never be warm again, no matter what I wore or how hot it became? I shivered, but then noticed a faint shimmer, like heat waves, around me, and suddenly realized Mab was tinting the air with glamour, manipulating my emotions and letting me imagine the worst fate possible. She didn't have to threaten or say anything; I was terrifying myself quite well.

In a lucid moment of distraction, I wondered if Ash had done the same to my emotions, manipulating me into falling for him. If Mab could do it, I'm sure her sons had the same talent. Were my feelings for Ash real, or some sort of fabricated glamour?

Now's not the time to wonder about that, Meghan!

Mab stared at me, gauging my reaction. I still shook in fear, but a part of me knew what the queen was doing. If I lost it and begged for mercy, I would find myself trapped in a faery contract before I knew what was happening. Promises are deadly serious among the fey, and I wasn't going to let Mab strongarm me into pledging something I would instantly regret.

I took a furtive breath to collect my thoughts, so that when I did answer the Queen of the Winter fey, I wouldn't start bawling like a two-year-old.

"Forgive me, Queen Mab," I said, choosing my words carefully. "I meant no harm to you or yours. I needed Ash's help to rescue my brother from the Iron King."

At the mention of the Iron King, the Unseelie fey behind me stirred and growled, glancing around warily. I felt hackles rise, teeth bare and claws unsheathe. For normal faeries, iron was deadly poison, draining their magic and burning their flesh. An entire kingdom made of iron was horrible and terrifying to them; a faery ruler called the Iron King was blasphemous. For a moment, I had the satisfying thought that the Iron fey had become the bogeys and bogeymen of the faery world, and bit down a vindictive smile.

"I would name you a liar, girl," Mab said calmly, as the growls and mutterings behind me died down, "if I had not heard the same from my son's own lips. Rest assured, the Iron King's minions are no threat to us. Even now, Ash and his brothers are scouring our territory for these Iron fey. If the abominations are within our borders, we will hunt them down and destroy them."

I felt a rush of relief, but not because of Mab's claim. Ash was out there. He had a reason not to be at court.

"And yet…" Mab regarded me with a look that made my stomach squirm. "I cannot help but wonder how you managed to survive. Perhaps Summer is in league with the Iron fey, plotting with them against the Winter Court. That would be terribly amusing, wouldn't it, Meghan Chase?"

"No," I said softly. In my mind's eye, I saw the Iron King, reeling back as I drove the arrow through his chest, and clenched my fists to stop them from shaking. I could still see Machina writhing in pain, felt something cold and serpentine slithering under my skin. "The Iron King was going to destroy Summer as well as Winter. He's dead, now. I killed him."

Mab narrowed her eyes to black slits. "And you would have

me believe that you, a half-human with virtually no power, managed to kill the Iron King?"

"Believe her," a new voice rang out, making my stomach twist and my heart jump to my throat. "I was there. I saw what happened."

Voices rose around me as the ranks of Unseelie fey parted like waves. I couldn't move. I was rooted to the spot, my heart pounding in my chest as the lean, dangerous form of Prince Ash strode into the chamber.

I shivered, and my stomach began turning nervous backflips. Ash looked much as he always did, darkly beautiful in black and gray, his pale skin a sharp contrast to his hair and clothes. His sword hung at his side, the sheath a luminous blue-black, giving off a frozen aura.

I was so relieved to see him. I stepped toward him, smiling, only to be stopped dead by his cold glare. Confused, I stumbled to a halt. Maybe he didn't recognize me. I met his gaze, waiting for his expression to thaw, for him to give me the tiny smile I adored so much. It didn't happen. His frosty eyes swept over me in a brief, dismissive glance, before he stepped around me and continued toward the queen. I felt a stab of shock and hurt; maybe he was playing it cool in front of the queen, but he could've at least said *hi*. I made the mental note to scold him later when we were alone.

"Prince Ash," Mab purred, as Ash went down on one knee before the throne. "You have returned. Are your brothers with you?"

Ash raised his head, but before he could answer, another voice interrupted him.

"Our youngest brother practically fled our presence in his haste to get to you, Queen Mab," said a high, clear voice behind me. "If I didn't know better, I would think he didn't want to speak to you in front of us."

Ash rose, his face carefully blank, as two more figures strode into the chamber, scattering fey like birds. Like Ash, they wore long, thin blades at their hips, and carried themselves with the easy grace of royalty.

The first, the one who had spoken, resembled Ash in build and height: lean, graceful and dangerous. He had a thin, pointed face, and black hair that bristled like spines atop his head. A white trench coat billowed out behind him, and a gold stud sparkled in one pointed ear. His gaze met mine as he swept past, ice-blue eyes glittering like chips of diamond, and his lips curled in a lazy smirk.

The second brother was taller than his siblings, more willowy than lean, his long raven hair tied back in a ponytail that reached his waist. A great gray wolf trailed behind him, amber eyes slitted and wary. "Rowan." Mab smiled at the first prince as the two bowed to her as Ash had done. "Sage. All my boys, home at last. What news do you bring me? Have you found these Iron fey within our borders? Have you brought me their poisonous little hearts?"

"My queen." It was the tallest of the three that spoke, the oldest brother, Sage. "We have searched Tir Na Nog from border to border, from the Ice Plains to the Frozen Bog to the Broken Glass Sea. We have found nothing of the Iron fey our brother has spoken of."

"Makes you wonder if our dear brother Ash exaggerated a bit," Rowan spoke up, his voice matching the smirk on his face. "Seeing as these 'legions of Iron fey' seem to have vanished into thin air."

Ash glared at Rowan and looked bored, but I felt the blood rush to my face.

"He's telling the truth," I blurted out, and felt every eye in the court turn on me. "The Iron fey are real, and they're still out there. And if you don't take them seriously, you'll be dead before you know what's happening."

Rowan smiled at me, a slit-eyed, dangerous smile. "And why would the half-blood daughter of Oberon care if the Winter Court lives or dies?"

"Enough." Mab's voice rasped through the chamber. She stood and waved a hand at the fey assembled behind us. "Get out. Leave, all of you. I will speak with my sons alone."

The crowd dispersed, slinking, stomping or gliding from the throne room. I hesitated, trying to catch Ash's gaze, wondering if I was included in this conversation. After all, I knew about the Iron fey, too. I succeeded in capturing his attention, but the Winter prince gave me a bored, hostile glare and narrowed his eyes.

"Didn't you hear the queen, half-breed?" he asked coldly, and my heart contracted into a tiny ball. I stared at him, mouth open, unwilling to believe this was Ash speaking to me, but he continued with ruthless disdain. "You're not welcome here. Leave."

I felt the sting of angry tears, and took a step toward him. "Ash—"

His eyes glittered as he shot me a glare of pure loathing. "It's *Master* Ash, or *Your Highness* to you, half-breed. And I don't recall giving you permission to speak to me. Remember that, because the next time you forget your place, I'll remind you with my blade." He turned away, dismissing me in one cold, callous gesture. Rowan snickered, and Mab watched me from atop her throne with a cool, amused gaze.

My throat tightened and a deluge pressed behind my eyes, ready to burst. I trembled and bit my lip to keep the flood in check. I would *not* cry. Not now, in front of Mab and Rowan and Sage. They were waiting for it; I could see it on their faces as they watched me expectantly. I could not show any weakness in front of the Unseelie Court if I wanted to survive.

Especially now that Ash had become one of the monsters.

With as much dignity as I could muster, I bowed to Queen Mab. "Excuse me then, Your Majesty," I said, in a voice that trembled only slightly. "I will leave you and your sons in peace."

Mab nodded, and Rowan gave me a mocking, exaggerated bow. Ash and Sage ignored me completely. I spun on my heel and walked from the throne room with my head held high, my heart breaking with every step.

CHAPTER TWO

A Declaration

When I woke up, the room was light, cold beams streaming in the window. My face felt sticky and hot, and my pillow was damp. For one blissful moment, I didn't recall the events of the past night. Then, like a black wave, memory came rushing back.

Tears threatened again, and I buried my head under the covers. I'd spent most of the night sobbing into my pillow, my face muffled so that my cries wouldn't be overheard by some fey in the hall.

Ash's cruel words stabbed me through the heart. Even now, I could hardly believe the way he'd acted in the throne room, like I was scum beneath his boots, like he truly despised me. I'd been hoping for him, longing for him, to come back, and now those feelings were a twisted nail inside. I felt betrayed, as if what we shared on our journey to the Iron King was only a farce, a tactic the cunning Ice prince had used to get me to come to the Unseelie Court. Or perhaps he had just grown tired of me and moved on. Just another reminder of how capricious and insensitive the fey could be.

In that moment of utter loneliness and confusion, I wished

Puck were here. Puck, with his carefree attitude and infectious smile, who always knew what to say to make me laugh again. As a human, Robbie Goodfell had been my neighbor and best friend; we shared everything, did everything, together. Of course, Robbie Goodfell turned out to be Robin Goodfellow, the infamous Puck of *A Midsummer Night's Dream,* and he was following Oberon's orders to protect me from the faery world. He'd disobeyed his king when he brought me into the Nevernever in search of Ethan, and again when I fled the Seelie Court and Oberon sent Puck to bring me back. His loyalty cost him dear when he was finally shot in a battle with one of Machina's lieutenants, Virus, and nearly killed. We were forced to leave him behind, deep within a dryad's tree, to heal from his wounds, and guilt from that decision still ate at me. My eyes filled with fresh tears, remembering. Puck couldn't be dead. I missed him too much for that.

A tapping came at my door, startling me. "Meghaaaan" came the singsong voice of Tiaothin the phouka. "Wake uuuup. I know you're in there. Open the doooor."

"Go away," I yelled, wiping my eyes. "I'm not coming out, okay? I don't feel good."

Of course, this only encouraged her further. The tapping turned to scratching, setting my teeth on edge, and her voice grew louder, more insistent. Knowing she'd sit there all day, scratching and whining, I leaped off the bed, stomped across the room and wrenched open the door.

"What?" I snarled. The phouka blinked, taking in my rumpled appearance, tear-streaked face and swollen, runny nose. A knowing grin came to her lips, and my anger flared; if she was here just to taunt me, I was so not in the mood. Stepping back, I was about to slam the door in her face when she darted into the room and leaped gracefully onto my bed.

"Hey! Dammit, Tiaothin! Get out of here!" My protests

went ignored, as the phouka bounced gleefully on the mattress, shredding holes in the blankets with her sharp claws.

"Meghan's in lo-ove," sang the phouka, making my heart stop. "Meghan's in lo-ove. Meghan and Ash, sitting in a tree—"

"Tiaothin, shut up!" I slammed the door and stalked toward her, glaring. The phouka giggled and came to a bouncing stop on my bed, sitting cross-legged on the pillow. Her gold-green eyes gleamed with mischief.

"I am not in love with Ash," I told her, crossing my arms over my chest. "Didn't you see the way he spoke to me, like I was dirt? Ash is a heartless, arrogant bastard. I hate him."

"Liar," the phouka retorted. "Liar liar, lying human. I saw the way you stared at him when he appeared. I know that look. You're smitten." Tiaothin snickered, flicking an ear back and forth as I squirmed. She grinned, showing all her teeth. "Not your fault, really. Ash just does that to people. No silly mortal can look at him and *not* fall head over heels. How many hearts do you think he's already broken?"

My spirits sank even lower. I'd thought I was special. I thought Ash cared for me, if only a little. Now, I realized I was probably just another girl in a long line of humans who'd been foolish enough to fall for him.

Tiaothin yawned, settling back against my pillows. "I'm telling you this so you won't waste your time chasing after the impossible," she purred, slitting her eyes at me. "Besides," she continued, "Ash is already is love with someone else. Has been for a long, long time. He's never forgotten her."

"Ariella," I whispered.

She looked surprised. "He told you about her? Huh. Well then, you should already know Ash would never fall for a plain, half-human girl, not when Ariella was the most beautiful sidhe in the Winter Court. He'd never betray her memory, even if the law wasn't an issue. You know about the law, don't you?"

I didn't know about any law, and I really didn't care. I got the feeling the phouka wanted me to ask about it, but I wasn't going to oblige. But Tiaothin seemed determined to tell me anyway, and went on with a sniff.

"You're Summer," she said disdainfully. "We're Winter. It's against the law that the two should ever be involved. Not that we have many incidents, but occasionally some star-struck Summer fey will fall in love with a Winter, or vice versa. *All* sorts of problems there—Summer and Winter are not meant to be together. If they're found out, the high lords will demand they renounce their love at once. If they refuse, they're banished to the human world forever, so they can continue their blasphemous relationship out of sight of the courts…if they're not executed right then.

"So, you see," she finished, fixing me with a piercing stare, "Ash would never betray his queen and court for a *human*. It's best to forget about him. Maybe find a silly human boy in the mortal world, if Mab ever lets you go."

By now I was so miserable I couldn't open my mouth without screaming or crying. Bile burned my throat, and my eyes swelled up. I had to get out of here, away from Tiaothin's brutal truths, before I fell to pieces.

Biting my lip to keep the tears at bay, I turned and fled into the halls of the Unseelie Court.

I nearly tripped over a goblin, who hissed and gnashed his teeth at me, jagged fangs gleaming in the darkness. Muttering an apology, I hurried away. A tall woman in a ghostly white dress floated down the corridor, eyes red and swollen, and I ducked down another hall to avoid her.

I needed to get out. Outside, into the clear, cold air, to be alone for just a few minutes, before I went crazy. The dark corridors and crowded halls were making me claustrophobic. Tiaothin had showed me the way out once; a pair of great double doors, one carved to resemble a laughing face, the other curled in a terrible snarl. I had searched for them on my own but could never find them. I suspected Mab put a spell on the doors to hide them from me, or maybe the doors themselves were playing a twisted game of hide-and-seek—doors did that sometimes in Faeryland. It was infuriating: I could see the sparkling, snow-covered city from my bedroom window, but could never get there.

I heard a clatter behind me and turned to see a group of redcaps coming down the hall, mad yellow eyes bright with hunger and greed. They hadn't seen me yet, but when they did, I'd be alone and unprotected, far from the safety of my room, and redcaps were *always* hungry. Fear gripped my heart. I hurried around a corner...

And there they stood, across an ice-slick foyer. The double doors, with their laughing face and snarling face, seeming to mock and threaten at the same time. Now that I'd finally found them, I hesitated. Would I be able to get back in, once I was out? Beyond the palace was the twisted, frightening city of the Winter fey. If I couldn't get back in, I'd freeze to death, or worse.

An excited whoop rang out. The redcaps had seen me.

I hurried across the floor, trying not to slip, as the tiles appeared to be made of colored ice. A pencil-thin butler in a black suit watched me impassively as I approached, his lank gray hair falling to his shoulders. Huge round eyes, like shiny mirrors, stared at me unblinking. Ignoring him, I grabbed the door with the laughing face and pulled, but it didn't budge.

"Going outside, Miss Chase?" the butler asked, tilting his smooth, egg-shaped head.

"Just for a while," I snapped, straining at the door, which, infuriatingly, started laughing at me. I didn't jump or scream, having experienced far stranger, but it did make me mad. "I'll be right back, I promise." I heard the jeering laughter of the redcaps, mingling with the howling of the door, and gave it a resounding kick. "Dammit, open up, you stupid thing!"

The butler sighed. "You are assaulting the wrong door, Miss Chase." He reached over and pulled open the snarling door, which scowled at me as it creaked on its hinges. "Please be careful in your excursion outside," the butler said primly. "Her Majesty would be most displeased if you…ahem…ran away. Not that you would, I'm sure. Her protection is all that keeps you from being frozen, or devoured."

A blast of frigid air blew into the foyer. The land beyond was dark and cold. Glancing behind at the redcaps, who watched me from the shadows with bright, pointy grins, I shivered and stepped out into the snow.

I almost went back inside, it was so cold. My breath hung on the air, and ice eddies stung my exposed flesh, making it tingle and burn. A pristine, frozen courtyard stretched before me, trees, flowers, statues and fountains encased in the clearest ice. Great jagged crystals, some taller than my head, jutted out of the ground at random intervals, spearing into the sky. A group of fey dressed in glittering white sat on the lip of a fountain, long azure hair rippling down their backs. They saw me, snickered behind their hands and rose. The nails on their fingertips glimmered blue in the half-light.

I went the other way, my boots crunching through the snow, leaving deep prints behind. A while ago, I might've wondered how it could snow underground, but I'd long accepted that things never made sense in Faeryland. I didn't really know where I was going, but moving seemed better than standing still.

"Where do you think you're going, half-breed?"

Snow swirled, stinging my face and blinding me. When the blizzard receded, I was surrounded by the four fey girls who had been sitting at the fountain. Tall, elegant and beautiful, with their pale skin and shimmering cobalt hair, they hemmed me in like a pack of wolves, full frosted lips twisted into ugly sneers.

"Ooh, Snowberry, you were right," one of them said, wrinkling her nose like she smelled something foul. "She *does* reek of a dead pig in the summer. I don't know how Mab can stand it."

Clenching my fists, I tried to keep my cool. I was *so* not in the mood for this now. *God, it's like high school all over again. Will it never end? These are ancient faeries, for Pete's sake, and they're acting like my high school pom squad.*

The tallest of the pack, a willowy fey with poison green streaked through her azure hair, regarded me with cold blue eyes and stepped close, crowding me. I stood my ground, and her gaze narrowed. A year ago, I might have grinned benignly and nodded and agreed with everything they said, just to get them to leave me alone. Things were different now. These girls weren't the scariest things I'd seen. Not by a long shot.

"Can I help you?" I asked in the calmest voice I could manage.

She smiled. It was not a nice smile. "I'm just curious to see how a half-breed like you gets off on speaking to Prince Ash like an equal." She sniffed, curling her lip in disgust. "If I were Mab, I would've frozen your throat shut just for looking at him."

"Well, you're not," I said, meeting her gaze. "And since I'm a guest here, I don't think she'd approve of whatever you're planning to do to me. So, why don't we do each other a favor and pretend we don't exist? That would solve a lot of problems."

"You don't get it, do you, half-breed?" Snowberry pulled herself up, staring down her perfect nose at me. "Looking at my prince constitutes an act of war. That you actually *spoke* to him makes my stomach turn. You don't seem to understand that you disgust him, as well you should, with your tainted Summer blood and human stench. We'll have to do something about that, won't we?"

My prince? Was she talking about Ash? I stared at her, tempted to say something stupid like, *Funny, he never mentioned you.* She might act like a spoiled, rich, mean girl from my old school, but the way her eyes darkened until there were no pupils left reminded me that she was still fey.

"So." Snowberry stepped back and gave me a patronizing smile. "This is what we're going to do. You, half-breed, are going to promise me that you won't so much as glance at my sweet Ash, ever again. Breaking this promise means I get to pluck out your wandering eyes and make a necklace with them. I think that's a fair bargain, don't you?"

The rest of the girls giggled, and there was a hungry, eager edge to the sound, like they wanted to eat me alive. I could have told her not to worry. I could have told her that Ash hated me and she didn't have to threaten to get me to stay away. I didn't. I drew myself up, looked her in the eye, and asked, "And what if I don't?"

Silence fell. I felt the air get colder and braced myself for the explosion. A part of me knew this was stupid, picking a fight with a faery. I would probably get my butt kicked, or cursed, or something nasty. I didn't care. I was tired of being bullied, tired of running into the bathroom to sob my eyes out. If this faery bitch wanted a fight, bring it on. I'd do my fair share of clawing, too.

"Well, isn't this fun." A smooth, confident voice cut through the silence, a second before all hell would have broken loose. We jumped as a lean figure dressed entirely in white materialized from the snow, his coat flapping behind him. The look on his pointed face glowed with haughty amusement.

"Prince Rowan!"

The prince grinned, his ice-blue eyes narrowed to slits. "Pardon me, girls," he said, slipping up beside me, making the pack fall back a few steps. "I don't mean to ruin your little party, but I need to borrow the half-breed for a moment."

Snowberry smiled at Rowan, all traces of hatefulness gone in an instant. "Of course, Your Highness," she cooed, as if she'd just been offered a wonderful gift. "Whatever you command. We were just keeping her company."

I wanted to gag, but Rowan smiled back as if he believed her, and the pack drifted away without a backward glance.

The prince's smile turned to a smirk as soon as they'd gone, and he gave me a sideways leer that made me instantly cautious. He might have saved me from Snowberry and her harpies, but I didn't think he'd done it to be chivalrous. "So, you're Oberon's half-blood," he purred, confirming my suspicion. His eyes raked me up and down, and I felt horribly exposed, as though he was undressing me with his gaze. "I saw you at Elysium last spring. Somehow I thought you were...taller."

"Sorry to disappoint you," I said frostily.

"Oh, you're not disappointing." Rowan smiled, his gaze lingering on my chest. "Not a bit." He snickered again and stepped back, gesturing for me to follow. "Come on, Princess. Let's take a walk. I want to show you something."

I really didn't want to, but I saw no way of politely refusing a prince of the Unseelie Court, especially since he'd just done me a favor by getting rid of the pack. So I followed him to another part of the courtyard, where frozen statues littered the snowy landscape, making it eerie and surreal. Some stood straight and proud, some were twisted in abject fear, arms and limbs thrown up to protect themselves. Looking at some of their features, so real and lifelike, made me shudder. *The Queen of Winter has a creepy sense of style.*

Rowan paused in front of one statue, covered in a layer of smoky ice, its features barely distinguishable through the opaque seal. With a start, I realized this wasn't a statue at all. A human stared out of his ice prison, mouth open in a scream of terror, one hand flung out before him. His blue eyes, wide and staring, gazed down at me.

Then he blinked.

I stumbled back, a shriek lodging in my throat. The human blinked again, his terrified gaze beseeching mine. I saw his lips tremble, as if he wanted to say something but the ice rendered him immobile, frozen and helpless. I wondered how he could breathe.

"Brilliant, isn't it?" said Rowan, gazing at the statue in admiration. "Mab's punishment for those who disappoint her. They can see, feel and hear everything that goes on around them, so they're fully aware of what's happened to them. Their hearts beat, their brains function, but they don't age. They're suspended in time forever."

"How do they breathe?" I whispered, staring back at the gaping human.

"They don't." Rowan smirked. "They can't, of course. Their noses and mouths are full of ice. But they still keep trying. It's like they're suffocating for eternity."

"That's horrible!"

The sidhe prince shrugged. "Don't piss off Mab, is all I can tell you." He turned the full brunt of his icy gaze on me. "So, Princess," he continued, making himself comfortable at the base of the statue. "Tell me something, if you would." Pulling an apple out of nowhere, he bit into it, smiling at me all the while. "I hear you and Ash traveled all the way to the Iron King's realm and back. Or so he claims. What do you think of my dear little brother?"

I smelled a hidden motive and crossed my arms. "Why do you want to know?"

"Just making conversation." Rowan produced another apple and tossed it at me. I fumbled to catch it, and Rowan grinned. "Don't be so uptight. You'd give a brownie a nervous breakdown. So, was my brother a complete troll, or did he remember his manners?"

I was hungry. My stomach growled, and the apple felt cool and crisp in my hand. Before I knew it, I'd taken a bite. Sweet, tart juice flooded my mouth, with just a hint of bitter aftertaste. "He was a perfect gentleman," I said with my mouth full, my voice sounding strange in my ears. "He helped me rescue my brother from the Iron King. I couldn't have done it without him."

Rowan reclined and gave me a lazy smile. "Do tell."

I frowned at his smirk. Something wasn't right. Why was I telling him this? I tried shutting up, clamping down on my tongue, but my mouth opened and the words rushed out of their own volition.

"My brother Ethan was stolen by the Iron King," I said, listening to myself babble on in horror. "I came into the Nevernever to get him back. When Ash was sent by Mab to capture me, I tricked him into making a contract with me, instead. If he helped me rescue Ethan, I would go with him to the Un-

seelie Court. He agreed to help, but when we got to the Iron
Kingdom, it made Ash horribly sick, and he was captured by
Machina's Iron Knights. I snuck into the Iron King's tower,
used a magic arrow to kill Machina, rescued my brother and
Ash, and then we came here."

I clapped both hands over my mouth to stop the torrent of
words, but the damage was already done. Rowan looked like
the cat who just ate the canary.

"So," he crooned, slitting his eyes at me, "my little brother
let himself be tricked—by a weakling half-blood—into rescuing a mortal child and nearly killing himself in the process.
How very unlike Ash. Tell me more, Princess."

I kept my hands over my mouth, muffling my words, even
as they began pouring out. Rowan laughed and hopped off
the statue base, stalking toward me with an evil grin. "Oh,
come now, Princess, you know it's useless to resist. No need
to make this harder on yourself."

I wanted to punch him, but I was afraid if I took my hands
from my mouth, I'd reveal something else. Rowan kept coming, his grin turning predatory. I backed away, but a wave of
dizziness and nausea swept through me and I stumbled, fighting to stay on my feet. The prince snapped his fingers, and
the snow around my feet turned to ice, covering my boots
and freezing me in place. Horrified, I watched the ice crawl
up past my knees, making sharp, crinkling noises as it inched
toward my waist.

It's cold! I shivered violently, tiny needles of pain stabbing
my flesh through my clothes. I gasped, wanting desperately
to get away from it, but of course I couldn't move. My stomach cramped, and another bout of nausea made my head spin.
Rowan smiled, leaning back and watching me struggle.

"I can make it stop, you know," he said, munching on the

last of his apple. "All you have to do is answer a few innocent questions, that's all. I don't know why you're being so difficult, unless, of course, you have something to hide. Who are you trying to protect, half-breed?"

The temperature was becoming unbearable. My muscles began to spasm from the awful, bone-numbing cold. My arms shook, and my hands dropped from my mouth.

"Ash," I whispered, but at that moment, the ice holding me in place shattered. With the sound of breaking china, it collapsed into thousands of crystalline shards, glinting in the weak light. I yelped and stumbled back, free of the icy embrace, as another lean, dark form melted out of the shadows.

"Ash." Rowan smiled as his brother stalked toward us, and my heart leaped. For a moment, I imagined Ash's gray eyes were narrowed in fury, but then he drew close and looked the same as he had the night before—cold, distant, slightly bored.

"What a coincidence," Rowan continued, still bearing that disgustingly smug grin. "Come and join us, little brother. We were just talking about you."

"What are you doing, Rowan?" Ash sighed, sounding more irritated than anything. "Mab told us not to bother the half-breed."

"Me? Bother her?" Rowan looked incredulous, blue eyes widening into the picture of innocence. "I'm never a bother. We were just having a scintillating conversation. Weren't we, Princess? Why don't you tell him what you just told me?"

Ash's silver gaze flicked to mine, a shadow of uncertainty crossing his face. My lips opened of their own accord, and I clapped my hands over my mouth again, stopping the words before they spilled out. Meeting his gaze, I shook my head, beseeching him with my eyes.

"Oh, come now, Princess, don't be shy," Rowan purred.

"You seemed to have a lot to say about our dearest boy Ash, here. Go on and tell him."

I glared at Rowan, wishing I could tell him exactly what he could do with himself, but I was feeling so sick and light-headed now, it took all my concentration to stay upright. Ash's gaze hardened. Striding away from me, he bent and plucked something out of the snow, holding it up before him.

It was the fruit I'd dropped, a single bite taken out of the flesh, like Snow White's poisoned apple. Only it wasn't an apple now, but a big spotted toadstool, the fleshy insides white as bone. My stomach heaved, cramping violently, and I nearly lost the bite I'd taken.

Ash said nothing. Glaring at Rowan, he held up the mushroom and raised an eyebrow. Rowan sighed.

"Mab didn't specifically say we *couldn't* use spill-your-guts," Rowan said, shrugging his lean shoulders. "Besides, I think you'd be most interested in what our Summer princess has to say about you."

"Why should I be?" Ash tossed the mushroom away, looking bored again. "This conversation isn't important. I made the bargain to get her here, and now it's done. Anything I said or did was for the purpose of bringing her to court."

I gasped, my hands dropping away from my face, to stare at him. It was true, then. He'd been playing me all along. What he told me in the Iron Kingdom, everything we shared, none of that was real. I felt ice spreading through my stomach and shook my head, trying to erase what I just heard. "No," I muttered, too low for anyone to hear. "It's not true. It can't be. Ash, tell him you're lying."

"Mab doesn't care how I did it, as long as the goal was accomplished," Ash continued, oblivious to my torment. "Which is more than I can say for you." He crossed his arms and shrugged, the picture of indifference. "Now, if we're quite done here, the half-breed should return inside. The queen will not be pleased if she freezes to death."

"Ash," I whispered as he turned away. "Wait!" He didn't even glance at me. Tears pressed behind my eyes, and I stumbled after him, fighting a wave of dizziness. "Ash!"

"I love you!"

The words just tumbled out of me. I didn't mean to say them, but the moment I did, my stomach twisted with disbelief and utter horror. My hands flew back to my mouth, but it was far, far too late. Rowan grinned his biggest yet, a smile full of terrible glee, like he'd been given the best present in the world.

Ash froze, his back still to me. For just a moment, I saw his hands clench at his sides.

"That's unfortunate for you, isn't it?" he said, his voice dead of emotion. "But the Summer Court has always been weak. Why would I touch the half-breed daughter of Oberon? Don't make me sick, human."

It was like an icy hand plunged into my body, ripping my heart from my chest. I felt actual physical pain lance through me. My legs buckled, and I collapsed to the snow, ice crystals biting into my palms. I couldn't breathe, couldn't even cry. All I could do was kneel there, the cold seeping through my jeans, hearing Ash's words echo through my head.

"Oh, that was cruel, Ash," Rowan said, sounding delighted. "I do believe you broke our poor princess's heart."

Ash said something else, something I didn't catch, because the ground began to twirl beneath me, and another wave of dizziness made my head spin. I could have fought it off, but I was numb to all feeling, and I didn't care at the moment. *Let the darkness come,* I thought, *let it take me away,* before it pulled a heavy blanket over my eyes and I dropped into oblivion.

CHAPTER THREE

The Scepter of the Seasons

I drifted for a while, neither awake nor asleep, caught somewhere between the two. Hazy, half-remembered dreams swam across my vision, mingling with reality until I didn't know which was which. I dreamed of my family, of Ethan and Mom and my stepdad, Luke. I dreamed of them going on without me, slowly forgetting who I was, that I ever existed. Shapes and voices floated in and out of my consciousness: Tiaothin telling me to snap out of it because she was bored, Rowan telling Queen Mab that he had no idea I would react so violently to a simple mushroom, another voice telling the queen that I might never wake up. Sometimes I dreamed that Ash was in the room, standing in a corner or beside my bed, just watching me with bright silver eyes. In my delirium, I might have heard him whisper that he was sorry.

"Humans are such fragile creatures, aren't they?" murmured a voice one night, as I drifted in and out of stupor. "One tiny nibble of spill-your-guts sends them into a coma. Pathetic." It snorted. "I heard this one was in love with Prince Ash. Makes you wonder what Mab will do to her, once she wakes up. She's none too pleased with the Summer whelp being all mushy-mushy with her favorite son."

"Well, she certainly picked an inconvenient time to go all Sleeping Beauty," added another voice, "what with the Exchange coming up and all." It snorted. "If she does wake up, Mab might kill her for the annoyance. Either way, it'll be entertaining." The sound of their laughter faded away, and I floated in darkness.

An eternity passed with few distractions. Voices slipping by me, unimportant. Tiaothin repeatedly poking me in the ribs, her sharp claws drawing blood, but the pain belonged to someone else. Scenes of my family: Mom on the porch with a police officer, explaining she didn't have a missing daughter; Ethan playing in my room, which was now an office, repainted and refurnished, all my personal items given away.

There was a dull throb in my chest as I watched him; in another life, it might have been sorrow, longing, but I was beyond feeling anything now and watched my half brother with detached curiosity. He was talking to a familiar stuffed rabbit, and that made me frown. Wasn't that rabbit destroyed…?

"They have forgotten you," murmured a voice in the darkness. A deep, familiar voice. I turned and found Machina, his cables folded behind him, watching me with a small smile on his lips. His silver hair glowed in the blackness.

My brow furrowed. "You're not here," I muttered, backing away. "I killed you. You aren't real."

"No, my love." Machina shook his head, his hair rippling softly. "You did kill me, but I am still with you. I will always be with you, now. There is no avoiding it. We are one."

I drew back, shivering. "Go away," I said, retreating into the black. The Iron King watched me intently, but did not follow. "You're not here," I repeated. "This is just a dream, and you're dead! Leave me alone." I turned and fled into the darkness, until the soft glow of the Iron King faded into the void.

Another eternity passed, or perhaps only a few seconds, when through the confusion and darkness, I felt a presence near the bed. *Mom?* I wondered, a little girl once more. Or maybe Tiaothin, come to bother me again. *Go away,* I told them, retreating into my dreams. *I don't want to see you. I don't want to see anyone. Just leave me alone.*

"Meghan," whispered a voice, heart-wrenchingly familiar, drawing me out of the void. I recognized it immediately, just as I realized it was a figment of my desperate imagination, because the real owner of that voice would never be here, talking to me.

Ash?

"Wake up," he murmured, his deep voice cutting through the layers of the darkness. "Don't do this. If you don't come out of this soon, you'll fade away and drift forever. Fight it. Come back to us."

I didn't want to wake up. There was nothing but pain waiting for me in the real world. If I was asleep, I couldn't feel anything. If I was asleep, I didn't have to face Ash and the cold contempt on his face when he looked at me. Darkness was my retreat, my sanctuary. I drew back from Ash's voice, deeper into the comforting blackness. And, through the layer of dreams and delirium, I heard a quiet sob.

"Please." A hand gripped mine, real and solid, anchoring me to the present. "I know what you must think of me, but…" The voice broke off, took a ragged breath. "Don't leave," it whispered. "Meghan, don't go. Come back to me."

I sobbed in return, and opened my eyes.

The room was dark, empty. Faery light filtered through the

window, casting everything in blue and silver. As usual, the air was icy cold. *A dream, then,* I thought, as the mist swirling around my head for so long finally cleared, leaving me devastatingly awake and aware. *It was a dream, after all.*

A sense of betrayal filled me. I'd come out of my lovely darkness for nothing. I wanted to retreat, to return to the oblivion where nothing could hurt me, but now that I was awake, I couldn't go back.

An ache filled my chest, so sharp that I gasped out loud. Was this what a broken heart felt like? Was it possible to die from the pain? I'd always thought the girls at school so dramatic; when they broke up with their boyfriends, they cried and carried on for weeks. I didn't think they needed to throw such a fuss. But I'd never been in love before.

What would I do now? Ash despised me. Everything he'd said and done was to bring me to his queen. He was a cheat. He'd *used* me, to further his own ends.

And the saddest part was, I still loved him.

Stop it! I told myself, as tears threatened once more. *Enough of this! Ash doesn't deserve it. He doesn't deserve anything. He's a soulless faery who played you every step of the way, and you fell for it like an idiot.* I took a deep breath, forcing back the tears, willing them to freeze inside me, to freeze everything inside me. Emotions, tears, memories, anything that made me weak. Because if I was going to play in the Unseelie Court, I had to be made of ice. No, not ice. Like iron. *Nothing will hurt me again,* I thought, as my tears dried and my emotions shriveled into a withered ball. *If the damned faeries want to play rough, so be it. I can play rough, too.*

I threw back the covers and stood tall, the cold air prickling my skin. *Let it freeze me, I don't care.* My hair was a mess, tangled and limp, my clothes rumpled and disgusting. I peeled them off and walked into the bathroom for a long soak in the tub—the only warm place in the entire court—before dressing in black jeans, a black halter top and a long black coat. As I was finishing lacing up my black boots, Tiaothin walked into the room.

She blinked, obviously astonished to see me on my feet, before breaking into a huge grin, fangs shining in the moonlight. "You're up!" she exclaimed, bouncing over and leaping onto my bed. "You're awake. That's a relief. Mab's been annoyed and cranky ever since you collapsed. She thought you were going to sleep forever, and then she'd have a devil of a time explaining your condition to the Seelie courtiers when they come for the Exchange."

I frowned at her, and for a moment, a tiny spark of hope flickered inside. "What Exchange?" I wondered. *Have they come for me? Has Oberon finally sent someone to rescue me from this hellhole?*

Tiaothin, in that guileless way of hers, seemed to know exactly what I was thinking. "Don't worry, half-breed." She sniffed, looking at me with slitted eyes. "They're not coming for *you*. They're here to pass on the Scepter of the Seasons. Summer is finally over, and winter is on the way."

I felt a pang of disappointment and quashed it. *No weakness. Show her nothing.* I shrugged and casually asked, "What's the Scepter of the Seasons?"

Tiaothin yawned and made herself comfortable on my bed. "It's a magical talisman that the courts pass between them with the changing of the seasons," she said, picking at a loose thread on my quilt. "Six months out of the year, Oberon holds it, when spring and summer are at their peak, and winter is at its weakest. Then, on the autumn equinox, it is passed to Queen Mab, to signify the shift in power between the courts.

The Summer courtiers will be arriving soon, and we'll have a huge party to celebrate the start of winter. Everyone in Tir Na Nog is invited, and the party will last for days." She grinned and bounced in place, dreadlocks flying. "It's a good thing you woke up when you did, half-breed. This is one party you don't want to miss!"

"Will Lord Oberon and Lady Titania be there?"

"Lord Pointy Ears?" Tiaothin sniffed. "He's much too important to go slumming around with Unseelie lowlifes. Nah, Oberon and his bitch queen Titania will stay in Arcadia where they're comfortable. Lucky thing, too. Those two stiff necks can really ruin a good party."

So I'd be on my own after all. Fine with me.

The Summer Court arrived in a hale of music and flowers, probably in direct defiance of Winter, whose traditions I was beginning to hate. I stood calf deep in snow, the collar of my fur coat turned up against cold, watching Unseelie fey mill about the courtyard. The event was to take place outside, in the courtyard full of ice and frozen statues. Will-o'-the-wisps and corpse candles floated through the air, casting everything in eternal twilight. Why couldn't the Winter fey hold their parties aboveground for once? I missed the sunlight so much it hurt.

I felt a presence behind me, then heard a quiet chuckle in my ear. "So glad you were able to make it to the party, Princess. It would've been terribly boring without you."

My skin prickled, and I squashed down my fear as Rowan's breath tickled the back of my neck. "Wouldn't miss it for the world," I replied, keeping my voice light and even. His eyes bored into my skull, but I didn't turn. "What can I do for you, Your Highness?"

"Oh ho, now we're playing the ice queen. Bravo, Princess, bravo. Such a brave comeback from your broken heart. Not what I expected from Summer at all." He shifted around me so that we were inches apart, so close I could see my reflection in his ice-blue eyes. "You know," he breathed, his breath cold on my cheek, "I can help you get over him."

I desperately wanted to back away, but I held my ground. *You are iron,* I reminded myself. *He can't hurt you. You're steel inside.* "The offer is appreciated," I said, locking gazes with the sidhe prince, "but I don't need your help. I'm already past him."

"Are you now?" Rowan didn't sound convinced. "You know he's right over there, don't you? Pretending not to watch us?" He smirked and took my hand, pressing it to his lips. My stomach fluttered before I could stop it. "Let's show dear Ash how much you're over him. Come on, Princess. You know you want to."

I did want to. I wanted to hurt Ash, make him jealous, put him through the same pain I had gone through. And Rowan was right there, offering. All I had to do was lean forward and meet his smirking mouth. I hesitated. Rowan *was* gorgeous; I could do worse in the casual make-out department.

"Kiss me," Rowan whispered.

A trumpet sounded, echoing over the courtyard, and the smell of roses filled the air. The Seelie Court was arriving, to the roars and shrieks of the Winter fey.

I started, wrenching myself out of the glamour-induced daze. "Dammit, stop doing that!" I snarled, yanking my hand from his grip and stumbling back. My heart slammed against my rib cage. God, I'd almost fallen for it this time; another half second and I would have been all over him. Shame colored my cheeks.

Rowan laughed. "You're almost attractive when you blush," he snickered, moving out of slapping range. "Until next time, Princess." With another mocking bow, he slipped away.

I glanced around furtively, wondering if Ash truly was nearby and watching us, as Rowan claimed. Though I saw Sage and his enormous wolf lounging against a pillar near Mab's throne, Ash was nowhere in sight.

Two satyrs padded through the briar-covered gates of the courtyard, holding pale trumpets that looked made of bone. They raised the horns to their lips and blew a keening blast, one that set the Unseelie Court to howling. Atop her throne of ice, Mab watched the procedures with a faint smile.

"Gotcha!" hissed a voice, and something pinched me painfully on the rear. I yelped, whirling on Tiaothin, who laughed and danced away, dreadlocks flying. "You're an idiot, half-breed," she taunted, as I kicked snow at her. She dodged easily. "Rowan's too good for you, and he's experienced. Most everyone, fey and mortal boys included, would give their teeth to have him to themselves for a night. Try him. I guarantee you'll like it."

"Not interested," I snapped, glaring at her with narrowed eyes. My butt still stung, making my words sharp. "I'm done playing games with faery princes. They can go to hell, for all I care. I'd rather strip naked for a group of redcaps."

"Ooh, if you do, can I watch?"

I rolled my eyes and turned my back on her as the Seelie Court finally made its appearance. A line of white horses swept into the courtyard, their hooves floating over the ground, their eyes as blue as the summer sky. Atop saddles made of bark, twigs and flowering vines, elven knights peered down haughtily, elegant in their leafy armor. After the knights came the standard-bearers, satyrs and dwarfs bearing the colors of the Summer Court. Then, finally, an elegant carriage pulled up, wreathed in thorns and rosebushes and flanked by two grim-faced trolls who growled and bared their fangs at the crowds of Winter fey.

Tiaothin sniffed. "They're being highly paranoid this year," she muttered, as a troll took a swat at a goblin that edged too close. "Wonder who the high-and-mighty noble is, to warrant such security measures?"

I didn't answer, for my skin was prickling a warning, though I didn't know why until a moment later. The carriage rolled to a stop, the doors were opened…

And King Oberon, Lord of the Seelie Court, stepped out into the snow.

The Unseelie fey gasped and snarled, backing away from the carriage, as the Erlking swept his impassive gaze over the crowd. My heart hammered in my chest. Oberon looked as imposing as ever: slender, ancient and powerful, his silver hair falling to his waist and his eyes like pale leaves. He wore robes the color of the forest, brown and gold and green, and an antlered crown rested on his brow.

Beside me, Tiaothin gaped, flattening her ears. "Oberon?" she snarled, as I watched the Erlking's gaze sweep the crowd, searching meticulously. "What's Lord Pointy Ears doing here?"

I couldn't answer, for Oberon's piercing stare finally found me. His eyes narrowed, and I shivered under that look. The last time I'd seen the Erlking, I'd snuck away from the Seelie Court to find my brother. Oberon had sent Puck to fetch me back, and I'd convinced him to help me instead. After our rebellion and direct disobedience, I imagined the Seelie king was none too happy with either of us.

My stomach twisted and a lump rose to my throat as I thought of Puck. I managed to swallow it down before any

Unseelie noticed my bout of weakness, but the memories still haunted me. I desperately wished Puck were here. I stared at the carriage, hoping his lanky, red-haired form would come leaping out, flashing that defiant smirk, but he did not appear.

"Lord Oberon," Mab said in a neutral voice, but it was clear that she, too, was surprised to see her ancient rival. "This is a surprise. To what do we owe the honor of your visit?"

Oberon approached the throne, flanked by his two troll bodyguards. The crowd of Unseelie fey parted quickly before him, until he stood before the throne. "Lady Mab," the Erlking said, his powerful voice echoing over the courtyard, "I have come to request the return of my daughter, Meghan Chase, to the Seelie Court."

A murmur went through the ranks of Unseelie fey, and all eyes turned to me. *Iron,* I reminded myself. *You are like iron. Don't let them scare you.* I stepped out from behind Tiaothin and met the surprised, angry looks head-on.

Oberon gestured at the carriage, and the trolls reached inside, dragging out two pale Winter sidhe, their arms bound behind their backs with living, writhing vines. "I have brought an exchange, as the rules dictate," Oberon continued, as the trolls pushed the prisoners forward. "I will return to you your own, in exchange for my daughter's freedom—"

Mab interrupted. "I'm afraid you misunderstand, Lord Oberon," she rasped with the faintest of smiles. "Your daughter is not a prisoner of the Unseelie, but a willing guest. She came to us on her own, after making a bargain with my son to do so. The girl is bound by her contract to Prince Ash, and you have no power to demand her return. Once a bargain is made, it must be honored by all."

Oberon stiffened, then slowly turned to me again. I gulped as those ancient-as-the-forest eyes pierced right through me.

"Is this true, daughter?" he asked, and though his voice was soft, it echoed in my ears and made the ground tremble.

I bit my lip and nodded. "It's true," I whispered. *I guess your wolf henchman didn't come back to tell you that part.*

The Erlking shook his head. "Then, I cannot help you. Foolish girl. You have doomed yourself to your fate. So be it." He turned from me, a deserting gesture that spoke louder than any words, and I felt like he had punched me in the stomach. "My daughter has made her choice," he announced. "Let us be done with this."

That's it? I thought as Oberon walked back toward the carriage. *You're not going to fight to get me out, bargain with Mab for my freedom? Because of my stupid contract, you're just going to leave me here?*

Apparently so. The Erlking didn't look at me a second time as he reached the carriage and gestured to his trolls. One of them shoved the Unseelie prisoners back into the carriage, while the other opened the opposite door with a grunt.

A tall, regal faery stepped out into the snow. Despite her size, she looked so delicate it seemed she would break at the slightest puff of air. Her limbs were bundles of twigs, held together with woven grass. Fragile white buds grew from her scalp instead of hair. A magnificent mantle covered her shoulders, made of every flower under the sun: lilies, roses, tulips, daffodils, and plants I didn't have a name for. Bees and butterflies flitted around her, and the smell of roses was suddenly overpowering.

She stepped forward, and the hoards of Winter fey leaped back at her approach, as if she had a disease. However, it wasn't the flower woman all eyes were trained on, but what she held in her hands.

It was a scepter, like kings and queens used to carry, only

this one wasn't just some decorated rod. It pulsed with a soft amber glow, as if sunlight clung to the living wood, melting the snow and ice where it touched. The long handle was wrapped in vines, and the carved head of the scepter continuously sprouted flowers, buds, and tiny plants. It left a trail of leaves and petals where the lady passed, and the Winter fey kept their distance, growling and hissing.

At the foot of the throne, the lady knelt and held out the scepter in both hands, bowing her head. For a moment, Mab did nothing, simply watching the faery with an unreadable expression on her face. The rest of the Winter Court seemed to hold their breath. Then, with deliberate slowness, Mab stood and plucked the scepter from the woman's hands. Holding it before her, the queen studied it, then raised it up for all to see.

The scepter flared, the golden aura swallowed up by icy blue. The leaves and flowers shriveled and fell away. Bees and butterflies spiraled lifelessly to the ground, their gossamer wings coated in frost. The scepter flared once more and turned to ice, sending sparkling prisms of light over the courtyard.

The faery kneeling before the queen jerked and then…she, too, shriveled away. Her gorgeous robe withered, the flowers turning black and falling to the ground. Her hair curled, becoming dry and brittle, before flaking off her scalp. I heard the snapping of twigs as her legs broke at the knees, unable to hold her up any longer. She pitched forward into the snow, twitched once, and was still. As I watched in horror, wondering why no one went forward to help, the smell of roses faded away, and the stench of rotting vegetation filled the courtyard.

"It is done," said Oberon, his voice weary. He raised his head and met Mab's gaze. "The Exchange is complete, until the summer equinox. Now, if you will excuse us, Queen Mab. We must return to Arcadia."

Mab shot him a look that was purely predatory. "You will not stay, Lord Oberon?" she crooned. "Celebrate with us?"

"I think not, Lady." If Oberon was disturbed by the way Mab looked at him, he didn't show it. "The ending of summer is not something we look forward to. I'm afraid we will have to decline. But, be warned, Queen Mab, this is not yet over. One way or another, I will have my daughter back."

I gave a start at those words. Maybe Oberon would come through for me after all. But Mab's gaze narrowed, and she stroked the handle of the scepter.

"That sounds uncomfortably close to a threat, Erlking."

"Merely a promise, my lady." With Mab still glaring at him, Oberon deliberately turned his back on the Winter Queen and strode to the carriage. A troll opened the door for him, and the Erlking entered without a backward glance. The driver shook the reins, and the Summer entourage was off, growing smaller and smaller, until the darkness swallowed them up.

Mab smiled.

"Summer is over," she announced in her raspy voice, raising her other arm as if to embrace her waiting subjects. "Winter has come. Now, let the Revel begin!"

The Unseelie went berserk, howling, roaring and screaming into the night. Music started from somewhere, wild and dark, drums pounding out a fast, frenzied rhythm. The fey swarmed together in a chaotic, writhing mass, leaping, howling and twirling madly, rejoicing in the coming of winter.

I didn't get into the party. One, I wasn't in the mood, and two, dancing with the Winter fey didn't seem like such a great idea. Especially after I saw a group of drunk, glamour-high redcaps swarm a boggart and tear it limb from limb. It was like a mosh pit from hell. Mostly I hung back in the shadows, trying to avoid notice and wondering if Mab would think me rude if I retreated to my room. Looking at the frozen statues of humans and fey scattered throughout the courtyard, I decided not to risk it.

At least Rowan was absent from the celebrations, or lurking somewhere I couldn't see. I had been bracing myself to fend off his advances all night. Ash was also mysteriously absent, which was both a relief and a disappointment. I found myself searching for him, scouring the shadows and mobs of dancing fey, looking for a familiar tousled head or the glint of a silver eye.

Stop that, I thought, when I realized what I was doing. *He's not here. And even if he was, what would you do? Ask him to dance? He's made what he thinks of you perfectly clear.*

"Excuse me, Princess."

For a moment, my heart leaped at the soft, deep voice. The voice that could either be Rowan's or Ash's, they sounded so much alike. Bracing myself, I turned, but it wasn't Ash standing there. Thankfully, it wasn't Rowan, either. It was the other brother, the oldest of the three. Sage.

Dammit, he's gorgeous also. What was with this family, that all the sons were so freaking handsome it hurt to look at them? Sage had his brothers' pale face and high cheekbones, and his eyes were chips of green ice, peering out beneath slender brows. Long black hair rippled behind him, like a waterfall of ink. His wolf sat a few paces away, watching me with intelligent golden eyes.

"Prince Sage," I greeted warily, prepared to fend off another assault. "Can I help you with anything, Your Highness?" *Or did you just come to push yourself on me like Rowan, or mock me like Ash?*

"I want to speak with you," the prince said without pre-amble. "Alone. Will you walk with me a bit?"

This surprised me, though I still hesitated, wary. "Where are we going?" I asked.

"The throne room," Sage replied, sweeping his gaze back to the palace. "It is my duty to guard the scepter this night, as only those with royal blood are allowed to touch it. With all the chaos from the Revel, it is best to keep the scepter away from the masses. It could get messy otherwise." When I paused, thinking, he shrugged a lean shoulder. "I will not force you, Princess. Come with me or not, it makes no differ-ence. I merely wanted to speak to you without Rowan, Ash, or some phouka trying to eavesdrop on the conversation."

He waited patiently as I struggled for an answer. I could refuse, but I wasn't sure I wanted to. Sage seemed straight-forward, almost businesslike. Different from his brothers. He wasn't making any attempt to be charming, but he wasn't being condescending, either. And unlike Rowan, who oozed charm and malice, he wasn't using glamour, and I think that's finally what sold me.

"All right," I decided, motioning with my hand. "I'll talk with you. Lead the way."

He offered me his arm, which surprised me again. After a moment's hesitation, I took it, and we started off, his wolf trailing silently behind us.

He led me back into the palace, down empty halls swathed in ice and shadow. All the Unseelie fey were outside, dancing the night away. My footsteps echoed loudly against the hard floors; his and the wolf's made no sound at all.

"I've seen you," Sage murmured without looking at me. He turned a corner, so smoothly I stumbled to keep pace. "I've watched you with my brother. And I want to warn you, you mustn't trust him."

I almost laughed, the statement was so obvious. "Which one?" I asked bitterly.

"Either of them." He pulled me down another corridor, one I recognized. We were close to the throne room now. Sage pressed on without slowing. "You do not know the enmity between Ash and Rowan, how deep the rivalry goes. Especially on Rowan's part. The jealousy he feels for his youngest brother is a dark poison, eating him from the inside, making him bitter and vengeful. He has never forgiven Ash for Ariella's death."

We entered the throne room in all its frigid, icy beauty. Sage released me and walked toward the throne, his wolf padding behind him. I shivered, huddling deeper into my coat. It was colder in here than it was outside. "But Ash wasn't responsible for Ariella's death," I said, rubbing my forearms. "That—" I stopped, not wanting to say it out loud. *That was Puck, who led them into danger. Who was responsible for the death of Ash's love.*

Sage didn't answer. He had come to a stop a few feet beside Mab's icy throne, staring at something on the altar beside it. A moment later, I realized that was the source of the ungodly chill in the room. The Scepter of the Seasons hovered a few inches over the altar, washing the prince's face in icy blue light.

"Beautiful, isn't it?" he murmured, running his fingers over the frozen handle. "Every year, I see it, and yet it never ceases to amaze me." His eyes glittered; he seemed to be in some sort of trance. "Someday, if Mab ever gets tired of being queen, it will be mine to accept, to rule with. When that happens…"

I didn't get to hear the rest, for at that moment, the wolf let out a long, low growl and bared its teeth.

Sage whirled around. In one smooth motion, he drew the

sword at his waist. I stared at it. It was much like Ash's, straight and slender, the blade throwing off an icy blue aura. I shivered, remembering what it was like to grasp that hilt, feel the awful cold bite into my skin. And for a moment, I was terrified. *He's going to kill me, that's why he brought me here alone. He was going to kill me all along.*

"How did you get in here?" Sage hissed.

I turned. There, against the back wall, several dark forms melted out of the shadows. Four were thin and lanky, almost emaciated, their frames nothing but wires twisted together to form limbs and a body, resembling huge puppets as they skittered over the ground on all fours. The wolf's growls turned into snarls.

My heart turned over as another form stepped into the light, dressed in segmented metal armor emblazoned with a barbed-wire crown. He wore a helmet, but the visor was up, showing a face as familiar to me as my own. There was no mistaking that pale skin, those intense gray eyes. Ash's face gazed out at me from under the helmet, his eyes as bleak as the winter sky.

CHAPTER FOUR

The Theft

"Ash?" Sage muttered in disbelief. I shook my head mutely, but the prince wasn't looking at me.

The knight blinked, giving Sage a solemn look. "I'm afraid not, Prince Sage," he said, and I shivered at how much he sounded like his double. "Your brother was simply the blueprint for my creation."

"Tertius," I whispered, and Ash's doppelgänger gave me a pained smile. The last time I'd seen the Iron knight was in Machina's tower just before it came crashing down. I couldn't imagine how he'd survived. "What are you doing here?"

Tertius's gaze met mine, his eyes blank and dead, looking so much like Ash's it made my heart ache. "Forgive me, Princess," he murmured, and made a sweeping gesture with his arm.

With shrieks like knives scraping against each other, the Iron faeries rushed me.

They were appallingly fast, scuttling gray blurs across the floor. I had the absurd image of being ambushed by a swarm of metallic spiders before they were upon me. The first attacker leaped up and slashed at my face with a twisted wire claw as sharp as any razor.

It met a gleaming blue sword instead, screeching off the blade in a volley of sparks, bringing tears to my eyes. Sage threw back one attacker and whirled to meet the next, ducking as wire talons slashed over his head. The Winter prince thrust out a palm, and a jagged ice spear surged out of the floor, stabbing toward the Iron fey. Lightning fast, they dodged, leaping back and giving us time to retreat. Grabbing my wrist, Sage yanked me behind the throne.

"Keep out of the way," he ordered, just as the faeries descended on us again, swarming over the chair and leaving deep gouges in the ice. Sage slashed at one, only to have it spring back. Another darted in from behind, lashing out with steel talons. The prince dodged, but he didn't move fast enough, and a bright splash of blood colored the floor.

My stomach twisted as the prince staggered, swinging his blade in a desperate circle to keep the assassins back. There were too many for him, and they were too quick. Frantically, I looked around for a weapon, but saw only the scepter, lying on the pedestal near the throne. Knowing I was probably breaking a dozen sacred rules, I lunged for the scepter and snatched it up by its frozen handle.

The cold seared my hands, burning them like acid. I gasped and nearly dropped it, gritting my teeth against the pain. Sage stood in the middle of a slashing whirlwind, desperately trying to keep them back. I saw lines of red on his face and chest. Trying to ignore the searing pain, I rushed up behind an Iron fey, raised the scepter over my head and smashed it down on the faery's spindly back.

It whirled with blinding speed. I didn't even see the blow until it backhanded me across the face, making lights explode behind my eyes. I flew back into a corner, striking my head on something hard and slumping to the floor. The scepter dropped from my grasp and rolled away. Dazed, I watched the faery scuttle toward me but suddenly jerk to a stop, as if yanked by invisible strings. Ice covered its body, pushing up through the seams in the wire as the faery clawed at itself frantically. Wire-thin fingers snapped off, and the faery's struggles slowed before it curled in on itself like a giant insect and stopped moving altogether.

I didn't have the breath to scream. I tried pushing away from the wall, but everything spun violently and my stomach lurched. I heard footsteps coming toward me and opened my eyes to see Tertius bend down and take the Scepter of the Seasons.

"Don't," I managed, trying to struggle to my feet. The ground swayed, and I stumbled back. "What are you doing?"

He observed me with solemn gray eyes. "Following the orders of my king."

"King?" I struggled to focus. Everything seemed to be moving in slow motion. A few feet away, Sage and the assassins fought on. The wolf had its jaws clamped around a faery's leg, and Sage pressed it unmercifully with his sword. "You don't have a king anymore," I told Tertius, feeling light-headed and numb. "Machina is dead."

"Yes, but our realm endures. I follow the commands of the new Iron King," Tertius murmured, drawing his sword. I stared at the steel blade, hoping it would be quick. "I bear you no ill will, this time. My orders do not include killing you. But I must obey my lord."

And with that, Tertius spun on his heel and marched away, still holding the Scepter of the Seasons. It pulsed blue and white in his hands, coating his gauntlets with frost, but he did not fumble. His face was grim as he strode up behind Sage, still locked in battle with the assassins. The wolf thrashed on the ground in a pool of blood, and Sage's breaths came in ragged gasps as he fought on alone. In horror, I saw what Tertius was going to do and screamed out a warning.

Too late. As Sage cut viciously at one of the Iron fey, he didn't see Tertius looming behind him until the knight was right there. Aware of the danger at last, Sage whirled, swinging his sword, cutting at Tertius's head. The knight knocked the blade aside and, as Sage staggered back, took one step forward and plunged his own sword through the Winter prince's chest.

Time seemed to stop. Sage stood there a moment, a look of shock on his face, staring at the blade in his chest. His own sword hit the ground with a ringing clang.

Then Tertius yanked the blade free, and I gasped. Sage crumpled to the floor, blood pooling from his chest and streaming onto the ice. The assassins tensed to pounce on him, but Tertius blocked them with his sword.

"Enough. We have what we came for. Let's go." He flicked blood off the blade and sheathed it, his eyes moving to the corpse of the frozen assassin. "Fetch your brother, quickly. We can leave no evidence behind."

The Iron fey scrambled to comply, lifting the dead faery onto their shoulders, careful not to touch the ice piercing its skin. They even grabbed the pieces off the floor. Tertius turned to me, his gaze bleak, as darkness hovered on the edge of my vision. "Farewell, Meghan Chase. I hope we do not meet again." He spun quickly to follow the assassins, marching out of my line of sight. I turned my head to follow them, but they were already gone.

My head throbbed, and darkness threatened at the edges of my vision; I took several deep breaths to drive it back. I would *not* pass out now. Gradually, the churning blackness cleared, and I pulled myself upright, looking around. The throne room had fallen silent again, except for the slow thudding of my heart, which sounded unnaturally loud in my ears. Blood flecked the walls and pooled along the floor, horribly vivid against the pale ice. The altar that had held the Scepter of the Seasons lay empty and bare.

My gaze wandered to the two bodies still in the room with me. Sage lay on his back, his sword a few inches from his hand, gazing up at the ceiling, gasping. A few feet away, the furry body of the wolf, gray fur streaked with blood, lay crumpled on the ice.

Limping, I ran over to Sage, passing the body of the poor wolf, sprawled out next to him. The wolf's jaws gaped open, and a tongue lolled out between bloody teeth. It had died protecting its master, and I felt sick at the thought.

Just as I reached Sage, a shudder went through the prince's body. His head arced back, mouth gaping, and ice crawled up from his lips, spreading over his face, down his chest, and all the way to his feet. He stiffened as the air chilled around us, the ice making sharp crinkling sounds as it encased the prince in a crystal cocoon.

No. I looked closer, and realized Sage's *body* was turning to ice. His clawed fingers flexed, losing their color, becoming hard and clear. His thumb abruptly snapped off and shattered on the floor. I put both hands to my mouth to keep from screaming. Or vomiting. Sage gave a final jerk and was still, a cold, hard statue where a live body had been a moment before.

The oldest son of the Winter Court was dead.

And that's how Tiaothin found us a moment later.

Later, I didn't recall much of that moment, but I did remember the phouka's screech of horror and fury as she fled to tell the rest of the court. I heard her shrill voice echoing down the corridor, and knew I should probably move, but I was cold, numb to all feeling. I didn't leave the prince's side until Rowan swept in with a platoon of guards, who pounced on me with angry cries. Rough hands grabbed me by the arms and hair, dragging me away from Sage's body, oblivious to my protests and cries of pain. I shouted at Rowan to tell him what had happened, but he wasn't looking at me.

Behind him, Unseelie fey crowded into the room, and roars of fury and outrage filled the chamber when they saw the dead prince. Fey were screaming and crying, tearing at themselves and each other, demanding vengeance and blood. Dazed, I realized the Unseelie were outraged at the murder of a Winter prince in their own territory. That someone had dared slip in and kill one of their own, right under their noses. There was no sorrow or remorse for the prince himself, only fury and demands for revenge at the audacity of it. I wondered if anyone would truly miss the eldest prince of Winter.

Rowan stood over Sage's body, his expression eerily blank as he stared down at his brother. Amid the roars and cries of the fey around us, he regarded his sibling with the curiosity one might show a dead bird on the sidewalk. It made my skin crawl.

Silence fell over the room, and a chill descended like an icy blanket. I twisted in my captor's grasp and saw Mab standing in the doorway, her gaze locked on Sage's body. Everyone backed away as she entered the throne room. You could hear a pin drop as the queen walked up to Sage's body, bending down to touch his cold, frozen cheek. I shivered, for the temperature was still dropping. Even some of the Winter fey looked uncomfortable as new icicles formed on the ceiling and frost crept over skin and fur. Mab was still bent over Sage, her expression unreadable, but her mulberry lips parted and mouthed a single word. "Oberon."

Then she screamed, and the world shattered. Icicles exploded, flying outward like crystallized shrapnel, pelting everyone with glittering shards. The walls and floor cracked, and fey screeched as they disappeared into the gaping holes.

"Oberon!" Mab raged again, whirling around with a terrifying, crazy look in her eyes. "He did this! This is his revenge! Oh, Summer will pay! They will pay until they are screaming for mercy, but they will find no pity among the Winter Court! We will repay this heinous act in kind, my subjects! Prepare for war!"

"No!" My voice was drowned out in the roar that went up from the Unseelie fey. Twisting out of my captor's grip, I staggered into the middle of the room.

"Queen Mab," I gasped, as Mab swung the full brunt of her terrible gaze on me. Madness warred with the fury in her eyes, and I shrank back in terror. "Please, listen to me! Oberon didn't do this! The Summer Court didn't kill Sage, it was the Iron King. The Iron fey did this!"

"Be silent!" hissed the queen, baring her teeth. "I will not listen to your pathetic attempts to protect your wretched family, not when the Summer King threatened me in my own court. Your sire has murdered my son, and you will be silent, or I will forget myself and give him an eye for an eye!"

"But, it's true!" I insisted, though my brain was screaming at me to shut up. I glanced around desperately and spotted Rowan, looking on with a faint smile. Ash would back me up, but Ash, as usual, wasn't here when I needed him. "Rowan, please. Help me out. I'm not lying, you know I'm not."

He regarded me with a solemn expression, and for a moment I really thought he would come through, before a corner of his mouth curled nastily. "It isn't nice to deceive the queen, Princess," he said, looking grim apart from the sneer in his eyes. "If these Iron fey were a threat, we would have seen them by now, don't you think?"

"But they do exist!" I cried, on the verge of panic now. "*I've* seen them, and they *are* a threat!" I turned back to Mab. "What about the huge, fire-breathing iron horse that almost killed your son? You don't think that's a threat? Call Ash," I said. "He was there when we fought Ironhorse and Machina. He'll back me up."

"*Enough!*" Mab screeched, whirling on me. "Half-breed, you go too far! Your line has already robbed me of a son, and you will not touch another! I know you seek to turn my youngest against me with your blasphemous claims of love, and *I will not have it!*" She pointed a manicured nail at me, and a flare of blue-white shot between us as I stumbled back. "You will be silent, once and for all!"

Something gripped my feet, holding them fast. I looked down to see ice creeping up my legs, moving faster than I'd seen before. In the space of a blink, it had flowed up my waist and continued over my stomach and chest. Icy needles stabbed my skin as I wrapped my arms around myself, just before they were frozen to my chest. And still, the ice came on, creeping up my neck, burning my chin. Panic gripped me as it covered my lower jaw, and I screamed as ice flooded my mouth. Before I could suck in another breath, it covered my nose, my cheekbones, my eyes, and finally reached the top of my head. I couldn't move. I couldn't breathe. My lungs burned for air, but my mouth and nose were filled with ice. I was drowning, suffocating, and my skin felt like it was being peeled away by the cold. I wanted to pass out, I longed for darkness to take me, but though I couldn't breathe and my lungs screamed for oxygen, I didn't die.

Beyond the wall of ice, everything had fallen silent. Mab stood before me, her expression torn between triumph and hate. She turned back to her subjects, who watched her with wary eyes, as if she might lash out at them, too.

"Make ready, my subjects!" the queen rasped, raising her arms. "The war with Summer starts now!"

Another roar, and the minions of the Unseelie Court scattered, leaving the room with raucous battle cries. Mab spared me one more glance over her shoulder, her lips curling into a snarl before she walked out. Rowan stared at me a moment longer, snickered, and followed his queen from the room. Silence fell, and I was left alone, dying but unable to die.

When you can't breathe, each second feels like an eternity. My entire existence shrank into trying to draw air into my lungs. Though my head knew it was impossible, my body couldn't understand. I could feel my heart thudding laboriously against my ribs; I could feel the hideous chill of the ice, searing my skin. My body knew it was still alive and continued its fight to live.

I don't know how long I stood there, hours or only a few minutes, when a shadowy figure slipped into the room. Though I could still see out, the ice made everything cracked and distorted, so I couldn't tell who it was. The shadow hesitated in the doorway, watching me for a long moment. Then, quickly, it glided across the room until it stood next to my prison, laying a pale hand against the ice.

"Meghan," a voice whispered. "It's me."

Even through my air-starved delirium, my heart leaped. Ash's silvery eyes peered through the wall separating us, as bright and soulful as ever. The torment on his face shocked me, as if he were the one trapped and unable to breathe.

"Hang on," he murmured, pressing his forehead to mine through the wall. "I'm getting you out of there." He leaned back, both hands against the ice, and closed his eyes. The air began to vibrate; a tremor shook the walls around me, and tiny cracks spider-webbed through the ice.

With the sound of breaking glass, the prison shattered, shards flying outward but somehow leaving me unscathed. My legs buckled and I fell, choking and coughing, vomiting up water and ice shards. Ash knelt beside me and I clung to him, gasping air into my starved lungs, feeling the world spin around me.

Somehow, through the dizzying rush of air, the relief at being able to breathe again, I noticed that Ash was holding me, too. His arms were locked around my shoulders, pressing me to his chest, his cheek resting against my wet hair. I heard his rapid heartbeat, pounding against my ear, and strangely, that calmed me down a little.

The moment ended too soon. Ash pulled away, dropping his black coat around my shoulders. I clutched at it gratefully, shivering. "Can you walk?" he whispered, and his voice was urgent. "We have to get out of here, now."

"W-where are we g-going?" I asked, my teeth chattering. He didn't answer, only pulled me to my feet, his gaze darting about warily. Grabbing my wrist, he started leading me from the room.

"Ash," I panted, "wait!" He didn't slow down. My nerves jangled a warning. With all my strength, I stopped dead in the middle of the floor and yanked my hand out of his grip. He whirled, eyes narrowing to slits, and I remembered all the things he'd said to Rowan, that everything he'd done was in service to his queen. I quickly backed out of his reach. "Where are you taking me?" I demanded.

He looked impatient, stabbing his fingers through his hair in an uncharacteristically nervous gesture. "Back to Seelie territory," he snapped, reaching for me again. "You can't be here now, not when a war is about to start. I'll get you safely over to your side and then I'm done with this."

It felt as if he'd slapped me. Fear and anger flared, making me stupid, making me want to hurt him all over again. "Why should I trust you?" I snarled, throwing the words at him like stones. I was completely aware that I was being an idiot, that we needed to get out of there before anyone saw us, but it was like I'd eaten spill-your-guts again, and words just kept pouring out. "You've misled me from the beginning. Everything you said, everything we did, that was all a ploy to bring me here. You set me up from the very start."

"Meghan—"

"Shut up! I hate you!" I was on a roll now, and had the vindictive pleasure of seeing Ash flinch as if I'd struck him. "You're a real piece of work, you know? Is this a game you like to play? Make the stupid human girl fall for you and then laugh as you rip her heart out? You knew what Rowan was doing, and you didn't do anything to stop it!"

"Of course not!" Ash snarled back, his vehemence startling me into silence. "Do you know what Rowan would do if he found out...what we did? Do you know what *Mab* would do? I had to make them believe I didn't care, or they would've torn you apart." He sighed wearily, giving me a solemn look. "Emotions are a weakness here, Meghan. And the Winter Court preys on the weak. They would've hurt you to get to me. Now, come on." He reached for me again, and I let him take my hand without protest. "Let's get out of here before it's too late."

"I'm afraid it's already too late," drawled a snide, familiar voice, making my heart stop. Ash jerked to a halt, yanking me behind him, as Rowan stepped out of the hallway, grinning like a cat. "I'm afraid your time just ran out."

CHAPTER FIVE

Brothers

"Hello, Ash." The older prince smiled gleefully as he sauntered into the room. His gaze met mine, and he raised a sardonic eyebrow. "And what, may I ask, are you doing with the half-breed? Could it be you're actually helping her escape? Oh dear, what a dreadfully treasonous idea you've come up with. I'm sure Mab will be quite disappointed in you."

Ash said nothing, but his hand on mine clenched tight. Rowan chuckled, circling us like a hungry shark. Ash moved with him, keeping his body between me and Rowan. "So, little brother," the older prince mused, adopting an inquisitive expression, "I'm curious. What made you risk everything for our wayward princess here?" Ash said nothing, and Rowan *tsked*. "Don't be stubborn, little brother. You might as well tell me, before Mab tears you limb from limb and banishes you from Tir Na Nog. What is the price of such loyal obedience? A contract? A promise? What is the little harlot giving you to betray your entire court?"

"Nothing." Ash's voice was cold, but I caught the faintest tremor below the surface. Rowan apparently did as well, for his eyebrows shot up and he gaped at his brother, before throwing back his head with a wild laugh.

"I can't believe it," Rowan gasped, staring at Ash in disbelief. "You're *in love* with the Summer whelp!" He paused and, when Ash didn't deny it, collapsed into shrieking laughter again. "Oh, this is rich. This is too perfect. I thought the half-breed was a fool, pining for the unattainable Ice prince, but it seems I was wrong. Ash, you've been holding out on us."

Ash trembled, but he didn't release my hand. "I'm taking her back to Arcadia. Get out of our way, Rowan."

Rowan sobered immediately. "Oh, I don't think so, little brother." He smiled, but it was a cruel thing, sharp as the edge of a blade. "When Mab finds out, you'll *both* be decorating the courtyard. If she's feeling merciful, maybe she'll freeze you two together. That would be tragically fitting, don't you think?"

I shuddered. The thought of returning to that cold, airless, living death was too much. I couldn't do it; I'd rather die first. And the thought of Ash having to endure it with me for hundreds of years was even more horrifying. I squeezed Ash's hand and pressed my face into his shoulder, glaring at Rowan for all I was worth.

"Of course," Rowan went on, scratching the side of his face, "you could always beg forgiveness, drag the half-breed to the queen, and still be in Mab's favor. In fact," he continued, snapping his fingers, "if you go to Mab right now and turn over the princess, I'll even keep my mouth shut about what I saw here. She won't hear a peep out of me, I swear."

Ash went rock still; I could feel muscles coiling beneath his skin, the tension lining his back.

"Come on, little brother." Rowan leaned against the door frame and crossed his arms. "You know it's for the best. There are only two choices here. Hand over the princess, or die with her."

Ash finally moved, as if coming out of a trance. "No," he whispered, and I heard the pain in his voice as he came to some terrible decision. "There is one more."

Releasing my hand, he took one deliberate step forward and drew his sword. Rowan's eyebrows shot up as Ash pointed his blade at him, a cold mist writhing along its edge. For a moment, there was absolute silence.

"Get out of the way, Rowan," Ash growled. "Move, or I'll kill you."

Rowan's face changed. In one instant, it went from arrogant, condescending and evilly smug, to something completely alien and terrifying. He pushed himself from the archway, his eyes gleaming with predatory hunger, and slowly drew his sword. It sent a raspy shiver echoing across the hall as it came into view, the blade thin and serrated like the edge of a shark's tooth.

"You sure about this, little brother?" Rowan crooned, flourishing his weapon as he stepped up to meet Ash. "Will you betray everything—your court, your queen, your own blood—for her? You can't change your mind once you start down this path."

"Meghan," Ash said, his voice so soft I nearly lost it. "Get back. Don't try to help me."

"Ash..." I wanted to say something. I knew I should stop this, this fight between brothers, but at the same time I knew Rowan would never let us go. Ash knew it, too, and I could see the reluctance in his eyes as he steeled himself for battle. He didn't want to fight his brother, but he would...for me.

They faced each other across the icy room, two statues each waiting for the other to make the first move. Ash had taken a battle stance, his sword out in front of him, his expression reluctant but unwavering. Rowan held his blade casually at his side, tip pointing toward the floor, smirking at his opponent. Neither of them seemed to breathe.

Then Rowan grinned, a predator baring his fangs. "All right, then," he muttered, sweeping up his blade in a blindingly quick move. "I think I'm going to enjoy this."

He lunged at Ash, his sword a jagged blur through the air. Ash brought his weapon up, and icy sparks flew as the blades screeched against each other. Snarling, Rowan cut viciously at his brother, advancing with a series of savage head strikes. Ash blocked, ducked, and suddenly lunged, stabbing at Rowan's throat. But Rowan spun gracefully aside, his sword licking out and back again. Ash whirled with inhuman speed, and would've cut him in two if the older prince hadn't leaped back.

Smiling, Rowan raised his weapon, and I gasped. The gleaming point was smeared with crimson. "First blood to me, little brother," he taunted, as a trickle of red began to drip from Ash's sword arm, speckling the floor. "There's still time to stop this. Turn over the princess and beg for Mab's mercy. And mine."

"You have no mercy, Rowan," Ash growled, and lunged at him again.

This time, they both moved so quickly, twisting, jumping, spinning aside and slashing with their blades, it was hard to see it as anything but a beautifully timed dance. In fast-forward. Sparks flew, and the sound of blades clashing echoed off the walls. Blood appeared on both swords, and red splattered the floor around the combatants, but I couldn't see who had the advantage.

Rowan suddenly knocked Ash's blade aside, then thrust out his hand, sending a jagged spear of ice at his brother's face.

Ash threw himself backward to avoid it, hitting the floor and rolling to his knees. As Rowan brought his sword down at his kneeling opponent and I screamed in fear, Ash ducked aside, letting the blade miss him by centimeters. Grabbing Rowan's arm, letting his brother's momentum carry him forward, Ash spun and threw him to the floor. Rowan's head struck the ice, and I heard the breath leave his body in a startled *whoof*. Quick as a snake, Rowan flipped over, sword in hand, but by that time, Ash had his blade at his throat.

Rowan glared at his brother, his face twisted into a mask of pain and hate. Both were panting, dripping blood from numerous wounds, yet Ash's grip was steady as he pressed the blade against Rowan's neck.

The older prince chuckled, raised his head and spit blood in Ash's face. "Go on then, little brother," he challenged, as Ash winced but didn't shy away. "Do it. You've betrayed your queen, sided with the enemy, drawn a sword against your own brother…you might as well add slaughtering your family to the list as well. Then you can run off with the half-breed and live out your sordid fantasy. I wonder how Ariella would feel, if she knew how easily she's been replaced."

"Don't talk about her!" Ash snarled, raising the hilt as if he really would thrust the sword through Rowan's throat. "Ariella is gone. Not a day goes by that I don't think of her, but she's gone, and there's nothing I can do about it." He took a deep breath to calm himself, the longing on his face plain to see. A lump caught in my throat, and I turned away, blinking back tears. No matter how much I loved this dark, beautiful prince, I could never match what he'd already lost.

Rowan sneered, narrowing his eyes. "Ariella was too good for you," he hissed, raising himself up on his elbows. "You failed her. If you'd really loved her, she would still be here."

Ash flinched, as if struck a physical blow, and Rowan pressed his advantage. "You never saw what a good thing you had," he continued, sitting up as Ash backed away a step. "She's dead because of you, because you couldn't protect her! And now you disgrace her memory with this half-breed abomination."

Pale, Ash glanced at me, and I saw Rowan's arm move a second too late. "Ash!" I cried, as the older prince leaped up and lunged with frightening speed. "Look out!"

Ash was already moving, the honed reflexes of a fighter kicking in even when his mind was elsewhere. Leaping back, his sword came up as Rowan slashed at him with a dagger that appeared from nowhere, and Rowan's lunge carried him right onto the point of Ash's blade.

Both brothers froze, and I bit down a scream. For a moment, everything ground to an abrupt halt, frozen in time. Rowan blinked and looked down at the blade in his stomach, his eyes wide and confused. Ash was staring at his hand in horror.

Then Rowan staggered back, dropping the knife and leaning against a wall, his arms around his gut. Blood streamed between his hands, staining the white fabric crimson.

"Congratulations...little brother." His voice came out choked, though his eyes were clear as he nodded at Ash, still frozen in shock. "You finally...managed to kill me."

Pounding footsteps echoed in the hall, and faint shouts carried into the throne room. I wrenched my eyes from Rowan's bloody form and ran to Ash, who was still staring at his brother in a horrified daze.

"Ash!" I grabbed his arm, snapping him out of his trance. "Someone's coming!"

"Yes, run away with...your half-breed, Ash." Rowan coughed, a line of blood trickling from his mouth. "Before

Mab comes in…and sees that her last son is dead to her. I don't think you can do anything more…to betray your court."

The voices were getting louder. Ash shot Rowan one last guilty, agonized look, then grabbed my wrist and ran for the door.

I don't remember how we made it out. Ash pulled me along like a madman, running through hallways I didn't recognize. It was a miracle we didn't run into anyone, as footsteps and sounds of pursuit echoed all around us. Maybe it wasn't coincidence at all, as Ash seemed to know exactly where he was going. Twice, he yanked me into a corner and pressed his body up against mine, whispering at me to be silent and not move. I froze as a gang of redcaps skittered past, snarling and waving knives at one another, but they didn't notice us. The second time, a pale woman in a bloody dress floated by, and my heart thudded so loudly I was sure she would hear, but she drifted past without seeing.

We fled down a cold, empty corridor with icicles growing from the ceiling like chandeliers, flickering with a soft blue light. Ash finally pulled me through a door with the silhouette of a bone-white tree emblazoned on the front. The room beyond was rather small and sparsely decorated with a tall bookshelf, a dresser made of polished black wood, and an impressive knife collection on the far wall. A simple bed sat in the corner, the blankets pulled tight, looking as if it hadn't been used in decades. Everything looked exceptionally clean, neat and Spartan, not like a prince's bedroom at all.

Ash sighed and finally released me, leaning against the wall with his head back. Blood soaked his shirt, leaving dark stains against the black material, and my stomach turned.

"We should clean those," I said. "Where do you keep the bandages?" Ash looked right through me, his eyes glassy and blank. The shock was taking a toll on him. I bit down my fear and faced him, trying to sound calm and reasonable. "Ash, do you have any rags or towels lying around? Something to stop the bleeding?"

He stared at me a moment, then shook himself and nodded to the corner. "Dresser," he muttered, sounding more weary than I'd ever heard him. "There's a jar of salve in the top drawer. *She* kept it…for emergencies…"

I didn't know what he meant by that, but I walked over to the dresser and yanked open the top drawer. It held an assortment of weird things: dead flowers, a blue silk ribbon, a glass dagger with an intricately carved bone handle. I rummaged around and found a jar of herb-scented cream, nearly empty, sitting on an old, bloodstained cloth. In the corner sat a roll of what looked like gauze made of spiderwebs.

As I pulled them out, a thin silver chain came with the gauze and slithered to the floor. Bending down to pick it up, I saw two rings attached to the links, one large and one small, and what Ash said finally sank in.

This—this drawer full of odds and ends—was Ariella's, where Ash kept all his memories of her. The dagger was hers, the ribbon was hers. The rings, exquisitely designed with tiny leaves etched in silver and gold, were a matching set.

I replaced the chain and shut the drawer, a cold knot settling in my stomach. If I ever needed proof that Ash still loved Ariella, here it was.

My eyes stung, and I blinked them angrily. Now was not the time for a jealous tantrum. I turned and found Ash watching me, his eyes dull and bleak. I took a deep breath. "Um, I think you'll have to take off your shirt," I whispered.

He complied, pushing himself away from the wall, leaving a smear of red. Removing his tattered shirt, he tossed it on the floor and turned back to me. I tried hard not to stare at the lean, muscular chest, though my mouth went dry and my face burned crimson.

"Should I sit?" he muttered, helping me along. Gratefully, I nodded. He moved to the bed, easing himself down on the mattress with his back to me. The wounds on his shoulder and ribs seeped crimson against his pale skin.

You can do this, Meghan. Carefully, I moved up behind him, shuddering at the long, jagged cuts across his flesh. There was so much blood. I dabbed at it gingerly, not wanting to hurt him, but he didn't make a sound. When the blood was gone, I dipped two fingers in the salve and touched it lightly to the gash on his shoulder.

He made a small noise, like an exhalation of breath, and slumped forward, head down and hair covering his eyes. "Don't worry about hurting me," he muttered without looking up. "I'm...fairly used to this."

I nodded and applied more salve to the wound, liberally this time. He didn't flinch, though his shoulders were taut and rigid beneath my fingertips; I could feel the tight coil of muscles beneath my hands. I wondered if Ariella used to do this for him, in this very bedroom, patching him up whenever he was hurt. Judging from the pale scars across his back, this wasn't the first time he'd been wounded in a deadly fight. Had she felt the same as me, angry and terrified whenever Ash put himself in mortal danger?

My eyes grew blurry. I tried blinking, but it was no use. Retrieving the gauze, I wrapped it around his shoulder, biting my lip to keep silent as tears streamed down my face.

"I'm sorry."

He hadn't moved, and his voice was so soft I barely heard it, but I still almost dropped the gauze. Tying it off, I didn't answer as I went to work on his ribs, winding the bandages around his waist. Ash sat perfectly still, barely breathing. A teardrop fell from my chin to land on his back, and he flinched.

"Meghan?"

"Why are you apologizing?" My voice came out shakier than I wanted it to, and I swallowed hard. "You already told me why you were being a bastard. You had to protect me from your family and the Winter Court. They were perfectly good reasons." *Not that I'm bitter or anything.*

"I didn't want to hurt you." Ash's voice was still soft, hesitant. "I thought that if I could make you hate me, it would be easier when you returned to your world." He paused, and his next words were almost a whisper. "What I said in the courtyard... Rowan would have tormented you even more if he knew."

I finished binding his ribs and pulled the wrappings tight around his waist. My eyes still streamed, but they were different tears now. I didn't miss the subtle phrasing: when you return to your world. Not *if.* When. As though he knew I would go back someday, and we would never see each other again.

Still silent, I picked up the jar and returned it to the dresser. I didn't want to face him now. I didn't want to think that he could be gone from my life forever, vanishing back into a world where I couldn't follow.

"Meghan." Ash turned and grabbed my hand, sending tingles up my arm. Against my will, I looked down at him. His face was desolate, his eyes pleading for understanding. "I can't...have feelings for you," he murmured, tearing a hole right through my heart. "Not in the way you want. Whatever happens, Mab is still my queen, and the Winter Court is my home. What happened in Machina's realm..." His brow knitted, and his expression darkened with pain. "We have to forget that, and move on. Once I take you to Arcadia's borders and you're safe with Oberon, you won't see me again."

The pain in my heart became a sick and fiery gnawing. I stared at him, hoping he would take it back, tell me he was kidding. He withdrew his hand and stood, facing me with a deeply sorrowful expression. "I'm sorry," he murmured again, avoiding my eyes. "It's…better this way."

"No." I shook my head as he drew away, brushing past me. I whirled to follow him, reaching for his arm, missing. "Ash, wait—"

"Don't make this harder." He opened his closet and pulled out a tight gray shirt, shrugging into it with barely a wince. "I…killed Rowan." He closed his eyes, struggling with the memory. "I'm a kinslayer. There's nothing left in my future now, so be glad you won't be around to see what happens."

"What will you do?"

He grimaced. "Return to court. Try to forget." Reaching into the closet, he pulled out a long black coat crossed with silver chains and drew it over his shoulders. "Throw myself on Mab's mercy and hope she doesn't kill me."

"You can't!"

He faced me fully, the coat swirling around him. Just like that, he became something cold and remote, a deadly beautiful faery, unearthly and unreachable. "Don't get involved in fey politics, Meghan," he said darkly, shutting the closet door. "Mab will find me, no matter what I do or how far I run. And with the war approaching, Winter will need every soldier it can get. Until Summer returns the scepter, Mab will be relentless."

He turned away, but mention of the war reminded me of something else. "The scepter. Ash, wait!" I grabbed his sleeve, ignoring the way he went perfectly still. "It wasn't the

Summer Court!" I blurted before he could say anything. "It was the Iron fey. I saw them." He frowned, and I leaned forward, willing him to believe me. "It was Tertius, Ash. Tertius killed Sage."

He stared at me blankly for a moment, and I held my breath, watching his expression. Out of everyone in the Winter Court, Ash was the only one to actually see the Iron fey. If he didn't believe me, I didn't have a chance of convincing anyone else.

"Are you sure?" he murmured after a few seconds. Relief flooded me, and I nodded vigorously. "Why? Why would the Iron fey steal the scepter? How did they even get inside?"

"I don't know. Maybe they want its power? Or maybe they took it to start a war between the courts. They accomplished that much at least."

"I have to tell the queen."

"No!" I moved to block him, and he glared at me. "Ash, she won't believe you," I said desperately. "I tried to tell her, and she turned me into an icicle. She's convinced it's Oberon's doing."

"She'll listen to me."

"Are you sure? With everything you've done? Will she listen to you after you saved me and killed Rowan?" His expression darkened, and I ignored the guilt stabbing holes in my chest. "We have to go after them," I whispered, suddenly sure of what we had to do. "We have to find Tertius and get the scepter back. It's the only way to stop the war. Mab will have to believe us then, right?"

Ash hesitated. For a moment, he looked terribly unsure, balanced between me and duty to his queen. He raked a hand through his hair, and I saw the indecision in his eyes. But before he could reply, a sudden scratching on his door made us both jump.

We exchanged a glance. Drawing his sword and motioning me back, Ash strode to the door and warily cracked it open. There was a streak of dark fur, and a cat darted through the opening. I yelped in surprise.

Ash sheathed his blade. "Tiaothin," he muttered, as the phouka shed the feline form for her more human one. "What's happening out there? What's going on?"

The phouka grinned at him, slitted eyes bright and eager. "The soldiers are everywhere," she announced, twitching her tail. "They've sealed all doors into and out of the palace, and everyone is looking for you and the half-breed." She spared me a glance and chuckled. "Mab is *pissed*. You should go now, if you're going. The elite guard are on their way right now."

I looked to Ash, pleading. He glanced at me, then back to the door, his expression torn. Then, he shook his head as if he couldn't believe he was doing this. "This way," he snapped, yanking open the closet. "Inside, now."

I crossed the threshold into the small, dark space and looked back for Ash. He paused at the frame, glancing at the phouka dancing in the middle of the room. "Lie low after this, Tiaothin," he warned. "Stay out of Mab's way for a while. Got it?"

The phouka grinned, mischief written on every inch of her smile. "And what fun would that be?" she said, sticking out her tongue. Before Ash could argue, her ears twitched backward and she jerked her head up. "They're almost here. Go, I'll lead them away. No one does a wild-goose chase better than a phouka." And before we could stop her, she ran to the door, flung it open and leaned into the hall. "The prince!" she screeched, her shrill voice echoing down the corridor. "The prince and the half-breed! I saw them! Follow me!"

We ducked into the closet as the sound of booted feet thundered past the door, following Tiaothin as she led them away. Ash sighed, raking a hand through his hair. "Idiot phouka," he muttered.

"Will she be all right?"

Ash snorted. "Tiaothin can handle herself better than anyone I know. That's why I asked her to keep an eye on you."

So that's why the phouka was so interested. "I didn't need babysitting," I said, both annoyed and thrilled that he'd thought to look out for me when he couldn't be there.

Ash ignored me. Putting a hand to the wall, he closed his eyes and muttered several strange, unfamiliar words under his breath. A thin rectangle of light appeared, and Ash pulled open another door, bathing the room in pale light and revealing an icy staircase plunging into darkness.

"Come on." He turned to me and held out a hand. "This will take us out of the palace, but we have to hurry before it disappears."

Behind us, a roar of discovery echoed through the hall, as something poked its head in the room and bellowed for its friends. I grabbed Ash's hand, and we fled into the darkness.

CHAPTER SIX

The Goblin Market

I followed Ash down the glittering staircase and through a narrow corridor studded with leering gargoyles and flickering blue torches. We didn't speak; the only sounds were our footsteps echoing off the stones and my ragged breathing. Several times, the tunnel split off in different directions, but Ash always chose a path without hesitation. I was glad for the long winter coat around my shoulders; the temperature here was frigid, and my breath clouded the air as we ran, listening for sounds of pursuit.

The passage abruptly dead-ended, a solid wall of ice blocking our path. I wondered if we'd taken a wrong turn, but Ash released me and walked forward, placing one hand against the ice. With sharp, crinkly sounds, it parted under his fingers, until another tunnel stretched away before us, ending in open air.

Ash turned to me.

"Stay close," he murmured, making a quick gesture with his hand. I felt the tingle of glamour as it settled over me like a cloak. "Don't talk to anyone, don't make eye contact, and don't attract any attention. With that glamour, no one will notice you, but it will break if you make a noise or catch someone's eye. Just keep your head down and follow me."

I tried. The problem was, it was difficult *not* to notice anything beyond the castle walls. The beautiful, twisted city of the Unseelie fey rose up around me, towering spires of ice and stone, houses made of petrified roots, caves with icicles dangling from the openings like teeth. I followed Ash down narrow alleys with eyes peering out from under rocks and shadows, through tunnels that sparkled with millions of tiny crystals, and down streets lined with bone-white trees that glowed with sickly luminance.

And of course, the Unseelie were out in droves tonight. The streets were lit up with will-o'-the-wisps and corpse candles, and swarms of Winter fey danced, drank and howled at the top of their lungs, their voices echoing off the stones. I remembered the wild Revel in the courtyard, and realized the Unseelie were still celebrating the official arrival of winter.

We skirted the edges of the crowds, trying to avoid notice as the Winter fey whirled and spun around us. Music rang through the night, dark and seductive, stirring the mob into frenzies. More than once, the dancing turned into a bloodbath as some unfortunate faery vanished under a pile of shrieking revelers and was torn apart. Trembling, I kept my head down and my eyes on Ash's shoulders as we wove our way through the screaming throngs.

Ash grabbed me and pulled me into an alley, his glare warning me to be silent. A moment later, a pair of knights cantered into the crowd on huge black horses with glowing blue eyes, scattering the Winter fey like a flock of birds. The dancers snarled and hissed as they leaped aside, and a goblin screeched once as it was trampled beneath a charging horse, falling silent as a hoof cracked its skull open.

The knights yanked their mounts to a halt and faced the mob, ignoring the growls and hurled insults. They wore black leather armor with thorns bristling from the shoulders, and the faces beneath the open helms were sharp and cruel. Ash shifted beside me.

"Those are Rowan's knights," he muttered. "His elite Thornguards. They answer only to him and the queen."

"By orders of Her Majesty, Queen Mab," one knight shouted, his voice somehow rising over the cacophony of music and snarling voices, "the Winter Court has officially declared war on Oberon and the Summer Court! For the crime of killing Crown Prince Sage and the theft of the Scepter of the Seasons, all Summer fey will be hunted down and destroyed without mercy!"

The Winter fey roared, screeching and howling into the night. It was not a roar of rage, but rather one of ecstasy. I saw redcaps laughing, goblins dancing for joy, and spriggans grinning madly. My stomach heaved. They wanted blood. The Winter Court lived for violence, for the chance to rip into their ancient rivals without mercy. The knight let them howl and carry on a few moments before holding up his hand for silence.

"Also," he roared, bringing the chaos to a murmur, "be aware that Prince Ash is now considered a traitor and a fugitive! He has attacked his brother, Prince Rowan, gravely wounding him, and has fled the palace with the half-breed daughter of Oberon. Both are considered extremely dangerous, so it would do you well to be wary."

Ash sucked in a breath. I saw relief cross his face, as well as guilt and concern. Rowan was still alive, though our escape through the city had become much more dangerous.

"If you see them, by order of Queen Mab, they are not to be harmed!" bellowed the knight. "Capture them, or report their whereabouts to any guard, and you will be greatly rewarded. Failure to do so invites the queen's wrath upon your head. Spread the word, for tomorrow we march to war!"

The knights spurred their mounts into action and galloped off, amid the roars of the Unseelie crowd. Ash looked deep in thought, his eyes narrowed to gray slits.

"Rowan isn't dead," he breathed, and I couldn't tell if he was pleased with this news or not. "At least, not yet. This will make things considerably more difficult."

"How will we get out?" I whispered.

Ash frowned. "The gates will be guarded," he muttered, looking past me into the street, "and I don't trust the regular trods if Rowan knows we're out here." He paused, thinking, then sighed. "There is one more place we can go."

"Where's that?"

He glanced at me, and I suddenly realized how close we were. Our faces were just inches apart and I felt his heartbeat quicken, matching my own. Quickly, he turned away, and I ducked my head, hiding my burning face.

"Come on," he whispered, and I thought I caught a tremor in his voice. "We're not going far, but we have to hurry. The Market keeps its own hours, and if we don't reach it in time, it will disappear."

A wild howl rang out of the darkness, and we looked back at the crowd. The Winter fey had gone back to their partying as if nothing had happened, but there was a meaner, desperate edge to their revels now, as if the promise of war had only whetted their appetite for blood. A pair of redcaps and a hag squabbled over the body of the dead goblin, and I turned away before I was sick. Ash took my hand and pulled me on, into the shadows.

We fled through the city, keeping to the shadows and darkness, somehow avoiding the mobs in the street. At one point, we very nearly tripped over a redcap exiting a hole in the wall. The creature snarled an insult, but then its beady eyes widened in recognition and it turned to shout a warning instead. Ash gestured sharply, and an ice dagger thunked into the creature's open mouth, silencing it forever.

We reached a circular courtyard on the banks of a huge underground lake, mist writhing off the water to drift along the ground. Colorful booths and tents stood empty as we passed through, flapping in the breeze like a dead, abandoned carnival. An enormous white tree stood in the very center, bearing fruit that looked like human heads. A narrow door was embedded in the thick trunk, and Ash quickened his pace as we approached.

"The Market is through here," he explained, pulling me behind the tree as an ogre lumbered past, its steps slow and ponderous. "Now, listen. Whatever you see in there, don't buy anything, don't offer anything, and don't accept anything, no matter how much you want it. The vendors will try to make a deal with you—ignore them. Keep silent, and keep your eyes on me. Got it?"

I nodded. Ash opened the narrow door with a creak and led me inside, shutting it behind him. The interior of the trunk glowed softly and had a putrid sweet smell, like decaying flowers. I looked around for another door or way out, but the trunk was empty except for the door we came in.

"Stay close," Ash whispered, and he pushed the door open again.

Noise exploded through the doorway. The circular court-yard now thronged with life; the booths overflowed with merchandise; music and faery fire drifted through the night, and fey milled about in huge numbers, buying, talking and haggling with the vendors. I shrank back against the trunk, and Ash gave me a reassuring smile.

"It's all right," he said, leading me forward again. "In the Market, no one questions why you're here or where you came from. The only thing they're concerned about is the deal."

"So, it's safe, then?" I asked, as a faery with a wolf's head stalked through the crowd, carrying a string of severed hands. Ash chuckled darkly.

"I wouldn't go that far."

We joined the throng who, despite the jostling, shoving and snarled insults, paid us little attention. Unearthly vendors stood beside their booths or tents, crying out their wares, beckoning to passersby with long fingers or claws. A warty goblin caught my eye and grinned, pointing to his display of necklaces made of fingers, teeth and bones. A hag waved a shrunken pig's head in my face, while a hulking troll tried handing me some kind of meat-on-a-stick. It smelled wonderful, until I noticed the crispy bird and rat heads stuck on the kebabs between other unidentifiable chunks, and hurried after Ash.

The oddities continued. Dream catchers made of spider silk and infant bones. Monkey Paws and Hands of Glory. One booth had a prominent display of still-beating hearts, while the tent beside it offered flowers of delicate spun glass. Everywhere I looked, I saw wonders, horrors, and the just plain weird. The vendors were incredibly persistent; if they caught you looking, they would leap in front of you, shouting the marvels of their wares and offering "a deal you can't refuse."

"A few locks of your hair," cried a rat-faced imp, holding

out a golden apple. "Be young and beautiful forever." I shook my head and hurried on.

"A memory," crooned a doe-eyed woman, waving a glittering amulet back and forth. "One tiny memory, and your greatest wish will be answered." Yeah right. I'd done the whole memory thing before, thank you. It wasn't pleasant.

"Your firstborn child," quite a few of them wanted. "Your name. A phial of your tears. A drop of blood." With every offer, I just shook my head and hurried after Ash, weaving my way through the crowds. Sometimes, a glare from the Ice prince would cower the more persistent vendors who followed us through the aisles or latched on to my sleeve, but mostly we just kept moving.

Near the lake, a row of wooden docks floated above the ink-black water. A weathered tavern crouched at the shoreline like a bloated toad. A goblin staggered out holding a tankard, puked all over the sidewalk, and collapsed in it with his face to the sky. Ash stepped over the groaning body and ducked through the swinging doors. Wrinkling my nose at the trashed goblin, I followed.

The interior was smoky and dim. Battered wooden tables were scattered about the room, hosting a variety of unsavory-looking fey, from the redcap gang in the corner to the single, goat-headed phouka who watched me with glowing yellow eyes.

Ash glided through the room, weaving his way to the bar, where a dwarf with a tangled black beard glared at him and spit into a glass. "You shouldn't be here, Prince," he growled in an undertone, wiping the tankard with a dirty rag. "Rowan's got half the city lookin' for you. Sooner or later, the Thorn-guards will show up an' tear the place apart if they think we're hidin' you."

"I'm looking for Sweetfinger," Ash said in an equally low voice, as I pulled myself onto a bar stool. "I need to get out of Tir Na Nog, tonight. Do you know where he is?"

The dwarf shot me a sidelong glance, his thick face pulled into a scowl. "If I didn't know you better, Prince," he muttered, polishing the glass again, "I would accuse you of goin' soft. Word is you're a traitor to the Winter Court, but I don't care about that." He plunked the tankard down and leaned across the counter. "Just answer me this. Is she worth it?"

Ash's face went blank and cold, like a door slamming shut. "Would this be considered payment for finding Sweetfinger?" he replied in a voice dead of emotion.

The dwarf snorted. "Yeah. Sure, whatever. But, I want a serious answer, Prince."

Ash was still for a moment. "Yes," he murmured, his voice so low I barely caught it. "She's worth it."

"You know Mab will tear you apart for this."

"I know."

The dwarf shook his head, giving Ash a look of pity. "You an' your lady problems," he sighed, putting the glass under the counter. "Worse than the satyrs, I tell you. At least *they're* smart enough not to get attached."

Ash's tone was icy. "Can you find me Sweetfinger or not?"

"Yeah, I know where he is." The dwarf scratched his nose, then flicked something away. "I'll send someone out to find him. You and the Summer whelp can stay upstairs until he shows up."

Ash pushed away from the counter. His face was still locked into that expressionless mask as he turned to me. "Let's go."

I hopped off the bar stool. "Who's Sweetfinger?" I ventured as we made our way across the room. No one stopped us. The other patrons either ignored us or gave us a very wide berth.

Which wasn't surprising; the cold radiating from the Winter prince was palpable.

"He's a smuggler," Ash replied, motioning me up a set of stairs in the corner. "A goblin, to be specific. Instead of smuggling goods, he smuggles living creatures. He might be the only one who can get us out of the city. If we can pay his price."

Goblins. I shuddered. My own experience with goblins hadn't been pleasant. A pack of them tried to eat me once, when I first came to the Nevernever.

Upstairs, Ash led me down a creaky hallway, past several wooden doors with strange noises coming from beyond them, until we came to the last one. Inside, a tiny room greeted us, with two simple beds along opposite walls and a flickering lamp in the far corner. I noticed the lamp was actually a round cage atop a gilded stand, and the light made desperate squeaking noises as it flitted from side to side. Ash shut the door, and I heard the click of a lock before he leaned back against it, looking utterly exhausted.

I longed to hold him. I wanted to melt into him and feel his arms around me, but his last words hung between us like a barbed-wire fence. "Are you all right?" I whispered. He nodded and ran his fingers through his hair.

"Get some sleep," he murmured. "I don't know if we'll get another chance to stop after this. You should rest while you can."

"I'm not tired."

He didn't press the issue, but stood there watching me with a weary, sorrowful expression. I gazed back, wishing I could bridge the distance between us, not knowing how to reach him.

An awkward silence filled the room. Words hovered on the

tip of my tongue, wanting to burst out, but I knew Ash didn't want to hear them. I teetered between silence and confession, knowing I would be spurned, still wanting to try. Ash stood quietly, his gaze wandering about the room. A couple times he, too, seemed about to say something, only to fall silent, stabbing his fingers through his hair. When words finally did come, we both spoke at the same time.

"Ash—"

"Meghan, I—"

Someone pounded on the door, making us both jump. "Prince Ash!" a squeaky voice shouted from the other side. "Are you there? Sweetfinger is downstairs, waiting for you."

"Tell him I'm on my way," Ash replied, and pushed himself off the door. "Wait here," he told me. "It should be safe. Lock the door and try to get some rest." He opened the door, revealing a leering goblin on the other side, and closed it softly behind him.

I sat down on one of the beds, which reeked of beer and dirty straw, and stared at the door for a long time.

Then I was being shaken awake. I blinked in the darkness; someone had put a black cloth over the caged light and the room was swathed in shadow. Sleep made my eyelids heavy and awkward, but I cracked them open to focus on the blurred form above me. Ash sat on the edge of the mattress, silver eyes bright in the gloom, holding me gently by the shoulders.

"Meghan," he murmured, "wake up. It's time."

Exhaustion pulled at me. I'd been more tired than I thought, and my thoughts swirled muzzily. Seeing I was awake, Ash started to rise off the bed, but I slid forward and wrapped my arms around his waist.

"No," I murmured, my voice still groggy with sleep. "Stay."

He shivered, and his hands came to rest over mine. "You're not making this any easier," he whispered into the darkness.

"Don't care," I slurred, tightening my hold on him. He sighed and half turned in my arms, smoothing the hair from my cheek.

"Why am I so drawn to you?" he muttered, almost to himself. "Why is it so hard to let go? I thought…at first…it was Ariella, that you remind me of so much. But it's not." Though he didn't smile, his eyes lightened a shade. "You're far more stubborn than she ever was."

I sniffed. "That's like the pot calling the kettle black," I whispered, and a faint, tiny grin finally crossed his face, before his expression clouded and he lowered his head, touching his forehead to mine.

"What do you want of me, Meghan?" he asked, a low thread of anguish flickering below the surface. Tears blurred my vision, all the fear and heartache of the past few days rising to the surface.

"Just you," I whispered. "I just want you."

He closed his eyes. "I can't do that."

"Why not?" I demanded. His face swam above me, blurring with tears, but I refused to release him to wipe my eyes. My desperation grew. "Who cares what the courts say?" I challenged. "We could meet in secret. You could come to my world, no one will see us there."

He shook his head. "Mab already knows. Do you think she would let us get away with it? You saw how well she reacted in the throne room." I sniffled, burying my face in his side, as his fingers gently combed my hair. I didn't want to let him go. I wanted to curl into him and stay there forever.

"Please," I whispered desperately, not caring about pride anymore. "Don't do this. We can find a way around the courts.

Please." I bit my lip as a shiver went through him, and I held him tighter. "I love you, Ash."

"Meghan." Ash's voice was tormented. "You don't…know me at all. You don't know what I've done…the blood on my hands, both faery and mortal." He stopped, taking a breath to compose himself. "When Ariella died, everything inside me froze. It was only through hunting—killing—that I could feel anything again. I cared for nothing, not even myself. I threw myself into fights I thought I would lose, if only to feel the pain of a sword blow, the claws tearing me apart."

I shivered and clung to him, remembering the scars across his back and shoulders. I could imagine him fighting, his eyes dead and cold, hoping that something would finally get lucky and kill him.

"Then you came along," he muttered, touching my wet cheek, "and suddenly…I don't know. It was like I was seeing things for the first time again. When I saw you with Puck, the day you came to the Nevernever…"

"The day you tried to kill us," I reminded him.

He winced, nodding. "I thought fate was playing a cruel joke on me. That a girl, who could have been Ariella's shadow, was keeping company with my sworn enemy—it was too much. I wanted to kill you both." He sighed. "But, then I met you at Elysium, and…" He closed his eyes. "And everything I thought I'd lost forever came trickling back. It was maddening. I thought about killing you several times during Elysium, just to stop what I knew would be my downfall. I didn't want this, to feel anything, especially with a half-human girl who was the daughter of the Summer King." He snorted ruefully, shaking his head. "From the moment you stepped into the Nevernever, you've been my undoing. I should never have agreed to that contract."

I sucked in a breath. "Why?"

He brushed a strand of hair from my cheek, his voice gentler than before. "Because no matter what I feel, I can't fight centuries of rules and traditions, and neither can you."

"We could try—"

"You don't know the courts," Ash continued softly. "You haven't been in Faery long enough to know what could happen, but I do. I've seen it, centuries of it. Even if we get the scepter back, even if we manage to stop the war, we'll still be on opposite sides. Nothing will change that, no matter how much you wish it wasn't so. No matter how much *I* wish it was different."

I didn't answer, too miserable to comment. His voice, though filled with regret, was resolved. He had made up his mind, and I wouldn't be changing it.

A strange peace settled through me, or perhaps my despair finally gave in to resignation. *So, this is it,* I thought, as numbness spread through my body, easing the sharp pain in my chest. *This is what breaking up is like.* Although, I was sure "breaking up" was the wrong expression. It seemed much too common and trivial for what was happening.

"Come on." Ash pried my hands from his waist and stood up. "We should go. Sweetfinger and I made a deal. He'll get us out of the city through the goblin tunnels that run beneath it. We'll need to hurry—Rowan's Thornguards are still scouring the streets for us."

"Ash," I said, struggling upright. "Wait. Just one more thing, before we go."

He frowned warily. "What do you want?"

I rose from the bed, my heart thudding in my chest. "Kiss me," I whispered, and saw his eyebrows arc in surprise. "Just once more," I pleaded, "and I promise it will be the last time.

I'll be able to forget you after that." A bald-faced lie. Even if I turned ninety, lost my mind and forgot everything else, the memory of the Winter prince would be a shining beacon that would never fade.

He hesitated, unsure, and I tried to make my tone light. "Last time, I swear." I met his gaze and tried for a smile. "It's the least you can do. I didn't get a proper breakup, you know."

Ash still wavered, looking torn. His eyes flicked to the door, and for a moment I thought he would walk away, leaving me to shrivel into a mortified heap. But then he let out a quiet sigh, and his shoulders slumped in resignation.

Meeting my gaze, he took one step forward, drew me into his arms, and brushed his lips to mine.

I think our last kiss was meant to be quick and chaste, but after the first touch of his lips fire leaped up and roared through my belly. My fingers yanked him close, digging into his back, and his arms crushed me to him as if wanting to meld us together. I knotted my fingers in his hair and bit down on his bottom lip, making him groan. His lips parted, and my tongue swept in to dance with his. There was nothing sweet or gentle in our last kiss; it was filled with sorrow and desperation, of the bitter knowledge that we could've had something perfect, but it just wasn't meant to be.

It ended much too soon. Ash pulled away, eyes bright, shaking with desire and passion. Both our hearts were thudding wildly, and Ash's fingers were digging painfully into my shoulders. "Don't ask me this again," he rasped, and I was too breathless to answer.

He released me and stalked through the door without looking back. I took a deep breath, halting the tears crawling up my throat, and followed.

A goblin waited for us at the foot of the stairs, his mouth

pulled into a toothy grin that showed missing fangs and gold teeth. He was decked out in jewelry: rings, ear studs, necklaces, even a gold nose ring. A milky glass eye sparkled as he turned to me, rubbing his claws and grinning like a gleeful shark.

"Ah, this is princess that turned prince traitor," he hissed, eyeing me up and down. "And now they need goblin tunnels out of city, good, good." He gestured with a ring-encrusted hand. "No time to speak. We leave now, before guards show up, ask too many questions. Need anything before we go, traitor prince?"

Ash looked pained, but shook his head. The goblin cackled, gold teeth flashing in the dim light. "Yes, good! Follow me, then."

CHAPTER SEVEN

The Ring

Sweetfinger led us out a back door of the tavern and along the edge of the lake. Past the docks, the ground dropped away sharply to a narrow coastline of jagged rock and stone. Hugging the breaker wall, we followed Sweetfinger to the water's edge, where two burlier goblins waited inside a small wooden boat.

"Quickly, quickly," Sweetfinger said, urging us inside. We took a cautious seat between the two hench-goblins, who picked up the oars as Sweetfinger shoved us into the water and leaped in. As they rowed us farther from shore, he turned to us with an apologetic smile.

"Goblin tunnels aren't far from here," he said, fingering one of his rings. "Only goblins know where they are, and only goblins are allowed to see them and live. Used to be, payment would be your lovely eyes, but times change. Point is, you not goblin, you cannot see our secret tunnels. Rules, you know. So sorry."

"Understood," Ash muttered as a goblin slid behind him

and pulled a blindfold over his eyes. I jumped as a black cloth covered my eyes as well, plunging me into darkness.

We drifted for a long while, the only sounds being the rhythmic sloshing of the oars in the water and Sweetfinger's occasional comment to his thugs. Ash's body was tense against mine, muscles coiled bands under his skin. The air grew colder, and I heard the squeaking of bats somewhere above us. The boat bumped and scraped against rocks, and a foul stench crept into the air, smelling of dung and rotten meat. Snickers and cackling laughter echoed in the darkness, and clawed feet skittered over the rocks.

Then, the noises and smells faded, and we floated in silence for a time. I heard Sweetfinger and his guards muttering among themselves, and it made me very nervous. Finally, the boat bumped against solid ground, and someone pulled it ashore.

I pulled off the blindfold and blinked in the dim light. We were in a small cave with a pebbly floor, bones and trash scattered about the room. In the distance, a circle of light glimmered invitingly. I breathed a sigh of relief. We'd made it.

Sweetfinger leered at us as Ash helped me out of the boat. "As promised," he said, gesturing to the exit at the back of the room. "Safe passage out of city. Now, I believe traitor prince owes me something, yes?" He held out a jewel-encrusted claw, and Ash dropped a small leather pouch into his waiting hand.

"Tell no one you've seen us," Ash said as the two hench-goblins shoved the boat back into the water.

"I'm afraid it's too late for that, Your Highness," came a harsh, gravelly voice at the other end of the cave. We spun, Ash's hand on his sword, as four Thornguards stepped into view, their boots crunching over the stones.

"Very intelligent, not going through the regular trods,

Ash," said one guard. His armor was thornier than the others', the barbs on his shoulders bristling like giant porcupine quills. "Mab has them all well guarded, but you knew that, didn't you? Unfortunately, Rowan already bribed every smuggler in the city by the time you found this one. Goblins are such disgusting opportunists, aren't they?"

Furious, I glared back at Sweetfinger, but the boat was already well out of reach, Sweetfinger grinning at me from the bow.

"Sorry, Princess," the goblin cackled. "Prince's offer was good. Other prince's offer was better. Nothing personal, yes?" He waved, and the boat drifted away into the dark. An icy stone settled in the pit of my stomach, and I turned back to the guards.

As one, the Thornguards drew their weapons. Their swords were spiky and black, with long thorns running the length of the blade, looking as sharp as razors.

"Stand down, Edgebriar," Ash commanded. He hadn't drawn his sword yet, but his posture was tense. "I don't want to fight you. You can walk away from this and Rowan would never know. We're not returning to the city."

"I'm afraid we weren't ordered to return you to the city, or Mab," Edgebriar said with the barest of smirks. "You see, Rowan knows you're going after the scepter, and he can't allow that. The new king wants the half-breed alive, but I'm afraid we're going to have to kill you, Prince. Like Sweetfinger said, it's nothing personal."

For a second, I didn't know who he was talking about. Then it hit me like a punch in the stomach. The new king. The new *Iron King.* They were working for the Iron Kingdom. Rowan must've let Tertius and the wiremen into the palace. He let them kill Sage and take the scepter, and convinced Mab that the Iron fey were not a threat!

Ash's face went blank with shock. "No," he said, as the blood drained from his face. "No, Rowan wouldn't sell us out. Not to them. What have you done?"

"We can't stop the Iron Kingdom," Edgebriar continued, his voice earnest. "The old ways have become obsolete. Mab can't protect us any longer. It is time to ally ourselves with the stronger power, to become greater than we are. Rowan will lead us to a new era, one where we will fear nothing. Not the touch of iron, not the fading of human imagination, nothing! Let the oldbloods wallow in their ancient traditions. They will fall soon, and we will rise up to take their place."

"Rowan will destroy us," Ash said grimly. "This war only hastens our destruction. If Summer and Winter stood together, we could stop the Iron Kingdom."

"For how long?" Edgebriar demanded, punctuating his words with a savage swing of his blade. "The humans dream their technology, their grand sweeping visions, and forget us. We can't turn back the clock, but we *can* evolve to survive. I will show you what I mean." He ripped off his gauntlet, holding up his bare hand. On his third finger, an iron ring gleamed in the light. The entire digit was blackened and shriveled, and my stomach turned as he shook his fist triumphantly. "Look!" he demanded. "Look at me! I do not fear the touch of iron, of progress. It burns me now, but soon I will be able to use it freely, like the humans. Soon, I will be like them."

"You're dying, Edgebriar." Ash's voice was full of horror and pity. "It's killing you slowly, and you don't even realize it."

"No! After the war, when both sides are weak and open, the Iron fey will sweep in and destroy all traces of the old. There will be no more Summer or Winter. There will be no more courts. There will be only the Iron Kingdom, and those strong enough to stand with it."

I stared at him. "Rowan let the Iron fey into the palace, didn't he?" I whispered, and his fevered gaze turned on me. "He sent them to steal the scepter, and he let them kill his own brother. How can you work for such a bastard? Can't you see he's using you?"

"Be silent, half-breed." Edgebriar glared at me. "Insult my prince again, and I will cut out your tongue and feed it to my hounds. Rowan is the only one who cares for the future of Tir Na Nog."

Ash shook his head. "Rowan wants power, and would sacrifice his entire court to achieve it. You don't have to be responsible for his insanity, Edgebriar. Let us pass. We can end this war, and if Summer stands with us, we can find a way to deal with the Iron Kingdom."

Edgebriar's face didn't change. "We have our orders, Prince Ash. We will be taking the half-breed with us, but I'm afraid your journey ends here. Rowan made it quite clear that he did not want you returning to Mab, for any reason." He gestured to the knights behind him, and they began to close in. "I apologize for the location. A prince's tomb should be a grander affair."

I backed away, knowing the violence that was coming next. For the millionth time, I tried desperately to do *something* with my glamour; pull up a root to trip the knights, throw a glowy ball of light to distract them, anything. It was like hitting a glass wall. I *knew* my power was on the other side, but I couldn't access it.

Ash faced the approaching knights calmly, though I could sense muscles coiling beneath his skin. "Rowan doesn't know me as well as he thinks," he murmured, seemingly unconcerned with the jagged blades closing in on him, "otherwise he never would've made such a mistake."

Edgebriar smiled, leering at Ash from behind the trio of knights, content to let his guards engage the Winter prince. "And what mistake would that be?"

"There's only four of you."

His arm whipped out, sending a flurry of ice shards at the oncoming Thornguards. The knights flinched, throwing up their arms to protect their faces, and Ash lunged into their midst.

The first one didn't stand a chance. Ash's blade sheared through his armor, and the faery crumpled before he could even raise his sword. Where he fell, his spiky armor seemed to unravel, flaring out into thick black briars, thorns curling into the air. In seconds, the faery's body had turned into a giant thornbush, growing right out of the rocks. A metal band glinted on one of the branches.

The screech of blades focused me on the current battle. I couldn't see Edgebriar, but the other two Thornguards had Ash pressed into a corner and were hounding him mercilessly. Ash parried and spun, blocking their attacks, his blade a blue-white streak through the air. I glanced around and picked up a fist-sized rock from the edge of the water. Maybe I couldn't throw fireballs, but that couldn't stop me from hurling other things.

Please don't hit Ash, I thought, winding back for the throw.

The first rock thumped off the back of a knight, doing nothing, but the second struck the side of his head, making him flinch for just a moment. It was enough. Ash's blade whipped out, ripping through his chest. The knight crumpled without a sound, and brambles erupted from his armor, covering the body in a cocoon of thorns.

I gave a shout of triumph, but a dark shape filled my vision. Edgebriar stepped out of invisibility and reached for me with taloned fingers. I tried to dodge, but the Thornguard latched on to my wrist and yanked me to him, twisting my arm behind my back. As I gasped in pain, his other arm came up to circle my throat. I squirmed and kicked at him, but only jabbed myself on his spiny armor as his arm tightened and cut off my air.

An explosion of brambles signaled the end of the last knight, and Ash came striding through the hedge toward us, a cold, murderous gleam in his eye.

"Stay where you are, Prince," Edgebriar spat, and pressed a cold black dagger against my cheek. "Not another step, or I will gouge out her pretty eyes. The Iron King doesn't care if she's a bit damaged when she comes to him."

Ash stopped, lowering his blade, his eyes never leaving the knight. Edgebriar's chokehold loosened just the tiniest bit, and I sucked in a much-needed breath, trying to be calm. This close, the knight smelled of sweat and leather, and something sharper, metallic. The ring on his hand glinted against his blackened finger as he held the knife point to my face.

"Now," Edgebriar panted, locking gazes with Ash, "I want you to put down your sword and swear you will not follow us." When Ash didn't move, Edgebriar stabbed the point of the knife into my cheek, just enough to draw blood. I gasped at the sudden pain, and Ash tensed. "I won't ask you again, Your Highness," Edgebriar growled. "You've lost this battle. Put down your sword, and promise you will not follow us."

"Edgebriar." Ash's voice was as cold as frozen steel. "Rowan has poisoned your mind, as surely as that iron is poisoning your insides. You can still walk away from this. Let me take the princess back to Arcadia, and then we can warn Mab about the Iron King and Rowan."

"It's too late." Edgebriar shook his head wildly. "They're already coming. You can't stop them, Ash. No one can." He chuckled, a note of madness coming to the surface, and tightened his stranglehold on my neck. *"All the king's army and all the king's men,"* he whispered, waving the knife in front of my eyes, *"came to Faery on the day it would end."*

All right, enough was enough. Edgebriar had lost it; he had taken a long walk off the short end. I had to do *something*. But without a weapon or glamour, what could I do?

Blood was trickling down my face, oozing a path over my skin like a giant red tear. My cheek throbbed, and pain brought everything into sharp focus. In my mind, I saw the metal ring glowing white, pulsing with energy. I felt the glamour around it, but it was different from anything I'd felt before—cold and colorless. Was this…iron glamour? Could I use it as the fey used the wilder magic of dreams and emotion? The ring shimmered, fluid and alive, eager to be worked upon. To be shaped into something new.

Tighten, I thought, and the metal band responded instantly, biting into the skin. Edgebriar jerked, looking startled, and I squeezed harder, twisting the ring so that it cut into his flesh, drawing blood. It hissed where it touched, and Edgebriar howled, jerking his arm from my neck as if burned. I twisted from his grasp and shoved him away.

Ash lunged for Edgebriar. The Thornguard saw him coming and at the last second went for his sword, too late. Ash stepped within his guard and plunged the blade through his chest, so hard that it erupted out of the knight's back.

Edgebriar staggered and fell away, hitting the water with a loud splash. He stared at the blood on his chest, then gazed up at us, his eyes blank and confused. "You don't…understand," he gurgled, as Ash looked down on him sadly. "We were going to become…like them. Rowan…promised us. He promised…"

Then his eyes rolled up in his head, and thorny creepers slithered over his body, hiding him from view.

I shuddered, torn between throwing up and bursting into tears. Strange how all my time in the Winter Court still hadn't desensitized me to blood and death. I felt Ash's gaze on me, curious and wary, like a stranger's.

"What did you do to him?"

I shook my head. The strange glamour was already fading, like it had never been. My body trembled from the aftermath of shock and adrenaline. "I don't know."

Ash glanced once more at the thornbush, at the iron ring dangling from a twig, and shuddered. "Come here," he sighed, motioning me to a large rock. "Sit down. Let me see your face."

The cut wasn't deep, more of a puncture wound than a gash, though it still hurt like hell. Ash knelt and studied it, then tore a strip from his sleeve and dunked it in a nearby puddle. As he raised it to my cheek, I instinctively flinched and jerked away, grimacing. He shook his head, and a corner of his lip twitched.

"I haven't even touched it yet. Now hold still."

He lifted the rag, and our gazes met. Ash froze. I saw a dozen emotions cross his face before he took a quiet breath and very carefully pressed the cloth to my cheek.

I was tempted to close my eyes, but kept them open, watching his face. To have him here, to have him this close, was worth the pain. I studied his eyes, his lips, the tiny silver stud in his ear, almost hidden by his dark hair. I memorized those

little details, searing his image into my brain, wanting to remember this moment. Though his expression was closed and
businesslike after that first glance, his fingers were gentle.

"Why are you staring at me?"

His voice made me jump. "What? I'm not."

"Liar." Ash took my hand and pressed it to the cloth, holding it to my cheek. "Here. The bleeding's stopped, but keep
pressure on it for a bit just to be sure." His hand lingered on
mine, cool and smooth, though he wouldn't meet my eyes.
"I'm sorry, Meghan."

"Why?"

"For Rowan. For all of this." He rose and walked to where
Edgebriar had fallen. Now only a black thorny bush marked
the place where he had died, and Ash glared at it as if it might
come back to life.

"Rowan," I heard him mutter. "What are you thinking?"

Dropping the cloth, I walked up to him. "What now?"

He was quiet a moment, brooding. The shock of discovering that his brother was responsible for betraying all of Faery
was still new, like a wound that wouldn't close. I could tell he
didn't want to believe it. "Nothing's changed," he said at last,
his voice cold and resolved. "The scepter is still out there, and
if Rowan knows where it is, he isn't going to tell us. When
this is over, Mab will decide what to do with Rowan, but the
scepter comes first."

Very lightly, I touched his arm. "I'm sorry. He's a jerk, but
I'm sorry it had to be him."

He nodded. "Let's get out of here."

Four horses stood waiting at the cave entrance; faery steeds
with jet-black coats, lightning-colored manes, and glowing,
white-blue eyes. Their slender hooves didn't quite touch the

ground as they stamped and shifted, regarding us with eerie intelligence.

Ash helped me into one's saddle, and the fey-horse swished its tail and rolled its eyes at me, as if sensing my unease. I gave it a warning glare.

"Don't try anything, horse," I muttered, and it pinned back its ears, which was not a good sign. Ash approached another mount and swung easily into the saddle, as if he'd done it a thousand times.

"Where are we going?" I asked, fumbling with the reins, which made the horse prance sideways. Dammit, I'd never get used to this. "We know Tertius stole the scepter, Rowan helped him into the palace, and they're both working for a new Iron King." I frowned as I thought of the implications. "Ash, do you think we'll have to go back to the Iron Kingd—"

My horse suddenly let out a shrill whinny and half reared, nearly throwing me off. As I shrieked and grabbed its mane, the other mount tried to bolt, but Ash pulled one rein short, and the horse spun in frenzied circles until it calmed down. As our mounts quieted, still prancing and tossing their heads, we gazed around for the source of their fear. We didn't have to look far.

Through the trees, silhouetted against the cloudy sky, a lone figure on horseback watched us atop a snowy rise. The single tree standing over it had curled its branches as far away from the figure as possible, its limbs twisted and warped, but the rider didn't seem to care. As we stared at each other, the sun peeked out from behind the clouds, glinting off its steel armor.

A faint metallic rustling drifted over the wind, like thousands of knives scraping together, making my blood run cold. As the Iron knight stood motionless on the hill, an enormous pack of spindly legged creatures appeared around him. Claws flashing, limbs jerking sporadically, the wire-fey crowded the hilltop like huge spiders, gleaming in the sun.

Ash went pale, and my heart contracted in horror as the knight raised a hand toward us, sending the entire pack skittering down the hill.

We ran.

The faery steeds ate up the ground as they charged through the forest, their hooves making almost no noise in the snow. The trees flew by at a terrifying speed as the horses plunged between trunks and over logs, reminding me of my first wild ride through Faery, when I had been running *away* from Ash, ironically. At least I had a saddle this time. I clung to the horse's neck, unable to do anything else, steering or otherwise. Thankfully, Ash seemed to know where he was going, and my horse followed his as we flew over the ground.

Behind us, the metallic skittering of the wire-fey echoed on the wind, never fading or falling behind.

The trees fell away, and a steep incline soared above us, jagged rocks covered in ice as smooth as glass. My stomach turned, imagining my horse slipping and rolling on top of me, but the hooves of the Winter-born faery steeds charged up the hill without hesitation. It felt like they were running up a wall, and I clung to my horse until my arms burned with liquid fire.

At the top of the rise, Ash pulled his mount to a halt, and my horse stopped as well, prancing in place. Arms shaking from the strain of keeping my seat, I straightened cautiously.

Ash was staring down the slope, eyes narrowed to slits. I followed his gaze, and my stomach lurched. The edge of the rise fell away into a dizzying vertical drop, jagged rocks jutting up like spines. I suddenly wished I knew how to steer my horse, just to move it away from the edge.

"They're coming," Ash muttered.

The wiremen fey flowed from the trees in a glittering swarm. Scuttling to the rise, they began to climb, digging their claws into the ice as they edged upward. Steel limbs flashing, they crawled up the icy slope like ants, barely slowing down.

"What are these things?" Ash whispered. He raised his arm, and the air around him sparkled as a glittering ice spear formed overhead. With a flick of his hand, he hurled it down the slope, into the ranks of oncoming fey.

The spear hit one directly in the face, punching through the wires and tearing it from the hill. It clattered down the slope, arms and legs flailing, but the other fey leaped over the body or skittered aside, and kept coming.

My horse snorted and backed away. I grabbed for its mane as Ash whirled his steed around, his face grim.

"We can't outrun them," he announced, and I caught the faintest hint of fear in his voice, which only made me more terrified. "They're faster than us, and will overtake the horses long before we reach a trod. We have to make a stand."

I looked down at the approaching swarm, and my voice squeaked with terror. "Here? Now?"

"Not here." Ash shook his head and pointed down the other side of the slope. "There's an abandoned fort on the edge of the wyldwood. Ariella and I used it as a hunting lodge. If we can reach it, we might have a chance."

The other side of the slope fell away into the same break-neck drop. Far, far in the distance, I saw where the snow-covered treetops met the writhing gray mist of the wyldwood.

A raven circled us, giving a harsh cry as it passed overhead as the first of the wire-fey clawed its way to the top. Ash kicked his steed into motion, and mine followed, charging for the edge of the rise. I screamed as my horse gathered its legs underneath it and leaped into empty space.

We fell for what seemed like an eternity. When we finally hit the ground, the horses landed with barely a jolt and immediately plunged into the forest.

Behind us, the wiremen poured down the slope in a glittering flood.

My body ached and my arms burned from clinging to the horse for so long. Every bump sent a lance of pain through my side, and my breath came in short, agonizing gasps. Finally, we burst through the trees into a snow-covered clearing. In the center of the grove, a crumbling tower rose skyward in a precarious upside down *L,* as if it might collapse any moment.

"Come on!" Ash leaped off his mount, ignoring it as it raced away into the trees. My horse tried to follow, but the prince grabbed its reins, yanking it up short. I half slid, half fell out of the saddle, and I barely took a gasping breath before Ash was dragging me through the snow.

We ran for the fort, hearing the scraping of claws behind us. I didn't dare look back. Ahead, through the great wooden doors, I saw the darkened interior of the room. Sunlight slanted through holes in the roof, spilling over a strangely luminescent floor. As we drew closer, I gasped. The ground was completely carpeted in white, bell-like flowers, which glowed softly in the dim light. They grew on the walls and even covered the ancient furniture lying around the room: a wooden table, a cupboard, a few simple cots. Everything was also covered in snow and ice, as the roof was full of holes, but I supposed that hadn't mattered to Ash and Ariella. Freezing temperatures never bothered the Winter fey.

Ash pulled us through the opening, crushing flowers underfoot, and threw his weight against the doors. They groaned, reluctant to move. I joined him, and together, we strained at the stubborn gates. They closed slowly, creaking with age and time, and the wiremen were no more than twenty yards away when they finally banged shut. Ash threw down the bolt, then pressed both hands against it and sheathed the entire gate with ice. No sooner had he finished than the first blows rattled the wooden door, resounding through the chamber. The ice shivered and tiny cracks radiated through the surface as more blows shook the gate. It wouldn't hold them for long.

Ash drew his sword. "Get back," he told me as the door rattled again. More cracks shot through the ice. "Find a place to hide. There's an alcove behind that statue against the wall—you should be able to fit."

I shook my head frantically, seeing Sage surrounded by the hideous wire-fey, dying on the floor of the throne room. I couldn't watch Ash be torn apart like that before my eyes. Ash glanced back at me and frowned.

"Meghan, there's nothing you can do. Go! I'll hold them as long as I can. Go, now!"

A great chunk fell out of the door as a curved wire claw tore it away. The hole widened, as metal talons ripped and clawed at the wood. Fear got the better of me. I ran to the crumbling statue of some forgotten hero, darting behind it as the first of the wiremen squeezed through the crack like a giant spider.

Claws flashing, it lunged at Ash, who was waiting for it. His sword arced through the air, shearing the spindly fey in half. Another skittered toward him, and he whipped his blade around to slice off a flailing arm. The wireman collapsed, twitching, in the flowers, shredding the delicate blooms like paper.

I bit my cheek, trying not to be sick. More fey poured through the opening as they tore the gate to shreds. Ash was forced back, giving ground to prevent the wiremen from flanking him. Finally, he stood against a broken pillar, his back to the stones, as the Iron faeries swarmed around him, slashing and clawing.

I heard a noise above us, and a shower of stones and ice tumbled to the ground. A metallic form suddenly crawled through a hole in the roof and crawled along the ceiling, making my blood run cold. "Ash, above you!" I yelled, as more fey slithered through the cracks. "They're coming through the roof!"

The wiremen surrounded Ash in a chaotic blur. I could barely see him through the forest of slashing claws. Suddenly he leaped straight up, over the heads of the Iron fey, to land on the upright half of a broken pillar. His coat was in tatters, one side of his face was covered in crimson, and more blood dripped from numerous wounds to the flowers below.

The wiremen resumed their attack, crawling up the pillar or dropping from the ceiling. Fear hammered against my chest. I tried reaching for that strange, cold glamour I'd felt earlier with Edgebriar, but came up with nothing. I tried drawing in regular glamour, but hit the glass wall again. I wanted to scream. What was wrong with me? I had once taken down the Iron King; where was that power now? Ash was going to die in front of me, and I couldn't do anything to stop it.

Something big and black hurtled through the smashed door, diving toward the battle. It screeched as it slammed into a wireman, knocking it off the column, and the rest of the fey looked up, startled at this newest threat. It wheeled around to land on the pillar across from Ash—a giant black raven with emerald-green eyes. My heart leaped in my chest.

With a harsh, laughing cry, the bird disintegrated, vanishing in a swirling black cloud. A new form rose up from the explosion, shaking feathers from his fiery red hair, a wide, familiar grin spreading across his face.

"Hey, Princess," Puck called, brushing feathers from his clothes and gazing around at the carnage. "Looks like I got here just in time."

The wire-fey paused just a moment, blinking up at this newcomer, then scuttled forward once more. Puck drew a furry ball from his pocket, winked at me, and tossed it into the ranks of Iron fey swarming below him. It hit the ground, bounced once, and erupted into a large black boar, which charged into the fey with a maddened squeal.

Puck threw Ash a mocking smile. "You look like crap, Prince. Did you miss me?"

Ash frowned, stabbing a faery that was clawing at his feet. "What are you doing here, Goodfellow?" he asked coldly, which only caused Puck's grin to widen.

"Rescuing the princess from the Winter Court, of course." Puck looked down as the wire-fey piled on the squealing boar, ripping and slicing. It exploded into a pile of leaves, and they skittered back in confusion. "Though it appears I'm saving your sorry ass, as well."

"I could've handled it."

"Oh, I'm sure." Puck brandished a pair of curved daggers, the blades clear as glass. His grin turned predatory. "Well, then, shall we get on with it? Try to keep up, Your Highness."

"Just stay out of my way."

They leaped down from their pillars directly into the ranks of wiremen, who instantly swarmed around them. Back to back, Ash and Puck sliced into their opponents with renewed vigor, neither giving an inch now that the other was there. The mob of Iron fey thinned rapidly. Through the mass of writhing limbs, I caught glimpses of Ash's face, taut with concentration, and Puck's vicious smile.

Silently, the last few wiremen broke from the whirlwind of death in the middle of the floor. Without looking back, they scuttled up the walls, clawed their way through the holes in the roof and were gone.

Puck, his shirt now a tattered mess, sheathed his daggers and glanced around with a satisfied smirk. "Well, that was fun." His gaze found me, still frozen behind the statue, and he shook his head. "Wow, icy reception here. And to think I came back from the dead for this."

I squeezed from my hiding place, my heart pounding against my ribs, and ran to him. His arms opened, and I threw myself against his chest, hugging him fiercely. He was real. He was here, not dying in a tree somewhere, left behind and forgotten. "I missed you," I whispered against his neck.

He held me tighter. "I'll always come back for you," he murmured, sounding so unlike himself that I pulled back and looked at him. For a moment, his green eyes were intense, and I caught my breath at the emotion smoldering within. Then he smirked, and the effect was ruined.

I was suddenly aware of Ash leaning against a pillar, watching us with an unreadable expression. Blood streaked his face, splattering the white flowers beneath him, and his sword dangled limply from his grasp.

Puck followed my gaze, and his grin grew wider. "Hey, Prince," he greeted, "word is you're a traitor to the Winter Court. You've got the entire wyldwood in an uproar—they say you tried to kill Rowan after he caught you escaping with the princess. Clearly, I've missed a few things."

"News travels fast," Ash replied wearily. He started to rake a bloody hand through his hair, then thought better of it, dropping it to his side. "It's been an interesting morning."

"To say the least." Puck gazed around at the bodies of the wiremen and wrinkled his nose. "What the hell are those things?"

"Iron fey," I said. "I've seen them before. They were in the throne room with Tertius when he stole the scepter."

"The Scepter of the Seasons?" Puck looked at me aghast. "Oh, man. So that's where the war rumors are coming from. Winter really *is* going to attack Summer." He glared at Ash. "So, we're at war. Perfect. Shall we save time and kill each other now, or did you want to wait until later?"

"Don't start, Goodfellow." Ash matched Puck's glare. "I didn't want this. And I have no time for a fight." He sighed, deliberately avoiding my gaze. "In fact, now that you're here, you can do us both a favor. I want you to take Meghan back to the Summer Court."

CHAPTER EIGHT

Partings and Memories

"That's it?" Puck asked, as I stared at Ash, unable to believe what I'd just heard. He still wasn't looking and me, and Puck rattled on without noticing. "Take her back to Court? That's easy. I was going to do that anyway, whether you liked it or not. Comes with the whole rescue thing, you know—"

"What are you talking about?" I yelled, making Puck jump. "The hell with going back to Summer! We need to get the scepter back from the Iron fey! It's the only way to stop the war."

"I'm aware of that." Ash finally met my eyes, and his gaze was cold. "But this is Winter's problem. Retrieving the scepter is my responsibility. I want you to return to your own court, Meghan. You'll be safer there. You can't help me this time. Go home."

Hurt and betrayal stabbed me in the chest. "You were going to dump me on Oberon all along, weren't you?" I spit at him. "You liar. I thought we were going after the scepter together."

"I never told you that."

Puck glanced from me to Ash and back again, looking

confused. "Erm, so you're saying you don't want to go back home?" he asked me. I glared at him, and he shrugged. "Wow, so that totally makes the whole rescue plan a wash. You wanna throw me a bone here, Princess? I feel somewhat out of the loop."

"We have to go after the scepter," I told Puck, hoping he would back me on this. "Ash can't do it by himself. We can help—"

"No, you can't," Ash broke in. "Not this time. You'd be no use to me, Meghan, not with your magic sealed—" He caught himself, looking guilty, and Puck's eyes narrowed.

"Sealed?" Puck stepped forward threateningly. "You put a binding on her?"

"I didn't." Ash stared him down, defiant. "Mab did. When she first came to Winter. Mab was afraid her power would be too great, so she sealed her magic to protect the Court."

I remembered the wall I kept hitting whenever I tried using more than the simplest glamour, and my temper flared. How dare she! "And you knew," I accused Ash. "You knew about the seal, and you didn't bother telling me?"

Ash shrugged, unrepentant. "Mab ordered us not to. Besides, what difference would it make? I can't do anything about it."

I turned to Puck, who glowered at the prince as though he might attack him right then. "Can you break it?"

Puck shook his head. "Sorry, Princess. Only Mab, or someone of equal power, can remove a binding once it's been placed. That makes your choices Oberon, or Mab herself."

"All the more reason that you should return to Summer." Ash pushed himself off the pillar, wincing. Behind him, the column was smeared with red.

"Where are you going?" I asked, suddenly afraid that he would walk out that door and not return.

He sheathed his sword without looking at me. "There's a spring a few yards behind this tower," he replied, walking slowly toward the door. I sensed he was trying hard not to limp. "Unless either of you object, I'm going to bathe."

"But you're coming back, right?"

He sighed. "I'm not going anywhere tonight," he promised, and swept a hand toward a far wall. "There's a trunk with blankets and supplies in that corner. Make yourselves comfortable. I think we're all going to be spending the night here."

The trunk held several quilts, a few canteens, a quiver of arrows, and a bottle of dark wine I didn't recognize and immediately left alone. Puck went hunting for firewood and came back with an armful, plus a branch bearing strange blue fruits he swore were safe to eat. Together, we cleared away flowers to make the campfire, though I felt a stab of guilt every time I yanked one up. They were quite beautiful, the petals so thin and delicate they were almost transparent.

"You're awfully quiet, Princess," Puck said as he arranged the firewood into a tepee. His slanted green eyes shot me a knowing look. "In fact, you haven't said a word since his royal iciness left. What's wrong?"

"Oh." I cast about for an excuse. No way was I telling Puck about my feelings for Ash. He'd probably challenge him to a duel the moment he walked through the door. "I...um...I'm just weirded out, you know, with all those wiremen bodies around. It's kinda creepy, like they might come to life and attack us while we're sleeping."

He rolled his eyes. "You and your zombie obsession. I've never understood your fascination with horror movies, especially when they freak you out so much."

"They don't freak me out," I said, grateful for the change of subject.

"Riiiight, you just sleep with your light on to scare away roaches."

His comment made me smile. Not because he was right, but because it reminded me of another time, a simpler time, when all I had to worry about was homework and school and keeping up with the latest movie trends. When Robbie Good-fell and I could sit on the couch with a huge tub of popcorn and watch a marathon of *Friday the 13th* movies until the sun came up.

I wondered how much I'd missed in the time I'd been gone.

When I didn't answer, Puck snorted and shook his head. "Fine. Watch this." And he made a quick gesture with his hand. The air shimmered, and the twisted corpses lying around the room turned into piles of branches. "Better?"

I nodded, though I knew it was only an illusion. The dead fey were still there, beneath the faery glamour. Out of sight, out of mind didn't quite work for me, but at least it kept Puck from asking too many hard questions.

For a little while, anyway. "So, Princess," he began, once a cheerful fire crackled in the center of the room. I didn't know how he'd started it, but I'd learned not to question such things, in case it turned out to be an illusion and I only *thought* I was getting warm. "It seems I've missed a lot since I've been gone. Tell me everything."

I gulped. "Everything?"

"Sure!" He sat down on a quilt, leaning back comfortably. "Like, did you find Machina? Did you ever get your brother back?"

"Oh." I relaxed a bit and sat down beside him. "Yeah.

Ethan is safe. He's home, and that stupid changeling is gone for good."

"What about Machina?"

I bit my lip. "He's dead."

Puck must've noticed the change in my voice, for he sat up and put his arm around my shoulders, pulling me close. I leaned into him, feeling his warmth, taking comfort in his nearness. "I'm sick of this place," I whispered, feeling like a little kid, as my eyes burned and the world went fuzzy. "I want to go home."

Puck was silent for a moment, just holding me as I leaned against him, fighting back tears. "You know," he said finally, "I don't have to take you back to the Summer Court. If you want, I can take you back to your world. If you really want to go home."

"Would Oberon let me go?"

"I don't see why not. Your magic has been sealed off. You'd be like an ordinary high school student again. Mab wouldn't consider you a threat anymore, so the Unseelie would probably leave you alone."

My heart leaped. Home. Could I really go home? Back to Mom and Luke and Ethan, back to school and summer jobs and a normal life? I missed that, more than I realized. I felt a bit guilty for ditching the plan to get the scepter back, but screw it. Ash didn't want me around. My contract with him was over, and I'd paid my dues to the Unseelie Court. Our deal said nothing about me *staying* in Winter.

"What about you?" I asked, looking up at Puck. "Weren't you ordered to bring me back to Summer? Won't you get in trouble?"

"Oh, I'm in hot water already." Puck grinned cheerfully. "I wasn't even supposed to let you go after the Iron King, remember? Oberon will skin me alive for that one, so I really can't dig myself any deeper."

His tone was light, but I closed my eyes, guilt tearing at me. It seemed everyone I cared about was getting hurt, risking so much, just to protect me. I was tired of it; I wished I had my magic back, so that I could protect them in return.

"Why?" I whispered. "Why do you hang around? You and Ash could've died today."

Puck's heartbeat sped up under my fingers. His voice, when it came, was very soft, almost a whisper. "I would've thought you'd've figured that out by now."

I looked up and found our faces inches apart. Twilight had deepened the room to shadow, though the carpet of flowers glowed brighter than ever. Firelight danced within Puck's eyes as we stared at each other. Though he still wore a tiny, lopsided smile, there was no mistaking the emotion on his face.

I stopped breathing. A tiny part of me, somewhere deep inside, was rejoicing at this newest revelation, though I think, deep down, I'd always suspected. *Puck loves me,* it whispered, thrilled. *He's in love with me. I knew it. I knew it all along.*

"You're kind of blind, you know?" Puck whispered, smiling to soften his words. "I wouldn't defy Oberon for just anyone. But, for you…" He leaned forward, touching his forehead to mine. "I'd come back from the dead for you."

My heart pounded. That tiny part of me wanted this. Puck had always been there: safe, reliable, protective. He was part of *my* Court, so there was no stupid law to get in the way. Ash was gone; he had already made up his mind. Why not try with Puck?

Puck moved closer, his lips hovering an inch from mine. And all I could see was Ash, the passion on his face, the look in his eyes when he kissed me. Guilt gnawed my insides. *No,* my mind whispered, as Puck's breath caressed my cheek. *I can't right now. I'm sorry, Puck.*

I drew back slightly, ready to apologize, to tell him I couldn't right now, when a shadow appeared in the doorway and Ash walked in.

He froze, silhouetted against the night sky, the flowers casting his features in a pale glow. His hair was slightly damp, and his clothes were mended, whether through glamour or something else I couldn't tell. For a moment, shock and hurt lay open on his face, and his hands fisted at his sides. Then, his expression closed, his eyes turning blank and stony.

Puck blinked at my expression and turned as Ash walked in. "Oh, hey, Prince," he drawled, completely unconcerned. "I forgot you were here. Sorry 'bout that." I tried meeting Ash's gaze, to show him this wasn't what he thought, but he was studiously ignoring me.

"I want you gone by morning," Ash said in cold, clipped tones, sweeping around the campfire. "I want you out of my territory, you and the princess both. According to the law, I could kill you where you stand for trespassing. If I see either of you in Tir Na Nog again, I won't be so lenient."

"Jeez, don't get your panties in a twist, Your Highness." Puck sniffed. "We'll be happy to leave, right, Princess?"

I finally caught Ash's gaze, and my heart sank. He stared at me coldly, no traces of warmth or friendliness on his face. "Yeah," I whispered, my throat closing up. This was it, the last straw. I'd been in Faery long enough. It was time to go home.

Ash began moving the piles of branches, really the dead Iron fey, and dumping them outside. He worked quickly and silently, not looking at either of us, almost feverish in his desire to get them out. When the bodies were cleared away, he grabbed the bottle of wine from the trunk and retired to a far corner, brooding into the glass. His entire posture screamed *leave me the hell alone,* and even though I wanted to go to him, I kept my distance. Thankfully, Puck didn't try to kiss me again, but he was never far, giving me secret little smiles, letting me know he was still interested. I didn't know what to do. My mind was spinning, unable to settle on one thought. Later that evening, Ash stood abruptly and left, announcing he was going to "scout around" for more Iron fey. Watching him stalk out the door without a backward glance, I was torn between running after him and sobbing on Puck's shoulder. Instead, I pleaded exhaustion and climbed into one of the cots, pulling the blanket over my head so I wouldn't have to face either of them.

It was hard to sleep that night. Huddled beneath the quilts, I listened to the sound of Puck snoring and fought back tears.

I didn't know why I was so miserable. Tomorrow, I was going home, at last. I could see Mom and Luke and Ethan again; I missed them all so much, even Luke. Though I had no idea how much time had passed in the real world, just the thought of returning home should've filled me with relief. Even if Mom and Luke were old and gray, and my four-year-old kid brother was older than I was, even if it *had* been a hundred years, and everyone I knew was...

I gasped and veered my thoughts from that path, refusing to think about it. Home would be the same as it always was. I could finally go back to school, learn to drive, maybe even go to prom this year. *Maybe Puck can take me.* The thought was so ridiculous I almost laughed out loud, choking on unshed tears. No matter how much I wanted a normal life, there would be a part of me that longed for this world, for the magic and wonder of it. It had seeped into my soul and shown me things I'd never thought existed. I couldn't be normal and ignorant ever again, knowing what was out there. Faery was a part of me now. As long as I lived, I would always be watching for hidden doors and figures from the corner of my eyes. And for a certain dark prince who could never be mine.

I must've fallen asleep, for the next thing I knew, I was opening my eyes and the room was bathed in hazy starlight. The flowers had opened completely and were glowing as if tiny moons nestled between the petals, throwing back the darkness. Ethereal moths and ghostly butterflies flitted over the carpet, delicate wings reflecting the light as they floated between blooms. Careful not to wake Puck, I rose and wandered into the flowers, breathing in the heady scent, marveling as a feathery blue moth landed on my thumb, weighing nothing at all. I breathed out, and it fluttered off toward a dark figure in the center of the carpet.

Ash stood in the middle of the room, surrounded by glowing white flowers, eyes closed as tiny lights swirled around him. They shimmered and drew together, merging into a luminescent faery with long silver hair, her features so lovely and perfect that my throat ached. Ash opened his eyes as she reached for him, her hands stopping just shy of his face. Longing shone from his eyes, and I shivered as the spectral faery moved right through him, dissolving into tiny lights.

"Is that…Ariella?" I whispered, walking up behind him.

Ash whirled around, his eyes widening at the sudden interruption. Seeing me, several emotions crossed his face—shock, anger, shame—before he sighed in resignation and turned away.

"No," he murmured, as the ghostly faery appeared again, dancing among the flowers. "It isn't. Not in the way you think."

"Her ghost?"

He shook his head, his eyes never leaving the specter as she swayed and twirled over the glowing carpet, butterflies drifting around her. "Not even that. There is no afterlife for us. We have no souls with which to haunt the world. This is... just a memory." He sighed, and his voice went very soft. "She was always happy here. The flowers...remember."

I suddenly understood. This was Ash's memory of Ariella, perfect, happy and full of life, a yearning so great it was given form, if only for a moment. Ariella wasn't here. This was only a dream, an echo of a being long departed.

Tears filled my eyes and ran down my face. The gash on my cheek stung where they passed, but I didn't care. All I could see was Ash's pain, his loneliness, his yearning for someone who wasn't me. It was tearing me apart, and I couldn't say anything. Because I knew, somehow, that Ash was saying goodbye, to both of us.

We stood in silence for a while, watching Ariella's memory dance among the flowers, her gossamer hair floating on the breeze as bright motes swirled around her. I wondered if she really was that perfect, or if this was what Ash remembered her to be.

"I'm leaving," Ash said quietly, as I knew he would. He finally turned to face me, solemn, beautiful, and as distant as the stars. "Have Goodfellow take you home. It isn't safe here any longer."

My throat felt tight; my eyes burned, and I took a shaky breath to free my voice. And even though I already knew the answer, even though my head was telling me to shut up, I whispered, "I won't see you again, will I?"

He shook his head, once. "I wasn't fair to you," he murmured. "I knew the laws, better than anyone. I knew it would end…like this. I ignored my better judgment, and for that, I'm sorry." His voice didn't change. It was still calm and polite, but I felt an icy hand squeeze my heart as he continued. "But, after tonight, we'll be enemies. Your father and my queen will be at war. If I see you again, I might kill you." His eyes narrowed, and his voice turned cold. "For real this time, Meghan."

He half turned, as if to leave. The glow of the flowers made a halo of light around him, only accenting his unearthly beauty. In the distance, Ariella danced and twirled, free from sorrow and pain and the trials of the living. "Go home, Princess," murmured the Unseelie prince. "Go home, and forget. You don't belong here."

I couldn't remember much of the night afterward, though I think it involved a lot of sobbing into my quilt. In the morning, I woke up to snow drifting in through the roof, coating the floor with heavy white powder. The flowers had faded, and Ash was already gone.

PART TWO

CHAPTER NINE

The Summoning

The evening following Ash's departure, Puck and I hit the edge of the wyldwood.

"Not far now, Princess," Puck said, giving me an encouraging grin. A few yards from where we stood, the snow and ice just…stopped. Beyond it, the wyldwood stretched before us, dark, tangled, trapped in perpetual twilight. "Just gotta cross the wyldwood to get you home. You'll be back to your old boring life before you can say 'summer school.'"

I tried smiling back, but couldn't manage it. Even though my heart soared at the thought of home and family and even summer school, I felt I was leaving a part of me behind. Throughout our hike, I'd kept turning around, hoping to see Ash's dark form striding through the snow after us, gruffly embarrassed and taciturn, but there. It didn't happen. Tir Na Nog remained eerily empty and quiet as Puck and I continued our journey alone. And as the sun sank lower in the sky and the shadows lengthened around us, I slowly came to realize that Ash wasn't coming back. He was truly gone.

I quivered on the verge of tears but held them back. I did

not want to have to explain to Puck why I was crying. He already knew I was upset, and kept trying to distract me with jokes and a constant string of questions. What happened after we left him to confront Machina? How did we find the Iron Realm? What was it like? I answered as best I could, leaving out the parts between me and Ash, of course. Puck didn't need yet another reason to hate the Winter prince, and hopefully he would never find out.

As we approached the colorless murk of the wyldwood, something moved in the shadows to our left. Puck spun with blinding speed, whipping out his dagger, as a spindly form stumbled through the trees and collapsed a few feet away. It was a girl, slender and graceful, with moss-green skin and hair like withered vines. A dryad.

The tree woman shuddered and gasped, clawing herself upright. One long-fingered hand clutched her throat as if she were being strangled. "Help…me," she gasped at Puck, her brown eyes wide with terror. "My tree…"

"What's happened to it?" Puck said, and caught her as she fell. She sagged against him, her head lolling back on her shoulders. "Hey," he said, shaking her a little. "Stay with me now. Where's your tree? Did someone cut it down?"

The dryad gasped for air. "P-poisoned," she whispered, before her eyes rolled up and her body turned to wood in his arms. With the sound of snapping twigs, the dryad curled in on herself until she resembled little more than a bundle of dry branches. I watched the faery's life fade away, remembered what Ash had said about the fey and death, and felt terribly, terribly sad. That was it for her, then. She'd simply ceased to exist.

Puck sighed, bowing his head, and gathered the lifeless dryad into his arms. She was thin and brittle now, fragile as spun glass, but not one twig snapped or broke off as he carried her away. With utmost care, he laid the body at the foot of a giant tree, murmured a few words and stepped back.

For a moment, nothing happened. Then, huge roots unfurled from the ground, wrapping around the dryad to draw her down into the earth. In seconds, she had disappeared.

We stood quietly for a moment, unwilling to break the somber mood. "What did she mean by poisoned?" I finally murmured.

Puck shook himself, giving me a humorless grin. "Let's find out."

We didn't have to search far. Only a few minutes into the wyldwood, the trees curled away, and we stumbled onto a familiar patch of dead ground in the middle of the forest. An entire swath of forest was sickened and dying, trees twisted into strange metal parodies. Metal lampposts grew out of the ground, bent over and flickering erratically. Wires crawled over roots and trunks, choking trees and vegetation like red and black creeper vines. The air smelled of copper and decay.

"It's spreading," Puck muttered, holding his sleeve to his face as the metallic breeze ruffled my hair and clothes. "This wasn't here a few months ago." He turned to me. "I thought you said you killed the Iron King."

"I did. I mean, yes, he's dead." I gazed out over the poisoned forest, shuddering. "But that doesn't mean the Iron Realm is gone. Tertius told me he served a new Iron King."

Puck's eyes narrowed. "*Another* one? You sort of failed to mention that before, Princess." Shaking his head, he scanned the wasted area and sighed. "Another Iron King. Dammit, how many of them are we going to have to kill? Are they going to keep popping up like rats?"

I squirmed at the thought of yet another killing. A sharp wind hissed over the wasteland, scraping the branches of the metal trees, making me shiver. Puck coughed and staggered away.

"Well, come on, Princess. We can't do anything about it now. Let's get you home."

Home. I thought about my family, about my normal life, so tantalizingly close. I thought of the Nevernever, dying and fading away bit by bit. And I made my decision. "No."

Puck blinked and looked back. "What?"

"I can't go home yet, Puck." I gazed around at the poisoned Nevernever, seeing echoes of Machina's realm looming over everything. "Look at this. People are dying. I can't close my eyes and pretend it isn't happening."

"Why not?" I blinked at him, stunned by his cavalier attitude. He just grinned. "You've done enough, Princess. I think you deserve to go home after everything you went through. Hell, you already took care of one Iron King. The Nevernever will be fine, trust me."

"What about the scepter?" I persisted. "And the war? Oberon should know Mab is planning to attack him."

Puck shrugged, looking uncomfortable. "I was already planning on telling him, Princess, provided he doesn't turn me into a rat as soon as he sees me. As for the scepter, the Ice prince is already looking for it. Not a lot we can do, there." At my protest, he waved a hand airily. "The war is going to start with or without us, Princess. It's nothing new. Winter and Summer have always been at odds. Not a century goes by that there isn't some kind of fighting going on. This will pass, like it always does. Somehow, the scepter will be returned, and things will go back to normal."

I frowned, remembering something Mab had said to Oberon

at the ceremony. "What about my world?" I demanded. "Mab
said there would be a catastrophe if Summer held the scepter
longer than it was supposed to. What will happen if the Iron
King gets it? Things will get really screwed up, right?"

Puck scratched the back of his neck. "Erm…maybe."

"Maybe, like how?"

"Ever wanted to go sledding in the Mojave Desert?"

I stared at him. "We can't let that happen, Puck! What's
wrong with you? I can't believe you'd think I'd just ignore
this!" He shrugged, still infuriatingly nonchalant, and I went
for the cheap shot. "You're just afraid, aren't you? You're scared
of the Iron fey and you don't want to get involved. I didn't
think you'd be such a coward."

"I'm trying to keep you safe!" Puck exploded, whirling on
me. His eyes glowed feverishly, and I shrank back. "This isn't
a game, Meghan! The shit is about to hit the fan, and you're
right in the middle of it without knowing enough to duck!"

Righteous indignation flared; I was sick of being told what
to do, that I should be afraid. "I'm not helpless, Puck!" I shot
back. "I'm not some squealing cheerleader you have to baby-
sit. I've got blood on my hands now, too. I killed the Iron
King, and I still have nightmares about it. I *killed* something!
And I'd do it again, if I had to!"

"I know that," Puck snapped, throwing up his hands. "I
know you'd risk everything to protect us, and that's what worries me. You still don't know enough about this world to be
properly terrified. Things are going to get screwed eight ways
from Sunday, and you're making goo-goo eyes at the enemy!
I heard what happened in Machina's realm and yes, it scared
the hell out of me. I love you, dammit. I'm not going to watch
you get torn apart when everything goes bad."

My stomach twisted, both from his confession, and what he'd said about me and Ash. "You...you knew?" I stammered.

He gave me a scornful look. "I've been around a long time, Princess. Give me a little credit. Even a blind man would see the way you looked at him. I'm guessing something happened in Machina's realm, but once you came out, our boy remembered he wasn't supposed to fall in love with Summer." I blushed, and Puck shook his head. "I didn't say anything because he'd already made up his mind to leave. You might not know the consequences, Princess, but Ash does. He did the right thing, much as I hate to speak well of him."

My lip trembled. Puck snorted, but saw me teetering on the brink of tears. His expression softened. "Forget about him, Meghan," he said gently. "Ash is bad news. Even if the law wasn't an issue, I've fought him enough times to know he would break your heart."

The tears finally spilled over. "I can't," I whispered, giving in to the despair that had followed me all morning. This wasn't fair to Puck, after he'd finally confessed that he loved me, but I couldn't seem to stop. My soul cried out for Ash, for his courage and determination; for the way his eyes thawed when he looked at me, as if I were the only person in the world; for that beautiful, wounded spirit I saw beneath the cold exterior he showed the world. "I can't forget. I miss him. I know he's the enemy, and we broke all kinds of rules, but I don't care. I miss him so much, Puck."

Puck sighed, either in sympathy or aggravation, and pulled me close. I sobbed into his chest, releasing all the pent-up emotions that had been building since I first saw Ash in the throne room. Puck held me and stroked my hair like old times, saying nothing, until the tears finally slowed and I sniffled against his shirt.

"Better?" he murmured.

I nodded and broke away, wiping my eyes. The ache was still there, but it was bearable now. I knew it would be a long time before the hurt went away, if ever, but I knew in my heart that I had said my last goodbyes to Ash. Now, maybe I could let him go.

Puck moved behind me and put his hands on my shoulders, leaning close. "I know it's too soon right now," he muttered into my hair, "but, just so you know, I'll wait. When you're ready, I'll be right here. Don't forget, Princess."

I could only nod. Puck squeezed my shoulders and stepped back, waiting quietly while I composed myself. When I turned around again, he was back to being normal Puck, perpetual grin plastered to his face, leaning against a tree.

"Well," he sighed, "I don't suppose I'll be changing that stubborn mind of yours, will I?"

"No, you won't."

"I was afraid of that." He leaped onto an old stump, crossing his arms and cocking his head. "Well then, my scheming princess, what's the plan?"

I wanted to smile at him, but something was wrong. My legs felt all tingly, and a strange pull tugged at my stomach. I felt restless, like ants crawled beneath my skin, and I couldn't hold still if my life depended on it. Without meaning to, I began edging away from Puck, toward the forest.

"Princess?" Puck hopped down, frowning. "You all right? Got ants in your pants or something?"

I had just opened my mouth to reply when some invisible force nearly yanked me off my feet, and I shrieked instead. Puck reached for me, but I leaped away without meaning to. "What is this?" I cried, as the strange force yanked on me again, urging me into the trees. "I can't...stop. What's going on?"

Puck grabbed my arm, holding me back, and my stomach felt like it was being pulled in two. I screamed, and Puck let go, his face white with shock.

"It's a Summoning," he said, hurrying after me as I walked away. "Something is calling you. Did you make a bargain or give anything personal away recently? Hair? Blood? A piece of clothing?"

"No!" I cried, grabbing a vine to stop myself. Pain shot up my arms, and I let go with a yelp. "I haven't given anything away! How do I stop it?"

"You can't." Puck jogged at my side, his gaze intense and worried, but he made no move to touch me. "If something is Calling, you have to go. It only gets more painful if you resist. Don't worry, though." He attempted a cheerful grin. "I'll be right behind you."

"Don't worry?" I tried to scowl at him over my shoulder. "This is like *Invasion of the Body Snatchers;* of course I'm worried!" Once more, I tried latching on to a tree to stop my feet from waltzing away without my say-so. No use. My arms wouldn't even obey me anymore. With a final glance at Puck, I gave in to the strange compulsion and let my body take me away.

I strode through the forest like I was on a mission, ignoring all but the greatest obstacles. I scrambled over rocks and fallen trees, charged headlong down gullies, and walked through brambles and briar patches, gasping as they tore at my skin and clothes. Puck followed close behind, his worried gaze at my back, but he didn't stop me a second time. My legs burned, my breath came in short gasps, and my arms bled from dozens of cuts and scratches, but I could no sooner make myself stop than fly. And so we continued our mad rush through the forest, getting farther away from Tir Na Nog and deeper into unknown territory.

Night was falling when the weird spell faded at last, and my feet stopped so abruptly that I fell, pitching forward and rolling in the dirt. Puck was beside me instantly, helping me up, asking whether I was okay. I couldn't answer him at first. My legs burned, and all I could do was suck air into my starving lungs and feel relieved that my body was finally my own again.

"Where are we?" I gasped as soon as I was able.

It seemed we had stumbled onto some sort of village. Simple mud and thatch huts lay in a loose semicircle around a fire pit, which was empty and cold. Bones, animal skins, and half-eaten carcasses lay scattered about, buzzing with flies.

"Looks like an abandoned goblin village," Puck muttered as I leaned against him, still gasping. He looked down at me, smirking. "Piss off any goblins lately, Princess?"

"What? No." I wiped sweat from my eyes and stumbled over to a log, collapsing on it with a groan. "At least, I don't think so."

"There you are," came a disembodied voice, from somewhere near the edge of the trees. I jumped up and looked around, but couldn't see the speaker. "You are late. I was afraid you had gotten lost, or eaten. But, I suppose it is only human failing that is to blame for the loss of punctuality."

My heart leaped. I knew that voice! I gazed around eagerly, but of course I couldn't see anything until Puck grabbed my arm and pointed me toward the edge of the trees. An old log lay in the shadows just outside the village border, dappled by moonlight. One moment, it was empty. Then, I blinked, or the moonlight shifted, and a large gray cat sat there, bottlebrush tail curled around his legs, regarding me with lazy golden eyes.

"Grimalkin!"

Grimalkin blinked at me, looking much as he always did, long gray fur blending perfectly into the moonlight and shadows. He ignored me as I rushed up, completely absorbed in washing his front paw. I might have swooped him up and given him a squeeze, if I didn't know his sharp claws would turn my face into hamburger and he would never forgive me.

Puck grinned. "Hey, cat," he greeted with an airy wave. "Long time no see. I guess you're the one responsible for our little Death March?"

The feline yawned. "That is the last time I put a Summoning on a human," he mused, raising a hind leg to scratch his ear. "I could have taken a nap instead of waiting for you to finally show up. What took you so long, human? Did you *walk?*"

I finally remembered: Grimalkin had helped me in the search for my brother, and in return, we had agreed that he could call on me, once, at a time of his choosing, though I'd had no idea what that entailed at the time. That was our bargain. Seems he'd finally gotten around to calling it in.

"What are you doing here, Grim?" I asked, torn between delight and aggravation. I was happy to see him, of course, but I wasn't thrilled about the forced march through goblin-infested woodlands, just to say hi. "This better be good, cat. Your stupid Summoning spell could've killed me. What is it you want?"

Grimalkin turned to groom his hindquarters. "*I* do not want anything from you, human," he said between licks. "I brought you here as a favor for someone else. You will have to take your business up with him. And, if you would, remind him that he now owes me a boon, since I wasted a perfectly good Summoning on you."

"What are you talking about?"

"HE MEANS ME, MEGHAN CHASE." The thunderous voice shook the ground, and the smell of burning coal drifted over the breeze. "I ASKED HIM TO CALL YOU HERE."

Something stepped out from behind a hut, a monstrous horse of blackened iron, with burning red eyes and flames smoldering through the chinks in its belly. Steam billowed from its nostrils as it swung to face me, huge and imposing and terrifyingly familiar.

Ironhorse.

CHAPTER TEN

Truth and Lies

"STOP!" Ironhorse bellowed as Puck immediately pulled out his dagger, shoving me behind him. "I DID NOT COME HERE TO FIGHT, ROBIN GOODFELLOW. PUT YOUR WEAPON DOWN AND LISTEN TO ME."

"Oh, I don't think so, Rusty," Puck sneered, as we began backing toward the edge of the village. "I have a better idea. You stay there until we get to Oberon, who will rip you apart and bury your pieces so far apart you'll never get put back together."

My heart pounded, both from fear and a sudden fury. Ironhorse was one of Machina's lieutenants, sent to capture me and bring me to the Iron King. We'd escaped him twice before, once in Tir Na Nog and once in the Iron Kingdom, but Ironhorse had a bad habit of popping up when we least expected it. I certainly hadn't expected to run into him *here*.

"Dammit, Grim!" I raged, shooting the cat a furious glare as we backed up. He blinked at me calmly. "You sold us out to *them*? That's low, even for you."

Grimalkin sighed and gave Ironhorse a chiding look. "I

thought you were to stay hidden until I could explain things," he said with an exasperated flick of his tail. "I told you they would overreact."

Ironhorse stamped a hoof, sending an explosion of dirt into the air. "TIME IS PRESSING," he boomed, tossing his head. "WE DO NOT HAVE THE LUXURY OF WAITING MUCH LONGER. MEGHAN CHASE, I MUST SPEAK WITH YOU. WILL YOU HEAR ME OUT?"

I hesitated. This was new. Normally, about this time, we'd be fighting for our lives. Ironhorse wasn't usually polite. And Grimalkin still watched calmly from the log, gauging our reaction. Curiosity got the better of me. I put a hand on Puck's arm to stop him from backing up farther.

"I want to talk to him," I whispered, ignoring his frown. "He came here for a reason, and maybe he knows about the scepter. Keep an eye on him, will you?"

Puck glared at me, then shrugged. "Fine, Princess. But the second he makes a move, he'll be upside down in a tree before he can blink."

I squeezed his arm and stepped around him to face Ironhorse. The huge Iron fey loomed over me, steam writhing from his mouth and nostrils. "What do you want?"

I'd forgotten how *big* Ironhorse was. Not just tall, but massive. He shifted his weight, gears clanking and groaning, and I took a wary step back. He might not be attacking, but I trusted him about as far as I could throw him, which was not at all. I also hadn't forgiven him for nearly killing Ash the last time we'd met.

Ironhorse lowered his head in what was almost a bow. "THANK YOU, MEGHAN CHASE. I CALLED YOU HERE BECAUSE WE HAVE A MUTUAL PROBLEM.

YOU SEEK THE SCEPTER OF THE SEASONS, IS THAT NOT CORRECT?"

I crossed my arms. "What do you know about that?"

"I KNOW WHERE IT IS," Ironhorse continued, swishing his tail with a clanking sound. "I CAN HELP YOU RETRIEVE IT."

Puck laughed. "Sure you can," he mocked, as Ironhorse snorted and pinned his ears. "And all we have to do is follow you like eager little puppy dogs, all the way into the trap. Sorry, tin can, we're not that naive."

Ironhorse snorted. "DO NOT MOCK ME, ROBIN GOODFELLOW," he said with a blast of flame from his nostrils. "MY OFFER IS GENUINE. I DO NOT SEEK TO MISLEAD YOU."

"Bull," I snapped, crossing my arms. Ironhorse blinked at me, astonished. "Tertius and a bunch of creepy metal assassins stole the scepter and killed Sage, knowing Mab would blame Oberon for it. The new Iron King designed this war. He plans to slaughter everyone when the courts are at their weakest. Why would you want to help us stop it?"

"BECAUSE—" Ironhorse stamped a hoof. "—THE NEW IRON KING IS A FRAUD."

It was my turn to blink at him. "A fraud? What do you mean?"

The lieutenant tossed his head disdainfully. "EXACTLY WHAT I SAID. THE KING CURRENTLY SITTING THE THRONE IS AN INTRUDER AND A FAKE. I FEEL NO LOYALTY TOWARD HIM." He swished his tail and raised his head imperiously. "I AM NOT LIKE THE IRON BROTHERHOOD. THE KNIGHTS WERE CREATED TO OBEY WHOEVER SITS UPON THE THRONE.

THEIR SENSE OF DUTY IS WARPED. I KNOW THE
TRUTH. AND I WILL NOT SERVE HIM."

I glanced at Puck. "What do you think of all this?"

"Me?" Puck smirked and crossed his arms. "I think all Iron
fey should be melted down into scrap metal. I wouldn't follow Rusty here if my life depended on it."

"How very predictable." Grimalkin's voice drifted up from
near my feet. I hadn't even heard him move. "Your prejudice
blinds you to what is really happening."

"Oh, really?" I glared at him. "Then why don't you tell us
what's going on, Grim."

Grimalkin yawned. "Is it not obvious? When you killed
Machina, the Iron fey lost their ruler. They needed someone
to sit upon the throne, give them direction. A false monarch
claiming to be the Iron King answered them, but not everyone accepted him. Now, the Iron fey are split into two camps,
one siding with the false king, and one that wishes to bring
him down. Ironhorse is part of the second. Is that not true?"

"THAT IS CORRECT."

"If the false king gets the scepter, he will become even more
powerful," Grimalkin continued, gazing at me with unblinking golden eyes. "If he is to be stopped, it must happen before he receives it. Ironhorse claims to know its location. You
would be foolish not to listen to him."

"What if he's lying?"

Ironhorse threw up his head with an indignant blast of
flame. "I DO NOT LIE," he boomed, and I shrank back from
the heat. "DESPITE WHAT YOU THINK OF ME, I AM
STILL FEY, AND NO FEY CAN TELL AN UNTRUTH."

Blinking, I looked at Puck. I hadn't heard that before, except in vague mentions of faery lore. "Really?"

Puck nodded. "Pretty much, Princess." He shot an evil

look at Ironhorse. "Though comparing Rusty to one of us is a bit of a stretch."

"But...you told lies all the time, when you were Robbie. Your entire life was a lie."

Grimalkin snorted. "Just because he cannot lie does not mean he cannot deceive, human. Robin Goodfellow is an expert at dancing around the truth."

"Oh, look who's talking. If you're not an expert at screwing people over, I'll eat my head."

Ironhorse snorted and shook his mane. "ENOUGH. TIME IS PRESSING. WE DO NOT HAVE TIME TO ARGUE. MEGHAN CHASE, WILL YOU ACCEPT MY HELP OR NOT?"

I looked him in the eye. His blank, rigid mask gazed back at me, expressionless and impassive. "Are you really here to help us?" I asked. "You really want to get the scepter back and stop the war?"

"YES."

"And, you aren't going to lead us into some kind of trap?"

"NO."

I took a deep breath and let it out again. "That seems to be all the questions I can think of right now."

"Here's an important one," Puck added. "Where *is* the scepter anyway, Rusty?"

Ironhorse blew a puff of steam at him. "I DO NOT ANSWER TO YOU, OLDBLOOD. MY BARGAIN IS WITH THE GIRL."

"Yeah?" Puck's grin grew dangerous. "What if I take you apart and turn you into a toaster oven? How'd you like that, tin can?"

"I WOULD LIKE TO SEE YOU TRY."

"Guys, please!" This was as bad as refereeing the frequent

threat-fests between Puck and Ash. "Enough with the posturing and testosterone. Ironhorse, if we're going to do this, we need to know where the scepter is. We can't follow you blindly into wherever."

Ironhorse bobbed his head. "OF COURSE, MEGHAN CHASE." I frowned at his compliancy, but he went on without pause. "THE SCEPTER OF THE SEASONS HAS BEEN TAKEN INTO THE MORTAL REALM. IT IS BEING HELD IN A PLACE CALLED SILICON VALLEY."

"Silicon Valley? That's in California."

"YES."

"Why there?"

"SILICON VALLEY WAS THE BIRTHPLACE OF LORD MACHINA," Ironhorse said gravely. "MANY OF HIS LIEUTENANTS, LIKE VIRUS AND GLITCH, ALSO HAIL FROM THAT AREA. IT IS A REGION OF IRON FEY, ONE THAT THE OLDBLOODS—" he shot a glance at Puck "—AVOID COMPLETELY. IT IS THE IDEAL PLACE TO HIDE THE SCEPTER."

"You can say that again," I mused. Silicon Valley wasn't just one city, it was every city in that area. "Finding the scepter will be like looking for a needle in a haystack—in a field of haystacks."

"I CAN FIND IT." Ironhorse raised his head, looking down his long nose at us. "I SWEAR IT. DO YOU WANT ME TO SAY THE WORDS? MEGHAN CHASE, I, IRONHORSE, LAST LIEUTENANT OF LORD MACHINA, WILL TAKE YOU TO THE SCEPTER OF THE SEASONS, AND I VOW TO PROTECT YOU UNTIL IT IS IN YOUR HANDS. THIS I SWEAR, ON MY HONOR AND MY DUTY TO THE TRUE MONARCH OF THE IRON COURT."

I drew in a breath, and even Puck looked surprised. An oath like that meant the speaker was bound to fulfill it. Ironhorse wasn't playing around. As I stood there gaping at him, Puck took my arm and turned me aside.

"What about Oberon?" he murmured. "He's the only one who can remove the seal. If we go gallivanting off to California, you won't have your magic to protect you."

"We can't worry about that now." I shook off his hand. "The scepter is more important. Besides, that's what I have *you* for." I smiled at him, and turned to Ironhorse. "All right, Ironhorse. We have a deal. Take us to the scepter."

"Finally." Grimalkin stood and stretched, bottlebrush tail curling over his back. "You make decisions as slowly as you answer Summonings, human. I do hope this will not become a habit."

"Wait. You're coming, too? Why?"

"I am bored." Grimalkin waved his tail languidly. "And you are always entertaining…except when I am waiting for you to arrive, of course. Besides, the lieutenant and I have business, as well."

"You do?" I waited, but he didn't elaborate. "What is it?"

He sniffed and half slitted his eyes. "None of your concern, human. And you will need my guidance, if you want to get the scepter as quickly as possible. I believe the closest trod to Silicon Valley is through the Briars."

Puck's eyebrows shot up. "The Briars? You're risking an awful lot, cat. Why don't we try a trod a little less, oh I don't know…lethal? If we double back, we can use the trod through the Frost Meadows. That will bring us close to San Francisco, and we can easily hitch a ride from there."

Grimalkin shook his head. "If we want to reach Silicon Valley, we must go through the thorns. Do not worry, I will not get you lost. The trod past the Frost Meadows has become inaccessible. It sits too close to Tir Na Nog."

"Still don't see the problem, cat."

Ironhorse snorted. "THE FROST MEADOWS HAVE BECOME A BATTLEFIELD, ROBIN GOODFEL-LOW," he said, making my stomach clench. "WINTER HAS ALREADY CUT A SWATH OF DESTRUCTION THROUGH THE WYLDWOOD, AND THEY ARE AD-VANCING ON SUMMER AS WE SPEAK. THERE IS A HUGE ARMY OF UNSEELIE BETWEEN US AND THAT TROD. THE CAITH SITH IS RIGHT—WE CAN-NOT TURN BACK."

"Of course I am," Grimalkin agreed. "We go through the Briars."

"I don't get it," I said, as Grim trotted off with his tail in the air, confident in his victory. "What are the Briars? Gri-malkin? Hey!"

Grimalkin looked back, his eyes bright floating orbs in the gloom.

"I am not here to chitchat, human. If you truly want your question answered, ask your Puck. Perhaps he will be able to soften the reality for you. I would not." He twitched his tail, and continued into the trees without looking back.

I looked at Puck. He grimaced and shot me a humorless smile.

"Right. The Briars. Just a second, Princess. Hey, Rusty," he called, motioning to Ironhorse, who pinned back his ears, "why don't you walk ahead of us, huh? I want your big ugly ass where I can see it."

Ironhorse glared at him balefully, tossed his head, and strode after the quickly vanishing Grimalkin. The Iron faery left a faint path of destruction in his wake; branches curled away from him, plants withered and grass shriveled under his feet, leaving burned-out hoofprints on the trail. Shaking his head, Puck muttered something very rude under his breath and followed, leading us deeper into the wyldwood.

CHAPTER ELEVEN

The Briars

Later, after a night of following Grimalkin through increasingly thick forest, I decided that some questions are better left unanswered.

"The Briars," Puck began, keeping a wary eye on Ironhorse walking in front of us, "or Brambles or Thorns, or whatever you want to call it, is a maze. No one knows how big it really is, but it's huge. Some say it encircles the entire Nevernever. There are rumors that if you're in the wyldwood and start walking in any direction, you'll eventually hit the Briars. You can find patches growing most anywhere, from the Greatwood and the Venom Swamps, to the courts of Arcadia and Tir Na Nog."

"Like the Hedge," I murmured, remembering the tunnel of thorns in Oberon's court and the brambly escape route Grimalkin had used to get us out of Faery. The bramble wall surrounding the Seelie Court had opened for the cat, revealing a maze of tunnels in the thorns, and I'd followed him as he led me back to the mortal world.

Puck nodded. "That's another name for it. Though the

Hedge is a tamer version of the real Briars. In Arcadia, the Hedge responds fairly consistently, taking you wherever you want to go within the court. Out here, in the wyldwood, the Briars are rather...sadistic."

"You make it sound like they're alive."

Puck gave me a very eerie stare. "They *are* alive, Princess," he warned in a low voice. "Not in the way that we're accustomed to, but do not take them lightly. The Briars are a force, one that cannot be tamed or understood, even by Oberon or Mab. And they're always hungry. It's easy to get in—getting out is the tricky part. Not only that, but the things that live in the Briars are always hungry, too."

I felt a chill run all the way down my spine. "And we're going through the Briars...why?"

"Because the Briars have the greatest concentration of trods in all the Nevernever," Puck replied. "There are doors hidden throughout the Briars, some constantly shifting, some only appearing at a special time under special circumstances. Rumors are that, within the Briars, there is a trod to every doorway in the mortal realm, from an L.A. strip club to some kid's bedroom closet. Find the right door, and you're home free." The grin grew wider, and he shook his head. "But you have to get to it first."

Rain hissed through the branches of the trees, a cold, gray rain that leeched color from everything it touched. Even Puck's bright auburn hair turned dull and colorless in the misty deluge. He'd rake his fingers through it, streaking his hair with red, only to have the rain soak through it once more, bleaching away the color. Grimalkin was nearly invisible; not even his eyes glimmered in the gloom.

Above us, the massive wall of black thorns rose into the air, tendrils creaking and curling about. Some of the thorns were longer than me, waving about like the spines of a sea urchin, and the whole thing bristled with eerie menace.

I shivered, even standing close to Ironhorse and the smoldering heat radiating from him. The Iron faery steamed in the rain, surrounded by writhing smoke, as water struck his hot metal skin and sizzled away. Ironhorse gazed up at the wall of thorns, craning his neck to stare at it, billowing like a small geyser in the storm.

"How do we get through?" I wondered.

No sooner were the words out of my mouth than the wall shifted. Branches creaked and moaned as they peeled away to reveal a narrow, spiky corridor through the thorns. Mist curled out of the hallway, and the space beyond was choked in shadow.

Puck crossed his arms. "Looks like we're expected." He looked down at Grimalkin, a gray ghost in the mist, calmly washing his front paws. "You sure you can get us through, cat?"

Grimalkin gave one paw a few more licks before standing up. Shaking himself so that water flew everywhere, he yawned, stretched and trotted forward without looking back. "Follow me and find out" were his last words before he vanished into the tunnel.

Puck rolled his eyes. Holding out his hand, he gave me an encouraging smile. "Come on, Princess. Don't want to get separated in here." I clasped his hand, and he curled his fingers tight around mine. "Let's go, then. Rusty can bring up the rear. That way, if we're jumped from behind, we won't lose anything important."

I felt Ironhorse's indignant snort as we entered the tunnel, and I pressed closer to Puck as the shadows closed in on us like grasping fingers. Around us, the corridor pulsed with life, slithering, creaking, unfurling with faint hissing sounds. Whispers and strange voices drifted down the hallway, murmuring words I couldn't quite understand. As we stepped in farther, the hole behind us shut with a quiet hiss, trapping us within the Briars.

"This way," came Grimalkin's disembodied voice up ahead. "Try to stay close."

The bristly walls of the corridor seemed to press in on us. Puck didn't release my hand, but we had to walk single file through the tunnel to avoid being scratched. A couple times, I thought I saw a thorn or creeper actually move toward me, as if to prick my skin or catch my clothes. Once, I glanced back at Ironhorse to see how he was faring, but the thorns, much like the rest of the Nevernever, seemed loath to touch the great Iron fey, curling back from him as he passed.

The tunnel finally opened up into a small hollow with tunnels and paths twisting off in all directions. Overhead, the canopy of bramble shut out the light, so thick you couldn't see the sky through the cracks. Bones lay here and there among the thorns, bleached white and gleaming in the darkness. A skull grinned at me from a tangle of brambles, empty eye sockets crawling with worms. I shuddered and turned my face into Puck's shoulder.

"Where's Grim?" I whispered.

"Here," Grimalkin said, appearing out of nowhere. The cat leaped atop a large skull and regarded each of us in turn. "We are going deep into the Briars now," he stated in a calm, very soft voice. "I would tell you what we might face, but perhaps it is better that I do not. Try to be silent. Do not separate. Do not go down another path. And stay away from any doors you come across. Many of the gates here are a one-way

trip; go through one and you might not be able to go back.
Are you ready?"

I raised my hand. "How do you know your way around
this place, Grim?"

Grimalkin blinked. "I am a cat," he said, and vanished down
one of the tunnels.

When I was twelve, my school took a field trip to a "haunted"
corn maze on the outskirts of town, a week or so before Hal-
loween. Sitting on the bus, listening to the boys brag about
who would find his way out first, and the girls giggling in their
own little groups, I made my own vow that I would do just as
well. I remember walking down the rows of corn all by myself, feeling a thrill of both fear and excitement as I tried finding my way to the center and back again. And I remembered
the sinking feeling in my gut when I knew I was lost, when I
realized no one would help me, that I was alone.

This was ten thousand times worse.

The Briars were never still. They were always moving,
slithering, reaching for you out of the corner of your eye.
Sometimes, if you listened just right, you could almost hear
them whisper your name. Deep within the tangled darkness,
twigs snapped and branches rustled as *things* moved through
the brambles. I never got a clear look, just glimpsed dark
shapes shuffling away into the undergrowth. It creeped me
out. Big-time.

The Briars went on, an endless maze of twisted thorns
and gnarled branches, shifting, creaking and reaching out for
us. As we ventured ever deeper, doors, frames and archways
began appearing at odd intervals in completely random places.
A faded red door hung perilously from an overhead branch, a
tarnished *216* glimmering in the dim light. A filthy restroom

stall, cracked and shedding green paint, stood near the edge of the path, so wrapped in thorns that it would be impossible to push the door open. Something lean and black slithered across our path and vanished through an open closet. As it creaked shut, I caught a glimpse of a child's bedroom through the frame, and a crib outlined in moonlight, before thorny vines curled around the door and pulled it back into the Briars.

Grimalkin never hesitated, leading us on without a backward glance, passing gates and doors and strange, random things stuck in the tangled web of thorns. A mirror, a doll and an empty golf bag dangled from the branches as we walked by, as well as the countless bones and sometimes full skeletons that littered the trail. Strange creatures watched us from the shadows, mostly unseen, just their eyes glowing in the dark. Black birds with human faces perched in the branches, observing us silently as we passed, like waiting vultures. At one point, Grimalkin pulled us all into a side tunnel, hissing at us to be quiet and not move. Moments later, a massive spider, easily the size of a car, crawled over the brambles directly overhead, and I bit my lip so hard that I tasted blood. Huge and shiny, with a splash of red across its bloated abdomen, it paused a moment, as if sensing warm blood and fluids were very close, waiting for the slightest tremor to betray its quarry.

We held our breath and pretended to be stone.

For several heart-pounding seconds, we crouched in the tunnel, feeling our muscles cramp and our hearts thud too loud in our chests. Above us, the spider sat perfectly still as well, patiently waiting for its prey to grow bored, to assume it was safe and make the first move that would be its last. Eventually, something rustled in the branches ahead, and it darted away, frighteningly quick for something that huge.

The scream of some unfortunate creature pierced the air, and then silence.

For a few moments after the spider left, no one dared to move. Eventually, Grimalkin crept forward, poking his head out warily, scanning the thorns.

"Wait here," he told us. "I will see if it is safe." Slipping into the shadows like a ghost, he disappeared.

I sagged to my knees as the adrenaline wore off and my muscles started to shake, leaving me weak and nearly hyperventilating. I could handle goblins and bogeymen and evil, flesh-eating horses, but giant freaking spiders? That's where I drew the line.

Puck knelt and put a hand on my shoulder. "You okay, Princess?"

I nodded, ready to make some snarky comment about the pest problem around here. But then, one of the thorns moved.

Frowning, I bent closer, squinting my eyes. For a moment, nothing happened. Then, the three-inch barb shivered and unfurled into a pair of pointed black wings, attached to a tiny faery with glittering eyes that glared with insectlike menace. Its spindly body was covered by a shiny black carapace. Spikes grew from its elbows and shoulders, and it clutched a thorn-tipped spear in one tiny claw. As we stared at each other, the faery curled its lip, revealing teeth as sharp as needles, and flew at my face.

I jerked back, swatting wildly, and hit Puck, causing us both to tumble back. The faery dodged my flailing hands, buzzing around us like an angry wasp. I saw it pause, hovering in the air like an evil hummingbird, then streak forward with a raspy cry.

A gout of flame seared the air in front of me. I felt the blast of heat on my face, bringing tears to my eyes, and the faery disappeared into the fire. Its tiny, charred body dropped like a stone to the earth, curling in on itself, the delicate black wings seared away. It gave an insectlike twitch, then was still.

Ironhorse tossed his head and snorted, looking pleased as smoke curled from his nostrils. Puck grimaced as he pushed himself to his feet, holding out a hand to help me up.

"You know, I'm really starting to hate the insect life around here," he muttered. "Next time, remind me to bring a can of Off!"

"You didn't have to kill it," I told Ironhorse, dusting off my pants. "It was like three inches tall!"

"IT ATTACKED YOU." Ironhorse sounded puzzled, cocking his head at me. "IT CLEARLY HAD AGGRESSIVE INTENT. MY MISSION IS TO PROTECT YOU UNTIL WE RETRIEVE THE SCEPTER. I WILL ALLOW NOTHING TO BRING YOU HARM. THAT IS MY SOLEMN VOW."

"Yeah, but you don't need a machine gun to kill a fly."

"Human!" Grimalkin appeared, bounding up with his ears flattened to his head. "You are making too much noise. All of you are. We must leave this area, quickly." He glanced about, and the fur on his back started to rise. "It might already be too late."

"Ironhorse killed this teensy little faery—" I began, but Grimalkin hissed at me.

"Idiot human! Do you think that was the only one? Look around you!"

I did, and my heart nearly stopped. The thorns around us were moving, hundreds upon hundreds of them, unfurling into tiny faeries with pointed, gnashing teeth. The air filled with the sound of buzzing, and thousands of tiny black eyes glimmered through the thorns.

"Oh, this isn't good," Puck murmured as the buzz grew louder, more frantic. "I really, really wish I had that Off!"

"Run!" spit Grimalkin, and we ran.

The faeries swarmed around us, the hum of their wings vibrating the air, their high-pitched voices shrieking in my ears. I felt the weight of their tiny bodies on my skin, an instant before the stings, and flailed wildly, trying to dislodge them. Puck snarled something unintelligible, swiping at them with his knives, and Ironhorse blasted flame from his mouth and nostrils, roaring. Charred, dismembered faeries dropped shrieking from the air, but dozens more buzzed in to take their place. Grimalkin, of course, had vanished. We charged blindly down a tunnel of thorns, through swarms of furious killer wasp-fey, with no clue of where we were going.

As I rounded a corner, a body appeared right in front of me. I had no time to react before I crashed into it, and we both went sprawling.

"Ow! What the hell!" someone yelped.

Swatting faeries, I looked into the face of a girl a year or two younger than me. She was tiny and Asian, with hair that looked as if she'd taken a machete to it, wearing a ratty sweater two sizes too big. For a second, my mind went blank with the shock at seeing another human, until I saw the furry ears peeking out of her hair.

We blinked at each other for a second, before the sting from a killer-wasp faerie snapped me out of my daze. Flailing, I scrambled to my feet as the swarm buzzed around the strange girl as well. She yelped and swatted wildly, backing away.

"What is this?" she hissed, as Puck came up behind me and Ironhorse charged in, blowing flame. "Who the hell are you people? Oh, never mind! Run!" She darted past us, looking back once to shout "Hurry up, Nelson!" over her shoulder. I barely had time to wonder who Nelson was when a kid built like a linebacker barreled through us, somehow dodging Puck and Ironhorse, and pounded after the girl. I caught a glimpse of gorillalike shoulders, muddy blond hair, and skin as green as swamp water. He clutched a backpack in his arms like a football and charged down the trail without a backward glance.

"Who were they?" I asked, over the buzzing of the swarm and my own frantic flailing.

"No time," Puck said, slapping at a faery on his neck. "Ow! Dammit, we have to get out of here! Come on!"

We had started down the path again when a roar shook the air ahead of us, causing the swarm of killer fey to freeze in mid-air. It came again, guttural and savage, as something rattled the wall of thorns, coming toward us with the sound of snapping wood. I sensed hundreds of creatures in the brambles fleeing for their lives.

The faeries scattered. Buzzing in terror, they vanished into the hedge, through cracks and tiny spaces between the thorns. In seconds, the whole swarm had disappeared. I peered through the branches and saw something coming down the trail, ripping through the wall of thorns like it wasn't there. Something black and scaly, and much, much bigger than the spider.

Is that what I think it is?

"Thiiiief!" roared a deep, inhuman voice, before a gout of flame burst through the hedge, setting an entire section on fire, making the air explode with heat. Ironhorse bugled, rearing up in alarm. Puck cursed, grabbed my arm, and yanked me back the way we came.

We fled down the trail after the strange girl and her muscle-necked companion, feeling the heat from the monster's fire at our backs. *"Thieves!"* the terrible voice snarled, staying right on our heels. *"I can smell you! I can feel your breath and hear your hearts. Give me back what is mine!"*

"Great," Puck panted, as Ironhorse cantered beside us, bellowing that he would shield me from the flames. "Just great. I hate spiders. I hate wasps. But, you know what I hate even more than that?"

The thing behind us roared, and another blast of flame seared the branches overhead. I winced as we ran beneath a rain of cinders and flaming twigs. "Dragons?" I gasped.

"Remind me to kill Grimalkin next time we see him."

The trail narrowed, then shrank down to a tight, thorny tunnel that twisted off into the darkness. Bending down and peering into it, I could just make out a door at the end of the burrow. And, I couldn't be sure, but I thought I saw the door shut.

"I think I see a door!" I called, looking over my shoulder. Puck nodded impatiently.

"Well, what are you waiting for, Princess! Go!"

"What about Ironhorse?"

"He'll have to squeeze!" Puck pushed me toward the mouth, but I resisted. "Come on, Princess. We don't want to be in the middle of that if Deathbreath decides to sneeze on us."

"We can't leave him behind!"

"WORRY NOT, PRINCESS," Ironhorse said, and I gaped at him, not believing my eyes. Where a horse had been, now a man stood before me, dark and massive, with a square jaw and fists the size of hams. He wore jeans and a black shirt that bulged with all the muscles underneath, the skin stretched tight over steely tendons. Dreadlocks spilled from his scalp like a mane, and his eyes still burned with that intense red glow. "YOU ARE NOT THE ONLY ONE WITH A FEW TRICKS UP YOUR SLEEVE, GOODFELLOW," he said, a faint smirk beneath his voice. "NOW, GO. I WILL BE RIGHT BEHIND YOU."

With a horrible cracking sound, the dragon's head rose above the briars on a long, snaking neck, looming to an impossible height. It was bigger than I'd imagined, a long toothy maw covered in black-green scales, ivory horns curling back from its skull to frame the sky. Alien, red-gold eyes scanned the ground impassively, gleaming with cunning and intelligence. *"I see you, little thieves."*

Puck gave me a shove, and I tumbled into the burrow, scratching my hands and knees and jabbing myself on the thorns. Cursing, I looked up and saw two familiar golden eyes floating before me in the dark.

"Hurry, human," Grimalkin hissed, and fled down the burrow.

The tunnel seemed to shrink the farther I went, scraping my back and catching my hair and clothes as I followed Grimalkin, bent over like a crab. I heard Puck and Ironhorse behind me, felt the glare of the dragon's eye at my back, and cursed as my sleeve caught on a thorn. We were going too slow! The red door loomed at the end of the tunnel, a beacon of light and safety, so far away. But as I got closer, I saw Grimalkin standing in front of it, ears flattened against his skull, hissing and baring his teeth.

"Saint-John's-wort," he snarled, and I saw a cluster of dried yellow flowers hanging on the door like tiny sunbursts. "The fey cannot enter with that on the door. Take it down, quickly, human!"

"Burn, little thieves!"

Fire exploded down the tunnel, writhing and twisting in a maelstrom of heat and fury, shooting toward us. I ripped the flowers off the door and dove through, Puck and Ironhorse toppling in after me. Flames shot over my head, singeing my back as I lay gasping on a cold cement floor. Then, the door slammed shut, cutting off the fire, and we were plunged into darkness.

CHAPTER TWELVE

Leanansidhe

For a few moments, I lay there on the concrete, my body curiously hot and cold at the same time. My neck, my shoulders, and the backs of my legs burned from the fire that had come way too close for comfort. But my cheek and stomach pressed into the cold cement, making me shiver. To either side of me, Puck and Ironhorse struggled to their feet with muffled curses and groans.

"Well, that was fun," Puck muttered, helping me stand. "I swear, if I ever see those two kids again, we're going to have a little chat. If you're going to steal from a fifty-foot, fire-breathing lizard with the memory of an elephant, you'd better have a damn impressive riddle, or you wait until it isn't home. And who the hell put Saint-John's-wort over the door? I'm feeling very unwelcome right now."

A flashlight clicked on in the shadows, blinding me. Shielding my eyes, I counted three silhouettes at the end of the beam. Two I recognized; the tiny girl with furry ears and the green-skinned boy we'd met in the Briars. The last, the one holding the flashlight, was tall and skinny, with thick dark hair, a scraggly goatee, and two ridged horns curling up from his brow. He held a cross in the other hand, raised in front of his face like he was warding off a vampire.

Puck laughed. "Hate to break it to you, kid, but unless you're a priest, that isn't going to work. Neither is the salt you have poured across the floor. I'm not your average bogey."

"Damn faeries," spit goatee boy, looking pale. "How did you get in here? You'd better leave right now, if you know what's good for you. *She'll* tear your guts out and make harp strings with them."

"Well, there's a problem with that," Puck continued with mock regret. "See, right outside that door is a very pissed off reptile who is eager to turn us into shish kebab, because *you three* were stupid enough to steal from a dragon." He sighed and shook his head in a disappointed manner. "You know dragons never forget a thief, don't you? So, what'd you take?"

"None of your business, faery," goat boy shot back. "And maybe I wasn't clear when I said you're not welcome here." He reached into his pocket and pulled out three iron nails, holding them between white, shaking knuckles. "Maybe a faceful of iron will convince you otherwise."

I stepped forward, shooting Puck a warning glare before he could rise to the challenge. "Take it easy," I soothed, holding up my hands. "We don't want any trouble. We're just trying to get through the Briars, that's all."

"Warren!" gasped the girl, staring at me wide-eyed. "It's her!" All eyes flashed to me.

"It *is* you," Warren breathed. "You're her, aren't you? Oberon's half-blood. The Summer princess."

Ironhorse growled and pressed closer, causing the trio to shrink back. I put a hand on his chest. "How do you know me?"

"*She's* looking for you, you know. Got half the exiles looking for you—"

"Whoa, slow down, goat-boy." Puck held up a hand. "Who is this remarkable *she* you keep talking about?"

Warren shot him a look that was half fearful, half awe. "*Her,* of course. The boss of this place. So…if this is Oberon's daughter, you must be him, aren't you? Robin Goodfellow? The Puck?" Puck smiled, which caused Warren to swallow noisily. His Adam's apple bobbed in his throat. "But—" he glanced at Ironhorse "—she didn't say anything about him. Who's he?"

"Stinks," rumbled the green-skinned boy, curling his lip to reveal blunt, uneven teeth. "Smells like coal. Like iron."

Warren's eyebrows shot up. "Aw, crap. He's one of *them,* isn't he? One of those Iron faeries! She won't be happy about this."

"He's with me," I said quickly, as Ironhorse drew himself up. "He's safe, I promise you. And who do you keep talking about? Who is this *she?*"

"Her name is Leanansidhe," Warren stated, as if I were an idiot for not figuring it out. "Leanansidhe the Dark Muse. Queen of the Exiles."

Puck's eyebrows arched into his hair.

"You're kidding," he said, his face caught between a grimace and a smirk. "So, Leanansidhe fancies herself a queen, now? Oh, Titania will love that."

"Who's Leanansidhe?" I asked.

The grimace won out. He shook his head and turned to me, his face grim. "Bad news, Princess. At one time, Leanansidhe was one of the most powerful beings in all the Nevernever. The Dark Muse, they called her, because she inspired many great artists, helping them produce their most brilliant works.

You might recognize some of the mortals she's helped—James Dean, Jimi Hendrix, Kurt Cobain."

"No way."

Puck shrugged. "But, as you should know, such help always comes with a price. None whom Leanansidhe inspires lives very long, ever. Their lives are brilliant, colorful, and very brief. Sometimes, if the artist was particularly special, she'd take him back to the Nevernever to entertain her for eternity. Or until she got bored. Of course, this was before..." He trailed off, giving me a sideways look.

"Before what?"

"Titania banished her to the mortal realm," Puck said quickly, as if he was really going to say something else. "According to some, Leanansidhe was growing too powerful, had too many mortals worshipping her, and there was talk that she wanted to make herself queen. Naturally, this made our good Summer Queen more than a little jealous, so she exiled the self-proclaimed Queen of Muse and sealed off all trods to her, so that Leanansidhe could never return to Faery. That was several years ago, and no one has seen or heard from her since.

"But, apparently," Puck continued, glancing at the three teenagers listening in rapt fascination, "Leanansidhe has a new following. A new little mortal cult ready to throw themselves at her feet." He smothered a laugh. "Pickings must be pretty slim nowadays."

"Hey," said the girl, narrowing her eyes at him. "What's that supposed to mean?"

"Why is Leanansidhe looking for me?" I asked, before an unpleasant thought drifted to mind. "You...you don't think she wants revenge, for what Titania did to her?" Great. That was all I needed, another faery queen who was out to get me. I must hold some sort of record.

We glared at Warren, who stepped back and raised his hands. "Hey, man. Don't look at me. I don't know what she wants. Just that she's been looking for you."

"WE CANNOT GO TO THIS LEANANSIDHE NOW," Ironhorse boomed, making the teens jump and the ceiling rattle. God, he couldn't speak quietly if his life depended on it. "OUR MISSION IS URGENT. WE MUST GET TO CALIFORNIA AS SOON AS POSSIBLE."

"Well, we're not going anywhere now, not with ol' Death-breath guarding the only way out."

"Come with us."

I looked up. Warren had spoken and was staring at me intently. The eager look in his eyes made me uncomfortable, as did his sudden change in mood. "Come with us to Leanan-sidhe's," he urged. "She could help. You want to go to California? She can get you there, easy—"

"Warren," said the girl, grabbing his sleeve and pulling him aside. "Come here a second, would you? 'Scuse us a sec, people." Surprisingly strong for her size, she dragged him into a far corner. Huddled against the wall, they whispered furiously to each other, casting suspicious glances at Ironhorse over their shoulders.

"What are we going to do?" I wondered. "Should we wait until the dragon leaves to find our way back through the Bri-ars? Or should we find out what Leanansidhe wants?"

"NO," thundered Ironhorse, his voice bouncing off the walls. "I DO NOT TRUST THIS LEANANSIDHE. IT IS TOO DANGEROUS."

"Puck?"

He shrugged. "Under normal circumstances, I'd agree with the toaster oven," he said, earning a hard glare from Iron-horse. "Leanansidhe has always been unpredictable, and she has enough power to make that dragon look like a cranky Gila monster. But...I always say the enemy you know is better than the enemy you can't see."

I nodded. "I agree. If Leanansidhe is looking for us, I think we should meet her on our own terms. Otherwise, I'd just worry about what she's sending after us."

"Besides..." Puck rolled his eyes. "I think we have another problem."

"What's that?"

"Our trusty guide has gone AWOL."

I looked around, but Grimalkin had vanished, and he didn't respond to my hissed calls for him to show himself. The street kids were watching us now, eager and hesitant at the same time. I sighed. There was no telling where Grimalkin was, or when he'd return. Really, there was just one option.

"So." I gave them a hopeful smile. "How far is Leanansidhe's?"

Turns out, we were in the basement of her mansion.

"So, Leanansidhe has you guys steal from dragons?" I asked the girl as we walked down the dimly lit corridors, torchlight flickering over the damp stone walls. Whatever the house looked like, the basement was huge. It reminded me of a medieval dungeon, complete with heavy doors, wooden portcullises, and gargoyles leering at us from the walls. Mice scurried over the floor, and other things moved in the shadows, just out of sight.

The girl, Kimi, grinned at me. "Leanansidhe has lots of clients with very unusual tastes," she explained. "Most of them are exiles, like her, who can't go back into the Nevernever for some reason. She uses us—" she gestured to herself and Nelson "—to fetch things she can't get herself, like that thing with the dragon. Apparently, a banished Winter sidhe in New York is paying a fortune for real dragon eggs."

"You stole its *eggs?*"

"Only one." Kimi giggled at my stunned expression. "Then the stupid lizard woke up and we had to book it." She giggled again, smoothing down her ears. "Don't worry, we're not going to decimate the dragon population. Leanansidhe told us to leave a couple behind."

Puck made a noise that might've been appreciation. "And what do you guys get out of this?"

"Free room and board. And the rep that goes with it. We'd be out on the streets, otherwise." Kimi and Nelson shared a secret glance, but Warren was staring at me. He'd been doing that since we left to meet Leanansidhe, and it was making me very uncomfortable.

"The pay's not bad, either," Kimi went on, oblivious to Warren's scrutiny. "At least, it's better than the alternative—being hunted down for what we are, getting stepped on by the exiles and the fey who just like it better in the mortal realm. Leanansidhe's made it safer for us—you don't screw around with the queen's pets. Even the redcap gangs know to leave you alone. For the most part, anyway."

"Why?" I asked. "You're exiles, too, right? Why should it be different for you?" I looked at her furry, tufted ears, at Nelson's swamp-water skin and Warren's horns. They weren't human, that much was certain. But then I remembered Warren holding out the iron cross, his fearful *damned faeries,* how they could get through the door when Grimalkin couldn't. And I knew what they were even before Kimi said it.

"Because," she said cheerfully, twitching her ears, "we're half-breeds. I'm half-phouka, Nelson's half-troll, and Warren

is part-satyr. And if there's one thing an exile hates more than
the fey who banished him, it's half-breeds like us."

I hadn't thought of that before, though it made sense. I suspected half-breeds like Kimi, Nelson and Warren had it pretty
tough. Without Oberon's protection, they would've been left
to the whims of the true fey, who probably made life very difficult for them. It wasn't surprising they would make a deal
with this Queen of the Exiles, in exchange for some degree
of protection. Even if it meant stealing dragon eggs right out
from under the dragon.

"Oh, and by the way," Kimi went on, with a quick glance
at Ironhorse, clanking along behind me. "Leanansidhe knows
about…um…*his kind*. They've been killing off lots of exiles
lately, and it's making her mad. Your 'friend' should be really careful around her. I don't know how she'll take an Iron
faery in her living room. I've seen her throw a fit for less."

"Shut up, Kimi," Warren said abruptly. We had reached the
end of the hall, where a bright red door waited for us atop a
flight of stairs. "I told you, it's not a big deal."

I frowned at him, but something caught my attention.
Strains of music drifted down the steps, the low, shivery chords
of a piano or organ. The music was dark and haunting, reminding me of a play I'd seen a long time ago, *The Phantom
of the Opera*. I remembered Mom dragging me to the theater
when the play came through our little town, shortly before
Ethan was born. I remembered thinking I'd have to sit through
three hours of absolute boredom and torture, but from the first
booming organ chords, I was completely entranced.

I also remembered Mom crying through several of the
scenes, something she never did, even with the saddest movies. I didn't think anything of it then, but it seemed a little
odd, now.

We stepped up and through the doorway into a magnificent foyer, with a double grand staircase sweeping toward a high vaulted ceiling and a roaring fireplace surrounded by plush black sofas. The hardwood floor gleamed red, the walls were patterned in red and black, and gauzy black curtains covered the high arched windows near the back of the room. Nearly every clear space on the wall was taken up by paintings—oil paintings, watercolors, black-and-white sketches. The Mona Lisa smiled her odd little smile on the far wall, next to a weird, disjointed painting that was probably Picasso.

Music echoed through the room, dark and haunting piano chords played with such force that they made the air vibrate and my teeth buzz. An enormous grand piano stood in the corner near the fireplace, the flames dancing in the reflection of the polished wood. Hunched over the keys, a figure in a rumpled white shirt beat and pounded the ivory bars, fingers flying.

"Who—?"

"Shh!" Kimi shushed me with a light smack on the arm. "Don't talk. *She* doesn't like it when someone's playing."

I fell silent, studying the pianist again. Brown hair hung limp and shaggy on his shoulders, looking as if it hadn't been washed in days. His shoulders were broad, though his shirt hung loose on a lean, bony frame that was so thin his spine pressed tightly against his skin.

The song ended with one last, vibrating chord. As the notes faded and silence descended on the room, the man remained hunched over the keys. I couldn't see his face, but I thought his eyes were closed, and his muscles trembled as if from exertion. He seemed to be waiting for something. I looked to the others, wondering if we should applaud.

A slow clapping came from the top of the stairs. I looked

up and saw none other than Grimalkin, sitting on the railing with his tail around his feet, looking perfectly at home. Any annoyance I felt with him disappeared at the sight of his companion.

A woman stood on the balcony, her gold and crimson gown billowing around her, though I was sure there'd been no one there a second ago. Her wavy, waist-length hair shimmered like strands of copper, almost too bright to look at, floating around her face as if it weighed nothing at all. She was pale and tall and magnificent, every inch a queen, and I felt my stomach contract. Forget Arcadia or Tir Na Nog; we were in her court now, playing by her rules. I wondered if she expected us to bow.

"Bravo, Charles." Her voice was pure song, made of poetry given sound, of every creative notion you've ever had. Hearing it, I felt I could sweep onto a stage and bring the masses roaring and screaming to their feet. "That was quite magnificent. You can go now."

The man rose shakily to his feet, grinning like a little kid whose finger painting had been praised by the teacher. He was younger than my stepdad, but not by much, the hint of a beard shadowing his mouth and jaw. When he turned and spotted us, I shivered. His face and hazel eyes were blank of reason, as empty as the sky.

"Poor bastard," I heard Puck mutter. "He's been here awhile, hasn't he?"

The man blinked at me, dazed for a moment, but then his eyes grew wide. "You," he muttered, shambling forward, jabbing at me with a finger. I frowned. "I know you. Don't I? Don't I? Who are you? Who?" He frowned, an anguished expression crossing his face. "The rats whisper in the darkness," he said, clutching at his hair. "They whisper. I can't remember their names. They tell me…" His eyes narrowed and he panted, glaring at me. "Rag girl, flying round my bed. Who are you? *Who?*" This last was a shout, and he lurched forward.

Ironhorse stepped between us with a rumbling growl, and the man leaped back, hands flying to his face. "No," he whimpered, cringing on the floor, arms cradling his head. "No one in here. Empty empty empty. Who am I? I don't know. The rats tell me, but I forget."

"That is enough." Leanansidhe floated down the staircase, her gown trailing behind her. Sweeping up to the human, she touched him lightly on the head. "Charles, darling, I have guests now," she murmured, as he gazed up at her with teary eyes. "Why don't you take a bath, and then you can play for us at dinner?"

Charles sniffled. "Girl," he whimpered, clutching at his hair. "In my head."

"Yes, I know, darling. But if you don't leave, I'll have to turn you into a harp. Go on, now. Shoo, shoo." She made little fluttery motions with her hands, and with one final glance at me, the man scuttled away.

Leanansidhe sighed and turned to us, then seemed to notice the trio for the first time. "Ah, there you are." She smiled, and their faces lit up in the glow of her attention. "Did you manage to get the eggs, darlings?"

Warren snatched the backpack from Nelson's arm and held it out. "We found the nest, Leanansidhe. It was just where you said. But the dragon woke up then, and…" He unzipped the pack, revealing a yellow-green egg the size of a basketball. "We were only able to get one."

"One?" Leanansidhe frowned, and shadows fell over the room. "Only one? I need at least two, pets, or the deal is off.

The former Duke of Frostfell specifically said a pair of eggs. How many is in a pair, darling?"

"T-two," Warren stammered.

"Well, then. I'd say you still have work to do. Go on, now. Chop-chop. And don't come back without those eggs!"

The trio fled without hesitation, following the human out the same door. Leanansidhe watched them go, then whirled on us with a bright, feral smile. "Well! Here we are at last. When Grimalkin told me you were coming, I was ever so pleased. It's so *good* to finally meet you."

Grimalkin descended the stairs with his typical indifference, completely unfazed by the Death Glares coming from me and Puck. Leaping onto a sofa, he sat down and began grooming his tail.

"And Puck!" Leanansidhe turned to him, clasping her hands in delight. "I haven't seen you in forever, darling. How is Oberon these days? Still being henpecked by that basilisk of a wife?"

"Don't insult the basilisks," Puck replied, smiling. Crossing his arms, he gazed around the room, moving ever so slightly in front of me. "So, Lea, looks like you've been busy. What's up with the crazies and the half-bloods? Building an army of misfits?"

"Don't be silly, darling." Leanansidhe sniffed, plucking a cigarette holder from a lamp stand. She took a puff and blew a hazy green cloud over our heads. It writhed and twisted into a smoky dragon before dissipating in the air. "My coup days are behind me, now. I've made a nice little realm for myself here, and overthrowing a court is so tedious. However, I'd ask you not to tell Titania that you found me, darling. If you went and blabbed, I might have to rip out your tongue." She smiled, examining a bloodred nail, as Puck inched closer to me. "Also, Robin dear, you needn't worry about protecting the girl. I mean her no harm. The Iron faery I might have to dismember and send its remains to Asia—" Ironhorse tensed and took a step forward "—but I have no intention of hurting the daughter of Oberon. So relax, pet. That's not why I called her here."

"Ironhorse is with me," I said quickly, putting a hand on his arm before he did something stupid. "He won't hurt anything, I promise."

Leanansidhe turned the full brunt of her glittering sapphire gaze on me. "You're so *cute,* did you know that? You look just like your father. No wonder Titania can't stand to look at you. What's your name, darling?"

"Meghan."

She smiled, vicious and challenging, appraising me. "And what's a cutie like you going to do if I want that abomination out of my home? That's quite the binding you've got there, dove. I doubt you can scrape up the glamour to light my cigarette."

I swallowed. This was a test. If I was going to save Ironhorse, I couldn't falter. Steeling myself, I looked into those cold blue eyes, ancient and remorseless, and held her gaze. "Ironhorse is one of my companions," I said softly. "I need him, so I can't let you hurt him. I'll make a deal with you, if that's what it takes, but he stays here. He's not your enemy, and he won't hurt you or anyone under your protection. You have my word."

"I know that, darling." Leanansidhe continued to hold my stare, smiling all the while. "I'm not worried about the Iron faery harming me. I'm worried I won't be able to get his stink out of my carpets. But, no matter." She straightened, releasing me from her gaze. "You've given your word, and I'll hold you to that. Now, come, darling. Dinner first, then we can talk. Oh, and please tell your iron pet not to touch anything while he's here. I don't want him melting the glamour."

We followed Leanansidhe down several long corridors carpeted in red and black velvet, past portraits whose eyes seemed to follow us as we walked by. Leanansidhe didn't stop talking, a mindless, bubbly stream, as she led us through her home, spouting names, places and creatures I didn't recognize. But I couldn't stop listening to the sound of her voice, even if all I heard was chipmunk chatter. In my peripheral vision, I caught glimpses of rooms through half-opened doors, drenched in shadow or strange, flickering lights. Sometimes, I thought the rooms looked weird, as if there were trees growing out of the floor, or schools of fish swimming through the air. But Leanansidhe's voice cut through my curiosity, and I couldn't take my eyes from her, even for a closer look.

We entered a vast dining hall, where a long table took up most of the left wall, surrounded by chairs of glass and wood. Candelabra floated down the length of the surface, hovering over a feast that could feed an army. Platters of meat and fish, raw fruits and vegetables, tiny cakes, candies, bottles of wine, and a huge roast pig with an apple in its mouth as the centerpiece. Except for the flickering candlelight, the room was pitch-black, and I could hear things scurrying about, muttering in the darkness.

Leanansidhe breezed into the room, trailing smoke from her cigarette, and stood at the head of the table. "Come, darlings," she called, beckoning us with the back of her gloved hand. "You look famished. Sit. Eat. And please don't be so rude as to think the food glamoured or enchanted. What kind of host do you think I am?" She sniffed, as though the very thought annoyed her, and looked away into the shadows. "Excuse me," she called, as we cautiously moved toward the table. "Minions? I have guests, and you are making me look impolite. I will not be pleased if my reputation is soured, darlings."

Movement in the shadows, muttering and low shuffles, as a group of little men edged into the light. I had to bite my lip to keep from laughing. They were redcaps, evil-eyed and shark-toothed, with their hats dipped in the blood of their victims, but they were also dressed in matching butler suits with pink bow ties. Sullen and scowling, they emerged from the darkness, glaring for all they were worth. *Laugh and die,* their eyes warned, but Puck took one look at them and started cracking up. The redcaps glared at him like they were going to bite his head off.

One of them caught sight of Ironhorse and let out a piercing hiss that sent all of them scrambling back. "Iron!" he screeched, baring his jagged fangs. "That's one of them stinking Iron faeries! Kill it! Kill it now!"

Ironhorse roared, and Puck's dagger flashed out, a devilish grin stretching his face at the thought of violence. The redcaps surged forward, snarling and gnashing their teeth, just as eager. I grabbed a silver knife from the table and held it ready as the redcaps lunged forward. One of them leaped onto the table, gathering his short legs under him to launch himself at us, fangs gleaming.

"That is *enough!*"

We froze. It was impossible not to. Even the redcap on the table locked up, then fell into a bowl of fruit salad.

Leanansidhe stood at the end of the table, glowering at us all. Her eyes glowed amber, her hair whipped away from her face, and the candelabra flames danced wildly. For a heart-stopping moment, she stood there, alien and terrifying. Then she sighed, smoothed back her hair and reached for her cigarette holder, taking a long drag. As she blew out the smoke, things returned to normal, including our ability to move, but no one, least of all the redcaps, had any aggressive thoughts left.

"Well?" she finally said, looking to the redcaps as if nothing had happened. "What are you minions standing about for? My seat isn't going to move itself."

The largest redcap, a burly fellow with a bone fishhook through his nose, shook himself and crept forward, pulling Leanansidhe's chair away from the table. The others followed suit, looking like they'd rather beat us to death with our own arms, but wordlessly drew out our chairs. The one attending Ironhorse growled and bared his teeth at the Iron faery, then darted away as quickly as he could.

"I apologize for the minions," Leanansidhe said when we were all seated. She touched her fingers to her temple, as if she had a headache. "It's so hard to find good help these days, darlings. You have no idea."

"I thought I recognized them," Puck said, casually reaching for a pear near the center of the table. "Isn't the leader Razor Dan, or something like that? Caused a bit of a stir during the Goblin Wars, when they tried selling information to both sides?"

"Nasty business, darling." Leanansidhe snapped her fingers twice, and a brownie melted out of the darkness with a wine flute and a bottle, scrambling onto a stool to fill her glass. "Everyone knows you don't cheat the goblin tribes if you know what's good for you. Like poking a stick down an ant nest." She sipped the wine the brownie poured her and sighed. "They came to me for asylum, after pissing off every goblin tribe in the wyldwood, so I put them to work. That's the rule here, darling. You stay, you work."

I glanced in the direction the redcaps left, feeling their hateful gaze staring out from the darkness. "But aren't you afraid they'll get mad and eat someone?"

"Not if they know what's good for them, darling. And you're not eating anything. Eat." She gestured at the food, and I suddenly realized how hungry I was. I reached for a platter of tiny frosted cakes, too hungry to care about glamours or enchantments anymore. If I was munching on a toadstool or a grasshopper, so be it. Ignorance is bliss.

"While you're here," Leanansidhe continued, smiling as we ate, "you leave all personal vendettas behind. That's my other rule. I can easily deny them sanctuary, and then where will they be? Back in the mortal realm, dying slowly or fighting it out with the Iron fey who are gradually infesting every town and city in the world. No offense, darling," she added, smiling at Ironhorse, implying the exact opposite. Staring blindly at the table, Ironhorse didn't respond. He wasn't eating anything, and I figured he either didn't want to be indebted to Leanansidhe, or he didn't eat regular food. Thankfully, Leanansidhe didn't seem to notice. "Most choose not to take the risk," she went on, stabbing her cigarette holder in the direction the redcaps had fled. "Take the minions, for example. Every so often, one will poke his nose back in the mortal realm, get it hacked off by some goblin mercenary, and come crawling back to me. Exiles, half-breeds and outcasts alike. I'm their only safe haven between the Nevernever and the mortal world."

"Which begs the question," Puck asked, almost too casually. "Where *are* we, anyway?"

"Ah, pet." Leanansidhe smiled at him, but it was a frightening thing, cold and vicious. "I was wondering when you would ask that. And if you think you should run and tattle on me to your masters, don't bother. I've done nothing wrong. I haven't broken my exile. This is my realm, yes, but Titania can relax. It doesn't intrude upon hers in any way."

"Okay, totally not the question I asked." Puck paused with an apple in hand, raising an eyebrow. "And I think I'm even more alarmed now. Where are we, Lea?"

"The Between, darling." Leanansidhe leaned back, sipping her wine. "The veil between the Nevernever and the mortal realm. Surely you've realized that by now."

Both Puck's eyebrows shot up into his hair. "The Between? The Between is full of nothing, or so I was led to believe. Those who get stuck Between usually go insane in very short order."

"Yes, I'll admit, it was difficult to work with at first." Leanansidhe waved her hand airily. "But, enough about me, darlings. Let's talk about you." She took a drag on her cigarette and blew a smoky fish over the table. "Why were you tromping around the Briars when my streetrats found you? I thought you were looking for the Scepter of the Seasons, and you certainly won't find it down there, darlings. Unless you think Bellatorallix is sitting on it."

I started. Ironhorse jerked up, sending a bowl of grapes clattering to the floor. Brownies appeared from nowhere, scurrying to recover the lost fruit as it rolled about the tile. Leanansidhe raised a slender eyebrow and took another drag on her cigarette as we recovered.

"You knew?" I stared at her, as the brownies set the bowl on the table again and scampered off. "You knew about the scepter?"

"Darling, please." Leanansidhe gave me a half scornful, half patronizing look. "I know everything that happens within the courts. I find it unforgivable to be so out of the loop, and it's terribly boring here otherwise. My informants clue me in on all the important details."

"Spies, you mean," Puck said.

"Such a dirty word, darling." Leanansidhe *tsked* at him. "And it doesn't matter now. What matters is what I can tell you. I know the scepter was stolen from under Mab's nose, I know Summer and Winter are about to go to a bloody war over it, and I know that the scepter is not in the Nevernever but in the mortal realm. And—" she took a long drag on her cigarette and sent a hawk soaring over our heads "—I can help you find it."

I was instantly suspicious, and I could tell Ironhorse and Puck felt the same. "Why?" I demanded. "What's in it for you?"

Leanansidhe looked at me, and a shadow crept into her voice, making it dark and ominous. "Darling, I've seen what's been happening in the mortal realm. Unlike Oberon and Mab, who hide in their safe little courts, I know the reality pressing in on us from every side. The Iron fey are getting stronger. They're everywhere: in computers, crawling out of television screens, massing in factories. I have more exiles under my roof now than I've had in the past century. They're terrified, un-willing to walk in the mortal realm any longer, because the Iron fey are tearing them apart."

I shuddered, and Ironhorse had gone very still. Leanansidhe paused, and nothing could be heard except the faint skitter-ing of things unseen in the pressing darkness.

"If Summer and Winter go to war, and the Iron fey attack, there will be nothing left. If the Iron fey win, the Nevernever will become uninhabitable. I don't know what that will do to the Between, but I'm sure it will be quite fatal for me. So you see, darling," Leanansidhe said, taking a sip of wine, "it would be advantageous for me to help you. And since I have eyes and ears everywhere within the mortal realm, it would be prudent of you to accept."

Ironhorse shifted, then spoke for the first time. To his credit, he tried to keep his voice down, but even then it echoed around the room. "YOUR OFFER IS APPRECIATED," he rumbled, "BUT WE ALREADY KNOW WHERE THE SCEPTER IS LOCATED."

"Do you now?" Leanansidhe shot him a vicious smile. "Where?"

"SILICON VALLEY."

"Lovely. *Where* in Silicon Valley, pet?"

A pause. "I DO NOT—"

"And how do you plan on getting to the scepter once you find it, darling? Walk in the front door?"

Ironhorse glowered at her. "I WILL FIND A WAY."

"I see." Leanansidhe gave him a scornful look. "Well, let me tell you what *I* know about Silicon Valley, pet, so the princess has an idea of what she's up against. It's the gremlins' spawning ground. You know, those nasty little things that crawl out of computers and other machines. There are literally thousands of them down there, perhaps hundreds of thousands, as well as some very powerful Iron fey who would turn you into bloody strips as soon as look at you. You go down there without a plan, darling, and you're walking into a death trap. Besides, you're already too late." Leanansidhe snapped her fingers, holding out her glass for more wine. "I've been keeping tabs on the scepter's movements ever since I heard it was stolen. It was being held in a large office building in San Jose, but my spies tell me it's been moved. Apparently, someone already tried to get in and steal it back, but didn't quite succeed. Now, the building has been cleared out, and the scepter is gone."

"Ash," I whispered, glancing at Puck. "It had to be Ash." Puck looked doubtful, so I turned back to Leanansidhe, a cold desperation spreading through my stomach. "What happened to him, the one who tried to take the scepter? Where is he now?"

"I've no idea, pet. Ash, you say? Am I right in assuming this is Mab's Ash, the darling of the Unseelie Court?"

"We have to find him!" I stood up, causing Puck and Ironhorse to blink at me. "He could be in trouble. He needs our help." I turned to Leanansidhe. "Could you get your spies to look for him?"

"I could, dove." Leanansidhe twiddled her cigarette lighter. "But I'm afraid I have more important things to find. We're after the scepter, remember, darling? The prince of the Winter Court, scrumptious though he is, will have to wait."

"Ash is fine, Princess," Puck added, dismissing the idea immediately. "He can take care of himself."

I sat back down, anger and worry flooding my brain. What if Ash wasn't fine? What if he'd been captured, and they were torturing him, like they had in Machina's realm? What if he was hurt, lying in a gutter somewhere, waiting for me? I became so worked up over Ash, I barely heard what Puck and Leanansidhe were discussing, and a small part of me didn't care.

"What do you suggest, Lea?" This from Puck.

"Let my people search the valley. I know a sluah who is simply fabulous at finding things that don't want to be found. I've sent for him today. In the meantime, I have all my minions scouring the streets, keeping their heads down and their ears to the ground. They'll turn up something, eventually."

"Eventually?" I glared at her. "What are we supposed to do until then?"

Leanansidhe smiled and blew me a smoke rabbit. "I suggest you get comfortable, darling."

It wasn't a request.

CHAPTER THIRTEEN

Charles and the Redcaps

I hate waiting. I hate standing around with nothing to do, cooling my heels until someone gives me the go-ahead to move. I hated it while I was at the Winter Court, and I certainly didn't like it now, in Leanansidhe's mansion, waiting for complete strangers to bring word of the missing scepter. To make things worse, there were no clocks anywhere in the mansion and, even weirder, no windows to see the outside world. Also, as most faeries did, Leanansidhe hated technology, so that of course meant no television, computers, phones, video games, *anything* to make time pass more quickly. Not even a radio, although the crazy humans wandering the mansion would often spontaneously burst into song, or start playing some kind of instrument, so the house was never without noise. The few exiled fey I saw either fled my presence or nervously told me that I was not to be bothered, Leanansidhe's orders. I felt like a mouse trapped in some kind of bizarro labyrinth. Add in my constant worry for Ash, and it started to drive me as crazy as Leanansidhe's collection of gifted but insane mortals.

Apparently, I wasn't the only one going nuts.

"THIS IS UNACCEPTABLE," Ironhorse announced one day—night?—as we lounged in the library, a red-carpeted room with a stone fireplace and bookshelves that soared to the ceiling. With an impressive collection of novels and mostly fashion magazines at my fingertips, I managed to keep myself entertained during the long hours that we waited for Leanansidhe's spies to turn something up. Today, I was curled on the couch with King's *The Dark Tower* series, but it was difficult to concentrate with a restless, impatient Iron faery in the same room. Puck had vanished earlier, probably tormenting the staff or getting into some kind of trouble, and Grimalkin was with Leanansidhe, swapping favors and gossip, which left me alone with Ironhorse, who was getting on my last nerve. He was never still. Even in a human body, he acted like a flighty racehorse, pacing the room and tossing his head so that his dreadlocks clanked against his shoulders. I noticed that even though he wore boots, he still left hoof-shaped burn marks in the carpet, before the glamour of the mansion could smooth it out again.

"PRINCESS," he said, coming around the couch to kneel in front of me, "WE MUST ACT SOON. THE SCEPTER IS GETTING FARTHER AND FARTHER AWAY, WHILE WE SIT HERE AND DO NOTHING. HOW CAN WE TRUST THIS LEANANSIDHE? WHAT IF SHE IS KEEPING US HERE BECAUSE SHE WANTS THE SCEPTER FOR HERSEL—?"

"Shh! Ironhorse, be quiet," I hissed, and he immediately fell silent, looking as contrite as his expressionless face would allow. "You can't say those things out loud. She could hear you, or her spies could rat us out. I'm pretty sure she has them watching our every move." A quick glance around the library revealed nothing, but I could still feel eyes on me, peering unseen from cracks and shadows. "She already has it in for all Iron fey. Don't add to it."

"MY APOLOGIES, PRINCESS." Ironhorse bowed his head. "I CANNOT ABIDE THIS WAITING. I FEEL AS IF I SHOULD BE DOING SOMETHING, BUT I AM USELESS TO YOU HERE."

"I know how you feel," I told him, placing a hand on his bulky arm. His skin was hot to the touch, and the tendons beneath were like solid steel. "I want to get out of here, too. But we have to be patient. Puck and Grim are out there—they'll let us know if anything turns up or if we have to leave."

He looked unhappy, but nodded. I sighed with relief and hoped Leanansidhe's spies found something soon, before Ironhorse started tearing down the walls.

The door banged open, and we both jumped, but it was only a human, the scruffy piano player we'd seen when we first came to the mansion. He ambled into the room, blank eyes scanning the floor, until they spotted me. With an empty smile, he stumbled forward, but stopped when he saw the huge Iron faery kneeling in front of me.

Ironhorse rose with a growl, but I smacked his arm, wincing as the rock-hard bicep bruised my knuckles. "It's all right," I told him when he gave me a puzzled look. "I don't think he'll hurt me. He looks pretty harmless."

Ironhorse gave the human a suspicious glare and snorted. "IF YOU NEED ME..."

"I'll yell."

He nodded, shot the man one last dark look, and retreated to the other side of the room to glower at us.

With Ironhorse at a distance, the man seemed to relax. He inched up to the couch and perched on the edge, staring at me curiously. I smiled at him over my book. He seemed much calmer now, not so crazy. His eyes were clear, though the way he stared at me, unblinking, was making me a bit uncomfortable.

"Hi," I greeted, squirming a bit under that unrelenting gaze. "You're Charles, aren't you? I heard your playing earlier. You're really good."

He gave me a confused frown, tilting his head. "You heard me…play?" he murmured, his voice surprisingly clear and deep. "I don't…remember that."

I nodded. "In the foyer. When we first came here. You were playing for Leanansidhe and we heard the end of it."

"I don't remember," he said again, scratching his head. "I don't remember a lot of things." He blinked and looked up at me, suddenly contemplative. "But…I remember you. Isn't that strange?"

I glanced at Ironhorse, hovering in the corner and pretending not to listen to us. "How long have you been here, Charles?"

He frowned, scrunching his forehead. His face, though lined and worn, was curiously childlike. "I…I've always been here."

"They can't remember anything." Grimalkin popped into existence on the back of the couch, waving his tail. I started and dropped my book, but Charles simply looked at the cat, as if he had seen far stranger. "He's been here too long," Grimalkin continued, sitting down and curling his tail around his legs. "That's what being in Faery does to mortals. This one's forgotten everything about his life before. Same as all the other mortals wandering around this place."

"Hi, kitty," muttered Charles, reaching a hand toward Grimalkin. Grimalkin bristled and stalked to the other end of the couch.

"How many of them are there?" I asked.

"Humans?" Grimalkin licked a paw, still keeping a wary eye on Charles. "Not so many. A dozen or so, I'd guess. All great artists—poets or painters or other such nonsense." He sniffed and scrubbed the paw over his face. "That's what keeps this place alive, all that creative energy and glamour. Not even the redcaps will lay a finger on them."

"How can she keep them here?" I asked, but Grimalkin yawned and settled down on the couch back, burying his nose in his tail and closing his eyes. Apparently, he was done answering questions. I'd poke him, but he would just swat me or disappear.

"Here you are, darlings." Leanansidhe breezed into the room, trailing a gauzy black dress and shawl behind her. "I'm so glad I caught you before I left. Charles, darling, I must speak with my guests now. Shoo shoo." She fluttered her hands, and with a last glance at me Charles slipped off the couch and out the door.

"You're leaving?" I eyed her dress and purse. "Why?"

"Have you seen Puck, darling?" Leanansidhe gazed around the library, ignoring my question. "We need to have a little chitchat. Cook has been complaining that certain dinner items keep going missing, the head maid is mysteriously in love with a coatrack, and my butler has been chasing mice around the foyer all evening." She sighed and pinched the bridge of her nose, closing her eyes. "Anyway, darling. If you see Puck, be a dear and tell him to reverse the glamour on my poor maid, and to please stop stealing cakes from the oven before Cook has a meltdown. I shudder to think of what I might return to, but I simply cannot stay."

"Where are you going?"

"Me? I'm off to Nashville, darling. Some brilliant young songwriter is in need of inspiration. It's horrible to be so blocked, but not to worry. Soon, everyone will be in love with his muuuusic." She sang the last word, and I bit my lip to kill the urge to dance. Leanansidhe went on without notice. "Also, I need to pay a visit to a night hag, see if she has any information for us. I'll be back in a day or two, human time. Ciao, darling."

She waggled her fingers at me and vanished in a swirl of glitter.

I blinked and fought the urge to sneeze.

"Show-off," Puck muttered, appearing from behind one of the bookshelves, as if he'd been waiting for her to leave. He crossed the room to perch on the armrest, rolling his eyes. "She could've left without all the sparkly. But then, Lea always knew how to make an exit."

"BUT SHE IS GONE." Ironhorse hurried over, looking around as if he feared Leanansidhe was really hiding behind one of the chairs in the room, listening to him. "SHE IS GONE, AND WE CAN FIND A WAY OUT OF HERE."

"And do what, exactly?" Grimalkin raised his head and gave him a scornful look. "We still do not know where the scepter is. We would only be announcing our presence to the enemy and lowering our chances of finding it."

"Furball's right, unfortunately," Puck sighed. "Lea's not the easiest fey to deal with, but she's true to her word, and she has the best chance of finding the scepter. We should stay put until we actually know where it is."

"SO." Ironhorse crossed his massive arms, his eyes smoldering heat and fury. "THAT IS THE PLAN FROM THE

GREAT ROBIN GOODFELLOW. WE SIT HERE AND DO NOTHING."

"And what's your brilliant plan, Rusty? Go clomping off to the city and poke our noses into every major corporation until the scepter falls on our heads?"

"PRINCESS." Ironhorse turned to me. "THIS IS FOOL-ISH. WHY WAIT HERE ANY LONGER? DON'T YOU WANT TO FIND THE SCEPTER? DON'T YOU WANT TO FIND PRINCE ASH—"

"Stop right there." My voice dropped a few degrees, and maybe Ironhorse heard the warning in it because he quickly shut up. I stood, clenching my fists. "Don't you dare bring Ash into this," I hissed, making him take a step back. "Yes, I want to find him—he's on my mind every single day. But I can't, because we have to find the scepter first. And even if the scepter wasn't an issue, I still couldn't do anything about Ash because he doesn't *want* to be found. Not by me. He made that perfectly clear last I saw him." My throat started to close up, and I took a shaky breath to fight it. "So, the answer to your question is, yes, I want to find Ash. But I can't. Because the damn scepter is more important. And I'm not gonna screw up just because you can't sit still for two damn minutes." Tears welled, and I blinked angrily, aware that all three were staring like my head was on fire. I couldn't tell what Ironhorse was thinking behind that expressionless mask, but Grimalkin looked bored, and Puck's face was balanced between jealousy and pity.

Which pissed me off even more.

"Meghan," Puck began, but I spun around and stormed out before I really started bawling. He called after me, but I ignored him, swearing that if he grabbed me or got in my way he would get an earful.

"Let her go," I heard Grimalkin say as I bashed the door open. "She would not hear you now, Goodfellow. She wants only him."

The door swung shut behind me, and I stomped down the hall, fighting angry tears.

It wasn't fair. I was tired of being responsible, tired of making the hard decisions because it was the right thing to do. I wanted nothing more than to find Ash and beg him to reconsider. We could be together; we could find a way to make it work if we tried hard enough, screw the consequences. And the scepter.

The hallways stretched on, each one similar to the last: narrow, dark and red. I didn't know where I was going, and I didn't really care. I just wanted to get away from Puck and Ironhorse, to be alone with my selfish wishes for a while. Statues, paintings and musical instruments lined the corridors; some of them vibrated softly as I passed, faint shivers of music hanging on the air.

Finally, I sank down beside a harp, ignoring a piskie that watched from the end of the hall, and buried my face in my hands.

Ash. I miss you.

My eyes stung. I swiped at them angrily, determined not to cry. The harp thrummed in my ear, sounding curious and sympathetic. Idly, I drew my finger across the strings, and it released a mournful, shivery note that echoed down the hall.

Another chord answered it, and another. I raised my head and listened as the low, faint strains of piano music drifted into the corridor. The song was dark, haunting and strangely familiar. Wiping my eyes, I stood and followed it, down the twisted hallways, past instruments that hummed and added their voices to the melody.

The song led me to pair of dark red doors with gilded handles. Beyond the wood, it sounded like a symphony was in full swing. Cautiously, I pushed the doors open and stepped into a large, circular red room.

Waves of music flowed over me. The room was full of instruments: harps and cellos and violins, along with a few guitars and even a ukulele. In the middle of the room, Charles sat hunched over the keys of a baby grand piano, eyes closed as his fingers flew over the instrument. Along the walls, the other instruments thrummed and trilled and lent their strains to the melody, turning the cacophony into something pure and wondrous. The music was a living thing, swirling around the room, dark and eerie and haunted, bringing new tears to my eyes. I sank onto a red velvet couch and gave in to my churning emotions.

I know this song.

But try as I might, I couldn't remember from where. The memory taunted me, keeping just out of reach, a gaping hole where the image should be. But the melody, mysterious and devastatingly familiar, pulled at my insides, filling me with sadness and a gaping sense of loss.

Tears flowing freely down my skin, I watched Charles's lean shoulders rise and fall with the chords, his head so low it almost touched the keys. I couldn't be sure, but I thought his cheeks were wet, too.

When the last note died away, neither of us moved for several heartbeats. Charles sat there, his fingers resting on the final keys, breathing hard. My mind was still spinning in circles, trying to remember the tune. But the longer I sat there, trying to recall it, the farther it slipped away, vanishing into the walls and carpet, until only the instruments remembered it at all.

Charles finally pushed the seat back and rose, and I stood with him, feeling faintly guilty for eavesdropping.

"That was beautiful," I said as he turned. He blinked, obviously surprised to see me there, but he didn't startle or jump. "What was the name of the song?"

The question seemed to confuse him. He frowned and cocked his head, furrowing his brow as if trying to understand me. Then a sorrowful expression crossed his face, and he shrugged. "I don't remember."

I felt a pang of disappointment. "Oh."

"But…" He paused, running his fingers along the ivory keys, a faraway look in his eyes. "I seem to recall it was a favorite of mine. Long ago. I think." He blinked, and his eyes focused on me again. "Do you know what it's called?"

I shook my head.

"Oh. That's too bad." He sighed, pouting a bit. "The rats said you might remember."

Okay, now it was time to leave. I stood, but before I could make my escape, the door creaked open, and Warren entered the room.

"Oh, hey, Meghan." He licked his lips, eyes darting about in a nervous fashion. One hand was tucked into his jacket, hiding it from view. "I…um…I'm looking for Puck. Is he here?"

Something about him put me off. I shifted uncomfortably and crossed my arms. "No. I think he's in the library with Ironhorse."

"Good." He stepped in farther, pulling his hand out of his jacket. The lights gleamed along the black barrel of a gun as he raised the muzzle and pointed it at me. I went stiff with shock, and Warren glanced over his shoulder. "Okay," he called, "coast is clear."

The door swung open, and a half-dozen redcaps poured

into the room behind him. The one with the fishhook in his
nose, Razor Dan, stepped forward and leered at me with a
mouthful of jagged teeth.

"You sure this is the one, half-breed?"

Warren smirked. "I'm sure," he replied, never taking the
gun, or his eyes, off me. "The Iron King will reward us hand-
somely for this, you have my word."

"Bastard," I hissed at Warren, making the redcaps snicker.
"Traitor. Why are you doing this? Leanansidhe gives you everything."

"Oh, come on." Warren sneered and shook his head. "You
act like it's a total shock that I want something better than
this." He gestured around the foyer with his free hand. "Being
a minion in Leanansidhe's sorry refugee cult hasn't exactly
been my life goal, Princess. So I'm a little bitter, yeah. But the
new Iron King is offering half-breeds and exiles part of the
Nevernever and a chance to kick the pure-blooded asses of all
the dicks who stomped on us if we just do him a teensy favor
and find you. And you were nice enough to drop into my lap."

"You'll never get away with it," I told him desperately.
"Puck and Ironhorse will come looking for me. And Leanansidhe—"

"By the time Leanansidhe gets back, we'll be long gone,"
Warren interrupted. "And the rest of Dan's crew is taking care
of Goodfellow and the iron monster, so they're a little busy
at the moment. I'm afraid that no one is coming to your rescue, Princess."

"Warren," snapped Razor Dan with an impatient glare.
"We don't have time to gloat, you idiot. Shoot the crazy and
let's get out of here before Leanansidhe comes back."

My stomach clenched tight. Warren rolled his eyes, swinging the barrel of the gun around to Charles. Charles stiffened,

seeming to grasp what was happening as Warren gave him a crooked leer.

"Sorry, Charles," he muttered, and the gun filled my vision, cold, black and steely. I saw the opening of the barrel like Edgebriar's iron ring, and felt a buzzing beneath my skin. "It's nothing personal. You just got in the way."

Tighten, I thought at the pistol barrel, just as Warren pulled the trigger.

A roar shattered the air as the gun exploded in Warren's hand, sending the half-satyr stumbling back. Screaming, he dropped the mangled remains of the weapon and clutched his hand to his chest as the smell of smoke and burning flesh filled the room.

The redcaps stared wide-eyed at Warren as he collapsed to his knees, wailing and shaking his charred hand. "What are you waiting for?" he screamed at them, his voice half shout and half sob. "Kill the crazy and get the girl!"

The redcap closest to me snarled and lunged. I shrank back, but Charles suddenly stepped between us. Before the redcap could dodge, he grabbed a cello off the wall and smashed it down over its head. The instrument let out a shriek, as if in pain, and the redcap crumpled the floor.

Razor Dan sighed.

"All right, lads," he growled, as I grabbed Charles's hand and pulled him back behind the piano. "All together now. Get them!"

"PRINCESS!"

Behind them, the door burst open with a furious roar, and two redcaps were hurled through the air, landing face-first into the wall. The pack spun around, their eyes going wide as Ironhorse barreled into them, swinging his huge fists and bellowing at the top of his lungs. Several redcaps went flying and the rest swarmed him with bloodthirsty cries, biting at his arms and legs. They fell back, shrieking in pain, teeth shattered, mouths blackened and raw. Ironhorse continued to hurl them away like he'd gone berserk.

"Hey, Princess." Puck appeared beside me, grinning from ear to ear. "Grimalkin said you were having redcap trouble. We're here to help, although I must say Rusty is doing fine on his own." He ducked as a redcap flew overhead, landing with a crunch against the wall. "I'll have to remember to keep him around. He'd be great fun at parties, don't you think?"

The redcap Ironhorse had thrown into the wall staggered to his feet, looking dazed. Seeing us, he bared a mouthful of broken teeth and tensed to lunge. Puck grinned and pulled out his dagger, but there was an explosion of light between them, and a ringing voice filled the hallway.

"Everyone freeze!"

We froze.

"Well," Leanansidhe said, striding over to me and Puck. "Turns out this game was a rousing success. Although, I must say, I was hoping to be surprised. It gets rather boring when you're right about everything."

"L-Leanansidhe," Razor Dan stammered, all the blood draining from his face as she regarded him with her fearsome smile. "H-how...? You're supposed to be in Nashville."

"Dan, darling." Leanansidhe shook her head and *tsked*. "Did you really think I was blind to what was going on? In my own house? I know the rumors circulating the streets, pet. I know the Iron King has been offering rewards for the girl. I had the feeling there was a traitor in my house, a so-called agent of the Iron King. What better way to flush him out than to leave him alone with the princess and wait for him to make his move? Your kind is so very predictable, darling."

"We…" Dan glanced around at his crew, clearly looking for someone else to blame. "This wasn't our idea, Leanansidhe."

"Oh, I know, darling. You're too dull to organize something like this. Which is why I'm not going to punish you."

"Really?" Dan relaxed a bit.

"Really?" I blurted, looking up at her. "But they attacked me! And they were going to kill Charles! You're not going to do anything about that?"

"They were only following their base instincts, pet." Leanansidhe smiled at me. "I expected nothing less of them. What I really want is the mastermind. Why don't you stick around… *Warren*."

We all turned to where Warren was trying to sneak down the corridor without being seen. He froze, wincing at the sound of his name, and gave Leanansidhe a feeble smile.

"Leanansidhe, I…I can explain."

"Oh, I'm sure you can, darling." Leanansidhe's voice made my stomach curl. "And you will. We're going to have a little chitchat, and you're going to tell me everything you know about the Iron King and the scepter. You're going to sing, darling. Sing as you've never sung before, I promise."

"Come on," Puck told me, taking my elbow. "You don't want to hear this, Princess, trust me. Lea will give us the information when she has it."

"Charles," I said, and he turned from Leanansidhe to me, his eyes blank and empty once more. "Come on. Let's get out of here."

"Pretty lady's sparkly," Charles muttered. I sighed.

"Yeah," I said sadly, taking his hand. "She is."

With Ironhorse glowering and Puck leading the way, we fled the music room and Leanansidhe's presence, leaving Warren to his fate.

CHAPTER FOURTEEN

Royal Treatment

"A software corporation?" Puck repeated, brow furrowing. "Really. That's where they've been hiding it all this time?"

"Apparently, darling." Leanansidhe leaned back in her chair, crossing her long legs. "Remember, the Iron fey aren't like us. They're not going to be hanging around parks and museums, singing to flowers. They like high-tech places that attract the cold, calculating mortals we care so little for."

I shared a glance with Puck. We'd been talking about that strange, cold glamour I'd used on the gun before Leanansidhe came in. Though we were only guessing, we'd both come to the conclusion that it had indeed been iron glamour that I'd used on Warren, and that Leanansidhe, with her obvious hate and contempt for the Iron fey, definitely should not know about it yet.

I wished *I* knew more about it. I had the feeling this had never happened in the faery world before, that I was a first, and there was no expert to talk to. Why did I have iron glamour? Why could I use it sometimes and not others? Too many questions, and no answers. I sighed and decided to focus on the problem at hand, instead of the one I had no hope of un-raveling yet.

"What's the name of this place?" I asked Leanansidhe, not pointing out that I was one of those cold, calculating mortals who liked gadgets and computers and high-tech. I still missed my poor drowned iPod, the victim of a river crossing the first time I came to Faery, and this was the longest I'd ever gone without television. If I ever got back to having a normal life, I'd have a lot to catch up on.

Leanansidhe tapped her fingers against the armrest, pursing her lips in thought. "Oh, what did they call it? They all sound the same to me, darling." She snapped her fingers. "SciCorp, I believe it was. Yes, in downtown San Jose. The heart of Sili-con Valley."

"Big place," I muttered. "I don't think we can just walk in. There's sure to be cameras and security guards and everything."

"Yes, a frontal assault is doomed to fail," Leanansidhe agreed, glancing at Ironhorse, who stood in the corner with his arms crossed. "And remember, it's not only mortals you have to worry about. There's sure to be Iron fey as well. You're going to have to be...sneakier."

In the corner, Ironhorse raised his head. "WHAT ABOUT A DISTRACTION?" he offered. "I COULD KEEP THEIR ATTENTION ON ME, WHILE SOMEONE GOES IN THROUGH THE BACK."

"Or I could glamour Meghan invisible," Puck added.

Grimalkin yawned from where he lay the couch. "It will be risky holding a glamour with all the iron and steel inside," he said, blinking sleepily. "And we all know how horribly in-competent the human is when it comes to magic, even with-out her glamour sealed off."

I threw a pillow at him. He gave me a disdainful look and went back to sleep.

"Do we know anything about the building?" I asked Leanansidhe. "Blueprints, security, that kind of thing?" I suddenly felt like a spy in an action movie. The image of me dangling over a net of trip wires, *Mission Impossible* style, sprang to mind, and I bit down a nervous giggle.

"Unfortunately, Warren didn't have much to say about the building, though he really wanted to at the end, poor boy." Leanansidhe smiled, as if reliving a fond memory, and I shivered. "Thankfully, my spies found out all we needed to know. They said they're holding the scepter on floor twenty-nine point five."

"Twenty-nine point five?" I frowned. "How's that work?"

"I've no idea, darling. That's just what they said. However—" and she produced a slip of paper with a flourish "—they were able to come up with this. Apparently, it's some sort of code, used to get into the Iron faeries' lair. They couldn't solve it, but perhaps you will have better luck. I've no head for numbers at all, I'm afraid."

She handed the paper to me. Puck and Ironhorse crowded around, and we stared at it for several moments. Leanansidhe was right—it was definitely part of a code.

3
13
1113
3113
132113
1...

"Okay," I mused, after several moments of racking my brain and not coming up with anything. "So, we just have to figure this out and then we're home free. Doesn't sound too hard."

"I'm afraid it's a bit more complicated, darling." Leanansidhe accepted a glass of wine from a brownie. "As you said before, SciCorp is not a place you can just walk into. Visitors are not allowed past the front desk, and security is fairly tight. You have to be an employee to get off the first floor."

"Well, what if we pretended to be the janitor or cleaning service, or something like that?"

Grimalkin snorted and shifted position on the couch. "Would you not need an ID card for that?" he said, settling comfortably on the pillow I'd thrown at him. "If the building is so well guarded, I doubt they let in common riffraff off the street."

I slumped, frowning. "He's right. We would need a fake ID, or the ID of one of the workers, to make it inside. I don't know anyone who can get us something like that."

Leanansidhe smiled. "I do," she said, and snapped her fingers twice. "Skrae, darling," she called, "would you come here a moment? I need you to find something."

A piskie spiraled into view, gossamer wings buzzing. Three inches tall, he had indigo skin and dandelion hair, and wore nothing but a razor-toothed grin as he fluttered by. His eyes, enormous white orbs in his pointed face, regarded me curiously, until Leanansidhe clapped her hands.

"Skrae, pet, I'm over here. Focus, darling." The piskie gave me a wink and a suggestive hip wiggle before turning his attention to Leanansidhe. "Good. Now, pay attention. I have a mission for you. I want you to find the streetrats. The half-phouka and the troll boy, I forget their names. Tell them to leave off the eggs for now, I have another job for them. Now go, darling. Buzz buzz." She fluttered her hand, and the piskie zipped away out of sight.

"Kimi and Nelson," I said softly.

"What, darling?"

"That's their names. Kimi and Nelson. They were with... with Warren, when we first met." I remembered Kimi's impish grin, Nelson's stoic expression. "You don't think they're involved with the Iron fey, too?"

"No." Leanansidhe leaned back, snapping at a brownie for wine. "They knew nothing of Warren's betrayal or plot to kidnap you. He made that very clear."

"Oh. That's a relief."

"Although," Leanansidhe mused with a faraway look, "the girl would make a lovely violin. Or maybe a lyre. The troll is more of a bass, I believe. What do you think, darling?"

I shuddered and hoped she was kidding.

Kimi and Nelson showed up a few hours later. When they walked into the foyer, Leanansidhe wasted no time in telling them what had happened to Warren, which left them shocked and angry but not disbelieving. No tears were shed, no furious accusations were hurled at anyone. Kimi sniffled a bit, but when Leanansidhe informed them they had a job, both perked up instantly. They struck me as very pragmatic kids, used to the school of hard knocks, which left little room for self-pity or wallowing.

"So," Kimi said, flopping back on the sofa, which almost swallowed her whole, "what do you want us to do?"

Leanansidhe smiled and gestured for me to take over. "This is your plan, dove. You tell them what you need."

"Um...right." The two half-breeds looked at me expectantly. I swallowed. "Um, well, have you heard of a company called SciCorp?"

Kimi nodded, kicking her feet. "Sure. Big corporation that makes software, or something like that. Why?"

I looked at Leanansidhe, and she waved her cigarette at me

encouragingly. "Well, we need to get inside the building and steal something. Unnoticed."

Kimi's eyes widened. "You serious?"

I nodded. "Yes. But, we need your help to get past the guards and the security. Specifically, we need an ID card from one of the workers, and Leanansidhe said you might be able to get us one. Could you do that?"

Kimi and Nelson shared a glance, and the half-phouka turned to me with a mischievous smile. "No problem." Her eyes gleamed, relishing the encounter. "When do you want it?"

"As soon as possible."

"Right, then." Kimi squirmed off the couch and tapped Nelson's huge bicep. "Come on, big guy. Let's go terrorize a human. Back before you know it."

As the two left the foyer, Puck glanced at Leanansidhe. "You sure those two can handle it?" he asked, and grinned mischievously. "Want me to help them out?"

"No, darling. It's best that you do not." Leanansidhe stood, green smoke swirling about her. "Half-breeds have it easier in Silicon Valley—they won't attract as much attention as normal fey, and they haven't our allergies to all the iron and steel. Those two will be fine, trust me. Now, then." She walked toward me, smiling. "Come with me, my pet. We have a big day ahead of us."

I stared at her nervously. "Where are we going?"

"Shopping, darling!"

"What? Now? Why?"

Leanansidhe *tsked*. "Darling, you can't expect to waltz into SciCorp looking like *that*." She regarded my jeans and sweater imperiously, and sniffed. "It doesn't exactly scream 'I'm a business professional.' More like, 'I'm a Goodwill junkie.' If we're going to get you into SciCorp, you'll need more than luck and glamour. You'll need an entire makeover."

"But we're running out of time. Why can't Puck just glamour me some clothes—"

"Darling, darling, darling." Leanansidhe waved her hand. "You *never* turn down a chance to go shopping, pet. Besides, didn't you hear Grimalkin? Even the most powerful glamour has the tendency to unravel if surrounded by steel and iron. We don't want you to *look* like a corporate worker, dove, we want you to *be* a corporate worker. And we're going shopping, no buts about it." She gave me an indulgent smile I didn't like at all. "Think of me as your temporary faery godmother, darling. Just let me get my magic wand."

I followed Leanansidhe down another long corridor that dumped us out onto a sunny sidewalk bustling with people, who didn't notice our sudden appearance from a previously empty alleyway. Even though the sun was shining and the sky was clear, there was a frigid bite to the air, and people hurried down the street in thick sweaters and coats, a sign that winter was on its way or had already arrived. As we passed a newspaper machine, I quickly scanned the date in the corner and breathed in a sigh of relief. Five months. I'd been stuck in Faery five months; a long time to be sure, but better than five years, or five centuries. At least my parents were still alive.

I spent the rest of the afternoon being dragged from shop to shop, following Leanansidhe as she plucked clothes from racks and shoved them at me, demanding I try them on. When I balked at the ungodly prices, she laughed and reminded me that she was my temporary faery godmother today, and that price was not an issue.

I tried on women's suits first, sleek jackets and tight, knee-length skirts that made me look five years older, at least to Leanansidhe's reckoning. I must've tried on two dozen different styles, colors and combinations before Leanansidhe finally announced that she liked a simple black outfit that looked like every other black outfit I had tried on.

"So, we're done now?" I ventured hopefully, as Leanansidhe had the store clerk take the suit away to be wrapped. The faery looked down at me in genuine surprise and laughed.

"Oh, no, darling. That was just a suit. You still need shoes, makeup, a purse, a few accessories…no, pet, we've only just begun."

"I didn't think faeries liked shopping and buying stuff. Isn't that a bit…unnatural?"

"Of course not, darling. Shopping is just another form of hunting. *All* fey are hunters, whether they admit it or not. It's in our nature, pet, nothing unnatural about it."

That made a strange sort of sense.

More stores. I lost track of all the places we visited, the aisles we stalked, the racks we pored over. Leanansidhe was a faery on a mission; the second she swept through the doors, all salespeople would drop what they were doing and flock to her side, asking if they could help, if they could be of service. I was invisible beside her; even when Leanansidhe announced we were shopping for *me,* the clerks would forget I existed the second they turned away. Still, they were eager to please, bringing out their best shoes in my size, showing us a staggering variety of purses I would never use, and suggesting earrings that would accent the color of my eyes. (This was also the time Leanansidhe discovered I didn't pierce my ears. Thirty minutes later, I sat with my earlobes throbbing as a bubbly clerk pressed cotton to my ears and cheerfully told me the swelling would go down in a day or two.)

Finally, as the sun was setting over the buildings, the Queen of Shopping decided we were finished. Relieved that the long day was over, I sat on a chair, staring at the stupid code, annoyed that I still couldn't solve it. I watched Leanansidhe chat up the clerk as she wrapped and bagged the merchandise. When she announced the grand total, I nearly fell out of my seat, but Leanansidhe smiled and handed her a credit card without blinking once. For just a moment, when the clerk handed it back, the card looked more like a piece of bark, but Leanansidhe dropped it into her purse before I could get a closer look.

"Well," my temporary faery godmother said brightly as we departed the store, "we have your clothes, your shoes, and your accessories. Now, the real fun begins."

"What?" I asked wearily.

"Your hair, my dove. It's just…not good." Leanansidhe made as if to pluck my bangs, but couldn't quite bring herself to touch them. "And your nails. They need help. Fortunately, it's almost time for the spa to open."

"Spa?" I looked at the glowing orange ball disappearing over the horizon, wishing we could go home. "But it must be six o'clock. Aren't most places like that closed?"

"Of course, darling. That's when all the humans leave. Don't ask such silly questions." Leanansidhe shook her head at my naïveté. "Come now. I know Ben will be dying to meet you."

Natural Earth Salon and Spa was crowded tonight. We passed a pair of giggling sylphs on the pebbled path to the salon. Petite and delicate, their razor-edged wings buzzing softly, they grinned at us as we walked by, teeth glinting like knives. A Winter sidhe, tall and cold and beautiful, brushed by us as we stepped through the door into the waiting area, leaving a trail of frost on my skin and a chill in my lungs. A trio of piskies landed in my hair, laughing and tugging, until Leanansidhe gave them a look and they buzzed out the door.

Inside, the lighting was dim, the walls hewn of natural stone, giving it a cavelike feel. A marble fountain with fish and mermaids bubbled in the center of the foyer, filling the room with the cheerful sound of running water. Orchids and bamboo flourished in natural planters, and the air was warm and damp.

"Why are there so many fey here?" I asked softly, as a huge black dog loped across the doorway in the back. "Is this a place for exiles? A salon and spa? That's kind of weird."

"Can't you feel it, dove? The glamour of this place?" Leanansidhe leaned down, gesturing to the walls and fountain. "Some places in the mortal world are more magical than others, hot spots for glamour, if you will. It draws us like a moth to a flame—exiles, solitary and court fey alike. Besides, darling—" Leanansidhe straightened with a sniff. "Even our kind appreciates a bit of pampering now and then."

A blond, well-dressed satyr welcomed Leanansidhe with a kiss on both cheeks, before turning to me with a dazzling smile.

"Ah, so this is the princess I've heard so much about," he gushed, taking my hand to press it to his lips. "She's absolutely adorable. But—" and he glanced at Leanansidhe "—I can see what you mean about her hair. And her *nails*." He shuddered and shook his head before I could say anything. "Well, leave it to me. We'll have her looking fabulous in no time."

"Work your magic, Ben," Leanansidhe said, wandering away toward a back door. "I'll be with Miguel if you need me, darling. Meghan dear, just do what Ben says and you'll be fine." She waved her hand airily as she sauntered through the door, and was gone.

Ben turned to me and clasped his furry hands. "Well, sweet-cakes, you're in luck. We have the rest of the evening booked for you."

"Really?" I couldn't help sounding dubious. I had never been to one of these places before, let alone one run completely by the fey, and didn't know what to expect. "How long can it take to do hair?"

Ben laughed. "Oh, sweet pea, you're killing me. Come, now. We've got a lot to do."

The next few hours flew by in a confused blur. The fey staff, mostly satyrs and a few brownies, were alarmingly attentive. They took my clothes away and wrapped me in a very white bathrobe. I was made to lie on my back while brownies in white suits slathered cream on my face and put cucumbers over my eyes, telling me to lie still. After maybe an hour of this, they sat me up, and a cute satyr named Miroku soaked my hands in a warm bath that smelled like cocoa and coffee beans. He massaged my hands with lotion before meticulously filing, polishing, and painting my nails. Then the whole procedure was done to my feet. After that, they whisked me away to the stylist, who shampooed, trimmed and styled my hair—with bronze scissors, I noted—chatting at me all the while. It was odd. I won't say I didn't enjoy all the attention and pampering, but I did feel a bit dazed through the whole process, and a little out of place. This wasn't me. I wasn't a princess or a superstar or anything special. I was a poor pig-farmer girl from Louisiana, and I didn't belong here.

They were adding the final touches of makeup to my eyes

and lips when Leanansidhe sauntered back into the room, looking so smug and relaxed that her skin glowed. She had dropped her more human glamour, and her ethereal beauty filled the room, red-gold hair nearly blinding under the artificial lights. Ben trailed behind her, gushing about how radiant she looked.

"Mmm yes, I swear that Miguel is a virtual musician with his fingers," Leanansidhe murmured with a catlike stretch, raising too-slender arms over her head. "If you didn't need him so badly, love, I'd kidnap him myself and take him home. That kind of talent is hard to find, believe me. Well now," she exclaimed when she saw me. "Look at you, darling. You're a completely different person. I barely recognize you."

"Isn't she cute?" Ben added, beaming at me. "Don't you love what they did with her hair? I adore the highlights, and Patricia does layering so well."

"It's perfect." Leanansidhe nodded, studying me with a half smile that made me very uncomfortable. "If I don't recognize her, no one in SciCorp will, either."

I wanted to say something, but at that moment, a strange odor cut through the smell of perfume, makeup and moisturizers, stopping me mid-breath. Leanansidhe and Ben stiffened, as did every faery in the room. A couple brownies went scurrying away in terror, and the faery patrons began to murmur and shift restlessly as the foreign smell grew stronger. I recognized it, and my heart sped up, beating against my ribs. Metal. There was an Iron faery on the premises.

And then, it walked through the door.

My stomach turned over, and some of the patrons gasped. The Iron faery was dressed in a dove-gray business suit, and an expressive-looking one at that. Short black hair didn't conceal the long pointed ears, or the Bluetooth phone near his jaw. His skin, green as circuit board, glinted with hundreds of blinking lights, wires and computer chips. Behind thick, wire-rimmed glasses, his eyes shimmered green, blue and red.

Smooth as glass, Ben sidled in front of me, blocking my view but also shielding me from the faery's gaze. I froze and tried to be as invisible as possible.

"Well." The Iron faery's voice, thick with mockery, cut through the room. "Isn't anyone going to invite me in? Give me a pamphlet? Tell me your services? For such a high-ranking business, the customer service leaves much to be desired."

For a moment, nobody moved. Then one of the satyrs edged forward, shaking but furious at the same time. "We don't serve your kind here."

"Really?" The faery put a hand to his chest, feigning astonishment. "Well, I must say, I'm rather embarrassed. Then again, I could probably kill you all without even thinking about it, so I suppose a little prejudice is acceptable."

Leanansidhe stepped forward, her hair coiling behind her like snakes. "What do you want, abomination?"

"Leanansidhe." The Iron faery smiled. "You are Leanansidhe, aren't you? We've heard of you, you and your little network of spies. Word is, you know the location of Oberon's daughter, the Summer princess."

"I know a lot, darling." Leanansidhe sounded utterly bored and disinterested. "It's my business to be informed, for my own amusement and safety. I don't make a habit of involving myself. Nor do I make a habit of conversing with iron abominations. So, if we're quite done here, I think you should leave."

"Oh, I'll be gone soon enough." The Iron faery didn't seem the least bit perturbed. "But, my boss has a message for you, and an offer. Give us the location of Oberon's daughter, and all your crimes will be abolished when we take the

Nevernever. You can go home. Don't you want to go home, Leanansidhe?" He raised his voice, addressing the rest of the assembled fey. "And that goes for every half-breed and exile, pure-blooded or not. Help us find the Summer princess, and your place in the Nevernever will be assured. The Iron King welcomes all who want to serve him."

He paused after this announcement, waiting for someone to step forward. No one moved. Probably because Leanansidhe, standing in the middle of the room, was throwing off some seriously scary vibes, flickering the lamps with her power. Which was a good thing, because everyone was looking at her and not me.

The Iron faery waited a moment longer, and when no one volunteered to piss off the Queen of the Exiles, he stepped back with a smile. "Well. If anyone changes his mind, just call us. We're everywhere. And we will come for you, in the end."

He spun on a heel and left, footsteps clicking over the tile. Everyone watched him go. Leanansidhe glowered at the door until the last traces of iron faded away, then spun on me.

"Party's over, darling. Let's go. Ben, you're a doll and your assistance today is much appreciated, but we really must dash."

"Of course, girl." Ben waved to us as we hurried out. "You bring that cutie back to see me soon, okay? And good luck infiltrating the megacorporation!"

When we returned to the mansion, we found Puck and Ironhorse discussing strategy with Kimi and Nelson, who had returned from their mission. All four were huddled around the library table, heads bent close together, muttering in low voices. When we came in, followed by several redcaps carrying our bags, they straightened quickly, and their eyes went wide. Even Ironhorse's glowing eyes got big and round when we swept through the door.

"Wow, Meghan!" Kimi bounced in place, clapping her hands. "You look awesome! I love what you did with your hair."

"PRINCESS." Ironhorse looked me up and down, nodding in approval. "TRULY, YOU ARE A VISION."

I glanced at Puck, who was staring at me in a daze. "Um…" he stammered, while I nearly went into shock with the novelty of actually rendering Puck speechless. "You look…nice," he muttered at last.

I blushed, suddenly self-conscious.

"Children." Leanansidhe clapped her hands, bringing our attention back to her. "If we are going to retrieve the scepter, we need to move quickly. You, streetrats." She snapped her fingers at Kimi and Nelson. "Did you get what I sent you for, darlings?"

Kimi nodded at Nelson, who dug in his pocket and held up a plastic ID card. The face of a bespectacled blond woman glared out from the right corner, lips pursed as if trying to kill the camera with a look. Nelson tossed the card to Leanansidhe, who studied it disdainfully.

"Rosalyn Smith. A bit old, but she'll have to do. Well, then." She turned to the rest of us. "Tomorrow is a big day, darlings. Don't stay up too late. I'll meet you in the foyer tomorrow morning. Meghan, dove, you really need to figure out that code before tomorrow. Operation Scepter begins at dawn. Ta!" She gestured dramatically and vanished in a swirl of glitter.

That night, I was too nervous to sleep. I lay on my bed, Grimalkin dozing beside me on the pillow, trying to figure out the code but really just staring at the numbers until my eyes glazed over. I kept visualizing everything that could go wrong during the mission, which was a rather lengthy list. In a few hours, we were going to sneak into SciCorp using some woman's badge, grab the scepter, and book out before anyone realized we were there. As if it would be that easy, like a walk on the beach. As if they wouldn't have the scepter guarded day and night.

There was a soft rap on my door, and Puck peeked his head inside.

"Hey, Princess. Thought you could use something to eat. Mind if I come in?"

I shook my head, and Puck entered with a plate bearing sandwiches and apple slices. "Here," he announced, setting it down on the bed. "You should eat something. I tried making something better, but Cook chased me out of the kitchen with a rolling pin. I don't think she's very fond of me." He snickered and fell across the bed, helping himself to an apple slice as he got comfortable.

"Appreciate it," I murmured, picking up a sandwich. Cheese and…more cheese; better than nothing, I guessed. "Where's Ironhorse?"

"Off with the two streetrats, discussing strategy," Puck replied, stuffing the whole apple wedge into his mouth. "You should hear them—they think they're in a James Bond movie or something." He noticed me fiddling with a corner of the paper square and sat up. "How's it going, Princess?"

I crumpled the paper into a wad and threw it across the room. Puck blinked. "Um, not well, I assume?"

"I don't get it," I sighed, drawing my hand across my eyes. "I've tried everything I can think of to make heads or tails of it—addition, multiplying the lines, division—and I still don't get it. And if I can't decrypt the stupid code, we won't get up to the right floor, which means we won't get the scepter, which means everyone will die because of me!"

"Hey." Puck sat up and put an arm around me. "Why are you freaking out? This is nothing, Princess. This should be cake for you. You're the one who took down the Iron King. You marched into the heart of enemy territory and kicked ass. This isn't any different."

"Yes, it is!" I put my sandwich down and stared at him. "This is worlds apart! Puck, when I faced Machina, it was to rescue Ethan, just Ethan. I'm not saying he wasn't important— I would've died to save him in a heartbeat. But it was only one person." I closed my eyes and leaned into Puck's chest, listening to his heartbeat for a few seconds. "If I screw this up," I muttered, "if I don't get the scepter back, *everyone* will die. Not just you and Ironhorse and the others, but everyone. Faery will be wiped out. No Summer, no Winter, nothing. Nothing but the Iron fey will be left. Now do you see why I'm a little jumpy?"

I didn't mention that I wished Ash was here. That he was the main reason I'd been brave in the Iron Kingdom. I missed him, his calm, unflinching determination, his quiet self-confidence.

Puck shifted so that he was facing me, tilting my chin to look at me square. I met his eyes and saw a hundred churning emotions in his emerald gaze.

"I'm here," he murmured, running long fingers through my hair. "Don't forget that. No matter what happens, I'll protect you." He leaned in, resting his forehead to mine. I smelled apples on his breath, saw my own reflection in his eyes. "I'll never leave your side, no matter what comes at us. Count on it."

My heart thumped in my ears. I knew I was standing on the edge of a vast precipice, looking down. I knew I should pull away, that if I stayed here, a line would be crossed, and we could never go back.

I closed my eyes instead. And Puck kissed me.

His lips were hesitant at first, brushing lightly against mine, giving me room to pull away. When I pressed into him, he cupped the back of my head and kissed me in earnest. I wrapped my arms around his neck and pulled him close, wanting to forget everything that was happening, to drown myself in feeling. Maybe now the gaping hurt and loneliness would go away for a little while. Puck shoved the plate off the bed and leaned back, pulling me down with him, his lips suddenly at my neck, tracing a line of fire down my skin.

"If you are going to do that, would you mind not jostling the bed so much?" came a sarcastic voice near the headboard. "Perhaps you could roll around on the floor."

Blushing furiously, I looked up. Grimalkin lay on the pillow, watching us with a bemused, half-lidded stare. Puck followed my gaze and let out an explosive sigh.

"Did I ever mention how much I hate cats?"

"Do not blame me, Goodfellow." Grimalkin blinked, managing to sound bored and indignant at the same time. "I was minding my own business long before you and the princess started humping like rabbits."

Puck snorted. Rolling to his stomach, he pushed himself off the bed and pulled me up with him, wrapping me in his arms. My face flamed, but whether it was from Grimalkin's ill-timed comments or something else, I couldn't tell.

"I'd better go," Puck sighed, sounding reluctant. "I told Ironhorse I'd look at some blueprints Kimi managed to swipe from somewhere." His gaze strayed to the scattered food on the floor, sandwiches and apple slices everywhere, and he bit down a sheepish grin. "Erm, sorry about the mess, Princess. And don't worry about the code, we'll figure something out. Try to get some sleep, okay? We'll be right outside."

He bent down, as if to kiss me, but I couldn't meet his eyes and looked away. He paused, then placed a light kiss on my forehead and left, shutting the door behind him.

I collapsed to the bed, burying my face in a pillow. What had I done? I kissed Puck, because he was there. Because I was scared and lonely for someone else. Puck loved me, and I had kissed him for all the wrong reasons. I'd kissed him thinking of Ash. And...I liked it.

Guilt gnawed at me. I missed Ash, and the longing was ripping my stomach to pieces, but I also wanted Puck to come back and kiss me some more.

"I am so screwed up," I muttered, flopping back on the bed. The cracks in the ceiling smirked at me, and I groaned. "What am I going to do?"

"Hopefully obsess in silence so I can get to sleep," Grimalkin said without opening his eyes. He flexed his claws, yawned, and burrowed deeper into the pillow. "Perhaps you can work on deciphering the code so that we can retrieve the scepter. I would hate to put in all this work for nothing."

I glared at him, but he was right. And, maybe it would take my mind off Puck for a while. "I mean, it's not like I'm cheating on Ash or anything," I reasoned, retrieving the crumpled ball of paper and climbing back onto the bed. "He was the one who dumped me and said to forget about him. We're over. Actually, I'm not sure we had anything in the first place."

Grimalkin didn't answer. I stared at the code and sighed again, heavily, as the numbers seemed to crawl across the paper like ants. "I'm never going to get this, Grim," I mut-

tered. "This is hopeless. You'd have to be a mathematical ge-
nius or something."

Grimalkin thumped his tail and shifted around so that his
back was to me. "Try looking at the code as a riddle, instead
of a mathematical equation," he muttered. "Perhaps you are
trying too hard to fit it to a formula. The Iron fey are still fey,
after all, and riddles are in our blood."

A riddle, huh? I looked down at the paper again and
frowned. I still couldn't make heads or tails of the stupid
code, no matter how much I looked at it.

3
13
1113
3113
132113
1…

"Grim, I don't—"

"Read it out loud, human." Grim sounded annoyed but resigned, as if he knew he wasn't going to get any sleep until he
helped me. "If you must make noise, at least try to be useful."

"Fine," I muttered. "But it's not going to help." Grim
didn't reply, so I started reading it from the top. "Three. One-
three. One-one-one-three. Three-one-one-three." I stopped,
frowning. It sounded different, reading it out loud. I tried the
third line again. "One-one, one-three."

One 1. One 3.

I blinked. Could it really be that simple? I ran through the
rest of the lines, just to be sure, and my eyes widened as it
all clicked into place. "I…I got it! I think. Wait a minute." I
scanned the paper again. "Yes, that's right! It's not just a num-

ber riddle, it's a language riddle, too! You were right, Grim! Look!" I shoved the paper at Grimalkin, who continued to ignore me, but I went on anyway. "Each of the lines describes the line before it. The first number is a three, so the second line goes, One 3. The next line is One 1, One 3, and so on. So, if that's the case, the last line of the riddle, and the answer to the code would have to be…" I counted the numbers in my head. "1-1-1-3-1-2-2-1-1-3." I felt a thrill of pride and excitement, somehow knowing I was right, and couldn't help the huge grin spreading over my face. "I figured it out, Grim! We can get the scepter after all."

Grimalkin didn't answer. His eyes were closed, and I couldn't tell if he was asleep or faking it. I considered tracking down Puck and Ironhorse to share in my victory, but on reflection I wasn't sure I wanted to face Puck just then. So I lay on the bed, listening to the brownies scurry back and forth, cleaning up apple slices, while my mind replayed Puck's kiss until the memory was seared into my brain. Guilt and excitement assaulted me by turns. One moment, I was ready to drag Puck back here to finish what we'd started, the next, I missed Ash so much my chest hurt. I stayed awake, too hyped up to sleep, until a brownie poked his head in to tell me it was dawn and Leanansidhe was waiting for me.

CHAPTER FIFTEEN

Operation Scepter

The woman stared at me over the gold rim of her glasses, lips pursed in a disdainful expression. She wore a black business suit that clung to her body, and her hair was pulled into a tight yet elegant bun, giving her a stern demeanor. Her makeup was perfect, and the towering black heels made her seem taller and even more imposing.

"What do you think, darling?" Leanansidhe asked, sounding pleased. "The glasses might be a bit much, but we don't want to take any chances today."

I stuck out my tongue at the woman, who did the same in the mirror's reflection. "It's perfect," I said, amazed. "I don't even recognize myself. I look like a lawyer or something."

"Hopefully enough to get you into SciCorp this afternoon," Leanansidhe murmured, and all the dread and fear I'd managed to suppress all morning rose up like a black tide. I swallowed hard to keep the nausea down, wishing I hadn't eaten that box of powdered doughnuts Kimi brought in for breakfast. I wouldn't look very professional if I puked all over my expensive shoes.

Puck, Kimi, Nelson and Ironhorse were in the foyer, hud-dled around a blueprint when we came in, me wobbling be-hind Leanansidhe in my flimsy heels. Grimalkin dozed on the top of the piano, his tail brushing the keys, ignoring us all. I saw Leanansidhe glance his way and wince, as if imag-ining scratch marks on the polished wood.

Puck glanced up at me and smiled. He held out a hand, and I tottered up to him, grabbing his arm for support. My toes throbbed, and I leaned into him, trying to take the weight off my feet. How did women do it, walking around in these things every day without snapping their ankles?

"How's that walking thing coming?" Puck murmured so that only I could hear.

"Shut up." I smacked his arm. "I'm still learning, okay? This is like walking around on toothpicks." He snickered, and I shifted my attention to the map spread out between them. "What are we looking at?"

"The plan," Kimi answered, standing on tiptoes to bend over the table. "This is the SciCorp entrance," the half-phouka continued, pointing to an obscure line near the bottom of the paper. I squinted, but I couldn't make it out from all the other lines spread over the blueprint. "According to Warren," Kimi went on, tracing a finger up to another line, "the scepter is being held here, between floors twenty-nine and thirty."

"I still don't know how that's possible," I muttered. "How can a building have a floor between floors?"

"The same way I can have a mansion between the mortal world and the Nevernever, darling," Leanansidhe answered, looking at Grimalkin as if she really wanted to shoo him off the piano. "The Iron fey have their horrible glamour, just as we have ours. We turn into rabbits, they eat bank accounts. Grim, darling, do you *have* to sleep there?"

"You, Puck and Ironhorse will come in here," Kimi continued, tapping the bottom of the blueprint. "Past the doors will be the security checkpoint, which will scan your ID card. Puck and Ironhorse will be invisible to mortal eyes, so we don't have to worry about them being seen."

"What if there are Iron fey on the first floor?" Puck asked.

"There aren't," Kimi replied, glancing at him. "Nelson and I checked it out. If the Iron fey are going into the building, they're not using the front doors."

That sounded ominous, like the Iron fey could have hidden doors or trods we didn't know about, but there was nothing for it now.

"Once you're past the checkpoint, the elevators are here," Kimi went on, tracing the path with her finger before giving us a grave look. "And this is where things get dicey. I don't know how you're getting up to floor twenty-nine and a half. They might have a certain button only those with Sight can see, or there might be a password, or you might have to press buttons in a certain sequence. I have no idea. Alternatively, you can take the stairs, here, but that will mean climbing up thirty floors from ground level, with no guarantee there will be an entrance to floor twenty-nine and a half."

"We'll burn that bridge when we come to it," Puck said, waving it away. "So, what about the floor with the scepter? What can we expect?"

"Wait a minute," I warned, putting a hand on his chest. "This sounds awfully risky. We don't know if we can even get up to the twenty-ninth floor? How is this good planning?"

"Twenty-nine point five," Puck corrected me. "And it's not. Good planning, I mean. But, look at it this way." He grinned. "We either go with our gut, or we don't go at all. Not a lot of choices, Princess. But, don't worry." He put an arm around my shoulders and squeezed. "You don't need a plan. You have the Puck with you, remember? I'm an expert at this. And I've never needed an elaborate plan to pull anything off."

There was a loud clank from the piano, as Leanansidhe finally convinced Grimalkin to sleep elsewhere. Annoyed, the cat had slid from his perch and landed with his full weight on the keys, then leaped to the bench. "Worry not, human," the cat sighed, giving himself a thorough shake. "I am going with you as well. With Goodfellow's exemplary planning, someone has to make sure you go through the right door."

"Huh." Puck snorted and glared at the feline. "That's awfully helpful of you, cat. What's in it for you?"

"Grimalkin and I worked something out, darling, don't worry about it." Leanansidhe gave the blueprint a cursory glance over Puck's shoulder before dismissing it with a sniff. "Remember, pets, when you get to the floor where the scepter is being held, you must be prepared for anything. Robin, it will be up to you and the iron thing to protect the princess. I'm quite sure they won't have the scepter lying around where anyone can snatch it. There will most likely be guards, wards, nasty things like that."

"I WILL PROTECT THE PRINCESS WITH MY LIFE," Ironhorse boomed, making Puck grimace and Kimi pin back her ears. "I SWEAR, WHILE I STILL LIVE AND BREATHE, NO HARM WILL BEFALL HER. WE WILL RETRIEVE THE SCEPTER, OR WE WILL DIE TRYING."

"And personally, I'd like *not* to do the dying thing," Puck added.

I was about to agree, when there was a commotion in the hall, and a moment later a human rushed into the room. It was Charles, the crazy piano player, looking as wild and panicked as I'd ever seen, even more than when we'd faced the redcaps. His anguished brown eyes met mine and he lurched forward, only to be stopped by Ironhorse stepping in front of me with a warning growl.

"She...she's leaving?" Charles looked utterly despondent, wringing his hands and biting his bottom lip. "No no no. Can't leave again. Can't disappear. Stay."

"Charles." Leanansidhe's voice made the air tremble, and the poor man gave her a terrified look. "What are you doing here? Go back to your room."

"It's all right, Charles," I said quickly, as he looked on the verge of tears. "I'm not leaving for good. I'm coming back, don't worry."

He stopped wringing his hands, straightened, and looked at me dead on. And for just a moment, I saw him without the crazy light to his eyes. The way he must have been...before. Young. Tall. Handsome, with laugh lines around his mouth and jaw. A kind yet weary face. One that was vaguely familiar.

"You'll come back?" he murmured. "Promise?"

I nodded. "Promise."

Then Leanansidhe clapped her hands, the sharp rap making us jump. "Charles, darling," she said, and was it my imagination, or did she sound a bit nervous? "You heard the girl. She'll be back. Now, why don't you find the other Charles and find something to play tonight? Go on, now. Shoo." She waved her hand, and Charles, with one last look at me, stumbled from the room.

I frowned at Leanansidhe. "Other Charles? There's more than one?"

"I call them all Charles, darling." Leanansidhe shrugged. "I'm horrible with names, as you've no doubt seen, and human

males look virtually the same to me. So they're all Charles,
for simplicity's sake."

Grimalkin sighed and leaped from the bench. "We are wast-
ing time," he announced, bottlebrush tail held straight up as
he trotted past. "If we are going to get this circus started, we
should leave now."

"Good luck, darlings," Leanansidhe called as we followed
Grim out of the room. "When you return, you must tell me
all about it. Meghan, dove, don't do anything I wouldn't do."

Kimi and Nelson led the way back to the outside world.
We followed them through several rooms, where groups of fey
and humans watched us leave, down a red carpeted hallway,
then up a long spiral staircase that finally stopped at a trapdoor in the ceiling. The trapdoor was oddly shaped: round,
gray and heavy looking. I peered closer and saw that it was
the bottom of a manhole cover. When Nelson pushed it up to
peek through, bright sunlight spilled through the crack, and
the smell of asphalt, tar and exhaust fumes assaulted my nose.
While the half-troll scanned the road overhead, waiting for a
clear spot, Kimi turned to me.

"This is as far as we go, I'm afraid." The little half-phouka
looked disappointed as she handed me a plastic ID card on a
string.

"You're not coming?"

She gave me an apologetic smile, nodding to Puck and Ironhorse. "Nah, you have your champions. Those two are pure-
bloods. They'll be invisible to humans just by virtue of being
fey. Nelson and I can't work glamour as well, and it would
look suspicious if you were seen with a couple of streetrats
in tow. Don't worry, though. We're really close to SciCorp,
and from here you can take a taxi or something. Here." She

handed me a slip of paper, scrawled on with bright green ink. "That's the address you're looking for. The trod back will be on Fourteenth and Maple, and you want the second manhole from the left. Got it?"

I nodded, as my stomach fluttered nervously. "Got it."

"Clear," Nelson grunted, and shoved the manhole cover out of the way. Puck scrambled out first, then pulled me up after him. As Ironhorse and Grimalkin crawled out, I gazed around the middle of a busy street.

A horn blared, and a bright red Mustang screeched to a stop a few feet away. "Get out of the road, you crazy bitch!" the driver yelled from the window, and I scrambled to the edge of the curb. The driver roared off, oblivious to the massive Iron faery who swung a huge fist at the hood, barely missing.

"You ran a light anyway, dickhead!" I yelled after him, as Puck and Ironhorse joined me on the sidewalk. People stared at me, shaking their heads or chuckling under their breath. I scowled, trying to calm my racing heart. They wouldn't laugh if they could see Ironhorse looming over me like a protective bodyguard, glaring at anyone who got too close.

"Are you all right?" Puck asked anxiously, standing so close that his breath tickled my cheek. I nodded, and he kissed the top of my head, making butterflies swarm through my stomach. "Don't scare me like that, Princess."

"Well, that was amusing." Grimalkin hopped lightly onto the sidewalk, making a show of taking his sweet time. "Are we quite ready to go, now? Human, you know where we are headed, correct?"

I looked down at the paper, still clutched in my hand. It trembled only a little. "You guys okay with taking a taxi?"

Puck made a face. "Now see, anyone else would have a few qualms about riding in a big metal box, but I've learned to deal." He smirked. "All those years I took the bus with you was good practice. Still, keep the windows open, Princess."

We found a pay phone, and I called for a taxi. Ten minutes later, a bright yellow cab pulled up, driven by a bearded man chewing a thick cigar. He kept glancing at me in the rearview window and smiling, oblivious to the two faeries pressed on either side of me, one glaring, one hanging his head out the window. I sat squashed between Puck and Ironhorse, with Grim on my lap and both windows rolled down, as we tore through the city streets. The smoke from the cabby's cigar stung my nose and made my eyes water, and Puck looked positively green.

At last, we pulled up in front of a gleaming tower, the sunlight reflecting off the mirrored walls as they rose into the sky. I paid the cab fare, and we piled out of the car. As soon as we were free of the cab, Puck started coughing. He looked pale and sweaty, and my heart lurched, remembering Ash in the wasteland of the Iron fey. Ironhorse watched him curiously, as though fascinated, and Grimalkin sat down to wash his tail.

"Ugh, that was unpleasant," Puck muttered when the harsh explosions finally stopped. He spit on the sidewalk and wiped his mouth with the back of his hand. "I don't know what was worse, the cab or the stench coming from the guy's cigar."

"Will you be all right?" I gave him a worried look, but he just grinned.

"Never better, Princess. So, here we are." He craned his neck, gazing up at the looming expanse of SciCorp towers. His eyes gleamed with familiar mischief. "Let's get this party started."

My heart behaved itself until we passed through the large glass doors. Then it started beating my ribs so forcefully I thought they would break.

"Oh, wow," I whispered, stopping to gape at the enormous lobby. A great vaulted ceiling soared above us, maybe eight or ten stories, with strange metallic designs dangling from wires, glittering in the sun. People in expensive suits rushed by us, designer shoes clicking over the sterile gray floor. I saw cameras in every corner, armed guards hovering by a turnstile security gate, and I locked my knees together to keep them from shaking.

"Steady, Princess." As I stood there, gawking like an idiot, Puck's firm hands came to rest on my shoulders. "You can do this. Keep your head up, your back straight, and it wouldn't hurt to sneer at anyone who makes eye contact." He squeezed my shoulders and bent close, his breath warm on my ear. "We're right behind you."

I gave my head a jerky bob. Puck squeezed my shoulders one last time and released me. Raising my chin, I took a deep breath, squared my shoulders and marched toward the security desk.

A guard in a slate-gray uniform eyed me with disinterest as I approached, looking the way I felt in algebra class, eyes glazed over and bored. The man in front of me muttered a quick, "Mornin', Ed," before passing his ID card under a scanner. The red light blipped to green, and the man swept through the turnstile.

My turn. Adopting what I hoped was an imperious expression, I sauntered up to the gate. "Good morning, Edward," I greeted, slipping Rosalyn Smith's badge under the flickering red scanner light. The guard bobbed his head with a polite smile, not even looking at me. *Ha,* I thought, triumphant. *That was easy. We're home free.*

Then the scanner let out a shrill warning beep, and my heart stood still.

Ed stood up, frowning. "Sorry, miss," he said, as ice water began creeping up my spine. "But I'll have to see your badge."

Puck, Grim and Ironhorse, already on the other side of the gate, looked back fearfully. I swallowed my terror, wondering if we should abandon the plan now and get the hell out. The guard held out his hand, waiting, and I forced myself to be calm.

"Of course." Thankfully, my voice didn't crack as I looped the badge from my neck and held it out. The guard took it and held it up to his face, squinting his eyes. I felt a dozen gazes on the back of my neck, and crossed my arms, trying to appear bored and irritated.

"Sorry, Ms. Smith." Ed finally looked up at me. "But did you know your card expired yesterday? You'll have to get a new one before tomorrow."

"Oh." Relief bloomed through my stomach. Maybe I could pull this off after all. "Of course," I muttered, trying to sound embarrassed. "I've been meaning to renew it, but you know how busy it's been lately. I just haven't had the time. I'll take care of it before I leave today. Thank you."

"No problem, Ms. Smith." Ed handed me the badge and tipped his hat. "You have a good morning." He pressed a button and waved me through.

I hurried around a corner and collapsed against the wall before I started hyperventilating.

"None of that, Princess," Puck said, pulling me to my feet just as a group of businessmen turned the corner, talking about reports and staff meetings and firing a junior executive. I avoided eye contact as they swept by, but they paid me no attention.

"By the way, you did great back there," Puck went on as

we made our way down the brightly lit corridor. "I thought you would lose it, but you kept it together. Nice job, Princess."

I grinned.

"First hurdle cleared," Puck continued cheerfully. "Now, all we have to do is find floor twenty-nine point five, grab the scepter, and get out again. We're halfway home."

Easy for him to say. My heart had gone into overdrive, and a cold sweat was still dripping down the backs of my knees. I was just about to say so, when I noticed we had another problem. "Um, where's Grimalkin?"

We glanced around hastily, but the cat had disappeared. Maybe his faith in the plan had been shaken by the little scene at the gate, or maybe he'd just decided "the hell with this," and had taken off. It wouldn't be the first time.

"WHY WOULD HE ABANDON US?" Ironhorse questioned, making me wince as his voice echoed down the hall. Thank goodness humans couldn't hear faeries, either. "I THOUGHT THE CAITH SITH HAD HONORABLE INTENTIONS. I WOULD NOT HAVE PEGGED HIM A COWARD."

Puck snorted. "You don't know Grimalkin very well, then," he commented, but I wasn't sure I agreed. Grimalkin had always come through for us, even when he disappeared with no explanation. Though Ironhorse looked stunned, I wasn't worried; Grimalkin would most assuredly pop up again when least expected.

"Never mind." I turned and continued walking. Ironhorse still looked confused, almost hurt that an ally could betray him like this. I gave him what I hoped was a reassuring smile. "It's okay, Ironhorse. Grim can take care of himself, and he'll show up if we need him. We should keep looking for the scepter."

"IF YOU SAY SO, PRINCESS."

At the end of the corridor, we came to a pair of elevators.

"Floor twenty-nine point five," I mused, pressing the up button. A few seconds passed before the doors opened with a *ding* and two women exited, passing us without a second glance. Peeking inside, I scanned the wall but, as I expected, there was no button 29.5.

I stepped over the threshold into the box, Ironhorse following at my heels. Cheerful orchestra music played at a muted volume over the speakers, and the floor was carpeted in red. Puck rushed inside and stood in the middle of the floor, away from the walls, arms crossed tightly to his chest. Ironhorse turned and blinked at him.

"ARE YOU ALL RIGHT, GOODFELLOW?" he asked, his voice nearly bringing tears to my eyes as it echoed within the box. Puck gave him a fearsome smile.

"Me? I'm fine. Big metal box in a big metal tube? Not a problem. Hurry and get us to the right floor, Princess."

I nodded and unfolded a piece of paper from my suit pocket, holding it up to the light. "Well, here goes nothing," I murmured, and started punching in the code on the elevator buttons. 1-1-1-3-1-2-2-1-1-3. The numbers lit up as they were punched, singing out a little tune like the buttons on a cell phone.

I hit the last *3* and stepped back, waiting and holding my breath. For a moment, nothing happened. Ironhorse's raspy breathing echoed off the metal walls, filling the box with the smell of smoke. Puck coughed and muttered something under his breath. I started to punch the code in again, thinking I'd pressed a wrong button, when the doors swooshed shut. The lights dimmed, the music ceased, and a large white button shimmered into existence, marked with a bold 29.5.

I shared a glance with my companions, who nodded.

"Floor twenty-nine point five," I whispered, and hit the button with my thumb. "Going up."

The elevator stopped, and the doors opened with a cheerful ding.

We peered out at a long, brightly lit hallway with numerous doors lining its walls and gray tiles leading to a single door at the very end. I knew we were in the right place. I could feel it in the air, a faint buzz, a sharp tingle just below my skin. It made my neck hairs stand on end, and was oddly familiar. Glancing at Puck and Ironhorse, I knew they could feel it, too.

We inched down the corridor, Puck in front and Ironhorse bringing up the rear. Around us, our footsteps echoed in the silence. We passed doors without hesitation, knowing they were the wrong ones. I could feel the buzzing getting louder the closer we got to the end of the hall.

Then, we were at the last door, and Puck leaned against it, putting his ear to the wood. *I don't hear anything,* he mouthed at us, and pointed to the handle. *Shall we?*

Ironhorse nodded, clenching his massive fists. Puck reached down and freed his daggers, gesturing to me with a point. Biting my lip, I reached out and carefully turned the handle.

The door swung forward with a creak, and a waft of frigid air hit me in the face. I shivered, resisting the impulse to rub my arms as my breath clouded the air before me. Someone had cranked the AC down to like zero degrees; the room was a freezer box as we stepped inside.

A dozen or so humans in expensive business suits sat around a long, U-shaped table in the center of the floor. From the looks of it, we had interrupted a business meeting, for they all turned and stared at me with various degrees of annoyance and confusion. At the end of the table, a swivel chair sat with its back to us, hiding the speaker or CEO or whoever was in charge. I suddenly remembered all the times I'd snuck into class late and had to scurry down the aisles to my desk while everyone watched. My face burned, and for a moment, you could hear a pin drop.

"Um, sorry," I muttered, backing away. The business suits continued to stare at me. "Sorry. Wrong room. We'll just... go."

"Oh, why don't you stick around, my dear." The buzzing, high-pitched voice made my skin crawl. At the front of the table, the figure swiveled the chair around to face us, smiling. She wore a neon-green business suit, radioactive-blue lipstick, and bright yellow glasses above a thin, sneering face. Her hair, a myriad of computer cables, was bound atop her head in a colorful mockery of a bun. She held the scepter in green-nailed hands, like a queen observing her subjects, and my stomach gave a jolt of recognition.

"VIRUS!" Ironhorse boomed.

"No need to shout, old man. I'm right here." Virus put her heels on the table and regarded us smugly. "I've been waiting for you, girl. Looking for this, are you?" She lifted her arm, and I gasped. The Scepter of the Seasons pulsed a strange, sickly green light through her fingers. Virus bared her teeth in a smile. "I was expecting the girl and her clown to come sniffing after it, but I never expected the honorable Ironhorse to turn on us. Tsk-tsk." She shook her head. "Loyalty is so overrated these days. How the mighty have fallen."

"YOU DARE ACCUSE ME?" Ironhorse stalked forward, smoke drifting from his mouth and nostrils. We hurried after him. "YOU ARE THE BETRAYER, WHO FOLLOWS THE COMMANDS OF THE FALSE KING. YOU ARE THE ONE WHO HAS FALLEN."

"Don't be so melodramatic," Virus sighed. "As usual, you have no idea what is really going on. You think I want to follow the wheezings of an obsolete monarch? I want that even less than you. When he put me in charge of stealing the scepter, I knew that was the last command I would ever follow. Poor Tertius, believing I was still loyal to his false king. The gullible fool handed me the scepter without a second thought." She smiled at us, fierce and terrible. "Now, *I* have the Scepter of the Seasons. I have the power. And if the false king wants it, he'll have to take it from me by force."

"I see," I said, coming to a stop a few feet from her. Around us, the men in business suits continued to stare. "*You* want to become the next ruler. You had no intention of giving it to the Iron King."

"Can you blame me?" Virus swung her feet off the table to smile at me. "How often have you disobeyed your king because his commands were rubbish? Goodfellow—" she pointed the scepter at Puck "—how often has the thought of rebelling crossed *your* mind? Don't tell me you've been a faithful little monkey, catering to Oberon's every desire, in all the years you've known him."

"That's different," I said.

"Really?" Virus sneered at me. "I can tell you, it wasn't difficult to convince Rowan. That boy's hatred and jealousy are inspiring. All he needed was a little push, a tiny promise of power, and he betrayed everything he knew. He was the one who told me you were coming for the scepter, you know." She snorted. "Of course, the claims of becoming immune to iron are completely false. As if thousands of years of history can be rewritten or erased. Iron and technology have been and will always be lethal to the traditional fey. That's why we're so inherently superior to you oldbloods. That's why you're going to fall so easily after the war."

Ironhorse growled, the furious rumble of an oncoming train. "I WILL TAKE THAT SCEPTER AND PLACE THE TRUE MONARCH OF THE IRON FEY ON THE THRONE," he vowed, taking a threatening step forward. "YOU WILL GIVE IT TO ME NOW, TRAITOR. YOUR HUMAN PUPPETS WILL NOT BE ENOUGH TO PROTECT YOU."

"Ah ah ah." Virus waggled a finger at him. "Not so fast. I didn't want my drones up here because they are delicate and rather squishy, but I'm not quite so stupid as to be unguarded." She smiled and gazed around the table. "All right, gentlemen. Meeting adjourned."

At that, all the humans sitting at the tables stood, shedding glamour like discarded jackets, filling the air with fraying strands of illusion. Human facades dropped away, to reveal a dozen faeries in spiky black armor, their faces sickly and pale beneath their helms. As one, the Thornguards drew their serrated black swords and pointed them at us, trapping us in a ring of faery steel.

My stomach twisted violently, wanting to crawl up my throat and make a break for the door. I heard Puck's exhalation of breath and Ironhorse's dismayed snort as he pressed closer to me. Virus snickered, leaning back in her chair.

"I'm afraid you've walked nose first into a trap, m'dears," she gloated as we tensed, ready to run or fight. "Oh, but you don't want to rush off now. I have one last little surprise for you." She giggled and snapped her fingers.

The door behind her creaked, and a dark figure stepped into the room, coming to stand behind the chair. This time, my heart dropped to my toes and stayed there.

"I'm sure you four know each other," Virus said, as my world shrank down to a narrow tunnel, blocking everything else out. "My greatest creation so far, I think. It took six Thornguards and nearly two dozen drones to bring him down, but it was *so* worth it. Ironic, isn't it? He nearly got away with the scepter the first time, and now he'll do anything to keep it here."

No, my mind whispered. *This isn't happening. No no no no no.*

"Ash," Virus purred as the figure came into the light, "say hello to our guests."

CHAPTER SIXTEEN

Traitor

I stared at Ash in a daze, torn between relief that he was alive and an acute, sickening despair. This couldn't be real, what was happening. I had stepped into a nightmare world, where everything I loved was twisted into something monstrous and horrible. My legs felt weak, and I had to lean against Puck or I would've fallen.

Ironhorse snorted. "AN ILLUSION," he mocked, staring at Ash in contempt. "A SIMPLE GLAMOUR, NOTHING MORE. I HAVE SEEN WHAT HAPPENS TO THE OLD-BLOODS YOU IMPLANT WITH YOUR FOUL BUGS. THEY GO MAD, AND THEN THEY DIE. THAT IS NOT THE WINTER PRINCE, ANY MORE THAN THESE GUARDS."

"You think?" Virus's grin was frighteningly smug. "Well, if you're so sure, old man, you're welcome to try to stop him. It should be easy to defeat one simple guard, although I think you'll find the task harder than you ever expected." She turned a purely sadistic smile on me. "The princess knows, don't you, my dear?"

Ironhorse turned, a question in his eyes, but I couldn't take my gaze off Virus's bodyguard. "It's not an illusion," I whispered. "It really is him." The way my heart fluttered around my chest proved this was real. I stepped forward, ignoring the bristling Thornguard weapons, and the prince's gaze sharpened, cutting me like a knife. "Ash," I whispered, "it's me. Are you hurt? Say something."

Ash regarded me blankly, no glint of recognition in his silver eyes: no anger, sorrow, nothing. "All of you," he said in a quiet voice, "will die."

Shock and horror lanced through me, holding me immobile. Virus giggled her hateful, buzzing laugh. "It's no use," she taunted. "He hears you, he even recognizes you, but he remembers nothing of his old life. He's been completely reprogrammed, thanks to my bug. And now, he listens only to me."

I looked closer, and my heart twisted even more. In the shadows of the room, the prince's face was ashen, the skin pulled so tight across his bones it had split in places, showing open wounds beneath. His cheeks were hollow, and his eyes, though blank and empty, were bright with unspoken pain. I recognized that look; it was the same look Edgebriar had turned on us in the cave, teetering on the edge of madness. "It's killing him," I whispered.

"Well, only a little."

"Stop it," I hissed, and Virus arched a sardonic eyebrow. My heart pounded, but I set my jaw and plunged on. "Please," I begged, stepping forward. "Let him go. Let me take his place. I'll sign a contract, make a bargain, anything, if that's what you want. But take the bug out of his head and let him go."

"Meghan!" Puck snapped, and Ironhorse stared at me in horror. I didn't care. I couldn't let Ash fade away into nothing, as if he had never existed at all. I imagined myself in a field of

white flowers, watching a ghostly Ash and Ariella dance together in the moonlight, together at last. Except it would be
a lie. Ash wouldn't be with his true love, even in death. He
wouldn't be anything.

Virus chuckled. "Such devotion," she murmured, rising
from the chair. "I'm terribly moved. Come here, Ash." Ash
immediately stepped up beside her, and Virus laid a hand on
his chest. "You should congratulate me," Virus continued, regarding the prince like a student with a winning science project. "I've finally discovered a way to implant my bugs in the
fey system without killing them outright, or driving them mad
within the first few hours. Instead of rewriting his brain—"
she stroked Ash's hair, and I clenched my shaking fists, fighting the urge to leap across the table and rip out her eyes "—I
had it take over his cervical nervous system, here." Her fingers dropped to the base of his skull, caressing it. "You're welcome to try to carve it out, I suppose, but I'm afraid that will
be quite fatal for him. Only *I* can order my bugs to willingly
release their hosts. As for your offer…" She threw me an indulgent smile. "You have only one thing I want, and I will
take that from you momentarily. No, I find that I prefer my
bodyguard as he is, for however long he has left."

My heart pounded. He was so close. I could reach over the
table, grab his hand and pull him to safety. "Ash!" I cried,
holding out my hand. "Jump, now! Come on, you can fight
it. Please…" My voice dropped to a whisper. "Don't do this.
Don't make us fight you…"

Ash gazed straight ahead, not moving a muscle, and a sob
tore free from my throat. I couldn't reach him. Ash was lost
to us. The cold stranger across the table had taken his place.

"Well." Virus took a step back. "This has grown tiresome.
I think it's time I took what I want from you, my dear. Ash."

She placed a hand on his shoulder. "Kill the princess. Kill them all."

With a flash of blue light, Ash drew his sword and slashed it across the table. It happened so quickly, I didn't even have time to scream before the icy blade streaked down at my face.

Puck lunged in front of me and caught the blade with his own, deflecting it with a screech and a flurry of sparks. I stumbled back and Puck grabbed my wrist, dragging me away even as I protested. "Retreat!" he yelled as the Thornguards leaped across the tables with a roar. I looked back and saw Ash jump gracefully onto the table, his terrible blank gaze fastened on me. "Ironhorse, fall back, there are too many of them!"

With a bellow and a blast of flame, Ironhorse reared up into his true form, breathing fire and lashing out with his hooves. The guards fell back in shock and Ironhorse charged, knocking several aside and clearing a path to the door. As the huge Iron fey thundered past, Puck shoved me toward the exit. "Go!" he shouted, and whirled to block Ash's sword, slicing down at his back.

"Ash, stop this!" I cried, but the Winter prince paid me no attention. As the Thornguards closed on us again, Puck snarled a curse and threw a fuzzy black ball into their midst.

It burst into a maddened grizzly, which reared up with a booming roar, startling everything in the room. As the Thornguards and Ash turned toward this new threat, Puck grabbed my hand and yanked me out of the room.

"Been saving that, just in case," he panted, as Ironhorse snorted with appreciation. "Now let's get out of here."

We ran for the elevator. The hallway seemed longer now, the steel doors deliberately keeping their distance. I looked back once and saw Ash stalking toward us, his sword radiating blue light through the corridor. The icy calm on his face sent a bolt of raw fear through me, and I wrenched my eyes from him.

Ahead of us, the elevator dinged. A second later, the doors slid open, and a squadron of Thornguards stepped into the hall.

"Oh, you gotta be kidding me," Puck exclaimed as we skidded to a halt. As one, the knights drew their swords and marched forward in unison, filling the corridor with the ring of their boots.

I looked behind us. Ash was advancing steadily as well, his eyes glassy and terrifying.

A click echoed through the hall and miraculously, one of the side doors swung open.

"How predictable," Grimalkin sighed, appearing in the doorway. We gaped at him, and he regarded us with amusement. "I thought you might need a second way out. Why is it always up to me to think of these things?"

"I would kiss you, cat," Puck said as we crowded through the doorway, "if we weren't in such a hurry. Also, the hair-balls could be unpleasant."

I slammed the door and leaned against it, gasping as we took in our newest surroundings. A vast white room stretched before us, filled with hundreds upon hundreds of cubicles, creating a labyrinth of aisles. A low hum vibrated in the air, accompanied by the rhythmic sound of tapping keys. Humans sat at desks within each cubicle, dressed in identical white shirts and gray pants, staring glassy-eyed at the monitors as they typed away.

"Whoa," Puck muttered, looking around. "Cubicle hell."

Simultaneously, the tapping stopped. Chairs shifted and groaned as every single human in the room stood up and, as one, turned in our direction. And, as one, they opened their mouths and spoke.

"We see you, Meghan Chase. You will not escape."

If I hadn't been filled with a hollow, bone-numbing despair, I would've been terrified. Puck cursed and pulled out his dagger just as a *boom* shook the door behind us. "Looks like we're going straight through," he muttered, narrowing his eyes. "Grimalkin, get moving! Rusty, clear us a path!"

Grimalkin bounded into the maze, dodging feet and weaving through legs as the hordes of zombie-drones shuffled toward us. Ironhorse pawed the tile, put his head down and charged with a roar. Drones flung themselves at him, punching and clawing, but they bounced off or were thrown aside as the angry Iron fey stampeded through the hall. Puck and I followed in his wake, leaping over downed bodies, dodging the hands that grabbed for us. Someone latched on to my ankle once, but I let out a shriek and kicked him in the face, knocking him back. He fell away clutching my shoe, and I quickly shook the other off, running barefoot through the hall.

The maze of aisles and cubicles seemed to go on forever. I glanced over my shoulder and saw the mob of zombie heads bobbing above the cubicle walls, following us.

"Dammit," Puck snarled, following my gaze, "they're coming fast. How much farther, cat?"

"Here," Grimalkin said, darting around a cubicle. The room finally ended with a stark white wall and a door in the corner, marked with an Exit sign. "The emergency stairs," he explained as we rushed forward in relief. "This will take us to the street level. Hurry!"

As we charged the door, Ash stepped out of an aisle next to us, appearing from nowhere. There was no time to think or scream a warning. I threw myself to the side, hitting the wall with a jolt that knocked the wind from my lungs.

Time seemed to slow. Puck and Ironhorse bellowed something from far away. A blinding stab of pain shot up my arm. When I grabbed for it, my palm came away slick and wet. For a second, I stared at my fingers, not understanding.

What happened? Did Ash...do this? Ash cut me?

Stunned, I looked up into the glassy eyes of the Unseelie prince, his sword raised for the killing blow.

For just a moment, he hesitated. I saw the sword waver as his arm trembled, a flicker of torment crossing his face. Just a moment, before the blade came flashing down, but it was enough time for Ironhorse to lunge between us, shoving Ash away. I heard the hideous screech of metal as the blade ripped into Ironhorse's side and he staggered, almost going to his knees. Then Puck was pulling me to my feet, yelling at Ironhorse to get moving, and I was being dragged through the door, screaming at Puck to let me go. Ironhorse lurched to his feet and followed, dripping a thick black substance behind him, his wheezing breaths echoing down the stairwell. As we escaped SciCorp and fled into the streets, the last thing I remembered was watching the door close behind me on the stairs and seeing Ash's face through the window, a single tear frozen on his cheek.

PART THREE

CHAPTER SEVENTEEN

Choices

In my dream, he was kneeling in the dead grass beneath a
great iron tree, head bent, dark hair hiding his face. Around
us, a swirling gray fog blanketed everything beyond a few feet,
but I could sense another presence here, a cold, hostile being,
watching me with cruel intelligence. I tried to ignore it as I
approached the figure beneath the tree. He was shirtless, his
pale skin covered in tiny red wounds, like punctures, down
his spine and across his shoulders.

I blinked. For a moment, I could see the glistening strings
of wire sunk into his body, coiling up and vanishing into the
fog. I quickened my pace, but with every step I took, the body
under the tree moved farther away. I started to run, stumbling
and panting, but the fog was drawing him back into its possessive embrace, claiming him for its own.

Desperately, I called to him. He raised his head, and the
look on his face was beyond despair. It was utter defeat, hope-
lessness and pain. His lips moved wordlessly, then the fog
coiled around him and he was lost.

I stood there shivering as the mist grew dark, and the other presence hovered at the edge of my consciousness. As the dream faded and I sank into oblivion, I could still see his final words, mouthed to me in desperation, and they chilled me like nothing else.

Kill me.

Consciousness returned slowly. I clawed myself up from sleep, feeling dizzy and confused as the world came into focus. Thankfully, I recognized my surroundings almost immediately. Leanansidhe's mansion: the foyer, if the huge fireplace was any indication. I lay on one of her comfortable sofas, dressed in slacks and a loose-collared shirt. Someone had taken off the slinky business suit, and of course I'd left my heels back in SciCorp.

"What happened?" I murmured, struggling to sit up. A blinding flare of pain stabbed up my arm and shoulder, and I gasped.

"Easy, Princess." Suddenly Puck was there, pushing me back down. "You lost a nice amount of blood—it made you woozy. You passed out on our way here. Just sit still for a minute."

I looked at the thick gauze wrapped around my arm and shoulder, a faint pink stain coming through the bandage. It hadn't even hurt until now.

A knot tightened in my stomach as hazy memories pushed their way to the surface. My throat closed up, and I suddenly felt like crying. Pushing those feelings away, I took a shaky breath and focused on the present.

"Where's Ironhorse?" I demanded. "And Grim? Did everyone get out okay?"

"I AM FINE, PRINCESS." Ironhorse, back in his more human form, peered over the couch at me. "A LITTLE LESS THAN WHEN WE STARTED, BUT I WILL LIVE. MY

ONLY REGRET IS THAT I COULD NOT PROTECT YOU FULLY."

"Really?" The door opened and Leanansidhe entered the room, followed by Grim and two brownies bearing a tray with mugs. "I would have a few more regrets than that, darling. Meghan, dove, try to drink this. It should help."

I struggled to sit up, gritting my teeth against the pain. Puck knelt beside the couch and eased me into a sitting position, then handed me the mug the brownies offered. The hot liquid smelled strongly of herbs, making my eyes water. I took a cautious sip, made a face, and swallowed it down.

"Kimi and Nelson?" I asked, forcing down more of the stuff. Gah, it was like drinking potpourri in hot water, but I could feel it working as it slid down my throat—a warm drowsiness stealing through my system. "Are they here, too?"

Leanansidhe swept around the couch, trailing smoke from her cigarette holder. "Haven't checked in yet, darling, but I'm sure they're fine. They're smart kids." With a flourish, she sat in the opposite chair and crossed her legs, watching me over her cigarette. "So, before that kicks in, dove, why don't you tell me what happened in there? Grimalkin told me some of it, but he wasn't there for the whole operation, and I can't get a cohesive story from this pair—" she waved her cigarette at Ironhorse and Puck "—because they're too busy worrying over you. Why couldn't you get the scepter, darling? What happened in SciCorp?"

The memories flooded in, and the despair I'd been hiding from descended like a heavy blanket. "Ash," I whispered, feeling tears prick my eyes. "It was Ash. She has him."

"The prince?"

"Virus has him," I continued in a daze. "She put one of her

mind-control bugs inside him, and he attacked us. He tried…
tried to kill us."

"He's the one guarding the scepter," Puck added, collapsing in a chair. "Him and about two dozen nasty Thornguards, and a whole building of Virus's little human drones."
He shook his head. "I've fought Ash before, but not like this.
Whenever we dueled, there was always a small part of him,
deep down, that wasn't serious. I know his royal iciness, and
I knew he really didn't want to kill me, no matter how much
he boasted otherwise. That's why our little feud has lasted so
long." Puck snorted and crossed his arms, looking grave. "The
thing I fought today wasn't the frosty Ice prince we all know
and love. There's nothing there anymore. No anger, no hate,
no fear. He's more dangerous now than he ever was before,
because he doesn't care if he lives or dies."

Silence fell. All I could hear was the faint sound of Grimalkin sharpening his claws on the sofa. I wanted to lie down
and cry, but the herbs were kicking in, and my depression
was giving way to a numbing exhaustion. "So," Leanansidhe
ventured at last, "what will you do now?"

I stirred, fighting the drowsiness. "We go back," I murmured, looking at Puck and Ironhorse, hoping they would
back me up. "We have to. We have to get the scepter and stop
the war. There's no other way around it." Both nodded gravely,
and I relaxed, grateful and relieved that they would follow
me on this. "At least we know what we're up against now," I
continued, grabbing for a faint ray of hope. "We might have
a better chance the second time around."

"And the Winter prince?" Leanansidhe asked softly. "What
will you do with him?"

I glanced at her sharply, about to tell her that we would

save Ash and I didn't like what she was implying, but Puck beat me to it.

"We have to kill him."

The world screeched to a halt. Slowly, I turned my head to stare at Puck, unable to believe what I just heard. "How could you?" I whispered. "He was your friend. You fought side by side. And now you want to cut him down like it was nothing!"

"You saw what he did." Puck met my eyes, beseeching. "You saw what he *is* now. I don't think I can fight him without holding back. If he attacks you again—"

"You don't want to save him," I accused, leaning forward. My arm throbbed, but I was too angry to care. "You don't even want to try! You're jealous, and you've always wanted him out of the way!"

"I never said that!"

"You don't have to! I can see it on your face!"

"HE'S DYING, PRINCESS."

Words froze in my throat. I stared at Ironhorse, silently pleading with him to be wrong. He gazed back with a sorrowful expression. "No." I shook my head, fighting the persistent tears that stung my eyes. "I won't believe that. There has to be a way to save him."

"I AM SORRY, PRINCESS." Ironhorse bowed his head. "I KNOW YOUR FEELINGS FOR THE WINTER PRINCE, AND I WISH I COULD GIVE YOU BETTER NEWS. BUT THERE IS NO WAY TO FORCEFULLY REMOVE THE BUGS ONCE THEY HAVE BEEN IMPLANTED. NOT WITHOUT KILLING THE HOST." He sighed, and his tone softened, though the volume did not. "GOODFELLOW IS RIGHT. THE WINTER PRINCE IS FAR TOO DANGEROUS. IF HE ATTACKS AGAIN, WE CANNOT HOLD BACK."

"What about Virus?" I pressed, unwilling to give up. "She's the one controlling the bugs. If we take her out, maybe her hold on him will—"

"Even if that were the case," Puck interrupted, "the bug would still be inside him. And with no way to get it out, he'll either go mad, or be in so much torment that he would be better off dead. Ash is strong, Princess, but that thing inside him is killing him. You saw it, you heard what Virus said." His brow furrowed, and his voice went very soft. "I don't think he has much time left."

The tears pressing behind my eyes finally spilled over, and I buried my face in the pillow, biting the fabric to keep from screaming. God, it wasn't fair! What did they want from me? Hadn't I given enough already? I'd sacrificed everything—family, home, a normal life—for the stupid greater good. I had worked so hard; I was trying to be brave and mature about everything, but now I had to watch while the thing I loved most was killed in front of me?

I couldn't. Even if it was impossible, even if Ash killed me himself, I would still try to save him.

The room had grown very quiet. I peeked up and saw that everyone except Puck had left, slipping from the room to let me come to terms with myself, and the decision looming over my head, in peace.

Seeing me glance up, Puck tried catching my gaze. "Meghan…"

I turned away, pressing my face into the cushions. Anger and resentment boiled; Puck was the last person I wanted to see, much less talk to. Right now, I hated him. "Go away, Puck."

He sighed and rose from the chair, coming to perch on the sofa next to me. "Well, you know that never works."

The silence stretched between us. I sensed that Puck wanted to say something but couldn't seem to find the right words.

Which was odd; I'd never known him to hesitate about any-thing.

"I won't let you kill him," I finally muttered after a few minutes of quiet.

There was a lengthy pause before he answered. "Would you ask me to watch you die?" he murmured slowly. "Stand by while he puts a sword through your heart? Or, maybe you want me to die instead. You could just tell me to stand still while Ash chops off my head. Would that make you happy, Princess?"

"Don't be stupid!" I bit my lip in frustration and sat up, wincing as the room spun for a moment. "I don't want anyone to die. But I can't lose him, Puck." My anger abruptly drained away, leaving only a hollow despair. "I can't lose you, either."

Puck put his arms around me and pulled me close, gently so as to not jolt my wounded arm. I laid my head on his chest and closed my eyes, wishing I were normal, that I didn't have to make these impossible decisions, that everything would be all right again. If wishes were horses...

"What do want me to do, Princess?" Puck whispered into my hair.

"If there's any way we can save him..."

He nodded. "I'll try very hard not to kill his royal iciness if we meet again. Believe it or not, Princess, I don't want Ash dead, any more than you do." He sniffed. "Well, maybe a little more than you. But..." And he pulled back to look me in the eye. "If he puts you in danger, I won't hold back. That's my promise. I won't risk losing *you*, either, understand?"

"Yeah," I whispered, closing my eyes. That was all I could ask. *I'll save you,* I thought, as drowsiness stole over me and my mind drifted. *No matter what, I'll find a way to bring you back. I promise.*

I was nearly asleep, surrendering to the exhaustion stealing all my coherent thoughts, when a slamming door jerked me awake and Puck's arms tightened around me.

"Meghan Chase." Kimi's voice cut across the room, clipped, flat and mechanical. I looked up and my stomach dropped away.

Kimi and Nelson stood beside the door like soldiers at attention, a posture so strange for both of them that I didn't recognize them at first. As one, their heads turned, and they gave me an empty stare. The same look Ash had turned on me back in SciCorp.

"Oh, no," I whispered. Puck went stiff with shock.

"Our Mistress has a message for you, Meghan Chase." Kimi took a short step forward, moving like a robot. "'Congratulations for breaking into SciCorp and, more impressive, breaking out again. You have my admiration. Unfortunately, I cannot have you running amok, making plans to return for the scepter, as I know you will. I'll be moving it tonight to a safer location. If you come back to SciCorp, I'm afraid you'll find it quite empty. Oh, and by the way, I'm also sending Ash to kill your family. They're in Louisiana, right?'"

I sucked in a breath, and the blood drained from my face. Kimi's expression didn't change, but her voice turned mocking. "'So you have a choice now, my dear. Come back for the scepter, or run home and try to stop Ash. You'd better hurry. He's probably halfway to the bayou by now.

"'One more thing!'" she added as I leaped to my feet, drowsiness forgotten. Heart pounding, I glared at her. Robot Kimi gave me an empty smile. "'I want you to remember, this is not a game, Meghan Chase. If you think you can waltz into my lair and try to take what is mine without repercussions, you'd best think again. People will get hurt because of you.'"

Kimi stepped forward and narrowed her eyes. "'Do not screw with me, child. Let this be a little reminder of what can happen when you play with the big girls.'"

Kimi spasmed, spine arching back, mouth open in a silent scream as she twitched and thrashed. A moment later, Nelson did the same, limbs jerking wildly, before they both collapsed to the floor.

Puck was beside Kimi instantly, rolling her over. The little half-phouka's eyes were open, gazing sightlessly at the ceiling, and she didn't move a muscle. I bit my lip, my heart pounding. "Are they…dead?"

He paused a moment before rising to his feet. "No. At least, I don't think so. They're still breathing, but…" He frowned, squinting at Kimi's slack expression. "I think their brains have short-circuited. Or the bugs are keeping them in some sort of coma." He shook his head, looking up at me. "Sorry, Princess. I can't do anything for them."

"Of course you can't, darling." Leanansidhe breezed through the doorway, her face a porcelain mask, eyes glowing green. "Fortunately, I know a mortal doctor who might be able to help. If he cannot revive the streetrats, then there is no hope for them." She turned to me, and I tried not to cringe under that unearthly gaze. "You are leaving, I presume?"

I nodded. "Ash is out there," I said. "He's going after my family. I have to stop him." I narrowed my eyes, staring her down. "Don't try to keep me here."

She sighed. "I could, darling, but then you would be a complete mess and of no use to us. If there is one thing I've learned about humans, it's that they become absolutely unreasonable when it comes to family." She sniffed and waved her hand. "So go, darling. Rescue your mother and father and brother and get it over with. My door will still be open when you come back. If we're still alive, that is."

"PRINCESS!" Ironhorse bashed the door open, skidding to a halt in the middle of the room, breathing hard. "ARE YOU HURT? WHAT HAS HAPPENED?"

I gazed around for my sneakers, wincing as a bright talon of pain clawed up my arm. "Virus sent Ash to kill my family," I said, dropping to my knees to peer under the couch. "I'm going to stop him."

"WHAT ABOUT THE SCEPTER?" he continued, as I pulled out my sneakers and stuffed my feet into them, gritting my teeth as my arm throbbed with every movement. "WE MUST RETRIEVE IT BEFORE VIRUS HAS IT MOVED. SHE IS VULNURABLE NOW AND WILL NOT BE EX-PECTING US. NOW IS THE TIME TO ATTACK."

"No." I felt pulled in several directions at once, and tried to stay calm. "I'm sorry, Ironhorse. I know we have to get the scepter, but my family comes first. Always. I don't expect you to understand."

"VERY WELL," Ironhorse said, surprising me. "THEN I WILL COME WITH YOU."

Startled, I looked up at him, but before I could reply, Gri-malkin interrupted me.

"A quaint idea," the cat mused, leaping onto the table, "and exactly what Virus is hoping for. We must have scared her quite a bit for her to react so dramatically. If we abandon the mission now, we might never find her again."

"He's right." I nodded, ignoring Ironhorse's scowl. "We have to split up. Ironhorse, you stay here with Grim. Keep looking for the scepter and Virus. Puck and I will go after Ash. We'll be back as soon as we can."

"I DO NOT LIKE LEAVING YOU ALONE, PRIN-

CESS." Ironhorse raised his head in a proud, stubborn manner. "I SWORE I WOULD PROTECT YOU."

"While we were looking for the scepter, you did. But this is different." I stood up and met his burning red eyes. "This is personal, Ironhorse. And your mission has always been the scepter. I want you to stay behind with Grim. Keep looking for Virus." He opened his mouth to argue, and I spit out the last words. "That's an order."

He blew smoke from his nostrils like a furious bull and turned away. "AS YOU WISH, PRINCESS."

His voice was stiff, but there was no time to dwell on feelings of guilt. I turned to Puck. "We have to get to Louisiana fast. How do we get out of here?"

He glanced at Leanansidhe. "Don't suppose you have any trods to Louisiana from here, do you, Lea?"

"There's one to New Orleans," Leanansidhe replied, looking thoughtful. "I just adore Mardi Gras, darling, though Mab tends to hog the spotlight every year. Typical of her."

"That's too far away." I took a deep breath, feeling time slip away from me. "Isn't there a trod that's closer? I need to get home *now*."

"The Briars." Puck snapped his fingers. "We can go through the Briars. That will take us there quickly."

Leanansidhe blinked. "What makes you think there is a trod to the girl's house through the Briars, dove?"

Puck snorted. "Lea, I know you. You can't stand to be out of the loop, remember? You must have a trod that goes to Meghan's house from the Briars, even though you can't use it. I know you'd want keep an eye on Oberon's daughter. What kind of gossip would you miss out on, otherwise?"

Leanansidhe pursed her lips as if she'd swallowed something sour. "You caught me there, darling. Though you don't hesitate to rub salt in the wound, do you? I *suppose* I can let you use that trod, but you owe me a favor later, darling." Leanansidhe sniffed and puffed her cigarette. "I feel I should charge *something* for letting you in on my greatest secret. Especially since I have no interest in the girl's family. Such a boring lot, except the little boy—he has potential."

"Done," I said. "You have your favor. At least from me. Now, will you let us use it or not?"

Leanansidhe snapped her fingers, and Skrae the piskie fluttered down from the ceiling. "Take them to the basement trod," she ordered, "and guide them to the right door. Go." Skrae bobbed once and zipped to my shoulder, hiding in my hair. "I will continue to have my spies monitor SciCorp," Leanansidhe said. "See if they can discern where Virus is moving it to. You should get going, darling."

I straightened and glanced at Puck, who nodded. "All right, let's go. Grim, keep an eye on Ironhorse, would you? Make sure he doesn't go charging the army by himself. We'll be back soon." I shook my hair, dislodging the piskie huddled against my neck. "All right, Skrae, take us out of here."

CHAPTER EIGHTEEN

Close to Ice

Our trip back through the Briars was less exciting than our trip in. We saw no dragons, spiders or killer-wasp fey, though truthfully I could've wandered straight into their hive without noticing. My mind was consumed with Ash and my family. Would he really...kill them? Cut them down in cold blood, invisible and unheard? What would I do then?

I pressed a palm to my face, trying in vain to stop the tears. I would kill him. If he hurt Ethan or Mom in any way, I would put a knife through his heart myself, even if I was sobbing my eyes out while I did it. Even if I still loved him more than life itself.

Sick with worry, fighting the despair that threatened to drown me, I didn't see Puck stop until I ran into him, and he steadied me without a word. We had reached the end of the tunnel, where a simple wooden door waited in the thorns a few feet away. Even in the tangled darkness of the Briars, I recognized it. This was the gate that had led me into Faery, all those months ago. This was where it all began, at Ethan's closet door.

Ahead of us, Skrae gave a last buzz and flew back down the tunnel, back to Leanansidhe to give his report, I assumed. There was no going back for me. I reached for the door handle.

"Wait," Puck ordered. I turned back, impatient and annoyed, when I saw the grim severity in his eyes. "Are you ready for this, Princess?" he asked softly. "Whatever lies beyond that door isn't Ash any longer. If we're going to save your family, we can't hold back now. We might have to—"

"I know," I interrupted, not wanting to hear it. My chest tightened, and my eyes started to tear, but I dashed them away. "I know. Let's…let's just do this, all right? I'll figure something out when I see him." And before Puck could say anything else, I wrenched the door open and walked through.

The cold hit me immediately, taking my breath away. It hung in the air as I shivered, gazing around in horror, my stomach twisting so painfully that I felt nauseous. Ethan's bedroom was completely encased in ice. The walls, the dresser, the bookshelf; all covered in a layer of crystal nearly two inches thick, but so clear so I could see everything trapped within. Outside the window, a cold, clear night shone through the glass, the moonlight sparkling lifelessly off the ice.

"Oh, man," I heard Puck whisper behind me.

"Where's Ethan?" I gasped, rushing to his bed. The horrific vision of him trapped in ice, unable to breathe, made me virtually ill, and I nearly threw up at the thought. But Ethan's bed was empty, the quilts flat and still beneath the frozen layer.

"Where is he?" I whispered, near panic. Then I heard a faint noise from beneath the bed, a soft, breathy whimper. Dropping to my knees, I peered into the crack, wary of monsters and bogeys and the things that lurked under the bed. A small, shivering lump stirred in the far corner, and a pale face looked up at mine.

"Meggie?"

"Ethan!" Relieved beyond words, I reached under the bed and pulled him out, hugging him close. He was so cold; he clung to me with frozen hands, his four-year-old body shaking like a leaf.

"You c-came back," he whispered, as Puck crossed the room and shut the door without a sound. "Quick! You have to s-save Mommy and Daddy."

My blood ran cold. "What happened?" I asked, holding him with one arm while pulling open the door we came through. Now it was just a normal closet. I yanked out a quilt that wasn't covered in ice and wrapped Ethan in it, sitting him on the frozen bed.

"*He* came," Ethan whispered, pulling the folds tighter around himself. "The dark person. S-Spider told me he was coming. He told me t-to hide."

"Spider? Who's Spider?"

"The m-man under the b-bed."

"I see." I frowned and rubbed his numb fingers between mine. Why would a bogey be helping Ethan? "What happened then?"

"I hid, and everything turned to ice." Ethan gripped my hand, big blue eyes beseeching mine. "Meggie, Mommy and Daddy are still out there, with him! You have to save them. Make him go away!"

"We will," I promised. My heart started an irregular thud in my chest. "We'll make this right, Ethan, I promise."

"He should stay here," Puck murmured, peering through a crack in the door. "Man, it looks like the whole house is iced over. Ash is here, all right."

I nodded. I hated to leave Ethan, but there was no way I wanted my brother to see what came next. "You wait here," I told him, smoothing down his curly hair. "Stay in your room until I come get you. Close the door and don't come out, no matter what, okay?"

He sniffled and huddled deeper into the quilt. With my

heart in my throat, I turned to Puck. "All right," I whispered. "Let's find Ash."

We crept down the stairs, Puck in front, me clinging to the railing because the stairs were slick and treacherous. The house was eerily silent, an unfamiliar palace of sparkling crystal, the cold so sharp that it cut into my lungs and burned my fingers as they gripped the railing.

We reached the living room, cloaked in shadow except for the light that came from the open door and the flickering static of the television. Silhouetted against the screen, Mom's and Luke's heads were visible over the top of the couch. Leaning together, as if asleep, they were frozen solid, encased in ice like everything else. My heart stood still.

"Mom!"

I rushed forward, but Puck grabbed my arm, holding me back. Snarling, I turned on him, trying to shake him off, until I saw his face. His eyes were hard, his jaw set as he pulled me behind him, a dagger appearing in his hand.

Trembling, I looked into the living room again just as Ash melted out of the shadows on the far wall, drawing his sword as he did. In the harsh blue light, he looked awful, his skin split open along his cheekbones and his eyes sunk into his face. There were new wounds over his arms and hands, where the skin had blackened along the openings, looking burned and dead. His silver eyes were bright with pain and madness as he stared at us, every inch a killer, but I couldn't be afraid of him. There was only grief now, a horrible, soul-wrenching pain knowing that, no matter what happened, I had to let him die. If I wanted to save my family, Puck would have to kill Ash. Tonight. Right here in my living room. I forced down a sob and stepped forward, ignoring Puck as he grabbed for me, my eyes only for the dark prince standing across the room.

"Ash," I whispered as his eyes flicked to my face, following my every move. "Can you hear me at all? Please, give us something. Otherwise, Puck is going to…" I swallowed hard, as he continued to regard me blankly. "Ash, I can't let you hurt my family. But…I don't want to lose you, either." The tears spilled over, and I faced him desperately. "Please, tell me you can fight this. Please—"

"Kill me."

I sucked in a breath, staring at him. He stood rock still, the muscles working in his jaw, as if he was struggling to speak. "I…can't fight this," he gritted out, closing his eyes in concentration. His arms shook, and his grip on the sword tightened. "You have to…kill me, Meghan. I…can't stop myself…"

"Ash—"

His eyes opened, glazed over once more. "Get away from me, now!"

Puck shoved me away as Ash leaped across the room, his sword coming down in a sapphire blur. I hit the floor, wincing as the ice scraped my palms and bruised my knees. With my back against the wall, I watched Puck and Ash battle in the middle of the living room, feeling dead inside and out. I couldn't save him. Ash was lost to me now, and worse, one of them was going to die. If Puck won, Ash would be killed. But if Ash emerged victorious, I would lose everything, including my own life. I guess I should've been rooting for Puck, but the cold despair in my heart kept me from feeling anything.

As Ash whirled away from a vicious upward slash, something glittered beneath his hair at the base of his skull. Scrambling to my feet, I narrowed my eyes and my senses, staring at it intently. A tiny spark of cold, iron glamour glimmered at the top of Ash's spine and I gasped. That was it! The bug, the thing that was controlling him and, ultimately, killing him.

As if it could sense my thoughts, Ash whirled, his eyes narrowing in my direction. As Puck's knife came down at his back, he spun, knocking it aside, and stabbed forward with his weapon. Puck twisted desperately, but it wasn't enough, and the icy blade plunged deep into his shoulder. I cried out, and Puck stumbled back, dark blood blossoming over his shirt, his face tight with pain.

Ash lunged at me, and I tensed, my heart hammering in my chest. All those times watching him fight gave me an inkling of what was coming. As the sword came slashing down at my head, I dove forward, hearing the savage *chink* of the blade against the ice. Rolling away, I glanced back, saw the sword coming and threw myself aside, barely avoiding the second swing that bit into the floor, pelting me with ice shards. I hit the wall and turned back to see Ash standing over me, weapon raised high. There was nowhere to go. I looked into his face, saw his jaw tighten and his arm tremble as he met my gaze. For a split second, the sword wavered, and he closed his eyes...

Just as Puck rose up from nowhere with a snarl and slammed the dagger into his chest.

Time stood still. A scream lodged in my throat as Puck and Ash stared at each other, Puck's shoulders heaving with breaths or sobs, I couldn't tell. For a moment, they stood there, locked in a morbid embrace, until Puck let out a strangled noise and wrenched himself away, yanking out the dagger in a spray of crimson. The sword fell from Ash's hand, hitting the ground with a ringing clang that echoed through the house.

Ash staggered back, managing to stay on his feet for a moment, arms curled around his stomach. He swayed, putting his back to the wall, as dark blood began to drip to the ice, pooling beneath him. As I finally found my voice and screamed his name, Ash raised his head and gave me a weary smile. Then those silver eyes dimmed, like the sun vanishing behind a cloud, and he crumpled to the ground.

CHAPTER NINETEEN

Sickness

"Ash!"

I rushed forward, shoving Puck out of the way. Puck stumbled aside, moving like a sleepwalker. The bloody dagger dropped limply from his hand. Ignoring him, I lunged toward Ash.

"Stay back!"

His voice brought me up short, sharp and desperate. Ash struggled to his knees, arms around his stomach, shaking with agonized gasps. Blood pooled around him as he raised his head, eyes bright with anguish. "Stay back, Meghan," he gritted out, a line of red trickling from his mouth. "I could…still kill you. Let me be." He grimaced, closing his eyes, one hand clutching at his skull. "I can still…feel it," he rasped, shuddering. "It's in…shock now, but…it's getting strong again." He gasped, clenching his teeth in pain. "Dammit, Goodfellow. You could've…made it clean. Hurry and get it over with."

"No!" I cried, flinging myself down beside him. He flinched away from me, and I caught his shoulder.

It was like touching an electric fence, without the shock. I felt a rush of sharp, metallic glamour coming from Ash, buzzing in my ears and vibrating my senses. I felt something inside me respond, like a current beneath my skin, rushing up to my fingertips, and suddenly everything was much clearer. If glamour was raw emotion and passion, this was the absence of it: logical, calculating, impassive. I felt all my fear, panic and desperation drain away, and I looked at Ash with a new curiosity. This was a problem, but how was I going to fix it? How would I solve this equation?

"Meghan, run." Ash's voice was strangled, and that was all the warning I had before his eyes went glassy and his hands fastened around my throat, cutting off my air. I gasped and clawed at his fingers, staring into his blank eyes as a sharp, droning voice echoed through my head.

Kill you.

I gasped airlessly, fighting to stay calm, to stay connected to that cold, impassive glamour buzzing under my skin. As I stared into his eyes, I could *see* the bug, its hateful glare peering back at me. I could see its round, ticklike body, clamped to the top of Ash's spine, the metal parasite that was killing him. I could hear it, and I knew it could hear me, too.

"Meghan!" Puck snatched the ice sword from where it lay, forgotten, and raised it over his head.

"Puck, don't." My voice came out raspy, but calm. I fought for air and felt Ash's grip loosen the tiniest bit. He closed his eyes, breaking my connection with the bug, but I could still feel the iron glamour, buzzing all around me. He was fighting its commands, his face tight with concentration, sweat running down his skin.

"Do it," he rasped, and I realized he spoke to Puck, not me.

"No!" I met Puck's conflicted gaze, saw the sword waver as he swept it toward Ash. "Puck, don't! Trust me!"

My vision was getting fuzzy. I didn't have much time. Praying Puck would hesitate a little longer, I turned back to Ash, laying my palm against his cheek. "Ash," I said, hoping my mangled voice would get through to him, "look at me, please."

He didn't respond at first, his fingers shaking as he fought the compulsion to crush my throat. When he did look up, the raw anguish, horror and torment on his face was agonizing. But, beyond his pain-filled eyes, I could see the parasite as it tightened its hold on him. My will rose up to meet it, iron glamour swirling around us. I shaped that glamour into a command, and sent it lancing into the metal bug.

Let go, I told it, putting as much force into the words as I could.

It buzzed furiously and clamped down hard, and Ash cried out in agony. His fingers on my throat tightened, crushing my windpipe and turning my world red with pain. I sagged, fighting to stay conscious, seeing darkness crawling along the edge of my vision. *No!* I told it. *I will not lose to you. I will not give him up! Let go!*

The bug hissed again…and loosened its hold, still fighting me all the way. I put my shaking hand against Ash's chest, over his heart, feeling it crash against his ribs. Ash's grip tightened once more, and the world started to go black. *Get out,* I snarled with the last of my strength. *Get out of him, now!*

A crackle and a flash of light, and Ash convulsed, shoving me away. I fell against the cold floor, striking my head against the ice, blackness momentarily blinding me. Fighting for consciousness, I saw a glint of light, of something tiny and metallic, fly up toward the ceiling, and Ash staring at his hands in horror. The metal spark hovered in the air a moment, then zipped toward me with a furious buzz.

Puck's hand shot out, snatching the bug from the air, hurling it to the floor. For a split second, it lay there glinting coldly against the ice. Then his boot smashed down and ground the bug into oblivion.

I struggled upright, breathing hard, waiting for the room to stop spinning. Puck knelt in front of me, one shoulder covered in blood, his whole body tense with concern.

"Meghan." One of his hands smoothed my cheek, rough and urgent. "Talk to me. Are you all right?"

I nodded. "I think so." My voice came out harsh and raspy, and my throat burned like I'd been gargling with razor blades. Something cold and wet dripped onto my knee. I glanced up and saw that the ceiling was beginning to crack and melt. "Where's Ash?"

Puck moved aside, looking grave. Ash was slumped against the wall in the corner, head down, one hand covering his still bleeding ribs. His eyes were open, staring at the floor, at nothing. Heart in my throat, I gingerly approached and knelt beside him, saw him shift, very slightly, away from me.

"Ash." My worry for him, for Ethan, for my family, was a painful knot in my stomach. I longed to help him, but the image of my mom and Luke, frozen on the couch, filled me with dread and fear. If Ash had hurt them, if they were…I could never forgive him. "My mom," I asked, staring into his face. "My stepdad. Did…did you…?"

He gave his head a small shake, a tiny movement in the shadows. "No," he whispered without looking at me, his voice flat and dead. "They're just…asleep. When the ice melts, they should be fine, with no memory of what happened."

Relief bloomed through me, although short-lived. I reached out to touch his arm, and he flinched as if my touch was poison.

"What will you do with me now?" he whispered.

Puck's shadow fell over us. I looked back and saw him holding Ash's sword, a grim, frightening look on his face. For a second, I was afraid Puck would stab him right there, but he tossed the blade at Ash's feet and turned away. "Think you can walk, Prince?"

Ash nodded without looking up. Puck pulled me reluctantly to my feet and drew me aside. "I'll deal with Ash, Princess," he murmured, holding up a hand to interrupt my protest. "Why don't you check on your brother before we go?"

"Go? Where?"

"I'd say Ash needs a healer, Princess." Puck glanced back at the prince and made a face. "I know I would, if I'd had a metal bug stuck inside my head. Probably screwed him up pretty bad. Luckily, I know a healer not far from here, but we should go *now*."

I looked back at Mom and Luke, at the water slowly dripping from their frozen silhouettes, and yearning twisted my stomach. I missed them, and who knew when I'd see them again. "We can't stay, just a little while?"

"What would you tell them, Princess?" Puck gave me a look that was sympathetic and exasperated at the same time. "The truth? That a faery prince froze the inside of the house in order to draw you here and kill you?" He shook his head, making sense even as I hated him and his logic at that point. "Besides, we need to get his royal iciness to a healer, and soon. Trust me, it's better if your folks never knew you were here."

I gave my parents one last look and nodded slowly. "Right," I sighed. "I was never here. Let me say goodbye to Ethan, at least."

Feeling old inside and out, I retreated up the steps, pausing once to look back. Puck was crouched in front of the Unseelie prince, his lips moving soundlessly, but Ash was looking straight at me, his eyes glimmering slits in the gloom. Biting my lips, I continued on to Ethan's bedroom.

I found him in the hallway, peering out between the railings, the blanket still draped over his shoulders. "Ethan!" I hissed, and he glanced up with big blue eyes. "What are you doing out here? I told you to stay in your room."

"Where's Mommy and Daddy?" he asked as I picked him up, carrying him back to his room. "Did you tell the bad person to go away?"

"They'll be all right," I told him with my own sense of relief. "Ash didn't hurt them, and as soon as the ice melts, they'll be back to normal." Though they would probably wonder why the whole house was wet. The ice was melting rapidly; I stepped around several puddles as I crossed the hall into his room.

Ethan nodded, gazing at me solemnly as I set him on his bed. "You're going away again, aren't you?" he asked matter-of-factly, though his lip trembled and he sniffled, trying to hold back tears. "You didn't come back to stay with me."

I sighed, sitting beside him on the frozen bed. "Not yet," I murmured, smoothing down his hair. "I wish I could. I really do, but..." Ethan sniffled, and I pulled him close. "I'm sorry," I whispered. "There are still some things I have to take care of."

"No!" Ethan clung to me, burying his face in my side. "You can't leave again. They won't take you again. I won't let them."

"Ethan—"

"Princesss." From the darkness under the bed, something latched on to my ankle, claws digging into my skin. I yelped, swinging my feet up onto the mattress, and Ethan gave a startled cry.

"Dammit, bogey!" My sore throat blazed with pain at the

outburst, making me even angrier. I leaped off the bed and stalked to Ethan's dresser, grabbing the flashlight still kept on top. Bogeys hated light, and the white beam of a flashlight could make them flee in terror. "I am so not in the mood for this," I rasped, flicking on the beam. "You have three seconds to get out of here before I make you leave."

"Meggie." Ethan hopped off the bed and padded up, taking my hand. "It's okay. It's only Spider. He's my friend."

I looked at him, aghast. Since when did bogeys make friends with the kids they terrorized? I didn't believe it, but a soft slithering sound came from under the bed, and two yellow eyes peered up at me.

"Fear not, Princesss," it whispered, keeping a wary eye on the flashlight in my hand. "I am here under ordersss. Prince Asssh told usss to watch thisss houssse. It isss under the protection of the Unssseelie Court."

"*Ash* ordered this? When?"

"Before he came to collect your bargain, Princesss. Before you went back with him to Tir Na Nog." The thing slithered to the edge of the crack, staying just out of the light. "The child isss in no danger," it rasped, "and neither are hisss parentsss, though they do not know we are here. Protect thisss houssse and work no missschief on thossse who live here, those are our ordersss."

"He tells me stories every night," Ethan said, looking up at me. "Most of them are pretty scary, but I don't mind. And sometimes there's a black pony in the front yard, and little man in the basement. Mommy and Daddy don't see them, either."

I closed my eyes. The thought of so many Unseelie fey hanging around my house did nothing to ease my nervousness, even if they were claiming to protect my family. "How did you know about Ash?" I finally asked.

"I sssmelled an Iron fey coming, and knew I mussst protect the boy, at leassst," Spider went on, oblivious to my conflicted feelings. "I pulled him under the bed, where I could hide him better. Imagine my sssurprissse when I dissscovered it wasss Prince Asssh himsssself, attacking thisss houssse. He mussst have been posssesssed, or perhapsss it wasss an Iron fey dissguisssed asss the prince. But, I followed my ordersss, and kept the boy sssafe."

"Well, I'm grateful for that," I muttered. And then a thought occurred to me, one that I almost didn't ask about, but couldn't leave alone. "Have…have my parents…mentioned me? Do they talk about me at all, or wonder where I am?"

"I know nothing of the adultsss, Princesss."

It didn't really matter now, but I suddenly wanted to know. Was I still a part of this family, or just a long-forgotten memory? How could I find out without asking Mom and Luke? I snapped my fingers. My bedroom. I had deliberately avoided it until now, unsure if I could handle seeing it turned into an office, or a guest room, proof that Mom had forgotten me. But with Ethan clutching my hand, his blanket trailing behind us, I walked down the hall to my room and pushed the door open.

It was exactly as I remembered it, frozen in ice, familiar and strange at the same time. A lump caught in my throat as I walked inside. Nothing had changed. There was my old stuffed bear sitting on my bed, a birthday present from long ago. My *Naruto* and *Escaflowne* posters were still on the wall. I ran my fingers over my dresser, scanning the photographs between my scattered collection of CDs, now probably ruined. Photos of me, Mom and Ethan. One family picture with Luke. One of me and Beau, our old German shepherd, as a puppy. And a small, single framed picture on my nightstand that I didn't recognize.

Frowning, I snapped it away from the ice and held it up, staring at the photograph. It was a picture of me as a little kid, no older than Ethan, being held by an unfamiliar man with short brown hair and a lopsided smile.

"Oh, my God," I whispered.

My knees crumpled, and I sat down on the bed, slush and frigid water seeping through my clothes. I barely felt it. Ethan stood on tiptoes to stare at the frame. "Who's that?" he whispered.

Puck appeared in the doorway, his shirt and hands smeared with blood. "Princess? We should get going. Ash says there's a tatter-colt outside who can give us a ride to the healer." He stopped when he saw my face. "What's wrong?"

I held up the frame. "Recognize him?"

Puck squinted at the photo, then his eyes got wide. "Hell," he muttered. "It's Charles."

I nodded faintly. "Charles," I whispered, pulling the frame back. "I didn't even know him. I don't know how I didn't recognize…" I stopped, remembering an old woman shifting through my mind, scattering memories like leaves, searching for the one she wanted. When we were first searching for Ethan and the Iron King, we'd asked an ancient Oracle, living in New Orleans, to help us find Machina's lair. The Oracle agreed to help us…in exchange for one of my memories. I hadn't given it any thought until now. "That was the exchange, wasn't it?" I asked bitterly, looking at Puck. "The Oracle's payment for helping us. This was the memory she took."

Puck didn't say anything. I sighed, staring at the frame, then shook my head. "Who is he?" I asked.

"He was your father," Puck murmured. "Or, at least, the

man you thought was your father. Before you came here, and your mom met Luke. He disappeared when you were six."

I couldn't take my eyes off the strange photo, at the man holding me so easily, both of us smiling at the camera. "You knew who he was," I murmured without looking away. "You knew who Charles was, didn't you? All that time we were at Leanansidhe's, you knew." Puck didn't answer, and I finally tore my gaze from the photo, glaring up at him. "Why didn't you tell me?"

"And what would you have done, Princess?" Puck crossed his arms and stared back, unrepentant. "Made a bargain with Leanansidhe? Dragged him home again, like nothing happened? Do you think your mom would take him back without a second thought?"

Of course she wouldn't. She had Luke now, and Ethan. Nothing would change, even if I did manage to bring Charles home. And the worst part was, I couldn't remember why I'd wanted to.

My mind spun. I was drowning in a torrent of confusing emotions, feeling my world turned upside down. The shock of discovery. Guilt that I didn't recognize my mother's first husband, the man who'd raised me as a child, and worse, couldn't remember anything about him. He was like a stranger on the street. Anger at Puck. He had known all along, and deliberately kept me in the dark. Anger at Leanansidhe. What the hell was she doing with my dad? How did he even get there? And how was I going to get him out?

Did I even want to get him out?

"Princess." Puck's voice broke through my numb trance. I glared poisoned daggers at him and he gave me a weak smile. "Scary. You can rip me to pieces later. His royal iciness isn't looking so good. We have to get him to a healer, now."

Ethan sniffed and clamped himself to my leg, his small body tight with determination. "No!" he wailed. "No, she's not leaving! No!"

I looked at Puck helplessly, torn in several directions and feeling I could scream. "I can't leave him here alone."

"He will not be alone, Princesss," came Spider's voice from under my bed. "We will defend him with our livesss, asss ordered."

"Can you promise me that?"

A soft hiss. "Asss you wisssh. We three of the Unssseelie Court, bogey, tatter-colt, and cluricaun, promissse to look after the Chassse boy until we are told otherwissse by Hisss Highnesss Prince Asssh or Queen Mab hersssself."

I still didn't like it, but it was all I could do for now. Once a faery says the word *promise,* it is an ironclad contract. Ethan, however, wailed and clung tighter to my leg. "No!" he cried again, on his way to a rare but intense temper tantrum. "You're not leaving! You're not!"

Puck sighed and placed his palm gently on Ethan's head, murmuring something under his breath. I saw a shimmer of glamour go through the air, and Ethan slumped against my leg, going silent mid-scream. Alarmed, I scooped him up, but a soft snore came from his open mouth, and Puck grinned.

"Did you really have to do that?" I said, bundling Ethan in the blanket and carrying him back to his room.

"Well, it was either that or turn him into a rabbit for a few hours." Puck was infuriatingly unrepentant as he followed me down the hall. "And I don't think your parents would've appreciated that."

Icy water dripped from the ceiling and ran rivulets down the walls, soaking his toys and stuffed animals. "This isn't going to work," I groaned. "Even if he is asleep, I can't leave him in here. He'll freeze!"

As if on command, the closet door swung open, warm and dark and, most important, dry.

"Come on, Princess," Puck urged as I hesitated. "Make a decision here. We're running out of time."

Reluctantly, I set Ethan's small body in the closet, pulling down several more blankets to make a nest around him. He remained deeply asleep, breathing easily through his nose and mouth, and didn't even stir as I piled the quilts around him.

"You'd better take good care of him," I whispered to the shadows around me, knowing they were listening. After smoothing his hair back one last time, pulling the covers over his shoulders, I finally rose and followed Puck down the stairs.

"I hope Ash doesn't object to us dragging his carcass outside," Puck muttered as we made our way down the steps, getting dripped on every few feet. "I patched him up as best I could, but I don't think he can walk very..." He trailed off as we reached the frozen living room. The front door creaked softly on its hinges, spilling a bar of moonlight across the floor, and Ash was nowhere to be seen.

I flung myself across the room, slipping on slush and ice, and burst onto the porch. Ash's lean silhouette was moving silently across the yard, stumbling every few feet, one arm around his middle. At the edge of the trees, barely visible within the shadows, a small black horse with glowing crimson eyes waited for him.

I leaped down the steps and raced across the yard, my heart pounding in my ears. "Ash!" I cried, and lunged, catching hold of his arm. He flinched and tried shrugging me off, but nearly fell with the effort. "Wait! Where are you going?"

"Back for the scepter." His voice was dull, and he tried

pulling away again, but I clung to him desperately. "Let me go, Meghan. I have to do this."

"No, you don't! Not like this." Despair rose up like a black tide, and I choked back tears. "What are you thinking? You can't face them all alone. You'll be killed." He didn't move, either to disagree or to shake me off, and my desperation grew. "Why are you doing this?" I whispered. "Why won't you let us help you?"

"Meghan, please." Ash sounded as if he was desperately clinging to the last shreds of his composure. "Let me go. I can't stay here. Not after..." He shuddered and took a ragged breath. "Not after what I did."

"That wasn't you." Releasing his arm, I stepped in front of him, blocking his path. He wouldn't meet my eyes. Steeling myself, I stepped closer, finding the courage to gently turn his face to mine. "Ash, that wasn't you. Don't go blaming yourself—you had no control over this. This is no one's fault but *hers*."

His silver eyes were haunted. "It doesn't excuse what I did."

"No." He flinched and tried drawing back, but I held firm. "But that doesn't mean you should throw your life away because you feel guilty. What would that accomplish?" He regarded me solemnly, his expression unreadable, and my throat ached with longing. I yearned to fling my arms around him and hug him close, but I knew he wouldn't allow it. "Virus is still out there," I continued, holding his gaze, "and now we have a real chance to get the scepter back. But we have to do it together this time. Deal?"

He regarded me solemnly. "Is this another contract?"

"No," I whispered, appalled. "I wouldn't do that to you again." He remained silent, staring at me, and I reluctantly let him go, raw desperation tearing at my stomach. "Ash, if you really want to leave, I can't stop you. But—"

"I accept."

I blinked at him. "Accept? What—?"

"The terms of our contract." He bowed his head, his voice somber and grim. "I will aid you until we get the scepter back and return it to the Winter Court. I will stay with you until these terms are fulfilled, this I promise."

"Is that all it is to you? A bargain?"

"Meghan." He glanced at me, eyes pleading. "Let me do this. It's the only way I can think of to repay you."

"But—"

"So, are we done here?" Puck sauntered up beside me, putting an arm around my shoulders before I could stop him. Ash stiffened, drawing back, and his eyes went cold. Puck looked past him to the tatter-colt, standing in the trees, and raised an eyebrow. "I guess that's our ride, then."

The black horse pinned its ears and curled back its lips in a very unhorselike snarl, baring flat yellow teeth at us. Puck snickered. "Huh, I don't think your friend likes me very much, Your Highness. Looks like you'll be riding to the healer's solo."

"I'll go with him," I said quickly, stepping out of Puck's casual embrace. He blinked at me and scowled as I pulled him aside. "Ash can barely keep his feet," I whispered, matching his glare. "Someone has to stay with him. I just want to make sure he doesn't go off on his own."

He gave me that infuriating smirk. "Sure, Princess. Whatever you say."

I resisted the urge to punch him. "Just get us to the healer, Puck." He rolled his eyes and stalked off, glaring at Ash as he swept by. Ash watched him leave without comment, his expression strangely dead.

Turning away, he stumbled over to the tatter-colt, which bent its forelegs and knelt for him so that he could pull himself onto its back with a barely noticeable grimace. A little nervously, I approached the equine fey, which tossed its head and swished its ragged tail but thankfully didn't lunge or bite. It didn't kneel for me, however, and I had to scramble onto its back the hard way, settling behind Ash and wrapping my arms around his waist. For a moment, I closed my eyes and laid my cheek against his back, content just to hold him without fear. I heard his heartbeat quicken, and felt a little shiver go through him, but he remained tense in my arms, rigid and uncomfortable. A heaviness settled in my chest, and I swallowed the lump in my throat.

A harsh cry made me glance up. A huge raven swooped overhead, so close that I felt the wind from its passing ruffle my hair. It perched on a branch and looked back at us, eyes glowing green in the darkness, before barking another caw and flapping away into the trees. Ash gave a quiet word to follow, and the tatter-colt started after it, slipping into the woods as silently as a ghost. I turned and watched my house getting smaller and smaller through the branches, until the forest closed in and the trees obscured it completely.

CHAPTER TWENTY

The Healer

We rode for a couple hours while the sky above us turned from pitch black to navy blue to the faintest tinge of pink. Puck kept well ahead of us, flitting from branch to branch until we caught up, then swooping away again. He led us deep into the swamps, through bogs where the tatter-colt sloshed through waist-deep pools of murky water, past huge, moss-covered trees dripping with vines. Ash said nothing as we traveled, but his head hung lower and lower the farther we went, until it was all I could do to hold him upright.

Finally, as the last of the stars faded from the sky, the tatter-colt pushed its way through a cluster of vine-covered trees to find the raven perched atop a rustic-looking shack in the middle of the swamp.

Before the tatter-colt stopped moving, Ash was sliding off its back, crumpling to the misty ground. As soon as he was off, the tatter-colt began tossing its head and bucking, until I half slid, half fell off its back into the mud. Snorting, the colt trotted into the bushes with its head held high and disappeared.

I knelt by Ash, and my heart clenched at how pallid he

looked, the abrasions on his face standing out angrily against his pale skin. I touched his cheek and he groaned, but he didn't open his eyes.

Puck was there suddenly, dragging Ash to his feet, grimacing at the pain of his own wound. "Princess," he gritted out, taking the prince's weight, "go wake up the healer. Tell her we've got an iron-sickened prince on our hands. But be careful." He grinned, his normal self once more. "She can be a little cranky before she's had her coffee."

I climbed the rickety wooden steps onto the porch, which creaked under my feet. A cluster of toadstools, growing right out of the wall near the door, pulsed with a soft orange light, and the shack itself was covered in various moss, lichens and mushrooms of different colors. I took a deep breath and knocked on the door.

No one answered right away, so I banged again, louder this time. "Hello?" I called, peering through a dusty, curtained window. My raw throat ached, bringing tears to my eyes, but I raised my voice and called out again. "Is anyone there? We need your help! Hello?"

"Do you have any idea what time it is?" yelled an irritable voice on the other side. "Do you people think healers don't have to sleep, is that it?" Shuffling footsteps made their way to the door while the voice still continued to mutter. "Up all night with a sick catoblepas, but do I get any rest? Of course not, healers don't need rest. They can just drink one of their special potions and stay up all night, for days on end, ready to jump at every emergency that comes banging on their door at five in the morning!" The door whooshed open, and I found myself staring at empty air.

"What?" snapped the voice near my feet. I looked down.

An ancient gnome stared up at me, her face wrinkled and

shriveled like a walnut under a frayed clump of white hair. Barely two feet tall, dressed in a once-white robe with tiny gold glasses on the end of her nose, she glared at me like a furious midget bear, black eyes snapping with irritation.

I felt a stab of recognition. "Ms....Ms. Stacy?" I blurted out, seeing, for just a moment, my old school nurse. The gnome blinked up at me, then pulled her glasses off and began cleaning them.

"Well now, Ms. Chase," she said, cementing my hunch. "It has been a while. Last I saw you, you were hiding in my office after that cruel trick that boy played on you in the cafeteria."

I winced at the memory. That had been the most embarrassing day of my life, and I didn't want to think about it. "What are you doing here?" I asked, amazed. The nurse snorted and shoved her glasses back atop her nose.

"Your father, Lord Oberon, bade me keep an eye on you with Mr. Goodfellow," she replied, looking up at me primly. "If you were hurt, I was supposed to heal you. If you saw anything strange, I was to help you forget. I provided Goodfellow with the necessary herbs and potions he needed to keep you from seeing us." She sighed. "But then, you went traipsing off to the Nevernever to find your brother, and everything unraveled. Fortunately, Oberon allowed me to keep my job as school nurse, in case you ever came back."

I felt a small prick of anger that this woman had blinded me for so long, but I couldn't think about that now. "We need your help," I said, turning so she could see Puck and Ash coming toward the porch. "My friend has been stabbed, but not only that, he's iron-sick and getting weaker. Please, can you help him?"

"Iron-sick? Oh dear." The gnome peered past me, staring at the two fey boys in the yard, and her eyes got wide behind her glasses. "That…is that…Prince Ash?" she gasped, as the blood drained from her face. "*Mab's* son? You expect me to help a prince of Winter? Have you gone mad? I…no!" She backed through the door, shaking her head. "No, absolutely not!"

The door started to slam, but I stuck my foot in the frame, wincing as it banged my knee. "Please," I begged, shouldering my way through the gap. The nurse glared at me, pursing her lips, as I crowded through the frame. "Please, he could be dying, and we have nowhere else to go."

"I don't make a habit of aiding the Unseelie, Ms. Chase." The nurse sniffed and struggled to close the door, but I wasn't budging. "Let his own take care of him. I'm sure the Winter Court has its share of healers."

"We don't have time!" Anger flared. Ash was getting weaker. He could be dying, and with every second, the scepter got farther away. I bashed my shoulder into the door, and it flew open. The nurse stumbled back, hand going to her chest, as I stepped into the room. "I'm sorry," I told her in my best firm voice, "but I'm not giving you a choice. You *will* help Ash, or things will get very unpleasant in a very short time."

"I won't be bullied by a half-human brat!"

I straightened and towered over her, my head just touching the ceiling. "Oberon *is* my father, you said so yourself. Consider this an order from your princess." When she scowled, her eyes nearly sinking into the creases of her face, I crossed my arms and glared imperiously. "Or, should I inform my father that you refused to help me? That I came to you for aid, and you turned me away? I don't think he'd be too pleased about that."

"All right, all right!" She raised her hands. "I'll get no peace otherwise, I see that now. Bring in the Winter prince. But your father will hear of this, young lady." She turned and shook a finger at me. "He will hear of this, and then we will see who will be the target of his ire."

I felt a small pang of guilt that I had to pull the daddy card like some spoiled rich kid, but it faded as Puck dragged Ash up the stairs. The prince seemed more wraith than flesh now, his skin a sickly gray except for the angry red wounds on his face and arms, where the skin seemed to be peeling off the bones. I shuddered and my heart twisted with worry.

"Put him in here," the nurse ordered, directing Puck to a small side room with a low-lying bed. Puck complied, laying Ash down on the sheets before collapsing into a chair that looked like an enormous mushroom.

The nurse sniffed. "I see the princess has you in on this, too, Robin."

"Don't look at me." Puck smirked and wiped a hand across his face. "I did my best to kill the guy, but when the princess wants something, there's no changing her mind."

I scowled at him. He shrugged and offered a helpless grin, and I turned back to Ash.

"Ugh, he doesn't just smell of iron, he reeks of it," the nurse muttered, examining the wounds on his face and arms. "These burns aren't normal—they've erupted from the inside out. It's almost like he had something metal inside him."

"He did," I said quietly, and the nurse shuddered, wiping her hands. She pulled up Ash's shirt, revealing a layer of gauze that was just beginning to seep blood onto the mattress. "At least the bandaging was done properly," she mused. "Very nice, clean work. Your handiwork, I presume, Goodfellow?"

"Which one?"

"The bandage, Robin."

"Yeah, that was mine, too."

The nurse sighed, bending over Ash, studying the cuts on

his face, peeling away the gauze to see the stab wound. Her brow furrowed. "So, let me get this straight," she continued, looking at Puck. "You stabbed Ash, prince of the Winter Court."

"Guilty as charged."

"And, judging by both of your conditions—" her eyes flickered to my throat and Puck's bloody shoulder "—I'm guessing the Winter prince did that to you, as well."

"Right again."

"Which means you were fighting each other." The nurse's eyes narrowed. "Which means he was probably trying to kill you, yes?"

"Well…" I stammered.

"So, why in the name of all that's sacred do you want me to heal him? Not that I won't," she added, holding up her hand, "but what's to stop him from attacking you again? Or me, for that matter?"

"He won't," I said quickly. "I promise, he won't."

"Are you planning to use him as a hostage, is that it?"

"No! It's just—" I sighed. "It's a long story."

"Well, you will have to tell me later," the nurse sighed, standing up. "Your friend is very lucky," she continued, crossing the room to take a porcelain jar off the shelf. "I don't know how he didn't die, but he is strong, to survive as long as he did. He must've been in terrible pain." She returned to his side, shaking her head as she knelt beside him. "I can heal his surface wounds, but I don't know what I can do about the iron sickness. He must recover from that himself. It is better if he returns to Tir Na Nog after this. His body will throw off the sickness faster in his own land."

"That's not really an option," I ventured. The nurse snorted.

"Then I'm afraid he will be quite weak for a long, long

time." She straightened and turned around, staring at us with her hands on her hips. "Now I need to work. Both of you, out. If you're tired, use the extra bed in the adjoining room, but don't disturb my other patient. The prince will be fine, but I can't be tripping over you every few seconds. Go on, now. Get."

Making shooing motions with her hands, she chased us from the room and slammed the door behind us.

Even exhausted, I was too worried to sleep. I wandered the healer's small cabin like a restless cat, checking the door every ten seconds, waiting for it to open. Ash was on the other side, and I didn't know what was happening to him. I drove Puck and the satyr with the broken leg crazy, drifting from one room to the next, until Puck threatened, only half jokingly, to put a sleeping spell on me if I didn't relax. To which I threatened, only half jokingly, that I would kill him if he did.

Finally, the door creaked open and the nurse stepped out, bloodstained and weary-eyed, her hair in disarray.

"He's fine," she told me as I rushed up, the question on the tip of my tongue. "Like I said before, he's still weak from the iron-sickness, but he's no longer in any danger. Though I must say—" and she glared at me fiercely "—the boy almost snapped my wrist when I tried sewing his wounds shut. Wretched Unseelie, the only thing they know is violence."

"Can I see him?"

She eyed me over her gold-rimmed glasses, and sighed. "I should tell you no, he needs his rest, but you wouldn't listen to me, anyway. So yes, you can see him, but keep it short. Oh, and Robin," she said, crooking a finger at Puck, "a word."

Puck gave me a grimace of mock terror and followed the

nurse from the room. I watched them leave, then slipped quietly into the darkened room, closing the door behind me.

Easing over to his bed, I sat beside him and studied his face. The cuts were still there, but they were faded now, less severe. His shirt was off, and clean bandages wrapped his stomach and torso. His breathing was slow and deep, his chest rising and falling with each breath. I reached down and gently placed a hand over his heart, wanting to touch him, to feel his heartbeat under my fingers. His face was peaceful, free of harsh lines or worries, but even in sleep, he looked a little sad.

Preoccupied with watching his face, I didn't see his arm move until strong fingers curled gently over mine. My stomach leaped as I looked down, seeing my hand trapped within his, and glanced back at his face. His silver eyes were open now, staring at me, his expression unreadable in the darkness. My breath caught in my throat.

"Hi," I whispered, for lack of anything to say. He continued to watch me, unmoving, and I rattled on. "Um, the nurse says you're going to be fine now. You'll be a little sick from the iron, but that should fade with time." He remained silent, his eyes never leaving my face, and my cheeks started to burn. Maybe he just had a nightmare, and I'd startled him by creeping into his room like a stalker. I was lucky he hadn't snapped my wrist like he almost did with the nurse. "Sorry if I woke you," I muttered, attempting to pull back. "I'll let you sleep now."

His grip tightened, stopping me. "Stay."

My heart soared. I looked down at him, wishing I could just melt into him, feel his arms around me. He sighed, and his eyes closed. "You were right," he murmured, his voice nearly lost in the darkness. "I couldn't do it alone. I should have listened to you back in Tir Na Nog."

"Yes, you should have," I whispered. "Remember that, so that next time you can just agree with whatever I say and we'll be fine."

Though he didn't open his eyes, one corner of his mouth curled, ever so slightly. It was what I was hoping for. For a moment, the barriers had crumbled and we were all right again. I squeezed his hand. "I missed you," I whispered.

I waited for him to say *I missed you, too,* but he grew very still under my hand, and my heart plummeted. "Meghan," he began, sounding uncomfortable. "I…I still don't know if…" He stopped, opening his eyes. "We're still on opposite sides," he murmured, his voice tinged with regret. "Nothing changes that, even now. Contract aside, you're still considered my enemy. Besides, I thought you and Goodfellow—"

I shook my head. "Puck is…" I began, and stopped. What was he? Thinking about him, I suddenly realized I couldn't say he was just a friend. "Just friends" didn't kiss each other in an empty bedroom. "Just a friend" wouldn't make my stomach squirm in weird, fluttery ways when he came through a door. Was this love, this strange, confusing swirl of emotion? I didn't have the same intense feelings for Puck that I did for Ash, but I did feel something for him. I couldn't deny that anymore.

I swallowed. "Puck is…" I tried again.

"Is what?"

I spun around. Puck stood in the doorway, a rather dangerous smile on his face, watching us with narrowed green eyes.

"…talking to the nurse," I said faintly, as Ash released my hand and turned his face away. Puck stared at me, hard and uncomfortable, as if he knew what I was thinking.

"Nurse wants to talk to you," he said at last, turning away. "Says to leave his royal iciness alone so he can sleep. Better go see what she has to say, Princess, before she starts throwing her coffee mug."

I glanced down at Ash, but his eyes were closed and he wasn't looking at me.

A little apprehensive, I approached the kitchen, where the nurse sat at the table with a steaming mug of what was probably coffee, since the whole room smelled like it. The nurse glanced up and waved me to the opposite chair.

"Sit down, Miss Chase."

I did. Puck joined us, plunking into the seat beside me, munching an apple he'd gotten from who knew where.

"Robin tells me you're going on a dangerous mission after this," she began, cupping her withered hands around the mug, staring into the coffee. "He wouldn't give me details, but that's why you need the Winter prince healthy, so he can help you. Is that right?"

I nodded.

"The problem is, if you go through with this plan, you'll almost certainly kill him."

I jerked up. "What are you talking about?"

"He is very sick, Miss Chase." She glared at me over the rim of her mug, steam writhing off her glasses. "I wasn't joking when I said he'll be weak. The iron was in his system too long."

"Isn't there anything else you can do?"

"Me? No. He needs the glamour of his own realm to heal, so his body can throw off the sickness. Barring that—" she took a sip of coffee "—if you could find a great influx of human emotion, in large quantities, that might help him. At the very least, he could begin to recover."

"Lots of glamour?" I thought a moment. Where would there be a lot of crazy, unrestrained human emotion? A concert or a club would be perfect, but we had no tickets, and I was underage for most clubs. But, as Grimalkin had taught me, that wasn't a problem when you could conjure money from leaves and a valid license from a Blockbuster card. "Puck—think you can sneak us into a club tonight?"

He snorted. "I can sneak us into anything, Princess. Who do you think you're talking to?" He snapped his fingers, grinning. "We can pay a visit to Blue Chaos again, that'll be fun."

The nurse blinked. "Blue Chaos is owned by a Winter sidhe who employs redcaps and is rumored to have an ogre in the basement." She sighed. "Wait. If you insist on doing this, I've a better idea, one not so…insane." She looked caught between reluctance and resignation as she turned to me. "The Winter Formal is tonight at your old school, Miss Chase. If there is one place that is sure to have an overabundance of emotionally charged, hormonal teenagers, that would be it."

"The Winter Formal? Tonight?" My stomach fluttered. Going back to my school would mean facing my former classmates, and all the gossip, rumors and stories that followed. I would have to wear a fancy dress in front of everyone, maybe even dance, and they would all snicker and laugh and whisper behind my back. *Think of an excuse, Meghan, quick.* "How will we get in? I haven't been to school in forever, and they're likely to be monitoring the tickets to make sure only students attend."

Puck snorted. "Please. How many of these things do you think I've crashed? Tickets?" He sneered. "We don't need no stinkin' tickets."

The nurse shot Puck an annoyed look and turned to me. "Your parents called off the investigation for you a few months ago, Miss Chase," she said solemnly. "I believe the excuse your mother used was that you had come home and that they sent you away to a boarding school out of state. I'm not sure what she told your father—"

"Stepfather," I muttered automatically.

"—but no one has been looking for you for a while," the nurse finished, as if I hadn't said anything. "Your appearance might seem odd at first, but I'm sure Robin can fix it so you aren't conspicuous. Either way, I doubt anyone will remember you."

I wasn't sure about that. "What about a dress?" I argued, still determined to find a loophole. "I don't have anything to wear."

This time, I received scornful looks from both the nurse and Puck. "We can get you a dress, Princess," Puck scoffed. "Hell, I can glamour you a dress made of diamonds and butterflies, if you want."

"That's a little extravagant, don't you think, Robin?" The nurse shook her head at him. "Do not worry, Miss Chase," she told me. "I have friends who can help us in that regard. You will have a beautiful dress for the formal, I promise you that."

Well, that would be a nice sentiment, if I wasn't absolutely terrified. I tried again. "The school is forty-five minutes away," I pointed out, "and I don't have a license. How will we get there?"

"I have a trod that leads directly to my office in the school," the nurse replied, crushing that hope. "We can be there in seconds, and you won't miss a thing."

Damn. I was fast running out of excuses. Desperately, I played my last card.

"What about Ash? Should we move him this soon? What if he doesn't want to go?"

"I'll go."

We all whirled around. Ash stood in the doorway, leaning

against the frame, looking exhausted but a little better than before. His skin had lost the gray pallor, and the wounds across his face and arms were not as striking. He didn't look good, by any means, but at least he wasn't at death's door.

Ash clenched a fist in front of his face, then let it drop. "I can't fight like this," he said. "I'd be a liability, and our chances of getting the scepter will diminish. If there's a chance for me to shake this off, I'll take it."

"Are you sure?"

He looked at me, and that faint, familiar smile crossed his lips. "I have to be on top of my game if I'm going to kill things for you, right?"

"What you need," the nurse replied, stalking toward him with a steely glint in her eye, "is to go back to bed. I did not spend the last few hours stitching you back together for you to fall apart because you refused to stay down. Go on, now. Back to bed!"

He looked vaguely amused, but let himself be herded back into the room, and the nurse shut the door firmly behind him. "Bullheaded youngsters," she sighed. "Think they're damned invincible." Puck snickered, which was the wrong thing to do.

She whirled around. "Oh, you think it's funny, do you, Goodfellow?" she snapped, and Puck winced. "I happened to notice your shoulder doesn't look well at all. In fact, it's bleeding all over my clean floor. I believe it needs stitches. Follow me, please."

"It's only a flesh wound," Puck said, and the nurse's gaze darkened. Stalking back across the floor, she grabbed him by one long ear and pulled him out of the chair. "Ow! Hey! Ow! Okay, okay, I'm coming! Jeez."

"Miss Chase," the nurse snapped, and I jerked to attention. "While I'm fixing up this idiot, I want you to get some sleep.

You look exhausted. Use the empty cot in the patient room, and tell Amano that if he bothers you, I'll break his other leg. After I'm done with Robin, I'll come by with something for your throat."

Doubts still nagged at me, but I nodded. Finding the empty cot, I lay down, ignoring the satyr who invited me to share his "much softer bed." *I'll just lie down for a minute,* I thought, turning my back on Amano. *Just for a minute, and then I'll check on Ash.*

"Come on, you sleeping beauty. We've got a ball to attend."

I woke up, embarrassed and confused, staring around blearily. The room was dark; candles flickered erratically, and mushrooms on the walls glowed with a soft yellow luminance. Puck stood over me, grinning as usual, the light casting weird, fluttering shadows over his face.

"Come on, Princess. You slept all day and missed the fun. Our lovely nurse got a few of her friends together to make you a dress. They refuse to show it to me, of course, so you have to march in there and come out wearing it."

"What are you talking about?" I muttered, before I remembered. The Winter Formal! I was supposed to show up at my old school after being gone for so long, and face all my former classmates. There would be pointing and rumors and whispers behind my back, and my stomach clenched at the thought.

But there was no going back now. If we were going to get the scepter, Ash needed to heal, which meant I had to endure the humiliation and just get on with it.

I trailed Puck out of the room, where the nurse was waiting for me in the hall, a small, pleased smile on her lips. "Ah, there you are, Miss Chase."

"How's Ash?" I asked before she could say anything else. With a snort, the nurse turned and beckoned me to follow.

"The same," she replied, leading me down the hall. We passed Ash's room, the door tightly closed, and continued without pausing. "The stubborn fool is walking now, and even challenged Robin to a sparring match this afternoon. I stopped them, of course, though Robin was only too happy to fight him, the idiot."

"Hey," Puck said behind us. "I'm not the one who offered. I was just doing the guy a favor."

The nurse whirled and fixed him with a gimlet eye. "You—" she began, then threw her hands up. "Go get ready, idiot. You've been hovering at the door like a lost puppy all day. Tell the prince we'll be leaving as soon as Miss Chase is ready. Now, get."

Puck retreated, grinning, and the nurse sighed. "Those two," she muttered. "They're either best friends or darkest enemies, I can't tell which. Come with me, Miss Chase."

She pushed open another door and stepped through, and I followed, ducking my head. We entered a small room with shelves and potted plants encircling the walls, and a sharp, almost medicinal tang filled the room, as if I had wandered into someone's herb garden. Which, I guess, I had. Two other gnomes, as shriveled and wrinkly as the nurse, looked up from three-legged stools and waved cheerfully.

My breath caught. They were working on a dress so gorgeous my mind stumbled to a halt for a moment. A floor-length, blue satin gown hung from a mannequin in the center of the room, rippling like water in the sun. The bodice was embroidered with silvery designs and glittering ribbons of pure light, and a gauzy blue shawl had been draped over the naked shoulders, so sheer that it was almost invisible. A sparkling diamond choker encircled the mannequin's neck, sending prisms of fragmented light across the walls. The entire outfit was dazzling.

I swallowed. "Is that...for me?"

One of the other gnomes, a short man with a nose like a potato, laughed. "Well, the prince certainly isn't going to wear it."

"It's beautiful."

The gnomes preened. "Our ancestors were shoemakers, but we've learned to sew a few other things, as well. This weave is stronger than normal glamour, and won't fray if you happen to touch anything made of iron. Now, come try it on."

It fit perfectly, sliding over my skin as if made for me. I caught a shimmer of glamour out of the corner of my eye as I pulled it on, and deliberately ignored it. If this dress was put together with leaves, moss and spider silk, I didn't want to know.

When I was done, I raised my arms and turned around for inspection. The tailor gnomes clapped like happy seals, and the nurse nodded approvingly.

"Take a look at yourself," she murmured, making a spinning motion with her finger. I turned to see myself in the floor-length mirror that appeared out of nowhere, and blinked in surprise.

Not only was the dress perfect, but my hair was styled into complex curls, my face lightly touched with makeup, making me look older than before. And, whether it was part of the dress's glamour or the nurse's doing, I looked *human* again, without the pointed ears and huge, unnatural eyes. I looked like a normal teenager, ready for prom. Illusion, I knew, but it still startled me a moment, this tall, elegant stranger in the mirror.

"The boys won't be able to keep their eyes off her," a gnome sighed, and all my fears came rushing back. Fancy dress or no, I was still me, the invisible Swamp Girl of Albany High. Nothing would change that.

"Come," the nurse said, putting a shriveled hand on mine. "It's almost time."

Back we went, through the door into the central room, where a handsome boy in a classic black tuxedo waited for us. I gasped when I saw it was Puck. His crimson hair had been spiked up so it didn't look quite as disheveled, and his shoulders filled out the jacket he wore. I hadn't realized how fit he was. His green eyes raked me up and down, very, very briefly before returning to my face, and he smiled. Not teasing or sarcastic, but a pure, genuine smile.

"Humph," said the nurse, not nearly as shocked as me. "I guess you can clean up when you want to, Robin."

"I try." Puck, looking very human now, crossed the room and reached for my hand, slipping a white corsage onto my wrist. "You look gorgeous, Princess."

"Thanks," I whispered. "You look nice, yourself."

"Nervous?" he asked.

I nodded. "A little. What will I say if someone asks me where I've been? How will I explain what I've done all year, especially after I come waltzing in like nothing has happened? What about you?" I looked up at him. "Won't they wonder where you've been all this time?"

"Not me." Puck's normal grin came flashing back. "I've been gone too long—long enough for anyone to forget that I ever went to high school. The most I'll get is a vague recollection, like déjà vu, but no one will really recognize me." He shrugged. "One of the perks of being me."

"Lucky you," I muttered.

"Are we ready?" the nurse asked, suddenly appearing in her

human mien, a short, stout woman in a white lab coat, with lined brown skin and the same gold glasses on the end of her nose. "And if you're wondering, yes, I am coming with you," she announced, peering at us over her glasses, "just to make sure my patient doesn't push himself so hard he collapses. So, are we done here?"

"We're still waiting for Ash."

"Not anymore," she replied, gazing over my shoulder. I turned slowly, heart pounding against my ribs, not knowing what to expect. For a moment, my mind went completely blank.

I'd daydreamed about Ash in a tuxedo, silly fantasies that crossed my mind every so often, but the image in my head was as far removed as a house cat was to a jaguar. His tuxedo wasn't black, but a dazzling, spotless white, the open jacket showing a white vest and an icy blue tie beneath. His cuff links, the silk handkerchief in his breast pocket, and the glittering stud in his ear were the same icy color. Everything else was white, even his shoes, but instead of appearing ghostly or faded, he filled the room with presence, a royal among commoners. He stood in the doorway with his hands in his pockets, the picture of nonchalance, and even as a human, he was too gorgeous for words. His dark hair had been combed back, falling softly around his face, and his mercury eyes, though they should've seemed pale against all the white, glimmered more brightly than anything.

And they were fixed solely on me.

I was unable to move or make a sound. If my knees hadn't already been locked, I would've been a satiny blue puddle on the floor. Ash's gaze held mine; his eyes didn't stray from my face, but I felt him looking at all of me, taking me in as surely as Puck had scanned the length of my dress in a glance.

I couldn't stop staring back. Everything around me—noise, colors, people—faded into the ether, losing all relevance and meaning, until it was only me and Ash in the entire world.

Then someone took my elbow, and my heart jolted back to normal.

"Okay," Puck said a little too loudly, steering me away, "the gang's all here. Are we going to this party, or not?"

Ash walked up beside me. He made no noise, but I could feel his presence as surely as my own. He didn't offer his arm or make any move to touch me, but my nerves buzzed and my skin tingled, just with him standing there. I caught a hint of frost and the strange, sharp smell that was uniquely him, and the memory of our first dance together came rushing back.

I didn't miss the subtle look that passed between Ash and Puck, either. Ash kept his expression carefully blank, but Puck's mouth twitched in a faint smirk—one of his dangerous ones—and his eyes narrowed a fraction.

The nurse must've seen it, too, for she clapped her hands briskly, and I jumped about three feet in the air. "May I remind you three," she stated in a no-nonsense voice, "that even though this is a party, we are there for a specific reason. We are not there to spike the punch, seduce the humans, glamour the food, challenge the males to a fight, or do anything pertaining to mischief. Is that understood?" She shot a piercing glare at Puck when she said this, and he pointed to himself with a wide-eyed, *who, me?* look. It did not amuse her. "I will be watching you," she warned, and even though she was barely four feet tall, white-haired, and shriveled like a prune, she made the threat sound ominous. "Do try to behave yourselves."

CHAPTER TWENTY-ONE

The Winter Formal

It was an eerie feeling, walking the hallways of my school after being gone for so long. Dozens of memories floated through my head as we passed once-familiar landmarks: Mr. Delany's classroom where I'd sat behind Scott Waldron in Classic Lit, the bathrooms I'd spent a lot of time in, crying, the cafeteria where Robbie and I had always eaten together at the last table in the corner. So much had changed since then. The school seemed different somehow, less real than before. Or maybe I was the one who had changed.

Clusters of blue and white balloons led the way to the gym, light and music pouring out from the double doors and windows. My stomach started turning nervous backflips the closer we got, especially when the doors swung open and two students walked out, holding hands and giggling. The boy pulled his date to him for a long, tongue-swabbing kiss, before they broke apart and began creeping behind the building.

"Mmm, smell the lust," Puck muttered beside me. The nurse snorted.

"They're not supposed to leave the gym without supervision," she growled, putting her hands on her hips. "Where are the chaperones? I suppose I'll have to deal with this. You three, behave." She stalked away, virtually bristling with indignation, following the pair around the gym and into the shadows.

The coast was clear. Swallowing my nervousness, I looked back at the boys to see if they were ready. Puck grinned at me, eager as always, mischief written plainly on his face. Ash regarded me with a solemn expression. He looked stronger already, his eyes bright, the cuts healed to just faint, thin scars across his cheeks. Our gazes met, and the depth of emotion smoldering within left me breathless.

"How do you feel?" I asked, to hide the longing I knew must show on my face. "Is this helping at all? Are you getting better?"

He smiled, very faintly. "Save me a dance," he murmured.

And then we were moving toward the gym. The music grew louder and the din of voices echoed beyond the walls. Puck and Ash each pushed open a door, and we swept through into another world.

The gym had been decorated with more blue and white balloons, crepe paper, and glittering foam snowflakes, though we never saw snow in Louisiana. We passed the ticket booth with a group of teens clustered around it, either buying tickets or waiting in line. No one seemed to notice us as we swept by, but my stomach lurched as I caught sight of a familiar figure, smiling as she handed tickets to another well-dressed couple. Angie the ex-cheerleader stood behind the table, minus the huge pig nose Puck had given her last year in a vengeful prank. She seemed perfectly happy, smiling and nodding as if she did this kind of work every day. I tried to catch her eye as we passed, but her attention was on the line in front of her and the moment was gone.

Beyond the ticket booth, blue and white tables lined one side of the room; only a few people sat there, the unfortunate ones who couldn't get a date but didn't want to miss the formal just because they were single.

Where I would be, I thought, *if I hadn't been pulled into Faery. Or, more than likely, I wouldn't have been here in the first place. I'd have been home, with a movie and a half-pint of ice cream.*

The room's other half was a sea of swirling gowns and tuxedos. Couples swayed to the music, some dancing casually with their partners, some so welded together you'd need a crowbar to pry them apart. Scott Waldron, my old crush, had his arms around a stick-thin blonde I recognized as one of the cheerleaders, his hands sliding below her waist to fondle her rear. I watched them dance, their hands roaming all over each other, and felt nothing.

And then the murmurs began, starting from the table where the Dateless sat, spreading to the dance floor and the corners of the room. People were staring at us, shooting furtive glances over their dates' shoulders, heads bent low to whisper to each other. My face burned and my steps faltered, wanting to beat a hasty retreat from the room to the nearest bathroom stall. Mr. Delany, my old English teacher, looked up from where he stood guard over the punch bowl and frowned. Breaking away from the table, he strode toward us, squinting through his thick glasses. My heart pounded, and I turned to Puck in a panic.

"Mr. Delany is coming toward us!" I hissed. Puck blinked and looked over my shoulder.

"Huh, it is old Delany. Jeez, he's gotten fat. Hey, remember the time I put itching powder in his toupee?" He sighed dreamily. "That was a good day."

"Puck!" I glared at him. "Help me out here! What do I say? He knows I haven't been in school for months!"

"Excuse me," Mr. Delany said, right behind me, and my heart nearly stopped. "Is that...Meghan Chase?" I turned to him with a sickly smile. "It *is* you. I thought so." He gaped at me. "What are you doing here? Your mother told us you were at a boarding school in Maine."

So that's where I've been all this time. Nice cover, Mom. "I'm... uh...home for Christmas vacation," I answered, saying the first thing that came to mind. "And I wanted to see my old school one more time before I went back."

Mr. Delany frowned. "But, Christmas vacation was several..." He trailed off suddenly, a glazed look coming over his face. "Christmas vacation," he murmured. "Of course. How lovely for you. Will you be coming back next year?"

"Um." I blinked at his sudden change of mood. "I don't know. Maybe? There's still a lot of things to work out."

"I see. Well, it was nice to see you, Meghan. Enjoy the dance."

"See you, Mr. Delany."

As he wandered back toward the punch bowl, I breathed a sigh of relief. "That was a close one. Nice save, Puck."

"Huh?" Puck frowned at me. "What do you mean?"

"The charm spell?" I lowered my voice to a whisper. "Come on, you didn't cast that?"

"Not me, Princess. I was about to turn his wig into a ferret, but then he went all sleepy-eyed before I could pull it off." Puck sighed, gazing at the retreating English teacher in disappointment. "Pity, really. That would've livened up the party. There's so much glamour here, it's a shame not to use it."

I looked over his shoulder. "Ash?"

The Winter prince gave me a faint smile. "Subtlety has

never been Goodfellow's forte," he murmured, ignoring Puck's scowl. "We're not here to cause a riot. And human emotions have always been easy to manipulate."

Like mine were? I wondered as we continued across the gym floor. *Did you just cast a charm spell to manipulate my emotions, like Rowan tried to do? Are my feelings for you real, or some sort of fabricated glamour? And do I even care if they are?*

At the tables, Puck stepped in front of me and bowed. "Princess," he said formally, though his eyes were twinkling as he held out a hand. "May I have the honor of the first dance?"

"Um." For a moment, I balked at the idea, on the verge of telling Puck that I couldn't dance. But then I felt Ash's gaze, reminding me of a moonlit grove and swirling around the dance floor with the Unseelie prince as scores of faeries looked on. *You're Oberon's blood,* his deep voice murmured in my head. *Of course you can dance.*

Besides, Puck wasn't exactly giving me a choice. Taking my hand, he led me toward the floor. I glanced at Ash in apology, but the prince had moved to a dark corner and was leaning against the wall, looking out over the sea of faces.

And then we were dancing.

Puck danced very well, though I don't know why this surprised me. He probably had loads of experience. I stumbled a few times at first, then closed my eyes and imagined my first dance with Ash. *Stop thinking,* Ash had told me that night as we swirled across the floor in front of several dozen fey. *The audience doesn't matter. The steps don't matter. Just close your eyes and listen to the music.* I remembered that dance, the way I'd felt with him, and the steps came easily once more.

Puck gave a soft chuckle. "Okaaaay," he murmured as we spun around the room, "I seem to remember a certain someone swearing that she couldn't dance at all. Obviously I must've been with her twin sister, because I was expecting you to step on my toes all night. Been taking lessons, Princess?"

"Oh…um. I sort of picked it up while I was in the Nevernever." *Not entirely a lie.*

As we moved around the dance floor, I caught glimpses of Ash, standing alone in the corner with his hands in his pockets. It was too dark to see the emotion on his face, but his gaze never left us. Then Puck pulled me into a twirl, and I lost sight of him for a moment.

The next time I glanced in Ash's direction, he wasn't alone. Three girls, one of them the skinny blonde who had been melded to Scott a few minutes ago, had trapped him and were very obviously flirting. Smiling coyly, they oozed close, flipping their hair and giving him sultry looks from beneath their lashes. My hand fisted on Puck's lapel. It took all my willpower not to stomp over and tell them to back the hell off, but what right did I have? Ash wasn't mine. I didn't have any claim to him.

Besides, he would probably just ignore them, or tell them to go away. But when I peeked at the corner again, I saw Ash smiling at the girls, achingly handsome and charming, and my stomach roiled. He was *flirting* with them.

The song came to an end and Puck drew back, frowning slightly, as though he knew my heart wasn't in it anymore. I fanned myself with both hands, feigning breathlessness, but really drying the tears that stung my eyes. Ash was still there in the corner, chuckling at something one of the girls had said. My throat closed up, and my chest felt tight.

"You okay, Princess?"

I wrenched my gaze from Ash and the girls, swallowing hard. "A little hot," I confessed, smiling as we edged our way off the dance floor, back to the tables. "And maybe a little dizzy." Puck chuckled, his old self again, and pulled out a chair for me.

"Sorry. I just have that effect on people." I smacked his stomach with the back of my hand as I sat down, and he grinned. "Hang on. I'll get you something to drink." He vanished into the crowd, making his way toward the refreshment table at the far wall. I hoped he wouldn't spike the punch with something that would turn everyone into frogs. Sighing at the thought, I let my gaze wander around the gym, deliberately keeping it from straying to the far corner.

"Hey." A body moved across my vision, blocking my view. A wide-shouldered body, in a perfectly tailored black tux. I glanced up past the vest and lapels and bow tie, and met Scott Waldron's smiling gaze.

"Hi," he greeted cheerfully, as my stomach did a backflip. Was I seeing this right? Was *Scott Waldron,* football jock extraordinaire, talking to me? Or was this another of his tricks, meant to embarrass and humiliate me, just like last time? I had to admit, he was still really cute—wide shoulders, wavy blond hair, adorable smile—but the memory of the entire cafeteria, roaring with laughter at my expense dampened my enthusiasm a bit. He wouldn't play me like that, ever again.

"Uh, hi," I returned cautiously.

"I'm Scott," he went on in the confident, self-assured way of someone who was used to being admired. "I haven't seen you around school before. You must go somewhere else, right? I'm the varsity quarterback for Albany High."

He didn't even recognize me. I didn't know whether to be relieved or annoyed. Would he be talking to me now if he knew who I was? Would he remember the shy, geeky Swamp Girl who'd crushed on him for two years and waited by his locker every day just to watch him pass her in the hall? Did he ever regret the horrible prank he'd pulled all those months ago?

"You wanna dance?" he asked, holding out his big, football-callused hand.

I glanced toward the drinks table to see that Puck had been cornered by the nurse, who, from his half annoyed, half contrite expression, appeared to have caught him doing some kind of mischief. Probably spiking the punch, exactly as I'd feared.

A high-pitched giggle came from the corner I wasn't looking at, and my stomach turned.

"Sure," I answered, putting my hand in his. If he heard the bitterness in my voice, he didn't let on as we swept out to the dance floor.

Scott put his hands very low on my waist as we swayed to the music, standing closer than I was really comfortable with, but I didn't protest. Here I was, me, Meghan Chase, dancing with the esteemed Golden Boy of Albany High. I tried to be excited; a year ago, I would've given *anything* for Scott to look at me and smile. Had he asked me to dance, I probably would have fainted. But now, feeling his hands on my hips, seeing his face not six inches from mine, I thought only that Scott seemed very young. Still handsome and charming, there was no mistaking that, but the intense fluttery feeling I used to get whenever I looked at him was gone.

"So," Scott murmured, running his hands up my back. I shifted uncomfortably, but at least they didn't slide in the opposite direction. "Did I mention I'm the varsity quarterback already?"

"You did." I smiled at him.

"Oh, right." He grinned back, wrapping a curl of my hair

around his finger. "Well, have you ever been to any of my games?"

"A few."

"Yeah? Pretty impressive, huh? Think we have a chance to make Nationals this year?"

"I really don't know much about football," I admitted, hoping he would drop the subject. Apparently, it was the wrong thing to say. He immediately launched into a full explanation of the sport, citing all the games he'd won, his teammate's flaws and shortcomings, and all the years he'd carried the team to victory. That led to his plans for college, how he'd gotten a scholarship to Louisiana State, how he'd been voted Most Likely to Succeed, and the brand-new Mustang his dad bought him just because he was so proud. I plastered a smile to my face, made appropriate noises of appreciation, and tried not to let my eyes glaze over.

"Hey," he said at last, as I secretly hoped he was wrapping up, "you wanna get out of here? I'm meeting a bunch of people at Brody's house later—his old man is out of town, and there's gonna be a party after the dance. Wanna come?"

Another shock. Scott was inviting me to a cool kids' party, where there would be drinking, drugs and other activities parents frowned upon. For just a moment, I felt a twinge of regret. The one night I got invited to a party would be the one night I couldn't go.

"I can't," I told him. "I'm sorry, I have other plans tonight."

He pouted. "Really?" he said, and his hands slid past my hips, definitely farther than I was comfortable with. "You can't break them, even for me?"

I stiffened, and he actually seemed to get the hint, sliding them back into neutral territory. "I'm sorry," I said again. "But I really can't. Not tonight."

He sighed in genuine regret. "All right, mystery girl, break my heart." Taking my hand, he pressed it to his chest and gave me a coy, little-boy smile. "But at least let me call you this weekend. What's your name?"

And there it was.

I could tell him. I could tell him, and watch the smile fade from his lips as he realized whom he'd been seducing so earnestly. Watch that cocky grin turn to horror and disbelief, and maybe just a little regret. I wanted to see regret. He deserved it, after what he'd done to me. I just had to say two words, two simple words, *Meghan Chase,* and the Golden Boy of Albany High would be laid lower than the bottom of my heels.

All I had to do was say my name.

I sighed, softly patted his chest, and whispered, "Let's keep it a mystery, okay?"

"Uh…" The grin faltered, and he blinked, looking so confused that I almost laughed out loud. "Okay. But…how will I get in touch with you? How will I know who to call?"

"Excuse me."

My stomach fluttered. I felt the smile stretching my face even before we turned around, though I tried to look severe and angry. It was no use. Ash stood there under the dim lights, solemn and beautiful as he extended his hand to me. "May I cut in?"

Knowing Scott, I expected him to refuse, to tell the competition to back off. But perhaps he was still off balance, or maybe it was something in the prince's steady gaze that made him take a step back. Still looking a bit confused, like he didn't know what had just happened, he wandered off the dance floor and into the crowd. And I suddenly had the feeling that would be the last time I ever saw Scott Waldron.

I suppose I should've been happy, but all I felt was relief

that he was gone. Ash smiled at me, and I forgot to be angry, forgot to be distant and coy and aloof as I'd planned. Instead, I took his hand and let him draw me close, breathed in the frosty scent of him, and was whisked away to our first dance under the stars, the first time I held his hand, looked into his eyes, and was completely lost.

Dancing with Ash was exactly how I remembered it.

The song was slow and sweet, so we swayed back and forth, barely moving, but the look on his face, the feel of his hand on mine, was all heart-achingly familiar. I laid my head on his chest and closed my eyes, content to touch him, to listen to his heartbeat. He sighed and rested his chin atop my head, and for a moment, neither of us spoke; we just swayed to the music.

Until I decided to be an idiot and open my mouth.

"So, you seemed to be enjoying yourself back there." I couldn't keep the accusation from my voice, even though I hated myself for sounding like a freaky-possessive girlfriend. "Those girls found you very interesting, I suppose. What were you talking about?"

He chuckled, sending a tingle down my spine. He laughed so infrequently, and it was a deep, marvelous sound when he did. "They invited me to a party after the dance," he murmured, pulling back to look at me directly. "I told them I was already with someone, so they spent the next few minutes trying to convince me to…ditch?…whomever I was with and join them. It was a rather interesting conversation."

"You could've just told them to go away." I'd seen that cold, *don't-bother-me-or-I'll-kill-you* glare. No one in their right mind would continue pestering the Ice prince once that chilling gaze was turned on them.

"That wouldn't have been very gentlemanly." Ash sounded amused. "And it was advantageous for me to have them stay.

There was enough glamour in that one corner to choke a dragon. Isn't that why we're here?"

"Oh." Relief and embarrassment colored my face. "Right. It is. I just thought…never mind. I'll shut up now."

Ash looked down at me, cocking his head with a puzzled frown. "What exactly are you accusing me of, Meghan Chase?"

"I wasn't accusing." I hid my face in his shirt, mumbling through the cool fabric. "I just thought…with how easy it is to manipulate human emotions…that you, I don't know. Might find something more interesting than me."

Wow, that had come out stupid and psycho possessive. My face burned even more. I kept my head down so he wouldn't see my crimson cheeks, and I wouldn't have to see his reaction either.

"Ah." Ash brushed my cheek with the back of his hand, catching a loose strand of hair between his fingers. "I've seen thousands of mortal girls," he said softly, "more than you could ever count, from all corners of your world. To me, they're all the same." His finger slid below my chin, tilting my head up. "They see only this outer shell, not who I really am, beneath. You have. You've seen me without the glamour and the illusions, even the ones I show my family, the farce I maintain just to survive. You've seen who I really am, and yet, you're still here." He brushed his thumb over my skin, leaving a trail of icy heat. "You're here, and the only dance I want is this one."

My heart skipped a beat. His nearness was overwhelming, his face and lips just inches away. We stared at each other, and I could see the hunger in his eyes. I trembled in anticipation, my lips aching to touch his, but a flicker of regret crossed his face and he silently drew back, ending the moment. Sighing, I laid my head against his shirt, my entire being buzzing with thwarted hope, a heavy disappointment settling in my chest. I heard his heart thudding against my cheek, and felt him tremble, too.

"Since we're on the subject," Ash murmured after a few minutes of silent dancing, as our hearts and minds composed themselves, "you never answered my question."

He sounded uncharacteristically unsure. I shifted in his arms and looked up, meeting his gaze. "What question?"

His eyes were deep gray in the dim light. Glamour shimmered around him, heavy in the air and in the dreams of those around us. For just a moment, the illusion of the human boy dancing with me wavered, revealing an unearthly faery with silver eyes, glamour pouring off of him in waves. Compared to the suddenly plain human dancers surrounding us, his beauty was almost painful.

"Do you love him?"

My breath caught. For the barest of seconds, I thought he meant Scott, but of course that wasn't right. There was only one person he could mean. Almost against my will, I glanced behind me, through the swaying crowd of dancers, to where Puck stood at the edge of the light. His arms were crossed, and he was watching us with narrowed green eyes.

My heart skipped a beat. I turned back, feeling Ash's gaze on me, my mind spinning several directions at once. *Tell him no,* it whispered. *Tell him Puck is just a friend. That you don't feel anything for him.*

"I don't know," I whispered miserably.

Ash didn't say anything. I heard him sigh, and his arms tightened around me, pulling us closer together. We fell silent again, lost in our own thoughts. I closed my eyes, wanting time to freeze, wanting to forget about the scepter and the faery courts and make this night last forever.

But of course, it ended much too soon.

As the last strains of music shivered across the gym floor, Ash lowered his head, his lips grazing my ear. "We have company," he murmured, his breath cool on my skin. I opened my eyes and looked around, peering through the heavy glamour for invisible enemies.

A pair of slitted golden orbs stared at me from a table, floating in midair above the flowery centerpiece. I blinked, and Grimalkin appeared, bushy tail curled around himself, watching me. No one else in the room seemed to notice a large gray cat sitting in the middle of the table; they moved around and past him without a single glance.

Puck met us at the edge of the dance floor, indicating he'd seen Grimalkin too. Casually, we walked up to the table, where Grimalkin had moved on to grooming a hind leg. He glanced up lazily as we approached.

"Hello, Prince," he purred, regarding Ash through half-lidded eyes. "Nice to see you are not evil…well…you know. I assume you are here for the scepter, as well?"

"Among other things." Ash's voice was cold; fury rippled below the surface, and the air around him turned chilly. I shivered. He didn't just want the scepter; he was out for revenge.

"Did you find anything, Grim?" I asked, hoping the other students wouldn't notice the sudden drop in temperature. Grimalkin sneezed once and stood, waving his tail. His gold eyes were suddenly serious.

"I think you had best see this for yourself," he replied. Leaping off the table, he slipped through the crowds and out the door. I took one last look around the gym, at my old classmates and teachers, feeling a twinge of sadness. I'd probably never see them again. Then Puck caught my gaze with his encouraging smile, and we followed Grimalkin out the doors into the night.

Outside, it was bitingly cold. I shivered in my thin gown, wondering if Ash's mood could spread to the entire district. Ahead of us, Grimalkin slipped around a corner like a furry ghost, barely visible in the shadows. We followed him down the corridors, past numerous classrooms, and into the parking lot, where he stopped at the edge of the sidewalk, gazing out over the blacktop.

"Oh, my God," I whispered. The entire lot—pavement, cars, the old yellow bus in the distance—was covered with a fine sheeting of white powder that sparkled under the moonlight. "No way. Is that...*snow?*" I bent and scooped up a handful of the white drifts. Wet, cold and crumbly. It couldn't be anything else. "What's going on? It never snows here."

"The balance is off," Ash said grimly, gazing around the alien landscape. "Winter is supposed to hold the power right now, but with the scepter gone, the natural cycle is thrown off. So you get events like this." He gestured to the snowy parking lot. "It will only get worse, unfortunately."

"We have to get the scepter back now," I said, looking down at Grimalkin. He gazed back calmly, as if snow in Louisiana was perfectly normal. "Grim, did you and Ironhorse find anything yet?"

The cat made a great show of licking his front paw. "Perhaps."

I wondered if Ash and Puck ever felt the urge to strangle him. Apparently, I wasn't asking the right questions. "What did you find?" Puck asked, and Grimalkin finally looked up.

"Maybe the scepter. Maybe nothing." He flicked his paw several times before continuing. "But...there is a rumor on the streets of a great gathering of Iron fey in a factory in downtown San Jose. We located it, and it looks abandoned, so per-haps Virus has not gathered her army yet."

"Where's Ironhorse?" I asked.

Ash narrowed his eyes.

"I left him at the factory," Grimalkin said. "He was ready to charge in, but I convinced him I would return with you and Goodfellow. He is still there, for all I know."

"You left him *alone?*"

"Is that not what I just said, human?" Grimalkin narrowed his eyes at me, and I gave the boys a panicked look. "I suggest you hurry," he purred, looking out over the parking lot. "Not only is Virus gathering a great army of Iron fey, but I do not think Ironhorse will wait very long. He seemed rather eager to charge in by himself."

"Let's go," I said, glancing at Ash and Puck. "Ash, are you all right for this? Will you be able to fight?"

He regarded me solemnly and made a quick gesture with his hand. The glamour fell away, the tuxedo dissolving into mist, as the human boy disappeared and the Unseelie prince took his place, his black coat swirling around him.

I looked back at Puck and saw his tux replaced with his normal green hoodie. He gave me a once-over and grinned. "Not exactly dressed for battle, are you, Princess?"

I looked down at my gorgeous dress, feeling a pang of regret that it would probably be ruined before the night was out. "I don't suppose I have time to change," I sighed.

"No." Grimalkin twitched an ear. "You do not." He shook his head and glanced skyward. "What time is it?"

"Um…I don't know." I'd long given up wearing a watch. "Almost midnight, I think. Why?"

He appeared to smile, which was rather eerie. "Just sit tight, human. They will be here soon."

"What are you talking…" I trailed off as a cold wind whipped across the parking lot, swirling the snow into eddies, making them dance and sparkle over the drifts. The branches rattled, an unearthly wailing rising over the wind and trees. I shivered, and saw Ash close his eyes.

"You called *Them,* caith sith?"

"They owed me a favor," Grimalkin purred, as Puck glanced nervously at the sky. "We do not have the time to locate a trod, and this is the fastest way to travel from here. Deal with it."

"What's going on?" I asked, as both Ash and Puck moved closer, tense and protective. "Who'd he call? What's coming?"

"The Host," Ash murmured darkly.

"What…" But at that moment I heard a great rushing noise, like thousands of leaves rustling in the wind. I looked up and saw a ragged cloud moving toward us at a frightening speed, blotting out the sky and stars.

"Hang on," Puck said, and grabbed my hand.

The black mass rushed toward us, screaming with a hundred voices. I saw dozens of faces, eyes, open mouths, before it was upon us, and I cringed back in fear. Cold, cold fingers snatched at me, bearing me up. My feet left the ground in a rush, and I was hurtling skyward, a shriek lodging in my throat. Icy wind surrounded me, tearing at my hair and clothes, numbing me to all feeling except a small spot of warmth where Puck still held my hand. I closed my eyes, tightening my grip as the Host bore us away into the night.

CHAPTER TWENTY-TWO

Ironhorse's Choice

I don't know how long the Host carried us through the sky, screeching and wailing in their unearthly voices. I don't know if they had trods that let them move between worlds, if they could bend space and time, or if they just flew really, really fast. But what should have been hours felt like only minutes before my feet hit solid ground and I was falling forward.

Puck's grip on me tightened, jerking me to a halt before I could fall over. I clutched his arm to regain my balance, looking around dizzily.

We stood on the outskirts of an enormous factory. Across a bright parking lot, lit with neat rows of glowing streetlamps, a huge glass, steel and cement monstrosity loomed at the edge of the pavement. Though the lot was empty, the building itself didn't look damaged in any way: no smashed windows, no graffiti streaking the sides. I caught glimpses of things moving along the walls, flashes of blue light, like erratic fireflies. A moment later, I realized they were gremlins—hundreds, if not thousands of them—scuttling over the factory like ants. The blue lights were the glow of their fangs, hissing, shrieking and baring teeth at each other. A chill ran through me, and I shivered.

"A gremlin nest," Grimalkin mused, watching the swarm curiously. "Leanansidhe said the gremlins congregate in places that have a lot of technology. It makes sense Virus would come here, too."

"I know this place," Ash said suddenly, and we all looked at him. He was gazing at the plant with a small frown on his face. "I remember Virus talking about it when I…when I was with her." The frown grew deeper, and a shadow crept over his face. He shook it off. "There's supposed to be a trod to the Iron Kingdom inside."

Puck nudged my arm and pointed. "Look at that."

I followed his finger to a sign at the front of the building, one of those big marble slabs with giant glowing words carved into it. "SciCorp Enterprises," I muttered, shaking my head.

"Coincidence?" Puck waggled his eyebrows. "I think not."

"Where's Ironhorse?" I asked, looking around.

"This way," Grimalkin said, trotting along the edge of the parking lot. We followed, the boys slightly blurred at the edges, telling me they were invisible to humans, and me in my very conspicuous prom dress and heels that were so not useful for raiding a giant factory, or even walking down a sidewalk. To my right, cars zoomed past us on the street; a few slowed down to honk at me or whistle, and my cheeks burned. I wished I could glamour myself invisible, or at least have had time to change into something less cumbersome.

Grimalkin led us around the factory, skirting the edges of the sidewalk, to a drainage ditch that separated one lot from the other. At the bottom of the ditch, oily black water pooled from a massive storm drain, trickling through the weeds and grass. Bottles and cans littered the ground, glinting in the moonlight, but there was no sign of Ironhorse.

"I left him right here," Grimalkin said. Looking around briefly, he leaped to a dry rock and began shaking his paws, one by one. "We appear to be too late. It seems our impatient friend has already gone inside."

A deep snort cut through the air before I could panic. "HOW FOOLISH DO YOU THINK I AM?" Ironhorse rumbled, bending low to clear the rim of the pipe. He was in his more human form, as there was no way he could have fit his real body inside. "THERE WAS A PATROL COMING, AND I WAS FORCED TO HIDE. I DO NOT BREAK THE PROMISES I GIVE." He glared at Grimalkin, but the cat only yawned and started washing his tail.

Ash stiffened, and his hand went casually to his sword hilt. I didn't blame him. Barring his brief stint with Virus, the last Ash had seen of Ironhorse, he was dragging us to Machina in chains. Of course, Ironhorse was wearing a different form now, but you had only to look closely to see the huge, black iron monster that lurked beneath the surface.

I switched to the problem at hand, not oblivious to the dark look he was receiving from Ash. "We're sure Virus is in there?" I asked, subtly moving between them. "So, how are we going to get inside, especially with the gremlins crawling all over the building?"

Ironhorse snorted. "THE GREMLINS WILL NOT BOTHER US, PRINCESS. THEY ARE SIMPLE CREATURES. THEY LIVE FOR CHAOS AND DESTRUCTION, BUT THEY ARE COWARDLY AND WILL NOT ATTACK A POWERFUL OPPONENT."

"I'm afraid I have to disagree," Ash said, a dangerous edge to his voice now. "You yourself lead an army of gremlins in

Machina's realm, or have you forgotten? They don't attack powerful opponents? I seem to recall a wave of them trying to tear me apart in the mines."

"That's right," I echoed, frowning. "And what about the time the gremlins kidnapped me and hauled me off to meet you? Don't tell me the gremlins aren't dangerous."

"NO." Ironhorse shook his head. "LET ME CLARIFY. BOTH TIMES, THE GREMLINS WERE UNDER MACHINA'S COMMAND. LORD MACHINA WAS THE ONLY ONE WHO COULD CONTROL THEM, THE ONLY ONE THEY EVER LISTENED TO. WHEN HE DIED, THEY REVERTED TO THEIR NORMAL, FERAL STATE. THEY ARE NO THREAT TO US, NOW."

"What about Virus?" Puck asked.

"VIRUS SEES THEM AS VERMIN. EVEN IF SHE COULD CONTROL THEM, SHE WOULD RATHER LET HER DRONES DO THE WORK THAN STOOP TO DEALING WITH ANIMALS."

"Well, this should be easy, then." Puck smirked. "We'll just stroll in the front door, waltz up to Virus, grab the scepter, have some tea and save the world before breakfast. Silly me, thinking it would be hard."

"What I think Puck is trying to say," I said, shooting Puck a frown, "is—what will we do about Virus when we find her? She's got the scepter. Isn't it supposed to be powerful?"

"Don't worry about that." Ash's voice raised the hairs on my neck. "I'll take care of Virus."

Puck rolled his eyes. "Very nice, Prince Cheerful, but there is one problem. We have to get inside first. How do you propose we do that?"

"You're the expert." Ash glanced at Puck, and his mouth twitched into a smirk of his own. "You tell me."

Grimalkin sighed and rose, his tail lashing his flanks. "The hope of the Nevernever," he said, eyeing each of us disdainfully. "Wait here. I will check the place out."

He hadn't been gone long when Puck stiffened and Ash jerked up, his hand going to his sword. "Someone's coming," he warned, and we scrambled into the ditch, my gown catching on weeds and jagged pieces of glass. Sloshing into the pipe, I grimaced as the cold, filthy water soaked my shoes and dress. At this rate, it wouldn't survive the night.

Two figures marched past our hiding spot, dressed in familiar black armor with spines growing from the shoulders and back. The faint smell of rot and putrefying flesh drifted into the tube at their passing. I stifled a cough and put my hand over my nose.

"Rowan's Thornguards," Ash murmured grimly as the pair moved on. Frowning, Puck peeked over his shoulder.

"Wonder how many are in there?"

"I'd guess a few squads at least," Ash replied. "I imagine Rowan wanted to send his best to take over the realm."

"You are right," Grimalkin said, suddenly materializing beside us. He perched on a cinder block so as not to touch the water, keeping his tail straight up. "There are many Thornguards inside, along with several Iron fey and a few dozen human drones. And gremlins, of course. The factory is crawling with them, but no one seems to pay them much attention."

"Did you see Virus or the scepter?" I asked.

"No." Grimalkin sat down, curling his tail tightly around his feet. "However, there are two Thornguards stationed at a back door who will not let anyone past."

At Virus's name, Ash narrowed his eyes. "Can we fight our way through?"

"I would not advise it," Grimalkin replied. "It appears some of them are using iron weapons—steel swords and crossbows with iron bolts and such. It would only take one well-placed shot to kill you."

Puck frowned. "Fey using iron weapons? You think Virus has them all bugged?"

"Something far worse, I'm afraid." Ash's face was like stone as he stared at the factory. "I was forced into service. Virus didn't give me a choice. The Thornguards are acting on their own. Like Rowan. They want to destroy the Nevernever and give it to the Iron fey."

Puck's eyebrows shot up. "*The hell?* Why?"

"Because they think they can become like Virus," I replied, thinking back to what Edgebriar had said, remembering the crazed, doomed look in his eye. "They believe it's only a matter of time before Faery fades away entirely. So the only way to survive is to become like the Iron fey. They wear a metal ring beneath their gloves to prove their loyalty, and because they think it will make them immune to the effects. But it's just killing them slowly."

"Huh. Well, that's…absolutely horrifying." Puck shook his head in disbelief. "Still, we have to get in there somehow, iron weapons or no. Can we glamour ourselves to look like them?"

"It won't hold up against all the iron," Ash muttered, deep in thought.

"I might have a better idea," Grimalkin said. "There are several glass skylights on the roof of the factory. You could map the layout of the building from there, maybe even see where Virus is."

That sounded like a good idea. But… "How do we get up

there?" I asked, staring at the looming glass-and-metal wall of the factory. "Puck can fly, and I'm sure Ash can get up there, but Ironhorse and I are a little more earthbound."

Grimalkin nodded sagely. "Normally, I would agree. But tonight, it seems the Fates are on our side. There is a window cleaner's platform on the far side of the building."

Even with Ironhorse's assurance that the gremlins wouldn't bother us, we approached with extreme caution. The memory of being kidnapped by the gremlins, their sharp claws digging into my skin, their freaky, maniacal laughter and buzzing voices, still burned hot in my mind. One had even lived in my iPod before it was broken, and Machina had used it to communicate with me even within the borders of Arcadia. Gremlins were sneaky, evil, little monsters, and I didn't trust them one bit.

Fortunately, our luck seemed to hold as we made our way around the back of the factory. A small platform hovered over the ground, attached to a pulley system that climbed all the way up to the roof. The wall was dark, and the gremlins were absent, at least for now.

Grimalkin hopped lightly onto the wooden platform, followed by Ash and Puck, being careful not to touch the iron railings. Ash pulled me up after him, and then Ironhorse clambered aboard. The wooden planks creaked horribly and bent in the middle, but thankfully held firm. I prayed the entire thing wouldn't snap like a matchstick when we were three stories in the air.

Puck and Ironhorse each grabbed a rope and began drawing the platform up the side of the building. The dark, mirrored walls reflected a strange party back at us: a cat, two elf-boys, a girl in a slightly tattered gown, and a monstrous black man with glowing red eyes. I contemplated how strange my life had become, but was interrupted by a soft hiss overhead.

A gremlin crouched on the pulleys near the top of the roof, slanted eyes glowing in the dark. Spindly and long limbed, with huge batlike ears, it flashed me its razor-blue grin and let out a buzzing cry.

Instantly, gremlins started appearing from everywhere, crawling out of windows, scuttling along the walls, swarming over the roof to peer at us. A few even clung to the pulley ropes or perched on the railings, staring at us with their eerie green gaze. Ash pulled me close, his sword bared to slash at any gremlin who ventured near, but the tiny Iron fey didn't make any move to attack. Their buzzing voices filled the air, like radio static, and their vivid grins surrounded us with a blue glow as we continued to inch up the wall, unhindered.

"What are they doing?" I whispered, pressing closer to Ash. He held me protectively with one arm, his sword between us and the gremlins. "Why are they just staring at us? What do they want? Ironhorse?"

The lieutenant shook his head. "I DO NOT KNOW, PRINCESS," he replied, sounding as mystified as I felt. "I HAVE NEVER SEEN THEM ACT IN THIS MANNER BEFORE."

"Well, tell them to go away. They're creeping me out."

A buzz went through the gremlins surrounding us, and the swarm began to clear. Crawling back along the walls, they disappeared through the windows, squeezed into the cracks or scrambled back over the roof. As suddenly as they'd appeared, the gremlins vanished, and the wall was dark and silent again.

"Okay." Puck cast wary looks all around us. "That was... weird. Did someone release gremlin repellant? Did they just get bored?"

Ash sheathed his sword and released me. "Maybe we scared them off."

"Maybe," I said, but Ironhorse was staring at me, his crimson eyes unfathomable.

Grimalkin reappeared, scratching his ear as if nothing had happened. "It does not matter now," he said, as the platform scraped up against the roof. "They are gone, and the scepter is close." He yawned and blinked up at us. "Well? Are you just going to stand there and hope it flies into your hands?"

We crowded off the platform onto the roof of the factory. The wind was stronger here, tugging at my hair and making my gown snap like a sail. I held on to Ash as we made our way across the roof. Far below and all around us, the city sprawled out like a glittering carpet of stars.

Several raised glass skylights sat in the middle of the roof, emitting a fluorescent green glow. Cautiously, I edged up to one and peered down.

"There," Ash muttered, pointing to a mezzanine twenty or so feet above the floor, and maybe thirty feet below us. Through the glass, I could pick out a blur of poison-green amid the stark grays and whites, surrounded by several faeries in black armor. Virus walked to the edge of the overhang and gazed out over a crowd of assembled fey, ready to give a speech, I supposed. I saw Thornguards and wiremen and a few green-skinned men in business suits, along with several fey I didn't recognize. The scepter pulsed yellow-green in Virus's hands as she swept it over her head, and a muffled roar went through the crowd.

"Okay, so we found her," Puck mused, pressing his nose against the glass. "And it looks like she hasn't gathered her whole army quite yet, which is nice. So, how do we get to her?"

Ash made a quiet noise and drew back.

"You don't," he muttered. "I will." He turned to face me. "For all she knows, I'm still under her control. If I can get close enough to grab the scepter before she figures out what happened—"

"Ash, no. That's way too dangerous."

He gave me a patient look. "Anything we try will be dangerous. I'm willing to take that risk." His hand came up, fingers brushing the spot where Puck had stabbed him. "I'm still not completely recovered. I won't be able to fight as well as I normally do. Hopefully, I can fool Virus long enough to get the scepter from her."

"And then what?" I demanded. "Fight your way out? Against those masses? And Virus? What if she knows you don't have the bug anymore? You can't expect to—" I stopped, staring at him, as something clicked in my head. "This isn't about getting the scepter, is it?" I murmured, and he looked away. "This is about killing Virus. You're hoping to get close enough to stab her or cut off her head or whatever, and you don't care what happens next."

"What she did to me was bad enough." Ash's silver eyes glittered as he turned back, cold as the moon overhead. "What she made me do, I will never forgive. If I am discovered, I will at least create a big enough distraction for you to slip in and grab the scepter."

"You could die!"

"It doesn't matter now."

"It does to me." I stared at him in horror. He really meant it. "Ash, you can't go down there alone. I don't know where this fatalistic crap is coming from, but you can stop it right now. I'm not going to lose you again."

"SHE IS RIGHT."

We looked up. Ironhorse stood on the other side of the

glass, watching us. His eyes glowed red in the darkness. "IT *IS* TOO DANGEROUS. FOR YOU."

I frowned. "What are you talking—"

"PRINCESS." Abruptly, he bowed. "IT HAS BEEN AN HONOR. WERE THINGS DIFFERENT, I WOULD GLADLY SERVE YOU UNTIL THE END OF TIME." He looked to Ash and nodded, as it suddenly dawned on me what he was implying. "SHE THINKS THE WORLD OF YOU, PRINCE. PROTECT HER WITH YOUR LIFE."

"Ironhorse, don't you dare!"

He whirled and took off, oblivious to my cries for him to stop. My heart clenched as he approached the second skylight, and I watched helplessly as he gathered himself and jumped...

The glass exploded as he crashed into it, shattering into a million sparkling pieces. Gasping, I looked through the skylight to see the glittering shards rain down on the crowd below. Screaming and snarling, they looked up, covering their eyes and faces as the massive iron horse smashed into their midst with a *boom* that shook the building. Roaring, Iron-horse reared up, blasting flame from his nostrils, steel hooves flailing in deadly arcs.

The room erupted into chaos. Once they recovered from their shock, Thornguards and wiremen surged forward to at-tack, flinging themselves at Ironhorse, ripping and clawing.

"We have to get down there!" I cried, rushing toward the broken skylight only to have Ash catch my arm.

"Not that way," he said, pulling me back to the unbroken window. "The distraction has already been launched. We can-not help him now. Our target is Virus and the scepter. You should stay here, Meghan. You have no magic and—"

I yanked my arm from his grip. "You did *not* just bring that excuse up again!" I snarled, and he blinked in surprise. I glared at him. "Remember what happened the last time you went off without me? Get this through your stubborn head, Ash. I'm not staying behind and that's final."

One corner of his mouth twitched, just a little. "As you wish, Princess," he said, and glanced at Puck, who was leering at us both. "Goodfellow, are you ready?"

Puck nodded and leaped onto the skylight. I scowled at them both and clambered onto the glass, ignoring Puck's hand to help me up. "How do you expect us to get down there?" I demanded as I clawed myself upright. "Go right through the window?"

Puck snickered. "Glass is a funny thing, Princess. Why do you think ancient people put salt along windowsills to keep us out?" I looked down and saw Virus directly below us, shouting and waving the scepter above her head, her attention riveted on the battle and Ironhorse.

Ash leaped onto the skylight, drawing his sword as he did. "Look after Meghan," he said, as glamour began shimmering around both him and Puck. "I'll take care of Virus."

"What—?" I started, but Puck suddenly swept me into his arms. I was so surprised I didn't have time to protest.

"Hold on tight, Princess," he murmured, as a shimmer went through the air around us, and we dropped straight through the glass like it wasn't there.

We plummeted toward the overhang, a shriek escaping my throat, but it was swallowed up in the chaos between Ironhorse and the rest of the fey. Ash dropped toward Virus like an avenging angel, his coat flapping in the wind, sword bared and gleaming as he raised it over his head.

At the last moment, one of the Thornguards surrounding Virus glanced up, and his eyes got huge. Drawing his sword, he gave a shout of warning, and amazingly, Virus whirled and looked up. Ash's blade slashed down in a streak of blue and met the Scepter of the Seasons as Virus swept it up to block him.

There was a flash of blue and green light and a hideous screech that echoed through the room and caused every eye to turn to the pair on the overhang. Sparks flew between the ice blade and the scepter, bathing the combatants' faces in flickering lights. Virus looked rather shocked to be facing her former soldier; Ash's mouth was tight with concentration as he bore down on her with his sword.

Puck set me down—I didn't even remember landing—and leaped between the Thornguards as they rushed up with drawn swords. Grinning, he threw himself at the guards, daggers flashing in the hellish light coming from Ash's blade and the scepter.

Then Virus started to laugh.

I felt a surge of cold iron glamour, and she shoved Ash away, pushing him back in a flash of green. He recovered immediately, but before he could rush her again, Virus retreated, stepping off the mezzanine to float several feet in the air. Her poisonous green eyes found me and she smiled.

"Well." She sniffed and cast bemused glances at the chaos spread at her feet. Ironhorse, surrounded by Iron fey, still kicked and raged at them, though his struggles were growing weaker. More Thornguards came rushing up the steps, but these held crossbows with iron bolts, pointed right at us. Ash and Puck drew back so that they were standing between me and the guards, who had us surrounded in a bristly black ring.

"Meghan Chase. You are full of surprises, aren't you?" Virus smiled at me. "I've no idea how you managed to free the Winter prince from my bug, but it doesn't matter now. The armies of the false king are ready to march on Summer and Winter. Once they have taken the Nevernever and killed off the oldblood rulers, it will be our turn. We will overrun their armies and kill the false king before he has a chance to savor his victory. Then, the Nevernever will belong to m—"

She didn't have a chance to finish. Ash drew back and hurled a flurry of ice daggers at her face, taking her by surprise. She flinched, holding up the scepter; there was a flash of green light and a surge of power. The icicles shattered, bursting apart before they reached her. With angry shouts, the crossbow men released their quarrels even as Virus screamed at them to stop.

The deadly storm of iron bolts flew toward us. I could *feel* them sailing through the air, *Matrix* style, leaving distorted ripples in their wake. Without thinking, I turned and flung out my hand. I didn't think how crazy it was, that at such close range the bolts would rip right through me like I was paper. That we would all most certainly die, peppered by lethal darts that could kill even if they weren't made of iron. I wasn't thinking of anything as I spun and gestured sharply, feeling a surge of electricity beneath my skin.

A ripple went through the air. The bolts flew to either side of us, thunking into the walls and pinging off metal beams to clatter to the floor. I heard Iron fey shriek as they were hit, but not one of the half-dozen bolts touched us.

The Thornguards gaped. Ash and Puck stared at me as if I had grown another head. I shivered violently, trembling from the strange cold glamour that writhed under my skin and buzzed in my ears.

"Impossible." Virus spun slowly to face me, her face draining of color. She shook her head, as if trying to convince herself. "You cannot be the one. A weakling human girl? You're not even one of us. It's a mistake, it must be!"

I had no idea what she was talking about, but it didn't seem to matter. Virus started to giggle, sticking a green-tinted nail in her mouth, her laughter growing louder and more hysterical, until she stopped and glared at me with wide, crazy eyes. "No!" she screamed, making even the Thornguards flinch. "It isn't right! I was his second! His power should have been mine!"

Her mouth opened, gaping impossibly wide, and the Thornguards backed away. Heart pounding, I pressed close to Ash and Puck, feeling their grim determination, their resolve to go down fighting no matter what. The air started to vibrate, a terrible buzzing filling the air, and Virus threw her head back. With the droning of a million bees, a huge swarm of metal bugs spiraled up from Virus's mouth, swirling around her in a frantic glittering cloud.

Her smile was savage as she looked down at us, extending a hand from the center of the buzzing tornado. "Now, my dears," she said, barely audible over the droning of a thousand bugs, "we will end this little game once and for all. I should have done this when I first saw you, but I had no idea you were the one I was searching for all along."

Everything grew very still. The cold glamour still buzzed beneath my skin, and I could taste metal on the air. I looked at the swarm and saw thousands of individual bugs, but also a single creature sharing one mind, one goal, one purpose.

A hive mind, I thought impassively, not knowing why I felt so calm. *Control one, and you control them all.*

Vaguely, I was aware that Virus was speaking, her voice seeming to come from very far away.

"Go," she screamed, sweeping her arm toward us. "Crawl down their throats and nostrils, into their eyes and ears and every open pore. Burrow into their brains and make them tear out their own hearts!"

The Swarm flew toward us, a furious, buzzing cloud. Ash and Puck pressed close; I felt one of them shaking but couldn't tell who. A droning filled my ears as the Swarm approached, glowing bright with iron glamour, melded into a single massive entity.

One mind. One creature.

I threw up both my hands as the Swarm dove forward to attack,

Stop!

The Swarm broke apart, swirling around us, filling the air with their deafening buzz. But they didn't attack. We stood in the middle of the screaming hurricane, metal bugs zipping around us frantically but moving no closer.

I felt the Swarm straining against my will, fighting to get past it. I saw Virus's face, first slack with disbelief, then white with fury. She made a violent gesture, and the Swarm buzzed angrily in response. I strengthened my hold, pouring magic into the invisible barrier, drawing glamour from the factory. My head pounded, and sweat ran into my eyes, but I couldn't break my concentration or we'd be torn apart.

Virus smiled nastily. "I have underestimated you, Meghan Chase," she said, rising higher into the air. "I did not think you would force me to use the scepter, but there you go. Do you know what this does, my dear?" she asked, holding it out before her. Ash looked up sharply. "It took me forever to puzzle it out, but I finally got it." She grinned, triumphant. "It enhances the power of the one who holds it. Isn't that interesting? So, for instance, I could make my darling bugs do this…"

The scepter glowed a sickly green, and in that light, the Swarm started to change. They swelled like ticks full of blood, becoming sharp and spiky, with long stingers and huge curved jaws. Now they were the size of my fist, a horrible cross between a wasp and a scorpion, and their wings scraped against each other like a million knives. And their *minds* changed, to something more savage, more visceral and predatory. I nearly lost my hold on them, and the whirlwind tightened, pressing closer to us, before I regained control and pushed them back.

Buzzing furiously, they turned on whatever living thing they could reach, including the guards surrounding us. The Thornguards screamed, reeling back and clawing at themselves as the metal bugs swarmed over them, biting and stinging, burrowing into their armor.

Virus giggled madly overhead. "Kill them!" she cried, as several bugs chewed their way into their victims, who fell thrashing and screaming to the ground. My stomach heaved, but I couldn't look away for fear of losing control of the Swarm. I didn't know what Virus thought she was doing until a moment later, when the Thornguards lurched to their feet again, crazed gleams in their eyes.

Raising their swords, they staggered toward us, blood pouring from their wounds and the holes in their armor, their eyes empty of reason. Ash and Puck met them at the edge of the whirlwind, and the clash of weapons joined the metallic drone of the Swarm.

We were lost. I couldn't keep this up forever. My head throbbed so much that I felt nauseous, and my arms were shaking violently. I could feel my strength draining with the amount of glamour I was using to keep the Swarm at bay.

Out of the corner of my eye, I saw a Thornguard, covered in bugs, stagger to the edge of the platform and pick up a crossbow. Raising it up, he loaded an iron bolt and swung it around at me. I couldn't move. If I dodged, the Swarm would break free and kill us. Puck and Ash were busy fighting off the other guards and couldn't help. I couldn't even shout a warning. In slow motion, I watched him raise the crossbow, unhindered, and take aim.

Later, I remembered the clanging footsteps charging up the steps only because they seemed so out of place. I saw Puck whirl around, saw his dagger whip out and soar end over end toward the Thornguard, just as he pulled the trigger. The dagger thunked into the guard's chest, hurling him off the mezzanine, but it was too late. The bolt was coming toward me, and I couldn't do anything about it.

Something huge and black lunged across my vision a split second before the bolt hit home. Ironhorse, covered in bugs and shedding chunks of iron everywhere, stumbled, fighting desperately to stay on his feet. He staggered toward the edge of the overhang, shaking his head as bugs swarmed him viciously. A hoof slipped off the edge, and he lurched sideways.

"No!" I screamed.

With a last defiant bellow and blast of flame, Ironhorse toppled from the edge, vanishing from sight. I heard his body strike the cement with a resounding boom that echoed through the building, and my vision went white with rage.

I arched my back, clenching my fists, and glamour rushed through me, exploding out in a wave. *"GET BACK!"* I roared at the Swarm, at Virus, at every Iron faery in the room. *"Damn you all! Back off, NOW!"*

The Swarm flew in every direction, scattering to all four corners of the room. The Thornguards flinched and stumbled backward; some even fell off the edge of the railing. Even Virus jerked in midair, reeling back like she had been sucker punched, her hands falling limply at her sides.

I slumped to the floor, all the strength going out of me. As the Swarm began coalescing again, buzzing angrily as they swarmed back together, and the Thornguards regained their senses, Virus put a hand to her temple and looked down at me, a smug grin stretching her blue lips.

"Well, Meghan Chase. Congratulations, you've managed to give me a pounding headache. But it is not enough to—aaaahhhhhh!"

She jerked, throwing up her hands as Ash launched himself off the edge of the railing and leaped at her, sword raised high. Still screaming, she tried to bring up the scepter, too late. The ice blade sliced down, through her collarbone and out the other side, cutting her clean in two.

If I wasn't so dizzy, I might've puked. Virus's halves fell away, wires and oily goo spilling from her severed body as both she and Ash dropped out of sight.

The Thornguards spasmed, then collapsed like puppets with cut strings. As I sat there, dazed by what had just happened, Puck hauled me upright and dragged me under a beam. Then it started raining insects.

The clatter of metal bugs brought me back to my senses. "Ash," I muttered, struggling to free myself. Puck wrapped his arms around me and held me to his chest. "I have to go to him...see if he's all right."

"He's fine, Princess," Puck snapped, tightening his grip. "Relax. He knows enough to get out of the rain."

I relented. Closing my eyes, I leaned into him, resting my head on his chest as the bugs clattered around us like glittering hail. He hugged me close, muttering something about Egyptian plagues, but I wasn't listening. My head hurt, and I was still trying to process everything that had just happened. I was so tired, but at least it was over. And we had survived.

Or, most of us had.

"Ironhorse," I whispered as the rain of bugs finally came to an end. I felt Puck tense. Freeing myself from his arms, I stumbled across the mezzanine, taking care to avoid the dead bugs and Thornguards, and groped my way down the stairs. I didn't know what I'd find, but I was hopeful. Ironhorse couldn't be dead. He was the strongest of us all. He might be terribly hurt, and we'd have to find someone to put him back together, but Ironhorse was near invincible. He had to have survived. He had to.

I'd almost convinced myself not to worry when Ash stepped out from beneath the overhang and stood at the foot of the stairs, gazing up at me. His sword was sheathed, and in one hand, the Scepter of the Seasons pulsed with a clean blue light.

For a long moment, we stared at each other, unwilling to break the silence, to voice what we both were thinking. I wondered if Ash would take the scepter and leave. Our contract was done. He had what he came for; there was no reason for him to stick around any longer.

"So." I broke the silence first, trying to quell the tremor in my voice, the stupid tears that pressed behind my eyes once more. "Are you leaving now?"

"Soon." His voice was calm but tired. "I'll be returning to Winter, but I thought I would pay my respects to the fallen before I go."

My stomach dropped. I looked behind him and saw, for the first time, the pile of mangled iron in the shadows of the mezzanine. With a gasp, I lurched down the rest of the stairs, pushed past Ash, and half ran, half stumbled to where Ironhorse lay surrounded by dead bugs and the smoking remains of Virus.

"Ironhorse?" For a split second, I thought I saw Grimalkin there, sitting at his head. But I blinked back tears and the image was gone. Ironhorse lay on his side, heaving with great raspy breaths, the fires in his belly burning low. One of his legs was shattered, and huge chunks of his body had been ripped away. Pistons and gears were scattered around him like broken clockwork.

I knelt beside his head, putting a shaking hand on his neck. It was cold, and his once burning red eyes were dim, flickering erratically. At my touch, he stirred, but didn't raise his head or look at me. I had a horrid suspicion he couldn't see any of us.

"Princess?"

Hearing his voice, so small and breathy, almost made me burst into tears. "I'm so sorry," I whispered, feeling Puck and Ash press behind me, gazing over my shoulder.

"No." The red in his eyes dimmed to tiny pinpricks, and his voice dropped to a whisper. I had to strain to hear him. "It was…an honor…" He sighed one last time, as the tiny spots of light flickered once, twice. "…my queen." And he was gone.

I closed my eyes and let the tears come. For Ironhorse, who had never wavered, never once compromised his beliefs or convictions. Who had been an enemy, but chose to become an ally, a guardian and, ultimately, a friend. I knelt on the cold tile and sobbed, unembarrassed, as Puck and Ash looked on gravely, until the faint rays of dawn began seeping through the broken skylights.

"Meghan." Ash's quiet voice broke through my grieving. "We should go." His tone was gentle but unrelenting. "The Iron King's army is ready to march. We have to return the scepter. There's not much time left."

I sat up and wiped my eyes, cursing the damned faeries and their eternal war. It seemed there was never enough time. Time to dance, or talk, or laugh, or even mourn the passing of a friend. Slipping off my corsage, I laid it on Ironhorse's cold metal shoulder, wanting him to have something natural and beautiful in this lifeless place. *Goodbye, Ironhorse.* Ash held out a hand, and I let him pull me to my feet.

"Where to now?" I sniffled.

"The Reaping Fields," answered a familiar voice, and Grimalkin appeared, perched several feet away on a cardboard box. He gingerly batted a metal bug off the surface, where it pinged to the floor, before continuing. "All the major battles between the courts have been fought on those plains. If I were looking for the armies of Summer and Winter, that is where I would go."

"Are you sure?" I asked.

"I did not say I was sure, human." Grimalkin twitched his whiskers at me. "I only said that is where I would look. Also, I am not coming with you."

Somehow, this didn't surprise me. "Why not? Where are you going this time?"

"Back to Leanansidhe's." Grimalkin yawned and stretched, arching his tail over his back. "Now that we are done here, I will inform her that Virus is dead, and that the scepter is on its way back to the Winter Court. I am sure she will want to hear about your success." The cat turned, waving his tail in farewell. "Until next time, human."

"Grim, wait."

He paused, looking back with unblinking golden eyes.

"What did Ironhorse promise you, that made you come along?"

He flicked his tail. "It is not for you to know, human," he replied, his voice low and solemn. "Perhaps you will find out, someday. Oh, and if you do make it to Reaping Field, look for a friend of mine. He still owes me a favor. I believe you have met him before." And with that cryptic message, he leaped off

the box and wove gracefully through the scattered hordes of
fey and metal bugs. Trotting behind a beam, he disappeared.

I looked at the boys. "How will we get to Reaping Field?"

Ash held up the scepter. It throbbed with icy blue light,
sparkling like it was made of crystal, as I'd first seen it back
in Tir Na Nog. "I'll use the scepter to open a trod," he murmured, turning away. "Stand back."

The scepter flared, filling the room with cold, making my
breath steam. The air around us shimmered, as though a veil
had been dropped over everything. A hazy circle opened up
in front of Ash; beyond it, I saw trees and earth and the foggy
twilight of the wyldwood.

"Go," Ash told us, his voice slightly strained.

"Come on, Princess. This is our stop." Puck gestured at
the portal, waiting for me to go through. I turned and cast
one final look at Ironhorse's body, lying cold on the cement,
and blinked back tears.

Thank you, I told him silently, and stepped through the
circle.

CHAPTER TWENTY-THREE

Reaping Fields

The wyldwood was in chaos. Wind and hail whipped around me as I stumbled off the trod, screaming through the branches and pelting me with shards of ice. Green lightning streaked overhead, slashing through massive clouds that roiled and churned above us, shaking branches and stirring debris into violent whirlwinds. Gouts of snow intermingled with the rain, gathering in mounds and drifts and then scattered by the wind. A violet-skinned piskie went hurtling by, caught in a savage tailspin, until she vanished into the trees.

"Dammit." Puck appeared behind me, crimson hair flying in all directions. He had to shout to be heard. "They started the war without us. I had an invitation, too."

Ash stepped through the circle, and it closed behind him. "Reaping Field is close." He raised his head to the wind, closing his eyes, and his brow furrowed. "The fighting is well underway. I can smell the blood. Follow me."

We hurried through the forest, Ash in front leading the way, the scepter a bright blue glow against the dark of the wyld-wood. Around us, the storm raged and howled, and thunder boomed overhead, shaking the ground. My shoes sank into the mud, and my gown snagged on a dozen thorns and branches that tore through the fabric and ripped what remained to shreds.

Finally, the trees fell away, leaving us staring over a vast, icy gulley flanked by rugged hills, their tops disappearing into the clouds. A frozen river snaked its way through the boulder-studded valley, coiling lazily around the ruins of an ancient castle in the center of the plains.

From here, the armies of Summer and Winter looked like swarming ants, a huge, chaotic blur of motion and color. Roars and screams filled the air, rising above the howl of the wind. Ranks of soldiers clashed against one another in a somewhat disciplined fashion, while other groups bounded across the field, ricocheting from one fight to the next, joyfully hurling themselves into the fray. Giant shapes lumbered through the masses, swinging and crushing, and swarms of flying creatures attacked from the air. It was a colossal, violent, crazy free-for-all that would be suicide to go through.

I gulped and looked to Ash and Puck. "We're going through that, aren't we?"

Ash nodded. "Look for Oberon or Mab," he said grimly, scanning the battlefield. "They'll likely be on opposite sides of the river. Try not to engage anything, Goodfellow. We don't want a fight—we just want to get the scepter to the queen."

"Don't kid yourself, Prince." Puck grinned and drew his daggers, pointing to Ash with the tip. "You're a traitor, Meghan's the Summer princess, and I'm Robin Goodfellow. I'm sure the ranks of Unseelie will just let us waltz right through."

And then, a shadow fell over us, and a blast of wind nearly knocked me down. Ash shoved me away as a huge, winged lizard landed where I'd stood in an explosion of snow and rock. The creature hissed and shrieked, beating tattered wings and churning the ground with two clawed forelegs. Its scales were a dusty brown, its yellow eyes vicious and stupid. A long, muscular tail whipped the air behind it, a wicked, gleaming barb on the end. Hissing, it stepped between me, Ash and Puck, separating us with its body, coiling its tail over its back like a massive scorpion.

A rider sat between the creature's shoulder blades, his white armor pristine and shining, not a drop of blood on him.

"Rowan!" I gasped.

"Well, well." The older prince sneered at me from the back of his lizard mount. "Here you are again. The wayward princess and our traitor prince. Don't move, Ash," he warned, shooting his brother a dark look. "One tiny move, and Thraxa will snap up your beloved half-breed faster than you can blink. You don't want to lose *another* girl to wyvern poison, do you?"

Ash already had his sword out, but at Rowan's threat he paled and shot me a haunted look. I saw the desperation in his eyes before he lowered his blade and stepped back.

"Good boy. This will be over soon, don't worry." Rowan raised his fist, and a dozen Thornguards emerged from the trees, weapons drawn, trapping us between them and Rowan. "It shouldn't be long now." The older prince smiled. "Once the courts are done tearing each other to pieces, the Iron King's armies will sweep in, and everything will be over.

"But first," he continued, turning to glare at Ash, "I'll need that scepter. Hand it over, little brother."

Ash tensed, but before he could do anything, Puck stepped between us, an evil grin stretching his face. "Come and get it," he challenged. Rowan looked over and sneered.

"Robin Goodfellow." He smiled. "I've heard so much about you. You're the reason Ariella is dead, aren't you?" Puck frowned, but Rowan went on without pause. "A pity Ash won't ever take his revenge, but believe me when I say this will be a pleasure. Thraxa," he ordered, sweeping his arm contemptuously toward Puck. "Kill."

The wyvern hissed and snaked its head down, baring needle sharp fangs. It was frighteningly quick, like a viper, and its jaws snapped shut over Puck's head.

I gasped, but Puck exploded in a swirl of leaves, leaving the wyvern blinking and confused. As it drew back, huffing and scanning the ground for its victim, a huge black raven swooped out of the trees, aiming right for its face. With a screeching caw, the bird sank its talons into the side of the wyvern's head and plunged its sharp beak into the slitted yellow eye.

The wyvern reared back with a scream, beating its wings and shaking its head, trying to dislodge the bird that clung to it. Rowan, nearly thrown from the saddle, cursed and yanked at the reins, trying to regain control, but the wyvern was panicked now, screeching and thrashing about in anguish. I ducked beneath the monster and ran to Ash, who caught me in an almost desperate hug, even as he kept his eyes on Rowan. I felt his heart racing beneath his coat.

The raven hung on, jabbing and clawing, until black ichor spattered the wyvern's face and the eye was a popped, useless mess. With a caw of triumph, it broke away and swooped back to us, changing to Puck in an explosion of feathers. He was still laughing as he rose to his feet, drawing his weapons with a flourish.

"Kill them!" Rowan screamed, as his mount decided it had had enough, and leaped skyward. "Kill them all and get that scepter! Don't let them ruin everything!"

"Stay back," Ash told me as the Thornguards started forward, closing their deadly half circle. There were a lot of them, seeming to melt out of the trees and bramble, more than I first thought. My eyes fell on Ash, holding both the scepter and his sword in a double-weapon stance. Could I just take the scepter and run? I shot a quick glance down the slope, into the valley, and my heart went cold with fear. No way. There was no way I'd get through that churning mass alive.

Lightning flickered, bright and eerie, and between one flash and the next, a white creature appeared at the edge of the slope. At first, I thought it was a horse. Only it was smaller and more graceful than any I'd seen before, more deer than equine, with a lion's tail and cloven hooves that barely touched the ground. Its horn spiraled up between its ears, beautiful and terrible at the same time, destroying any preconceived notions I had of the word *unicorn*. It regarded me with eyes as ancient as the forest, and I felt a shiver of recognition, like a memory from a dream, but then it was gone.

Grimalkin sent me. The voice whispered in my head, soft as a feather's passing. *Hurry, Meghan Chase.* With a toss of its head, the unicorn turned and vanished down the slope. In that moment, I knew what I had to do.

That whole encounter seemed to have taken place in an instant. When I turned back to the boys, they were still waiting for the Thornguards, who approached slowly, as if they knew we weren't going anywhere. "Ash," I murmured, placing a hand on his arm. "Give me the scepter."

He shot me a look over his shoulder. "What?"

"I'll get it to Mab. Just hold them off until I can get across the field." Ash stared at me, his expression torn. I closed my hand over the scepter, gritting my teeth as the cold burned like fire. "I can do this."

"Hey, Prince," Puck called over his shoulder, "uh, you can join in anytime, now. Whenever you're ready."

A shriek echoed over the valley, and a dark shape wheeled toward us on leathery wings. Rowan was coming back.

"Ash!" The Thornguards were almost upon us, and Ash still held the scepter tightly. Desperately, I met his eyes, saw the indecision there, the doubt, and the fear that he was sending me to my death. "Ash," I whispered, and put my other hand over his, "you have to trust me."

He shivered, nodded once, and released his grip. Clutching the scepter, I backed away, holding his worried gaze as the Thornguards got closer and the wail of the wyvern echoed over the trees. "Be careful," he said, a storm of emotion in those two simple words. I nodded breathlessly.

"I won't fail," I promised.

The Thornguards charged with a roar. Ash spun toward them, blade flashing, as Puck gave a whooping battle cry and plunged into their midst. Feeling the scepter burn in my hands, I turned and fled down the slope.

The unicorn waited at the bottom of the hill, almost invisible in the mist, its horn more real than the rest of it. My heart pounded as I approached. Even though the unicorn stood perfectly still, watching me, it was akin to walking up to a tiger that was tame and friendly, but still a tiger. It could either kneel and lay its head in my lap, or explode into violence and skewer me with that glimmering horn. Thankfully it did neither, standing motionless as a statue as I walked up close enough to see my reflection in its dark eyes. *What do I say? Do I have to ask permission to get on its back?*

A piercing wail rent the air above us, and the shadow of the wyvern passed overhead. The unicorn jumped, flattening its ears, trembling with the effort not to bolt. *Screw it, I don't have time!* As the wyvern's howl rang out again, I heaved my-self awkwardly onto the unicorn's back and grabbed its mane.

As soon as I was settled, the unicorn made a fantastic leap over the rocks and landed at the edge of the icy field, making my stomach lodge in my throat. For a moment, it hesitated, looking this way and that, trying to find an easier way in. A red-eyed hound sprang at us with a snarl, tongue lolling. The unicorn leaped nimbly aside, lashing out with its hooves. I heard a crack and a yelp, and the hound fled into the mist on three legs.

"There's no time to go around!" I yelled, hoping the uni-corn could understand me. "Mab is on the far side of the river! We have to go straight through!"

A bellow sounded behind us. I glanced back to see the wyvern dive from the slope and glide toward the ground, straight for us. I saw Rowan on the wyvern's back, sword drawn, his furious gaze fixed on me, and my stomach clenched in terror. "Go!" I shrieked, and with a desperate whinny, we plunged into the heart of the battle.

The unicorn bounded through the chaos, dodging weap-ons, leaping over obstacles, moving with terrifying speed. My hand gripped the mane so hard that my arm shook; the other hand burned with the scepter. Around us, Summer and Winter fey tore and slashed at each other, screaming in fury, pain and pure, joyful bloodlust. I caught flashes of the battle as we sped through. A pair of trolls pounded stone clubs into a swarm of goblins, their shoulders and backs bristling with spears. A trio of redcaps dragged a wailing sylph from the air, ignoring the razor edge of her dragonfly wings, and buried her under their stabbing knives. Seelie knights in green and gold armor clashed swords with Unseelie warriors, their movements so graceful it looked like they were dancing, but their unearthly beauty was twisted with hate.

The roar of the wyvern sounded directly above us, and the unicorn leaped aside so quickly I nearly lost my seat. I saw the wyvern's hooked, grasping talons slam into a dwarf, and the bearded man screamed as he was torn away and lifted into the air, struggling weakly. The wyvern soared upward, and I watched in horror as it dropped the still struggling dwarf to the rocks below. Wheeling in a lazy circle, it came for us again.

My mount started weaving, a frantic, zigzag pattern that jostled me from side to side and made me sick with fear. I pressed my knees into the unicorn's sides so hard that I felt its ribs through my gown. The wyvern wavered in the air, confused, then dove with another chilling wail. My nimble steed dodged once more, but this time the wyvern passed so close I could've slapped its claws with the back of my hand.

We were in the middle of the field, still nowhere near the river, when the unicorn went down.

The fighting was thicker in the center of the battleground, where soldiers from both sides clashed together over the dead and the dying. The unicorn darted between the crowds, seeming to know exactly when a hole would open up, slipping through without slowing down. But Rowan was still on our tail. As the unicorn dodged the wyvern's pass for the third time, a huge, rocklike monster reared up from beneath the snow, swiping at us with a massive club. It clipped the unicorn's front legs, and the graceful animal collapsed with a shrill whinny. I went flying off its back and hit a snowbank with a landing that drove the air from my lungs.

Dazed, I lay there as the world spun like a carousel, flickering in and out of view. Blurred, shadowy figures raged around me, screaming, but the sounds were muffled and distorted, coming from a great distance away.

Then the white shape of the unicorn reared up, pawing the air, slashing with its horn, before it was pulled under the black mass. I pushed myself to my knees, calling out to it, but my arms shook, and I collapsed, sobbing in frustration. Once more, the unicorn reared up, its white coat streaked with crimson, several dark things clinging to its back. I cried out, crawling forward desperately, but with a shrill cry, the unicorn disappeared into the churning mass once more. This time, it didn't resurface.

As I gasped for breath, fighting tears, something wet and slimy dripped onto my arm. I looked up into the warty face of a goblin, its crooked teeth slick with drool as it grinned at me, flicking a pale tongue over its lips.

"Tasty girl dead yet?" it asked, poking my arm with the butt of its spear.

I lurched upright. Nausea surged through me and the ground twirled. I concentrated on not passing out. The goblin scuttled back with a hiss, then edged forward again. I frantically gazed around for a weapon, and saw the scepter, lying in the snow a few feet away.

The goblin grinned, raising its spear, then vanished under several tons of wyvern as the monstrous lizard landed on it with a boom that shook the ground, sending snow flying. Roaring, it reared back to strike, and I lunged for the scepter.

My hand closed over the rod, and a jolt of electricity shot up my arm. I felt the wyvern's hot breath on my neck and rolled back, bringing up the scepter. In that split second, I saw the gaping, tooth-filled maw of the wyvern fill my whole vision, and the scepter in my hand glowing, not blue or gold or green, but a pure, blinding white.

Lightning shot from the rod, slamming into the wyvern's open mouth. The blast flung the lizard's head back, filling the air with the stench of charred flesh. At the same time, I felt something inside me break, like a hammer striking glass, shattering into a million pieces. Sound, color and emotion flooded my mind, a bottled-up wave of glamour pouring outward, and I screamed.

A pulse ripped through the air, flying outward. It knocked the nearest fighters off their feet and continued, spreading across the field. Fighting a wave of dizziness, I staggered to my feet, swaying like a drunk sailor in a torn and filthy gown. I couldn't see Mab or Oberon through the indistinct shadows around me, but I did see hundreds of glowing eyes, shining blades and bared teeth, ready to tear me apart. I certainly had everyone's attention now.

The scepter pulsed in my hand. Gripping the handle, I raised it over my head. A flickering light spilled over the crowd, making them mutter and draw back.

"Where is Queen Mab?" I called, my voice reedy and faint, barely rising above the howl of the wind. No one answered, so I tried again. "My name is Meghan Chase, daughter of Lord Oberon. I am here to return the Scepter of the Seasons." I hoped someone told Mab quickly; I didn't know how much longer I could stay conscious, much less speak in coherent sentences in front of the queen.

Slowly, the crowd parted, and the air around us dropped several degrees, making my breath steam before my face. Mab came through the crowd on a huge white warhorse, her gown trailing behind her, her hair unbound and flowing down her back. The horse's hooves didn't quite touch the ground, and great gouts of steam billowed from its nostrils, wreathing the Winter Queen in a ghostly halo of fog. Her lips and nails were blue, her eyes as black as a starless night as she peered down at me.

"Meghan Chase." The queen's voice was a hiss, her perfect features terrifyingly blank. Her gaze flicked to the rod in my hand, and she smiled, cold and dangerous. "I see you have my scepter. So, is the Summer Court finally admitting their mistake?"

"No," came a strong voice before I could answer. "The Summer Court had nothing to do with stealing the scepter. You are the one who jumped to conclusions, Lady Mab."

And Oberon was there, sweeping through the crowd on a golden-bay stallion, flanked by a squad of elven knights. His faery mail glittered emerald and gold, bright links woven around protrusions of bark and bone, and an antlered helm rose above his head.

I felt a surge of relief at seeing him, but it shriveled when the Erlking looked at me, his green eyes cold and remote. "I told you before, Queen Mab," he said, speaking to Mab but still glaring at me, "I knew nothing of this, nor did I send my people to steal the scepter from you. You have started a war with us over a false pretense."

"So you say." Mab gave me a predatory smile, making me feel like a trapped rabbit. "But, it seems the Summer Court is still at fault, Erlking. You might have known nothing of the scepter, but your daughter admits her guilt by trying to return what is mine, hoping perhaps, that I will be merciful. Is that not correct, Meghan Chase?"

I noticed crowds of both Winter and Summer fey edging back from the rulers, and wished I could do the same. "No," I blurted out, feeling the glare of both rulers burning holes through my skull. "I mean…no, I didn't steal it."

"Lies!" Mab leaped from her warhorse and stalking toward

me. The mad gleam was back, and my stomach contracted in fear. "You are a filthy human, and all you speak is lies. You turned Ash against me. You made him fight his own brother. You fled Tir Na Nog and sought sanctuary with the exile Leanansidhe. Is this not true, Meghan Chase?"

"Yes, but—"

"You were in the throne room when my son was murdered. Why did they let you live? How did you survive, if it was not the Summer Court behind it all?"

"I told you—"

"If you did not steal the Scepter of the Seasons, who did?"

"The Iron fey!" I shouted, as my temper finally snapped. Not the smartest move, but I was hurt, dizzy, exhausted, and could still see the body of Ironhorse, sprawled lifelessly on the cement, the unicorn torn apart before my eyes. After everything we'd done, everything we'd gone through, to have some faery bitch accuse me of lying was the last straw. "I'm not lying, dammit!" I screamed at her. "Stop talking and just listen to me! The Iron fey stole the scepter and killed Sage! I was right there when it happened! There's an army of them out there, and they're getting ready to attack! That's why they stole the scepter! They wanted you to kill each other before they came in and wiped out everything!"

Mab's eyes went glassy and terrifying, and she raised her hand. I figured I was dead. You don't shout at a faery queen and expect to walk away scot-free. But Oberon finally stepped forward, interrupting Mab before she could turn me into a Popsicle. "Hold, Lady Mab," he said in a low voice. The Winter Queen turned her mad, killing glare on him, but he faced her calmly. "Just a moment, please. She is my daughter, after all." He gave me a measuring look. "Meghan Chase, please return the scepter to Lady Mab, and let us be done with this."

Gladly. I approached Mab and held out the scepter in both hands, anxious to be rid of the stupid thing. For all its power, it seemed such a small, trivial item, to cause so much hate and confusion and death. For a moment, the Winter Queen stared at me, her features cold and blank, letting me sweat. Finally, and with great dignity, she reached out and took the scepter, and a great sigh of relief spread across the battlefield. It was done. The Scepter of the Seasons was back where it belonged, and the war was over.

"Now, Meghan Chase," Oberon said as the ripple died down, "why don't you tell us everything that happened?"

So I did, summarizing as best I could. I told them about Tertius stealing the scepter and killing Sage. I told them about the Thornguards, and how they wanted to become Iron fey themselves. I described Grimalkin leading us through the Briars, and how we met Leanansidhe, who agreed to help us. And finally, I told them about Virus, her plans to invade the Nevernever, and how we were able to track her down and get the scepter back.

I left out the parts with Ironhorse. Despite his help and noble sacrifice, they would only see him as the enemy, and I didn't want to be accused of guilt by association. When I was done, an incredulous silence hung in the air, and for a moment only the wind could be heard, howling over the plains.

"Impossible." Mab's voice was chilly, but it had lost the crazy edge, at least. My handing over the scepter seemed to placate her for now. "How did they get into the palace, and out again, without anyone seeing them?"

"Ask Rowan," I shot back, and a mutter went through the ranks of surrounding fey. "He's working with them."

Mab went absolutely still. Goose bumps rose along my arms as ice began creeping over the ground, snapping and crinkling, spreading out from the feet of the Winter Queen. When she spoke, her voice was soft, almost a whisper, but it scared me more than when she was crazy and shouting. "What did you say, half-breed?"

I glanced at Oberon, but he looked disbelieving, as well. I could feel his patience and support wearing thin; if I was going to accuse a son of Mab's of treason, I'd better be able to prove it. Else he wouldn't be able to protect me much longer.

"Rowan is working with the Iron fey," I repeated, as the ice spread around me, sparkling in the snow. "Him and the Thornguards. They...they want to become like them, immune to iron. They think—"

"Enough!" Mab's shriek made everyone but Oberon flinch. "Where is your proof, half-breed? Do not expect me to accept these blasphemous claims without proof—you are a human and can lie so easily! You say my son has betrayed his court and kin, to side with these iron abominations that none have seen? Very well! Show me proof!" She pointed a finger at me, eyes narrowed in triumph. "If you have none, you are guilty of slandering the royal family, and I will punish you as I see fit!"

"I don't—" But the sounds of a struggle interrupted us. The crowds shifted, looking around, then stepped out of the way as a trio of faeries came through. Ash and Puck, bleeding, grim faced and dirty, dragging the spiky frame of a Thornguard between them. Staggering into the circle, they threw the faery at Mab's feet.

Panting, Puck straightened, wiping blood from his mouth with the back of his hand. "There's your proof."

Oberon raised an eyebrow. "Goodfellow," he said, and that one word sent shivers down my spine and made Puck wince. "What is the meaning of this?"

Mab smiled. "Ash," she purred, but it wasn't a friendly

greeting. "What a surprise to find you here, in the company of the Summer girl and Robin Goodfellow. Would you care to add anything more to your list of crimes?"

"My queen." Ash stood before Mab, breathing heavily, his expression bleak and resigned. "The princess speaks the truth. Rowan is a traitor to us. He sent his elite guard to bolster the armies of the Iron fey, he allowed them access into the palace, and he is responsible for the death of Prince Sage. Were it not for Robin Goodfellow and the Summer princess, the scepter would be lost, and the armies of the Iron King would overwhelm us." Mab narrowed her eyes, and Ash stepped back, nodding to the moaning Thornguard. "If you doubt my word, my queen, just ask him for the truth. I'm sure he would be happy to tell you everything."

"Screw it," Puck snapped, stalking past me. "Or you could just do this."

He pounced on the guard, driving his knee into the faery's armored chest. The Thornguard's arms came up to protect himself, and Puck grabbed one of his gauntlets, ripping the glove away and holding up his wrist.

The sharp tang of metal filled the air, and the circle of curious onlookers leaped back with cries of horror. The Thornguard's entire hand was blackened and shriveled, the skin flaking off like ash. And on his long, gnarled finger, the iron ring gleamed brightly against the withered flesh.

"There!" Puck snapped, throwing the arm down and stepping away. "That proof enough for you? Every one of these bastards has one of those rings on, and it's not a fashion statement. If you want more proof, check the brambles at the top of the hill. We left this one alive to explain his little coup ambitions to his queen."

Mab turned her cold, cold gaze on the Thornguard, who cringed and started babbling.

"My queen, I can explain. Rowan ordered us to. I was acting on his command. He said it was the only way to save us. Please, I never wanted to...please, no!"

Mab gestured. There was a flash of blue light, and ice covered the guard, encasing him in frozen crystal. He drew a breath for one last scream, but the ice closed over his face and smothered it. I shivered and looked away.

"He will tell me everything later." Mab smiled coldly, speaking more to herself than to us. "Oh, yes. He will be begging to tell me." She looked up, her eyes as terrible as her voice. "Where is Rowan?"

As the crowds began muttering and looking around, I glanced over at the dead wyvern lying several yards away, smoke still curling from its open mouth. I shivered and turned away, already knowing the answer. Rowan was gone. They wouldn't find him in the Nevernever; he would flee to the Iron fey, continuing his quest to become like them.

After a long moment, it became clear that Rowan was no longer on the field. "Lady Mab," Oberon said, drawing himself up. "In light of this newest revelation, I propose a temporary truce. If the Iron King does plan to attack us, I'd prefer to meet him with my forces strong and ready. We will speak on this later, but for now I will be taking my people back to Arcadia. Meghan, Goodfellow." He nodded to us stiffly. "Come."

I looked at Ash, and he gave me a faint smile. I saw the relief on his face. But Mab wasn't about to let me go just yet. "Not so fast, my dear Oberon," she purred, and the smug satisfaction in her voice made my skin crawl. "I believe you are forgetting something. The laws of our people apply to your daughter, as well. She must answer for turning my son against me." Mab pointed the scepter at me as angry murmurs went through the crowd. "She must be punished for tricking him into helping her escape Tir Na Nog."

"That wasn't Meghan's decision." Ash's deep voice cut through the muttering. I looked at him sharply and shook my head, but he ignored me. "It was mine. I made the choice. She had nothing to do with it."

Mab turned to him, and her gaze softened. Smiling, she crooked a finger, and he approached at once, never wavering, though his hands were clenched at his sides. "Ash," Mab crooned as he drew near. "My poor boy. Rowan told me what happened between the two of you, but I know you had your reasons. Why would you betray me?"

"I love her."

Softly, and without hesitation, as if he'd already made up his mind. My heart turned over and I gasped, but it was lost in the ripple of horror and disbelief that went through the crowd. Whispers and muttering filled the air; some faeries snarled and hissed, baring their teeth, as if they wanted to mob Ash, but kept their distance from the queen.

Mab didn't look surprised, though the smile curling her lips was as cold and cruel as a blade. "You love her. The half-breed daughter of the Summer lord."

"Yes."

I ached for him, my stomach twisting painfully. He looked so desolate standing there alone, facing a mad queen and several thousand angry fey. His voice was flat and resigned, as if he'd been pushed into a corner and had given up, not caring what happened next. I started to go to him, but Puck grabbed my arm, his green eyes solemn as he shook his head.

"Ash." Mab placed a palm on his cheek. "You're confused. I can see it in your eyes. You didn't want this, did you? Not

after Ariella." Ash didn't reply, and Mab drew back, regarding him intently. "You know what comes next, don't you?"

Ash nodded once. "I swear an oath," he whispered, "never
to see her again, never to speak to her again, to sever all rela-
tionships and return to the Winter Court."

"Yes," Mab whispered back, and a sick despair tore at my
heart. If Ash spoke those words, it would be over. A faery
couldn't break a promise, even if he wanted to. "Swear the
oath," Mab continued, "and all is forgiven. You can come back
to Tir Na Nog. Return to the palace, and take your place as
heir to the throne. Sage is gone, and Rowan is dead to me."
Mab placed a kiss on Ash's cheek and stepped back. "You are
the last prince of Winter. It is time to come home."

"I..." For the first time, Ash hesitated. His gaze met mine,
bright and anguished, begging forgiveness. I choked on a sob
and turned away, my throat aching with misery, not wanting to hear the words that would take him from me forever.

"I can't."

Silence fell over the field. Puck stiffened; I could feel his
shock. Biting my lip, I turned back, hardly daring to believe.
Ash faced Mab calmly, the queen staring at him with a terrible, blank expression on her face. "Forgive me," Ash murmured, and I heard the faintest of tremors beneath his voice.
"But I can't...I won't...give her up. Not now, when I've just
found her."

I couldn't take it anymore. Breaking away from Puck,
I started toward Ash. I couldn't let him do this alone. But
Oberon stepped in front of me, holding out his arm, as un-
movable as a mountain. "Do not interfere, daughter," Oberon
said in a voice meant only for me. "This is between the Winter prince and his queen. Let the song play to its conclusion."

Distraught, I looked back to Ash. Mab had gone very still,

a beautiful, deadly statue, the ground beneath her coated with ice. Only her lips moved as she stared at her son, the air around them growing colder by the second. "You know what will happen, if you refuse."

If Ash was afraid, he didn't show it. "I know," he said in a weary voice.

"Their world will eat at you," Mab said. "Strip you away bit by bit. Cut off from the Nevernever, you will not survive. Whether it takes one mortal year or a thousand, you will gradually fade away, until you simply cease to exist." Mab stepped closer, pointing at me with the scepter. "She will die, Ash. She is only human. She will grow old, wither and die, and her soul will flee to a place you cannot follow. And then, you will be left to wander the mortal world alone, until you yourself are only a memory. And after that—" the queen opened her empty fist "—nothing. Forever."

Ash didn't react, but I felt the queen's words punch me in the stomach. Bile rose in my throat. How could I be so blind and stupid? Grimalkin had told me once that faeries banished from the Nevernever would die, that they would fade away until nothing was left. Tiaothin had told me that in the Winter palace, when I was trying to ignore her. I'd known all along, but refused to believe. Or perhaps I just hadn't wanted to remember.

"This is your final chance, Prince." Mab stepped back, her voice stiff and icy, like she was talking to a stranger. "Give me your solemn vow, or be damned to the mortal world forever. Make your choice."

Ash looked at me. I saw pain in his eyes, and a little regret, but they shone with such emotion I felt breathless. "I already have."

"So be it." If Mab's voice was cold before, it was in the

sub-zero range now. She waved the scepter and, with a sharp crack, a rip appeared in the air. Like ink spreading over paper, it widened into a jagged archway. Beyond the arch, a flickering streetlamp glimmered, and rain pounded the road, hissing. The smell of tar and wet asphalt drifted through the opening. "From this day forth," Mab boomed, her voice carrying over the field, "Prince Ash is considered a traitor and an exile. All trods will be closed to him, all safe holds are barred, and if he is seen anywhere within the Nevernever, he is to be hunted down and killed immediately." She looked at Ash, fury and contempt curling her lips. "You are not my son. Get out of my sight."

Ash stepped back. Without a word, he turned and walked toward the archway, shoulders back and head high. At the edge of the trod, he hesitated, and I saw a shadow of fear cross his face. But then his expression hardened, and he swept through the door without looking back.

"Ash, wait!"

Darting around Oberon, I rushed for the trod. Faeries hissed and snarled, and Puck yelled for me to stop, but I ignored them all. As I approached Mab, her lips curled in a cruel smile and she stepped back, giving me a clear shot at the open trod.

"Meghan Chase!"

Oberon's voice cracked like a whip, and a roar of thunder shook the ground. I stumbled to a halt a few feet from the doorway, so close that I could see the road and darkened street, the blurry outline of houses through the rain.

The Erlking's voice was ominously quiet, and his eyes glowed amber through the gently falling snow. "The laws of our people are absolute," Oberon warned. "Summer and Winter share many things, but love is not one of them. If you make this choice, daughter, the trods will never open for you again."

My stomach dropped. There it was. Oberon would banish me from the Nevernever, as well. For a split second, I almost laughed in his face. This wasn't my home. I hadn't asked to be half-fey. I'd never wanted to be caught up in their problems, or their world. Let him exile me; what did I care?

Don't kid yourself, I thought with a sudden sick feeling in my gut. *You love this world. You risked everything to save it. Are you really going to walk away and forget it ever existed?*

"Meghan." Puck stepped forward, pleading. "Don't do this. I can't follow you this time. Stay here. With me."

"I can't," I whispered. "I'm sorry, Puck. I do love you, but I have to do this." His face clouded with pain, and he turned away. Guilt stabbed at me, but in the end, the choice had always been clear.

"I'm sorry," I whispered again to Puck, to Oberon, to everyone, and turned back to the doorway. *I don't belong here. Not really. Time to wake up and go home for real.*

"Are you sure, Meghan Chase?" Oberon's voce was cold, remorseless. "Walk out of Faery with him now, and you're never coming back."

Somehow, the ultimatum made it that much easier.

"Then I'm never coming back," I said softly, and went through the arch, leaving Faery behind me forever.

EPILOGUE

Second Homecoming

As I stumbled through the trod and onto the sidewalk, the rain hit me like a hammer, cold, wet and comfortingly unpleasant. Like normal rain. Lightning flickered overhead; regular, white lightning that didn't respond to the whims of a faery king's mood. My gown clung to my body; the drenching would be the finishing touch to ruining it completely, but I didn't care. My time in Faery was over. No more faery glamour, faery food or faery tricks. I was done.

With one exception, of course.

"Ash!" I called, squinting through the rain and darkness, through the glow of the streetlamps that made it impossible to see more than a few feet. "Ash, I'm here! Where are you?"

The empty road mocked me. Didn't he think I'd come after him? Was he already gone, fading into the rain without a backward glance, believing himself alone in the world? Tears muffled my voice. "Ash!" I yelled, taking a few steps down the sidewalk. "Ash!"

"You'll wake everyone up if you keep shouting like that."

I whirled around. He stood where the portal had been, hands in his pockets, the rain drumming his shoulders and making his hair run into his eyes. Lamplight fell around him, shining off his slick coat, surrounding him with a faint nimbus of light. But to me, he'd never looked so real.

"You came after me," he murmured, sounding awed, incredulous, and relieved at the same time. I walked up to him, smiling through my tears.

"You didn't think I'd let you go off alone, did you?"

"I was hoping." Ash stepped forward and hugged me, pulling me close with desperate relief. I slid my arms beneath his coat and held him tight, closing my eyes. The rain pounded us, and a lone car passed us on the road, spraying us with gutter water, but I felt no urge to move. As long as Ash held me, I could stay here forever.

He finally pulled back but didn't release me from the circle of his arms. "So," he murmured, his silver eyes boring into mine. "What do we do now?"

"I don't know," I said, shivering as he brushed a strand of wet hair from my cheek. "I think…I should go home soon. Mom and Luke are probably going nuts. What about you?"

He shrugged, a casual lift of one shoulder. "You tell me. When I left the Nevernever, I didn't have any plans other than being with you. If you want me around, just say the word."

My eyes watered. I thought of Rowan, of Ironhorse, and the armies of the false king, still on the move. I thought of Leanansidhe and Charles, trapped in the Between. I would have to get him out someday, and confront Leanansidhe about stealing my dad so long ago. But for now, the only thing I wanted was standing right here, looking at me with an expression so open and unguarded that I thought my heart would burst out of my chest. "Don't leave," I whispered, tightening my hold. "Never leave me again. Stay with me. Forever."

The Winter prince smiled, a small, easy smile, and lowered his lips to mine. "I promise."

★ ★ ★ ★ ★

ACKNOWLEDGMENTS

One would think the second book in a series would be easy to write, now that you've finished the first one and gotten all the hard stuff out of the way. Ha ha ha! No. The second book is just as difficult, if not more so, as the first, and so the list of people I have to thank has not diminished in the slightest. My family, of course, for being so supportive and always believing I could do the impossible. My newfound friends online: Khy and Sharon and Kristi and Liyana, and all the wonderful YA book bloggers of the blogosphere, whose excitement and love of this genre makes me grateful and humbled at the same time. I cannot begin to express my thanks for all they have done. My agent, Laurie McLean, who always has time to answer my questions even though I spell her name wrong sometimes. Natashya Wilson and Adam Wilson, the perfect tag team of Super Editors, and all the wonderful, hardworking folks at Harlequin Teen. I cannot thank you all enough.

And again, I must express my deepest, heartfelt gratitude to my husband, Nick, the greatest listener of all time. I still couldn't have done it without him.

Be sure to read all of the books in the
New York Times bestselling series

THE IRON FEY

Book 3

Book 4

Book 5

COMING NOVEMBER 2013!

Book 6

"Julie Kagawa is one killer storyteller."
—MTV's *Hollywood Crush* blog

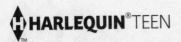
HTIFONETR3